D1807542

23035

MARKETING IN THE

Fifth Edition

▶ Music Industry

CHARLES W. HALL • FREDERICK J. TAYLOR

PEARSON

Custom
Publishing

PEARSON CUSTOM PUBLISHING
75 Arlington Street, Suite 300, Boston, MA 02116
A Pearson Education Company

Contents

Acknowledgments

We would like to dedicate this book to our wives, Rosemary Hall and Gloria A. Taylor for their enduring patience and understanding in the preparation of this book and to all of our children and grandchildren.

Among the many colleagues and friends that have assisted us, we would like to especially thank Chip Hall (Eurpac), Jimmy Starks (Sony Music), Jeff and Beverly Scheible (Rock Bottom Distribution), Julie Dillon, Jive Records, Steve Savoca, Jive Records, and Frederick Taylor Jr. (Tomorrow Pictures).

In addition, we appreciate the help given us by Gwen Kesler, Tom O'Flynn, George Rosenjack, Jim Hall, Dr. George Butler, Fred Traub, Larry Gallagher, Fred Love, Sue Roop, Norman Hunter, David Doolittle, Debra Wagnon, Lou Tatulli, Shachar Oren, and the students enrolled in Music Marketing classes at Georgia State University.

We also wish to thank the Recording Industry Association of America (RIAA), the National Association of Recording Merchandisers (NARM), the Recording Academy (NARAS), the Video Software Dealers Association (VSDA), the National Music Publishers Association (NMPA), the Music Entertainment Industry Education Association (MEIEA), International Federation of Phonographic Industries (IFPI), and the NARAS Awards Guide for many of the figures and other material included in this book.

Finally, we wish to thank the staff at Pearson Publishing for helping facilitate the many changes required in each edition because we are dealing with a constantly changing, very volatile industry.

Introduction

The way consumers are buying music is changing daily, as is the way they listen, store and share music. From vinyl to CD to MP3 to iPod, it is a new world. Broadband adoption, combined with digitalization and the introduction of so many portable players is changing many of the fundamental ideas of how you produce and market music.

The recording industry is one of the most competitive, most treacherous, most demanding, yet most exciting and potentially lucrative careers you can pursue these days. At the same time it *is one of the most misunderstood*. But possibly more important, recent events in the industry are making it far more difficult to break in and more difficult to succeed. Recent data from Nielsen/NetRatings tells us that almost 62 million people visited online music sites in April of 2005. Approximately 60% of those visitors were under 45 years of age and the majority has a household income of over $50,000.

A year ago there were over 230 music services online where consumers could purchase music, and the number has kept growing. These services are making their presence known worldwide. By mid-2005, record companies had digitized and licensed over a million songs. Music subscription services have given music listeners unprecedented access, value, and most important, flexibility. Because of the "star power" generated by recordings and recording artists, the industry receives far more than the normal share of public attention. Media coverage is intense and this trend will only intensify in the future, especially in light of the many problems hounding the music business. Along with the public's appetite for information about the major recording personalities, a much larger share of media attention is now being directed at the problems brought on by the rapidly expanding technology that allows for easier downloading and rapid "burning" (copying) of CD product.

The business pages of the major newspapers such as the *New York Times*, *USA Today*, *Washington Post* and *The Wall Street Journal* are highlighting these problems with front page articles several times each week.

The new millennium brought on the biggest problems the industry had ever faced. The Internet and computer revolution created problems that have remained insolvable to this day. The new computer technologies have had a major impact on everyone's activities and this will be discussed at great length later in the text. The four major distribution companies have different ideas on how to approach the problems, but so far none have worked. The morass has just continued to worsen. This is not to say that the industry has not faced problems in the past and been able to work out of them.

In the 1980s and into 1990, the music industry saw very slow growth (See Charts I-1 and I-2). Dollars increased slightly, but sales rode an up-and-down roller coaster. The introduction of Compact Disc and its higher wholesale and retail price kept the dollar volume from declining. The actual "penetration rate," considering the number of turntables, cassette decks and CD players that were in the hands of the consumers, was not very good. With playback equipment numbering well into the millions in the United States alone, the industry was still considering a "million seller" as a successful project. That has changed now, with the projections for "hit" product now well into multiplatinum ranges (Chart I-4).

In 1992 the surge came in both dollars and units, but this was still significantly behind the curve of the economy and population growth, both of which had tremendous increases in the 1980s. The music industry did start to catch up, however, when in 1993 the industry topped $10 billion for the first time to be followed by 1994's 20% growth to over $12 billion (Chart I-2). This meant that growth had almost tripled in a decade. Some of this was fueled by consumers converting their record libraries to CD, some by the entry into the record retailing market of stores like Best Buy and Circuit City. Some of the increases came because the number of record stores had increased by over 1500 outlets from the mid 1980s to the early 1990s.

But then in 1995, primarily in the last months of the year, some very serious problems clouded this bright outlook and the trend was reversed. Total sales for 1995 were really flat, with only a $252 million increase over 1994 (Chart I-2). The pipelines were getting filled as record buyers had pretty much converted their old LPs to CDs. However, the really disturbing figures were that even though the increase in units was fairly small, a 2.2% increase, the increase in dollars was even smaller at 1.7% which indicates that price erosion was starting. It also indicated the impact of retailers like Best Buy and Circuit City entering the market. While 1996 saw an upturn in units and total dollars, it was not very large (Chart I-2). The trend in 1997 was even more disturbing and both units and sales fell below 1996 levels, and this in a booming economy, which made it even more catastrophic. This caused a number of retail chains to declare Chapter 11, with some not emerging, and caused those that survived to cut back drastically on the number of stores they were able to operate. It also accelerated the move toward more consolidations, which makes it far more difficult for record companies to operate. As major accounts become fewer, they can make more demands. For example, Blockbuster Video got into the audio market by buying a number of major chains, two of the most notable being Record Bar, a national chain and Turtles, a large regional chain.

Chart I-1
The Recording Industry Association of America's
Year-end Statistics
1020 Nineteenth Street, N.W., Suite 200,
Washington, D.C. 20036 (202) 775-0101
Manufacturers' Unit Shipments and Dollar Value
(in Millions, Net After Returns)

1982–1991 Unit Shipments and Dollar Value

	1982	1983	1984	1985	1986	1987	1988	1989	1990	1991
CD	NA	0.8	5.8	22.6	53.0	102.1	149.7	207.2	286.5	333.3
	NA	$17.2	$103.3	$389.5	$930.1	$1593.6	$2089.9	$2,587.7	$3,451.6	$4,337.7
CD Single	NA	NA	NA	NA	NA	NA	1.6	−0.1	1.1	5.7
	NA	NA	NA	NA	NA	NA	9.8	−0.7	6.0	35.1
Cassette	182.3	236.8	332.0	339.1	344.5	410.0	450.1	446.2	442.2	360.1
	1384.5	1810.9	2383.9	2411.5	2499.5	2959.7	3385.1	3,345.8	3,472.4	3,019.6
Cassette Single	NA	NA	NA	NA	NA	5.1**	22.5	76.2	87.4	69.0
	NA	NA	NA	NA	NA	14.3**	57.3	194.6	257.9	230.4
Vinyl LP/EP	243.9	209.6	204.6	167.0	125.2	107.0	72.4	34.6	11.7	4.8
	1925.1	1689.0	1,548.8	1,280.5	983.0	793.1	532.2	220.3	86.5	29.4
Vinyl Single	137.2	124.8	131.5	120.7	93.9	82.0	65.6	36.6	27.6	22.0
	283.0	269.3	298.7	281.0	228.1	203.3	180.4	116.4	94.4	63.9
Music Video	NA	NA	NA	NA	NA	NA	NA	6.1	9.2	6.1
	NA	NA	NA	NA	NA	NA	NA	115.4	172.3	118.1
Total Units	577.4*	578.0*	679.8*	653.0*	618.3*	706.8*	761.9	806.7	865.7	801.0
Total Value	3641.6*	3814.3*	4370.4*	4378.8*	4651.1*	5567.5*	6254.8	$6,579.4	$7,541.1	$7,834.2

*Reflects inclusions of discontinued configurations.

Reprinted courtesy of RIAA.

Chart I-2
The Recording Industry Association of America's
1992 to 2001 Yearend Statistics
1330 Connecticut Avenue, NW, Suite 300, Washington, D.C. 20036
202-775-0101

Manufacturers' Unit Shipments and Dollar Value
(In Millions, net after returns)

	1992	1993	1994	1995	1996	1997	1998	1999	2000	% CHANGE 1999-2000	2001	% CHANGE 2000-2001
CD (Units Shipped)	407.5	495.4	662.1	722.9	778.9	753.1	847.0	938.9	942.5	0.4%	881.9	-6.4%
(Dollar Value)	5,326.5	6,511.4	8,464.5	9,377.4	9,934.7	9,915.1	11,416.0	12,816.3	13,214.5	3.1%	12,909.4	-2.3%
CD Single	7.3	7.8	9.3	21.5	43.2	66.7	56.0	55.9	34.2	-38.8%	17.3	-49.4%
	45.1	45.8	56.1	110.9	184.1	272.7	213.2	222.4	142.7	-35.8%	79.4	-44.4%
Cassette	366.4	339.5	345.4	272.6	225.3	172.6	158.5	123.6	76.0	-38.5%	45.0	-40.8%
	3,116.3	2,915.8	2,976.4	2,303.6	1,905.3	1,522.7	1,419.9	1,061.6	626.0	-41.0%	363.4	-41.9%
Cassette Single	84.6	85.6	81.1	70.7	59.9	42.2	26.4	14.2	1.3	-90.8%	-1.5	-215.4%
	298.8	298.5	274.9	236.3	189.3	133.5	94.4	48.0	4.6	-90.4%	-5.3	-215.2%
LP/EP	2.3	1.2	1.9	2.2	2.9	2.7	3.4	2.9	2.2	-24.1%	2.3	4.5%
	13.5	10.6	17.8	25.1	36.8	33.3	34.0	31.8	27.7	-12.9%	27.4	-1.1%
Vinyl Single	19.8	15.1	11.7	10.2	10.1	7.5	5.4	5.3	4.8	-9.4%	5.5	14.6%
	66.4	51.2	47.2	46.7	47.5	35.6	25.7	27.9	26.3	-5.7%	31.4	19.4%
Music Video	7.6	11.0	11.2	12.6	16.9	18.6	27.2	19.8	18.2	-8.1%	17.7	-2.7%
	157.4	213.3	231.1	220.3	236.1	323.9	508.0	376.7	281.9	-25.2%	329.2	16.8%
DVD Audio	-	-	-	-	-	-	-	-	-	N/A	0.3	N/A
	-	-	-	-	-	-	-	-	-	N/A	6.0	N/A
DVD Video*	-	-	-	-	-	-	0.5	2.5	3.3	32.0%	7.9	139.4%
	-	-	-	-	-	-	12.2	66.3	80.3	21.1%	190.7	137.5%
Total Units	895.5	955.6	1,122.7	1,112.7	1,137.2	1,063.4	1,123.9	1,160.6	1,079.2	-7.0%	968.5	-10.3%
Total Value	9,024.0	10,046.6	12,068.0	12,320.3	12,533.8	12,236.8	13,711.2	14,584.7	14,323.7	-1.8%	13,740.9	-4.1%

	1997	1998	1999	2000	% CHANGE 1999-2000	2001	% CHANGE 2000-2001
Total Retail Units	817.5	850.0	869.7	788.6	-9.3%	733.1	-7.0%
Total Retail Value	10,785.8	12,165.4	13,048.0	12,705.0	-2.6%	12,388.8	-2.5%

* While broken out for this chart, DVD Video Product is included in the Music Video totals

Permission to cite or copy these statistics is hereby granted, as long as proper attribution is given to the Recording Industry Association of America.

Chart I-3
2002 to 2004 Yearend Statistics
1330 Connecticut Avenue, NW, Suite 300, Washington, D.C. 20036
202-775-0101

Manufacturers' Unit Shipments
(In Millions, net after returns)

	2002	% CHANGE 2001–2002	2003	% CHANGE 2002–2003	2004	% CHANGE 2003–2004
(Units Shipped) CD	803.3	−8.9%	746.9	−7.1%	766.0	2.8%
(Dollar Value)	12,044.1	−6.7%	11,232.9	−6.7%	11,446.50	1.9%
CD Single	4.6	−74.1%	8.3	85.5%	3.1	−62.2%
	19.6	−76.4%	36.9	84.0%	14.9	−58.4%
Cassette	31.1	−30.9%	17.2	−44.7%	6.2	−69.6%
	209.8	−42.3%	108.1	−48.5%	23.6	−78.1%
Cassette Single[a]	−0.5	−68.0%	N/A	N/A	N/A	N/A
	−1.8	−70.3%	N/A	N/A	N/A	N/A
Digital Single[aa]	—	—	—	—	139.40	N/A
	—	—	—	—		N/A
Digital Albums[aa]	—	—	—	—	4.6	N/A
	—	—	—	—		N/A
LP/EP	1.7	−23.7%	1.5	−11.5%	1.3	−11.9%
	20.6	−25.2%	21.7	6.1%	19.2	−11.3%
Vinyl Single	4.4	−20.8%	3.8	−142%	3.5	−7.3%
	24.9	−20.6%	21.5	−140%	19.8	−7.3%
Music Video	14.7	−17.2%	19.9	36.0%	32.7	66.0%
	288.4	−12.4%	399.9	38.7%	607.2	61.8%
DVD Audio	0.4	63.8%	0.4	0.8%	0.35	−20.6%
	8.5	41.3%	8.0	−5.3%	6.4	−19.2%
SA CD	—	—	1.3	N/A	0.79	−39.6%
	—	—	26.3	N/A	16.6	−36.9%
DVD Video[aaa]	10.7	34.8%	17.5	64.1%	29.01	66.0%
	236.3	23.9%	369.6	56.4%	561.1	51.8%
Total Units	859.7	−11.2%	798.4	−7.2%	814.1	2.0%
Total Value	12,614.2	−8.2%	11,854.4	−6.0%	12,154.70	2.5%
	675.7	−7.8%	658.2	−2.7%	686.9	4.4%
	11,549.0	−6.8%	11,053.4	−4.3%	11,422.90	8.3%

Manufacturers' Unit Shipments and Dollar Value (In Millions, net after returns)
Reprinted courtesy of RIAA.

Chart I-4
How Records Achieve Gold, Platinum and Multi-Platinum

	Gold	Platinum	Multi-Platinum
Single	500,000 units	1 million units	2 million units
Album	500,000 units	1 million units	2 million units
Short-Form	250,000 units	500,000 units	1 million units
Multi-Box	500,000 units	1 million units	2 million units
Video Single	25,000 units	50,000 units	100,000 units
Video Long-Form	50,000 units	100,000 units	200,000 units
Video Multi-Box	50,000 units	100,000 units	200,000 units

Reprinted courtesy of RIAA.

However, in 1999, Blockbuster's parent company, Viacom, opted to get out of the audio retailing business and sold to a West Coast retail chain, Wherehouse. Blockbuster Video stores remain as they were, but the audio stores are all re-signed as Wherehouse Stores (It should be noted that the problems and consolidations noted above also hit Wherehouse). However, this meant that record companies had to deal with one giant instead of having three chains to approach. The sales curves finally righted themselves in 1998 with a $1.5 million increase, and everyone breathed easier. Much of the turn-around came from good product, product that was appealing to all generations of record buyers.

But even with the sales trends back on a positive note, all levels of the music industry were battling major problems. Labels and distribution companies were very actively exploring new ways to expose product and artists and to find more avenues into the consumers' homes. The Internet was certainly not the least of these explorations.

The industry had had turndowns in the past, but in most of these periods the lack of good product has been a major contributing factor. Some in the industry felt this was the case again, but others were concerned that there were too many other entertainment products siphoning off the consumers' dollars, especially the dollars of the younger consumers, always the primary base of prerecorded music. Games and other distractions associated with computers has certainly drawn off some of the income usually spent on recorded music. The industry also needs a new configuration that is even more portable than the CD, to compliment today's lifestyles.

Technology will have a major effect on how the music industry positions itself for the future. How the industry addresses the problems of copying and downloading will determine if the business survives as it is known today.

CHART I-5

2005 RIAA Mid-year Statistics
Phone: 202/775-0101

Manufacturers' Unit Shipments and Dollar Value
(In millions at suggested retail list price, net after returns)

Six Months Ended June 30

Format	2005				2004				Percent Change			
	Units to Retail	Dollars to Retail	Total Units	Total Dollars	Units to Retail	Dollars to Retail	Total Units	Total Dollars	Retail Units	Retail Dollars	Total Units	Total Dollars
CD[1]	257.9	$4,189.3	307.7	$4,486.3	270.2	$4,429.9	329.0	$4,778.7	−4.6%	−5.4%	−6.5%	−6.1%
Cassette	0.7	$4.4	1.2	$5.7	2.1	$10.7	3.0	$13.2	−68.1%	−58.4%	−62.2%	−57.1%
Vinyl LP/EP	0.5	$7.4	0.6	$8.0	0.6	$9.0	0.7	$9.3	−16.7%	−17.8%	−3.8%	−13.6%
CD Single	2.0	$7.3	2.0	$7.3	2.6	$11.6	2.6	$11.6	−23.8%	−37.0%	−23.8%	−37.0%
Vinyl Single	1.4	$7.7	1.4	$7.7	1.9	$10.9	1.9	$10.9	−30.4%	−29.1%	−30.4%	−29.1%
Music Video	4.3	$46.6	4.7	$50.0	0.5	$7.8	0.8	$10.8	720.9%	498.2%	457.9%	362.0%
SACD	0.3	$5.6	0.3	$5.6	0.3	$6.7	0.3	$6.7	−18.1%	−17.3%	−18.1%	−17.3%
DVD Video	11.6	$213.9	11.6	$213.9	11.2	$206.3	11.2	$206.3	3.3%	3.7%	3.3%	3.7%
DVD Audio	0.1	$1.7	0.1	$1.7	0.3	$4.8	0.3	$4.8	−63.7%	−64.2%	−63.7%	−64.2%
Total Albums[2]	**275.3**	**$4,469.1**	**326.1**	**$4,771.1**	**285.3**	**$4,675.2**	**345.4**	**$5,029.7**	**−3.5%**	**−4.4%**	**−5.6%**	**−5.1%**
Total Singles[3]	**3.3**	**$15.1**	**3.3**	**$15.1**	**4.5**	**$22.5**	**4.5**	**$22.5**	**−26.7%**	**−33.2%**	**−26.7%**	**−33.2%**
Total Physical	**278.6**	**$4,484.2**	**329.4**	**$4,786.2**	**289.8**	**$4,697.7**	**349.9**	**$5,052.3**	**−3.8%**	**−4.5%**	**−5.8%**	**−5.3%**
Digital Single[4]	148.7	$147.3	148.7	$147.3	58.6	$58.1	58.6	$58.1	153.6%	153.6%	153.6%	153.6%
Digital Album	5.1	$50.6	5.1	$50.6	1.5	$15.2	1.5	$15.2	231.7%	231.7%	231.7%	231.7%
Total Digital	**153.8**	**$197.8**	**153.8**	**$197.8**	**60.2**	**$73.3**	**60.2**	**$73.3**	**155.6%**	**169.9%**	**165.6%**	**169.9%**

[1]Includes DualDisc
[2]Includes CD, Cassette, Vinyl LP/EP, Music Video, SACD, DVD Video, and DVD Audio
[3]Includes CD Single and Vinyl Single
[4]Digital Sales Based On Estimated Current Retail Prices of $0.99 per Single And $9.99 per Album
Reprinted courtesy of RIAA.

For almost 50 years, the RIAA has tracked sales throughout the industry. In 2003, RIAA issued a report indicating cumulative sales by all artists that have sold over 20 million units (See Chart I-6)

Chart I-6
gold & platinum

Top Artists

Totals are derived from cumulative album sales totals (U.S. only)

Artist	Certified Units (in Millions)
BEATLES, THE	166.5
PRESLEY, ELVIS	117.5
LED ZEPPELIN	106.0
BROOKS, GARTH	105.0
EAGLES	88.0
JOEL, BILLY	78.5
PINK FLOYD	73.5
STREISAND, BARBRA	71.5
JOHN, ELTON	67.5
AEROSMITH	64.0
ROLLING STONES, THE	63.5
AC/DC	63.0
SPRINGSTEEN, BRUCE	61.5
MADONNA	60.0
JACKSON, MICHAEL	58.5
METALLICA	57.0
CAREY, MARIAH	57.0
STRAIT, GEORGE	54.5
HOUSTON, WHITNEY	54.0
VAN HALEN	50.5
ROGERS, KENNY	50.5
DIAMOND, NEIL	50.0
FLEETWOOD MAC	48.5
U2	48.0
KENNY G	47.5

Artist	Certified Units (in Millions)
ALABAMA	46.0
DION, CELINE	45.5
SANTANA	43.5
TWAIN, SHANIA	42.0
JOURNEY	40.0
NELSON, WILLIE	39.0
CLAPTON, ERIC	38.5
SIMON & GARFUNKEL	37.5
CHICAGO	37.0
SEGER, BOB/SILVER BULLET BAND	37.0
2 PAC	36.5
MC ENTIRE, REBA	36.5
PRINCE	36.5
FOREIGNER	36.0
BACKSTREET BOYS	36.0
GUNS N ROSES	35.5
JACKSON, ALAN	35.5
DYLAN, BOB	34.5
BON JOVI	33.5
DENVER, JOHN	33.5
STEWART, ROD	33.0
DEF LEPPARD	32.0
COLLINS, PHIL	32.0
RONSTADT, LINDA	31.5
BOSTON	31.0
TAYLOR, JAMES	30.5
QUEEN	30.5
DOORS, THE	29.5
MATTHEWS, DAVE BAND	29.0
PEARL JAM	28.5
DIXIE CHICKS	28.5
PETTY, TOM & THE HEARTBREAKERS	28.0
SPEARS, BRITNEY	28.0
'N SYNC	28.0

Artist	Certified Units (in Millions)
BOLTON, MICHAEL	28.0
KELLY, R.	28.0
OSBOURNE, OZZY	27.5
BOYZ II MEN	27.0
MELLENCAMP, JOHN	26.5
BEE GEES	25.5
SINATRA, FRANK	25.5
LYNYRD SKYNYRD	25.0
ZZ TOP	25.0
MC CARTNEY, PAUL	25.0
RUSH	24.5
JACKSON, JANET	24.0
MILLER, STEVE BAND	24.0
MANILOW, BARRY	24.0
NIRVANA	24.0
CARPENTERS, THE	24.0
CARS, THE	23.5
BROOKS & DUNN	23.0
CREED	23.0
EARTH, WIND & FIRE	23.0
HILL, FAITH	23.0
GILL, VINCE	22.5
VANDROSS, LUTHER	22.5
MANNHEIM STEAMROLLER	22.5
MOTLEY CRUE	22.5
SADE	22.5
ESTEFAN, GLORIA	22.0
MC GRAW, TIM	22.0
TLC	22.0
ENYA	22.0
POLICE, THE	22.0
DOOBIE BROTHERS	22.0
CREEDENCE CLEARWATER REVIVAL	22.0
R.E.O. SPEEDWAGON	21.5

Artist	Certified Units (in Millions)
GENESIS	21.5
EMINEM	21.0
RICHIE, LIONEL	21.0
BEASTIE BOYS	21.0
MEAT LOAF	20.5
BUFFETT, JIMMY	20.5
HEART	20.5
MORISSETTE, ALANIS	20.5
HENDRIX, JIMI	20.0
HOOTIE & THE BLOWFISH	20.0
BEACH BOYS, THE	20.0
WHO, THE	20.0
JAY-Z	20.0

This chart was generated on 8/25/2003

Reprinted courtesy of RIAA.

The Recording Industry Association of America (RIAA) in releasing the figures for the year 2001 commented strongly on how Internet piracy and CD-burning impacted the negative trend. Specifically, the total U.S. shipments dropped from 1.08 billion units shipped in the year 2000 to 968.58 million units in 2001—a 10.3 percent decrease. Figures for 2002 versus 2001 were no better. Depending upon what survey you use, sales dropped another 9% to 10% with a decrease of over one million CD's. The numbers for the first six months of 2002 were no more promising, with CD sales off over 7%. (See Chart I-5) Meanwhile, the slumping singles market continued a slide that had started a year earlier.

Even though the economy was slow, RIAA feels very strongly that the large drop in shipments was primarily due to online piracy and CD-burning. RIAA commissioned a survey of 2,225 music consumers between the ages of 12 and 54. The results showed that 23 percent of these consumers said they did not buy more music in 2001 because they downloaded or copied most of their music for free. Coinciding with the increase in copying, the study found that ownership of CD burners had increased at a staggering pace. The IFPI, the international association representing the recording industry worldwide, reported that "global piracy on the physical side cost the recording industry billions every year."

The RIAA figures for 2001 tell the whole sordid story. (Chart I-2) At this point, CD's are still the format of choice with 87 percent of units shipped in 2000 and 91 percent of the units shipped in 2001. But, presently, with CD the format of choice, the results for 2001 showing a 6.4 percent decrease in CD shipments and a 2.3 percent decrease in dollar shipments of CD, it is obvious how much trouble the industry faces. Throughout this dismal period, DVD had been a savior, with both DVD music video and DVD movies showing incredible growth. But DVD music video dollar gains cannot attempt to compete with CD losses. In addition, DVD sales are slowing and being hurt by copying and piracy.

There has always been an undercurrent among consumers that CD prices are too high and they did inch up both at wholesale and retail after 1999. Some labels are trying to fight this trend by keeping the new release price lower and not raising it until a product has gained widespread acceptance. However, an analysis on CD prices as compared to the recent increases in movie theater prices, book prices, concert prices and the prices of other popular pastimes, shows music prices running concurrent with the increases of other prices in entertainment.

Another factor could be the product. When retail fell off in late 2002 and early 2003, many analysts questioned if the consumer was not happy with the choices in all types of products being offered for sale. However, the results for 2004 show an upswing for the first time in the new millennium, with a 4.4% "surge."

The first half of 2005 saw another dip in sales through retailers, about 5.1% (See Chart I-5), but songs sold over the Web through paid downloads had tripled. According to Nielsen SoundScan, Internet users in the United State downloaded 158 million individual songs in the first half of the year, compared with 55 million for the same period a year previous.

For a long time, globalization was picking up most of the slack in domestic profitability. But that is no longer the case. However, it still does help tremendously (see chapter 15).

Record companies have to think globally when signing artists since a new act can cost up to, and possibly over, $2 million to "bring to the street." The global surge, however, is not helping the retailers and subdistributors in America. The number of outlets for prerecorded music is shrinking domestically, even more incentive for companies to look to the overseas markets. Fortunately, music is universal and thus "hits" from America can be moved to other countries, while an overseas product can become a hit in the United States.

The lifeblood of the industry is "baby acts," new artists or groups that must be brought to "hit" status constantly for a record company to keep showing profits and growth. If all you could do was purchase products by recording acts that have been popular for at least five or more years, you could readily realize the reason why new acts are the primary source of energy for the music business.

In the seventies and early eighties, just about all record activity, label and distribution, was distilled down to six major companies. However, in 1999 even that changed as Universal bought out Polygram and then there were only five: BMG, Sony, WMG, EMD and Universal. But that changed again in 2004 & 2005 when Sony and BMG merged, leaving four companies.

These four majors also face another problem, as the onset of rap has increased the market share of the independent distributors. However, keep in mind that the majors are all multinational organizations with far more than music as their sources of revenue.

This concentration of so many labels and operations within so few companies offered small, new labels far fewer options. Fortunately, in the late eighties, while the number of major companies did not increase, the major companies offered opportunities for small, new labels via distribution deals which also came with financing. However, not all small labels could or would join forces with the major companies. The new genres of music that were emerging in a network of independent distributors have been part of the business for years, but had fallen to a point where they accounted for a very small percentage of domestic sales. This was quickly reversed and "Indies," as they are termed, suddenly accounted for just under 20% of the overall volume, putting them ahead of four or five of the major distribution organizations. By 2005, "Indies" were responsible for between 20% and 25 % of the volume. Numbers in the music industry fluctuate rapidly since just a couple of "megahits," records way up in the multiplatinum galaxies, can change the order almost overnight.

Once the music or video tracks are "put down" and the process of bringing the final product to market commences, many traditional marketing concepts come into play. However, many non-traditional methods must also be employed. What might be considered a normal progression for most products from manufacture to eventual sale to consumers will not always apply for recorded music or video. In addition, the marketing strategies for established artists are quite different from those used to introduce and establish new artists. This is also the area where the costs are very high and the chances of success very low. While the odds are not good, every company must "roll the dice" constantly. Fortunately, when you are successful, the payoff is extremely high.

Meanwhile, there are marketing steps for recordings and videos that other products do not require, while some of the traditional marketing activities for most other products can be eliminated from music marketing when everything falls in place properly. Knowing the timing of all the activities is vital to success.

With a recorded product, you are not really selling a physical item. Except for some graphics, all recordings and videos look pretty much alike. You market the information encoded on that product. You sell the sounds; you sell what the music or visual does to the buyers' inner selves; you feed the buyers' souls; you sell a dream. Music and videos are not really required to sustain life, but they make life more bearable and far more pleasant, and everyone needs a different beat to nourish them. We take the music in our lives for granted most of the time. We only realize its importance when it goes silent.

Unquestionably, the industry is facing monumental problems and the landscape has changed drastically in a short period of time, with many more changes to come.

We know times have changed when "ring tones" can actually top the charts. We know times have changed when millions of songs are being downloaded and paid for on iPod as well as other sites.

In the first half of 2005, digital music accounted for 6% of the total business or about $790 million.

We know times have changed when Podcasts come from nowhere to being all over in a few months. About two years after Podcasts started there were at least 7000 available for downloading to Apple's iPods. But they too, are subject to a major shakeout. When iPod got involved only the biggest meant anything. How Podcasts will impact the airplay culture is still up for grabs.

The global platform created by computers and the Internet will continue to create major changes in the way music is made and delivered to the consumer. However, making them want to buy certain product will not change that much.

How times have changed will be addressed in far more detail in a separate chapter in this book.

A great many people are required to bring a recorded product to the marketplace, just as a great many people are required to record, edit, mix and refine the creation of the product. Many of these people are highly specialized and most feel they are "on call" constantly, since the difference between success and failure can sometimes be measured in hours.

This book will examine in detail the activities of all the people required to raise a recording to "hit" status. "Hits" and your involvement in them, are how you measure success in the music business. Association with successful recording and video projects is a bankable asset. However, the successful people in the music industry will tell you that the main benefit is helping to create the excitement that can propel an unknown musician or group from obscurity to the "top of the charts" with record sales in the millions and live appearances in the major arenas of the world. Each time you see the act perform or hear the product aired, you realize you helped make it all happen. Very few people are fortunate enough to have so visible a means to measure their success.

Chapter 1

The Nature of Marketing

Learning Objectives

After studying this chapter, you should be able to:

1. Define marketing

2. Describe the core concepts of marketing

3. Identify biological and psychological needs and wants

4. Recognize the role of demographics and psychographics in predicting consumer behavior

5. Define and correctly use the terms in the glossary

Marketing has been defined in various ways by various writers. Gilbert A. Churchill Jr. and J. Paul Peter define marketing as the process of planning and executing the conception, pricing, promotion, and distribution of ideas, goods and services to create exchanges that satisfy individual and organizational goals. Philip Kotler in *Marketing Management: Analysis, Planning, Control* defines it in this manner:

> *Marketing is a social and managerial process by which individuals and groups obtain what they need and want through creating and exchanging products and value with others.*

This definition of marketing rests on the following core concepts: needs, wants, and demands; products; value and satisfaction; exchange and transactions. These concepts are illustrated in Figure 1-1 and are discussed below.

Core Concepts of Marketing

People *need* food, shelter, air, water, clothing, sex, safety, belonging, esteem, love, self-fulfillment, knowledge, understanding and aesthetic experiences in order to survive physiologically and psychologically. A *need* is a state of felt deprivation of some basic satisfaction.

Figure 1-1
The Core Concepts of Marketing

Needs, Wants and Demands	>	Products	>	Value and Satisfaction	>	Exchange and Transaction

The basic needs in their order as stated by Abraham Maslow are as follows:

(1) *Physiological needs* include the needs for oxygen, water, food, temperature control, elimination, shelter, exercise, sleep, sensory stimulation, and sexual activity;

(2) *Safety needs* include the needs for security, dependency, consistency, stability, fairness, structure, order and limits; protection from immediate or future danger; freedom from fear, anxiety, and chaos; a certain amount of routine; and an orderly and structured environment;

(3) *Love and belonging needs* derive from societal factors and include a need to be cherished, a need for identification with significant others, affection from and affiliation with others, recognition and approval, companionship, and group interactions. Love is not synonymous with sexual needs, but sexual needs may be motivated by a need for love and affection;

(4) *Self-esteem and esteem for others* are concerned with the concept of self as a worthwhile person and an awareness of individuality and uniqueness. Included are needs

for self-respect and respect from others; a sense of confidence, dignity, competence, independence, prestige, status, and success; recognition from others for accomplishments; and a desire to attain certain standards of excellence;

(5) *Self-actualization needs* include needs for self-fulfillment and ongoing emotional and spiritual development; and for reaching individual potentialities, using talents, being productive and having peak experiences. They involve experiencing something fully, vividly, with full concentration and without self-consciousness;

(6) *Knowledge and Understanding needs* involve curiosity; a desire to know as much as possible; attraction to the mysterious, unknown, and unexplained; a desire to understand, systematize organize, and to analyze, and look for relations and meanings; and a desire to construct a value system;

(7) *Aesthetic needs* include needs for beauty, harmony, and order, and are expressed in our efforts to appreciate all of the artistic forms of art, literature, dance, and music.

These basic needs are the process by which consumers buy products and services. The recognition of a need may come from an internal feeling such as hunger, fatigue or it may come from external stimuli such as music being played on the radio. When consumers perceive that they have a need, the inner drive to fulfill the need is called a motivation. Music marketers want to know what motivates consumers so that they can appeal to those motives. Motivation to purchase a music product is influenced by social, marketing and situational forces.

Social Influences	Marketing Influences	Situational Influence
Culture	Product	Physical Surroundings
Subculture	Pricing	Social Surroundings
Social Class	Placement	Time
Reference Groups	Promotion	Task
Family		Monetary Conditions

Beyond this, people have a strong desire for other goods and services that are categorized as wants. A *want* is a desire for specific satisfiers or "deeper" needs such as music and designer clothes which are continually shaped and reshaped by societal forces and mass media. Our musical wants constantly change due to changing musical styles and technological innovations. The technology side of the industry has presented new products such as the Walkman, CD player, DAT recorder, video disc, DCC recorder, mini disc, CD Plus, DVD, MP3 and iPod. Many people want to upgrade to the new technology but only a few are really able and willing to do so. Therefore, the music industry must measure not only how many people want their product but, more importantly, how many would actually be willing and able to buy it. How do marketers create demand?

Demands are wants for specific products that are backed up by an ability and willingness to buy them. Wants become demands when backed up by purchasing power. Marketing departments do not create needs; needs preexist them. They, along with other factors in the society, influence wants by suggesting to music consumers that a new DVD player is technologically superior to any other configuration on the market. In essence, they try to influence demand by making their products attractive, superior, affordable and easily available.

A *product* is anything that can be offered to someone to satisfy a need or want. The importance of a product lies in its ability to satisfy, i.e., its ability to provide a service to satisfy needs and wants. We do not buy a piano to look at, but to perform on for the purpose of producing music. Normally the word "product" brings to mind a physical object, such as a musical instrument, video cassette player, or synthesizer. However, recorded music is an intangible product, musical sound, that provides an *aesthetic experience* for the listener. This musical sound is packaged in a compact disc, (CD), cassette, cassette single, vinyl LP/EP, vinyl single (7" & 12") video audio disk, dual disc, DVD-audio, super audio compact disc and digital downloads.

How does a consumer choose among the many packaged musical products that might satisfy a given need or want? When walking into a music retail chain, what is the deciding factor that would make you purchase one product over another, or any at all? The guiding concept is *value*. You will form an estimate of the value of each product in satisfying your goal. You might rank the music products in the outlet from the most desirable to the least desirable. Value is the consumer's estimate of the product's capacity to satisfy a set of goals. After value is established in the mind of the consumer, exchanges and transactions must take place. Exchanges and transactions describe the act of obtaining a desired product from someone by offering something in return.

Five conditions must exist before an exchange can take place:

1. There are at least two parties.
2. Each party has something that might be of value to the other party.
3. Each party is capable of communication and delivery.
4. Each party is free to accept or reject the offer.
5. Each party believes that it is appropriate or desirable to deal with the other party.

A transaction consists of a trade of value between two parties. In the example below, the seller offers musical goods or services in exchange for money.

Bases for Segmentation	Criterion	Examples
Demographic	Gender	Male; female
	Age	Under 6; 6–12; 13–19; 20–29; 30–39; 40–49; 50–59; 60+
	Race or ethnicity	White; black; oriental; other
	Income	Under $10,000; $10,000–$14,999; $15,000–$24,999; $25,000–$34,000; $35,000 or over
	Education	Grade school or less; some high school; graduated high school; some college; graduated college; some graduate work; graduate degree
	Occupation	Professional and technical; managers, officials and proprietors; clerical, sales; foremen; operatives; farmers; retired; students; homemakers, unemployed
	Family size	1–2; 3–4; 5+
	Family life cycle	Single; married, no children; married, youngest child under 6; married, youngest child 6 or over; married, no children under 18
Geographic	Region	Pacific; Mountain; West North Central; West South Central; East North Central; East South Central; South Atlantic; Middle Atlantic; New England
	Population density	Urban; suburban; rural
	Climate	Warm; cold
Psychographic	Lifestyle	Traditionalist; sophisticate; swinger
	Personality	Compliant; aggressive; detached
Buyer thoughts and feelings	Attitudes	Positive; neutral; negative
	Benefit sought	Convenience; economy; prestige
	Readiness stage	Unaware; aware; informed; interested; desirous; intend to purchase
	Innovativeness	Innovator; early adopter; early majority; late majority; laggard
	Perceived risk	High; moderate; low
	Involvement	Low; high
Purchase behavior	Usage rate	Light; medium; heavy
	Source loyalty	Purchase from one, two, three, four or more suppliers
	User status	Nonuser; ex-user; potential user; current user

Reprinted with permission.

Figure 1-2
Example of Exchange Transaction

Musical Transaction

Musical Goods or Services

Seller — — — — — — — — — — — — — — —> Buyer

Money

Seller <— — — — — — — — — — — — — — Buyer

The final process, called point of sale, takes place when the music consumer purchases the product with money and the sale is recorded in the cash register. How can the music industry measure qualitatively or quantitatively what music and how much music the consumer will spend of their money?

Demographic segmentation, dividing the market into segments based on demographic variables of age, sex, family size, occupation, income, family life-cycle, religion, race, nationality and social class is one way of measuring consumer's behavior. The RIAA identifies important market segments and target markets, because consumer wants and needs are often closely associated with demographic variables which are measurable. The 2004 RIAA Consumer Profile shows this information in detail in Chart 14-1. The survey indicates that appetite for music remains high.

The data gathered based on segmentation is market research which is the function that links the consumer, customer and public to the marketer through information. In other words, to anticipate or respond to customer needs, you must have knowledge about current and prospective customers. Music businesses often hire outside firms that specialize in music marketing research to perform this function or they will perform it in-house. Regardless of who performs the research function, the goal is to provide information that improves marketing decisions. Historically, the music industry gathered data which were simply facts and statistics. Music marketers today want data that is presented in a manner that is useful for decision making. This means that data are presented to indicate the presence or absence of a trend, relationship, or pattern. Instincts, hunches, guesses about customers music preferences should be supported by hard data. The table represents the kind of questions marketing research can help answer.

Even more crucial to music marketing objectives are differences in buyer attitudes, motivations, values, patterns of usage, aesthetic preferences, self concepts, activities, attitudes, feelings and personality traits. Marketers' attempts to quantify these intangibles are called "*Psychographics*." The traditional definition of psychographics is that it is quantitative research that attempts to measure consumer behavior on psychological constructs as opposed to strictly demographic segmentation.

Increasingly in today's music markets, demand turns on elusive factors like how the music product fits a consumer's self-concept or how it makes them *feel*. Ideally, the psychographic study utilizes the consumer's measurable demographic characteristics with the more intangible aspects of attitudes, opinions, emotions and interests. There are five types of psychographic studies that can be utilized for our purpose and they are lifestyle profile, product-specific psychographic profile, general lifestyle segmentation, personality traits as descriptors and product-specific segmentation. All of these studies have two common qualities in that they add the extra dimension of psychology and/or lifestyle to a demographic inquiry and they use quantitative survey techniques. These tools give music marketers objective and quantifiable information in which to readily identify potential consumers of music products.

Focus groups are one of the tools used to provide insight into beliefs and attitudes that underlie behavior. The focus group technique is especially well suited for music marketing research where complex psychological and sociological issues are often best explored through a qualitative approach. Underlying this technique is the rationale that with proper guidance from the focus group leader, group members can describe the rich details of complex experiences and the reasoning behind their actions, beliefs, perceptions and attitudes.

Focus groups are a data collection technique that capitalizes on the interaction within a group. It is a set of procedures for the collection and analysis of qualitative data that may help us gain an enlarged sociological and psychological point of view. Specifically, a focus group is 6 to 12 individuals who are similar in some way and come together to discuss an issue of specific interest. Focus groups rely on the dynamics of the group interactions to stimulate the thinking and thus the verbal contributions of the participants to provide the music marketing researcher with a rich, detailed perspective that could not be obtained through other methodological strategies. Once it has been determined that focus groups are an appropriate strategy, the population that is able to provide the sought-after perspective must be identified. It is important that potential participants have the common experience that is key to the research focus. Further, it is often important that potential group members have similar cultural experiences. In this context, culture should be interpreted quite broadly to include not only ethnicity, but also age, gender, socioeconomic status, or other factors that may have bearing on the group interaction. It is this similarity that facilitates the initial bonding and makes participants feel free to offer their input.

Some have suggested that it is better if participants do not know one another prior to the focus group. However, that is not always possible, and should not be perceived as an insurmountable obstacle in using focus groups.

Questions about Markets

Buyers	Demand	Channels
What kind of people buy our product?	Is demand for our product increasing or decreasing?	Do channels of distribution for our products need changing?
Where do they live?	Are there promising new markets that we have not yet reached?	Are new types of marketing institutions likely to evolve?
How much do they earn?		
How many of them are there?		

Questions about Marketing Mix

Product	Pricing	Placement	Promotion
Which product is likely to be most successful?	What price should we charge for our new product?	Where, and by whom should our products be sold?	How much should we spend on promotion?
What kind of packaging should we use?	Should the price of existing products be changed?	What kind of incentives should we offer the trade to push our products?	How should our budget be allocated to products and to geographic areas?
			What combination of media, newspapers, radio, television, magazines should we use?

Questions about Performance

Market Share	Customer Satisfaction	Reputation
What is our market share overall?	Are our customers satisfied with our products?	How are we perceived?
What is our share in each geographic area?		What is our reputation with music retailers?
What is our share by customer type?	How is our record for service? Are there many product returns?	

Preparing for the Focus Group

Prepare a semistructured interview guide or list of questions to help focus the discussion. Probe questions or subquestions are generally helpful in the event that the primary questions are not posed in a way that the participants can relate to, and to further explore a comment that is not clear or is inconsistent with previous comments. Probes are also useful to help refocus the group when the discussion wanders too far afield. It is often helpful if this guide includes an initial question to which all participants are asked to respond, such as describing some aspect of their experiences that they have in common with other group members. This not only emphasizes the similarities between the participants, but also brings all participants into the discussion and suggests that all contributions are equally valued.

Focus Group Session

During the actual focus group session, a leader or facilitator moderates the discussion. The major role of the leader is to pose questions, encourage the input of all participants, and keep the discussion on track as much as is appropriate. When the moderator can clearly anticipate what will be said next, that is an indication that the research is done. This usually takes three to four groups, although more may be required if the topic is complex or the goal is detailed analysis by group.

In analyzing focus group data, it is important to think of the context of group interaction, not individual comments. Credibility and usefulness of results will be enhanced through a careful documentation of steps and decisions in the analysis as raw data are transformed into understandable themes and patterns.

The perceptions, opinions, beliefs and attitudes (POBAs) collected in focus groups are subjective. Subjectivity is not a dirty word, but an inherent part of the qualitative process. Qualitative practitioners have different backgrounds, both academic and experiential, which provide a conversion mechanism through which what respondents said is converted into what respondents meant and furthermore, what conclusions or actions this indicates. This subjective process is the heartbeat of qualitative report writing.

The following list indicates some of the types of information that are collected in a focus group and processed through the subjective experience of the analyst: (1) Statements made by respondents in response to moderator questions; (2) unsaid information; (3) untrue statements stated as fact; (4) results of an counts; (5) nonverbal cues; (6) freewheeling discussions; (7) reactions; and (8) voting among choices.

In order to learn about others' experiences and perspectives active interviewing skills and knowledge of guidelines are essential. A focus group was conducted in the class "Current Problems in the Music Industry" at Georgia State University involving the use of bass music as recorded by artists from LaFace Records in Atlanta, GA. The following procedures were established from those preceding.

Procedure

1. A moderator and recorder will conduct the sessions

2. Group will comprise 6–12 participants, ideally 8

3. Three to four groups will be used

4. Two-hour focus group using fifteen questions

5. Population will consist of male and females ages 13–25

6. Groups will consist of mainly urban participants

7. College students will conduct the sessions

8. Topic will center around urban participants' attitudes, belief opinions, buying and listening habits as related to bass music

9. The active interview is a conversation, but not without a guiding purpose or plan

10. A conversational agenda rather than procedural directive

11. Cultivate the respondents' narrative activity and let the respondents' responses determine whether questions are necessary or appropriate as frames of references

12. The task of the active interviewer involves encouraging subjective relevances, promoting interpretive possibilities, facilitating narrative linkages, suggesting alternative perspective and appreciating diverse horizons of meaning

Focus Groups

Questions

1. Do you like this music?

2. What is it about this music that you like?

3. What does it motivate you to do?

4. Have you ever listened to this type of music?

5. Where did you listen to this type of music?

    home_____   car_____   radio_____   club_____   friend_____   other_____

6. What kind of setting would you like to or expect to hear this type of music in?

2. Industries that use "Psychographics" are those with new products to market, or those that are scrambling for market share. How can this tool benefit the music marketers on the internet?

3. What is the "typical" psychographic and demographic profile of the following music consumers: Purchasers of Country music; Pop; and Urban contemporary?

4. What are the important features of a focus group and how is it used in the music industry?

Chapter 2

Wholesale Distribution

Learning Objectives

After studying this chapter you should be able to do the following:

1. Define distribution

2. Define retail and wholesale

3. Describe the record distribution process

4. Define rack jobber and one stops

5. Describe independent distribution

6. Describe the structure, staffing and functions of a record distribution company

History of Record Distribution

Proper distribution is the most critical element in any record company's attempt to introduce a product and sustain sales once a project proves successful. Over the past nine decades, distribution of recorded products has worked through many stages. The first figures available (see Chart 2-1) showing total industry sales are for the year 1921 when sales reached just over $1,000,000. For a number of years after that, sales either dropped or were stagnant. In the mid 1930s, the industry almost perished. However, a few companies persisted, the Big Bands came into prominence, and sales started to edge upward. Innovations in recording techniques and sound quality certainly helped. The next surges came with the advent of long play and 45 RPM, high fidelity and stereo. Even so, the growth was nominal considering the economic explosion happening in so many other industries after World War II. It was not until 1967 that the music business reached the billion dollar plateau.

At the outset, records were distributed by organizations that handled a variety of products. After World War II into the early 1960s just about all prerecorded products —in those days primarily 78 RPM discs—were sold to consumers through a handful of small, independent record stores or in the record departments of major department stores. The companies that wholesaled record players, TV sets, and other products in that family of home entertainment products could handle the distribution process since they had experience in selling this type of account with most of their other products. These distributors also warehoused the record product for each geographical area.

Even then, and in those days the industry was still really quite small, radio airplay played a key role in building a record hit. Record companies had to employ large groups of "field representatives" and "promotion people" whose jobs were to create a demand from consumers via airplay and marketing at retail. The responsibility of promotion remains pretty much the same today as it was then, and most mainstream recorded products must still have heavy exposure on radio. Today, however, there are many other responsibilities delegated to promotion people as they work with their label marketing people to create a demand. In the past, the field representatives were responsible for assuring complete attention to each project by the distributor. They also let the record stores and department stores know what was happening and what they should be sure to stock. Field representatives made frequent contact with the retailers. The distributor, in those days, had no real stake in the product except as a channel to retailers.

Since the volume generated by records was quite small in comparison to that coming from a burgeoning television set market, and all the other "big ticket" home products handled by distributors, it was difficult to keep people focused on record product. The marketing of records was not easily understood by people and organiza-

Chart 2-1
Manufacturers' Dollar Shipments of Phonographic Records
Manufacturers' Dollar Shipments of Phonographic Records 1921–1966 (in millions)

Year	Dollars	Year	Dollars	Year	Dollars	Year	Dollars	Year	Dollars	Year	Dollars	Year	Dollars
1921	$105.6	1928	$72.6	1935	$ 8.8	1942	$ 55.0	1949	$173.0	1956	$377.0	1963	$698.0
1922	92.4	1929	74.8	1936	11.0	1943	66.0	1950	189.0	1957	460.0	1964	758.0
1923	79.2	1930	46.2	1937	13.2	1944	66.0	1951	199.0	1958	511.0	1965	862.0
1924	68.2	1931	17.6	1938	26.4	1945	109.0	1952	214.0	1959	603.0	1966	959.0
1925	59.4	1932	11.0	1939	44.0	1946	218.0	1953	219.0	1960	600.0		
1926	70.4	1933	5.5	1940	48.4	1947	224.0	1954	213.0	1961	640.0		
1927	70.4	1934	6.6	1941	50.6	1948	189.0	1955	277.0	1962	687.0		

* First year in which RIAA began reporting unit as well as dollar shipments figures, and providing a breakdown between shipments of singles and LPs.

** Other tapes include quadraphonic and reel-to-reel.

Reprinted courtesy of RIAA.

Chart 2-1 (cont.)

Manufacturers' Dollar Shipments of Phonographic Records 1967–1982 (in millions)

Year	Singles Units	Singles Dollars	Disc Albums Units	Disc Albums Dollars	Total Discs Units	Total Discs Dollars	8-Track Cart. Units	8-Track Cart. Dollars	Cassettes Units	Cassettes Dollars	Other Tapes Units	Other Tapes Dollars	Total Tapes Units	Total Tapes Dollars	Grand Total Units	Grand Total Dollars
1967		$190.0		$1,246.0		$1,051.0		$ 60.0		$6.0		$56.0		$ 122.0		$1,173.0
1968						1,124.0		155.0		17.0		62.0		234.0		1,358.0
1969						1,170.0		300.0		75.0		41.0		416.0		1,586.0
1970						1,182.0		378.0		77.0		23.0		478.0		1,660.0
1971						1,251.0		385.0		96.0		12.0		493.0		1,744.0
1972						1,383.0		425.0		102.0		14.0		541.0		1,924.0
*1973	228.0		280.0		508.0	1,436.0	91.0	489.0	15.0	76.0	2.2	15.6	108.2	580.6	616.0	2,046.0
1974	204.0	194.0	276.0	1,256.0	480.0	1,550.0	96.7	549.2	15.3	87.2	1.9	13.3	113.9	650.2	539.9	2,200.2
1975	164.0	211.5	257.0	1,485.0	421.0	1,696.0	94.6	588.0	16.2	98.8	1.5	10.2	112.3	695.0	533.3	2,391.0
1976	190.0	245.1	273.0	1,663.0	463.0	1,908.0	106.1	678.2	21.8	145.7	0.7	5.1	128.6	829.0	591.6	2,737.0
1977	190.0	245.1	344.0	2,195.1	534.0	2,440.2	127.3	811.0	36.9	249.6	—	—	164.2	1,060.6	698.2	3,500.8
1978	190.0	260.3	341.3	2,473.3	531.3	2,733.6	133.6	948.0	61.3	449.8	—	—	194.9	1,397.8	726.2	4,131.4
1979	212.0	353.6	290.2	2,057.0	502.2	2,411.2	102.3	684.3	78.5	580.6	—	—	180.8	1,264.9	683.0	3,676.1
1980	157.0	250.0	308.0	2,200.0	465.0	2,450.0	85.0	527.0	99.0	705.0	—	—	184.0	1,232.0	649.0	3,682.0
1981	147.0	246.0	273.0	2,113.0	420.0	2,359.0	50.0	313.0	124.0	954.0	—	—	174.0	1,267.0	594.0	3,626.0
1982	137.2	283.0	241.5	1,894.0	378.7	2,177.0	13.7	30.0	183.2	1,379.0	—	—	196.9	1,415.0	575.6	3,592.0

Reprinted courtesy of RIAA.

tions that were used to the usual methods of moving products: announce it, advertise it, run it on sale, and the consumer will react. There was very little "feel" for the music and what it could produce in the way of sales volume. Thus, the field rep had a difficult and frustrating assignment.

Propelled by the technical advances in recording (high fidelity monaural) and new configurations to play it on (long playing records, 45 RPM records), the industry realized it had to greatly expand the locations where consumers could buy prerecorded products. About this time many entrepreneurs saw the potential of making hit records as well as the financial rewards associated with those hits, and many successful "independent" record labels were launched. These "independents" had no ties with the companies that had always wholesaled records, and there evolved a network of independent record distributors who had no other products to sell but records. Therefore they could concentrate all their energies and activities in the direction of exposing, promoting, and selling hit records.

The advent of larger retailers, some with multiple locations, subdistributors (rack jobbers and one stops) also meant that the distributors who had been wholesaling the product from the old established labels would have to start selling to organizations that were totally foreign to their traditional business. These "discount houses" as they were termed in those days, were making marked changes in the retail landscape. The record industry desperately needed more and more outlets to expose its product, and this new segment of retail was the perfect answer.

Many major record companies realized that to tap the potential of accounts that could buy large quantities of hit products and thus compete with the new smaller labels that were taking advantage of a new form of distribution, they would have to drop the structure currently in place and initiate company owned distribution. These organizations would create the demand via airplay and "in store" activities, and these same organizations would contact and sell the product to the accounts that either serviced the large mass merchandisers or the retailers who sold to the consumers.

One by one, with the then Columbia Records leading the way, major labels started distributing their own product. Many of the independent labels like Warner, Electra, and Atlantic grew so big that they were able to form a group and start their own distribution company. Meanwhile, the independent labels grew and the companies distributing their products became very successful. By the 1980s, some of the more successful independent labels were being distributed by companies that were largely owned by the independent labels as well as by the independent distributors. That started to change as these labels needed the financial stability major label distributing companies could provide. The independent labels became so large now that they too had to project, plan, and have an assured cash flow, even in the dry spells between hits.

As more and more labels looked for this type of financial umbrella, the distribution of prerecorded music was narrowed down to six major distributing organizations who were responsible for handling the lion's share of all the product sold in the United States. There are many small labels that have retained the independent distribution mode, and, according to a recent Billboard Survey, account for between 19% and 20% of the overall volume done through accounts. Not too many years ago, this figure was at 5% or less. But "rap" and other music forms have created success for small labels that prefer using independent distribution. However, the now four "majors" handle most of the labels, large and small, those specializing in a limited type of product as well as those going after the mass market. These four distribution giants, EMD, Universal, Sony-BMG, and WMG, handle a vast array of record labels which cover the whole spectrum of music available to consumers in prerecorded formats today. (See Appendix for partial lists of labels marketed by the major distributors.)

The large distribution companies are constantly making changes in structure to accommodate the ever changing organization of the major customers, the rack jobbers, retailers, and one stops. In 1996 and 1997, three of the then "Big Five" made structural adjustments while the others entered the "downsizing derby" that all business has adopted.

Major Distribution Structure and Staffing

All of the four distribution organizations listed above have large home office and field structures. Located in either New York or Los Angeles, these major distributors have many levels of management, both in the home office and out in the field. "The Field" means branch offices, sales offices, whatever you might want to call them, that are located around the country.

National

Looking first at the structure and staffing of the headquarters or home office, you will usually find the following executive positions at most major distribution companies:

President
Vice President
Vice President—Marketing VP (optional)
Director—Label Liaison
Director—Sales Administration
Director—Distribution

President, Vice President, VP Marketing

The activities of the President, Vice President, and Vice President of Marketing at a distributing company can be characterized as follows:

Managerial
Motivational
Informational
Developmental

Each of these, in turn, can be broken down into the following broad responsibilities:

Managerial

Develop company policies covering terms of sale, returns, and payment terms.
Determine, clarify priorities.
Allocate operational funds; monitor their use.
Allocate advertising funds; monitor their use.
Oversee field operations.
Work with distributed labels in planning marketing activities.
Maximize sales of all product.
Develop strategies to attain both long range and short range goals.
Attain and surpass the goals set by the overall business plan.
Assign quotas and goals.

Motivational

Provide branch organization with proper incentives to create and maximize sales.
Stimulate creativity.
Set goals.
Maintain high morale level.

Informational

Present proper company image to customers and industry.
Monitor and maintain link between branch organization and major customers.
Create new strategies to sustain health of the company.
Create strategies to aid the growth of the entire industry.
Maintain link with all distributed labels.
Provide all levels with data required to perform duties.
Analyze information received about competitive activities.

Keep company highly competitive.

Develop marketing strategies for each type of product distributed, for catalog programs and other sales opportunities.

Developmental

Evaluate people; identify those qualified for future promotion.

Train people for increased responsibility.

Identify people outside the organization who can contribute if openings arise.

Identify and correct problems rapidly.

Director—Label Liaison

As more and more small labels are opting for arrangements with major distribution companies to get their product to accounts and consumers, the job of the **Director —Label Liaison** takes on added importance. It is best to have just one channel for all the information that must be disseminated to the various levels in the distribution company.

The Director—Label Liaison is the main contact between distribution and everyone involved in any aspect of producing and marketing products at each of the labels that come under any major distribution umbrella.

This position must help with a label's initial setup so that it can be easily integrated into the distribution system. This entails first being certain that whatever computer capabilities they have are totally compatible and that the necessary software is in place. The **Label Liaison** must be certain that everyone also knows how to work with distribution.

On a continuing basis, **Label Liaison** will:

Schedule new and catalog releases.

Acquire advance music and distribute it to distribution people as well as to some key account buyers and marketing people.

Help labels formulate marketing plans that will coordinate with all other projects being handled at the distribution level.

Help labels prepare and produce advertising material, display material and marketing products.

Condition labels to set up records in front and inform distribution of how this is being done.

Prepare sales forecasts in concert with label executives and distribution representatives that will satisfy the needs of both.

Integrate sales programs (hits, catalog, restocking, midline, etc.) into overall distribution plans for all labels so that everyone can participate in these important selling events.

As the number of distributed labels grows, the coordination with distribution becomes increasingly more difficult. Timing, types of releases, and assurance of attention to product has to be handled very tactfully, but firmly. Getting the maximum attention for each label is the main objective.

Sales Administration

The **Sales Administration Department** and its director must coordinate daily interaction between the distribution company and all other departments within the record company. This means working with:

Marketing
Promotion
Advertising
Business Affairs
Legal
Human Resources
Purchasing
Information Systems
Scheduling
Public Affairs
Financial

This department provides administrative services, financial analysis and all reports. Information received by everyone in the field is supplied by Sales Administration. Programs, dating, and other sales tools are disseminated and monitored by Sales Administration, as are reports necessary to compensate everyone in the field.

Sales Administration also maintains account contact for pricing changes and special sales programs.

Distribution and Warehousing

The physical handling of orders, returns, and the product itself is done by the **Distribution/Warehousing** function. This department maintains the warehouses, accepts and processes all the orders, and ensures that the product gets to the accounts on time.

This function is becoming very automated as computerization takes over. This end of the business is not very glamorous. It deals with manufacturing the product (pressing or duplicating) and storing it, warehouse square footage, contract carriers and telecommunications. However, distribution must of course show a profit; this means utilizing new methods and systems that can help the bottom line.

Each distribution company has a different philosophy of how and where to establish shipping facilities; this aspect of the industry has been changing rapidly over the last few years. Some organizations ship everything to every account from one central location. Others want their warehouses to be "full line" and located in more than one geographical area. Some supply catalog products from a central location, while "hits" come from regional depots.

Most shipping is done by contract carriers (truck lines) who specialize is transporting prerecorded product.

Warehouse configuration is also dependent upon the distribution company. Some are in an alphanumeric order, others just fill empty slots as the product is released and manufactured, and the computer finds it when it is time to ship it.

Inventory control is highly critical. The life of an album can be very long, but also can be very short. Not having too much stock on hand when the recording slips from favor is a way you help show a profit.

The order service department accepts, inputs, and separates all orders. Some come from distribution sales people and others come directly from the accounts. As technology advances, so does this aspect of distribution. Use of facsimile machines and direct computer interfacing is quite widespread.

Over 50% of the "line items" in regular orders coming into the order service department of a major distribution company will be computer to computer. However, these orders are only about 20% of the dollar volume. Close to 30% of the orders and about 20% of the volume comes in via facsimile machines. The rest are from mail and phone orders.

Manufacturing and duplicating is also done differently by each company. Some have their own facilities, while others buy this service from outside contractors. Even the labels that have entered into distribution or joint venture agreements with major companies are free to buy their duplicating where they get the best deal.

Field

It takes a great many people to handle all the above responsibilities. It also takes a great many people in "the field" to handle and complete all the assignments being set out constantly. This is done through a Branch Office Structure.

The importance of the Branches cannot be overemphasized, because this is the group that will have to implement all the plans, support all the activity of marketing and promotion. In short, these people SELL THE PRODUCT. They deal with the accounts.

Sales Branches have their own personality. You do not see this in the dry organizational chart that covers every similar organization. In the music business, the sales organization must convey the ambiance of the record labels they represent. That feeling that they bring to the street is highly critical to their success and the success of the product they must sell. The volume required is substantial, and not all of it can be done with "hits."

Branches are usually located in major cities such as:

New York	Atlanta
Chicago	Dallas
Los Angeles	

While all companies have their own organizational charts and nomenclature for all the jobs in the field, what follows is a reasonable example of how most companies work. These are the job descriptions at a typical field office for Universal Music and Video Distribution.

National Assortment Rep
Reports to: Account Executive/SAE
Department: Sales (Field)

Job Summary:

Focus on the assortment and inventory of current priorities and handle all customer service aspects of the account.

Job Functions:

- Present BDS, SoundScan, media, and tour information along with analysis of how this might impact sales at the account
- Utilize information available through UMVD and the account's systems
- Responsible for the overall UMVD assortment and weeks of supply.
- Active knowledge of current priorities and best selling catalog
- Follow the customer's system information, rankings, and market share
- Communicate and manage ongoing discount programs
- Understand UMVD systems and procedures
- Advanced understanding of UMVD policies regarding terms of sale, return procedure, ongoing programs, invoicing, inventory management, etc . . .

Minimum Qualifications:

- Understanding of statistics, mathematical formulas, and customer service
- Attention to detail
- Strong product knowledge
- Excellent communication, presentation, and interpersonal skills
- Excellent analytical skills
- Excellent organizational skills
- Knowledge of BDS, SoundScan, and Legacy systems

Account Director/Team Leader
Reports to: VP of National Sales
Department: Sales (Field)

Job Summary

Director must work with all facets of UMVD (sales, marketing, e-commerce and finance) to develop critical sales, marketing and business plans. Person will lead, guide and direct a small team of sales and marketing reps who will handle specific sales & marketing roles related to specified account(s). Person must also manage excellent relationships with labels and customers, be able to hit sales objectives, and manage advertising and marketing funds.

Job Functions:

Account Director will manage entire business plan for specified high volume account(s), to include:

- Marketing strategies and planners
- Sales strategies and planners
- Business development plans
- Goals to sales volume
- Creation and implementation of third-party promotions, merchandising, brand awareness and advertising campaigns
- Implement sales driven promotions designed to develop new artists

Minimum Qualifications:

- Solid experience selling / marketing in high level environments with a track record of exceeding assigned quotas (at least 3-5 years experience).

- Outstanding presentation/group presentation skills using various media including presentation software.
- Excellent communication and relationship skills with all levels of executives, management, administrative staff
- Ability to troubleshoot and provide feedback, guidance and solutions for plans involving marketing, advertising and sales promotion.
- Proven knowledge of sales and marketing strategies and concepts
- Solid analytical skills, strong business acumen and result-oriented
- Ability to foster key accounts and develop new business
- Sales and budget forecasting experience and knowledge
- Inherent skills in good judgment, creativity, high energy and integrity.
- Some experience in managing people
- Some experience in the entertainment business

National Accounts Coordinator
Reports to: VP National Sales
Department: Sales (Field & Home Office)

Job Overview:

Administrative support to sales teams in the area of account support and service. NAC's are assigned to specific accounts.

Job Functions:

- Sales and Reporting Support:
  - a) Point person for new release reporting and information, to include solicitation materials, SoundScan, BDS, and Legacy
  - b) Report first day numbers and projected weekly sales
  - c) Distribute account weekly charts
- Customer Service:
  - a) Follow up on order, shipping, and backorder inquiries
  - b) Provide artwork
  - c) Provide merchandising materials
  - d) Manage promotional product orders
- Advertising Administration:
  - a) Follow up on getting authorizations into Fastrac

      b) Follow up on ensuring outstanding adv. Authorized is not missing from the system

      c) Provide necessary advertising reports to team

Note:

The Regional Marketing Coordinators will continue to distribute general SoundScan and BDS reports regionally and distribute to all marketing and sales teams. The NAC should only pull account team specific reports needed.

Senior Account Executive
Reports to: Vice President of National Sales
Department: Sales (Field)

Job Overview:

Senior Account Executives oversee all marketing, sales, and strategic initiatives to UMVD's largest volume accounts. Reporting directly to Home Office - SAE's have the highest profile and expectation of all sales positions. SAE's manage a team consisting of UMVD genre experts and/or administrative support.

Job Functions:

- Primary liaison between labels and account to create marketing plans and advertising strategies for new releases. Solicit new releases to account
- Communicate on-going label priorities and catalogue opportunities utilizing SoundScan, BDS, and publicity data and create action plans to maximize sales
- Lead account team, delegate tasks as appropriate
- Communicate and manage ongoing discount programs to account
- Oversee special promotional opportunities such as in-store appearances, 3rd party retail promotions, in-store merchandising promotions, etc
- Communicate account corporate announcements, stock fluctuations, changes to policy, etc to appropriate UMVD executives
- Analyze account weekly sales activity versus national activity. Create action plans to maintain optimum market share
- Oversee all advertising and marketing plans for UMVD titles

Minimum Qualifications:

- Ability to operate in a highly collaborative manner and work in pressure situations
- Excellent negotiating and people skills. Polished presentation skills
- Ability to craft and deliver executive-level presentations
- Advanced knowledge of UMVD policies regarding terms of sales, return procedures, ongoing programs, invoicing, pricing and inventory management
- Advanced utilization of BDS and SoundScan
- Superior knowledge of OrderLink, Legacy and Fastrac systems
- Solid understanding of retail fundamentals including inventory and systems management, open to buy, profit margins, etc.

Market Director
Reports to: Sr. VP Marketing and Sr. VP Sales
Department: Sales and Marketing (Field)

Job Summary:

Manage the activities of Sales and Marketing of the Regional staff to maximize sales and direct and implement marketing activities within the entire region.

Job Functions:

- Develop and train staff
- Maintain and enhance relationships with all accounts in the region (sold & non-sold as well as local and National)
- Nurture the ongoing relationship with all UMVD label partners, both local, Regional and National
- Communicate with same as above
- Monitor sales and stock levels, and implement activities to achieve sales and marketing goals, with the intent of maintaining and enforcing company policies
- Work with the sales and marketing staffs to identify and implement sales opportunities as well as opportunities for artist development across the region

- Communicate direction from Home Office to Sales and Marketing staffs to ensure proper focus in all areas with National direction. (Compliance checks, price checks, etc.)
- Analyze and discuss weekly SoundScan and BDS activity as it pertains to all Regional activity
- Conduct weekly meetings with Sales and Marketing staff to discuss Regional activities of touring artists, sales priorities and any opportunities to better expose our artists. Also, hold bi weekly or monthly meetings with label partner staff to discuss N/R as well as to ensure coverage on all priority items
- Communicate with Home Office
  a) Communicate with Sr. VP of Mktg and Sr. VP of Sales on trends of sales & marketing within the region
  b) Inform Home Office of competitive information, Account activity and any and all activity of local, regional and national accounts
  c) Communicate with Label liaisons on ADR activities and label direction

Marketing Assistant
Reports to: Market Director
Department: Marketing (Field)

Job Summary:

Responsible for P.O.P. maintenance, artist visibility, marketing staff administrative support, and assisting the Marketing Director in the planning and implementation of all events and marketing campaigns

- Assist ADR staff with special event coordination and kit mailings
- Create, maintain, and distribute BDS and SoundScan reports as needed
- The creation and allocation of custom flyers, pop, bin clips, "On tour" bin cards and local lifestyle events
- Provide feedback to ADR and MD regarding an artist promotion and visibility status from lifestyle accounts and Webmasters
- Work with staff members on ways to tap into alternate marketing resources through new media and new product affiliation
- Design promotion give-away, sample, and added value marketing tools

- Develop contest motifs and lifestyle account survey
- Compile & distribute field staff schedules and reports
- Distribution of Current & Key Tracking
- Create Weekly Visibility Check Sheet
- Research artboard availability for media planners
- Book Tower Visual Concepts Visibility
- Create New Release Street Sheet
- Create and allocate custom pop on a local level for visibility, flyers, advertising events, 3 × 3 artboards etc.
- Coordinate College Rep Activities
- Order P.O.P. for marketing staff for mailings out of the UMVD office or for direct shipment to accounts
- Compile and distribute promotion calendar
- Create and maintain complete database of retail, press, radio, demographic, genre, P.O.P., and publication information for region
- Weekly Artist & Artistry Focus Sheet
- Maintain Merchandising Room

Regional Market Coordinator
Reports to: Market Director
Department: Admin (Field)

Job Summary:

This is a Pivotal position in terms of importance to the region. RMCs are Responsible for the day-to-day administrative operations of the branch office as well as advertising coordination and office communication. They work closely with the Market Director.

Job Functions:

- Manage the day-to day operations of the regional office, supporting the sales staff
- Maintain office equipment and operation, including telephones, faxes, copiers, and repairs
- Primary liaison with UMVD home office administrative staff
- Supervise Mailroom Manager, Mailroom Clerk, and Office Assistant /Receptionist

- Communicate to regional staff office related information, sales meeting schedules, and any other pertinent issues regarding the staff
- Oversee all office related invoices for supplies, stationary, resident UPS, telephone invoices, and sales related functions
- Coordination of fixed assets with UMVD home office
- Coordinate and oversee advertising through Fastrac for sales staff
- Oversee Timekeeper
- Set up new employees and interns with work related needs
- Answer phones and assist Market Director
- Run various reports as needed

Minimum Qualifications:

- Excellent organizational skills and ability to manage multiple tasks
- Proficient in MS Excel, Word, and Outlook
- Knowledge/training in Legacy, JD Edwards, Fastrac, and Adtrac
- Excellent verbal and written communication skills
- Ability to prioritize and meet deadlines

Mailroom
Reports to: Regional Market Coordinator
Department: Admin (Field)

Job Summary:

The Mailroom Clerk is in charge of sending and receiving all mail through UPS and US mail for UMVD and keeping the backroom functioning.

Job Functions:

- Receive and distribute all incoming mail to the proper w/in the region—label and UMVD personnel
- Maintain Office Depot account and order supplies to keep the region fully stocked
- Order all current P.O.P. and maintain a current list of P.O.P. when it arrives
- Maintain shipping computer so that all addresses and account lists are current

- Answer phones when Office Assistant is unavailable
- Assist FMRs and ADRs coordinate mail-outs for their accounts
- Mail new release books in the weekly mailer
- Package overnight pouches to the various regions/labels

Minimum Qualifications:

- High level of organization
- Ability to prioritize
- High customer service/people skills
- Ability to move and/or carry somewhat heavy items

Office Assistant
Reports to: Regional Market Coordinator
Department: Admin (Field)

Job Summary:

Office Assistant/Receptionist is an entry-level position that will allow the right person to learn the basics of music sales, marketing, and distribution. This on-the-job learning position may be a "stepping stone" for possible future advancement to FMR, ADR and/or other responsibilities in the regional office for the right candidate.

Job Functions:

- Receptionist for incoming calls and visitors to the office
- General clerical assistance, including typing and filing
- Responsible for running and distributing SoundScan and BDS reports weekly
- Maintain and track various operating budgets
- Track vacation and other personnel information
- Act as support to Marketing staff and Marketing Manager
- Support sales staff and Regional Coordinator
- Special event coordination/RSVP list maintenance
- Order office supplies and maintain inventory

Minimum Qualifications:

- Excellent communication and people skills
- Must be extremely organized and have the ability to multitask effectively

- Knowledge/training SoundScan and BDS systems
- Proficient in MS Excel, Word, and Outlook
- Fluent in Spanish (varies with region)

Office Assistant "First Things to Do" list

- Unlock front door for the day and check/disarm office alarm system
- Ensure that the phone is transferred over from any "night" message button that you would have on to take calls after normal business hours
- Familiarize yourself with the extension list and switchboard
- Learn all Label and Distribution staff
- Handle all incoming calls and distribute accordingly
- Check voice mail for both office general mailbox and self
- Make sure PC is working properly
- Familiarize yourself with Outlook
- Familiarize yourself with the mailroom and everyone's inbox
- Check faxes and distribute accordingly
- Meet with Regional Market Coordinator
- Go over bill coding and filing with RMC
- Change back-up tape
- End of the day; make sure fax/Xerox machines have paper. Put the phone on "night," lock the front door

Sales Rep
Reports to: Market Director
Department: Sales (Field)

Job Summary:

A Sales Representative will generally manage a diverse customer base, which may include customers with different classifications including retail and wholesale components.

Job Functions:

- Gather competitive information for dissemination to management keeping company up-to-date of new developments or strategies

- Be aware of trends that develop, for example in clubs, retail, radio, schools, etc . . .
- Capitalize on in-store opportunities in terms of positioning, displays, contests or local promotions
- Responsible for presentation and set-up of new releases to accounts
- The ability to increase sales of newer releases as well as Catalog by providing the latest marketing, promotion, Radio & TV, analysis
- Gain a working knowledge and understanding of the customer's business and its needs
- Coordinate and manage discount programs and finding new ways of marketing and selling our JumpSTART titles
- Present special promotional opportunities I.E. artist in-store appearances, consumer contests, sales contests, web tags, e-mail Blasts, etc . . .
- Understand UMVD customer service systems and procedures
- Advanced understanding of the order entry process
- Advanced knowledge of UMVD polices regarding terms of sales, return procedure, ongoing programs, invoicing, pricing, and inventory management

Minimum Qualifications:

- Self starter, motivated to work on your own without direct supervision
- Strong Relationship Skills "People Skills"
- Strong marketing skills
- Strong Sales Skills
- Excellent negotiation skills
- Excellent communication and analytical skills
- Knowledge of BDS, SoundScan, Legacy, and Fastrac systems, Excel, Retail Detail, UMVD.Com, UMVD Tools, E-Gratis, OrderLink and be internet savvy
- Advanced product knowledge
- Excellent organizational skills
- Ability to troubleshoot and provide feedback to our Label partners for plans involving marketing, advertising and sales promotion

- Solid understanding of retail fundamentals including inventory and systems management, open to buy, profit margins, etc. Be able to relate to and understand diversity and philosophic differences between various customer types

Sales Rep-Catalog
Reports to: Market Director
Department: Sales (Field)

Job Functions:

- Present new catalog titles, reissues, Hip-O, and UTV product to accounts with all relevant information pertaining to each release
- Communicate and manage deals, discount programs, and price changes to accounts
- Follow customer charts and national catalog charts
- Be prepared for any opportunity that will affect catalog sales, such as catalog artists on tour, soundtracks new to the rental market or with a current sequel, television specials, VH-I/MTV programming, etc . . .
- Provide labels with accurate New Release planners detailing the costs of account programs and potential orders while working within budget parameters set by label
- Work with Catalog Group Regional on setting up select releases such as new reissues, Hip-O, UTV and compilations
- Present special promotional catalog opportunities such as value adds, "theme" events, and consumer/label contests
- Target customers' area of potential growth I.E. midline, frontline, or genre
- Prepare quarterly account planners for top 1-3 customer base
- Look for new business opportunities beyond traditional customer base

Sales Rep Classics/Jazz
Reports to: Market Director
Department: Sales (Field)

Job Summary:

Deal with a diverse group of accounts and be a member of the sales teams for those accounts. Work closely with "team leader" for each account. Assist regional staff and sales teams to sell in and understand the repertoire and artists

Job Functions:

- Presentation of new releases
- Priority title and catalog maintenance
- Responsible for titles in the classical, jazz, new age, Broadway, and other genres
- Active knowledge of current priorities and best-selling catalog
- Communicate and manage ongoing discount programs
- Set up marketing plans for key new releases at accounts
- Secure co-op funding from the labels to maximize exposure
- Responsible for administration co-op budgets
- Keep label priorities and catalog titles present in accounts' marketing plans
- Organize special promotional opportunities such as artist in-stores, consumer contests, etc . . .
- Understand UMVD customer service systems and procedures
- Understand accounts' infrastructure including distribution systems, shipping and packaging requirements
- Advanced understanding of the order entry process
- Advanced knowledge of UMVD policies regarding terms of sale, return procedures, ongoing programs, invoicing, pricing, and inventory management

National Tour Coordinator
Reports to: Market Director
Department: Admin (Field)

Job Summary:

Purchase tickets nationally for assigned label groups as well as communicate to the field all information pertaining to ticket buys and ticket distribution.

Job Functions:

- Work closely with each label regarding ticket buys for artist tours (nationally)
- Call promoters to hold tickets, find out prices and their payment requirements

- Input promoter information, ticket price and payment information into ticket buy system for routing to all label departments
- Review approved ticket grid, contact promoters to release any extra tickets and process credit card purchases by fax to promoters
- Follow up with promoters and make sure tickets are sent out on a timely basis
- Send tickets out to label/field and provide emails to them with tracking information
- Update national tour spreadsheet each Friday with current tour dates for each artist
- Communicate to field all approved ticket quantities they will receive
- Reconcile monthly MasterCard statement matching label CTS numbers to individual charges

National Tour Coordinator
"First Things to Do" list

- Call your label contacts that will funnel all ticket buy communication to you from the label
- Set up all the email addresses for each promoter in your personal address book
- Set up group codes for:
  - a) Labels
  - b) UMVD label groups
  - c) Promoters
- Email the UMVD field and your promoter database to introduce yourself and what labels you will be doing ticket buys for
- Make plenty of room in your file drawers to make files for each tour that you will be buying tickets for. You will need to have them close by because you will be in each file several times a day when promoters are calling or emailing you back
- Learn how to place a hold on tickets with promoters, what information they need from you, if they have a deadline, etc. Be sure to have good notes if you place a hold by phone rather than email
- Update any promoter information in your database that may have changed. Ask promoters to make sure you are notified of any personnel changes—very important to keep updated!

- Log into the ticket buy system online and take some time to review how it works
- Familiarize yourself with downloading tour updates from the Music Mart site
- Put all of your ADR, RMC and label contacts (name, address, phone, email, etc) into a 3-ring binder so that you have it handy when you need to find out who covers what markets, who to send tickets to and where they want them sent to. Some of the ADR's and promotion people work from their home and that is where they want to receive their tickets

Artist Development
Rep Reports to: Market Director
Department: Marketing (Field)

Job Summary:

An ADR is responsible for marketing artists at retail and lifestyle accounts, also as an information source for the sales department and label

Job Functions:

- Build working relationships with the accounts
- Understand and build relationships with the coalitions (LINCS, CIMS, UIMRA, etc . . .)
- Understand accounts in territory (which ones report to trades, SoundScan, etc . . .)
- Knowledge of each priority project (tour dates, video play, airplay, competitive artists, etc . . .)
- Responsible for merchandising venues
- Set up advertising and/or promotions to create visibility around tour dates
- Provide sales staff with information regarding priority releases (BDS, tour, video, sales, etc . . .)
- Provide sales staff with account information (personnel changes, program changes, store openings and closings, etc . . .)
- Generate and maintain awareness and enthusiasm for priority artists within the branch
- Keep accounts aware of current tour information and ticket availability

Minimum Qualifications:

- Excellent written, presentation, and communication skills
- Excellent organizational skills
- Knowledge of Legacy, BDS, and SoundScan systems
- Advanced product knowledge
- Excellent analytical skills

Artist Development Rep
"First Things to Do" list

When you become an Artist Development Rep here at Universal Music Video and Distribution, you become the focal point of our developing artists.

Territory

- Know all the DMAs in your region, and any obvious music trends in each (i.e. "Cash Money" artists break from the South, hard rock sells great in Phoenix)
- Know the radio stations for each genre in every DMA. Learn which stations are most likely to affect sales at your stores
- Know the venues in each market, and make note of the promoters for each venue/city as you interact with them. They'll be great help down the line

Account Knowledge: Indie, chain, lifestyle

- This includes building working relationships with the District Managers, Assistant Managers, General Managers, buyers, etc.
- Understand and build relationships with the coalitions (i.e. LINCS, CIMS, UIMRA), and know which accounts belong to which organizations
- Know which stores are SoundScan, and each store's approximate SoundScan "weight"
- Know which retailers report to trades (i.e. Album Network, CMJ)
- Know which genres are appropriate at each account
- Learn where each key account buys their UMVD product

- Understand the basic advertising opportunities at the different independents (listening station programs, pricing & positioning, print, etc.), since you will be asked to set up advertising for a variety of records with varying budgets. Monitor the sales during the period in which you advertise a record, so you will be able to gauge the effectiveness of the program for future records

- Call key stores weekly for tracking on your priority records (i.e. call on Wednesday for first day tracking of a priority record, and call on Monday to get first week/regular weekly sales

Regional Office

- Meet your counterparts; FMR's, Sales Reps and Mailroom personnel. Remember you are part of a team and you must all be on the same page. Make time to reach out to your Home Office label liaison on a regular basis

Label and Regional Contacts

- Get to know them, since you will be the point person between the record label and Distribution Company. Building trust with your label will make your job more productive

Artist/Release Knowledge (we won't call this "Product Knowledge")

Try to keep a list of all the various things happening with each priority project you work (tour dates in your market, video play, airplay, past releases, sales on past releases, competitive artists, etc.) This will help you immensely when it comes time to share key information with the sales reps or accounts. It sounds basic, but when an artist comes to town, don't just go watch their show. Arrive at the venue performing before sound-check, and take time to introduce yourself to the band and their tour manager. This is an incredible boost to artist/label relations. It also gives you new insight into the artists you're trying to help, and it will provide an incredible resource when it comes time for an in-store or other event down the line. Whenever possible, bring retailers to meet the band (schedule a meet & greet with the label before the show, and follow up with the tour manager when you meet him/her in person). Know where each artist is from—they will likely have a fan base in their hometown, which is a great source to tap into wherever possible.

Marketing Tools

Learn the following computer programs: Publisher; PowerPoint; and Photoshop. In this position you will constantly be creating awareness material (bin cards, counter bin tops, laminates, and fliers) on your current priorities.

Sales Tools

BDS (radio analysis) and SoundScan (sales analysis) are two of your most powerful tools. Learn to pull reports and analyze the information they provide, including: Correlating airplay to sales in a market, monitoring how your promotions impact sales in the region, watching how an artist's tour affect sales in each market as it moves across the country to gauge how it will impact your market, check store strata reports to help plan in which accounts—indie, chain, mass merch—to set up a promotion. SoundScan has an incredible array of specific reports you can pull to help analyze the sales, or lack of sales, in your market. BDS includes a feature to track the time periods in which a song is played ("Day parts"). Understand sales and deal information. This is key information to share with sales reps when talking about your records, and is also important to accounts that buy direct from UMVD. Price is a huge tool—we have several very competitive price points for developing artists (Listen Up, Combustion, and the Launch Pad program), and this information is paramount for stores.

Reports

Get with your Marketing Manager or fellow ADRs to discuss report structure: show wrap-ups, in-store wrap-ups, planners (media/marketing), snapshots (weekly or bi-weekly), and templates for first day numbers. After a few weeks in your new position you should create an ADR one sheet with the following info: key video & radio adds, account P&P programs, tour dates, and publicity. Focus on titles that are on the current sales release book, ADC titles, and regional break-out titles.

College and Lifestyle Rep
Reports to: Market Director
Department: Marketing (Field)

Job Summary:

Responsible for marketing priority developing artists in assigned college market and serving as an informational source for college campus and general vicinity

Job Functions:

- Create awareness on campus and within local demographic by utilizing label-supplied tools (point of purchase materials, samplers, added value items, etc . . .) and creating various tools (flyers, bin cards, etc . . .)
- Work within the guidelines provided by the National Director and Marketing Manager with the implementation of promotions, listening parties, and other related events
- Monitor SoundScan numbers to determine effectiveness of promotions
- Establish relationships with activity committees, on-campus clubs, and lifestyle accounts to secure outlets for artist marketing ideas and programs
- Keep up-to-date of priority artists' tour itineraries and potential marketing opportunities
- Secure data base on lifestyle accounts for promotional opportunities
- Work in conjunction with ADR and/or Sales Rep to tie in retail promotions, coupons, and tags with retail accounts
- Assist resident Sales Reps with in-stores, merchandising venues, and store promotions

Minimum Qualifications:

- Excellent communication and people skills
- Excellent organizational skills
- Excellent written and communication skills
- Knowledge of Legacy, BDS, and SoundScan systems
- Strong marketing skills

Divisional Country Marketing Manager
Reports to: Market Director
Department: Marketing (Field)

Job Summary:

Responsible for maximizing the sales of all Universal Country products, via sales and marketing campaigns-internally AND with accounts

Job Functions:

- Responsible for presentation of new releases
- Participate in the creation of marketing plans
- Knowledge of each priority project (tour dates, video play, airplay, competitive artists, etc . . .)
- Provide sales staff with information regarding priority releases (BDS, tour, video, sales, etc . . .)
- Work with Marketing Managers to implement merchandising priorities and stock checks by the FMR's Build relationships with regional account personnel
- Maintain adequate stock levels and merchandising
- Create campaigns around key tour dates and/or strong airplay markets
- Pursue marketing opportunities at consumer focused event outlets (county fairs, bars, western wear shops, etc . . .)
- Coordinate artist visits and in-stores with label and artist management
- Distribute weekly recap of all activity on priority product
- Control and manage an advertising budget
- Create new release solicitation sheets
- Coordinate the inclusion of country priorities at account conventions

Minimum Qualifications:

- Sales and marketing experience
- Advanced product and systems knowledge
- Ability to work in pressure situations
- Understanding of BDS, SoundScan, Legacy, and Fastrac systems
- Excellent negotiating, communication, and analytical skills

Field Marketing Rep
Reports to: Market Director
Department: Marketing (Field)

Job Overview:

UMVD FMR's are primarily responsible for merchandising artists at music retail.

Job Functions:

- Achieve maximum in store merchandising visibility on priority projects
- Upload photos of displays to UMVD website
- Develop and maintain relationships with retail locations within their assigned DMA's
- Coordinate kit mailings via Lee Marketing to accounts outside of reachable DMA's
- Educate retail personnel about activity on assigned priorities
- Achieve maximum merchandising opportunities for product of touring artists, at retail and venues
- Merchandise venues for touring artists
- Monitor competitive retail merchandising opportunities and ideas and report back to Marketing Director and Director of Visual Merchandising in UMVD home office
- Participate in marketing activities at the retail level to increase artist awareness and visibility on assigned priorities
- Manage merchandising material inventory
- Provide feedback on most useful merchandising tools to Director of Visual Merchandising
- Work in conjunction with ADR's and College Reps on priority initiatives per Marketing Director's instructions

Minimum Qualifications:

- Enthusiasm and love for music
- Excellent follow through
- Ability to manage constantly changing label priorities with a positive and aggressive outlook
- Advanced product knowledge
- Ability to adapt to changing priorities
- Ability to complete all requested projects in a timely manner
- Ability to creatively utilize merchandising space with provided tools
- Knowledge of computer graphics programs (i.e. Photoshop) to create special items locally

- Aggressive and outgoing personality to do "cold calls" at lifestyle accounts

Field Marketing Rep
"First Things to Do" List

- Ensure your desktop/laptop are fully operational
- Ensure e-mail is operating and that you are on the FMR group code
- Ensure that you have access to upload photos onto the Tools website
- Obtain your retail account list
- Obtain maps and learn your way around your territory
- Obtain a digital camera
- Obtain supplies — staple gun, staples, tape gun
- Reach out to key retail stores to begin building relationships
- Organize your office/cubical
- Ensure proper tools are available — P.O.P., promos, chart checks, etc.
- Familiarize yourself with your regional office
- Meet with your Market Director
- Learn your FMR priorities
- Visit stores with one of your FMR counterparts
- Learn the types of marketing opportunities available at your accounts
- Learn your way around UMVD Tools/B2B site/Retail Detail
- Learn your regions DMAs and Sub DMAs
- Learn the formats of your region's radio stations

In addition to the list above, the following applies to resident FMR's:

- Designate a specific work space within your residence — enough room for your computer, docking station, printer, etc.
- Organize your promos and P.O.P.
- Obtain the necessary phone line, cable modem and fax line through Home Office
- Contact Home Office about UPN to access e-mail
- Contact your Regional Coordinator to get set up with UPS service at your residence

- Locate the nearest UPS drop off center (Staples, Office Depot, Office Max)
- Obtain a storage unit (if one is approved by your Regional Director)

When you become a Field Marketing Representative at Universal Music and Video Distribution, you become the liaison between our label groups and our retail accounts.

Territory

- Know all the DMAs in your region, and any obvious music trends in each
- Know the radio stations for each genre in every DMA
- Become familiar with your accounts' customer bases and what titles will sell at different locations
- Know the venues in your market

Account Knowledge

- Build relationships with District Managers, General Managers, Assistants, buyers, etc. These relationships will assist in obtaining maximum retail merchandising space, securing promotions and achieving the largest sale and visibility market share for UMVD
- Know which genres are appropriate at each account
- Learn where each account gets their product from and be aware of lead times to fill stock requirements for advertising or tour dates
- Learn the types of marketing opportunities that are available at each of your accounts (discretionary listening stations, custom boards, light boxes, etc.)

So obviously it takes quite a staff to cover all the activities necessary to breaking and selling product. What has just been outlined is the type of staff utilized by Universal Music and Video Distribution.

Independent Distribution Companies

As the music industry evolved, wholesale distribution went from companies that sold many types of products, not just records, to a large number of companies that specialized in marketing recorded products only as independent distribution organizations, to what we have today with five major distribution companies all tied directly into major record labels. However, this arrangement does not cover 100% of the product sold to retailers, rack jobbers and one stops, the organizations that put it before the consumers. There are still independent distributors selling small, specialty labels to the retailers, racks and one stops. There are literally hundreds of small, and even some fairly large labels, that are marketed through a network of independent distributors. These distributors are not large entities, are not tied into major corporations, and with some types of products, are actually closer to what it takes to get the product exposed.

Recently, even the major distributors have realized this. Thus, even if they have distribution rights, or are in joint ventures to produce and distribute labels that specialize in emerging music forms, alternative products, or other targeted markets, they are joining forces with independent distributors to promote and sell these innovative labels.

Most independent distributors have a better "feel" for this type of product. They can deal with small retailers and specialty retailers better than the majors. They know where these outlets are, and they know the people who own and run them. Usually, when someone owns and runs a single outlet, this person is really into music, really pays attention to what is emerging, and wants to be in on the start of something new. These "record freaks" play a big part in bringing new ideas before the consumer.

The "indies," as they are called, have a history of taking this type of record label, or experimental product, and getting it marketed well enough for it to enter the mainstream of today's tastes. Their whole history, even when they handled some of today's major labels when they were in their infancy, has been to "break" unknown acts on unknown labels. But, as we have seen, once those unknown acts and unknown labels became big sellers, the economics of the industry forced them to the major distribution structures.

However, with recent developments, the independent distributors can once again play a major role in starting product and thus being able to reap the rewards of that initial sales surge. Meanwhile, they are still in a position to break products they distribute exclusively and do not have to share with the major distributors.

In many instances when labels do break acts through their independent distributors, they immediately try to arrange distribution with the major companies. Once again, economics motivates that move.

The Independent Distributors live in a highly competitive world. There are no regional boundaries limiting their scope of operation as there are with the four major distributors. In an effort to solidify their position and remain competitive, many independent distributors are trying to become national companies with branches of their own, or by combining with others in similar circumstances in a distribution network.

Exercises

1. In just a few short years, the share of products being sold through independent distributors has grown rapidly (from about 5% of the total to almost 20%). Why has this happened?

2. When a record company refers to "the field," what segment of the organization is it referring to?

3. If you ran a record company, how would you identify future trends in music before your competitors?

4. The rash of mergers among retail chains in the music industry has changed the way companies are staffed. What adjustments have had to be made?

5. What was the most important factor in forcing the major record companies into company owned distribution? Why did so many successful independent labels abandon their own independent distribution to sign on with the majors?

Chapter 3
Marketing Organization

Learning Objectives

After studying this chapter you should be able to:

1. Understand how music marketing differs from marketing other products

2. Define marketing management

3. Outline and identify functions of a typical music marketing department

4. Define marketing concept and strategic planning

5. Describe the strategy employed by a record label in the release of a musical product

Structure and Development of the Recording Industry

Marketing organizations should identify and satisfy consumer needs through an integrated effort. Once a record company has made a commitment to release a musical product, a strategy must be employed that will eventually touch the music consumer. This strategy involves several departments in a music marketing organization. The process by which recorded music is brought to the consumer embraces packaging, merchandising, product management, advertising, distribution, sales, promotion, publicity, label, distribution marketing and market research.

Marketing Management

Marketing management occurs in the organizational structure because each department must set objectives and develop strategies for reaching the music consumer.

Marketing management involves the analysis, planning, implementation, and control of programs to create, build and maintain beneficial exchanges and relationships with target markets for the purpose of achieving organizational objectives. Each position in a music marketing organization is well defined and carries with it a set of responsibilities.

Marketing Concept

The marketing concept holds that the key to achieving organizational goals consists of determining the needs and wants of the target markets so as to deliver the desired satisfactions effectively and efficiently. The only hope a record company has of attracting attention with a new record is to conceive a unique marketing plan.

The actual structure of a marketing plan depends upon the department creating it. It must mesh with the overall marketing plan created by product management.

Once a record company, production company or group of investors has made a commitment to release an album or video, a marketing strategy must be prepared that covers all aspects of the exposure, promotion, and selling of the product. This requires the involvement of large departments within the record company and the record label, groups of people within the artists' management company, and even the artists themselves.

What follows is an overview of all the activities and pieces that must come together for a successful music marketing strategy.

Much of the activity planned depends upon the type of music being performed, the particular target audience, and very important, whether you are dealing with a new artist or an established artist. As noted, the recording business devotes the most time, money, and activity toward "breaking" new artists or "baby acts," as they are termed. The initial investment in establishing new artists can be very costly, but the return on that investment can be awesome, especially when you consider the contractual arrangements usually negotiated with new acts as opposed to those negotiated with major, established artists.

The major impetus behind new artist development is the buying public. Consumers' tastes change rapidly, and their allegiance moves so quickly that the recording world must constantly offer new types of music, faces, beats, and combinations. This can be extremely costly as record companies and artists attempt to predict the trends. But, this is also one of the aspects that adds not only to the excitement of the industry, but also to the monetary potential when the predictions are on target. While most major artists take much longer to develop star status than is generally realized by their fans, they can become very profitable artists for the record company in a comparatively short period of time. Part of that is due to a record's ability to "break" rapidly and sell large quantities in a reasonably short time. However, most of the profit is a result of the contracts usually given new artists with lower royalty rates and stipulations about who is responsible for "recoupable" costs. "Recoupable" costs can include marketing, tour support, studio and engineering time, plus some others.

There are some constants, no matter the type of act, type of music, past history, or target audience. There are some elements of the marketing strategy that must come into play with every release, activities or departments that must successfully complete their assignments for each project. Even if everyone completes assignments as expected, the music has to make the public react. Record companies allocate tremendous sums to ensure that the potential target market hears or sees the album or video often enough to have it make an indelible impact on their mind, an impact that can translate into a purchase. This aspect of why people buy recorded products cannot be emphasized enough. Even when everyone does his/her job perfectly and the exposure is tremendous, a profitable project is still not guaranteed. One of the saddest terms in the music industry is: "turntable hit." Record companies recoup nothing from tremendous airplay until this is translated into sales. So in the final analysis, the public still makes the final impact on the profit and loss statement.

The key is making sure the public does hear or see the product over and over again. Audio releases must be heard and video releases, seen and heard. Once that type of exposure has been achieved, the traditional "pipelines" must be filled. They include:

RETAIL RECORD STORES—These include large and small chains of stores with outlets all over a region or all over the country, as well as individually owned stores, usually referred to as "mom and pop" stores, and a type of outlet that is growing rapidly, known as "alternative stores." The most recent growth is with large, national electronics and appliance stores and superstores handling recorded products (audio and video), computer software and books.

RACK JOBBERS—Service organizations that supply recorded products as well as expertise to large discount operations, catalog houses, and other mass merchandisers.

ONE STOPS—Companies that sell to all types of retailers, allowing them to bypass the usual distributors when a specialized product is required, or the product is needed very quickly.

CLUBS, MAIL ORDER, PREMIUM SALES—A great deal of product manages to be sold through these activities. But they have little or no impact on "breaking" an album or recording. These activities merely use the success of all the other marketing activity to generate additional sales volume.

Since most album purchases are done on impulse it requires a large number of departments and many, many people to make the public aware of a recording and, of far greater importance, to make sure the consumer can buy it easily. These are the most commonly utilized groups that make it all happen:

> *Product Management.* The person or persons assigned an act by the record company releasing the product. This entity is responsible for devising a detailed plan of all activity necessary for at least the first 90 days of release with contingency plans for longer should sales and airplay warrant. The plan thus devised gives each department particular assignments.

> *Label Marketing.* Field activity by label representatives to steer all activities on behalf of the product in every market. This group coordinates with distribution as each ingredient of the plan comes due for implementation.

> *Promotion.* Radio and Club Airplay and Video Programming responsibilities are assigned and monitored. This remains the best way to expose the product to the most people in the shortest period of time.

> *Publicity.* This activity has taken on much added importance as the number of publications and avenues for TV exposure has grown. The market for recorded products is increasingly "celebrity conscious," and thus publications and television shows that exploit this are becoming more and more popular.

> *Distribution Marketing.* The activity required from a distribution company to sell and expose the album. Done in concert with all the other departments charged with a portion of the plan.

> *Market Research.* Backup information to guide each move as the album or video develops play and sales. This is provided by the distribution network as well as the label representatives.

Financial. Budgeting and allocation of funds to support all activity directed at establishing the product in the minds of consumers.

Each activity has its budget, a mandate to perform its job according to a schedule and a staff of experienced people. All have the resources of Market Research and can call on the artists' cooperation and participation. Everyone is dependent on airplay or MTV and MTV-like exposure; all depend on distribution and sales getting complete coverage.

Each department or group has a full agenda and there are a number of marketing ploys that can be utilized by each of them. A partial list of the "gimmicks" that can be put into play include:

Bios. Biographies of the act or artist with backgrounds, previous successes, insights into the music—in short, the rationale behind releasing this particular piece of product.

Press Kits. Contain the bios, pictures and information on all previous activity. They are a starting point for publicity and any other type of exposure or awareness.

Brochures. When budgets allow, these are a slicker, more exciting version of the press kit or bio. In some cases can become part of a display later on.

Mailers. Can be utilized before or after release. Traditional direct mail approach. "Teasers" can be distributed this way.

Flyers. Different from mailers in that certain types of accounts (wholesale primarily) solicit their customers on a regular basis via this method. Once again, builds awareness among those who bring the product to the consumer.

Radio and TV Activity. Airplay, of course, remains the major thrust with radio, and in addition to the traditional activity surrounding acquiring airplay, there are other approaches that can be used. Contests highlight the recording for listeners.

The most natural activity is time purchases on the broadcast outlets to advertise the product. Radio and TV alone can bring the sound and picture, which is what you are promoting, to the consumer.

Print Advertising. Once some activity has been generated, print advises the consumer where to buy and what the price will be.

Incentives. Merchandise, apparel, small, inexpensive items that are termed "tchotches" in the industry, and that relate to an artist, group, or song title can be given to people within the industry to raise their awareness. Some can be distributed to potential consumers in any

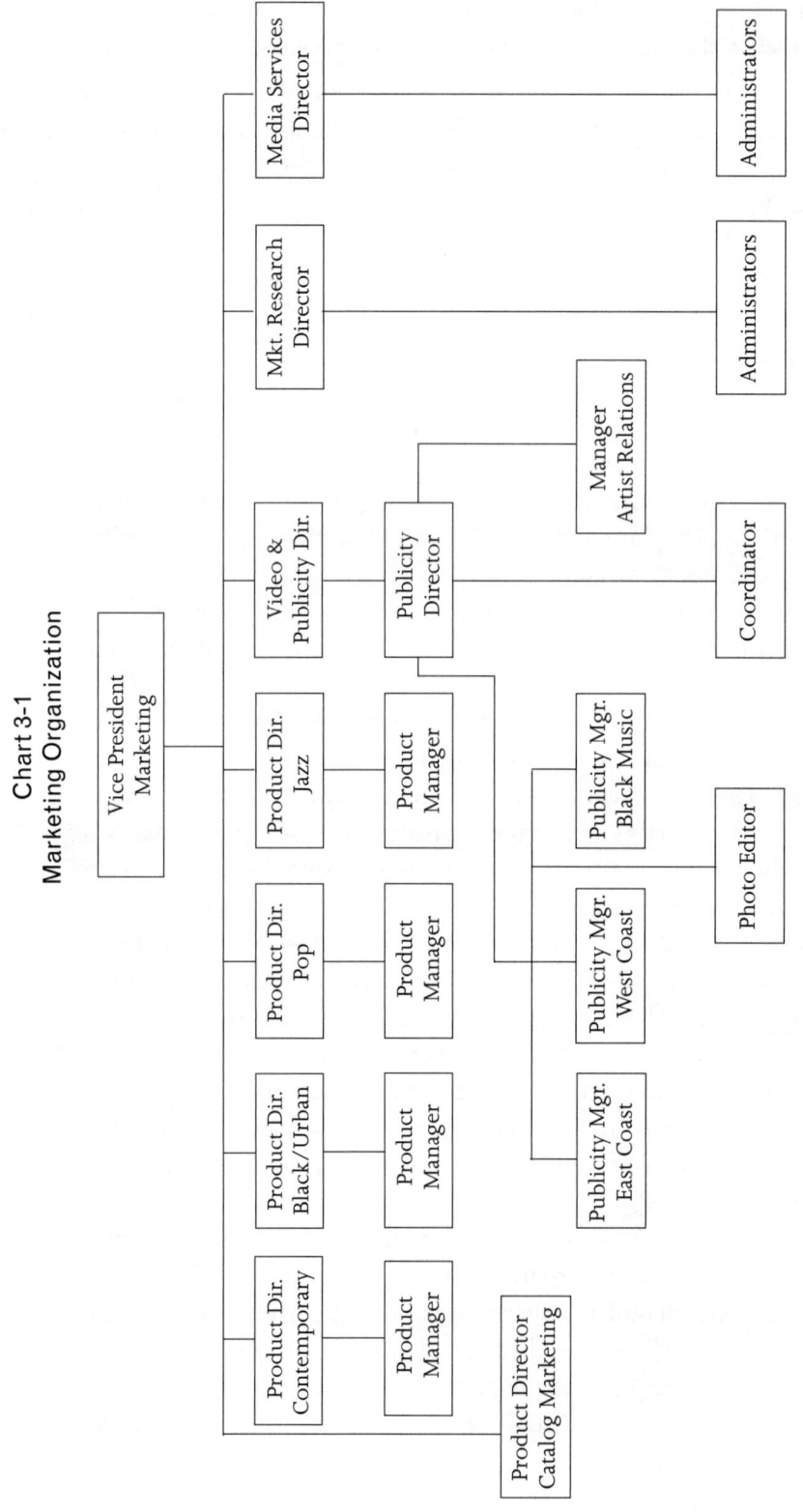

Chart 3-1
Marketing Organization

number of ways such as at retail outlets, via radio and TV, direct mail, through 800 and 900 numbers.

Incentives can also be utilized by those who sell, those who bring the product to the consumer and those who sell to the consumer. This is done via "spiffs," merchandise awards, or additional commission.

Discount, Dating and Guarantee Programs. These incentives make it more profitable for retailers and wholesalers to stock and expose the product. They also cut down on the risk involved with handling a product by lesser known acts.

Merchandise Tie-In. Cross promotions with other well-known products to heighten awareness.

Tours. Since you are marketing a look and a sound, what better way to expose these aspects of the product to both consumers and industry people than via appearances? The type of tour is determined by how far an act's career is advanced at that point.

Promotion Records. An obvious, but sometimes underutilized method to achieve "in-store" play, awareness among retail chain buyers, prizes for radio contests, consumer giveaways and airplay.

Listening Sessions. Playing the product for groups of industry people to aid the ordering process.

Buy It and Try It. Some retailers will allow consumers to buy an album and return it if not what they expected.

Those are some of the tools available to each department. There is room for variety in every marketing plan. The structure of a marketing plan depends upon the department creating it, and at the same time it can be part of an overall marketing plan. We will examine the responsibilities and activities of each department along with the elements of their plans.

PRODUCT MANAGEMENT—This department starts the whole process by creating an overall plan, lobbying for the budget necessary to carry the plan forward, and monitoring everyone's activities once the recording is released.

A marketing organization can be structured many ways, with one possible alignment shown in Chart 3-1. The main thrust of any music marketing organization is to have people in place to take responsibility for exposure once a decision has been reached to release the product.

The Product Management Department has all the elements required: product directors for each type of music that will be handled, publicity people, media buyers, video experts, artist relations people, creative service people, and marketing people to specialize in the types of product being released.

The key to the whole process is the product director. Once he or she has been assigned an act and an album, there are a number of actions that must be taken. The product director must:

- Get to know the group, find out what motivates them, and ascertain the level of cooperation you can expect. You will be spending a great deal of time with this act and assignment, so get the rules established early.

- Listen to the album, and listen, and listen, and listen and then listen some more.

- Target the market you want to penetrate with radio exposure in mind.

- Put together your budget request for at least the first 90 days that the album will be on release.

- With the help of other departments (promotion, sales) pick the first, and what you hope will be second and third singles.

Once the product director has gotten this far and is completely immersed in the career of the artists, he or she must generate enthusiasm for the act on all levels within the record company, and then among consumers. To do this the product director must:

- Maintain a close relationship with all other functions of a record company—Sales, Creative Services, A&R, Business Affairs, Publicity, Market Research, Media, Promotion, and Video Production.

- Develop a close relationship with the act being marketed.

- Develop the initial marketing plan that keys all departments into what is expected, how this is to be accomplished, and how it is to be funded.

- Monitor all phases of the plan as it is implemented, and have further plans ready when and if the product looks like it can be carried to the next level of sales and exposure.

- Act as focal point for upper management, the artists, and artist management.

- Be the proactive "champion" of his/her act throughout the entire organization.

- Utilize market research where appropriate to aid in decision-making. Take an active role in setting packaging objectives, interfacing with the artists and artist management, and creative services.

- Maintain all the paperwork essential to scheduling and funding advertising, promotion, tours, display, videos, and packaging.

Everything is based on the original marketing plan devised by the product manager. This plan goes to just about everyone who will have even the remotest part in implementation. Once this is accomplished, the other departments are then able to devise plans of their own to help the overall plan be successful. The plans initiated by all the other departments are usually quite specific, while the product manager's plan is usually all inclusive.

The product manager's plan should include information and detail on the following:

- Background: Contains biographical information, past experience as an artist, songwriter or backup player, and reason or concept of the album. Highlights past successes, associations with hit product or groups.

- Positioning: By this time the first, second, and possibly third single have been chosen. The plan explains the rationale behind the choice of the first and possibly second single and the target audience.

- Sales History: Established acts have a past sales history, while new acts have none. However, the type of product usually has a sales history via other performers.

- Forecast: Using any sales history that might be available, discussions with the sales department, and a "feel" for the project's potential, a forecast for the first 90 to 120 days of the life of the album is determined. At the same time, the suggested retail price structure of the album is determined, along with any wholesale discounts, dating or other incentives that will aid the sales department's efforts to book good initial orders.

- Scheduling: A time schedule is set up for sending advance samples or excerpts from the album to sales people, buyers for retail chains, other stores, and rack jobber companies. Decisions are made regarding when to send samples of the singles to radio, and what types of radio formats will be covered. Lastly, actual release dates for commercial copies that consumers can purchase are established.

- Merchandising, Point-of-Purchase Material: Depending on budgets acquired, display material is described, both type and quantity.

- Video: If the budget allows, a video to help promote the album is scheduled to be made along with dates it will go to MTV and others.

- Advertising: The publications to be used and dates are listed. This covers consumer publications as well as those read only within the industry. Advertising plans also include the type and number of radio and possibly TV spots that will be created for use on stations when airplay activity warrants the expenditure.

- Tours: Most releases are scheduled to coincide with some sort of tour. Unknown acts will either open for other acts, or just go around to major markets to meet people and pick up performing dates where possible.

- Publicity: The publicity department generates a plan of its own which is then incorporated into the master marketing plan.

DISTRIBUTION MARKETING—This is the activity that must sell the product to retailers, subdistributors, and others who make the albums available to the consumers. As noted previously, there are four major distribution organizations which market just about all the labels with any appreciable sales volume. These five are:

WMG

Sony-BMG

EMD

Universal

In each case, these distribution companies market a number of labels. Chart 3-2 shows the number of labels handled by just one company, Universal Music and Video Distribution.

The distribution organizations have the largest staffs and thus offer the best avenues into the business. The basic training at the distributor level can prepare you for just about any post in a record operation.

The Field Marketing Manager must coordinate, direct, and oversee all the interrelated activities of the distribution staffs. To do so, a close working relationship with key retail outlets and all retail home offices in the territory is key. This position requires close cooperation from Product Directors and Regional Label Marketing Managers.

A marketing plan for Distribution Marketing is usually targeted at a retail chain, rack jobber, or one stop and will contain most or all the following elements:

Product—album or albums specifically listed.

Sale Price—should have an incentive for consumer.

Dating—extended payment terms.

Guarantees—eliminate the risk to the accounts.

Time Frame—exact dates of the promotion.

CHART 3-2
UMVD LABEL INFORMATION

19 Recordings

ABKCO Records

ARK 21
Bungalo
Mondo Melodia
Pyramid

Concord Records
Concord Jazz
Concord Picante
Peak Records
Playboy Jazz

Disa
Procan

DreamWorks Nashville

DreamWorks Records

Fonovisa
DMY
Garmex
Oro Musical
Platino

Hollywood Records
Lyric Street
Mammoth
Skaggs Family
Ceili Music

Geffen
Drive Thru
Geffen Records
Chess
DGC
Experience Hendrix
Fiddler
Flawless
Flicker
Never So Deep
Radioactive
Rawkus

Interscope/A&M
A&M
Interscope Records
  Aftermath
  Amoru
  Beat Club
  Flip
  Nothing
  Shady

Island/Def Jam Music Group
American Recordings
Def Jam
Def Jam South
Def Soul
Murder, Inc.
Roc-A-Fella
Island
Mercury
Roadrunner

Lideres Records
Ole Music

Thump Records
B-Dub
Discos Fama
Thump Street

UMG Nashville
Lost Highway
Mercury Nashville
MCA Nashville
Rounder
Bullseye
Heartbeat
Marsalis Music
Philo
True North
Unitone
Zoe

Universal Classics & Jazz
Classics
Decca
Argo
L'Oiseau Lyre
London
Decca U.S.
Decca Broadway
GTSP
Deutsche Grammophon
  Archiv
  Westminster
ECM
Philips
  Mercury
  Point

Universal Motown Group
Bad Boy
Blackground
Casablanca
Cash Money
Cherry
D Block
Enjoy
Fo' Reel
Moonshine Conspiracy

Names in **bold** type
are Universal-owned divisions

The label names listed under each major label heading are those for which UMVD distributes a substantial amount of product. This list does not purport to be a complete listing of every sub-label, joint venture or other label relationship which has produced recordings included in the vast UMVD catalog.

Universal Motown, continued
Motown
Polydor
Republic
SRC
Strummer Recordings
Universal

Universal Music Enterprises
Chronicles
Hip-O Records
Universal Special Products
UTV

Universal Music Latino
Gold Star
Karen
Mas Flow
Metrix
Musimex
Perfect Image
Pimienta
Pina Records
Planet Rhythm
Platano | Big World | Music Up
Protel | Revolú
Regio
RMM
Universal Music Latino

Universal South

Univision Music Group
Ramex

Varese Sarabande Records
Fuel 2000
Fynsworth Alley
Sunswept Music
Water Music

Verve Music Group
Blue Thumb
GRP
Impulse
Verve

VI Music
Empire

Walt Disney Records
Buena Vista

Universal Music & Video Distribution/Visual Entertainment
Atkins Complete
Trinity
Palm Pictures
Xenon

Merchandising/P.O.P. Support—complete description of what display is available, the amount, how stores are to be supplied, where in the stores it should be used.

In Store Play—how audio cassettes or CDs will be supplied to play the promoted selections in the store. Will videos be made available for the same purpose?

Radio Play—frequent updates on local stations in each store's area playing the product.

Advertising Support—complete schedules of radio, print, and TV advertising that will be purchased to support the program.

These elements and others will be discussed in more detail when covering specific marketing plans.

LABEL MARKETING—Most record companies have regional label representatives in major markets who are responsible for a group of cities or markets. These representatives work with the distribution people to be sure everyone is focused on the particular pieces of product that are the labels' priorities at that time. As noted, all major distribution organizations have any number of labels attempting to get attention for their releases and thus the Label Marketing Representative must have a solid relationship with the people who sell the product in his or her markets, in addition to having firm information about how an album is really progressing.

The Regional Label Representative must update the distribution force constantly about sales, radio station ads, breakouts in other markets, chart position, and anything else that will draw attention to the album.

The label marketing representative's major responsibility is that of assuring the company that the Product Director's marketing plans are being implemented on schedule.

However, in addition to implementing the plans set forth by the record company's home office, label marketing people should also put together plans for specific retail chains. These should spell out:

- Objectives
- Product Available to Achieve Them
- Strategies
- Outlet by Outlet Analysis
- Commitment and Support Expected from Record Label
    Advertising
    People
    Systems and Information
- Support and Cooperation Expected from the Retailer
- Incentives to be Offered to the Retailer
- Time Frame to Measure Results.

Just about all major labels and distribution companies are making sure that their marketing teams are adapting to each particular account's structure and position in the business. Media Play is different from Best Buy, for example.

This outline can be used as a basis for a general plan to increase business for both parties, or can be tailored to help promote and expose one piece of product or a group of releases.

PROMOTION—There are any number of activities that enhance a recording's chances for success, but none even approaches the need for broadcast exposure for audio product and videos. Radio and Club airplay along with MTV-type video exposure is really the foundation for all other activities. The Promotion Department of any label is very powerful. Huge sums are allocated to this activity, all pay large staffs, and everyone is under tremendous pressure to succeed. The first activity to indicate an album has a chance for success is in the airplay charts. This is where the product gains credibility among other radio people, among retail executives, and among all those working on the overall Marketing Plan.

Each step within the Marketing Plan is predicated on airplay developing as planned. And it is planned. Progression of airplay is mapped out very carefully, with key radio stations expected to "make the add" on schedule. When this happens according to the blueprint, then most of the other elements can become more effective and bring greater results. Promotion has a plan just like every other department.

PUBLICITY— The major ingredient of a Publicity Plan is to identify what segment of the record buying public you wish to impress. Then, zoom in on the publications and TV shows that attract that group of consumers and set up appearances, interviews, and other contacts.

The consumer has always been celebrity conscious. But now that consumer is offered far more opportunities to feed the hunger via television, magazines, and newspapers. As a result, publicity is playing an ever larger part in building recording careers. More outlets mean more exposure and a better chance to make an impression on the minds of the consumer. TV, especially, creates an immediate impact. What took weeks of radio airplay just a few years ago can now be accomplished in a matter of days if the TV exposure is heavy enough. The proliferation of entertainment-oriented TV shows and magazines as well as expanded "Living" sections of daily and Sunday newspapers has been a tremendous help.

MARKET RESEARCH—As the stakes get higher, and as the methodology of obtaining market research information becomes more sophisticated, record companies are relying on their market research people more and more. A few years ago, it would have been unheard of to employ "focus group" companies, but now this is a common occurrence. The old way was to just listen to what radio people had to say and then act accordingly. Radio reaction remains very important, but now the consumer is being asked about the product before it is released, and in some cases, before it is even created.

The list of types of market research available now continues to grow (see chapter on Market Research). Industry trade associations like RIAA (Record Industry Association of America) and NARM (National Association of Recording Merchandisers) are just two of the trade groups that gather and make available research from consumers about:

What they buy
Where they buy
How often they make a music purchase
What motivates the purchase
What they will pay for product
What each age group thinks
Is the industry serving their needs today

Market Research has become a very vital activity. The investments are far too great to leave it all up to "gut feeling" as was the case some years ago. Today's recorded music market dictates that you take advantage of all the tools available to increase the odds for success. Market research has become so very sophisticated that, while it certainly cannot predict a "hit," it can tell a company what should have the best chance of being accepted by the greatest number of people, and where to have the product when airplay and other exposure has started to make the impact that everyone has been striving so hard to create.

FINANCIAL—Bringing any new recording, whether by an established artist or group, or by a "baby act," to the marketplace is a very expensive procedure. In the case of new acts, it can cost up to a million dollars or more. A large portion of that falls into the "recoupable" realm, but it is a bill that must be paid eventually whether the project fails or succeeds.

The financial department allocates the funds necessary to perform each function, tries to keep each department within the budget proposed for each project and each step, and advises everyone of the profitability or lack of it for each release. Most releases lose money, but since new acts are the lifeblood of the industry, and profits are great on those that do attain "hit" status, the money is committed on a regular basis. The financial department is responsible for the profitability of the company and plays a vital role in all decisions.

This is an overview of the music industry as well as the organization, the tools, and the type of activity required to take a recorded product from an idea to something that people can own and enjoy any time they wish. Most of these elements will be examined in far more detail.

Summary

Music marketing requires many specialists and the complete cooperation of everyone involved in making consumers aware of a recording or video, and aware enough to make them want to purchase it. There is no way to really "legislate" a hit (make consumers purchase music that does not touch them some way). All the activity possible will not really bring a venture "home" profitably. But, not doing all the right things can very easily result in what could have been a big selling hit never getting started. With the percentage of releases that actually make it so low, losing a good piece of product due to inattention is a real crime.

Terms

Label: Record Company, different from Distribution Company. Label has artists under contract, responsible for releasing recordings.

Distribution: Company responsible for getting the recorded product to the stores and organizations that sell to the consumer.

Marketing Management: Activity that determines when and how the product is to be presented to consumers and organizations that deal with consumers.

Marketing Concept: Approach to be taken with the product depending upon type, popularity, needs of consumers.

Target Market: Usually segmented by age, but also by musical preferences.

Promotional Videos: Videos made expressly to expose an audio product to consumers. Not for sale as music videos.

Positioning: Assuring that the product is up front in bins and display racks easily seen by customers at an attractive sale price.

Retail Chains: Groups of national or regional retail audio and video stores. Usually with only one central buying office and their own distribution facility. Usually carry very extensive inventories with selection count in the thousands. Now includes large national electronic and appliance chains, as well as superstores carrying all types of informational products.

Alternative Stores: Relatively new type of outlet. Smaller, specialized stores catering to consumers looking for vinyl LPs, as well as new releases by lesser known acts in any configuration. Will carry limited selection of major name act releases, but might have items not carried by big chain retailers.

Rack Jobbers: Organizations that service the record departments in national and regional mass merchandisers, such as Wal-Mart, Kmart, and Sears.

One Stops: Originally started supplying records to juke box operators, now service small non-chain retailers. Will sell regional product and fill-ins to major chain locations that cannot wait for own distribution centers to supply needs.

P.O.P. (Point of Purchase): Display material such as posters, reproductions of cover art, or other printed material used in arrangements on walls and elsewhere in outlets to attract attention to a specific product.

MTV (Music Television): Carried on cable, shows music videos 24 hours daily. Television version of music-oriented radio stations.

Spots: Commercials played on radio and TV to sell product.

Accounts: Customers sold by distribution companies. Retailers, rack jobbers, one stops referred to as "accounts."

"Adds": When radio station puts a single or album in rotation, meaning it will be played.

Radio Airplay: Exposure on radio stations with music formats.

Club Play: Exposure in dance clubs, at times as important as radio airplay.

"Recoupable": Costs incurred in recording, marketing, and supporting releases that will come out of future royalties earned by the act.

Bibliography

Kotler, Philip. *Marketing Management: Analysis, Planning, Control.* Prentice-Hall, Inc., Englewood Cliffs, New Jersey, Fifth Edition, 1984.

Exercises

1. How do you define Marketing Management?

2. List the three most important factors in your own decision to purchase a recording that thus should be part of any marketing plan.

3. How do you see "recoupable" costs impacting a company's profits and an artist's royalties?

4. List six specific outlets or media where publicity can gain imme-
    diate recognition of an act or record.

5. Of all the actions a Product Manager must take when assigned an
    act, what do you consider the three most important and why?

Chapter 4
Selling Strategies

Learning Objectives

After studying this chapter you should be able to:

1. Define discount and dating

2. Explain "functional discount" and returns

3. Define announced standard price

4. List the steps necessary in determining final cost of the product for an account other than the "published price"

5. Explain the "box lot" pricing system

6. Define "anticipation"

7. Explain the "incentive-disincentive" policy

8. Illustrate a good music related sales meeting

9. Demonstrate the nature and importance of good salesmanship

To properly market recorded products, it is important that you be very familiar with the usual terms of sale and return. These factors have a major impact on profit or loss and thus also impact the level of cooperation you receive from the companies that bring the product to the consumer. How you must deal with these accounts is very important to carrying a project to a successful completion. As you learn more about the strengths and weaknesses of each type of account, you will understand how the terms of sale can be used to your advantage.

The examples in this chapter relate mainly to the way the four major distributors do business with their accounts. The "Indies" have many diverse ways to deal with their customers based on credit history, past return history and a myriad of other factors. Their policies change frequently and are too numerous to attempt to list.

Pricing, Dating, Returns

Pricing of recorded products is unlike that of other products because basically all companies charge the same, with a cent or two difference here and there. Special discounts or "deals" change from time to time, but everyone is flexible enough to match deals.

An account's method of supplying stores, having distribution companies ship individual locations, or having the product shipped into central warehouses, where it becomes the account's responsibility to transfer it to stores, can have a slight impact on the published price with some distribution organizations. This practice has been initiated only recently.

Record distributors and labels can aim discount programs at individual segments of the business, as long as they offer them to everyone in a specific customer category. This approach is used frequently for particular types of products. For example, a black/urban product starts in a limited fashion so that accounts that handle that product can be targeted with extra incentives.

Since about 85% to 90% of the record business done through retail accounts is done by 10 or fewer accounts, their requirements and input have a great impact on pricing decisions. There has been much fine tuning over the years, but now it seems things have settled down. For some time, pricing was very difficult to explain and justify. At one time *subdistributors* were given a "functional discount" for the services they performed. Pricing then became a major disaster when companies attempted to justify pricing by what their competitors were doing. There were more ramifications, but suffice it to say, it really did not work.

Now, after many years of experimentation and changes in the way business has to be done, all companies have gone to a "box lot" pricing system. This means that if an account buys products in increments of what comes in full, sealed boxes, you get a lower price. This price is about 2-1/2% to 3% lower than if you buy loose quantities, less than a full box, or "shorts" as they are referred to in the industry.

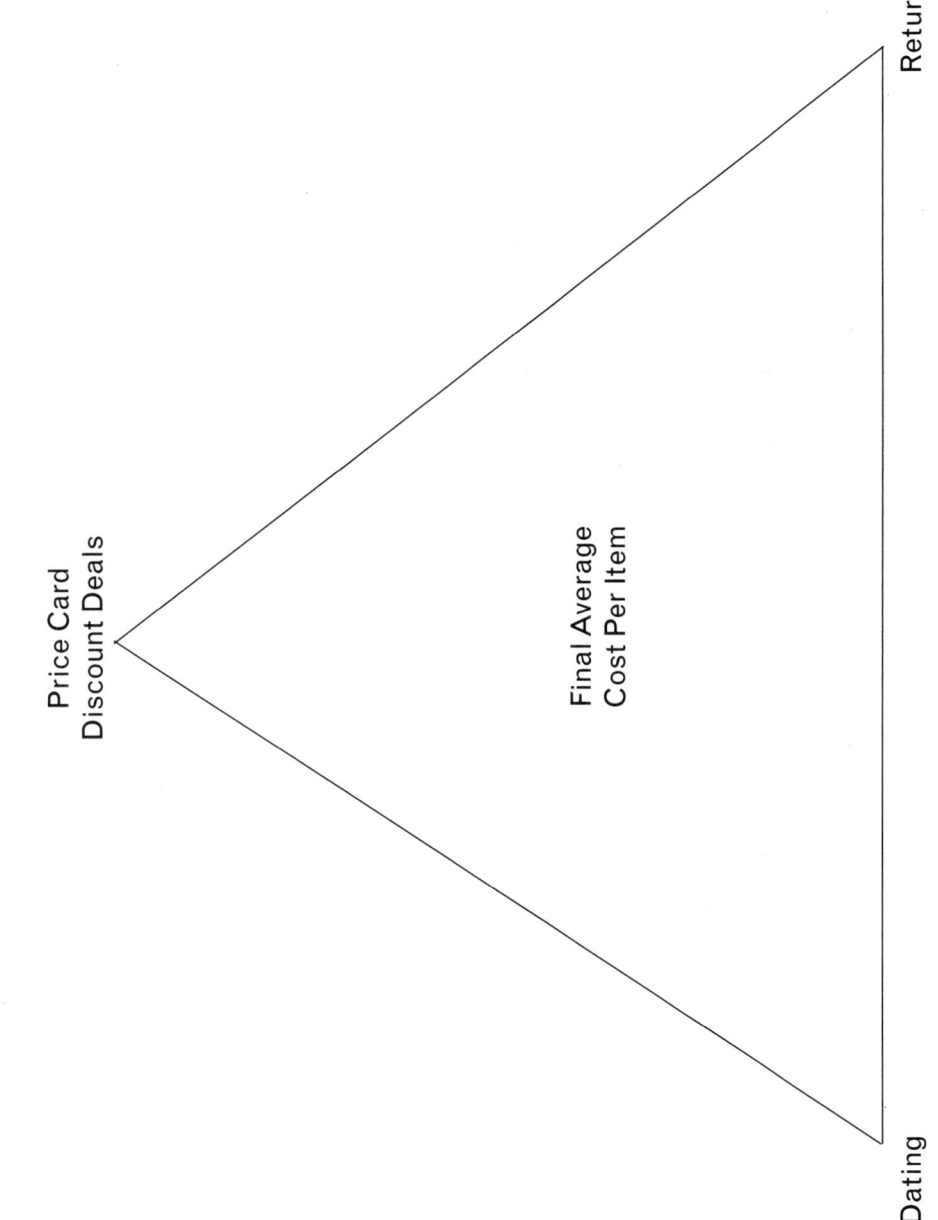

Chart 4-1
Final Cost of Goods to an Account

Price Card
Discount Deals

Final Average
Cost Per Item

Returns

Dating

There is more to determining the final cost of a product for an account than the "published" price. *There are, in fact, three major factors in the final cost to any account, be it retailer, one stop, or rack jobber.*

These are:

The **Announced standard price** that would appear on a price card but would include special discount programs and incentives. Distribution companies will offer ongoing incentive plans with each category of account on certain types of product. The discounts offered are different depending upon the product (full line, midline, budget, classical, etc.). These programs will sometimes change or eliminate the extra charge for not buying in box lots. Some products like jazz, Latin, and classical do not lend themselves to box lot orders.

Dating that can be offered to increase the time period in which a bill becomes due for payment.

Returns which are a major expense to everyone; by minimizing them, profits can be increased.

Look upon these three factors as a triangle. (See Chart 4-1.)

How an account uses the elements of this triangle—price, dating, and returns—determines what their real cost of goods is over any given period of time. In other words, since everyone is using the same deck, how you run your business, the amount of capital you have at your disposal, and your ability to take advantage of what is offered in the way of incentives really controls your ability to end up with a better price than your competitor. Here is how it works.

Price

Everything starts with the published price or price card that is issued by all distributors. This lists the regular price for each category of product, each configuration, and is usually noted by the "box lot" price. This published price list is the starting point for what each particular selection costs. Additionally, accounts are offered special discount programs and other incentives to bring that price down. The amount of cash or credit available to an account has a major impact on how frequently and to what extent an account can take advantage of these special prices. The programs are usually for limited periods and in many cases run during a period when a selection has its greatest potential for sales. Well run, successful businesses have the resources to maximize their use of programs.

Dating

To understand all the ramifications of pricing, what types of additional incentives can be offered, and how buying must be planned, you must know what are "normal" payment terms of sale for most recorded products.

Normal terms are 60 days to pay after the purchase in order to get a 2% cash discount. Any time payment terms longer than 60 days are offered, it is called "dating." Dating can stretch payment as far as 180 days, or six months, with the same 2% cash discount still earned.

Recently some companies have gone to "anticipation." Anticipation, which is used in many industries, means you get an extra discount if you pay early. Since normal terms are 2% discount if you pay within 60 days, an additional 1% or even 2% discount can be earned if you pay in 30 days or less.

For a variety of reasons, distributors and labels will offer extended terms for payment, or as it is termed, "dating." This means additional time, usually in 30-day segments, before a bill becomes due. The product can stay in an account's inventory longer before it must be paid for; and this is an incentive to buy.

Why do labels and distributors offer dating? Keep in mind, it costs a company money to extend dating since it really means the accounts are using your money. Thus the company loses use of the money or even worse, must borrow to support the dating program. There are a number of cases where it is necessary to extend dating. For example:

Catalog Programs: This is product that has been on the shelves for a long time, but continues to sell at a reasonable rate, but certainly not as rapidly as a hit product. It has a sales potential and will continue to move at a profitable rate; however, to assure it being stocked in record departments, it is necessary to share some of the financial burden of the slow rate of movement.

Classical: Product that is quite profitable from a profit and loss standpoint, but does move slowly. Once again, account and supplier share the cost of this slow sales rate via dating. At times, some labels have offered to extend payment dates as much as six months. In this way, dealers can order twice yearly for a standard catalog and not fear that the inventory will depreciate too rapidly.

Seasonal goods: Most records devoted to Christmas repertoire are solicited in the summer for shipment to arrive prior to Thanksgiving. These carry dating programs that call for payment right after Christmas or into the following January. This way, products can be produced when convenient, orders stockpiled, and shipments made during a specified time period. This is a convenience and cost saving procedure for everyone.

Get around "open to buy": Since many companies restrict the amount of products their buyers can purchase each month, an offer of extended dating can move a purchase out of one month's billing into another, and ease that pressure.

Make buyers feel more secure: If buyers know that the product they order for their stores will have a chance to sell and bring in receipts before payment must be made to the distributor, they are far more comfortable in placing large orders. This helps the ever-present problem of being out of stock on all types of product. Dating being offered on hit products is a major incentive because you can buy big and in most cases have sold it to your consumer before payment comes due.

However, the most important use is:

To get exposure on new acts: This is by far the most important use since it takes time to get a new artist established, and the odds are very slim that will even happen. But with new acts being the lifeblood of the industry, all labels and distributors are more than willing to extend payment terms on new artists. This is a type of protection for the account. It gives them time to see if anything will develop before payment, and in many cases, as will be discussed when covering returns, will offer an opportunity to send the product back before having to pay.

Offers of extended dating are attractive to all accounts primarily because they add money to the account's bottom line for the following reasons:

Dating saves borrowing money to pay bills and thus saves interest.

Depending upon the type of product being offered with dating terms, the product will sell and the account will have the cash before having to pay for it.

Cash on hand makes money for well-run companies. Money managers are a vital and profitable part of any financial department.

Average savings per month vary as interest rates vary. But for example, if it costs 12% annually to borrow, that means a 1% savings each month when dating is available. Even if interest rates were much lower and the savings were only .05%, a major account's purchases are well into the multimillions of dollars and that adds up to a sizable addition to profits each year.

Returns

A very effective cost cutter in the music industry is proper handling of returns. The handling of returns by accounts and manufacturers has traditionally been one of the most controversial subjects in the industry. Returns have created more acrimony and been the reason behind the failure of many accounts, distributors, and labels. Overshipments and irresponsible selling practices glutted the market with unsold products. For too long this unsold product could be returned for credit, but the financial impact was too great for many companies to withstand. This was an area where experimentation went on for years before the procedure in place now, the "incentive-disincentive policy," evolved. Just about every major supplier in the business presently handles returns with this policy.

The "incentive-disincentive" policy assigns an additional percentage of discount to most purchases, while assigning a penalty to all products returned under the policy. The actual percentages and penalties assigned are quite numerous and vary from distributor to distributor, and by type and configuration of product.

There are products sold with a full guarantee, which means that what does not sell can be sent back at a later date for full credit, without penalty, this does not get into the "incentive-disincentive" system. Much product, usually new acts, special projects and experimental products might be sold that way, but the bulk of any account's album purchases are purchased under the "incentive-disincentive" rules. Simply put, an additional discount is given the account when the purchase is made, but a larger penalty is assigned when something is returned. The numbers used here will reflect the original, simple programs that most companies initiated a few years ago. In all cases, numbers have changed to keep up with the changes in configuration and buying habits of the consumer. **However, the policies remain pretty much the same; just the percentages change.**

Keep in mind, you are dealing with album products bought on a day in and day out basis, with no special return deals. These are the bulk of what an account buys. The figures and example reflect a 1% incentive when purchases are made, and a 5% penalty when the product is returned. The 1% incentive appears as an added discount; the 5% disincentive is taken from the credit issued.

Assume you are a record dealer and you buy $1000 worth of product. Since you get 1% incentive it means you pay $990 for it for a gain of $10.

If you only have to send back $100 worth, you will be charged $5, which means you pocket $5.

If you send back $200, you are charged $10, and this means you break even.

If you send back $300, you are charged back $15, and this is a loss to you of $5.

With this example, it means keeping returns no higher than 20%. Handling the returns will still cost you, so good operators will keep that return percentage even lower and help defray the cost of handling returns. This example is an oversimplification to illustrate how the system works. In the real world, the incentive percentage and the disincentive percentage are manipulated by the type of product, configuration, and company to achieve more or less exposure to returns. This method also manipulates the "break even" point. The basic principles apply although the numbers change. For example, placing a 1.5% incentive on purchases of some types of product and adding a 10% disincentive brings the "break even" point to 15%. Depending on the type of account and type of product, most "break even" points in today's market are between 15% and 18%.

It should be quite plain that returns have a tremendous impact on that triangle of price, dating and returns.

Therefore, for every retailer, rack jobber, and one stop there is a way to gain an advantage over your competitor and bring your cost of product below that of a competitor:

1. Can you take advantage of deals, discount programs by having a well run business?
2. Can you take advantage of dating when it is offered?
3. Can you keep your returns at or possibly below the "break even" percentage?

Sales Meetings

When working out any selling strategy, and when compiling any marketing plan, the place it must all come together and be presented to the people who will be responsible for selling the plan and the product, is the weekly distributor sales meeting. The deals, the dating and the return problems must all be discussed fully, and everyone must be keyed in to everything that is happening with all projects, both current and proposed.

   Modern technology now makes it possible to hold sales meetings at which an entire company can be present either in person or via conference calling, and now teleconferencing. No matter what the format, this is where the marketing people get their message across and this is where they sell their plan first. In many cases, this is the most important sale of any record project's life. No matter how much technology advances, nothing can replace face to face contact, even confrontation, and a personal explanation of why a project can and must succeed.

   Why a meeting? Perhaps it is a good idea to revisit an activity that has been in our business culture for so long and examine what everyone can get from it.

   First, a suggested format for a music distributor related sales meeting:

Agenda:

Only with distributor people
   Cover general notes
   All priorities
   General status report on how total business is doing
   Discuss advertising needs, plans
Labels (each individually)
   Promotion
         airplay
         problem areas
         priorities
         feedback
         play new product
   Label Marketing people
         sales priorities
                status report-sales, display

advertising plans
retail promotion plans
new product
play
Assign objectives
Deals and dating programs
update ongoing deals
announce new ones

Remember, you are dealing with a product that is highly emotional; therefore the approach to explaining it has to be charged and emotional.

In writing in *The Harvard Business Review* some years ago about the functions of a meeting, Anthony Jay pointed out some of these facts.

1. In the simplest and most basic way, a meeting defines the team, the group, or the unit. Selling that unit is critical.

2. A meeting is the place where the group revises, updates, and adds to what it knows as a group. (Events happen so fast in the record industry that the constant need for immediate updating grows ever more important.)

3. A meeting helps every individual understand both the collective aim of the group and the way in which his or her own and everyone else's work can contribute to the group's success.(Timing is vital to a record project. If someone fails to handle an assignment at the proper time, it can be disastrous.)

4. A meeting is a status arena. It is no good to pretend that people are not or should not be concerned with their status relative to other members of the group. (The music industry is very competitive. It is an endeavor where you must think fast, have ideas ready at all times. Meetings are where you display your prowess.)

Salesmanship

No matter what the title and what the activity, everyone in marketing is really a salesperson. Marketing people not only sell the actual customer, but must sell the entire distribution and sales function. The key, however, is how the sales representative on the street handles the responsibilities of breaking and selling the product.

The following discussion applies to the actual sales representative as well as to the marketing people. In the case of marketing people, some of what is discussed relates to activities with the distribution personnel, but in many cases can apply to activities with the buyers in major accounts. In all cases, the same principles apply and the same advice should be followed.

The first responsibility **is to sell yourself.** This is where it all starts. Gaining the confidence of the buyer is possibly more vital in selling records than with other products in that aspects like price, quality, size, etc. that can determine another product's appeal, are not a factor. The relationship and confidence you build is your strongest asset.

This requires that you listen to your product over and over. You must learn all there is to know about the recording and the act, even though it might not be the type of music you like personally. Do not let personal tastes get in the way. You sell it all, and you are as enthusiastic about each and every project.

Know what is right for a particular market or account. Be very aware of who they sell to and what market they are trying to capture. Listen for opportunities either in the content of the product or possible promotional openings offered by the outlet.

Note that this means being a good listener. Do not feel you must do all the talking.

Your next most important asset is your ability to **"read the customer."** Reading that buyer can be the key because when you are selling new, emerging products, in particular, you are selling untried music. Finding the opening, finding the "nerve," is the key to success. Make note of some of the following precepts:

1. You have to know when to press, when to back off, and plan a strategy for another day.

2. You must be aware of your contact's problems and help, if you can, with those problems.

3. If you make promises, be 100% sure you can deliver as promised. People soon learn who they can count on to follow through, especially when helping with a problem.

4. You must keep your appointments. Sounds simplistic, but too many people feel that because the music business is part of the entertainment world, it operates on a different time schedule. This is not the case. The business end of music, where the money must change hands, **is a business.**

5. You might not like a person, but you cannot let that cloud your approach or judgment. Some buyers will be friends, others not.

6. You must know how to work around people's prejudices.

7. Have as much backup information as possible before any presentation, including:
    a. Chart action
    b. Sales elsewhere in the area or nation
    c. Radio play
    d. Any other "buzz" that will help your case

Not all salesmanship is just writing orders. A sales representative or marketing manager must also handle advertising paperwork, return paperwork, and order tracking. In the case of advertising:

1. You must know the most effective type for your purposes and the account's purposes.

2. You must know the costs involved.

3. You must know how much is actually available and be sure you have the money before commitment.

Paperwork is a mundane aspect of any business, especially when you get caught up in the excitement of music. But the paperwork keeps the industry on the right track. Some points to remember about paperwork are:

1. You must always stay up-to-date. You never get a slow time to "catch up." The industry moves too fast.

2. Keep track of your market and your contacts so you can answer questions accurately and rapidly.

3. You should try to cultivate a few good sources for competitive information. The music industry is very sensitive to what competitors are doing so you must be aware of the latest changes, latest policies.

4. If your paperwork is current, you can service your accounts' needs quickly.

The music industry places a great emphasis on "creativity." This factor must be paramount in all phases of the process. Creativity is what builds what you have to sell, so you have to expect this to drive all other aspects of the activity. You cannot have too many ideas, and you must have them ready at all times. Have promotional suggestions ready for your company and your accounts. You must always have a segment of your catalog ready to pitch when the hits dry up. And you must stay alert for tie-ins of all sorts to keep the product flowing.

The above includes some of the highlights. There is much more that can be said on the subject, but let us close with one admonition. **Be tactful.** Work out the problems you have with the people you usually contact and see frequently. Going to their superior or the owner can produce a very short-term success. You lose in the long run.

Summary

Determining the final cost of music products for an account (retailers, one stop, rack jobber) is embedded in special discounts, dating programs, and return policies and how they are utilized. This substantially lowers the overall average price eventually paid.

Good inventory control reduces penalties paid on returned product.

Catalog, classical, and seasonal product have a longer shelf life than "hits;" therefore, dating serves to extend payment dates.

Releases by new acts almost demand dating. Implementation of selling strategies are determined by effective sales meetings and good salesmanship.

Terms

Box lot pricing: Purchases made in increments of what comes in full, sealed boxes receive a lower price.

Discount: Special program for temporary lower price on particular product to account.

Dating: Extended terms (delayed billing) to accounts for selected product.

Returns: Unsold recordings shipped by the retailer back to the manufacturer for credit.

Normal billing terms: 2% cash discount if paid in 60 days.

Anticipation: An extra discount for paying in full prior to the normal 60 day terms.

Classical and Catalog programs: Musical product with longer shelf life in which accounts and suppliers share the cost by dating.

Midline: Catalog albums with a suggested list price generally $2.00 to $3.00 below that of brand new "Front Line."

Front Line: New album releases by current artists at the top of the industry's pricing tier.

Open to buy: An account's limits on how much can be spent on product purchases within a given period, usually a month.

Incentive-disincentive: A policy in which an additional percentage of discounts are assigned to purchases and a penalty to returns.

Exercises

1. What are "normal" terms for payment in the record industry?

2. Explain "anticipation" and who foots that bill.

3. Explain "box lot" pricing.

4. The most important use of dating is to help what type of product?

5. When trying to "read" a buyer, what signs does a good sales rep look for?

6. Explain the "incentive-disincentive" policy used by most distribution organizations.

Chapter 5

One Stops

Learning Objectives

After studying this chapter you should be able to define:

1. Retail

2. Wholesaler

3. One Stop

4. Subdistribution

5. Mom and Pop Stores

6. Telemarketing

Subdistribution 1—One Stops

All prerecorded products start with the artist. The creative powers of the performers, writers, engineers and producers must come together to mold a recording that has the potential to satisfy the inner desires of a large segment of the buying public. This is truly "a labor of love" on the part of all those involved. But no matter how well that is done at the outset, unless there is a channel to the buying public, no one will ever know that this marvelous creation ever existed. To market this creation, everything that started with the artist must go to the label, then to distribution, and on to subdistribution and retail as outlined below:

Songwriter/Artist
  |
Artist/Producer
  |
Label—A&R
  |
    Promotion
    Sales
  |
Distribution
  |
Accounts   Retail
    Rack Jobbers
    One Stops
  |
Tie Ins—Major companies
    Big Advertisers
  |
Media
  |
Consumer

While there are other avenues to the consumer, the three major players are basically as outlined above: one stops, rack jobbers, and retail stores. The importance of these three areas is far more than just making the product available to the consumer. They are an integral part of making just a recording a "hit" recording and, therefore, a big enough seller to make a profit for everyone.

From a marketing angle, there is far more that must be known about each type of account. While each has its own significant place in the chain, each also has strong points and weak points. You have to know what motivates and creates profit for each and understand how you exploit these factors to expedite your precious marketing plans. Each must be approached with full knowledge of the account's:

Goals
Problems
Competitive Situation
Segment of Market Served

This requires you to look at the type of music you are marketing and determine where you go first and what approach you must take with each type of account. **In short, you must know what is the "history" and "function" as well as the "strengths" and "limitations" of each type of account.**

Just as marketing techniques and approaches are changing constantly in the music industry, so too have evolved the organizations and avenues available to the distribution network to get the product before the consumer. Success is measured in sales to consumers, and for most recorded products, there are one and sometimes two levels that come into play before the music purchaser can make the decision to buy. Retail record stores sell about 50% of the products produced, and of that figure, most of the sales are through major retail chains, both regional and national. However, the small, independent record retailer is a vital link in not only supplying the consumer, but also in getting new products exposed in the market place. In recent years, the small dealer has taken on a much more important role due to the vast diversity of the products being recorded and released. Just about all of these small dealers are supplied by a subdistributor or middleman between the record company's distribution arm and locations that sell to the consumer. In just about all cases, this is the **one stop**.

Since you will need the one stop to some degree at the outset of your activities on just about every project, this type of account will be covered first.

In addition to supplying the product, the one stop is vital in terms of developing a "hit" product and moving large quantities when a piece of a product reaches a highly saleable level. This segment of the industry plays a significant role in aiding the marketing activity in creating an acceptance for a recording and then supplying the outlets that have access to the public and, ultimately, the public's buying decision.

One stops were originally developed to service coin operators, organizations that serviced juke boxes. At one time juke box activity was very vital to the success of a recording. In just about all cases, juke boxes would only offer "singles" or one song for the money deposited in the coin slots. Since the public's interest in singles changed very quickly, coin operators were required to change the selections offered very frequently. Not only did the public require this, but the people who owned the establishments where the juke boxes were located and who shared in the money deposited in each machine demanded that the selections be updated constantly. Juke boxes do not play anywhere near the role they played years ago when the record industry started a period of tremendous growth, but they still have an impact.

The need for an ever-changing mix on the juke boxes meant coin operator personnel had to go to each of the many distribution locations and buy their needs among the particular selections offered by each individual company. As recently as 25 years ago, there were 12 major distributors, plus far more "independent" distributors, and in the more distant past, those numbers were much higher, so the process was time consuming and expensive. This gave the impetus to developing one of the most aptly named organizations in any business, the **one stop**. Early one stops were put in place to sell the coin operators **ALL** their needs each week in *one stop*. At the outset the operators paid $.05 per record over normal wholesale cost, the cost they normally paid the distributors they had been patronizing.

As noted previously, the music industry has changed. To survive, those who are part of it must make constant adjustments. One stops have certainly done this. Now they are far more active with small dealers who cannot deal with major distribution organizations because of restrictions on credit, minimum orders, shipping distances, returns, and coverage. Coverage is one of the most important aspects of a one stop's activity. One stops have access to **all** retail outlets.

By far their main activity is that one stops help the product flow into the "Mom and Pop" stores which are independent, often small, single outlet stores. This particular segment of the retail business is very vital to new, developing product and to getting new trends started in the industry. Good one stops know how a record's popularity with consumers spreads through an area. They know how radio play can and must develop for the sales to follow. As will be discussed when concentrating on the retail portion of the industry, many retail stores cannot afford to experiment with all the new selections as they are released. However, one stops usually do try to stock something of everything since they service so many aspects of the retail establishment. The buyer at an average one stop will be presented with hundreds of new selections **weekly**. That is why a normal one stop inventory can be in the millions of dollars. While one stops do sell a lot of "fill-ins" to major chains, the most important aspect of their activity is servicing small dealers. This does not minimize the importance of supplying major chains with regionalized or "local" hits.

To do what they do well, and even though they are working on short profit margins, the one stop must maintain a large staff and very large warehouse and shipping facilities. Staffing must include:

Sales Management
Telemarketing Sales
Buyers

Accounting—receivables, payables
Inventory Control
Warehousing
Shipping

Since small dealers have little or no contact with the five major distributors, the type of contact afforded major chains because of their dollar volume, they turn to the one stop. In most cases, the operator of a small, single outlet store has the entire, or certainly the major, financial stake in the business. Available money precludes buying too far in advance. Basically, the small dealers, alternative stores, and specialty outlets work out of a one stop's inventory. Proximity to supply and thus availability is also a factor. Since owners of small dealerships are involved in everyday operation, they know their customers personally and pride themselves on being able to supply everyone's needs rapidly. This is what holds their customer base. Not too long ago, the four major distributors had over 30 servicing warehouses or distribution points throughout the United States. Today there are less than ten. Having your one stop positioned to get the product to you in a timely fashion is critical.

In addition, aside from all the product available through the five major distributors, there are at least a couple of hundred or more selections that are marketed through independent distributors. A one stop is really the only reasonable source for this type of merchandise, and with the new role being played by the "Indies," this aspect of a one stop's role becomes even more critical.

To survive and prosper, a good one stop must be able to provide its customers with the best:

Service
Fill
Price

Elaborating on each of these aspects of the way one stops perform their function, consider **service** first. Service usually means timely and accurate information about the progress and sales potential of all types of products, quick shipment after an order is placed, advertising money and display material. However, quick shipment is the major factor in service, since the accounts serviced by one stops buy their needs on what really translates into a daily basis. To offer quick shipment, just about every successful one stop retains staff and keeps working until every order received that day has been shipped and is on the way to the customer. The critical period for service is Friday, since weekend business is vital to any retailer. Receipts from the weekend usually dictate buying patterns for the next week.

Another aspect of service offered by one stops is mailings to their customers (usually done with distributor help) that list new releases, recordings that are starting to sell well, and other information. In many cases, this information is now being distributed via fax and the Internet. This way, the stores will have something in front of them when called for orders, or when they are preparing to place an order. And, more important, as with any type of promotion or advertising, it keeps a particular one stop's organization in the accounts' minds almost daily.

Telemarketing has been used by one stops since long before it became such a major component of the selling process in so many other industries. One stops have people who call regular customers on a schedule and solicit orders. The credibility of these telemarketing people is very vital. The telemarketing people must be as unbiased as possible because they deal with a product known for a high level of "hype." In addition, labels and distribution people are constantly contacting all segments of the industry to get their message across.

Good distributor organizations will keep one stop people advised on everything. This is very important because the information flows both ways. Making sure everyone maintains their credibility is difficult but it can be done and is done most of the time. You cannot underestimate the importance of the "credibility factor," since hits spread quickly and mistakes become costly.

Keep in mind that unlike the individual branches of the four major distribution companies, one stops do not have a protected territory. If most of your business is solicited by phone, any one of your competitors can contact your customer list. This is done constantly. Every one stop knows who the customers are and has phone people soliciting them. Your customer must have confidence in the information you offer, as well as your being competitive with the fill and price factors.

Many times phone people will solicit orders on product for future release and shipment. One stops are solicited on new releases as far as six weeks in advance of initial shipments. By soliciting their customers, one stops become a very accurate barometer of what overall national requirements might be prior to shipment. This is a major service to distributors and record labels since one stops are usually solicited early due to the two-step nature of their activity. In addition, good one stops will take special orders for merchandise not usually carried in stock.

For the amount of volume they represent, one stops do not usually demand too much advertising. Where required by their accounts to provide advertising, one stops will acquire it. But it is not something that fits the rapid nature of their business.

There are also one stops who, in cooperation with the major distributors, will prepare special CDs of new material for retailers to play "in store" in an effort to create an interest among consumers. As will be covered in more detail when discussing major retail, "in store" play can be a major assist in launching new product.

Good one stops are very close to their customers and provide many other services. It is not uncommon for a one stop to give financial advice to a good account to help them avoid the pitfalls that befall so many small businesses. Once again, remember, one stops deal with small business, usually undercapitalized, and run completely by their owners. There are a number of other services one stops provide as noted in Chart 5-1.

The second aspect of a successful one stop's activity is **fill**. This refers to just how much of every order placed is actually in a one stop's inventory and thus can be shipped promptly. Good one stops will be able to ship at least 90%, and most times more, of everything ordered that day unless their suppliers, the major distribution companies, have not been able to keep up with demand. By working with a good one stop, small retailers can cover their needs within 24 hours in most situations. Because of their nature, major chains with centralized warehouses rarely can do this, so most major chains allow their stores to order from local one stops, another reason one stops must maintain such large and varied inventories in their warehouses.

Successful one stops use people and computers to constantly monitor their own "out of stock" positions, as well as sales. Their buyers try to stay as close to on-target with demand as possible. This is not easy due to the volatile nature of recorded

Chart 5-1

Services	Other Products
Items are grouped in descending order according to frequency of response	*Items are listed in descending order according to frequency of response*
POP	Accessories
Regular mailer	• • • •
• • • •	Apparel
Credit Line	CD-ROM
Full-line Catalog Listing	Full-Line Video
"Next Day Air"	• • • •
Pick-Up	Books
Promotional Support	Computer Software
• • • •	Database
Advertising Support	• • • •
EDI	Video Games
• • • •	
Computerized Inventory Info	
• • • •	
Fixtures	
In-store Play Service	
Rack Services	
Week-End Sales	

All data in this section unweighted.
Reprinted by permission of NARM.

products. When a recording starts to break out, everyone wants it immediately. Accounts and consumers are not willing to wait. Meanwhile, while trying to maintain an inventory to satisfy everyone, the one stop must have the financial backing to pay for its inventory.

It is common in many commercial ventures to try to use price as the major enticement to any customer. Many one stops will sell price first, trying to be slightly lower than competitors. However, if in order to offer a better price, **service and fill** suffer, a one stop's customer soon realizes the diminishing return and looks for a one stop with a fair price and one that is the same for all customers, so as not to put some retailers at a disadvantage with their competitors.

One aspect of the music industry is that there are really no secrets. Information about policies, prices, and other activities travels very rapidly. The only situation in which a one stop will vary price, and this is done very openly, relates to the amount of return percentage offered a customer. Some customers have an option to receive a better price, but lose the ability to return unsold product. This equation is far more important than one might suspect. Smart operators know that returns must be handled well and promptly. Merchandise that will never sell is too great a burden to ignore.

Keep in mind that through all of this, any retailers who can order the minimum quantities, fulfill the credit requirements, and absorb the product can buy directly from the distributors. By buying from one stops, they pay anywhere from 10% to 15% more. But, be assured, that penalty is well worth it, when you analyze the benefits accrued and the drawbacks of trying to buy direct. Once again, regarding returns, good one stops give their dealers credit for returned merchandise in about a week. Major distributors, on the other hand, issue the credits in anywhere from 45 to 60 days and require a great deal of paperwork.

One stops are a vital link in breaking a new product. The stores they service are critical to exposure and sales of new and breaking acts. Getting a product into the market place when airplay starts is the key. Since airplay usually starts in smaller markets, the one stop is your only conduit to the retailers in those markets.

One stops are extremely important to black/urban/rap products since this is mainly cash business, the products have short life spans, and releases are plentiful. Urban dealers require a working relationship with a supplier who can react quickly and who are in close proximity since so many small dealers in these areas personally pick up their product needs frequently, at least twice weekly or even more often. Most of this business is done on a cash basis. Major distributors are not set up to handle COD shipments. Small dealers would rather deal with one stops on a daily, "hand to mouth" basis. That way, the risk of creating overstocks is minimized, especially considering the short life of so much of the product.

There is a somewhat similar situation with country records since that product

Exercises

1. What three elements must a one stop provide its customer base to survive and prosper? Explain each.

2. What is the main role played by one stops in today's record climate?

3. One stop telemarketing people call accounts on a regular schedule. What is one of the most important factors in their relationship?

4. What are the pitfalls for a small dealer if all they expect from a one stop is a better price?

5. Urban/black product is very dependent on one stops for breaking it as well as selling it after it hits. Why?

Chapter 6
Rack Jobbers

Learning Objectives

After studying Chapter 6, you should be able to:

1. Define the term, "rack jobber"

2. Explain the functions of rack jobbing

3. Discuss the history of rack jobbing

4. Explain how a rack jobber supports hits

5. Describe the advantages and disadvantages of rack jobbing

6. Discuss the challenges of rack jobbing

Subdistribution II—Rack Jobbers

A second major type of subdistributor that plays a vital role in getting product to the consumer is the **rack jobber**. This role is even more important when dealing with "hit" product and certain other types of products, in particular, country, budget or lower priced product. The single largest company selling recorded products acquired from record companies is the Handleman Company, a *rack jobber*.

Rack jobbers service mass merchandisers, discount stores and chain operations— **Wal-Mart, Kmart, Target, Roses, Hills, Sears, Kroger, TG&Y, and many, many others**—large, multi-product stores, where records and tapes are a very small part of the overall mix in terms of dollars, but a very important factor in terms of creating store traffic. They also service smaller outlets. See Chart 6-1 for a profile of how and where rack jobbers do business and how they fit into the overall marketing structure.

One cannot overestimate the value of having a major "hit" by a major artist in a mass merchandiser's record department for drawing people to the location where they can buy many other products. This also works the other way in that the impulse shopper has a source for music purchases while in the store for another reason.

It is no accident that the introduction of rack jobbing to the music industry ran concurrent with a tremendous increase in the overall industry volume. Until the 1950s most record sales were through record dealers and department stores, a comparatively small number of outlets that fulfilled the needs of a fairly small segment of the population. To some degree, the market was small because access to the product was limited. Impulse buying really could not exist with that type of exposure.

It was then that the record companies started looking to expand the consumer base by making recorded products available in far more than the traditional record and department stores. This push came at about the same time that a new type of mass merchandising, the "discount house," was becoming the phenomenon of retailing. At that time, and throughout the early 1960s, one record company in particular, RCA Records, made a concerted effort to help a number of entrepreneurs start rack jobbing operations to take advantage of this new type of retailing as well as being able to gain access to other outlets that had heavy customer traffic. One of the first companies approached was the Handleman Company, which until that time was a major drug and sundries wholesaler. The Handleman Company had access to thousands of outlets and all their customers, and even though it meant starting from the bottom with music, the transition proved to be so successful, that within a short period of time, the company was out of its previous business and into records 100%. The Handleman Company is over 70 years old, but has been in the record business only since the early 1960s. Today, they are also very important to the computer software business and the video business as are other rack jobbers. In short, a major rack jobber is in the "home entertainment"

Chart 6-1

Types of Retail Outlets Serviced	Types of Products Racked
Discount Dept. Store	Items are listed in descending order according to frequency of response
Drug Stores	Budget audio
Retail Music Stores	Budget video
Convenience Stores	Christmas music
Supermarkets	Front line audio
Video Stores	Front line video
Other	Singles
Book Stores	Cut-outs
Traditional Dept. Stores	Books
Service PXs	CD-ROM
Wholesale Clubs	Computer software

---

business (something we will find to be true of retailing also). This is a natural transition since computer software and video product are similar in appearance as well as acceptance because the consumer is primarily the same person. The inventory control and physical warehousing and distribution of all these types of products are the same.

An executive with RCA Records, Irwin Tarr, was the impetus behind this effort by the industry. He put together a special staff of marketing people who covered the country to find businesses whose activities were similar to what would be required for record rack jobbing. This staff convinced businesses that supplying their customers with music could be very profitable for them as well as their accounts. At that time, news wholesalers were one of prime businesses to approach since their activities with books, magazines, and newspapers paralleled the way they would eventually distribute records and tapes. Tarr saw the potential of having small record departments in supermarkets, the new "discount houses," drug stores and other outlets that had heavy shopper traffic, as well as in the record stores and department stores where people expected to find music products. In this way, the industry was able to expose records to a far greater buying audience. It made buying music so much easier and available to just about every consumer.

The success of this strategy is evidenced by the fact that by the early 1970s rack-jobber supplied outlets were selling almost 80% of all recorded products. That has changed now because of the tremendous growth of retailing, a phenomenon that can be credited to the activities of rack jobbers in that they brought music to everyone and made it a necessity in just about everyone's life.

The major distributors and the independent distributors really do not want to sell to the stores serviced by rack jobbers directly, and for the most part, these stores would much rather be supplied by a rack jobber for a number of reasons. It takes a very large staff, with a major rack supplier having hundreds of employees, about half of them field service representatives who go into each store being racked on a regular basis. The rack jobbers must maintain huge warehouses and huge inventories in those warehouses to be able to supply the thousands of accounts they service. Successful rack jobbers must be heavily financed to be able to maintain those inventories, warehouses, and employees. They also require an expertise about the industry and record product that their accounts cannot expect to match. But, the overriding factor for all these mass merchandisers in retaining the services of a rack jobber is that the **rack jobber takes the risk**. This means that what does not sell is returned to the rack jobber eventually.

There are many other ramifications to how a rack jobber is forced to operate. Remember, the rack jobber does not have the control over the merchandising and placement of the product that the average retail outlets might exercise. This is just one of the many problems inherent in a rack jobber's doing business. Being highly computerized is almost a necessity.

Some years ago, the Handleman Company developed the RIMS system. This is an acronym for Retail Inventory Management System. This system tracks all aspects of a store's inventory. Service people count what is in stock by "wanding" each selection. This information is used many ways. To oversimplify the procedure, by sending it to a central location via phone lines, another computer with the help of product analysis people can determine what has been sold since the last count, what has to be replaced, or what should be deleted from that store's inventory. Space in each department is limited so the product mix is very vital, and this information gathering is keyed to keep it at its most saleable level. With some rack operations, this information is gathered manually, with field route people actually counting and filling out inventory sheets which are submitted and used to generate new orders for shipment to the stores. The information coming from any system not only dictates replenishment levels, but also helps to spot trends and is helpful when talking to the management of the mass merchandiser chains. As with all products today, the music industry is looking into the "radio" tags to make inventory management even faster and more accurate.

The average inventory in a racked outlet can run to almost 10,000 units. Multiply that by the thousands and thousands of stores serviced by rack jobbers and it is quite apparent that control and reliable information are mandatory. Also, keep in mind that of those 10,000 units, the rack jobber has to be reasonably sure it is the right "mix" of selections.

Keep in mind that not all rack operations deal in a full spectrum of products. Some knowingly limit their business to certain types of product, such as low-priced or budget goods. This product is put into stores in bulk and left there a prearranged period of time and then taken out to be replaced later by more bulk shipments.

Just about all the racked departments serviced by this type of subdistributor are unmanned, which means they have no clerks on duty, and it is agreed by most in the industry that self-service does not help record sales. Lack of people to supervise a department makes it difficult to keep any department looking inviting. The rack jobber's field people can only make periodic visits, so must count on personnel in each store to help keep the racks looking inviting between visits. Lack of clerks also creates problems in keeping inventory levels where they should be, especially on a fast selling product. With no one there to place orders as a selection sells down, you are going to be "out of stock" frequently. This is a major disadvantage, and while sending heavy quantities into stores can help to keep a store in stock longer, the rack jobber risks eventual overstocks that must be taken back, and it also requires what could be a precarious financial investment. Remember, the rack jobber takes the risk. With so many selections (tens of thousands) available to the consumer, and with limited space and infrequent opportunities to track sales, it becomes more obvious why multiproduct stores would rather use a rack jobber. It is obvious why they frequently need help and direction.

It is also why most racked departments are geared to the impulse shopper, stocking easily recognized products that should sell fairly quickly. It is estimated that in most racked departments, about 65% of the sales are on impulse. An additional reason for having to concentrate on fast moving selections is that there is precious little space for anything else. Once again, remember, space is tight and a rack jobber's performance is rated by the sales the department generates per square foot of space they have in each store serviced. The space limitations are a major obstacle in terms of what is stocked and how many pieces are stocked, and as well restrict display options. Not having supervision adds to the problem.

As with all segments of the industry that help deliver the product to the consumer, the racks also recognize the need to help "break" products. While they do not have the space or control that a chain of retail record stores might have, racks are trying to play a part in developing hits and artists by using their vast number of outlets to promote certain records they deem as possible hits. They go slow, but they do work at it. Appearances in the stores by the artists, use of what display space is available, and special sections for emerging acts, are some of the ways the rack jobber and their accounts are attempting to play a part in keeping the industry growing.

There is very little opportunity for display and in-store merchandising, which limits promotions to what are termed "endcaps," or bins at the ends of the fixtures holding most of the product. "In store" play is certainly not as readily available as in regular retail stores. However, some rack operations have been making inroads into this problem. Many outlets play music videos specifically compiled for their stores. This is even more effective than just audio play, since music video is a growing segment of the business and you get sound and picture to help sell a product. However, racked departments have traditionally been quite effective for the sale of certain types of products. For example, rack jobbers play a major role in the sale of hits from country artists. The location of racked departments is often in small towns where the local Wal-Mart or Kmart is the only source for recorded material. This demographic tends to be heavily oriented to country acts. However, good rack jobbers use the inventory information they gather to rate their stores not only on their capacity to sell the product, but just what type of product they can sell. This relates to having that proper "mix" needed to maximize sales. While country music has a great potential at the rack level, pop and black/urban are still a major part of their sales history. When a record attains real "hit" status, the rack jobbers give you the "tonnage." They move those hits in huge quantities because of the number of consumers they reach. A record just about must have heavy rack sales to move into the multiplatinum stage.

Advertising costs are very high since you cannot pick and choose markets. If you wish to do a promotion with Wal-Mart, you have to advertise in all the stores in a particular region. This makes the cost of advertising very high, since you must be in a number of publications. There is very little chance to "cluster" your advertising dollars and thus economize. In addition, the type of accounts usually supplied by rack jobbers do their advertising primarily in supplements in newspapers, usually the Sunday paper. This situation also tends to limit advertising to hit products because the sales expected must generate sizable advertising budgets.

The nature of a rack jobber's activity and customer base makes them very susceptible to heavy returns for a number of reasons. Foremost is the number of accounts serviced. As noted, if a record or video appears to have a big potential, rack jobbers are tempted to ship very heavy initial quantities to be sure that the stores do not run out. If the product does not live up to its potential, there is a very large residue of unsold product. Since racks usually play a lesser role in helping push a product to the hit level, they sometimes make big buys only to see the record stop. Then, there is no longer a market. Timing on records can be treacherous. Even good sellers have an abnormally high return percentage from rack jobbers because of the nature of their business. You have to overstock to make sure you get any sales at all.

To run major promotions you need long lead times since the rack jobber is locked into the advertising and promotion plans of large mass merchandisers. Once again, timing comes into play since it is impossible to predict when and if a record will peak. Unlike most everything else carried by mass merchandisers, advance planning is difficult. There are also a number of levels of management at these retailers so the rack job-ber and label have to guide the project through a very involved process.

The rack jobber operates in a constant price squeeze. Their outlets are very price con-scious and they keep constant pressure on their suppliers when it comes to pricing. As is the case with the one stop, there is very little room to maneuver. The rack jobber must pay all costs from a very small markup, since the stores want to be competitive with reg-ular record retailers and that leaves very little room. Major accounts shop the competi-tion and in many situations a rack jobber is supplying most of a big outlet's competition at the same time. They must be very careful in how they handle each.

There are a number of other pitfalls for rack jobbers. For example, consider that when dealing with a major chain of big discount stores, a great percentage of the rack's volume is tied up with just a handful of customers. Lose one and it has a tremendous impact. More than one rack jobber has been forced out of business just from losing one major account.

Major stores like Wal-Mart, Kmart and Sears usually buy most of their product directly. They do not like having a middleman. Records are about the only product in the store handled that way. While they are smart enough to know they need a rack jobber because the product is volatile, it goes against their normal way of doing business. It also means they have to share some of the profit. Because most big chains do not understand music and records, the rack jobbers are constantly reeducating them and explaining why music sales are always on a roller coaster. When some product gets big enough that everyone knows it is a hit, and supplies from the dis-tributors are backordered, it is very difficult to explain.

Because of the huge volume they generate for most of their suppliers, big chains are used to getting their own way. This makes them very difficult to deal with and come out ahead. They are very conscious of what their competitors are doing, so the rack jobber can get "the call" anytime. Their very large national chains are used to dealing in big sales figures. Records are not a high ticket item and it takes many sales to bring in appreciable dollars. But records give them something they want very badly: <u>TRAFFIC</u>.

Major chains are also an easier sell for a rack's competitor. You can always find something wrong with any racked department, so you have a story to tell. If you are a competing rack jobber you claim you can do better; while this is not always true, everyone does it.

Major chains also like to have more than one rack supplier that so they can play one against the other and ask for more advertising dollars, and also to make sure they're getting the best program available. Since the rack jobber supplies the fixtures in all their outlets, this can be a very big yearly bill. The need to reconfigure a store can come for many reasons:

The industry introduces new configurations.

Their accounts redesign or upgrade their stores.

The industry makes changes in packaging.

Traffic flow wears out fixtures and some break.

But not everything is on the "downside." While dealing with a large chain can mean you must convince many levels, it also means that when you make the "sale" you will see very strong billing.

When the industry is having a run of big hits, the rack jobbers will benefit most. Their outlets are the outlets where the big sales accrue and as long as the labels can produce and break acts, the racks will have a good supply of the hit product to run through their stores. The surge in popularity in country product and country radio in the early 1990s resulted in the rack jobber share of overall business going up substantially from previous years.

Handled properly, the racks can make any marketing plan very successful, because that is the fastest way to blanket the whole country with the product when a hit starts to sell. The racks are the best and most efficient way to distribute the product to every corner of a region or the nation, at exactly the time when the need for speed is paramount. Remember, rack jobbers take the risk, so they do not have to sell their accounts on specific titles. One sales call on the part of the distributor or label can result in very heavy orders and very wide distribution.

Racked outlets are excellent locations to sell budget goods, or low-priced records. In most cases, this type of goods has been amortized by its label, and about all it pays are low royalties and pressing or duplication costs. The shopper in rack jobber-supplied stores is usually very price conscious and this product is very attractive.

Military Sales

There are two other major customers that we should discuss when we talk about rack jobbers, because they are really large racks. One is Eurpac and the other is AAFES, the Army and Air Force Exchange Service. These two accounts are totally different from traditional rack suppliers in that they deal exclusively with the military. Overall (all types of product) military sales are presently a $15 billion business, and home entertainment is one of the top three categories. There are currently about 1.6 million retired and active duty military personnel which translates to a market of about 10 million consumers.

Navy post exchanges, commissaries and ships are supplied primarily by an organization called Eurpac, based in Virginia Beach, Virginia. Unlike AAFES, the Navy is not appropriated funds to support their activity. In addition to PXs, commissaries, and Navy ships, Eurpac has programs for putting large, full service home entertainment stores on Navy installations. The Navy's attitude is why should their people spend their money off the bases, especially when they can get a better deal on the

Exercises

1. In the 1970s what percentage of domestic record sales went through rack jobbers? This has changed; who does the major share now and why?

2. Mass merchandisers do not necessarily like having a "middleman" handle a particular type of product in their stores. But in the case of records and videos it makes sense. Why?

3. Advertising through racked accounts (mass merchandisers) is more difficult than through retail record chains. What are the problems?

4. While rack-jobber serviced outlets have few options for helping break hits, what can they do for a major hit and why?

5. Rack jobbers are susceptible to very heavy returns. Why?

6. What type of product sells better in racked outlets and why?

Chapter 7

Retail

Learning Objectives

After studying this chapter you should be able to define:

1. The word "retail"

2. The word "retail" as it applies to record distribution

3. The role of a "Mom and Pop" operation in retail record distribution

4. The role of an alternative music store in retail record distribution

5. The role of a major chain in retail record distribution

6. The roles of people, product, merchandising, marketing, and theft prevention in the success of a retail operation

7. Why effective computerization is so necessary to a large retail operation

Retail

Retail: most dictionaries will say it means "to sell goods in small quantities to the ultimate consumer." But when talking about music retail, it could be better defined by saying *"to sell dreams in large quantities to the ultimate consumer."* As has been pointed out previously, what the music retailer sells is not necessary to sustain life nor to afford the means to sustain health and guard against the elements. But, music does have a major impact on just about everyone's daily life.

Retail Stores: According to an RIAA survey, from 1992, when the earliest surveys were available, to 2001, most prerecorded product was sold in traditional record stores. (See Chart 7–1). In 2001 and 2002, there was a notable increase in product going through "other stores." These were the Best Buys, Circuit City's, and other mass merchandisers and "entertainment superstores." The "other store" category just about matched record store activity.

Then in 2003, a NARM study shows the balance swinging away from record stores as noted in Chart 7–2 and Chart 7–3. Mass merchandisers and electronics stores increased their share considerably during that period. As expected, online sales also increased dramatically.

Even though record stores (or CD stores as they are termed in the NARM study— Charts 7–2 and 7–3) had given way to another form of retail, they still command a great deal of attention from record companies. They are far more capable of becoming partners in helping to push and expose product—new artists in particular. Both record labels and record stores need "hits" as well as hit artists to survive.

There is more to the increase in the growth of record stores than just an area to find new products. Record purchasing is really entertainment. Record stores provide an environment that not only sells entertainment, but is also entertainment in itself. The music being showcased, the color, the variety of choices, the excitement of hav-

Chart 7-1

	1992	1993	1994	1995	1996	1997	1998	1999	2000	2001
RECORD STORE	60.0	56.2	53.3	52.0	49.9	51.8	50.8	44.5	42.4	42.5
OTHER STORE	24.9	26.1	26.7	28.2	31.5	31.9	34.4	38.3	40.8	42.4
TAPE/RECORD CLUB	11.4	12.9	15.1	14.3	14.3	11.6	9.9	7.9	7.6	6.1
TV, NEWSPAPER, MAGAZINE AD OR 800 NUMBER	3.2	3.8	3.4	4.0	2.9	2.7	2.9	2.5	2.4	3.0
INTERNET[6]	NA	NA	NA	NA	NA	0.3	1.1	2.4	3.2	2.9

% purchases; they are not assigned a particular category by Hart Research.

Permission to cite or copy these statistics is hereby granted as long as proper attribution is given to the Recording Industry Association of America.

Reprinted courtesy of RIAA

Chart 7–2
Market Summary: Channel shift continues

CD Stores continued to concede dollar share to Big Box and Online retailers, dropping another 4 ppts in 2004.

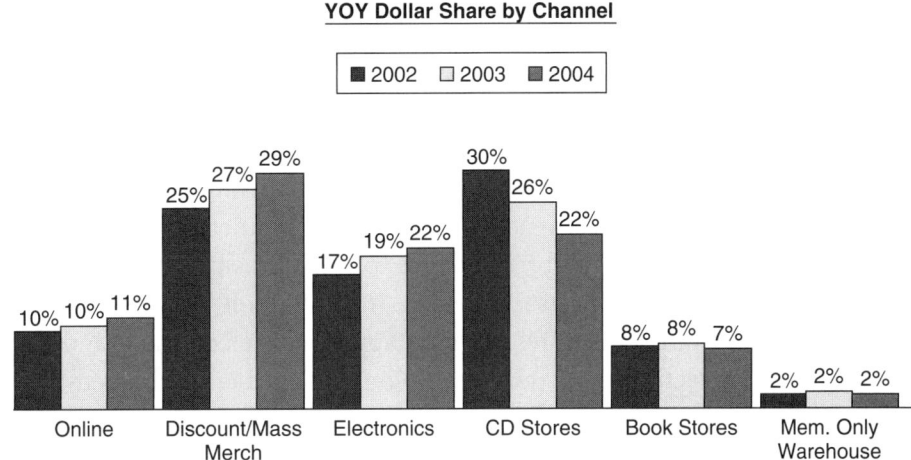

YOY Dollar Share by Channel

■ 2002   □ 2003   ■ 2004

Source: NPD MusicWatch; Full-length CD

Chart 7–3
Market Summary: Channel shift continues

Online's unit share is slightly higher than its dollar share.

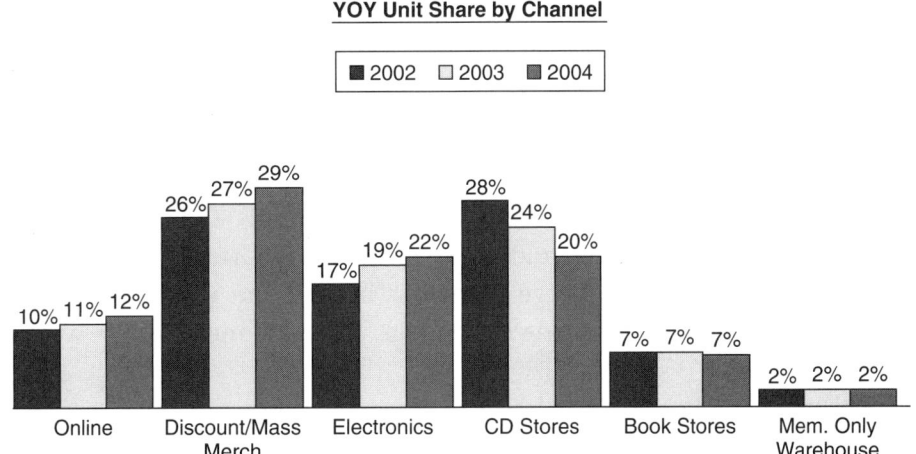

YOY Unit Share by Channel

■ 2002   □ 2003   ■ 2004

Source: NPD MusicWatch; Full-length CD

ing bins and bins of music, all help to create an aura that leaves you with a feeling of being entertained whether you make a purchase or not. Today's consumers are used to excitement surrounding just about everything they purchase as the interior design of stores becomes as important as the inventory in those stores. All-inclusive shopping malls provide something for all types of consumers, and the record stores are prominently placed in these malls. The record store is our present society's "candy store." This is where the people, usually young people, congregate, and the environment provided them is the drawing card.

The number of outlets continued to grow into the early to mid 1990s, as all major chains continued to open new stores, while the growth of a fairly new aspect of retailing, the alternative stores, added to the growth. In some areas, another type of specialty retailer has had an impact. This is the retail outlet devoted primarily to dance music. People hear it in clubs and dance to it in clubs but really want to have it at home for a variety of reasons. But by the mid 1990s it became apparent that added competition from superstores carrying appliances, electronics, and software as well as records, "electronic superstores" if you will, had created an environment where there were too many outlets. That is when a number of major retail record chains started closing hundreds of stores in order to survive. This came at a time when the entertainment dollar was being stretched very thin. Young people were spending more time in front of computer screens and not listening to music.

Major retailers started to close stores in the late 1990's, but the really heavy attrition came in 2002, 2003, and on into 2004, when due to bankruptcies, declining per store sales, and the threat from the digital world, major chains started to close stores with a vengeance. In many locations the real estate was more valuable than the sales activity.

To add to the malaise, the youth market disposable income is also being siphoned off for games to feed Playstations and X-Cubes. In-theater movie viewing, as well as videos are taking their toll too, as movie theaters, which had been hurting very badly, so badly that many chains were in or near bankruptcy, started to see daylight with a number of blockbuster releases. However the motion picture industry does not come close to the volume generated by recorded music. The major siphon from record stores was the explosion of DVD. Granted, many music chains sold or rented DVD, but many dollars went to video stores and other outlets, rather than to audio. As the millennium started so did a huge surge in interest in DVD, but mostly movies. Music DVD's could not approach the movie excitement, and non-music outlets were moving so many movie DVD's.

The debate about how much "burning" (copying), downloading, and product being available via "e" commerce and other digital means, has hurt the retail store will rage for some time. But everyone agrees, something has hurt store sales. That is why the need to keep that environment in record stores as exciting as possible becomes even more important. As is the case with so much of our culture today, this phenomenon has its roots in the past. Music retailing is no different. Years ago the "listening booth" was an integral part of any record store. As more and more nontraditional music outlets opened, primarily in discount stores and other locations being serviced by rack jobbers, the listening booth was phased out. Even the few regular record stores that survived this period were anxious to phase them out to eliminate the cost, the use of space, the need to have opened product available to be previewed in an era when shrink wrapping records was mandatory, and the added labor costs. Now this aspect of music retailing has come full circle as retailers are opening larger and larger stores with a far more extensive selection. Having a way for consumers to hear products is now a primary requirement for major retailers, and listening stations, in one form or another, are quite common.

This rebirth of an old gimmick has also created another source of income for retailers. The record companies pay to have their product featured in the list of selections that can be heard this way by the consumer before making a purchasing decision.

There were some other significant changes in retailing in the late 1980s and into the 1990s. Stores became larger and larger. The small stores were the domain of the "Mom and Pop" outlets and the alternative stores.

At one time radio was the major advertising medium for major retailers, but according to a recent NARM study, print has edged ahead, and every major chain reports that it uses print advertising. It is still the best way to advertise price, a major factor in the market.

While the number of stores might be diminishing, the size of the stores continues to grow, giving the major chains the ability to make their stores more exciting, giving them space to carry larger and more diversified inventories and providing the consumer with all the visual and auditory choices possible. Existing retail chains have embraced this philosophy with their newer, much larger stores, but the entry of chains like Circuit City and Best Buy into offering prerecorded music, has hastened the transition.

But no matter what level of retailing we will be discussing, the backbone of good retail can be summed up in five categories:

1. People
2. Product
3. Merchandising
4. Marketing
5. Loss Prevention

Depending on the level of direct management of a store by the owner, these five basics will take on additional or diminished importance.

"Mom and Pop" Stores

This category of a retail music store is run directly by the owner, therefore the first of the above categories is well represented. You have to assume that as the owner and operator, you have most of your people problems covered. However, there is usually a need for additional help, full time or part time, but your being in the store most of the time allows you to observe and supervise. This is certainly a major factor in keeping loss prevention at an absolute minimum. As owner/operator, you or perhaps a close family member is in the store most of the time and keeping an eye on the investment. There is usually one store involve; although there can be additional stores, that number will be very small. The owner is involved in every single aspect of the store's operation, and it is the owner who takes all the financial risk. However, the small store does have an advantage in that the markup requirements are lower than that of the major chains.

In most cases, these stores are owned by people who are very committed to music, the music "junkies" if you will. They are totally involved in the music, either love it or hate it and have complete autonomy over what they will keep in inventory and what they will try to sell. No matter how opinionated they might be, their expertise is the very best. They live with the music daily, and they learn all there is to know about it. This is very instrumental in knowing what product to stock.

In addition, they usually know their customers' music preferences very well and use this edge to keep them coming back. They can advise them of upcoming releases that they know will be desirable, or at the very least, acceptable, and they have frequent contact with customers. This high level of emotional involvement in particular types of music is very beneficial to the industry in getting certain types of products started toward the top of the charts. New genres of music, such as urban music and international music, all get their start in these small stores that service a comparatively small group of consumers. The small dealers can be very zealous about their music preferences. The investment is theirs, they know their customer and they can physically watch the inventory levels constantly. Their most important advantage over other types of more impersonal retailers is that they talk face-to-face with their customers frequently. No matter what the product, surveys about what are the most effective means to sell a product usually put "word of mouth" way up on the list. There is no way to put a price on the advertising impact of people talking positively about a product, and it is even more of a factor when you consider the nature of recorded music or video. Music is one of the most subjective items offered for sale, and therefore the inspired recommendation of someone whose opinion you respect has a major impact on your buying decision. This impact is magnified when the product is right there in the store and available for purchase. The operator of a small store can merchandise on a one-on-one basis far less expensively than major chains and far more effectively.

The primary conduit to the "mom and pop" stores is the one stop. No small record retailer has more than adequate financing. If money were readily available, most would use it to expand out of the "mom and pop" category and into more and larger stores, which means being a chain retailer. Since cash is always a consideration, it is much easier, much wiser, and much safer to deal with a reliable one stop. In practice, a small record store works out of the one stop's inventory since product requirements can be purchased on a daily basis in many instances. However, the usual routine is to buy twice weekly, unless something breaks very unexpectedly, and even then the one stop is right there to supply the product in a very short time. Small retailers do not have the financial resources to buy ahead and have stock sitting in inventory. As discussed when outlining the role of the one stop, small retailers cannot buy enough to qualify for the minimum purchases that the five major distribution companies impose on them. Consumer's desires, especially in music, change very quickly. It is imperative to have what they want in stock at that precise moment and available for sale right then and there. Should the consumer leave without that item, your chances of getting that sale diminish tremendously. Not only do you run the risk of the consumer going to another store, but it is quite possible that the consumer will hear something else being played and the buying decision will certainly be altered.

Alternative Stores

This segment of the retail world is similar in many respects to the "mom and pop" operations but with some definite differences. Alternative outlets can be small chains and more than one store, but not regional or national. If there is a chain, it will be in one city. The nature of their business is such that once again, close contact with customers is the rule, but even closer contact and involvement with the product is also the rule. Alternative stores are usually located in low rent strips and have none of the "glitz" of regular retail outlets. Alternative stores are usually found near colleges and other entertainment areas of cities where people go to eat, drink, and have fun. The stores are jammed with products, signing is usually fairly basic, and it is where you go to find vinyl versions and other "gems" and hard to locate releases since much of the inventory in alternative stores is used records. This is where the consumers trade in product. There is quite a market for used CDs that are traded in and then resold. However, the used CD trade has been expanded beyond alternative stores. There are stores devoted to used CDs exclusively, and now major players are entering that market.

The clientele at alternative stores is very much into music and many feel that chain operations are far too sterile and do not have knowledgeable staffing. This consumer will dig through the crowded bins and will ask what new trends are emerging and what products are being released to fan the flames of those trends.

Alternative outlets are vital to the success of new acts and new releases. Any experimental product pretty much has to be started at the alternative level of retailing. After being part of the music business "underground" for many years, record companies realized their importance and appointed marketing people to cover these stores and work with the owners and staffs. This attention paid off handsomely since alternative stores had the interested consumer as customers and their staffs were interested in the music themselves and were anxious to see experimental product break into the mainstream. Rap had its small urban stores; new age, and new rock had alternative outlets.

This type of store became even more vital to breaking hits as Billboard went to Nielsen SoundScan system for its charts, a procedure where an actual piece count of what was being sold over the counters determined a record's chart position. Alternative stores became part of this procedure and that gave any new product a better chance to be recognized.

Like the smaller dealers, alternative outlets have the same limitations on what they can afford to carry in inventory. Once again, purchasing is done primarily through one stops; however, a larger percentage of purchases goes to the major distributors than is the case with small, single outlet generalized record stores. In the mid 1990s, small dealers and small dealer chains have been uniting into what has been termed "coalition stores." By presenting a unified approach, the "coalition stores" feel they can compete for distributor attention and advertising as well as one stop attention. The label marketing people responsible for alternative stores keep in close touch and make sure there is at least adequate inventory on the "work" projects on hand. But the main focus is to see what type of movement is taking place to judge the strength of a new release and the timing for bringing it to the mainstream retailers.

The evolution of record retailing has followed the rules of selective process whereby when a void appears, someone will be ready to fill it. As the diversity of products being made available to the consumer increases, the industry must find new outlets that can concentrate on specialized segments of the releases and make sure they have a fair hearing.

Major Chains

By far, the greatest volume of sales and the most activity dollarwise takes place in chain retail outlets. There are a number of national and regional chains of retail music stores devoted largely to audio and video products.

The overriding factor for all chain operators is to be where the people are. A great deal of time and money is spent on market research to almost guarantee a demographic that is close enough, passes by often enough, and has enough income to support a store. Therefore, the primary locations for large record chain outlets are in malls, strip centers and freestanding buildings. There are benefits and drawbacks to each type of location as noted below.

Comparison: Mall Versus Strip Retail Location

Factors	Mall	Strip
Rent	Very high, growing	Lower
Traffic	Heavy, mall attracts	Consumer drives must attract
Advertising	Tell price, features	Same, but also must draw traffic
Use Clause	Mall protects tenants	No restrictions
Image	Mall must approve	Fewer limitations
Promotion	Mall must approve	Few limitations
Video Rental	Terrible in malls	Great traffic builder
Competition	Some mall protection but decreasing	Very little in same strip
Visibility	Destination location	Consumer choice
Renewing leases	Tied in to other malls	Less pressure
Markup Required	*40% to 44% overall	35% to 40% overall

* Stores with both mall and freestanding look for 41% average

For the past few years, the trend has been to open in freestanding locations or strip centers. The number of malls being built has diminished due to lack of available space for development, an uncertain economy and other factors. Meanwhile, malls have long lists of restrictions that retailers would rather avoid. However, many chains are tied in very closely with mall developers and therefore are almost mandated to go into a mall when that particular developer completes a project. In addition, at one time mall operators protected music retailers from too much competition within the same mall. This protection is not as strong as it once was, nor is it as important in this era of megamalls.

Rents are usually much more attractive in strip centers and with the research done by major retailers on new locations, it is much easier to place the new store in just the right area. There are strip locations available just about everywhere, either through new building or empty slots in existing strip centers. Freestanding locations are just as plentiful, and offer some other advantages, such as really being able to pinpoint a location and the most convenient parking, and no restrictions as a result of other tenants nearby.

Meanwhile, as the record store chains close stores, the mass merchandisers and electronics stores are increasing their locations and at the same time increasing their share of the market.

In retail, the five major concepts noted above, **People, Product, Merchandising, Marketing,** and **Loss Prevention** really become the backbone of the operation. No longer do we have a situation where the owner is there to watch everything. Now you have layers and layers of management making the decisions and supervising a large cadre of people. As you work your way up or down the table of operations, just about every activity must be directed at the consumer, where the money changes hands.

People: No computer program, no procedure, or no amount of cheerleading can replace good people. These aspects can make good people operate better, but you need the right raw material. Then the operative words become "well trained, well supervised." All the people involved—employees, customers, and vendors—are valuable assets. Your employees must be shown that there are higher goals to be attained in your company if they perform well, and you must reward them when the opportunities arise. Motivation, leadership training and good recruiting are key factors in having the right people. Labor costs are a very high percentage of operating overhead. Only good people give you the proper return on that investment. **Even with good people, how they are managed eventually determines success or failure.**

Product: Just about all major outlets have central buying offices and most also have centralized warehousing. The product is ordered by the purchasing people and shipped to a central location where it is then made available to the individual stores. All major chains attempt to purchase 100% of their needs centrally, but this is rarely possible. That is why even the major stores utilize the one stops for fill ins of local bands or localized hits, some backorders, releases from small independent labels, and in some cases, all singles because of their volatile nature. Specialty items are growing as part of the retail store inventory mix and not all of these can be purchased centrally. Therefore, more and more local autonomy might have to be given to individual store managers or at least their district supervisors.

Keeping track of inventory requirements and inventory positions takes the combined expertise of people and the phenomenal ability of computers to sort and hold information. That is the only way to stay abreast of what must be in the stores and in the warehouses with the tens of thousands of SKUs (stock keeping units) in retail stores today. The rapidity of the way a product suddenly becomes very saleable or totally unsalable, as is the case with a recorded product, mandates sophisticated and very expensive computers and computer programs being directed by very experienced and knowledgeable people to maximize the dollars an outlet invests in product. We speak frequently about the "record junkies" in relation to small owner-operated stores and alternative stores. But the "record junkies" really excel as buyers for the major chains. These are the people who listen to just about everything that is released. Hard to imagine, but they find time. However, the most important factor is their absolute love of music. It is a passion that is very hard to describe.

Another major factor is the buying philosophy of each retail organization, not only in the overall scheme of buying, but also regarding the needs of each store as dictated by size and location (consumer demographics). Each differs in how it reacts to new artists, what percentage of the inventory is in catalog, what percentage in hits. The feedback from the computerized cash registers, the store personnel, radio charts in the area and sales histories elsewhere must all be carefully considered when buying and stocking decisions are being made. The investment is staggering. A fairly small (2500 to 5000-square-foot) location can have almost 39,000 units in inventory in records, tapes and video. This translates into millions of dollars in the superstores with tens of thousands of square feet of selling space. In addition, each category of inventory—hits, catalog, budget, cutouts and nonrecorded items (accessories)—have different profit margins. Even configurations must be factored in, since cassettes and CDs have different markups due to wholesale pricing, while as has been explained, how accounts take advantage of discount programs, dating and returns also has an impact on the overall margins.

However, video rental, which was a major moneymaker for freestanding and strip center locations in the 1980s, fell off somewhat in the early 1990s but appeared to recover by mid-decade. It is still a factor to some retailers, but is no longer the salvation it once was when the audio industry could not deliver the hits. Some major players are moving away from video rental. The video rental market is running into a saturation situation, is running out of titles (movies cannot be released as frequently as records) and video viewing is really not portable, a factor that has helped the audio industry immeasurably in the past decade. DVD is addressing this, however. DVD's can be played on laptops, and while not as many of those are in circulation as are Walkmans, it is the start of portability. Early in the new century, DVD really gave the video market something to cheer about, but about that time, equipment to copy DVD's was hitting the consumer market. Throughout the '90's and into the new millennium, TV viewing has increased, but rentals have been somewhat stagnant. Competition from more and more cable channels being available as well as "pay per view" is not helping the rental market. As with all aspects of the entertainment world, every few months, consumers are offered more choices.

For decades, the record business considered itself recession proof, but that is no longer the case. However, it still remains more recession proof than many other areas since product is a comparatively inexpensive item that generates a great deal of excitement and entertainment. The industry must continue to deliver major hits and bring major new acts into prominence, a reality that is not lost on the retailers. Therefore they try to do everything they can to help break in new products. Until recently, most slowdowns in the music industry could be related directly to a lack of product that the consumers wanted. This will never change. The music industry is one of the most "product driven" businesses you will ever find.

Merchandising: Merchandising is the development of new products and bringing them to the forefront. The factors that impact on how successfully stores are merchandised are the "look" of a store and the ambiance it creates for the shopper. This ambiance is created by the imaginative use of:

Display
Signing
Cleanliness
Lighting
Video screens
Header cards
Display bins
Traffic flow
Window display (if available)
Color
Special merchandise pyramids or tables
Sale product areas, step downs
Ease of locating product
Playing product in the store
. . . and more.

This is all part of the visual and audio overload that has become almost mandatory in today's retailing. Retail growth is being sparked by the better education levels and ever widening and more detailed musical tastes of consumers all over the world. This trend will continue and retail must remain innovative and offer larger and more diverse stores to succeed, especially in the major cities of the world. Most merchandising is a joint effort between the stores, the labels, and distribution companies. Since the labels pay for 95% of the display and advertising, they play an important part in what is displayed, what is featured in the stores and what is advertised. The labels and distribution companies maintain merchandising staffs that spend most of their time in stores placing and creating displays. A large portion of any label's advertising and promotion budget is spent on display material. Some display can be planned and generated in advance of releases while other material must wait for the development of a project. Therefore, some is very elaborate and some is very basic and can be produced quickly.

Just acquiring the space for that display can be very costly also. The *Wall Street Journal* reports that for windows in large stores in the busy midtown blocks in Manhattan, the major record companies can pay up to $200,000 per year, a major source of revenue for these stores. The *Wall Street Journal* goes on to report that some record executives suggest that the top four companies spend at least $10 million a year this way.

There are a number of other schemes worked up by all segments of the business—retailers, rack jobbers, and one stops—to be rewarded for their ability to get to the consumers and to tell them the story the record companies want told.

Marketing: Successful major outlets spend heavily to market their stores. In today's world perception is the key. Perception is what makes a particular store a consumer's favorite store. All advertising, though usually used to feature a specific product, also devotes much of the space or airtime to selling the particular chain and its locations. The stores work very hard at selling the particular type of ambiance they have created. This is why major stores are returning to methods and equipment that allow consumers to preview the product before purchasing. Much of the technology incorporates computerization and cellular technology, and makes tens of thousands of selections available for preview. Marketing personnel know their customers and tailor everything they do in the stores to those customers' preferences and lifestyles. A large investment is made in researching potential locations, the specifics of which will be explained when discussing market research in general. Once this investment is made and a decision reached about where to open a store, the marketing starts, so it can be said that marketing begins by knowing the demographics.

Having fair, competitive prices is part of the marketing process, as is matching what is played in the store with the type of customer usually present at that time of the day. Offering trading stamps, frequent buyer programs, or other incentives can create positive consumer reaction and return visits. Getting repeat customers is one of the absolute requirements of successful retailing. A very large percentage of tickets to concerts, theaters, sports events, and other entertainment locations are sold in record stores via automated equipment. This brings customers into the stores, another marketing ploy.

Good retailers are always looking for "events" to have in their stores to build traffic, image and repeat customers. The product mix is vital to success as is tying in with whatever is "hot" at a given time. With the success of Disney video products a number of years ago came merchandising ideas for many other Disney products. Wherehouse, which operates around the country, is very successful with entire Disney sections in the audio sections in their bigger stores as they take advantage of a major marketing trend.

Training store people in telephone technique certainly has a place, but the most important training is to teach people how to handle the customers. Many successful retail chains have extensive training programs in these subject areas. This is not a new ploy. For some time, many major department stores have been trying to emulate the customer service record of Nordstroms. They are not reluctant to spend the money since the return is certainly worth it.

Loss Prevention: Loss exists at every level of retail, small store or large operation. It also exists at every level of the entire industry, no matter what the activity. There are figures that indicate the overall industry loss to shrinkage is between 4% and 4.5%. Good retail companies usually can keep it to around 1.5% to 2%, but it takes a lot of effort and expense. There is much more to shrinkage than what is attributable to shoplifting by consumers. This aspect is a small portion. Much more theft is attributable to employees. At one time it was estimated that almost 50% of chain employees were guilty of theft. The methods are almost endless. The amount of paperwork in keeping track of orders, shipments, receipts, shipping errors, listing discounts and dating is far more costly than what can be spirited out of a store.

All the types of accounts explained to this point play a part in the marketing of product, but by far, major retail plays the most important role. There are aspects of retail that lend themselves to the exposure and heavy sale of product, be it new acts or established artists. A simple comparison of the square footage of selling space available with retail would appear to tell the whole story. But that is not the case. There are a number of other benefits to the marketing people in dealing with national and regional groupings of stores.

Major retailers bring the widest range of selection to the consumer, such as deep catalog, classical and jazz. With the proliferation of not only specialty labels, but also "niche" type products, only chain retailers can expose these records in fairly large quantities. Changing lifestyles, changing income levels, and changing methods of recorded music exposure continue to feed the growth of major chains. Major stores usually have new releases in place first since in most cases, while they are usually supplied out of central warehouses, new releases are drop shipped to individual stores to be in place as soon as the release date arrives.

Majors advertise heavily and create excitement for the recorded product. You can be sure they will advertise major releases first. A small dealer can tell a small group of loyal customers about new product, but chains put it in the paper, on the radio, and now on TV. All retail helps by playing the music in stores. Major chains that span a region or the country can really give you more advertising impact for each dollar expended. "Cluster" advertising makes it possible for labels to allocate advertising dollars for use in areas where a chain is a dominant factor due to the number of stores in a city. However, they can get chainwide placement and even possibly a sale price as a result of that expenditure. Retail chains also have the ability to run far more selections on sale due to their financial condition and their access to advertising and promotional monies from the labels and distribution companies.

When stores are staffed as are record stores, they can give much more service to a consumer and have a far greater chance of making the sale than the type of outlet that caters to the impulse shopper only. Additionally, retailers have more display space and can create more of a desire to buy.

One the most effective methods to expose music is through playing it within a store. It is so effective that even mass merchandisers are experimenting with many methods of doing the same to help music sales in their stores. There are a number of examples of "in store" play actually starting new acts on the road to a major hit. It has become a major part of the marketing mix.

All major retailers with a substantial presence in a community are very close to the radio stations in that area. Radio and retail combine for many effective promotions, remote broadcasts or other means of bringing the stations' call letters and the name of the store before the public. Being aware of this can help the marketing people get cooperation all the way around.

Retailers are all going to point of purchase or point of sale computerization. This is very necessary to increase sales, TRACK SALES, and cut down on returns. This process has a number of other benefits to the labels and their marketing people. With reporting to *Billboard* for chart information being done via the Nielsen SoundScan system and thus being highly computerized, trends and sales outlooks can be obtained almost daily. This is very important to the marketing people as they make advance plans and allocate funds. Marketing plans are now being made for just about every stage of a record's life.

No matter where or how a project gets started, and no matter what the type of product, major retailers will work with labels on new acts and help get the record on the charts and into the mainstream. You must have the record stores to build a record, to build an act and certainly to get the volume to make it all highly profitable. This activity helps keep the industry healthy. When the product is there, when there are hits to be broken, retail will be at the forefront.

Until a short while ago, this is where the growth in the industry took place. Then came the introduction of the "entertainment superstore." While retail record chains have drastically slowed the opening of new stores and many are closing existing stores, many of the newer stores opening in the past few years are much larger than the stores opened previously, and some of the older stores, when renovated, are expanding into larger spaces or moving to larger spaces in the same mall or strip center. Most chains have started to diversify in their selection of new store sites. This gives them access to the best of each type of outlet.

No one really knows what the Internet has in store for consumers of prerecorded music. As has been seen, traditional retailers of music are heavily invested in Web sites. Other companies in the "e-business" are selling records to consumers. Meanwhile, the frantic search to figure out a sensible (and profitable for record companies) way to download music continues to heat up. Record company executives know what they have to sell, and they will use every avenue available. The changes in marketing approach are developing as rapidly as the new technologies. The fact that the largest group of record consumers is young and very computer friendly means that this whole process will be accelerated. The record companies, publishers, and artists will overcome the copyright, piracy, and billing issues, possibly not to everyone's satisfaction, but certainly to most segments of the creative and marketing process. However, the Internet will be addressed in far more detail later in this text.

Summary

Prerecorded music products are not necessary to sustain health or life but make daily living emotionally bearable and esthetically comprehensible. In 1994, 59% of all recorded music products were sold in retail stores with the growth continuing as major chains open new stores. The growth of retail outlets depends heavily upon the following:

(1)   People

(2)   Product

(3)   Merchandising

(4)   Marketing

(5)   Loss Prevention

The largest volume of sales and the most activity dollarwise occurs in chain retail outlets. The remainder is in single proprietorship or partnership business arrangements known as Mom and Pop and alternative stores.

Everything about retailing recorded products must be designed and implemented so that the consumer is entertained during every phase of the marketing process. The success of any marketing approach depends upon an appealing, exciting environment in the retail outlet, the knowledge and attitude of the people who are serving the customer, the product that is chosen for sale, the congruence of the

4. What are some of the factors that determine the ambiance of a record store?

5. How can retail record stores be more of a help in breaking product than one stops and rack jobbers?

6. Explain "cluster advertising."

7. Explain economy of advertising.

Chapter 8
Music Products Industry

Learning Objectives

After studying this chapter you should be able to do the following:

1. Discuss overall trends in retail and merchandising

2. Explain the kinds of business skills necessary in starting a music retail outlet

3. Describe the legal and business environment under which a retail music business must operate

4. Describe the organizational structure, marketing strategy and dollar value of the Music Products Industry 2005 market

5. Describe the method of distribution of music products to sellers

6. Explain the process of printed music distribution and organizational structure

7. Identify the sales trends in each product category

8. Describe the global marketing strategy of the Music Products Industry

Retail Trends

Retail is the most vulnerable sector of the U.S. economy. In retail business consumers rather than business-to-business purchases make up the bulk of income. Customers are more immediately affected by economic fluctuations and retail operations are often the first to feel the strength or weakness of consumer confidence.

Retail shopping has changed dramatically over the last 20 years. Shoppers once preferred large metropolitan or suburban department stores offering a broad range of both apparel and household merchandise. Stores such as Sears, Montgomery Ward and J. C. Penney were the dominant examples of this type of retail operation. This type of retail operation was supplemented by local merchants who were able to provide greater convenience at prices only slightly higher than department stores charged. Shoppers now want greater selection and more competitive prices than this general department store/neighborhood merchant model can provide. Successful stores today tend to fall into two formats: Superstore or Microspecialist. Many of the chain record retail outlets tend to utilize the superstore concept in upscale communities.

The characteristics of the microspecialist include: (1) carefully edited, broad assortment within a narrow product segment; stores tend to be small, and carry lifestyle merchandise which satisfies emotional needs, and the consumer perceives the assortment as unique (2) quality service and upscale ambiance; (3) high-margin, full-priced oriented; and (4) convenience with a carefully edited assortment.

The need for microspecialist such as music specialty stores are needed in the public schools, as baby boomers age, as rock bands continue to set trends and newer types of electronic instruments and equipment continue to revolutionize the industry. The music specialty store or music retail outlet consist of four main categories according to the National Music Merchants Association. The following is a brief description of each:

1. Piano—Majority of sales derived from pianos, organs and electronic keyboards.

2. School music—Band and orchestral instrumental sales but percussion, guitars, amplifiers, electronic keyboards, combo-sound reinforcement and recording equipment would be included.

3. Rock/combo-sound reinforcement—Stores which carry acoustic guitars, electronic guitars, instrument amplifiers, electronic keyboards.

4. Full-line—All acoustical and electronic instruments; percussion, sound reinforcement equipment, print music and accessories.

Music Business Skills

To become an owner or part-owner of a music retail outlet there are certain basic business skills you need to know that will help you in starting and maintaining a successful music business. The following are basic skills needed in starting and structuring any music business.

Basic Skills in Starting Your Own Music Business

1. Music education background and experience

    Do what you know best and enjoy it (music?)
2. Knowledge of basic recordkeeping and sound financial management skills
3. Knowledge of market and breakeven analysis
4. Knowledge of product and/or service
5. Federal, state and local tax knowledge
6. Legal environment in which your business operates
7. Start-up capital (money)
8. Business plan with short- and long-term goals
    a. Include a financial plan with projections
9. Excellent communication skills

*Remember 95 percent of all businesses fail due to poor financial management and undercapitalization (those without enough cash to carry them through the first six months or so before the business starts making money).

Types of Business Ownership

Sole Proprietorship

A. Advantages
    1. Low start-up costs
    2. Simplicity/easy to form and dissolve
    3. Few regulatory/reporting requirements
    4. Owner makes decisions
    5. Credit extended beyond balance sheets
    6. You retain all profits

  7. Easy entrance to other states
B. Disadvantages
  1. Unlimited liability
  2. Owner is taxed
  3. Limited working capital
  4. Management deficiencies
  5. Potential lack of continuity of operation
C. Start-Up
  1. Fictitious name
  2. Permits and licensing
  3. Tax number
  4. Lease or franchise agreement
  5. Location problems
D. Taxes
  1. Schedule C—taxed only once
  2. Individual tax rates
  3. Self-employment taxes

Partnerships

An association of two or more persons for the conduct as co-owners of a business enterprise for profit (general and limited)
A. Advantages
  1. Pass through of losses
  2. Simplicity of adding new partners
  3. Combined talents of partners
  4. Fewer regulations and reporting requirements than corporation
  5. More credit extended in relation to partner's personal resources
B. Disadvantages
  1. Unlimited liability of each partner
  2. Fiduciary obligation of each partner to each other
  3. Conflicts of authority and personality
  4. Financial condition of partner limits the ability to raise capital
  5. Partner can bind partnership
C. Start-Up
  1. Same as sole proprietorship
  2. Partnership agreement
  3. Certificate of limited partnership
D. Taxes
  1. Losses and gains personal

      2. Can allocate

      3. Taxed on income, distributed or not

      4. Not an entity—file 1065

  E. General Partnership

      1. Two owners responsible for business

      2. All income after expenses passes through to the individual partners

      3. Personally liable for debts of business and those of partner

  F. Limited Partnership

      1. Limited liability for limited partners

      2. Capital raising vehicle

Corporations

  A. Advantages

      1. Limited liability

      2. Spread the risk

      3. Capital raising vehicle

      4. Centralized management

      5. Continuity of existence

      6. Easy transfer of ownership interests

      7. Various types of interests (common stock, preferred stock)

  B. Disadvantages

      1. Expensive, formalities, complicated

      2. Regulation and reporting

      3. Consensus of directors/shareholders for decisions

      4. Expense of organization and maintenance

  C. Taxes

      1. Lower rate

      2. Regulations, excessive salary as dividend

      3. Double taxation (taxed at corporate and then again at individual rates)

  D. S Corporation

      1. Liability protection

      2. Profit and losses deductible on individual tax returns

      3. Income taxed at the shareholder's individual rate

Once you have acquired the basic skills necessary in starting a music business, written a business plan and decided on the legal structure in which the entity may operate, then it is time to look at how the business will be financed. Most start-up businesses are financed through family, friends, personal loans, banks, credit and venture capital. Most retail music stores are family owned in which the owner raises

the capital to start the business. This type of business is passed on from one generation to the next. The partnership is the other most-used form of structure in this
business, utilizing two or more individuals with different areas of expertise. The
partners complement each other when one is skilled in business (sales, finance,
human resources, administration, strategic planning, market analysis, banking etc.)
and the other has a record of making a living as a professional musician.

The next step in this process is to learn as much as there is to know about the
Music Products Industry both domestically and internationally. The majority of the
retail musical instrument business is based on elementary and secondary music programs. Most instruments are sold to students who are members of school band,
orchestra or other ensembles. Through rental, lease-purchase or outright buy students are able to afford front-line instruments such as flutes, clarinets or oboes while
schools purchase the larger band instrument such as French horns, trombones and
tubas.

The Selmer Corporation is a global music products company whose organizational structure and managerial responsibilities reflect the need to respond to changing conditions. The managers' responsibilities and organizational structure of the
company are as follows:

The Selmer Company, Inc.

National Sales Managers Responsibilities

Responsible for planning and controlling the company sales goals, policies, procedures, and activities.

- Prepare an annual and monthly sales forecast for the company and each sales territory.
- Monitor the progress toward achieving company goals.

Supervision of District Sales Managers

- Assist District Managers with territory sales planning, including the establishment of goals, strategies, marketing plans, and a plan of action for their assigned territory.
- Review and evaluate District Manager's progress in sales performance, call activity, product knowledge, attitude, health, etc., and submit findings and conclusions to the Vice President of Sales.
- Evaluate established territories and make recommendations for possible changes.
- Hiring, training, coaching, and termination of sales people.

Planning, organizing, and running of National and Regional Sales Meetings. (1 to 3 each year)

Review and make recommendations for approval or disapproval of new dealers, status changes of present dealers, and the termination of dealers.

Assist other departments in developing and implementing policies and procedures toward meeting the company's sales and performance goals;

- Marketing/Advertising Department
- Credit Department
- Customer Service
- Order Entry
- Manufacturing/Distribution
- Information Systems

The Selmer Company, Inc.

Marketing Managers Responsibilities

Development and implementation of a strategic marketing plan for the company.
- They must research the Strengths, Weaknesses, Opportunities, and Threats to determine the marketing goals and objectives.
- Prepare an annual budget for their product area.

Assist manufacturing in planning annual and monthly production schedules
- Prepares a monthly and annual production schedule by product model for manufacturing to product based on market demand and sales objectives.
- Involved with engineers in R & D and product development.
- Works with manufacturing in resolving warranty issues.

Works with Advertising Agency in developing product and company advertising materials, promotions, price lists, and related materials
- Supervises all advertising for their product area.
- Prepare press releases of new products, promotions, announcements, etc.
- Schedules advertising in all publications (Magazines, journals, news print, video, CD ROM, etc.)

Responsible for Artist Relations.
- Works with all professional musicians, endorsers, clinicians, and agents in scheduling clinics, promotions, concerts, etc.

Assists National Sales Managers and District Managers in training, educating, and promoting our products to music dealers, music educators, and the end users.
- Assists in developing promotions, specials, support materials for sales.
- Assists in developing support materials for dealers, educators, and consumers.
- Travels in the field conducting product and training sessions for music dealers, educators, and consumers.
- Assists District Managers through their presence at major National and State Music Educator Conferences and Conventions.

Assists Sales Department in meeting the company sales and performance goals.

Chart 8-1
The Selmer Company Inc. Organization

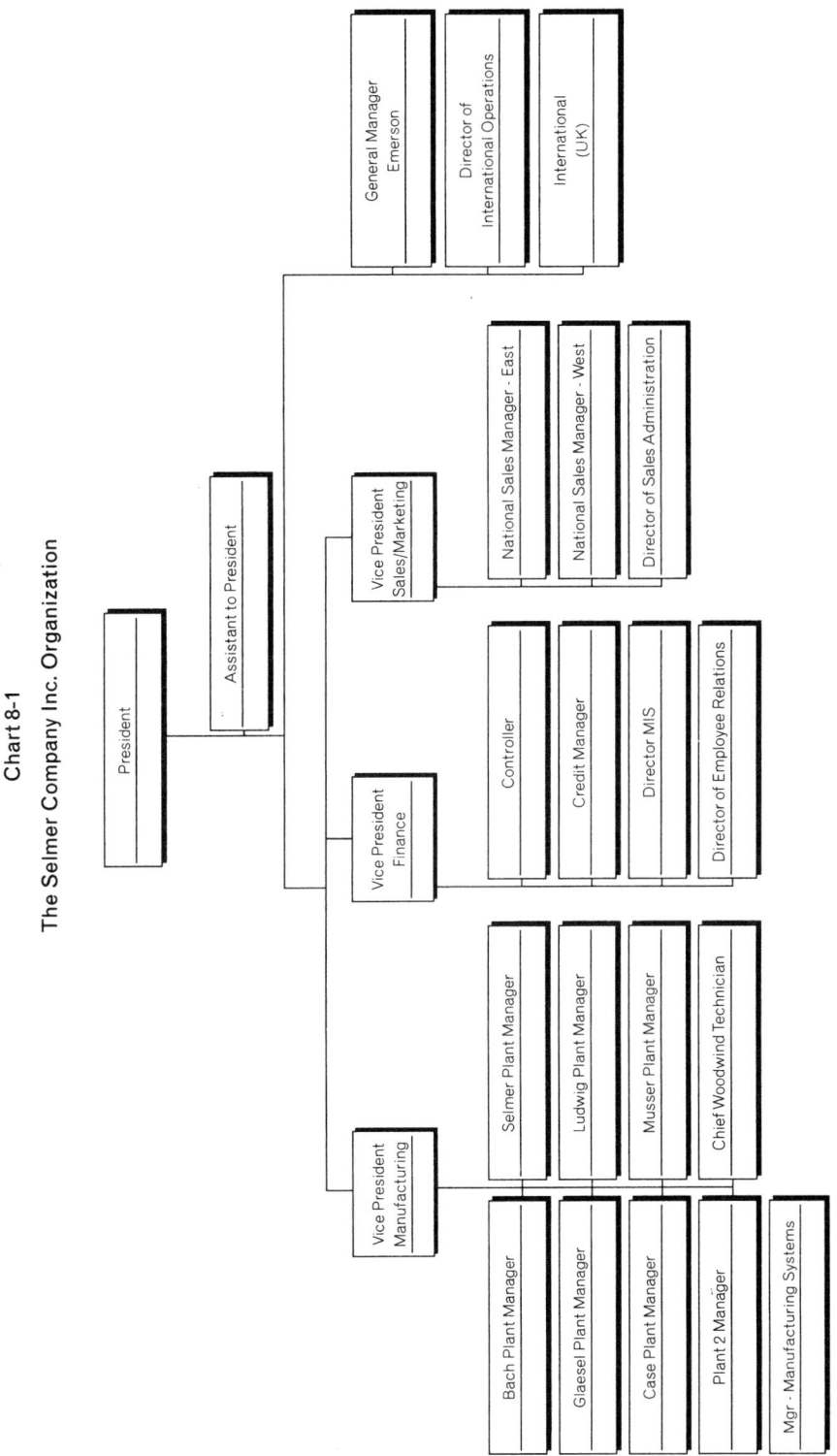

Chart 8-2

Sales/Marketing Organization

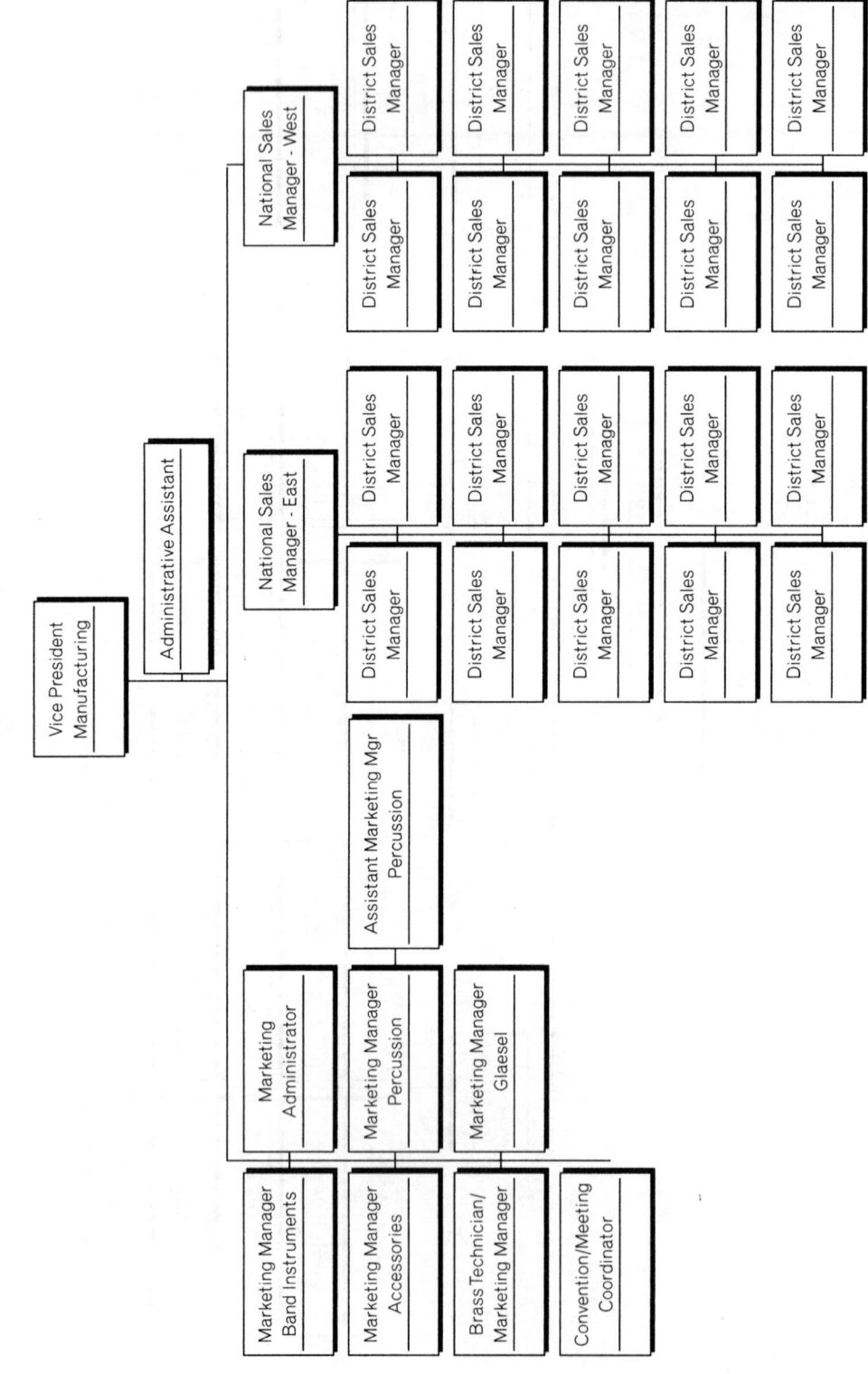

Chart 8-3

Customer Service Organization

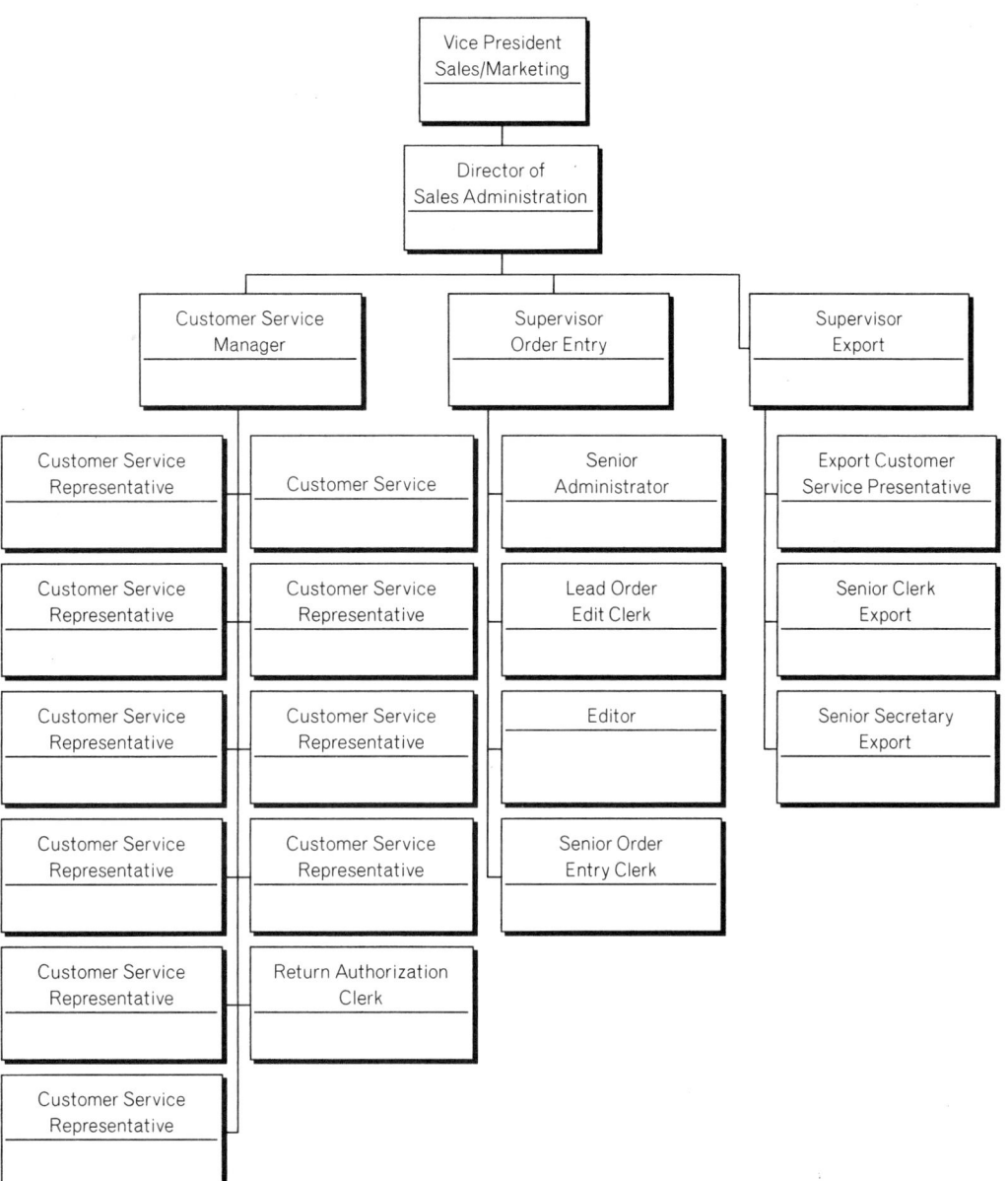

The method of distribution in the Music Products Industry is direct, or a one- or two-step process involving manufacturer, retailer and consumer. Selling directly to manufacturers is called "one-step" distribution and is the most common method. It involves a pattern in which suppliers receive orders from dealers, and merchandise is then shipped to them. Direct distribution involves smaller manufacturers and importers selling directly to consumer through magazine advertisements or direct mail. Vito Pascucci, Chairman and Chief Executive Officer of the G. Leblanc Corporation, says:

> "The field sales force of a music retailer must provide customer assistance and add value to the retailer, and must function as much more than order takers to survive in today's high-cost business world. Direct selling may provide the manufacturer with the maximum control of distribution of his products and is the means to keeping him closest to his actual customers. Direct selling allows the retailer to call on his customers, extend credit terms, co-sponsor clinics, and master classes, etc."

Two-step method of distribution involves the manufacturer receiving orders from independent distributors who sell music products to retailers. Similar to the regional warehousing and distribution in the recording industry, the music products industry maintains regional warehouses to move instrument and equipment product closer to distributors and provide faster service. Smaller producers sell directly to dealers through independent "manufacturers representatives," who handle a multitude of lines and perform some of the functions of a distributor without actually purchasing or warehousing the products themselves. Many of the manufacturers use both the one-step and two-step methods in various parts of the country.

In the retail music business credit and rental are essential to its survival and financial health. Credit may allow a customer to make larger purchases than he/she could for out-of-pocket purchases. The balance due on this kind of an account is usually thirty to ninety days. Sometimes collecting on overdue accounts must be handled by a collecting agency; however, on larger purchases and those requiring more than four payments, some stores will turn credit accounts over to a bank or another lending institution. Many larger stores will view this as an opportunity for additional revenue through self-financing.

The music retail outlet instrument policy is not purely rental or leasing but a rental-purchase agreement termed "credit sales." Under this plan the customer agrees to rent the instrument for an amount of money equivalent to the value of the instrument plus a small finance charge. The customer then has the option to own the instrument or continue renting it. Rental-purchase agreements are made with individuals, schools and organizations that support school music.

The music industry conference, an auxiliary of the Music Educators National Conference, represents music instrument manufacturers, educational music publishers, music retailers, textbook publishers, audiovisual aids/computer software and other music-related companies. Their business guide provides information covering music products and services. For additional information concerning the Music Products Industry, consult the Music Industry Conference, 1806 Robert Fulton Drive, Reston, Virginia 22091, or listing in Appendix.

Summary

The music products industry sales increased to a record $7.354 billion in 2004. Fretted instruments, drumkits, portable keyboards, and digital pianos all posted double digit gains. This increase is due to the segment of the market with discretionary income. Baby boomers (post WWII, 1944–1964 births) and Generation Xers age 35 to 50 year olds who are purchasing strictly for themselves typify this demographics. Low cost imports from China continue to force selling prices and profits down. In 2004 Chinese imports of pianos, band instruments, guitars, and audio products rose by more than 20 percent, largely at the expense of Korean, Japanese, and Taiwanese producers. It took 25 years for the Japanese to increase their portion of U.S. market share; 15 years for Korean manufacturers and less than ten years for the Chinese to carve out market share in the U.S. music products market.

Terms

Microspecialist: Small group of music retail outlets with a narrow product line emphasizing quality, convenience and accessibility (keyboards etc.).

Sole Proprietorship: Individually owned company.

Partnership: An association of two or more persons for the conduct as co-owners of a business enterprise for profit. (General and Limited).

Corporation: A legal business entity according to federal and state laws.

Export: Shipping American goods and products to other countries.

Fretted Instruments: String instruments such as guitars, banjo, mandolin, ukulele, dobro dulcimer and balalaika.

Import: Other countries shipping goods and products to America.

Karaoke: Prerecorded background music used as a sing-along for customers in karaoke bars to produce euphoria of instant stardom.

Modem: Device used to provide telephone access to computer networks.

One step distribution: Method in which supplier receives orders from dealers and merchandise is then shipped to them.

Direct distribution: Method that involves smaller manufacturers and importers selling directly to consumer through magazine advertisements or direct mail

Two-step distribution: Method that involves the manufacturer receiving orders from independent distributors who sell music products to retailers

Exercises

1. Chart and describe the overall retail sales performance of the 2003–2004 music products industry.

2. Describe the method of distribution, credit, compensation and rental purchase agreements in the music products industry.

3. Describe and explain the skills and knowledge needed in order to start and operate a small retail music outlet.

4. What are the trends and global forecast of the music products industry?

References

Statistical Review of the U.S. Music Products Industry, International Music Products Association, 5790 Armada Drive, Carlsbad, California. ISBN 0-9641677-3-5.

Music Industry Conference, *Business Guide*, Auxiliary of MENC, 1801 Robert Fulton Drive, Reston, VA.

Music Industry Conference, *Alphabetical Listing of Music Industry Conference Members*, 1801 Robert Fulton Drive, Reston, VA.

Fink, Michael, *Inside the Music Business*, Simon & Schuster, Macmillan: 2nd Edition, New York, 1996.

Chapter 9
Label Marketing

Learning Objectives

After studying this chapter you should be able to:

1. Explain the duties and responsibilities of a label representative

2. Define the terms "label marketing" and "label representative"

3. Discuss how a label representative might use his/her advertising budget

4. Explain how a label representative might take advantage of an artist's visit

5. Discuss the role of a label representative in the specialty product market

---

Major Labels

There has been quite an evolution in the recording industry over the last three or more decades. In this time period we have seen record distribution evolve from distribution by companies which handled many diverse lines to company owned distribution where prerecorded music was the only product. We have seen the rise of independent labels with their own distribution networks, only to have them be forced to become part of a consolidation of distribution where five major companies control about 80% of the business in product sold to retailers, rack jobbers and one stops. It is very difficult to ascertain just how much these segments of the industry are responsible for sales to consumers. The Internet and digital commerce have clouded that. However, these segments are very instrumental in "breaking" records and establishing hit acts. No one can really gauge the impact of the Internet on exposing new acts and obviously, record clubs and mail order play no part at all.

This evolution has also created new approaches to exposing new products. Years ago the distribution networks handled all aspects of marketing the product. This has changed. Now, the labels have taken on the responsibility for exposing and promoting the product. This is done in conjunction with distribution, but the main responsibility remains with the individual labels. Label marketers take what the songwriter and artist have created and move the product through a difficult process that ends with the consumers, ideally enough of them to make the product a hit and, if the artist is just starting out, a new hit act. A simplified progression would look like the outline below:

Label to Consumer

Label
Marketing Staff
+
Distributor
Sales Organization
+
Product
New artists, established acts
+
Media
Broadcast, print, other
+
Accounts
Record store, rack jobber, one stop
+

Consumer
Buys because of desire, price, convenience

To accomplish this, most labels have marketing representatives located strategically around the country, usually in major or regional market distribution offices. For the most part, label marketing people work on three types of artists:

1. Established: those artists with a sales history and track record at radio and with the retail trade.

2. Known: those artists who either have been cold for a while or are new to the labels so their past performances are not as well known.

3. New acts: those acts that are critical to the health of any label and the industry as a whole.

The initial impetus for a new release at all levels is provided by the label marketing staff. These are the people who advise and work with all aspects of the marketing chain, distribution, subdistribution, retail and radio to bring the product to the street.

Once a label commits to the release of a piece of product, the label marketing people are given samples. This could be two weeks to six months prior to the scheduled release. That is precisely when label marketing staffs start their campaigns.

Keep in mind, label marketing staffs only get the finished product. A label marketing manager or marketing director cannot change the label policy on a product and cannot pick and choose among the projects. The label dictates marketing priorities, and the label marketing people are required to accept decisions made by the label. Label marketing staffs are assigned a sales objective or quota, and an idea of how the marketing plan or plans will work; then they begin the label marketing process.

Marketing staffs determine when to contact and "sell" accounts, but first they must sell their distribution organization. In some cases, even though everyone is part of the same company, this can be the most difficult aspect of the job. With the ever growing number of labels handled by all the five major distribution companies, competition for attention gets fierce. Regional marketing people need strong relationships and excellent marketing plans to succeed.

A label marketing representative breaks down the numbers and assigns the distribution branch and its people their sales quotas. The label marketing representative works with the Branch Manager, Sales Manager and Marketing Manager at the branch sales office, and their plans are based on figures determined by the labels on a national level. These national figures are eventually broken down into regional areas, and these numbers are broken down again for each sales office.

It is never too early to start approaching accounts with information about a new project, hoping to create a "buzz" early. This can have a major impact on opening orders. There was a time when you waited for some airplay to develop, but that is no longer the case. Now you must create excitement before play might develop and have accounts primed when the product eventually hits the street. This buzz must not only be created at the account level, but also within your distribution staffs. (You can be sure that once the record hits the street, you will work with distributor people on that release daily, constantly feeding them information about station ads, breakouts elsewhere, sales activity and other hot spots.)

Meanwhile, depending on the level of acceptance expected of a project, label representatives are also working up special promotions and advertising programs with the accounts that are deemed right for that particular type of product.

Major retailers usually buy products in all categories while one stops are slightly more selective and rack jobbers are very selective. Therefore label representatives must be very careful about when and who they contact at each stage of product development.

Advertising campaigns and advertising allocations comprise much of a label marketer's responsibility. People in this business get "price and position," which to a large degree is the ultimate aim for most of a label marketer's activities. "Price and position" are extremely important in this phase of marketing. The product must be out front where consumers can see it and must be priced low enough to make them willing to buy. Only by obtaining both exposure and optimal pricing do label marketers maximize advertising expenditures and make product distribution financially feasible for everyone, including the consumer.

There are a number of advertising options, and these will be discussed in more detail later on. Depending on when you make the plans and thus how much or how little time you have to implement them, the label marketing people have many choices.

Radio	Billboards
Newspapers	Flyers
Magazines	Circulars
Tip Sheets	Direct Mail
Network TV	Shelf Cards
Cable TV	Bin Cards
Internet/Web sites	Coupons
Bus Boards	800/900 Phone Numbers
Taxi Boards	Snipes

However, by far, the best is "word of mouth." Label marketers never underestimate what having people talk about a project can do for its success. Black/urban product marketing plans now all include "taking to the streets" activity. The buzz is started months before release with copies leaked to deejays, both radio and club, and display showing up all over. This will be discussed in greater detail when illustrating specific marketing plans. However, this approach is not only being used with "rap" or "hip-hop" product but with many other genres. In many cases, the "street teams" are full time employees of the record labels. They deliver released and unreleased singles to the Club DJ's and have a relationship with these DJ's like radio promotion people have with radio programmers. They also deliver these singles to the people who make compilation CD's which are sold on the street. "Street Teams" are not new, having started over 15 years ago when radio and MTV would not play rap music.

It must be understood that just about all the advertising and promotion money required to start working a record, be it an established act or a new artist, is supplied by the label. Even though consumers see ads that appear to advertise a store rather than products, if some product is included in the ad, they can be sure the record labels represented paid for the ad.

When label marketing representatives commit advertising funds they try to project the very best time and best media so they can take advantage of radio rotation. This means that in many cases you have to be able to see into the future, because most well planned, viable promotions do take advance planning. With the way product can either break out or stop cold in a very short time, you can get caught at the wrong time on either side of the curve. With radio and newspapers, advertising can be arranged very close to when it actually runs, and since that type of advertising makes sense anyway, it is used most frequently.

In addition, most plans will include radio spot purchases since supporting airplay remains the most important strategy, even though many other avenues of exposure are being developed. Radio certainly is the key medium for emerging acts, while print can help you sell tonnage on established acts or newly broken acts. The marketing people are not only responsible for plans to help records get started, but must also be ready to drive a hit product to higher and higher sales levels. It is the multimillion-piece sales that really support the whole structure. When a piece of product reaches that plateau, advertising costs as compared to sales are very, very low. At this point, the label's main cost is manufacturing. The rest is high profit. This is an industry where one, two or three megahits can turn any record company's fortunes around overnight.

Label marketing people work very closely with all accounts, and the radio and print buys are bought through these accounts. All major retailers have contracts with the broadcast media and newspapers that guarantee them a lower rate in return for committing to buying a predetermined amount of advertising for a long period, usually a year. Not only are these rates less expensive, but the accounts must use these commitments, so they are anxious for every supplier to work through them. Label marketing people have to know what these costs are when planning promotions. In carrying out assignments, marketers not only work closely with the distribution people but also with the accounts. Label representatives do not write orders, but work with sales people to make sure product is ordered to cover the advertising which is allocated to a specific product. Any major advertising expenditure must carry stock requirements as well as other commitments, since the label representative is charged with getting value for advertising dollars spent.

Label representatives might not always initiate a promotion. It can be done by distribution personnel, but distribution personnel will come to a label representative for final approval since it is the label's advertising money that will drive a product home. So, no matter where or how an idea starts, label representatives will be completely involved in the marketing process as long as marketing strategies involve one or more of the artists on a label. Distribution has advertising money, but this is usually used when a record hits, and distributors are looking to move tonnage. Even so, label representatives will still be actively involved in the planning, no matter who is footing the bill. While distribution has to keep watch over many releases, a label representative has relatively few to monitor. Therefore, it is easier to keep track of progress, and a label representative will have the best feel for when and if money should be spent. Label representatives have more than one project, of course, so they become adept at juggling them all properly and being sure not to miss an opening. And, once again, advertising gives you "price and position."

A label representative will contact 40 to 50 store buyers, clerks and managers weekly. The idea is to push records up the charts gradually. But just as important is the need to make sure everyone is following through on the promotions in progress and make sure that the label is getting something in return for advertising expenditures. And, of course, you need to be constantly updated on progress so you can plan your next move or moves. As has been noted so many times, good relationships with customers are critical to success.

The label marketing staffs are also very deeply involved in artist relations. When acts are in their physical area of responsibility, label representatives must make contact and try to arrange promotional opportunities. In many instances, they have artists come to their area for prearranged activities of that type. Considering the number of venues available to recording acts today, this segment of a label representative's activities can be very time consuming. Adept label people make artist's visits work for them in order to generate excitement and sales.

As part of the artist relations, label marketing staffs are extremely aware of publicity opportunities. Publicity is becoming as important as any other avenue of promotion and exposure. Knowing the people and places to contact when label representatives have a story, or even if they are trying to get a story started, is extremely important.

Once again, and it cannot be emphasized too strongly, priorities are determined nationally. Label representatives must be prepared to run with the decisions they are given by the label, and they are responsible for making sure that the label's product is VISIBLE AT RETAIL.

Specialty Labels

Not all the product released is expected to achieve hit status. There are many specialty labels and special genres that have a very profitable niche in the industry today, especially with the growth of larger and larger record stores. The ability to carry more extensive stock and give the consumer greater choices has fostered the growth of this segment of the industry.

As has been seen, there are hundreds of labels and tens of thousands of selections available to the consumer. The distribution and marketing of these labels are structured in a variety of ways. In many instances, they are owned totally by one of the major record operations. This can mean that marketing is done by its label's staff. Usually specialty labels do not have large staffs, and much of what is accomplished by this staff is done by phone and fax. Some arrangements are joint ventures with other larger, more well established labels and marketing can be done either by the parent label's marketing staff or a combination of parent label and individual label. Many labels have only a distribution arrangement with one of the five major companies. The distribution arm of the company handles the selling and the label is paid a percentage. With the case of specialty products, marketing and promotion are the label's responsibility. These three situations cover most of the arrangements for small and specialty labels that are connected with the five major distribution organizations.

There are of course, hundreds of small labels that are distributed by independent distributors. In just about all cases, marketing is done by the individual labels.

Then there are small labels that attempt to sell directly to the public, via mail order, magazine advertising and even TV ads. These are specialty labels that have their own niche, usually not too large, but large enough to be very profitable. Some of these niches are growing quite rapidly. For example, there are scores of labels devoted to International Product, more than there are countries on our planet. However, Latin is now almost as big as some mainstream lines, and the projections are that it will grow even larger in the next decade. This product is no longer marketed only to the Hispanic consumer through specialty stores. Major chains, rack jobbers and one stops carry many Latin titles. This type of product does not just have to be part of the "niche" market. The soundtrack to *Selena* was a big seller. Estimates vary since large numbers of albums are purchased by the Latin community in non-Nielsen Sound-Scan outlets, but be assured the total sales are substantial. The sales are so substantial that not long ago, RIAA started compiling figures on **Latin music** as a separate category (Chart 9-1). Similar to overall market trends at mid-year 2001, though to a far smaller degree, the Latin music genre experienced a slight decline in the number of net shipments compared to mid-year 2000. However, the $329.3 million value at mid-year 2001 was well above the full year total for 1996, and almost equal to full-year 1997. This has been an explosive growth and will continue as the Hispanic population continues to grow, now the largest minority in the United States, and the music

Chart 9-1
2004 RIAA Year-End Statistics
LATIN MUSIC
Phone: 202/775-0101

January–December 2004 vs. January–December 2003
MANUFACTURERS' UNIT SHIPMENTS AND DOLLAR VALUE
(In thousands, at suggested list price, net after returns)

Format	2004		2003		Percent Change 2004–2003	
	Units	Dollars	Units	Dollars	Units	Dollars
CD	46,820	621,090	37,895	523,284	23.6%	16.7%
Cassette	−94	−802	232	2,356	−140.4%	−134.0%
Music Video	−3	−55	29	566	−109.8%	−109.6%
DVD	1,808	30,555	478	8,830	−278.2%	−246.0%
TOTAL	**48,531**	**650,788**	**38,633**	**535,036**	**25.6%**	**21.6%**

Latin music is defined as product 51% or more Spanish language
Genre Breakout (% based on suggested list price)

Regional Mexican/Tejano	60%
Pop/Rock	31%
Tropical	9%

Reprinted courtesy of RIAA

attracts mainstream buyers from the entire population. While unit shipments were down, the dollar value was higher for mid-year 2001 versus mid-year 2000 by almost $5 million, a 1% increase. In light of the decreases the overall industry is showing, this is a remarkable feat. As with all genres, CD growth was substantial, but cassette sales diminished. Meanwhile, among the many departments you will see in any major outlet will be **children's records, jazz, new age, acoustic** or **folk, bluegrass,** other international, **gospel** (black gospel and white gospel), **Christian rock, blues, rap, heavy metal, easy listening, oldies, beach music,** alternative and many others. One of the others is classical. Some major labels have classical labels or departments. However, there are a number of small labels doing the classical product and marketing it to stores in a variety of ways, as do other specialty labels.

Children's music and jazz are almost big enough on their own to be part of the mainstream product. It is difficult to overstate the loyalty children have for certain artists as they move from toddler, to preschool, to school age. Their capacity to listen to the same album over and over and over again is limitless, just as is their ability to watch the same video constantly and never tire.

A new wrinkle was introduced in the early 1990s, when some of the then six majors made arrangements with a network of independent distributors to handle the initial offerings of experimental product, some black/urban product and releases far out of the mainstream, mostly via single releases. Just when the majors would take over again should a record start to sell is a bit hazy. One can assume that if and when an album is released, the major company would then assume sales responsibility. The "indies" were much closer to the markets of alternative and urban accounts that knew and catered to the consumers attracted to that product and therefore had a better chance of getting something started. This also afforded the major labels room in keeping track of the progress of so many releases.

Summary

The importance of the label marketing team in the production of a hit record cannot be minimized. The advertising dollars spent wisely by label representatives can make the difference between a record becoming a hit or not, between a new group becoming a hit group or not, and between a cold artist becoming a hot artist. Just about all direction as to field activity and priorities come from the national office, but the ultimate success of a project can be traced to the label marketing staff.

Terms

Break: To "break" a record is to market a record to hit status.

Price and Position: Placement of product at retail so that it is easily seen by consumer and is priced low enough so that the consumer will purchase it.

Sales Quota: Forecast of units to be sold by a specified date, or in case of catalog, dollar figure to be attained.

Buzz: The talk on the street about a record which creates excitement about its potential.

Label Marketing Representative: Field personnel assigned to market all product that the label releases or assigned specific types of music to market.

Advertising: Monies allocated through accounts to sell and expose product.

Specialty Labels: Companies with their own niche in the market.

Exercises

1. Label marketing people can be assigned to work on an artist in any of three categories. What are those categories?

2. Label representatives must take direction from the home office as to priorities. Why must everyone follow those priorities at all times?

3. If you were a label marketing representative how would you go about getting a "buzz" started on a record weeks before its release?

4. All activity is directed at obtaining "price and position." What is that?

5. Out of the dozen or more choices of places to advertise, name eight.

Chapter 10
Marketing Tactics–1

Learning Objectives

After studying this chapter you should be able to:

1. Define product management

2. Explain product manager activities

3. Be able to list the elements necessary to a good marketing plan

4. Be able to create a marketing plan

5. Know what activities lead to breaking a hit record

6. Be familiar with the tools available to make a marketing plan successful

7. Know when and how to use advertising in music marketing

Marketing

There have to be thousands of bands around the world that deserve to have recording contracts, but only a relatively small number actually do. It takes a particular set of circumstances to become one of the "anointed" and have a label ready to invest in your music and talent and, thus, your future.

1. The act has to be in the right place at right time, and be heard or recommended by someone with access to the people who sign acts.
2. The act has be right on target with the type of product the public wants at that time.
3. Every act has to learn its craft. "Overnight sensations" usually take years to develop.
4. The act has to be lucky.

Countless numbers of bands are being showcased constantly in clubs, bars, stages and venues everywhere. When lightning strikes and they get a contract the marketing people usually have one shot to bring the project home and develop a hit, but even more important, establish a strong-selling act. The latter is what it is all about. Hits are important, but establishing the act is what really brings in the dollars release, after release, after release.

You cannot "legislate a hit." The product must be something the consumers want, but you can lose a potential hit because something or someone dropped out at a critical juncture. You rarely get a second chance to recoup lost ground in the development of recorded product.

Before looking at the specifics of marketing plans, it is important to review the conditions of sale, since knowing the specifics of how accounts buy will make it easier to create plans that will make them buy.

*   Basically, all product is returnable for credit.
*   All shipments to accounts are prepaid by the distributor.
*   All returns to distributors are prepaid by accounts.
*   All advertising is paid by labels and distributors, even the portion that advertises stores, store locations and price.
*   All display is paid by labels or distributors if the display involves product and promotions.
*   Terms: usually 60 days net for 2% cash discount.
*   Pricing and deals: same to all customers in the same class. The ability to buy box lots.

Artist-Oriented Marketing Plans

There are two types of record projects—**new acts and established acts.** To a large degree, the most important is new acts since, as has been outlined, the profit in having new acts hit is quite high. Do not minimize the dollar impact of established, big name acts. The major volume generated brings in tremendous sums, but the profit is certainly not as high as with hits by new acts with attractive (from the label standpoint) contracts. However, just as important is the need for having new acts emerging constantly. The public's appetite is endless, and offers an insatiable market for new and different music and people to perform it.

With **established acts** you can work off a percentage of expected sales for expenditures for, among other costs:

- Videos
- Independent promotion
- Time buys (TV and radio)
- Print advertising
- Display
- Tour support
- Publicity, TV exposure
- Listening sessions
- Street teams

All these ingredients can be budgeted fairly accurately since, if nothing else, initial orders can be forecast fairly easily. Granted, if the album misses, returns can be high, but even with a mediocre product, a major act's sales net out quite well. When the music is accepted, the sales are huge, and when albums hit the multiplatinum stage, the profits are monumental, no matter what the contract.

Marketing tactics for both established acts and new acts will be examined, especially since there are some similarities. The major point remains: Every act, no matter how big, **requires a marketing plan.** You cannot just release any product without a definitive plan and without implicit instructions to everyone in the organization who is responsible for making the product sell. Every project requires that the consumer know about it. Past history and previous success just takes a great deal of the guesswork out of the plans. Timetables can be almost mandated since airplay and other exposure can be predicted with far more accuracy, and acceptance at all stages is far more liable to be guaranteed.

But no matter what type of act, no matter what level of acceptance is present at the outset, every project has at its very heart one major goal. **This is to get "price and position" at retail,** no matter where the outlet. "Price and position" means that the product, in all configurations, is where the consumer can see it easily and is being offered at a retail price that will entice the consumer to purchase it. Just about all marketing tactics are geared to making "price and position" a reality.

Established acts can gain price and position fairly easily: however, discounts and advertising, as will be discussed, play a major role in this process. New acts are a whole different story. You have no history and you are just "rolling the dice." If the decision is made to bring a new act to the marketplace, you have to make a major commitment. In other words, you have to gamble big. Depending upon the act and the size of the marketing plan, it can take net sales of from 500,000 to 750,000 pieces and higher even to start to see some profit from a release today. Up until that point the label is spending 100% or more of what is coming back in profit, and even then it is quite small. The real profit does not start until the product hits the platinum plateau, and then the cost of promotion and sales has been reduced to practically nothing.

A marketing plan can be as simple or as elaborate as the author wants it. Much of the amount of detail included depends on the type of product, overall objectives and availability of funds to drive the project. However, there are some basic ingredients that every Product Manager or Product Director must have in his or her file before creating the "master plan" that so many people must follow. Some of the basic elements that the national people must have at their fingertips, although not all will be used in every plan, are:

Price

This refers to the list price that this product will carry when it is offered for sale to the consumer.

Deals (if any)

This refers to any special discounts offered accounts on their purchases. Product by new artists usually carries extra discount since accounts must have an added incentive to gamble on an unknown.

Dating (if any)

New acts might require dating, while established acts would not.

Guarantees

In the case of new acts, guarantees might have to be used, to leave the gamble with the label, not the account.

Schedule (target dates each step)

A very large number of people at all levels of label and distribution will have to carry out a number of actions on any project. Ensuring that each is done when expected so that it can be a foundation for future requirements is very important.

Bios and Background

Everyone needs to know just who the act is and why there is all the excitement.

Target Market

With radio, and to some degree, even with retail so segmented today, it is mandatory to know where your activity must be concentrated.

Display

Display production and usage is changing. Most chains either do not allow display or the space must be paid for (Light boxes, foam board blowups). The industry is experimenting with formats to accommodate this lack of display space in "mini easels," die cuts, and small hanging banners.

Ad Mats

If any print advertising is planned or expected, the ads have to be created and put into a form that accounts can easily use when scheduling the buys.

Radio and TV Spots

Commercials have to be created for either radio or TV so that time buys can be scheduled to be run very quickly. The accounts must have copy prepared in advance.

Forecast (30–60–90 days)

Sales figures and attainment of quotas drive any industry, music included, and every staff has to know what is expected.

Budget Breakdown (30–60–90 days)

Financial parameters are set for every project.

What distribution expected to do and fund

Since the label has its budgets set, it must know what additional help it can expect from other sources.

Best singles, or if the product will only be released as an album, which will be the target cut or cuts.

There must be concentration to be effective. If radio were allowed to pick cuts, you would not get anywhere near the total play you require to start a record. It takes many plays before the consumer starts to pay attention.

Track Listing

Want to know titles of all the cuts.

Management

Very important to know exactly which group is handling an act. The management company's track record can be even more important than the act's, especially a new act.

Tours

More and more, tours are a major consideration in launching any new album.

Booking Agent

You will be dealing with a booking agent frequently since tours are now a vital part of every project.

Producer

Once again, especially with a new act, the production team's track record is a major factor in getting people to pay attention. Buyers, press, radio will pay more attention to a piece of product when the producer has been responsible for prior hits, no matter who the artist.

Publicity

Publicity is becoming more and more important with so many outlets available for exposure today. The number of fanzines, entertainment related consumer press sections, other media, Web sites, entertainment-oriented TV shows, and talk shows are increasing constantly. They all have an insatiable appetite for information that you will be delighted to supply.

This list will grow in the future as technology and demand will create more and more ways to communicate with the consumer.

By far the most important element that must be understood by all is the rationale for the whole plan and for anything else that might excite people.

A great deal of experience, background and research of all types is required before any plan can go to the drawing board. Product Management people must do their "homework," some of which is unique. Two of the activities that are so vital are to meet the act and really get to know the act. This means practically living with them, and more or less getting inside their head or heads. It is important to gauge the level of cooperation that can be expected.

Perhaps the most important first step is to listen to the music, and listen, and listen, and listen some more.

With a new act, the Product Manager will literally live with the act for weeks to months before the album is actually released for sale. Getting to know the act and getting to know the music is vital to being able to do a complete, effective job in bringing it to the street. This helps in other ways since not only is the product manager or product director responsible for creating the means to get everything started, but is the **champion for the act throughout the company.** The competition for everyone's attention and effort is fierce. As has been pointed out, the number of labels handled by every major distribution company is vast, and every one of those labels has product management staffs vying for attention from the sales and marketing forces throughout the country.

Once the Product Manager has done the research, knows the act, and knows the music, the marketing plan will be generated and distributed. The size of the plan, the approach, and the concentration of money and activity is determined by the product and the faith that the label has in the act. The length of the plan depends on how detailed the Product Manager wants to be and exactly what he or she has in mind to help launch the project. Some plans are just a page or so (Chart 10-1) and give the basic thrust.

Another type of plan (Chart 10-2) has some successful history with the act to build on and makes use of more detailed information. **The Loggers** represents a country act that has had big selling albums in the past and thus warrants more initial attention from radio and the press. The project can also expect better account participation and this has to be covered completely. Knowing who you can expect to help launch the album and how it will be done must be listed in detail.

A very large number of publicity outlets are included in this plan. Getting the act on all of those shows will not be easy, but you go for them all.

The activity planned with accounts has a rack jobber leading the list. Normally, you wait before going to the racks, but this is a well known country act, so you can expect rack jobber activity immediately.

Chart 10-1

THE NONENTITIES—*Go For It*

Imaging Statement/Project Objective

Imaging Statement

The Nonentities are New York-based, beat intensive rappers with a strong liking for fun. Their sound, according to members of the group, is "bi-coastal" real hip-hop, with no gimmicks. Their audience, the street, those who go to clubs well after midnight and move until the early hours when the sun comes up. Those who swear by baggy, oversized jeans, SUVs and some kind of funky, phat hat. Those who stay in touch with what's happening in the underground hip-hop press.

Project Objective

To take advantage of **The Nonentities'** reputation from working with many major rap groups and to work the market from the streets up. This will obtain the initial forecast and develop a core sales base for the group.

Sales Objective

Initial Forecast: _____units
Full Year: _____ units

Strategies

Promotion

- The street campaign will begin before the single release with massive stickering, postcard and advance cassette giveaways, via street teams.
- Rap radio will be worked by label and independent promotion teams.

Internet

- Utilize on line "street teams," fans contacting other fans.
- Hit satellite radio, Podcasts.

Media

- Underground hip-hop publications will be worked, like The Bomb, One Nut Network.
- Rap publications—The Source, Rappages, Rap Sheet.
- Urban fanzines—Right On, Black Beat.

Artist Development

- Schedules advertising to coincide with single and album release dates.
- Run a snipe campaign at least two weeks before release in eight markets.
- Schedule visits to radio and retail in New York, Los Angeles.

Sales

- Full album advance will go to label and distribution staffs.
- Flyers have gone to label singles reps and Urban PDC's.

- Promotion package will be made up and be distributed prior to release dates.
- P.O.P.—4 color, double sided flat.
- One-stop coverage right out of the box.

Video
- Video has been shipped to all national, regional and local outlets.
- FOCUS will be placed on getting BET Rap City and The Box.
- Video is being worked by label staffs.

Chart 10-2

THE LOGGERS—"Cuttin' Fine"

Album Selection Number:	CD7890-0978
Album Street Date:	10/7/97
Forecast:	175,000 (90 days)
Producers:	Van Reve and Al McElvane
Management:	Ray Martin
	Nashville, TN
Booking Agent:	Major Artists
	Nashville, TN
Price Point:	CD—$0.00
Solicitation Dates:	8/15 to 9/25

Cuts:

Cuttin' Fine	*Racing Heart*
Serious Trouble	*She Knows It*
Timeless Tune	*Why Try Now*
Backwoods Banter	*Can't Handle It*
Goin' Home	*Don't Answer*

Al McElvane (guitar and vocals) met Randy Woods (drums) in the northwestern mountain town of Clayton, Georgia back in 1992. They were both working odd jobs, but really wanted to perform. Randy's brother Mark (bass guitar) joined the enterprise and very soon after, Ed McKee (guitar) came aboard. They put together **The Loggers,** and started writing, rehearsing, and making demos.

Luck was with them when Nashville producer Ray Martin heard them play at a mountain fair he was attending as part of his wife's family reunion. He took the demo to Nashville, decided the group had potential and signed them. The first album, aptly titled "Lucky Music," took off and **The Loggers** started a string of CMA and ACM awards. Widespread media attention was the order of the day, and "Lucky Music" was followed by "Heaven Loves Us" and "The Touch," both going gold.

Now with *Cuttin' Fine*, **The Loggers** are planning a major tour and the label has the boys set to make a number of major TV appearances.

Chart 10-2 (continued)

Radio Promotion:
- *Cuttin' Fine* promotional mailers sent to radio right after July Fourth
- Regional Promotion Managers will start talking up initial single, *Cuttin' Fine*
- Bios, press kits to radio and retail mid August
- Same time schedule to send snippets of initial single to radio.
- Single add dates 9/26

Other Radio:
Radio Showcase Weekends: Dallas 9/5
                             Atlanta 9/12
                             Ft. Worth 9/19

Syndicated Radio:
(To be taped just prior to CMA week in Nashville)
SW Networks
ABC
Westwood One
Clear Channel
Infinity
Satellite radio, Podcasts
Offer streams on websites

Targeted Media

Print:

Country Music	Country America	New Country
TWANG	Tune In	Time
Country Song Roundup	Spin	Newsweek
Music City News	Guitar Player	Guitar World
Modern Screens Country	Music Replay	Rolling Stone
Entertainment Weekly	Request	Musician

Trades:

Gavin	Music Row
Billboard	CMA Close-up
R&R	Performance

Television:

Entertainment Tonight	Conan
Leno	Today
Letterman	Regis and Kathy Lee
GMA	CMA Awards Show
CNN Showbiz Today	

Chart 10-2 (continued)

Sales:

Have single debut on Top Country Singles Chart after first week of release
National accounts—**"Price and Position"**
Advance product and flyers to buyers in all major accounts
Video to all major accounts

Account Activity:

Handleman	Endcaps
Target	Country Endcap
Musicland	Follow Feature
Transworld	Heavy Hitter
Best Buy	Feature
Wherehouse	Sale Pricing
Hastings	Country Feature/Sale Pricing
Eurpac	Feature
AAFES	Feature

The marketing plan for **Steel Magnolias** (Chart 10-3) goes into even more detail. Once again, you are dealing with an established act. This means that while the basics remain fairly constant, some of the avenues taken are different. Also keep in mind, there is more funding available with an established, successful act and this gives the Product Manager more choices. When dealing with an act that has a track record as good as **Steel Magnolias**, you can be sure that the Financial Department will allocate just about all of the money you request. The sales forecast of 400,000 units is for the first 90 to 120 days. Total will be far more than that. There is every reason to expect big things from *Going It Alone*.

In just about all cases, a timetable accompanies any marketing plan (Chart 10-4). This is a chart that defines the time frames within which many of the aspects of a plan will go into effect. This timetable is essential to keeping everyone focused and on schedule. Remember, you are dealing with many people, many departments. Each move has to be orchestrated.

Chart 10-3

STEEL MAGNOLIAS—*Going It Alone*

Marketing Plan

Consumer Profile

The **Steel Magnolias** have a huge following among urban youth and young adults. With the release of *Going It Alone* they are taking it back to the streets and giving all their fans exactly what they want.

Overview

The **Steel Magnolias** are back, better than ever. With *Going It Alone* they will maintain their reputation as one of the premier groups of the 90s. Their complementary harmonies have carved a very profitable niche in contemporary hip-hop/R&B. *Going It Alone* goes back to their roots and collaborations with some of the hottest producers around. Producers like Gee Marcus, Tammy Hot, Kyle Andrews, Brave Moss, Tinsel, Honee Lar and Ratso Blue are represented on this album. *Going It Alone* fits into urban, rhythm crossover, and Top 40 genres.

Executive Producers: Honee Lar and Shadow Tinsel
Management: Timeless Entertainment
Release Date: (Date)
Sales Forecast: 400,000 units
Price Structure: CD: $0.00

Tracks:

Time Now	*Timeless*
Could Be	*Final Love*
Going It Alone	*Cry Now*
Don't Cry	*Don't Lose Me*
Let's Get Hot	*How Can We*
Oh No!	*Want Me Now*

Packaging

Cover art has girls in Versace gowns. Foldout insert of glamour shots, also in Versace gowns.

Radio Promotion Singles:

First Single: *Final Love* produced by Shadow Tinsel

- *Final Love*—Radio Edit
- *Final Love*—Album Edit
- *Final Love*—Instrumental
- *Final Love*—Acappella
- Radio Call-Out Hook

12"—Tracklisting Side A (Radio Edit and Album Edit)
       Tracklisting Side B (Instrumental and A Cappella)

Chart 10-3 (continued)

Impact Date at CHR and R&B (Date)
    Product to Staff (Date)
    Digital Download to Radio (Date)
    Satellite radio, create and produce own Podcasts

Promotions will be set with major stations with product as prizes

Tipsheet Campaign
Major tipsheet advertising will be set initially featuring *Going It Alone* and then follow up with advertising featuring all **Steel Magnolias** product. Will use the following tipsheets:
    Hits
    Gavin
    Urban Network
    R&B Monitor
    Impact
    Behind the Scenes

The second single will be *Going It Alone* produced by Tammy Hot.

Video
First video will be *Final Love* and will be their most ambitious video to date. MTV, BET, and The Box will get it hand delivered, other outlets, regional shows will also be serviced.

Street Awareness
Snipes will be posted at least a week before release date in Los Angeles, New York, Washington, DC, Baltimore, Chicago, Atlanta, Houston, and Philadelphia. The snipe poster will highlight the major contributing producers.

A 12" mega-mix disk will be produced as a consumer giveaway.

Press
There are features, reviews, and interviews scheduled already for major market dailies, weeklies, and national magazines. Publications include, among others:
    Essence
    Black Essence
    Upscale
    The Source
    Rhythm and News
    One World
    Remix
    Vibe

TV appearances will be set with Letterman, Leno, Conan, and others.

Websites
A **Steel Magnolias** Web site had been set up previously and it has had over a million hits. The website will be updated with new photos, video and audio samples.

Publicity interviews, offer digital live performance streaming, downloads of reviews

Advertising
The first advertising phase will consist of TV spots on BET and MTV tagging outlets for national accounts as well as some local accounts. The second phases will be print ads.

Chart 10-3 (continued)

Retail Activity

Samplers will go to retail buyers via PDC's and college reps. The lyric content is such that in-store play can be encouraged. Arrangements will be made to have this album available on the in-store listening posts. Advertising with stores will be set up not only at release time but for the life of the album. Catalog will also be included in some of the store ads.

Tools

> Flats
> Posters
> Coming Soon Streamers
> Snipes
> Ad mats and minis
> Mixtapes
> Radio spots—30 second/60 second
> TV spots—30 second/15 second

Tour

Steel Magnolias will do a major urban tour. Details to come. Tour will target most successful markets and the arenas where last year's tour was so well received.

International

Going It Alone will be released worldwide at the same time it is released domestically.

Wrap-Up

Steel Magnolias has worldwide acceptance, and an excellent track record of three previous hit albums. The tools are there, and if you need any assistance, the Marketing Manager for this project is:

> Ed Rollins
> 770-660-0000 (o)
> 770-660-0001 (f)

As has been noted, there are a number of levels of commitment to new acts. When the commitment is high, the marketing plans are very extensive. Needless to say, they require a major budget, but when a plan is as detailed as the one for **Ajax** (Chart 10-5) and the expectations so high, the budget will be forthcoming. This is about as much detail as a product manager can offer as everyone associated with the plan is given specific instructions on what is expected of them. They must know who will be contacted, how they will be contacted, and exactly when they will be contacted. Keep in mind a very important feature of this plan. It covers a time period of many months prior to release of the product, as well as the time frame immediately after release.

Merchandise and event tie-ins are usually very productive. In the **Ajax** plan, the events, activities, and soft drink tie-ins are aimed right at the heart of the market for this music. While product managers have to be on the lookout for products and activities that can be used in plans like these, the products also have people contacting the record companies and trying to arrange mutual promotions. It is not difficult to get them together.

Chart 10-4

STEEL MAGNOLIAS TIMETABLE

February 22 through April 4

Sunday	Monday	Tuesday	Wednesday	Thursday	Friday	Saturday
Feb 22	Feb 23 Single "Going It Alone" to radio	Feb 24 Single released– Blitz One Stops with discount deal	Feb 25 Start solicit album	Feb 26 12" megamix available for consumer giveaway	Feb 27	Feb 28
Mar 1	Mar 2 Go To Tip Sheets: Hits Gavin, R&R	Mar 3 U/C adds, Dance adds	Mar 4	Mar 5	Mar 6	Mar 7
Mar 8	Mar 9 Solicit Tip Sheets: Urban Network, Impact, Behind the Scenes	Mar 10	Mar 11	Mar 12 Major Consumer Press Blitz: (See mkt'g plan for list)	Mar 13 Snipes Posted	Mar 14
Mar 15	Mar 16 Video available: Hand Deliver	Mar 17 More radio adds	Mar 18	Mar 19	Mar 20	Mar 21
Mar 22	Mar 23	Mar 24 Album arrives in stores	Mar 25	Mar 26	Mar 27 TV Advertising starts	Mar 28
Mar 29	Mar 30 Hit Talk Shows, Late Night Shows this week	Mar 31	Apr 1	Apr 2 Features, with reviews, interviews	Apr 3	Apr 4 Tour Starts: Details to follow

January							February							March							April							May						
S	M	T	W	T	F	S	S	M	T	W	T	F	S	S	M	T	W	T	F	S	S	M	T	W	T	F	S	S	M	T	W	T	F	S
				1	2	3	1	2	3	4	5	6	7	1	2	3	4	5	6	7				1	2	3	4						1	2
4	5	6	7	8	9	10	8	9	10	11	12	13	14	8	9	10	11	12	13	14	5	6	7	8	9	10	11	3	4	5	6	7	8	9
11	12	13	14	15	16	17	15	16	17	18	19	20	21	15	16	17	18	19	20	21	12	13	14	15	16	17	18	10	11	12	13	14	15	16
18	19	20	21	22	23	24	22	23	24	25	26	27	28	22	23	24	25	26	27	28	19	20	21	22	23	24	25	17	18	19	20	21	22	23
25	26	27	28	29	30	31								29	30	31					26	27	28	29	30			24	25	26	27	28	29	30
																												31						

Chart 10-5

AJAX—Time Was

Album title:	*Time Was*	
Producers:	AJAX	
Selection #:	CD3467-22	
Street date:	4/7/98	
Musicians:	Ed Freeble	guitar & singing
	Ted Paxton	guitar & singing
	Mel Markhouse	bass
	Charles Passiglia	drums
Label:	Hoot	
Management:	Ted Allgood	
	(address)	
	(phones)	
Booking agent:	Success	
	contact:	Art James
	(address)	
	(phone)	
Publishing:	Givens	
Marketing:	Timely Tunes	phone:
		fax:
A&R:	Mel Heat	phone:
		fax:
Publicity:	Implementation Associates	phone:
	Ray Goins	fax:
Songs:	*Going Fast*	*Who Can Tell*
	Why Now	*When You Know*
	Take a Chance	*Raging*
	Little Things	*Caught in the Web*
	Time Was	*Reveal It*

Background:

We released *We're Here* in the U.S. in mid-1997 to create an awareness of **Ajax** and to set the stage for the release of *Time Was*:

1. 7,200 units in the marketplace
2. #33 on the CMJ charts
3. Tour dates on the East Coast
4. Very strong showing at SXSW
5. Positive reviews in fanzines and alternative publications nationwide

Marketing:

Ajax has a unique sense of self-marketing and visual creativity:

1. They built a highly interactive and visually compelling Web site and CD-ROM.
2. They designed their own eye-catching, exciting merchandising P.O.P. and album network.

Chart 10-5 (continued)

We will expand on their vision and what they have created through:

1. *Cross-promotions/lifestyle marketing*
   A. Wakeboarding tie-in
      1. Wakeboarding is the hot, new "extreme" sport. It's a combination of surfing and waterskiing and it was born from the ingenuity of skate kids that were landlocked, couldn't surf, and had to turn to the lakes for their fun.
      2. This is Hoot Records' chance to get in on the ground floor of this sport much like Interscope did with skateboarding.
      3. **Ajax** and **Hoot Records** will be tying in with exhibitions across the U.S. and will be very visible at the World Championships in October.

   B. Glug tie-in
      Glug is a new soft drink targeted to a young alternative demographic. We have combined efforts and created a cassingle to give away at the following:
      1. Tour dates
      2. X-Games
      3. Rollerblade events
      4. Indie retail outlets
      5. Alternative publications
      6. Website

   C. AEI Programming
      1. Complete package sent 2/10

   D. Urban Outfitters programming
      1. Complete package sent 2/12

   E. We have purchased snipe posters and will be sniping select markets surrounding the street date and select shows.

Interactive:

AJAX has added an exciting dimension to the marketing campaign through their website (http://ajax.com) and their 3-hour CD-ROM.

Hundreds of flyers posted in college computer labs and libraries nationwide advertising a contest that will draw students into the website.
Link to several "alternative" websites.
• Glug soft drink
• Sega game?
Live Internet broadcasts of their shows on website
Online "chats" after their shows

Will spread word in other ways. In addition to interviews and reviews, will gather mailing lists of fans. Will go after websites like "pitchforkmedia.com" and other Internet taste makers for positive comments. Will offer promotional streams of live performances, interviews, etc.

Chart 10-5 (continued)

Will tie in wakeboarding websites and wakeboard manufacturer's websites.

Website address to be listed on admats, tip sheets, window clings, and other display and mailers.

Radio:
- S1: *Raging*
- S2: *Why Now*
- S3: *Reveal It*

Ajax is a Modern Rock band. Our strategy is to set this record up at College radio, and then hit Modern Rock and Active Rock radio very aggressively.

College radio:
We built a base at College radio through the release of *We're Here*, and will build upon that base with *Raging*.

Shipped *We're Here*, a bio, and a sticker to College radio and Modern Rock Specialty shows
Impact Date
Fax college stations a "thank you" from the band for their support
Mail out sticker/postcards written by the band to all of the college stations that added the record
Send autographed posters to key stations.

Specialty Shows:
The full album, bio and sticker will be serviced to Specialty Shows on 2/12/98. We are attacking the Specialty Shows aggressively to create a buzz at this level and have it crossover into the mainstream Modern Rock programming.
- Mailings including the band's newsletter, t-shirt, stickers, signed posters, window clings, etc.

Modern Rock:
We will start a "buzz" at the specialty shows and carry it over into the mainstream Modern Rock programming.

Ship *Raging* CDPRO
Impact date at Modern Rock Radio

Active Rock:

Ship *Raging* CDPRO
Impact date at Active Rock Radio

AAA Radio:
Because AAA has evolved into more of a "song driven" format, we will test *Raging* but our emphasis will probably be on *Reveal It*.
Satellite radio, Podcasts

Video:
The **Ajax** videos from *We're Here* were very well received at the local, regional and national level and have given us a strong foundation for the new video.

Chart 10-5 (continued)

Ship a full package to the local, regional and national video outlets which will include:

Raging *video*
bio & photo
band's newsletter
sticker

Send a sticker/postcard from the band to all of the video stations that have added the video.

Ship an autographed poster to the key stations.

Shoot interview footage of the band.

MuchMusic, which now airs in the U.S. and Canada, will add *Raging* into heavy rotation on 3/6. MuchMusic is seen in the following markets:

Arkansas, California, Florida, Ohio, Indiana, New Jersey, Connecticut, Massachusetts, Michigan, Virginia, Texas, New York, Kansas, Oklahoma. MuchMusic is also seen on DirecTV, SuperStar Connection/Netlink, Prime Time 24, Turner-Vision, Consumer Satellite Systems, HBO Direct, Satellite Receivers, Programmers Clearing House, American Programming Service, Programmers Warehouse, Adelphia Home Satellite and Burly Bear Network serving 136 U.S. colleges and 1.5 million students.

Touring:

Ajax has begun to establish a touring base on the East Coast. They have developed a good relationship with the promoters and club personnel and have made friends and fans along the way. They will resume touring in the U.S. We will set up the following surrounding each tour date wherever possible: (Tour dates to follow)

1. Radio visits (College, Modern Rock and Active Rock)
2. In-stores (visits and/or performance in both traditional and non-traditional retail outlets)
3. Contests with the following available as prizes:
   A. tickets
   B. t-shirts
   C. signed "firecracker" posters
   D. **Ajax** skate decks (limited)
4. Video interviews
5. Local press/tv
6. Sales of band's merchandise and CDs at the venues
7. Cassingle and sticker giveaways

Retail:

Street date: 4/7
Solicitation: 3/5 to 3/25
Forecast: 60,000 units

Tools:

Ad mats, minis, flats, posters, window clings and stickers are available.

Because there will be only four weeks of Modern Rock airplay before we street this record, we will need to create a buzz on this record in additional ways:

Chart 10-5 (continued)

1. High CMJ chart position
2. Early ads at Modern Rock radio
3. Heavy video play (including 120 Minutes, M2, and MTV)
4. Features and reviews in major publications
5. Tour dates

Press:

The band has established a following in Buffalo, Rochester, the Northeast, and to some degree the midwest; we will build from that base. Their first tour in the U.S. put the band in front of a number of important critics and garnered the band some impressive fans:

The Bob	National fanzine out of Philadelphia
Freelancer	*Feature in Manhattan Mirror*
Media America	
CBS Eye on People	
Musician	*New Singings piece*

We will focus on mainstream press which includes:

fashion magazines and high brow teen magazines, guitar/bass/drum magazines, alternative magazines including some skate publications, key Internet outlets, fanzines and regional magazines, dailies and weeklies

On-Line

Addicted to Noise	Music Universe
All Star	Omnibus
Blender (CD-ROM)	People on-line
BTR	Pepsi World
Launch (CD-ROM)	Rock Around the World
Microsoft	*Sonic Net*
Mr. Showbiz	The End Net

Mainstream/National

Advocate	Glamour	People
Allure	GQ	Replay
Audio Magazine	Harper's Bazaar	Request
Billboard	In Style	Rolling Stone
Build	Interview	*Seventeen*
Car Audio and Electronics	Live	Smoke
Cosmopolitan	Mademoiselle	Spin
Details	Maxium	Teen
Elle	MTV News	Tower Pulse
Entertainment @ Home	*Musician*	Us
Esquire	Newsweek	Vogue
Genre	Paper	YM

Chart 10-5 (continued)

Alternative/Regional/Fanzine

Alternative Press (national)
Aquarian (NYC)
Baby Sue (Atlanta, GA)
Big Brother (skate magazine)
Big Shout (Wilmington, DE)
Big Takeover (New York)
Bikini (national)
Boston Phoenix (Boston)
Cake (national)
Carbon 14 (Philadelphia, national)
Cheeseball (Boston)
Chicago Reader (Chicago)
Cleveland Free Times (Cleveland)
Dig (Nashville)
Elixir (Eugene, OR)
Extreme (Buffalo)
Fad (San Francisco)
Fizz (National)
Freeze (National)
Graffiti (Charleston)
Heckler (Sacramento)
Ink 19 (Tampa)
Insider (Chicago)
Insite (Atlanta)
Instant (Boston)
Jam (Florida)
Juice (North Carolina)
Lollipop (Boston)
Magnet (national)
Mean Street (LA)
Metronome (Boston)
Moo (monthly in Columbus, OH)
Music Monitor (North Carolina)
Music Paper (NYC)
New York Press
Night Times (monthly in St. Louis)
Orchstar (monthly in Florida)

PC (Austin)
Plow (national)
Plush (national)
Pop Watch (Boston)
Popsided (Orange County)
Popsmear (NYC)
Powerbunny (NJ)
Puncture (national)
Raygun (National)
Rayolux (Chicago)
Rocket (Seattle)
Scram (NYC)
Scrawl (NYC)
Seconds (National)
Slug (Salt Lake City)
Smash (Buffalo)
Soma (San Francisco)
Speed Kills (Chicago)
Squealer (Minneapolis)
Strength (national)
Strobe (LA)
Suburban Voice (Boston)
Surface (San Francisco)
Swing (national)
Tail Spins (Chicago)
The Bob (national)
The Fritz (Tampa)
The Noise (Boston)
Thicker (San Francisco)
Thora-zine (Austin)
Time Out (NYC)
Tough Trax (Boston)
Tribe (New Orleans)
Velocity (Chicago)
Your Flesh (national)
Zoom (Boston)

Guitar/Bass/Drums Music Magazines

Bass Player
Drum Magazine
Guitar
Guitar Magazine

Guitar Player
Guitar World
Modern Drummer
Performing Songwriter

Chart 10-5 (continued)

Dailies

A few of the dailies will be serviced ahead of time, but the majority will get the album three to four weeks before release.

Boston Globe	New York Times
Baltimore Sun	Philadelphia Daily News
Chicago Tribune	Philadelphia Inquirer
Detroit Free Press	USA Today
Grand Rapids Press	Washington Post
LA Times	

In all examples, the marketing plans must be finished long before the actual release of the product, and for that matter, in some cases some of the activity requested in the plan will take place before release of the product. In today's market, that preliminary "buzz" is quite important. At least three to four months prior to the "street date" many campaigns can be started with:

Teasers: Mailers or even personal contact that advises buyers, radio, etc. that something big is coming.

One Sheet: This is a single page of information aimed at buyers of particular types of product (see Chart 10-6). This is not a teaser, since all the information is presented and possibly other material about the artist will be attached.

Bios: If the act is new or the members have experience from having performed on or with major product, this must be pointed out.

Samplers: Product is usually ready at least three to four months in advance, and by this time, key cuts have been identified. Start letting people hear them.

Display: Start getting this arranged. Make sure you will have space when the time comes.

Publicity: This is very important at this stage. You have an act, and publicity can start even without the consumer hearing the music. Once again, much depends on who is in the band you are hyping. But publicity people are very creative, and they can squeeze a story out of very little.

All this activity prior to release is geared to implant the name of the act in people's minds, so that when the record is actually released, the trade will feel there is really something of substance there, and you have better opportunities for airplay and better initial orders.

There are a number of other aspects of a plan that might not be spelled out in the original plan, but come into play before release or as the record develops with airplay and sales. These should be examined also.

Chart 10-6

ATTENTION: GOSPEL BUYER

atlanta international records

PRESENTS
THE NEW RELEASE
BY

Dottie Peoples
God Can & God Will - Live In Atlanta

STREET DATE: MARCH 23

Dottie Peoples returns with her first live project in two years. Having successfully harnessed her explosive performing style in the studio with "Testify", it was time for her to spread her wings once again in front of an audience. And the results speak for themselves.

All the elements that made "Dottie Peoples ... Live" (AIR 10187) and "On Time God" (AIR 10200) such tremendous successes at radio and retail are present, including most of the same musicians and many of the same songwriters. No one "takes you to church" like Dottie Peoples, and this latest release will have her many fans ready to go along. Recorded at New Birth Missionary Baptist Church in Atlanta the performance is available as an audio and video release.

Song Titles:

Faith	There's A Brighter Day
Compassion	I Lift The praise Up
Oh What A Time we Had	We Give You Praise
God Can	Nobody But You
All My Help	More Than Enough
Show Some Sign	Testify

KEY SELLING POINTS

- Dottie People's visibility is at an all time high thanks to her performance on the Power 2003 Tour and her Dove & Stellar Nominations / Awards
- She is the recipient of the James Cleveland Lifetime Achievement Award
- Songs from "On Time God", "Testify" and "The Collection" are still receiving Heavy Airplay
- There will be a full national media blitz surrounding this release

LABEL / NUMBER: AIR 10250
CATEGORY: Gospel
LIST PRICE: $15.98 CD / $9.98 CS / $19.95 Video
UPC: 0-8992-10250-2-6 / 0-8992-10250-4-0 / 08992-10250-3-3
    30 count boxes on CD & CS

As part of publicity's campaign, you might want press kits produced. Since publicity is so important, making information available to the media in an exciting format can be very useful in getting and keeping that "buzz" going prior to and after release.

Time Buys

Newspaper Ads

Promotion Records

For "in store" play.
For the buyers at the accounts.
For radio contests.
For consumer giveaways.

Mailers and Flyers

One stops send out mailers to all their accounts. However, retailers send to consumers, usually to support holiday sales.

Brochures

Can be used by labels to inform accounts and press. These might differ from press kits in approach.

Other Radio Activity (in addition to getting airplay)

Contests.
Concert ticket giveaways.
Trip contests (cruises, weekends, trips to out-of-town concerts for listeners).
Supplying acts for special promotions being done by radio stations, such as charity softball games, special concerts, etc.

Listening Sessions (with or without artist)

Play the product for radio and retail, rack jobber and one stop people.
Do acoustic performances before a similar audience.

Tours

Perform as opening act (can be larger venue).
Perform as headliner (usually small venue).
Meet the accounts (can be tied in with listening sessions).
Work with sales department.

Incentives

T-shirts, sweatshirts, other labeled apparel.
Merchandise "tchotchkes" that relate to the product or act in some way to draw attention to the record.

Contests

For accounts.

Internal, within the company for distribution, promotion or other departments.

For consumers via tie-ins with other products at radio or in print. Gives labels access to merchandise, trips, vacations etc. This stretches advertising funds since all involved share spots and cost, but still get the exposure necessary. This tactic can be used in stores selling other types of products within the same mall or strip center.

Merchandise tie-ins

"Piggyback" advertising with other non-record products.

"Buy It and Try It" Type Promos (each account has own name)

Most retail chains have some sort of program where consumers can buy certain records and if not satisfied, return them for refund or credit. This pertains only to a limited list of selections, usually being advertised and promoted by the stores and labels. This is another incentive to get price and position.

Corporate Sponsorship

Many major companies, especially soft drink and beer companies, sponsor record artist tours. This usually has to be a major act, but if a new act is opening for the headliners, they get some of the benefit.

Marketing staff at all levels keep these and other possible actions at hand and either write them into the original plan, or roll them out as the record develops.

Once these initial plans have been honed and written plans have been distributed to everyone involved, a process starts that everyone hopes will develop the project to "hit" status. The first step has to be deciding on the single or album cut that will be the major initial focus. Once this has been accomplished, a release date is set; and once that date is reached, everything planned is set in motion.

Assuming the project is focused on a new act, ideally what happens next will be a steady progression of successes that will develop loosely along the following lines:

1. Some sales coverage on the single or album, in as many stores as possible, will be attained. This is where the one stop is critical. Assume there will not be a heavy outlay, but hopefully enough to sustain any play that might be obtained.

2. One approach at initial stages of a campaign is to attempt to get in store play, possibly have a listening party for retailers and radio, and even arrange a tour. The tour does not necessarily have to include performing in front of paying audiences, but can be just to meet the people who will be critical to breaking the record—retail, distribution, and radio.

3. Try to get some display at retail.

4. Starting in small markets (remember this is a new act) work for some airplay on the single or album cut.

5. When and if airplay does come, no matter how light, *BE SURE THERE IS STOCK IN THAT RADIO MARKET*. As noted, the one stop really is key to making this happen.

6. Contact all retail and one stops to ensure *STORE REPORTS*. **Keep in mind, these reports are to local stores from local radio, not Billboard, SoundScan, or other trade publication reports at this stage.** The marketing staffs must make frequent, almost constant, contact with retail in the area where play has started to ensure reports to the station or stations playing the record.

7. This could well be the stage when some small time buys are made to support the play. Obviously, the buys will be on stations playing the product.

8. Once these buys have been made and aired, it is mandatory to go for more store reports, once again to local radio, still not major industry trades.

9. Certainly in the area where play has developed, it should be possible to get more display in place at retail.

10. If play continues, and the chances are good that it will if all the follow-up has been completed on time, more time buys are in order. That play can be sustained and spread this way.

11. As this happens, the next step is to obtain more complete coverage of stock at retail with heavier quantities wherever possible. It is mandatory that stock be in most stores so the consumer can find it, buy it, and generate store reports (still mainly to radio). But now it is reasonable to look for some trade reports, so be sure one stops have stock and their phone people are talking it up.

12. If a performing tour has not been scheduled yet, certainly start scheduling one now.

13. Get money for a promotional video, if one has not already been made. **This step could well be even sooner than this. Depending on commitment from company, it could well have been in the original budget.**

14. By now airplay should be spreading to other areas and regions, and everyone in those markets is going after store reports. With the latest changes in reporting, namely the advent of the SoundScan sys-

tem, you now have to generate those reports via heavy promotions **(aimed at Price and Position)** in the chain outlets that report their sales figures.

15. When the release has attained this level of success, it requires massive additions to stock at retail all over, especially the major chains, large additions to display and chainwide promotions geared to print advertising. This is when it is necessary to use the "cluster" advertising approach with major chains, either nationally or regionally (depending on their strength).

16. Now is the time to **get the next single ready**.

17. If all these steps, plus some others that have been improvised throughout the building process, are working, it is time to start making plans to sell to the rack jobbers. This record warrants complete coverage in all types of outlets.

18. **Also, now it is obvious that the consumer likes the music,** so it is imperative that additional advertising and promotion plans are put into motion that will ensure the record will go "multiplatinum."

19. Start chilling the champagne for when the record goes "#1 with a bullet" on the Billboard charts, and most important, add this success story to your resume.

Of course, this is an oversimplification, since so many things can go wrong and each plateau is not so easily reached. However, to keep the project alive, much has to be improvised to take care of the glitches that appear along the way. But it is a road map and any detours taken can help make the trip more pleasant.

Advertising

In addition to airplay, which must start the whole process rolling, the next most important ingredient is **advertising. There are a number of general precepts about advertising that pertain to recorded music; however, there are some deviations.**

Advertising is a huge part of the marketing of any product, and especially in the United States. However, advertising expenditures are growing in other parts of the globe as more and more media choices are being offered. Advertising grew so fast in the United States because of the large number of radio stations available to the public. This generated huge advertising activity and revenues.

Advertising is successful and useful in any country where people have discretionary income, are offered a wide selection of products, and there are enough media to support it all. In the United States, advertising has an added aid in that advertisers can pretty much make any claims they wish with little or no government intervention. This is not necessarily the case in other countries. But this is changing ever so slightly as more and more advertisers and advertising agencies are being fined for deceptive practices.

The media, outlets, and locations to place advertising are mushrooming, and to some extent, people are starting to feel it is becoming more and more intrusive. But the trend will accelerate as more and more products come on the market, and more and more people are out there as possible consumers.

As Dr. Fred Allvine of Georgia Tech has pointed out in his marketing texts that before the industrial revolution buyers and sellers interacted directly. This is no longer possible in today's economies. In addition, manufacturing capacities have grown tremendously and this means more and more products must be sold. Nowhere is this more applicable than in the record industry. Until returns were brought under control, cutouts were almost as important as new releases.

As people become better educated and major retailers can offer a wider selection of product, advertising takes on added importance. In the music industry to a large extent, and to some extent with other products, the need to presell has grown as more and more retailers go to self-service. Sales people have little contact with customers as they make their choices these days and only see them when they want to pay. Some years ago, CBS (now Sony) used the philosophy at Christmas that there would be no ad money allocated to accounts. CBS would advertise heavily in each local market and in all media and create the demand. As long as all outlets stocked the product, every outlet would get a fair share of the sales volume. This was abandoned as pressure from the accounts demanded the advertising funds not only be used to sell the product but also be used to sell their particular outlets.

Not all advertising is directed at the ultimate consumer. There is **trade advertising**, and the record industry does use it. McGraw-Hill suggests that there are six stages in successfully selling to the "trade" or nonconsumer:

1. Making contact.
2. Arousing need.
3. Creating preference.
4. Making a proposal.
5. Closing the order.
6. Keeping the account sold.

The number of trade publications is staggering. There are hundreds of computer publications, some just for the trade, some aimed at consumers, and that industry is comparatively young. Both trade and consumer publications directed at music and its personalities continue to grow at a rapid rate.

The recording industry uses trade advertising for all for the same reasons as noted above, with some additional objectives thrown in. For example:

1.   Massage "tip sheets"

"Tip sheets" are publications that are circulated throughout the industry relating to sales, airplay, reviews, etc. The information is useful to all aspects of the business and many feel it is far more reliable than what is found in the regular trade papers, and since many "tip sheets" do accept advertising, they prosper.

2.   Appease artists and managers

In an industry where ego plays such an important part, this is a necessary activity. Attracting good acts is highly critical to any label. Artists and their management are very cognizant of who gets the exposure at the trade level.

3.   Get to small accounts that never see a sales representative

Small retailers are very anxious to have all the information possible. Not only do they want information about a new product, but many times their only exposure to what special deals are available can be found in trade publications.

4.   Massage accounts that have magazines or flyers

As has been noted previously, one stops in particular send mailers to their accounts. Advertising supports this sales tool.

The most important type of advertising and the one that commands the largest expenditures is "consumer advertising." This is where the marketing staffs must place their emphasis.

Unlike so many products, in records there is really no brand name advertising, since few people buy because of the record label. Over the years classical labels did promote their origin, and some jazz labels promote that way, but the buyers of most of the product are hardly aware of the label. To them, **the artist is really the only brand name they look for**. Record advertisers want to go directly to consumer with the actual product. It boils down to **play the music or show the cover and tell people about the price.**

For a long time, the advertising choices remained stagnant with the media choices listed by Dr. Allvine just about covering all the options. But Podcasting and the Internet have changed all that.

Podcasts are blanketing the nation (even General Motors has one) and will continue to grow. Advertising on the Internet has been with us for some time and it also continues to grow.

Clear Channel, a major billboard provider, is experimenting with giant electronic billboards using state-of-the-art LED (Light emitting diodes) that will change the message as often as desired. The advertiser will be buying time as opposed to buying space (something Clear Channel is familiar with being the largest radio chain in the country). This technology allows advertisers more control over what to feature and when.

Media Choices *

MEDIA	ADVANTAGES	DISADVANTAGES
Television	Wide reach Sight and sound Attention getting Prestigious High info content Pick audience (cable)	Short life High cost Clutter of ads Button (remote) pushers Not "TiVO" proof
Magazines	High quality ads High info content Long life Choose audience	Long lead time Position uncertain
Newspapers	Good local coverage Good for price info Can place quickly Groups ads by product Good demographic Cost effective	Poor quality presentation Short life Poor attention getting
Radio	Music, reinforce airplay Fair cost Can place quickly Can get high frequency Audience selectivity	Audio only Short attention span "Button pushers" Annoys young audience
Billboards	High exposure frequency Low cost "TiVO" proof	Message may not be read Shortness of message Environmental blight
Direct Mail	Best selectivity Large info content No interference from other ads Gets noticed	High cost per contact Associated with junk mail

* Adapted from *Marketing Principles and Practices*, Fred C. Allvine, HBJ.

The six media choices noted list advantages and disadvantages of each, and additions have been made to reflect how record advertising fits into the sequence. The media choices have to be considered in more detail. (Add Podcasts and the Internet to the above list. Meanwhile 800 and 900 phone numbers play a small part also.)

First, newspapers and print advertising are used extensively by all types of businesses that sell to the consumer.

Newspapers are used to promote a product, to promote stores, and to promote price. Newspapers allow the advertiser to display multiple covers which is an advantage over radio, and to some degree, television. Rarely do chains only show one title. This is done to highlight a major release or a tour, but in most cases previously released catalog product is also listed.

Print is becoming better equipped to sell record product through the use of flyers, circulars, and better reproduction of covers. Additionally, as pricing becomes more competitive among outlets, print is the best way to tell the story.

The use of magazine advertising in the music industry is mainly limited to running ads in the trade papers or "fanzines," publications that are devoted to records and record artists. The deadlines for trade papers and "fanzines" readily accommodate the immediacy of music products, and record advertisers find mass media consumer magazine ads expensive for their available funds. Mass media like *Newsweek*, *Cosmopolitan*, network television, etc. are not only far too expensive, but do not fit the needs of recorded music. Record ads must target specific audiences with specific musical tastes, and in localized areas where there is airplay. This accurately describes radio.

It should be noted that a new type of "fanzine" has evolved, and as expected, it is on the Internet. Websites like "Pitchfork.com" review and tout certain types of bands and get tens of thousands of "hits" per day. Getting a digital push from sites like these can result in very impressive sales increases.

Billboards are being used for record and especially video advertising. The product must be from major artists and the labels and accounts must feel that the records will stay popular for a long time. In the video business, movies have these attributes. However, if the LED billboard technology works well, deadlines will be immaterial and any product can be featured.

Direct mail is used in record advertising, but to a very small degree. It is very expensive, the lead times required are far too long, and if it is to be used, it will be for a holiday promotion that can be designed far enough in advance.

Television revolutionized the advertising industry. When sight and sound were combined it created an impact never before experienced. Records certainly use television, primarily through MTV, BET, CMT, VH1 and others. But this is not really advertising. This falls under the promotion banner. However, the proliferation of cable stations has been a boon to record advertising. For the longest time, the stations available were far too expensive for record advertising budgets. Only in rare cases could the potential accommodate the rates. But now, and certainly in the future, record advertising will be seen more and more on the television screens.

And last, but still very important is radio advertising. The price is still at a point where it is possible to expose the consumer to the music. Radio promotion for airplay and radio time buys for sales go hand in hand. People must hear the product repeatedly before they will make the decision to buy. Radio is still a critical medium choice. Previous data has shown us that newspaper advertising is still the major way many accounts will go, but be assured that radio is not very far behind.

Another aspect of record advertising that must be considered when making the media choice is available funds. Records must spend so much on getting the product played that the allocations remaining for advertising, no matter what media, are usually far less than what is available for other products. Also, keep in mind that all advertising allocations are based on the price of the product. Records are a low priced item compared to most other products, whether you use a wholesale or retail pricing structure.

This is what marketing managers have at their disposal when putting together the plans that can possibly be creating the next superstar. These marketing plans must not just be geared to breaking one particular record, but hopefully are geared to creating a major act in the process. Creating acts is what sustains record companies. This is what their marketing activities are all about.

Summary

Product management at the national level is where everything must start when introducing a piece of recorded music or video to the buying public, and in many cases they hold the fate of every new artist in their hands.

Marketing plans must be created for every record released, no matter how major or unknown the artist or group might be. A plan is necessary to coordinate and focus everyone's activity.

Marketing plans can be short or very extensive, depending upon the author.

Having everyone follow the timetable will result in far better success rates and keep everyone focused better.

While not every plan must incorporate all the actions available, the list is large.

Knowledge of advertising and how to incorporate it into all plans is vital to success.

Terms

Marketing Plan: The master plan prepared by label representatives to guide each project from release of each record.

Venue: Locations where artists can perform for the paying public or for promotional purposes to radio and retail people.

Conditions of Sale: Rules and terms under which product is sold to accounts by the six major distributors and independent distributors.

Platinum: When sales reach 1,000,000 units net.

Price and Position: Necessary ingredients for success of project whereby the record is where consumers can see it easily and the price is such to attract the buyer.

Product Manager (or Product Director): Person responsible for initial marketing plan and for steering project through to success.

Guarantees: When account is sold on 100% return basis with no penalty to incentivize their purchases.

Deals: Extra discount or better price to make buying the product more profitable should it sell well.

Dating: An extension of time to pay for product.

Time Buys: Purchase of radio or TV spots.

"Piggyback" Advertising: Sharing an ad with another type of product to extend advertising allocations.

In-Store Play: The music played in retail locations exposing what they have for sale.

Store Reports: Reports to radio about sales history of product stations are playing.

Bibliography

Allvine, Fred C. *Marketing*, Harcourt, Brace, Jovanovich Publishers 1987, p. 553.

Exercises

1. Established artists have a track record and potential sales level. Thus you can assume funding for marketing plans. What are five of the basic activities you would put in your plan?

2. List six of the dozen or so basic elements of any marketing plan, no matter what the level of acceptance of the artist.

3. More money is spent on advertising in the United States than anywhere else in the world. What are the two major factors that contribute to that?

4. What are the major media choices these days?

5. As seen in previous discussions, what are the two major media choices made by record marketers?

Chapter 11
Marketing Tactics–2

Learning Objectives

After studying this chapter you should be able to:

1. Understand other types of marketing plans

2. Understand their use and structure

3. Learn why not all marketing plans are geared to one piece of product

4. Learn how label representatives must interact with Distribution and Accounts

Other Types of Marketing Plans

While marketing plans devised by product managers at the national level and devoted to specific releases and artist development are the most critical to a label and demand the most time, attention, and money from all staff members, there are still a number of other areas where marketing plans must be devised and implemented. Anyone involved in marketing music must be able and willing to formulate plans that might not have the specific focus of a single release, but are vital to the profitability and growth of a label or a distribution company.

Recorded product certainly has a glamorous side that intrigues everyone, whether within the industry or on the outside as consumers. But sales objectives tick off constantly, quotas never take a vacation, and while it takes a minimum level of sales to support the entire operation, no company can accept a minimum sales level. There are too many variables and the financial history of the industry is peppered with examples of labels that are major players one day, and out of existence the next. Growth is mandatory for survival, but a predictable sales level also has its benefits.

Not all activity surrounds new, emerging artists or well known megaselling superstars. Every major label has an important catalog, both full priced and budget priced that sells at a consistent level day in and day out and can be counted on to produce revenue on a steady, predictable basis. The vaults are a very profitable source of revenue, as is the catalog of every artist who has a current hit on the charts or is touring and playing major venues. Being able to accurately forecast this revenue has a major impact on budgeting the expenditures for the new act's experimental product and planning for campaigns on major artists.

In addition, the marketing staffs at the local level must be able to devise plans that are targeted to specific accounts, most focused on particular releases. All of these activities must maintain constant pressure on the distribution structure and the account structure not only to maintain but also to increase the sales rate of all product.

Assortments or Groups of Product

Perhaps one of the best examples of wanting to market a group of records took place when compact disc became a reality. As more and more product was being newly mastered to CD, it was necessary to have plans to expose all of these selections so that the consumer would know what was available and where to find their favorites. Certainly this was not as glamorous as some of the projects, but as has been noted in survey after survey, the advent of CD helped maintain a dollar volume in the industry while unit sales were falling. Selections can be marketed a number of ways:

Particular type of music: Plans like this are done frequently since music of the same genre will attract a greater group of buyers. A consumer who likes one of the acts in the group of acts being marketed might be persuaded to try the music of another artist.

Entire catalog from a single major artist: Many times done in conjunction with a major new release from that artist. A promotion can increase catalog sales.

Seasonal selections: Back to school, holidays, etc.

Groups of selections at the same price point: Usually budget records.

Support for major tours and award show winners: Winning major honors from TV award shows has proven to spur sales of the winners' new releases and catalog.

These are more or less generic groupings in that they should be geared to a wide cross section of consumers. All such plans are geared to focus attention on what is being worked. Depending upon the grouping, marketers have the option of employing discounts or dating or advertising. The main thrust is to make sure that the distribution organization will give the product added attention and that the accounts will perceive the benefits of cooperating and giving the product the exposure it deserves. The mechanics are not elaborate, but they must be creative enough to get the attention of everyone, especially the consumer. The plans must be worked to include the largest number of outlets possible since these promotions should appeal to the largest group of record lovers.

In some cases, if you are focusing on jazz, classical, children's product, Latin, or some other more limited genre, you tailor the marketing plan for a smaller, but perhaps more loyal, segment of the buying public. In these cases, you pick and choose the outlets, the methods of exposure, and the incentives.

In either situation, the plan will list all the product being promoted, the time frame for the added activity, what incentives (if any) are being offered, and most important, the reason why this should command someone's attention in the midst of trying to break hits and new acts.

Field Marketing Manager Plans

These plans are usually in conjunction with the national plans explained previously. To really implement a national plan, there must be a coordinated effort at the local level to keep rolling whatever momentum has been generated. In this type of plan key accounts are selected for special advertising allocations and discount deals, with an emphasis on timing each promotion to maintain a high level of sales. A typical plan is outlined on the next page.

Field Marketing Manager Plan—Specific Title

Account	Media	Dollars	Run Dates	Special Promo
One Stop	Flyer	$800 page	7–15 to 7–22	
Chain Retail	Print	$4000	8–1	Sound Insurance*
Retail Chain	Radio	$3000	8–7 to 8–10	No Risk*
Retail Chain	Print	$3000	8–15	Sure Shot*
Racked Account	Circular	$500 a cut	8–22	

*Indicates chain's name for a "Buy It and Try It" promotion.

The dates for each segment are geared to keep the project in front of the consumer for over a month.

Specific Account, Specific Act

It is quite common in the business today for acts to schedule tours to coincide with the release of a new album. This way, all the promotional forces can be brought into focus and far greater mileage can be obtained from any expenditures. The excitement of a tour highlights the act, the tour showcases the new product and the retail community is anxious to tie in and cash in on the excitement. In this instance, the field marketing people will go to a specific account which has to be a chain that has enough stores in a particular region where the tour might be concentrated to make it worthwhile and tailors a promotion to just that chain.

The label people will usually write up the particulars of the promotion, with the approval of the merchandising manager of the chain of stores, and the details will be distributed to all stores involved. (See Chart 11-1)

It is the responsibility of the retail chain's supervisors to make sure that all the directed stores participate and do what is expected of them by the label that is paying the bills. But it is also important for the distribution people to monitor this. When multiple stores are involved, you can be sure there are some that will not follow through. With a promotion of this sort, the dollars allocated can be substantial and that money should not be wasted. That is why the whole plan is outlined as seen below so that there can be no misunderstanding.

However, in defense of store managers and chain supervisors, it is quite difficult to cover every detail completely. The label people realize that their promotion is usually not the only one of its kind in progress. This could be the case, however, and that is when you push it to the maximum. With any project of this sort, you must try to cover as many details as possible and leave nothing, or at least very little, to chance. Store managers and clerks like it better this way also. It saves asking questions.

Chart 11-1

Promotion for Specific Account, Specific Product

TO: All Store Managers

             Assistant Store Managers

             Record Department Supervisors

FROM: Record and Tape Merchandise Manager

DATE:

SUBJECT: Focus Promotion—[insert dates]

One area in which our chain has distinguished itself in the past year was in our single-minded devotion to breaking new product. I believe that your enthusiasm in supporting our special *"Focus"* promotions is something about which we have every right to feel great pride.

Once again we are being given an opportunity to exert the power of intense and imaginative merchandising which will *lead to sales.* The (distribution company) and (label) is totally committed to support us in our biggest *"Focus"* promotion of the year and our first ever dual promotion, since we are tying in with a tour that features two artists from the same label. The tour is geared very heavily to the markets where our stores dominate, and we must take advantage of this.

Product: (Can insert new release by both artists and, if everyone will agree, possibly a previous release)

Dates: (Coincide with tour, attempt to get two to four weeks)

Sale Price: $0.00 CD, *except during ad period,* when price drops to $0.00 CD.

Buy It and Try It

Both new releases will be sold as "Buy It and Try It." (See attached store policy information sheet rules). "Buy It and Try It" double bin signs are to be used for this promotion. Check NOW to be sure you have these signs, call if any are needed. Check now to make sure you have "Buy It and Try It" refund forms and call if any are needed.

Merchandising, Display and Display Material

The product is to be displayed in front stepups, four rows wide. Three rows will hold CD's.

Each store will be supplied with display materials and each store will be responsible for creating *very dominant displays.* Every store with a window must do a window, while within the store, sign frames, hanging displays, stacked displays will be used to call attention to this product. Storefront lattice work is to be devoted to this product for the full run of the promotion. Contact your local (distributor) if additional display material is needed for your store.

Display photos are to be sent to me and must reach me by (date). Every manager is responsible for seeing that this is done and each Regional Merchandising Manager is

Chart 11-1 (Continued)

charged with followup in the stores. (Distributor) sales and merchandising people will also be there to help obtain display, and will be checking the followup.

Please remember this is not a case of one sign frame being the display. This is a *"Focus" Promotion and the impact on this product must be felt by the consumer.*

In-Store Play

Both the new releases will be supplied to you and must be in *heavy rotation* on your in-store play list for the duration of the promotion.

Video

All stores equipped with video players will receive promotional videos to use during the course of this promotion. You are charged with seeing to it that the video is played.

Radio Play Lists

Play lists will follow weekly as they become available.

Advertising

Radio, TV and print will be utilized with this project, including multimedia MTV buys. *Please pay very careful attention to all advertising department bulletins. They will outline when advertising will affect your area.*

Product Buys

All product will be allocated from the warehouse. Should an immediate fill in that cannot be supplied from the warehouse be required, normal procedure with your local one stop will be followed.

_____

(Signed)

Merchandise Manager

Attachment: Complete Tour Schedule
        (Changes will be sent immediately)

Plans from Label Departments to Increase Sales on
Particular Types of Product—Long Term

Plans of this type work quite well when you have a separate department such as most labels have with country product. Usually based in Nashville, the country area is run separately with its own staff, budgets, promotion, and A & R. It is not uncommon for a well-run department like this to put together a plan that usually targets the distribution segment of the company. It sets goals, specifies time frames and is monitored constantly. The idea of this type of project is to bring a certain product into the spotlight and solicit special attention from everyone marketing and selling for the distributor. (See Chart 11-2)

Some of the ingredients are: plenty of advance warning about what will be released; overall goals on what size sales increases you require; goals on specific releases; and most important, ways of implementing the program and what support can be expected from the label. With plans such as this you build on experience, market research, knowledge of the account base in each market, strength of the artist roster, advance knowledge of what will be released and your ability to gain and maintain everyone's attention over a long period of time.

Plans for Accounts to Increase Business Over a Long Period of Time

Any plan geared to the distribution network can certainly be modified to target a chain of stores. The principles are very similar; however, you must also enlist the participation of the distribution people since they have the most direct access to the accounts. By outlining goals, spelling out the type of support you intend to offer and having the account commit time and display space, you take the ingredients and put them into a similar recipe, this time with a major retail chain.

National Plans for National Accounts

There are accounts that blanket the country with either retail stores (Transworld, for example) or racked accounts (Handleman Company, for example). When a major new release is scheduled, the marketing people at headquarters will want to go to these accounts and make sure that a major impact is guaranteed in all their outlets right from the initial release and shipment of the product. These plans always include advertising funds, "in store" commitments, and a large initial buy in, the latter required to support the large advertising and display commitments.

It is also not uncommon for the roles to be reversed and an account will devise a Marketing Plan to be used to acquire greater cooperation and more advertising funds from the labels and distributors. These plans extol the virtues of that account,

Chart 11-2

Plan to Increase Overall Business—Long Term

Objectives

Internal

1. Develop systems to provide greater information flow between Distribution Branches and Label.
2. Build on historical distributor/label relationship to foster a stronger partnership and utilization of individual strengths and resources.

External

1. Create and implement a 12 month marketing campaign with distribution branches to develop greater product focus, placement, positioning, promotion, and perception at optimum times.
2. To yield a business level of $ _____ gross and $ _____ net, which will yield a **___% increase in gross and a ***___% increase in net.

** based on last year's business
*** based on 15% return

Strategies

1. Research and develop plans for those accounts within the branch not currently covered by such.
   a. Put the responsibility into the hands of the people closest to the accounts— sales representatives and merchandisers.
   b. Research three year trends with accounts.
   c. Research product mix with accounts.
2. Develop a greater manpower and dollar focus on mid level projects to insure unit growth. (Specific numbers can be inserted)
   a. Greatest weakness is inability to drive many acts past the mid chart, mid level stage. This frustration also creates unwarranted returns.
   b. Key projects will be announced well in advance and everyone will be given ample opportunity to plan positioning and promotion with accounts.
   c. Releases will be scheduled to avoid major conflicts with other work projects.
3. Develop an understanding of and exploit the predictability of product and to insure correct timing of promotions and programs.
   a. Employ "Patience Marketing"— let history dictate each move.
   b. Artist development projects require more than one single to build recognition and sales.
   c. Creating advance "buzz" becoming more and more important.
   d. Product coverage in every market where play develops.
   e. Advertising support will be preallocated so can be placed immediately.
   f. A & R will realize necessity for three to four strong singles per album.

Chart 11-2 (Continued)

4. Establish specific unit and dollar goals to insure timely plan development utilizing the 12 month business forecast.
   a. Base on past performance or market research on similar product.
5. Create and implement timely reviews to insure the plan is working and cement communication between the distribution company and the label.
   a. Advise national label representatives of branch meeting schedules so they can attend to discuss progress.
   b. Enlist national label people in meetings with major accounts.
   c. Monitor ongoing numbers against plan.

---

* The above plan can be modified to be used with a distribution company and an account, or a label and an account.

quantify the potential to move product, and generally explain exactly what all the resources of that account can mean in extra business. Using charts documenting past buying history and projected buying patterns, an account, be it retailer, rack jobber or one stop, can convince the labels and distributors to afford them more attention and increased advertising allocations.

Marketing plans are not limited to what has been discussed thus far. Any time an idea is proposed, funded, and implemented, it is considered a marketing plan. The plans touched on are examples of what might be expected of anyone joining the marketing department of a label or distribution company. Not all plans are geared to just breaking one piece of product or one act. The financial base of any company depends on more than chart toppers, because every label is subject to business cycles, changes in the music, and "cold" periods.

Summary

Marketing Plans are not just devised to work one specific selection. The business demands that certain sales levels be attained and other plans must be devised to achieve these requirements. A marketing plan can take on just about any form, depending upon who creates it, where it is to be implemented, and how much of a commitment in time and money will be made.

Distribution companies also devise and implement plans to increase sales.

Terms

Sales Objectives, Quotas: A level of sales that must be attained by either label or distribution to support the company.

Budget Goods: Lower priced records that have been in the catalog for some time and are reissued at a cheaper price to reactivate sales.

Vaults: A term used to indicate the archives where all the previous product released by a label is stored, usually on tape, and now being transferred to CD.

Incentives: Anything used to further the implementation and success of a project.

"In Store" Commitment: A commitment made to support a promotion with display and other activity at the point of sale, the retail store.

Exercises

1. Some marketing plans are built around groups of products. What are four examples of what could be covered?

2. Explain what would be covered in a long term marketing plan.

3. What would be included in a plan to support a tour by a major act?

4. What types of accounts would you approach with a plan as outlined in question 3?

Chapter 12

Promotion

Learning Objectives

After studying this chapter you should be able to:

1. Understand the role of radio promotion in breaking a record

2. Know the various types of radio formats

3. Understand what drives radio, why it needs a niche

4. Identify the role of the promotion representative in the whole scheme

5. Understand how best to handle the activities of a radio promotion representative

Airplay

Even though the last few years have seen alternative methods to expose recorded music, such as clubs and MTV, bringing music "to the streets," radio airplay remains the primary way to get the most consumers to become familiar with a record in the shortest period of time. Airplay remains the primary goal of every record company and distribution organization. People will not buy what they have not heard, and no matter what the alternative outlets claim, nothing blankets the universe like a radio signal.

Not too long ago, while radio play was never easy to obtain, at least the landscape was fairly well defined. Formats were well delineated and promotion departments knew which records were aimed at which radio stations.

That has all changed. Satellite radio (XM and Sirius) the iPod, Podcasts, and Internet broadcasting have changed that landscape.

Researchers claim that the audience for Podcasts was less than a million in 2004, but by 2010 it is predicted to be 56 million. Theoretically independent podcasters cannot podcast music, but radio stations can and the number of stations podcasting is gaining exponentially. Meanwhile, in late 2005, Apple and Motorola combined the iPod and the cell phone to create another way to listen. Re the Internet, surveys show that consumers over 14 years old listen to music on the Internet over 76% of the time.

This is all creating a major backlash in broadcast radio listenership. In 2005, compared to the previous year, people were listening to radio at least three hours less per week and that trend is accelerating.

Part of the problem is radio itself. Clear Channel and Infinity control most of the stations in America. Surveys show that listeners are tired of the same songs being played in too tight a rotation, as well as the use of generic voices as DJ's on many stations at once. These trends are reflected in advertising revenues being down, and stations are fighting back by reducing spots from 60 seconds to 30 seconds and cutting the amount of commercial content per hour.

Radio, while late to get on board, has finally joined in selling music downloads. By late 2005, over 100 stations were doing it with more being added daily.

No matter what the media or the means of transmission, it takes special skills to obtain exposure for recorded product.

The Promotion Department of any company is the key link between the people who produce the music and those who market it to the trade for eventual sale to consumers. The airplay ingredient is what makes marketing music so different from marketing other products. It is what makes the succession of moves different from the marketing of cereal or soap.

The promotion organizations have to balance the need to expose the music against the broadcast industry's need to be profitable. Promotion must serve its own music releases; radio must serve the listeners in order to remain competitive.

Both the promotion people and the radio operate in what has to be the most complex and competitive atmosphere to be found in any business endeavor. To do their job well, promotion representatives must not only know their own product, but must understand radio formats and the fragmentation and programming challenges in a market that changes rapidly. Format changes are a daily occurrence in radio throughout the country. Radio stations are changing formats to stay with the trends. Radio attempts to serve the demographics they have chosen to target, and certainly cannot risk subjugating this goal to start serving record companies. The agendas have to conflict in many instances, but a proper relationship between the two forces can be beneficial to both. The key to good, effective radio relationships is for the promotion staffs to be able to properly manage the often conflicting agendas of their own record companies and those of the media whose cooperation they need so desperately for exposure. A great deal of research and preparation is mandatory when preparing a good promotion presentation, and those who learn this lesson well will have the competitive edge in their efforts to get airplay and thus expose the consumer to their company's music product. But it does not end there. There is a tremendous amount of work and maintenance required to ensure that the exposure a good presentation generates continues. Once a record is added, it does not end. Then the aim is heavy "rotation." The station will play the record often and in a time period when the station has the most listeners.

In the mad scramble to carve out a niche in every market, radio is constantly refining formats, changing the emphasis on format, and attempting to combine the elements of one or more formats in hopes of attracting a larger audience. The list of formats is almost endless.

Music Stations can be classified as offering:
Mainstream AOR (Album Oriented Rock)
    Heavy Metal
    Classic Rock
    New Wave
    Eclectic AOR
    Top Tracks
    Classic Hits
    Alternative
    Adult Alternative
Mainstream A/C (Adult Contemporary)
    Oldies Based A/C

Contemporary A/C (Adult CHR)
High Energy CHR
CHR/Rhythm and Blues
Mainstream Urban
Urban Contemporary
Gospel
Dance Oriented
Quiet Storm
Jazz
Heart & Soul
Mainstream Country
Modern Continuous
Renegade
Traditional
New Country
Beautiful Music
Soft A/C
New Age Jazz
Smooth Jazz
M-O-R
Nostalgia/Big Band
Easy Listening
Religious
Christian
Christian Contemporary
Classical (Fine Arts)
Popular Classical
NPR – National Public Radio
Oldies
Meanwhile, **all-talk radio** has become quite popular.
All News
All Sports
All Comedy
Call In

Meanwhile XM and Sirius can offer many more formats, further fractionalizing the options. However, traditional radio is fighting back. It is called "Jack Radio." The format—no DJ's and a wide selection of songs played with no regard to smooth transitions—has been likened to the shuffle feature on MP3 and iPod players. The format is all across the country now and the play list can come from a library of

1200 or more songs. To make that library, songs have had to make the top 40 lists over the past few decades.

That leaves only those stations that combine talk and music in some proportions.

From that list, it is quite apparent that radio is reaching for just about every demographic possible, every lifestyle possible, and every age group. It is all reduced to broadcasting's economic need to deliver consumers to their advertisers. The record industry's share in this quest is to provide music that each particular demographic will want to hear and thus stay tuned.

It is impossible to discuss promotion without starting with **singles.** This format remains the driving force for the charts as well as for album sales. The changes in how singles are handled, marketed and released has changed drastically in recent times. For years, since the early to mid 1950s, singles were the 45 RPM format, with one song on each side of a seven inch disc. But by the mid 1980s it was apparent that a major change had to be made.

Arista Records was one of first companies to delve into the problem via a study that showed conclusively that the 45 RPM format was obsolete. The findings were simple. Young people, the singles buyers, no longer had turntables; they listened on cassette players, primarily the famous Walkman. Research shows that singles are bought by consumers 12 to 24 years of age; that's the age group the market targets.

The cassette single was started by BMG (now SONY-BMG), WEA (now WMG) and UNI, (now Universal). With most of the testing done in the south, a region which for decades had always been a good singles market. One of the major reasons the south was always a good singles market was that the buyer of urban/black product appeared far smarter than most other buyers. When LP's had only one decent cut that buyer bought the hot selection only, in single format.

Now the industry is trying to come up with other singles formats. It is taking some time, but it will happen. That is, if singles themselves survive, since many labels would like to see them fade away as a commercial entity. However, singles will not fade away as a means to get airplay. Singles are necessary for airplay and even though many are not released commercially, singles versions are made available to radio for airplay. This airplay and what sales are left for singles sales still drive the charts and thus drive album sales.

After so many years of singles being such an important part of the business, now some companies no longer release singles for sales to consumers. Special versions are made available, but only for airplay. This is the way most product is handled today. However, it does not take much to make the record business reevaluate and make changes.

For a while, even the pop side of the industry was going in the direction of no more singles. However, if someone comes up with a huge selling single, many companies will start reevaluating the whole question. Another aspect of the whole singles issue is that for years, singles really lost money. The returns were staggering and singles sales became a nightmare. However, the industry continued to pursue singles sales and wrote them off as an advertising or promotional cost.

In today's market, the formats used leave room for a profit. (It might also be somewhat correct to label selections sold for iPods as singles). However, return policies have to be adjusted to make sure the profit remains, even with a new, higher price.

Even though many companies still release singles, many of them now cut off their availability for sale when they get into the top 10 or "power rotation." This enrages many accounts, but it is an economic move and an intelligent business move. Cassette format singles do cut into cassette album sales as the buyers start to outmaneuver the labels once again.

Singles that are available are sold primarily to the one stops as many retailers and many racked outlets have long since taken them off their shelves. The initial impact via one stop availability should airplay start, remains a vital factor in the whole process of getting product moving.

Another aspect of the singles picture is that companies have to "pull" (as it is termed) a single from an album so play can be concentrated. If you send an album to radio, every station will play a different cut; and there will be no concentrated effort or chance to saturate the consumers with the best cuts.

However, no matter how the single is available, it must get airplay to create excitement and recognition. Getting this airplay is the responsibility of the promotion force maintained by all labels, as well as some powerful independent promotion companies. The competition for airplay is fierce, to say the least, so only the best prepared, best informed, and most credible practitioners can hope for consistent success. Once again, be reminded that radio is not really interested in a record except to analyze it for **their** audience. If they feel their audience will want to hear it and stay tuned, you have a chance since radio makes or loses money based on audience size. **Radio needs records, records need radio, but radio sells time.** Radio lives by the rating services. Promotion's goal is to convince the stations that the audience does, indeed, want to hear certain product, and it takes a wealth of background information, statistics, and personal relationships to get your story even heard, let alone be accepted.

That is why promotion has become a very intricate process that requires detailed tracking of products as well as elaborate, well documented presentations to music directors each week. Music directors are bombarded with impassioned pleas regarding at least 100 records weekly. Sifting through all the information means they must receive presentations that are distilled, honed, and contain only important facts. A good presentation will usually be structured somewhat like the following:

First: A thorough analysis of the product being promoted, giving weight to the target audience, club play (if any), acceptance in other markets, trade paper (*Billboard* and *Radio & Records*) activity, sales activity, other radio activity, and MTV action, all done in an objective and businesslike manner.

Second: A convincing and specific analysis of the strengths, weaknesses, opportunities and dangers inherent in a station's playing the record.

Lastly: A plan to "close" that record at radio. Just as in sales, "closing" is the key.

All this requires much research, a great deal of knowledge about radio, the many formats, the idiosyncrasies of each market, competition from other stations in the market and the goals of each station contacted.

To prepare for a presentation the promotion representative must sift through a wealth of information. Much of what will be used in the presentation to a station will come from the "tracking" activities during the week. This tracking consists of:

- Knowing exactly what chart activity on a record has been during the last week, primarily from *Billboard*, *Radio & Records*, Nielsen Sound-Scan and BDS. (See Chart 14-2)

- It is also necessary to have chart and movement information from other radio stations with the same format in other cities. Radio is very sensitive to what it being played in other markets.

- Sales activity from local stores must be tracked either through phone calls or information supplied by the sales people in the local branch operation. Making your own calls pays a special benefit in that you can pick up other pertinent information to strengthen your case.

You must be accurate. With Nielsen SoundScan and BDS available, everyone's information can be checked easily. Once again, this is part of the importance of building credibility.

You must be prepared and become an expert on all aspects of the station and the product. Complete preparation will not only give you an edge in presenting the positive aspects of your record, but prepare you to counter the negatives that will most certainly be brought up. Radio likes to dwell on those negatives, rather than the positives. This also means knowing more than just the numbers. It can be very frustrating to put everything into the research and the presentation and be rejected, as happens so many times. But good promotion representatives will come back again and again if the product warrants it.

Years ago, personal relationships were the whole key to success in promotion. This is still true to a certain extent, but now research is so sophisticated, the stakes for stations so high, that personal relationships can only go so far. Add to that the new technology of BDS which electronically tracks if, when, and how frequently a record is actually played in hundreds of markets, and you have to realize that "doing your homework" before a call on the music director is still the best approach.

Without minimizing the importance of radio, promotion people have other avenues of exposure available in today's market, including club play, TV and print. It should be noted that while 7-inch (45 RPM) vinyl is gone, the 12-inch versions remain in distribution. Chances are they will be for some time, although Billboard has written that even this is under consideration by big companies. Small companies will keep them, as will some of the bigger organizations and this brings club play into focus. A large part of a promotion staff's activity is directed at club play. Supplying the record pools and people who spin records in the clubs is vital to having consumers hear the product. Club activity is also a great barometer of acceptance on so much of the product geared for that market.

Album promotion follows the same rules as those for singles, for even with albums, promotion is choosing specific cuts and working just those. Eventually, if the album hits, the album stations will play more than the target track, but everything has to start with concentration on what is hoped will be the major reason people like the whole album.

Video Exposure

Just as television appears to overshadow all aspects of our lives, it has certainly had an impact on music sales and exposure. The advent of MTV and its offspring, VH1, expanded the promotional opportunities for records many times. Country has its TNN and CMT, Urban has BET. These are such a major force because they are really the only situations where music is being broadcast **nationally,** not just locally. However, every market has its own locally broadcast video shows, either on regular broadcast channels or on cable channels. The promotion staffs have to use all these outlets.

Music videos started as a promotional tool only, but then took on another life as salable product within their own right. However, the transition for music videos from an exposure device to important salable product took a long time. Sales of music videos, with the exception of releases by some blockbuster artists, has lagged behind the sale of the audio counterparts.

Video itself has had a phenomenal ride in a very short time. It took video overall, movies, rental, music video, only a short time to overtake the audio industry in total dollars. But the part that the music industry was watching, music videos, was just a small part of that growth. Music video is growing, but it takes an audio hit to sell it, and perhaps the video's part in making the audio a hit is still its most important function. The combination of sight and sound has changed the promotional landscape forever, and while very costly, has created another avenue to get to the consumer. The list of ways to expose product to potential buyers can never be large enough when the competitive situation is so fierce.

Video product as a separate entity for sale will be discussed later.

The advent of television and some of the changes it has brought about with other media have greatly enlarged the number of places to take your promotional story via publicity. Publicity has always been a major consideration in the entertainment world, but in recent years this activity has been expanded.

Publicity

Entertainment related news, the music industry included, is now regularly included in network news, local news and cable news. Programming devoted exclusively to entertainment news is available all over the television schedule now, while the print media have jumped on this with scores of new publications. The public wants to hear and see what is going on within the recording industry. The print and broadcast media have so many publications, so many outlets, that they use up material at an alarming rate.

All the national news magazines devote a great deal of space to the music industry and recording artists. Just about every daily and even weekly newspaper has an entertainment section with a large portion of the space devoted to records and record acts. Therefore, they are very open to any idea that will interest their audience while at the same time the record company has the opportunity to tell a story about an artist or a recording.

As the concert business increases, as it has done in recent years, more and more opportunities are created to inundate the public with music related stories. Tours create an invaluable wedge for the marketing departments and promotion departments to expose the public and the trade to their acts.

To some degree, Podcasts and the Internet can be construed to be a form of publicity.

Summary

There are any number of radio formats and those that are devoted to music are very vital to the success of a new record.

There are a number of other avenues for promotion, but airplay still is the major way to get product exposed. However, a radio station is interested in acquiring and keeping an audience and their playlists reflect that audience.

Stations have very distinct niches in each market and target just a small segment of the listening public for concentration. Radio needs records to play, records need radio play, but radio sells time.

The Promotion Representative's duties and responsibilities have changed drastically over the past few years. Gathering and distilling information is now the primary means for convincing radio stations to add a record. New and far more accurate methods to track sales and actual airplay make this all necessary.

Meanwhile, television and publicity have become very important to promotion. As have the Internet, Podcasts, XM, and Sirius radio.

Terms

Airplay: Records in rotation on radio station and being played either frequently or even infrequently, but at least daily.

Rotation: the number of times a record is played by a station during a 24 hour period.

"Power" Rotation: When a record makes it into top 10 of a station chart and thus is played far more often than non top 10 records.

Format: The type of audience a station wishes to get and hold via the type of music played.

Demographic: The age group, gender, economic situation of a radio station's listeners.

Tracking: By radio, this is research to determine popularity of product via sales to consumers, call-ins. Determining movement up or down on radio station charts by record labels.

Exercises

1. When dealing with radio, what is a record company's goal?

2. What are radio stations' top priorities?

3. In preparing a presentation to a music director at a radio station, what information should a good promotion person present?

4. The concert business continues to grow. How do good promotion people use live appearances by an act to enhance a record's acceptance at radio?

5. Why is it mandatory to choose a specific single or album cut and make sure it, and it alone, is the focus of all activity?

Chapter 13

Video

Learning Objectives

After studying this chapter you should be able to:

1. Understand the background of video, especially music video, and how it evolved

2. Understand why video has had such a meteoric increase in sales over a short period of time

3. Know what types of outlets sell what types of video product

4. Know why video is part of just about any marketing plan today

History, Development, and Use of Video

The video market is relatively young, but it has grown very, very fast. This is one child that has outgrown its clothes every few weeks since 1978, when it first became a product for sale to the general public when the film studio 20th Century Fox contracted to have its films put on video and sold to consumers. By 1980, all the major studios had gotten into video and set up their own distribution.

Video volume grew very rapidly after that break through. It took the video industry ten years, or until 1996, to match the audio industry's sales of $14 billion, a level that took audio 50 years to attain. The Video Software Dealers Association (VSDA) tell us that by the year 1999 VCRs were in 84% of U. S. households, from a start that saw only a 6% penetration in 1982. But with the new millennium, came a new configuration, DVD (the Digital Versatile Disc), and it really energized the industry. By the year 2001, the video industry had its best year ever with total consumer spending rising to $18.7 billion. The rental market accounted for 45% of the revenue or $8.4 billion. This matched movie box office receipts for the year. 2001 brought in DVD rental revenues totaling $58.8 million.

DVD has not been on the scene for very long, which makes the growth statistics all the more impressive. The format was not introduced into the U.S. until second quarter 1997, when the first players were shipped. Four years later this no-rewind format, boasting digital picture clarity along with additional user options like "easter eggs" (hidden scenes), film out-takes, subtitles, and interviews with directors and cast, was in 24 million of the 103 million U.S. televisions households.

For a format less than ten years old, the growth has been fantastic. Chart 13-1 shows how fast releases have multiplied, along with information on price points.

But the growth in DVD players continued at a record pace. By mid-2005, 80% of all American households had players and consumers were buying large screen TV sets by the truckload. The push into HDTV also had a direct bearing on this surge. The DVD format was so far superior to the VHS reproduction, that consumers had to have it.

Meanwhile, the movie industry was suffering through almost two years of constant monthly declines in movie theater ticket sales. The total sales of DVD's in 2005 approached $20 billion, which was twice the $10 billion done at theaters. This prompted Hollywood to release movies on DVD earlier and earlier. A night at the movies could cost a small family $50 or more, while selling prices for DVD's have been dropping.

When to release movies on DVD has become a contentious issue in movieland. For years studios had adhered to a strict set of "windows." DVD retailers waited until at least six months after theater openings. In 1998, for example, the average time a DVD was held was 200 days. By 2005, that was down to 140.8 days. (See Chart 13–2)

Chart 13-1

DVD Releases By Year

Year	New DVD Releases	New Theatrical	All Other Releases
1997	528	18	510
1998	1,522	166	1,356
1999	2,742	289	2,453
2000	3,958	354	3,604
2001	5,630	366	5,264
2002	7,357	387	6,970
2003	10,126	455	9,671
2004	11,587	445	11,142
2005*	9,343	391	8,952
Combined	52,793	2,871	49,922

Year	Total DVD Cost	Theatrical DVD Cost	All Others
1997	$13,012.29	$469.60	$12,542.69
1998	$38,565.10	$4,548.75	$34,016.35
1999	$69,979.96	$8,214.75	$61,765.21
2000	$89,504.49	$9,829.46	$79,675.03
2001	$115,516.49	$9,792.86	$105,723.63
2002	$154,456.54	$10,571.72	$143,884.82
2003	$203,095.15	$12,353.80	$190,741.35
2004	$231,726.19	$12,115.79	$219,610.40
2005	$198,151.10	$10,394.90	$187,756.20
Combined	$1,114,007.31	$78,291.63	$1,035,715.68

Number - All DVD releases for the period, including titles that have subsequently been discontinued.

Theatrical - Those titles with a domestic theatrical run after Jan. 1, 1997.

Catalog - The difference between the total releases and new Theatrical product, regardless of genre.

Cost - Suggested manufacturer retail price, adjusted for price reductions/changes during the year of the price change. The total for Theatrical and Catalog reflects the current consumer cost to purchase all releases (including discontinued) as of Oct. 14, 2005.

DVD Price Points By Year

Year	Overall	Theatrical	Others	Premium
1997	$24.64	$26.09	$24.59	$1.50
1998	$25.34	$27.40	$25.09	$2.32
1999	$25.52	$28.42	$25.18	$3.25
2000	$22.61	$27.77	$22.11	$5.66
2001	$20.52	$26.76	$20.08	$6.67
2002	$20.99	$27.32	$20.64	$6.67
2003	$20.06	$27.15	$19.72	$7.43
2004	$20.00	$27.23	$19.71	$7.52
2005*	$21.21	$26.59	$20.97	$5.61
Combined	$21.10	$27.27	$20.75	$6.52

Overall - The average of all consumer costs for all DVD titles released during the period, adjusted for price reductions/changes during the year of the change.

Theatrical - The average consumer cost of new theatrical releases.

Catalog - The average consumer cost of all other DVD releases regardless of genre.

Premium - The difference in the average price of new Theatrical DVD releases and all other (Catalog releases).

Results through Oct. 14, 2005

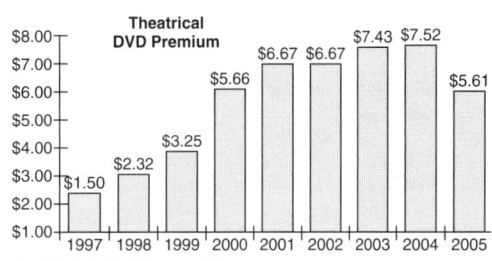

Theatrical DVD Premium
$8.00 / $7.00 / $6.00 / $5.00 / $4.00 / $3.00 / $2.00 / $1.00
$1.50 $2.32 $3.25 $5.66 $6.67 $6.67 $7.43 $7.52 $5.61
1997 1998 1999 2000 2001 2002 2003 2004 2005

Results through Oct. 14, 2005

DVD Pricing	Titles Purchased	Adjusted Cost	Average Price	Net Change
As of 10/14/05	52,793	$1,114,007.31	$21.10	+ $0.01
13 Weeks (Rolling Quarter)				
13-Weeks 10/14	2,971	$64,064.96	$21.56	+ $0.14
13-Weeks 07/15	3,006	$64,396.03	$21.42	

DVD Pricing - Yearly Price Grid

Price	1997	1998	1999	2000	2001	2002	2003	2004	2005	Combined
Under $10	1	119	115	372	949	1,208	1,824	2,581	1,607	8,776
$10 - $15	30	187	217	554	1,088	1,308	2,594	2,531	2,093	10,602
$15 - $20	105	107	403	1,104	1,608	2,290	3,039	2,849	2,265	13,770
$20 - $25	289	569	1,075	988	997	1,291	961	1,271	1,085	8,526
$25 - $30	92	391	684	821	790	846	1,162	1,461	1,521	7,768
$30 - $35	4	42	105	49	50	106	48	266	220	890
$35 - $40	0	20	43	52	114	144	204	241	253	1,071
$40 - $45	1	16	31	3	7	13	8	18	16	113
$45 - $50	6	68	60	(30)	(31)	24	89	120	99	405
Over $50	0	3	9	45	58	127	197	249	184	872
Combined	528	1,522	2,742	3,958	5,630	7,357	10,126	11,587	9,343	52,793
Average	$24.64	$25.34	$25.52	$22.61	$20.52	$20.99	$20.06	$20.00	$21.21	$21.10

Taken from www.homemediaretailing.com. Reprinted courtesy of Ralph Tribbey.

Chart 13-2

Theatrical On DVD

Asset Rollover Rate
Results Through: 10/14/05

Quickest To Market—Key Theatrical Titles
1997–2005*—$25-Million Plus

DVD Source	1997 #	1997 Ave.	1998 #	1998 Ave.	1999 #	1999 Ave.	2000 #	2000 Ave.	2001 #	2001 Ave.	2002 #	2002 Ave.	2003 #	2003 Ave.	2004 #	2004 Ave.	2005 #	2005 Ave.	Combined #	Combined Ave.
Lions Gate/Artisan					1	159.8			1	163.3	1	167.0	1	151.0	2	144.0	3	118.3	9	133.1
SONY Pictures	2	193.0	15	201.2	7	140.0	8	144.6	16	146.4	15	140.6	14	126.5	18	114.8	9	113.7	104	142.8
MGM Home Ent.			2	147.5	1	151.0	4	179.0	4	161.5	5	159.6	5	137.6	5	141.2	3	137.0	29	152.1
Warner	9	143.2	10	165.0	9	167.2	14	157.8	10	168.3	14	159.6	11	150.6	10	156.1	12	163.9	99	159.1
New Line	1	172.0	8	164.4	4	159.8	5	163.6	4	163.3	6	168.8	6	169.7	5	155.2	6	146.7	45	161.9
Universal			5	191.6	9	165.0	15	165.0	7	174.1	13	174.5	11	170.9	15	154.9	9	136.4	84	164.7
Paramount			3	305.0	10	174.3	10	184.7	11	157.5	13	159.6	10	148.2	8	148.4	8	142.3	73	166.0
Dreamworks SKG			2	252.5	4	186.0	5	190.4	6	175.3	4	186.0	7	147.6	4	157.5	2	144.0	34	174.9
20th Century-Fox			2	242.0	8	237.0	7	194.0	9	167.3	11	185.2	13	156.0	13	147.0	9	154.9	72	175.2
Buena Vista	1	146.0	10	231.6	15	179.3	17	200.2	18	179.3	19	203.3	17	157.5	21	156.0	11	131.9	129	178.7
USA Home Ent.			2	182.5	2	217.5			2	178.5									6	192.8
HBO Home Video													1	298.0					1	298.0
Sling Shot					1	348.0													1	348.0
Total By Year	13	153.3	59	200.4	71	179.1	85	175.7	88	165.4	101	171.4	96	153.0	101	145.8	72	140.8	686	164.5

The ARR (Asset Rollover Rate) measures the length of time (in days) between a motion picture's initial theatrical release and its debut in the DVD market.

Only those films released beginning in January of 1997 are included in the grid. Box Office performance and release dates have been compiled from Daily Variety and Hollywood Reporter charts published each week.

*$25,000,000+ theatrical release with an ARR of less than 365-days are defined as new. Those released after one year are considered catalog.

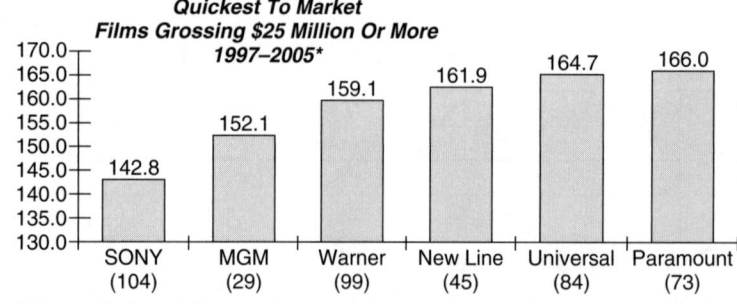

Quickest To Market
Films Grossing $25 Million Or More
1997–2005*

Theatrical releases with a box office gross of $25-million or more that have been released domestically after Jan. 1, 1997. Released on DVD as of Oct. 14, 2005.
**ARR—Asset Rollover Rate: Number of days between a film's initial theatrical release and its subsequent debut on DVD.*

*2005 results through Oct. 14—Average number of days (Asset Rollover Rate—ARR) for new theatrical releases to debut on DVD within one-year of their theatrical debut and a domestic box office gross of at least $25,000,000.

Chart 13-3
The Entertainment Consumer: DVD share

Mass Merchants hold the largest piece of the market, with Electronic Stores as number two, at less than half the share of the market leader.

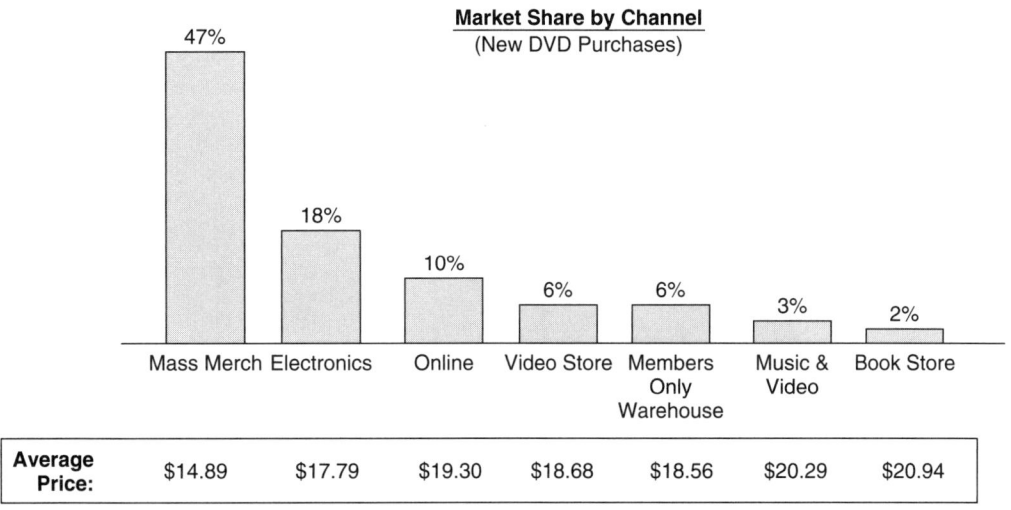

Market Share by Channel
(New DVD Purchases)

	Mass Merch	Electronics	Online	Video Store	Members Only Warehouse	Music & Video	Book Store
Market Share	47%	18%	10%	6%	6%	3%	2%
Average Price:	$14.89	$17.79	$19.30	$18.68	$18.56	$20.29	$20.94

Source: NPD VideoWatch; 2004 Unit Share, New DVD Purchase

In addition, profits for the studios from DVD's are huge. According to *Business Week* studios get about $12.00 per disk, no matter how little the mass merchandisers charge the consumer. (Chart 13–3). With so many movies touted as "blockbusters" not living up the hype and losing money, those worldwide DVD sales are the studios' salvation. Meanwhile, cable and satellite are clamoring for releases sooner and sooner for VOD (video on demand) as are outlets like HBO, Showtime, etc.

The market is also experimenting with allowing downloads for a price with limits on viewing and restrictions on shipping elsewhere. The movie industry is also feeling the cold breath of illegal downloading and other forms of piracy.

DVD is primarily devoted to theatrical product, which means movies. Comedy and drama make up almost half of all the genres. (Chart 13–4) The audiences for DVD varies somewhat from the CD audience. The younger demographic buys more CD's than DVD's, but that changes as consumers age. (For additional research on demographics and buying habits, see the Appendix). Do not, however, underestimate the value of video in the promotion and exposure of music and artists.

The promotional value of music videos cannot be underestimated. Just about every marketing plan must have a slot for a music video. These can eventually

Chart 13-4
The Entertainment Consumer: DVD genre share

Comedy and Drama comprised almost half of Industry sales this year

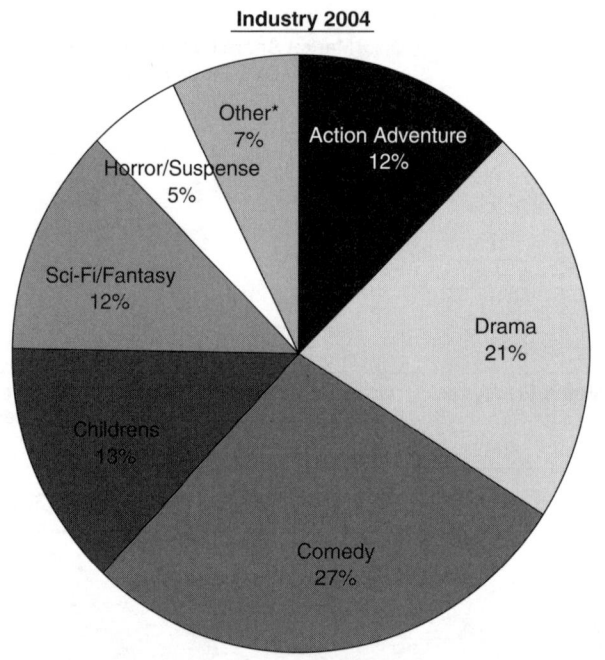

Industry 2004

Other* 7%

Action Adventure 12%

Horror/Suspense 5%

Sci-Fi/Fantasy 12%

Drama 21%

Childrens 13%

Comedy 27%

*Includes: Educational, Foreign Films, Musical, Religious, Sports and Westerns

Source: NPD VideoWatch; Unit Share, New DVD Purchase

become commercially released music videos, but unless they first do their job in helping to break a record or an act, there will be no demand. While all videos offered for sale have an impact on the retail aspect of the music industry, only promotional music videos impact what will eventually sell on records.

If one wishes to understand the true origins of music video, one may look no further than one's own television and stereo. Sit down in front of your television set and turn to your favorite music video channel. Turn down the volume of your set until all audio is muted. You now have moving images and no sound. Next, turn on your stereo and play your favorite genre of music—classical, jazz, rap, rock and roll or techno. Once again, it does not matter which. Sit back and begin to observe the visual material within your set. Slowly you will notice images will directly correlate with beats of music. The more you watch the program, the more the images and music will synchronize together. Suddenly, you will realize that you are having a unique auditory and visual experience. When looking at the impact of music videos on the promotion of records, this experience becomes even more meaningful.

True logic lies in the subconscious minds, not the consciousness of awareness. Music and images fused together are a unique type of experience.

In the early part of the twentieth century, major changes were taking place in the American culture. America was celebrating the dawn of the entertainment industry. Music, dance, sport and film were the true topics of discussion. In those days you could walk into a nickelodeon (movie theater) pay a nickel and see the latest in moving pictures. The images on the screen appeared to be seamless, animated and lifelike. The experience was overwhelming, for now people, places, and things moved as they do in real life. The experience was incredible but the experience was still two dimensional, something was missing. Suddenly, music was heard. In a small corner of the theater from a lone piano player providing music accompaniment for the images on the screen. Magically, the images took on a new form. Not only was your sense of hearing tantalized, but your sense of sight as well.

The music majestically swept you into the action and created a synthesized three dimensional reality that was indescribable. The more you simultaneously listened to the music and watched, the more the images appeared to seamlessly flow together in your consciousness. Slowly the mixed media seeped into your subconscious and you had a unique auditory and visual experience.

What people did not know at the time was that they had just experienced the law of eternal synchronized auditory and visual media (the law of eternal sync). The human brain is constantly attempting to create order out of chaos. Media A plus media B equals new media C (A+B=C). This formula is the basic framework for the assembly of music and motion pictures.

The law of eternal sync is based on the principle that all music and images propel themselves at a rhythmic pace. Music moves at beats per second as film moves at frames per second. They both travel on a linear path that has a beginning and theoretically no end. The longer they travel on the same parallel linear plain, the more they appear to coexist together. Eventually, within the subconscious of the viewer, one can not exist without the other.

Can you hear the song "Beat It" by Michael Jackson without thinking of the music video?

The viewers' romance with moving images and music has engulfed American society for almost a century. However, until 1927 these artistic elements were only synchronized within the mind of the viewer.

That year Hollywood changed moving cinema forever when Al Jolson starred in the first Hollywood talkie called, "The Jazz Singer." This film ushered in the romance of the synchronized image with emotionally charged music.

By the 1930s synchronized music and images were also standard fare in motion pictures. The public could not hear the song, "Somewhere over the Rainbow," without thinking of Judy Garland as Dorothy (*Wizard Of Oz*, 1939) Music correlated with images helped make songs within American society standards.

These standards in movies brought music to those who could not afford phonograph players, records, or radios. During the depression of the 1930s, Hollywood experienced its greatest economic boom. Movies were the cheapest form of entertainment during this era. With the aide of motion pictures music emerged as a part of popular American culture. Anyone could appreciate good music: rich, poor, black and white.

In the 1940s there was another upheaval in the way entertainment was delivered. Radio began to decline slightly with the upper-class as a new medium was introduced that changed the landscape of popular culture. Television emerged as the new and exciting source of entertainment and information. Radio adjusted as well as the Billboard hot 100 was introduced. Now all popular music in America was charted for all to see and hear.

Count Basie, Duke Ellington, Benny Goodman and others flooded the airwaves and popularized what was known then as swing, but today as jazz, the first breed of indigenous music to the American sociological landscape. Hollywood quickly followed suit on the musical band wagon by producing musical shorts.

Shorts were small information films produced by major studios and news outlets that informed film audiences about current events. These events ranged from what was new with your favorite Hollywood celebrities, to cartoons. Additionally, these shorts presented works of your favorite musical artist. During intermission or between shows one could catch a film short of Cab Calloway's latest hit song. Many of these stars such as Calloway went on to star in feature length films highlighting their music. These musical shorts helped to propel the emerging teenage population toward the 1950s with an insatiable appetite for music. The record industry was ready to handle the audio aspects.

Musical shorts of the 40s helped to reinforce the idea that African-Americans are woven into the fiber of American society as songs by Little Richard, The Platters and Nat King Cole climbed the charts. The achievements of Althea Gibson, Martin Luther King Jr. and Thurgood Marshall carved a new landscape for Black America.

Many of the record artists began to appear on a variety of television shows in the 1950s to perform their popular chart topping songs. By this time television was accessible to all. Most households had at least one set and the infusion of rock and roll with the pop cultural visual icon emerged. Record artists like Elvis Presley became as big on TV as on radio.

By the end of the 1950s television was the number one form of entertainment in America with music right on its heels. These two became interesting bedfellows in the 1960s. Marches and protests grew in epidemic proportions across the face of America. Visually, America grew as television captured all the major news events. This new visual medium that was bringing the Vietnam War into our living rooms began to influence our national psyche. Bob Dylan, Jimmy Hendrix and the Rolling Stones became overnight musical media heroes. African-American music took a new turn in the '60s as American society redefined itself. "Dancin' in the Street" by Martha Reeves and the Vandelas ushered in a string of hits by Berry Gordy and the Motown hit factory. By the end of the decade, Motown made Diana Ross, Marvin Gaye, Stevie Wonder, Smokey Robinson and Michael Jackson household names all over the world. Additionally, Berry Gordy's company, originally known as *Hitsville USA* went down in history as the number one recording company of the 1960s.

The Beatles touched down in America on February 12, 1964 and changed the landscape of American pop music forever. Their records soared up the charts and their concerts sold out to thousands. As a result, their popularity in Europe and American inspired a new genre in filmmaking, the rock and roll film. "Help" and "A Hard Days Night" ensured Paul McCartney, Ringo Starr, John Lennon and George Harrison musical and sociological immortality. In their films the group frolicked, joked and played their music to interpretive visuals. Little did they know at the time, (MTV was still 16 years away), but the Liverpool legends had ushered in a new era of music and filmmaking, the music video.

Television once again seized the opportunity to fuse images with music. Variety shows were no longer the only visual outlet for music. America produced its own version of the fab four but this time they were known as the Monkees. Once a week for a half hour these four romped and frolicked about to their latest release. Needless to say, the Monkees became a huge sensation in America. Viewers could now get their auditory and musical fix every week watching the Monkees, rather than every year watching the Beatles.

Teen dance shows also filled the air waves in the '60s as well. Leading the way was *American Bandstand* hosted by teen idol Dick Clark. Every week Bandstand presented new and established artists in their natural habitat, performing in front of an audience. Another front running show from this era was *Shindig* hosted by Jimmy O'Neill. Once again the acts were front running artists ranging from the Righteous Brothers to Aretha Franklin.

By the end of the '60s black/urban music had its own television outlet as well. *Soul Train*, better remembered as a national 70s program hosted by Don Cornielius, emerged as a regional television show in Chicago.

The seventies emerged on the landscape of political, social and sexual freedom. Women, minorities and the gay community had their voices and were being heard. The old groups were gone or fading. The Beatles all had solo careers and Diana Ross sang without the Supremes. All of the groups that had made the word Motown a verb were gone. Rock and roll sputtered and dance music turned into a mode of expression within the gay community. The music industry had its first serious downturn. For almost two years the numbers were frightening to most record company executives, and while many reasons for the drop in sales were offered, it was not until after the period was over that it became clear that the product just was not there. Once again it was film and television to the rescue.

In 1977, a teen idol from the popular television show burst onto the music and movie scene simultaneously, John Travolta in the title role of Tony Manero in the film, "Saturday Night Fever." The film and the movie's soundtrack rejuvenated record sales all over the world.

With the help of sixties pop group the Bee Gees, Travolta breathed new life into the music/visual genre. The 15–35 demographic was here to stay and they were ready to support their music. Not the '50s and '60s music of their parents.

It was ironic that Travolta's next breakaway hit movie was a rehashing of the musicals of the 1950s. With "Grease," the last commercially successful Hollywood musical. Travolta enjoyed international success that catapulted him to permanent Hollywood stardom. Television and music had once again saved the entertainment business.

Television and music were inseparable during the '70s. The syndicated program, *Soul Train*, peaked as a cross cultural entertainment and dance show. Any African-American act that was anybody was on *Soul Train*. Don Cornielius almost single-handedly kept rhythm and blues alive during this era as groups ranging from the Jackson Five to Tina Turner to Parliament thrilled millions of viewers every week. Even blue eyed soul acts such as David Bowie used the program's broad base as a vehicle to attain cross cultural appeal. The appeal of entertainment and dance on *Soul Train* inspired new syndicated dance shows in the seventies.

Dance Fever and *Solid Gold* burst onto the scene with vigor in the late seventies. Both weekly shows, *Dance Fever* and *Solid Gold* entertained as well as updated the audience on the latest in chart topping songs and dance moves.

Also in the late seventies, radio personality Casey Casem made the leap from the radio to television. His weekly syndicated show *America's Top Ten* informed music listeners not only about chart topping songs but showed music clips as well. Music clips had been shown on *Soul Train* and *Solid Gold* but they were not the focus of those shows. Dancing was the prime spectacle. Casem's show was designed to highlight chart topping music clips.

In those days only major act groups with almost guaranteed sales strength were producing clips. Record companies had not been convinced yet that music shorts were a viable means by which to promote an artist. Some established groups such as the Rolling Stones, Queen, David Bowie, and the Jacksons were producing music videos.

Initially, music clips were shot on videotape because the cost of film and skilled film personnel was too high. By today's standard the word music video is a misnomer. The correct term would be classified as music film. Unlike today, in the '70s most videos were produced on shoestring budgets with only visionary artists footing the bill. Not until the emergence of an established music video outlet did record companies realize the investment potential of the new visual genre. However, even then most record company and radio executives still believed video would kill the radio star.

One of the few that did not believe this was radio executive Bob Pittman and former Monkee guitarist Michael Nesmith. While running an NBC flagship station in New York in the late '70s Pittman discovered the listeners wanted more from their music. The new radio listener was no longer fixated with his or her own demographic. Everyone listened to everything (AOR, black music, top forty). This new listener landscape laid the groundwork and foundation for MTV, which certainly revolutionized record promotion and record sales potentials. It also meant that just about every act was demanding a music video as part of their marketing plans to help expose their latest releases.

With the existence of the elusive 18 to 34 audience and the great music depression of the late seventies, it was only a matter of time until someone was going to try something revolutionary. That someone was John Lack. John Lack, the executive vice-president of the American Express-Warner cable division in 1981, felt that the music video clip's time had come. Lack decided that a joint venture between him as a broadcaster and record companies could do nothing but help sell records again. He initially looked toward Nickelodeon to create a half hour program called Pop Clips. Lack then brought in ex-Monkee Michael Nesmith (the tall guy who wore the ski cap) to produce the show. Nesmith was a huge advocate of music video and felt that the genre could help revitalize sagging record sales. To him music videos were the most important event in the history of rock 'n roll music. Nesmith delivered thirteen episodes of Pop Clips to Nickelodeon that proved a music video program was a viable idea in America.

In Europe however, music videos have long been considered an acceptable form of music marketing and artistic expression. Music video shows such as, "Top of the Pops," ruled the television airwaves in the seventies. Television air waves can travel at a higher altitude than regular radio waves. As a result many parts of Europe were only exposed to new music through their television. As a result, many industrialized countries in Europe, such as Germany, England and France, had their own version of the popular video show. By the time MTV was gearing up in America thousands of music videos had already been produced in Europe.

Lack had decided that networks were still programming for viewers who had never seen television before. MTV was going to change all of that. He was programming for the viewer who grew up with the TV as their baby-sitter.

The labels still possessed little faith in the innovative television concept. They wanted MTV to buy the clips from them to safeguard any financial loss. Despite the odds MTV pushed on and launched their cable outlet at the dawn of the Reagan era. The formal announcement came March 3, 1981 and the first official broadcast came August 1st of that same year.

Compared to the news events of the day, the launching of a 24-hour music video cable network seemed insignificant. The Manhattan home office of the fledgling network could not even obtain media coverage for the now historical event. With so much emphasis on socio-political events and so little interest in MTV and music videos in general, the time was right for the dawn of a new genre of filmmaking.

Initially, in the early 80s in America not all artists produced clips. However, artists who did, specifically new and fringe artists, MTV offered them the opportunity to infiltrate radio playlists. Australian born artist Rick Springfield was a relative unknown until his single "Jessie's Girl" hit the air and television waves during the summer of '81. Up to that point, Springfield's only claim to fame was as Dr. Noah Drake on the ratings-hot daytime soap *General Hospital*. Springfield starred in the series during the storied Luke and Laura era of the program. The soap aired late in the afternoon daily. This enabled teenage females to become very familiar with Springfield's good looks and cool charm. This transferred very nicely to his first music video project. With a built-in audience (if you watched *General Hospital*, you watched MTV in those days), Springfield's video clip topped the MTV playlist. Shot on film (which was still unusual in those days), "Jessie's Girl" possessed a very simple and classic premise. Boy wants girl, girl is with boy's friend and boy sings about it. There is nothing earth shattering or groundbreaking here except for one minor detail. Springfield is continuously shot in close-up. To teen females of the early eighties Rick was hot and possessed soulful penetrable eyes. Springfield laments at the sink in his bathroom as he longs for Jessie's girl. He appears hurt as he sees Jessie with the only girl for him. The energy builds as Springfield sings and struts with his band under lights and a star filter. He wears expensive suits, has a great haircut and the editing is moderately paced by today's standards.

On MTV that went a long way in the eighties and it took his album "Working Class Dog" to the top of the charts. Springfield helped to usher in the power suit performer of the era. Good looks and charisma always was and always will be the ultimate standard for success in the music video genre. Music is a distant second.

By the end of 1981, MTV showcased the stark blue-eyed soul looks of Daryl Hall and the soft dainty cute persona of Olivia Newton-John. With moderate success in the '70s, Hall and Oates escalated to new heights on MTV. The reason was simple: the camera loved Daryl Hall. His sleek chiseled features picked up where Springfield left off. The clip was "Private Eyes" and unlike "Jessie's Girl," and regardless of the fact that it was shot on video, it dared to be different. The track was smart, infectious and very much '80s pop. Its surreal fast-paced images tantalized the virgin music video viewers of that era. You could not help but think that Daryl Hall and John Oates (the window dressing of the group) were cool and hip. Early videos of the '80s possessed an artistic interpretation of the song and the artistic interpretation of the artist. Despite this during its early era, music videos were still not for everyone.

While other artists broke big during the fourth quarter of '81—Diana Ross and Lionel Richie ("Endless Love"), Christopher Cross ("Arthur's Theme") and Kim Carnes ("Bette Davis Eyes")—none of these artists received any fanfare on MTV. Not because their songs were not popular (but MTV was desperate for programming and they would have taken anything); however, they elected not to produce clips for their tracks.

In the era of trickle-down economics, you were making history if you were on MTV—and even if you weren't. By the mid-80s, the rules had changed and an era in music ended. As the economy inflated, so did the spending power at record companies. This trickle-down effect elevated the status of entertainers to corporate pop icons. Like the '80s and corporate America, bigger became better. They were no longer music videos, they were short pop films.

Superstar acts such as Madonna ("Like A Virgin" and "Like A Prayer") and Michael Jackson ("Thriller" and "Bad") changed the landscape of music video by producing big-budget film clips. These well-marketed productions had price tags that exceeded many independent and low budget movies of their time. In the mid '80s MTV had exploded as a cultural sign post and a rite of passage for teens. If you wanted to market to youth culture you had to have a video on MTV. This cultural phenomenon attracted major advertisers to the 15–25-year-old crowd for the first time. Once the marketing platform was secure, anyone who had something to say to America's youth culture ended up on MTV. Whether it was acne products such as Clearasil, an anti-violence message, a voter registration movement, or the presidential campaign of Bill Clinton in the early nineties, MTV was the gatekeeper. With its new found cultural status and the beginning of corporate merger, it was only a matter of time until music video influenced other arms of the entertainment industry.

Prince rode the wave of his music all the way into your local movie theatre with "Purple Rain," "Under the Cherry Moon," and "Sign of The Times." The success of these soundtracks and music videos associated with the films help to solidify a direct marketing campaign for youth culture films that started with heavy saturation of a music video on MTV.

Guns n' Roses explored the epic/episodic music video with "November Rain." The clip explored the rise and fall of a pop icon. In haunting fashion, it later closely reflected the ascension and descension of the group's lead singer Axl Rose. Music videos in the '90s started to less imitate art and more imitate the life of the artist.

Gone was the artistic expression and freedom of the early '80s, as it was replaced by the show-stopping showmanship of the performer. Madonna continued her run of big-budget extravaganzas with "Vogue" and "Express Yourself." Michael Jackson was beginning to slip in record sales but he was still dominating the music video budgets with clips such as "Black or White" and "Scream."

The '80s pop star George Michael of the bubblegum group WHAM, who had a very successful late '80s solo career dropped out of the music video rat race. His clip "Freedom 90," directed by music video visionary David Fincher, showcased attractive supermodels but not him. Supermodels Linda Evangelista, Naomi Campbell and Cindy Crawford lip-synced George's cool tune. The video proved you did not need a star in the video to create a video hit, but no one cared.

A late '80s experiment that spilled over into the '90s would by the end of the decade become industry standard for teen formula. Maurice Starr, a record executive who produced the '80s teen black group called New Edition, came up with a new idea. He decided to develop a group that was all white but they sang and danced to black music. This late '80s hybrid was known as "The New Kids on the Block." Their first video was a very urban and stylized love ballad (à la New Edition) called "Please Don't Go Girl." With their good looks and dance moves they were a "can't miss" group that set the stage for today's bubblegum white groups. The Starr formula is the blueprint for all of the late '90s teen groups that are marketed through video.

The countercultural pop sensation of the late '80s was not even a black group. It was three Jewish teens from Brooklyn who acted black and hung out with rap artists. The Beastie Boys with their Hip Hop/Rap and rock influenced late '80s cut "Fight For your Right to Party," began the absorption of the rap world into mainstream society. Beastie Boy clips would entertain and influence white rap throughout the '90s. Similar to beliefs in the industry's past, it was still believed easier to sell a white image to white kids rather than a black one.

Videos in the '90s had finally sold their way into the development meetings at major production companies. Executives now wanted to use music video directors as feature film directors in order to create a more stylized look for their films. David Finch, director of "Vogue" and "Express Yourself," has found success on the big screen with "Seven" and "The Fight." Michael Bay, director of the Dyvinals clip "I Touch Myself," has found success in Hollywood with "Armageddon" and "The Rock." Bret Ratner ("Wu-Tang" and "Rush Hour"). Hype Williams ("Busta Rhymes" and "Belly") and Mark Pellington ("Pearl Jam" and "Arlington Road"), and Tamara Davis ("Sonic Youth" and "Happy Gilmore").

Executives continued their cross pollination of the industry by making movie stars out of music video stars. By marketing a music video star such as Ice Cube in the low-budget cult classic "Friday," directed by music video director F. Gary Gray ("TLC," "Waterfalls"). They assured themselves a movie with a built-in audience, name recognition and cutting-edge style. The marketing of music videos for the first time was reflecting the overall movement within the industry to consolidate and merge companies and talent. Successful early '90s films such as "Boyz in the Hood," "Singles" and "Pulp Fiction" all started with marketing campaigns that began with cool videos on MTV.

The one big difference in music in the '90s and the '80s was the emergence of a marketable underground music scene. Known as *grunge*, or alternative music, this anti-establishment art form exploded in 1991 through the medium of music video.

When Kurt Cobain and Nirvana released their single, "Smells Like Teen Spirit," on MTV they collectively killed off the '80s styled over-budget video that seemed like it would never die. The clip for "Smells Like Teen Spirit" was very simple. Kurt and the band at a pep rally in a high school dimly lit, punk style. No fancy lighting, no fancy makeup, no special effects, no dance sequences and no corporate tie-ins. The unsalable became salable. With Madonna's career in turnaround, Michael Jackson's entanglement with the law and Prince searching for a new name, the time was right for the down and dirty.

Exploding simultaneously with grunge was *gangsta rap*. Like grunge it was anti-establishment but unlike its counterpart it was uniquely Urban. These two genres briefly were bedfellows in the late '80s with the Run DMC/Aerosmith remake, "Walk This Way." The video was a hit. Aerosmith revived their career and Run DMC became a pop giant but it would take another ten years before record companies would package this style to a mass audience through music video. No one music video clip has created another genre of music but it would be hard to imagine the "Kid Rocks" (Nookie) and "Fat Boy Slims" (Funk Soul Brother) of today if it were not for "Walk This Way." Steven Tyler, in the video crashing through a wall that divides Aerosmith and Run DMC and screaming "Walk This Way," in one visceral moment set the stage for the marketing of rap/rock music videos for years to come. In the final decade of the century rap and rock have been the backbone of the music industry.

In the '90s the days of party rap were a distant memory. Rap somehow has always reflected the disposition of the country and in the media-drenched violence-filled '90s Hip Hop/Rap videos projected that mood. Rap was no longer friendly or even from New York. West coast rap dominated video airwaves in the early '90s with its anti-establishment call to arms video vibe. In a violence and media-crazed decade, music video and gangsta rap left their metaphor of society right on the doorstep of America. Gangsta rap videos became a part of the great debate on violence in the '90s with the children of the '60s. Rap clips could be seen on the news and talk shows as much as MTV or BET. Music videos were now advertising outside of their original outlets.

For the first time urban Hip Hop/Rap was in middle America via music video. More white suburban kids listen to Hip Hop/Rap than any other group in the world.

Their daily fix comes from the music video outlets not necessarily radio stations, for many white alternative stations only play white rap artists like the Beastie Boys.

With the death of Kurt Cobain, Tupac Shakur and Biggie Smalls in the mid-90s, grunge and gangsta rap took a nose dive. Through music video the mid- to late-nineties has seen a resurgence in party rap and glam rock groups. Alleged Hip Hop/Rap artist Sean "Puffy" Combs and so-called alternative groups like Matchbox 20 and Third Eye Blind dominated the video airwaves in the latter half of the nineties with big budgets, glamorous sets and special effects.

The late nineties music video scene has no rhyme or reason to it. It is a flavor of the month content as the music video demographic sinks even lower. Groups that satisfy the video palate of ten-year-olds were all the rage. Britney Spears, Christina Aguilera, The Backstreet Boys and 'N Sync dominated video airplay because little kids buy CDs. Like New Kids on the Block in their music videos, they have perfected the art of synthesizing a black bravado and personality. This cultural synthesis that is marketed through music video had helped to pull Hip Hop/Rap into the mainstream with groups like Kid Rock, Everlast, Insane Clown Posse, Fat Boy Slim and the original white rappers the Beastie Boys.

As the '90s came to a close the music video platform was wide open. VH1 controlled the kids of the '80s taste in pop culture and had successfully marketed to the baby boomer generation by creating visual essays of music icons from the '60s and '70s with its show "Behind the Music." Music video outlets were not only advertising new music they were reinventing the old cuts as well. As soon as a kid can watch television they are now watching MTV. MTV is the cultural tutor for today's youth. Within youth culture BET is no longer seen as "that black station." It is another outlet for anyone's favorite rap or R&B hit.

The Internet has created a potentially limitless new platform for broadcasting clips. Within a very short time after the turn of the millennium you were able to log on to your favorite music video and access the clip for the purposes of downloading it and playing it. CD-Rom and DVD are also multi-media platforms that can sell music to listeners through video.

Pop culture and the entertainment business are all uniquely American and 20th century occurrences. Music video in this millennium will continue to be a catalyst for launching new music, new movies and new ideas.

The recording industry has made good use of music videos for promotion primarily. Sales of music videos at retail have not had much of an impact. Needless to say, the cable and satellite industry has also jumped on the bandwagon. Music videos featuring all genres of music are available 24 hours a day to all viewers. These performances have to have an impact on commercial product sold in stores and on the Internet.

Chart 13–5
The Entertainment Consumer: DVD audience

CD sales skew slightly younger than DVD sales.

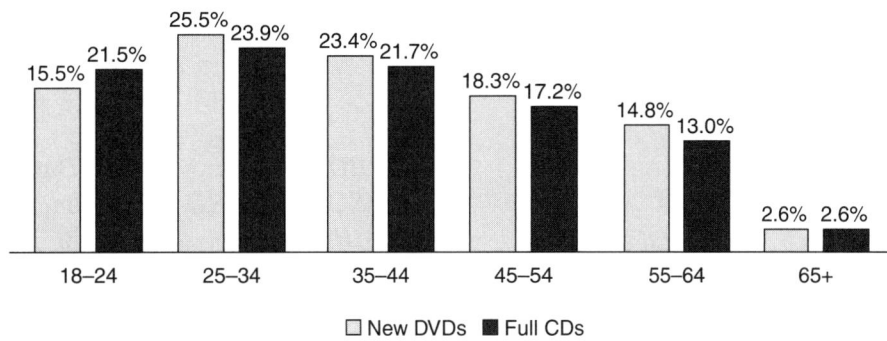

Share of CD/DVD Sales By Age Group

Source: NPD VideoWatch, NPD MusicWatch—2004

Both NARM and VSDA offer a great deal of information about video buying and rental, while Charts 13-6, 13-7, 13-8, and 13-9 show typical budgets for music videos.

The appendix contains a number of reports and charts relating to all aspects of the DVD environment.

Chart 13-6

TRISHA YEARWOOD
SUMMERTIME

MUSIC VIDEO: Production Cost Summary

DATE:	5 October	*PRODUCER:*	Jim Davis
JOB #:	MV-709	*PROD. COORD.:*	Michael O'Neill
SONG:	*Heartbeat*	*DIRECTOR:*	David Bryant
CLIENT:	Trisha Yearwood	*PROD. MGR:*	Greg Lucas
CONTACT:	Maria Eckhart / FORCE	*SOUND:*	Tim Sharp
ADDRESS:	1505 16TH Avenue South	*POST PROD.:*	MusicLand
	Nashville, TN 37212		Post Production
PHONE #:	615/385-4646		

SUMMARY OF PRODUCTION COSTS:	*TOTALS:*
Pre-Production	$ 2,500.00
Shooting Crew Labor	24,985.50
Location / Travel Expenses	9,679.00
Props, Wardrobe & Special Effects	5,997.00
Studio & Set Construction	6,024.50
Equipment Rental	12,846.50
Film & Video Stock	10,431.00
Miscellaneous	4,272.00
Director / Creative Fee	15,000.00
On-Camera Extras	3,700.00
Post Production	22,451.19
Production Fee	23,833.41
TOTAL:	141,690.10
TAXES:	9918.31
GRAND TOTAL:	**$151,608.41**

Chart 13-7

TOMORROW PICTURES, INC.		Label:	Restless Records
1720 Peachtree St., Suite 119, Atlanta GA 30309		Group:	Hi-Town DJS
Phone (404) 892-8923 fax (404) 892-9006)		Clip:	Ding-a-ling
Job #: MV-025-8			
Production Contact: Ellen Barnard 4/892-8923			
Director: Frederick J. Taylor			
Director of Photography: Frederick J. Taylor			
Set Designer: Shaunan Wood			
Editor: TBD			
No. of pre-prod. days: Pre-light:			
No. build/strike days: 1			
No. studio shoot days: 1			
No. Location shoot days:			
Location sites:			

SUMMARY OF ESTIMATED PRODUCTION COSTS		ESTIMATED	ACTUAL		
1. Pre-production and wrap costs	Totals A & C	4,450	0		
2. Shooting crew labor	Total B	7,530	0		
3. Location and travel expenses	Total D	0	0		
4. Props, wardobe, animals	Total E	1,250			
5.Sudio & Set Construction Costs	Total F, G & H	4,475	0		
6.Equipment costs	Total I	6,225	0		
'.Film stock devl. & print - #ft.	Total J	5,456	0		
8. Miscellaneous	Total K	450	0		
9.	Sub- Total A to K	29,836			
10. Director/creative fees (not incl. in Direct Costs)	Total L	2,900	0		
11. Insurance					
12.	Sub-Total Direct Costs	32,736	0	#######	
13. Production fee		3,000			
14. Talent costs and expenses	Total M & N	865	0		
15. Editorial and finishing per:		10,750			
16.					
17.	Grand Total (including director's fee)	47,351	0		
18. Contingency (Weather Day $ per day)					

Comments:
Hi Paul --
Here's the first crack at things. The editorial includes off-line, CGI, On-line and Effects.
I also included stylist and wardrobe. Let me know what you think!

Thanks- EB

Taken from Tomorrow Pictures, Inc.

Chart 13-8

TOMORROW PICTURES, INC.		
1720 Peachtree St., Suite 119, Atlanta GA 30309		
Phone (404) 892-8923 fax (404) 892-9006)		
Job #: MV-100-99		
Production Contact: Ellen Barnard 4/892-8923		
Director: Frederick J. Taylor		
Director of Photography: F. J. Taylor		
		1.
No. of pre-prod. days: 5 Pre-light:		2.
No. build/strike days: 0		3.
No. studio shoot days: 0		4.
No. Location shoot days: 2		5.
Location sites: 4		Agency Supplies:

SUMMARY OF ESTIMATED PRODUCTION COSTS		ESTIMATED	ACTUAL		
1. Pre-production and wrap costs	Totals A & C	2,065	1,585		
2. Shooting crew labor	Total B	6,018	5,785		
3. Location and travel expenses	Total D	2,435	1,973		
4. Props, wardobe, animals	Total E	150	109		
5. Studio & Set Construction Costs	Total F, G & H	0	0		
6. Equipment costs	Total I	4,650	5,925		
. Film stock devl. & print - #ft.	Total J	3,890	3,480		
8. Miscellaneous	Total K	450	200		
9.	Sub- Total A to K	19,658	19,056		
10. Director/creative fees (not incl. in Director Costs)	Total L	2,000	1,183		
11. Insurance		393			
12.	Sub-Total Direct Costs	22,051	20,239	($1,813)	
13. Production fee		5,000	5,000		
14. Talent costs and expenses	Total M & N	0	1,000		
15. Editorial and finishing per:	Total O & P	4,810	4,800		
16.					
17.	Grand Total (including director's fee)	31,861	31,039		
18. Contingency (Weather Day $ per day)					

Comments:	Total contract price: 33,000

Taken from Tomorrow Pictures, Inc.

Chart 13-9
Production Cost Summary for Music Video

Date:	4-Apr
Job #	MV-002
Production:	Don't Ever Touch Me (Again)
Client:	Dionne Farris
Contact:	Paul Robinson (PosAct Inc.)
Address:	530 Means Street Suite 400
	Atlanta, GA 30318
Phone #:	404-524-0030
Fax:	N/A
Producer:	To Be Determined
Prod. Coord:	Ellen Barnard
Director:	Frederick J. Taylor
Prod. Mgr.:	Bob Basher
Sound:	Peter Redding
Post:	Magick Lantern Post Production

Summary of Production Costs:

		Total
A.	Pre-Production	$1,150.00
B.	Shooting Crew Labor	$20,128.50
C.	Location/Travel Expenses	$4,440.00
D.	Props, Wardrobe & Special Effects	$1,550.00
E.	Studio & Set Construction	$1,125.00
F.	Equipment Rental	$8,975.00
G.	Film & Video Stock	$6,591.50
H.	Miscellaneous	$1,850.00
I.	Director/Creative Fee	$10,000.00
J.	On-Camera & Voice-Over Talent	$900.00
K.	Post Production	$14,412.50
L.	Production Fee	$16,358.18
	Total	$87,480.68
	Payroll Taxes (Payroll South)	$5,480.82
	Equipment Taxes	$2,225.64
	Grand Total	$95,187.13

Thank you for your consideration . . .

Reprinted by permission of Tomorrow Pictures

Terms

Theatrical: Video product primarily of movies and animated features.

Non-Theatrical: Most other video product.

Music Video: Video of performance or performances of music also being released on CDs and cassettes.

Law of Eternal Sync: Basic framework for assembly of music and motion picture.

Music Shorts: Forerunners of today's music videos.

MTV: Just what it implies, "Music Television," on cable TV, the most popular of that format.

BET: Black Entertainment Channel.

VH-1: Outgrowth of MTV, plays softer product.

CMT: Country Music Television.

Nickelodeon: First place to exhibit film.

"Talkies": First movies to incorporate sound and music.

Exercises

1. At the outset of music videos, what types of acts usually made them, and what made it possible?

2. How has MTV revolutionized the exposure of recorded product?

3. What part did the "dance shows" have in the development of music video?

4. What type of product brings in the most volume in sellthrough product and where is most of it sold?

Chapter 14
Market Research

Learning Objectives

After studying this chapter you will be able to:

1. Understand the place of market research in record marketing

2. Know what types of research are used in the record industry

3. Know what organizations can supply market research for marketing uses

4. Understand how trade paper charts, radio charts are now being compiled

5. Learn about recent changes in chart compilation

Market Research

Market research is a very important factor in all aspects of bringing products to the consumer. Each level—creation, manufacturing, distribution and retailing—make full use of market research. While later than some industries in the use of this information, the music industry, now takes full advantage of market research in all activities.

The music industry has been using the "focus group" concept for many years. Using a cross section of the consumer profile, these focus groups are asked to rate and comment on not only new recordings prior to release, but also on the appearance of an act as well as how they come across in videos and live performances. This type of market research is far more useful in trying to ascertain how an act will be accepted rather than how a specific recording will be accepted. A focus group hears the product once or twice before being asked to make a judgment. The ultimate consumer usually hears the record many, many times before making the subconscious decision to commit to a purchase.

Record labels and their distribution companies are always making use of research when planning new projects, planning tours and planning advertising campaigns. When attempting to determine where to put efforts and money, each potential market comes in for a great deal of scrutiny. It is important to know:

- the advertising costs in each area
- market conditions
- growth or lack of it in an area
- who has major outlets
- what retailers and racks say about area and business
- the size of music categories
- outlook
- type of radio market
- and possibly the most important factors, just how cooperative are the retailers and whether there is enough in an area to have an impact.

Over the years, a market's complexion has had a major impact on where the human and financial investments were made. In the 1960s, when singles were the dominant configuration and main driving force for hits, markets like Cleveland and Detroit were vital to making it big. The population in what were then referred to as "blue collar" markets bought the records. The radio stations in those markets were absolutely indispensable in making a hit. It was in these markets that all the major "disc jockeys" were on the air, and they could really create excitement since they had complete control over what they exposed during their shows.

Soon after this, with what was to be the first major impact of TV on the music industry, the markets with the "dance shows," like Pittsburgh, Baltimore and Philadelphia, became the major target of activity in trying to establish hits.

Later, with the emergence of country as a big selling category, markets like Atlanta and Dallas became target areas. However, a market like Atlanta was still very important to pop and rock and roll since the radio structure in the late 1970s and early 1980s was very conducive to getting exposure and thus getting records started. The Midwest had its day as the hotbed of rock; Detroit was the home of what was termed "Rhythm and Blues," and the South and Southwest, along with Northern and Midwestern urban areas saw tremendous surges in the sale of this genre. In the 1990s, with "R & B" known as "urban product," Atlanta is being touted as the "new Motown" because of the number of records being recorded there.

The West Coast had its run with special genres such as "new wave" and other pop types. Each market, each area could boast of having the edge on starting a particular type of music on its way to the top of the charts. To some extent, this still is the case, but not anywhere near what it was some time ago. The consumer is more mobile, more aware of what is important in music at all times and has a greater selection of all types to choose from in the ever expanding retail and radio structure. No particular markets are able to command too much attention at the expense of other areas.

Hits can break out of any area of the country, and depending on the type of music, certain cities might have a better chance to ignite the hit, but every part of the country has that potential, especially in light of the fact that demographics are constantly changing. Keeping track of these trends is a part of market research that all facets of the industry watch very closely. This is done through all companies' research staffs with sales and airplay information supplied by the industry's many trade papers, and with particular emphasis on *Billboard*, and the industry's own trade organizations. As the industry becomes more sophisticated, more computerized, everyone has available very good information on what configurations and what types of products are selling, which type or types of outlets are moving the most product, and possibly most important, who is buying the product by age, gender and income level.

The industry has three very important trade organizations that are constantly doing surveys to aid their members do a better job and increase profits. They are:

- NARM—National Association of Recording Merchandisers
- RIAA—Recording Industry Association of America
- VSDA—Video Software Dealers Association

NARM, RIAA, and VSDA produce many reports, but possibly the most inclusive and thus most effective are their annual reports that identify important trends, as well as the overall health of the industry.

RIAA, primarily, is the association for manufacturers and thus their annual "Statistical Overview" is geared to the segment of the industry that produces the product and sells to retailers, rack jobbers and one stops. Based in Washington, D.C., the RIAA is a trade organization whose member companies create, manufacture or distribute approximately 90 percent of all legitimate sound recordings sold in the United States. To briefly review record sales activity over the last few years, as outlined in the Introduction to this textbook and Charts I-1 and I-2, it was not until 1993 that the industry finally attained the $10 billion volume mark. The next year growth was very healthy at 20% to $12 billion, but then activity leveled off. Finally, in 1998 the barrier of no growth or very slow growth was eliminated and the industry had a good year. Unit sales were up 5.7%, but the really significant increase was in dollar volume, up 12.1%. Price erosion had been a problem for a few years, but that has been corrected. The increase in CD as a percentage of overall configuration sales, with cassettes losing ground, also helped the dollar figure. Price erosion stopped as list price for CD's went up and that configuration became a larger percentage of the overall mix.

As shown in Chart I-2 Increases were recorded again in 1999 as CD sales went up about a million units and dollar value rose $1.5 million dollars. However, overall dollars were up less than a million dollars as cassette sales really tailed off. This was about when the industry decided to eliminate cassettes from the mix.

CD's just about hung on into the new millennium, but dollars fell off due to more erosion in cassette sales. Then in 2001, all major configurations slid drastically with the exception of DVD, that showed dramatic increases. But as a percentage of overall business DVD was still not that large to make an major impact on overall volume.

Then, as outlined in the Introduction and Chart I-3, in the first half of 2002 only DVD showed growth but not nearly enough to eclipse the loss in CD sales. The final tally for 2002 showed a drop in units of almost 8% (7.8%). This falloff slowed the following year to 2.7%, but this time the dollar slippage was higher at 4.3%. The industry was getting desperate, until in 2004 there was finally a turnaround, no matter how slight. That year saw units increase by 4.4% and dollars by 3.3%.

One of the most important reports available each year from RIAA is the Consumer Profile. (See Chart 14-1.) It contains a great deal of valuable information about what type of music sells, who it sells to, where it is sold and what configurations it sells.

Except for 2003, where there was a slight rebound, rock sales have been slipping for about ten years. Even with some ups and downs in recent years, hip-hop/rap has been growing.

Chart 14-1

The Recording Industry Association of America

2004 Consumer Profile

Phone: 202/775-0101   Web: www.riaa.com

	1995	1996	1997	1998	1999	2000	2001	2002	2003	2004	
Rock	33.5	32.6	32.5	25.7	25.2	24.8	24.4	24.7	25.2	23.9	%
Rap/Hip-hop[2]	6.7	8.9	10.1	9.7	10.8	12.9	11.4	13.8	13.3	12.1	
R&B/Urban[3]	11.3	12.1	11.2	12.8	10.5	9.7	10.6	11.2	10.6	11.3	
Country	16.7	14.7	14.4	14.1	10.8	10.7	10.5	10.7	10.4	13.0	
Pop	10.1	9.3	9.4	10.0	10.3	11.0	12.1	9.0	8.9	10.0	
Religious[4]	3.1	4.3	4.5	6.3	5.1	4.8	6.7	6.7	5.8	6.0	
Classical	2.9	3.4	2.8	3.3	3.5	2.7	3.2	3.1	3.0	2.0	
Jazz	3.0	3.3	2.8	1.9	3.0	2.9	3.4	3.2	2.9	2.7	
Soundtracks	0.9	0.8	1.2	1.7	0.8	0.7	1.4	1.1	1.4	1.1	
Oldies	1.0	0.8	0.8	0.7	0.7	0.9	0.8	0.9	1.3	1.4	
New Age	0.7	0.7	0.8	0.6	0.5	0.5	1.0	0.5	0.5	1.0	
Children's	0.5	0.7	0.9	0.4	0.4	0.6	0.5	0.4	0.6	2.8	
Other[5]	7.0	5.2	5.7	7.9	9.1	8.3	7.9	8.1	7.6	8.9	
Full-length CDs	65.0	68.4	70.2	74.8	83.2	89.3	89.2	90.5	87.8	90.3	%
Full-length cassettes	25.1	19.3	18.2	14.8	8.0	4.9	3.4	2.4	2.2	1.7	
Singles (all types)	7.5	9.3	9.3	6.8	5.4	2.5	2.4	1.9	2.4	2.4	
Music videos/Video DVDs	0.9	1.0	0.6	1.0	0.9	0.8	1.1	0.7	0.6	1.0	
DVD audio	NA	NA	NA	NA	NA	NA	1.1	1.3	2.7	1.7	
Digital Download	NA	NA	NA	NA	NA	NA	0.2	0.5	1.3	0.9	
SACD	NA	NA	NA	NA	NA	NA	NA	NA	0.5	0.8	
Vinyl LPs	0.5	0.6	0.7	0.7	0.5	0.5	0.6	0.7	0.5	0.9	
10–14 Years	8.0	7.9	8.9	9.1	8.5	8.9	8.5	8.9	8.6	9.4	%
15–19 Years	17.1	17.2	16.8	15.8	12.6	12.9	13.0	13.3	11.4	11.9	
20–24 Years	15.3	15.0	13.8	12.2	12.6	12.5	12.2	11.5	10.0	9.2	
25–29 Years	12.3	12.5	11.7	11.4	10.5	10.6	10.9	9.4	10.9	10.0	
30–34 Years	12.1	11.4	11.0	11.4	10.1	9.8	10.3	10.8	10.1	10.4	
35–39 Years	10.8	11.1	11.6	12.6	10.4	10.6	10.2	9.8	11.2	10.7	
40–44 Years	7.5	9.1	8.8	8.3	9.3	9.6	10.3	9.9	10.0	10.9	
45+	16.1	15.1	16.5	18.1	24.7	23.8	23.7	25.5	26.6	26.4	
Record Store	52.0	49.9	51.8	50.8	44.5	42.4	42.5	36.8	33.2	32.5	
Other Store	28.2	31.5	31.9	34.4	38.3	40.8	42.4	50.7	52.8	53.8	%
Tape/Record Club	14.3	14.3	11.6	9.0	7.9	7.6	6.1	4.0	4.1	4.4	
TV, Newspaper, Magazine Ad Or 800 Number	4.0	2.9	2.7	2.9	2.5	2.4	3.0	2.0	1.5	1.7	
Internet[6]	NA	NA	0.3	1.1	2.4	3.2	2.9	3.4	5.0	5.9	
Concert	NA	NA	NA	NA	NA	NA	NA	NA	NA	1.6	
Female	47.0	49.1	51.4	51.3	49.7	49.4	51.2	50.6	50.9	50.5	%
Male	53.0	50.9	48.6	48.7	50.3	50.6	48.8	49.4	49.1	49.5	

Total U.S. Dollar Value

The figures below (in millions) indicate the overall size of the U.S. sound recording industry based on manufacturers' shipments at suggested list prices.

1995	$12,320.30
1996	$12,533.80
1997	$12,236.60
1998	$13,723.50
1999	$14,584.50
2000	$14,323.00
2001	$13,740.89
2002	$12,614.21
2003	$11,854.40
2004	$12,154.70

Methodology

This profile represents a combination of music-consumption data collected by Peter Hart Research and The Taylor Research & Consulting Group, Inc., during calendar year 2004. The data for the period from the beginning of 2004 through the end of July 2004 were collected by Peter Hart Research, while the data from August through the end of December were gathered by The Taylor Research & Consulting Group.[1]

Data based on telephone survey of past month music buyers (over 2,000 per year). The reliability of the data is +/2 2.2% at a 95% confidence level. With respect to genre, consumers were asked to classify their music purchases.

Permission to cite or copy these statistics is hereby granted as long as proper attribution is given to the Recording Industry Association of America.

[1]Calendar year 2004: data based upon a combination of survey data collected by Peter Hart Research and The Taylor Research & Consulting Group, Inc. Includes only partial-year data, as Hart did not interview during the months of March, April, June, and July of 2004. Channel data derived safely from Taylor August-December interviews.

[2]"Rap": Includes Rap and Hip-Hop.

[3]"R&B": Includes R&B, Blues, Dance Disco Funk, Fusion, Motown, Reggae, Soul.

[4]"Religious": Includes Christian, Gospel, Inspirational Religious, and Spiritual.

[5]"Other": Includes Big Band, Broadway, Shows, Comedy, Contemporary, Electronic, EMO, Ethnic, Exercise, Folk, Gothic, Grunge, Holiday Music House Music, Humor, Instrumental, Language, Latin, Love Songs, Mix. Mellow, Modern, Ska, Spoken word, Standards, Swing, Top-40, Trip-hop.

[6]Internet does not include record club purchases made over the Internet.

Reprinted courtesy of RIAA.

The section on which age groups are the biggest buyers contains some very interesting information. The average age of the record buyer is definitely getting older. Record companies and labels have been avoiding acknowledging this for many years, but can no longer do so. Buyers in the 40 to 45 year old age group have increased from 7.5% to 10.9% in ten years. Meanwhile the 45 and over group has just about doubled in that period. That has a bearing on the slippage in sales. More attention has to be given to the demographic that has the disposable income.

The record industry follows the thinking of the advertising establishment, who are obsessed with getting to a very young demographic, teens and "twenty-somethings." The philosophy behind this is to get people started on a product young and they will stay with it for the rest of their lives. This is a fallacy with today's young people. They are part of the "clicker" generation and have little loyalty to anything for any length of time today. It is even more pronounced in the music industry. Young people stay with acts for a very short time, and to survive labels must build acts, not just records.

One last note from the Profile. It shows that for four years female buyers have topped this category, as it swings back and forth.

This type of statistical information from NARM, RIAA, and VSDA is invaluable for any marketing force. All these data must be considered when planning to invest in any project.

VSDA information is included in the discussion on video in the previous chapter.

There are a number of Marketing Firms that are utilized by record companies. These marketing firms augment the marketing staffs of the labels. It is part of the "checks and balances" process that labels wish to have. They also make it possible to concentrate on certain projects without diminishing activity on others due to lack of field people. These firms also supply some data, usually by way of an annual questionnaire to the accounts they deal with that cover the health of the industry, attitudes toward projected changes and what is necessary for a strong future.

In addition to the information and exchange of ideas made available by these organizations, they, along with The Recording Academy (National Academy of Recording Arts and Sciences) are also very active in lobbying for initiatives vital to a healthy music business at both the federal (Congress) and state levels.

Retail Chains do a great deal of market research, especially when they are looking for new locations. One could call it "market market research." Before putting money into rent, fixtures, people and inventory, they look things over very carefully.

Mall locations are not determined by the individual retailers. That market research is done by the mall developers, and then the retailers determine, from the information provided by the developer, if they want to be part of the complex. In many cases, they do not have a choice. Most are tied in with major mall builders and must take locations to protect future opportunities in projected malls. However, freestanding or strip center locations are another story. Here, the retailers do most of their own research. Strip builders will provide some information, but the retailer has many ways to determine the feasibility of a location.

One of best and most used is the information created by the census taken every ten years. Chart 14-2 is a Profile of General Demographics Characteristics: 2000. This report is very detailed and offers a tremendous amount of information to anyone contemplating a business move in a given area. Chart 14-2 runs many pages but the data is confined to just one county, Fulton, in Georgia.

Some information is available from the local Chambers of Commerce, various city and town offices and even libraries. In many cases, they actually "fly over" a potential site and get a first hand look at what the area offers. In looking for a new location, retailers will look for:

- density of traffic (number of cars that will pass since strip centers are aimed at automobile traffic)

- easy access (once again automobile traffic is the key)

- population density (they usually want at least 30,000 residents within a three mile radius of the store, although the growth in some cities is so rapid, that many retailers will take locations based strictly on what the population will be in the future)

- income level (would like it to be at least $35,000 annually)

- education level (as much college level as possible)

The trend for some time now has been to free standing or strip centers for chains, while "Mom and Pop" locations look to fill a niche in a neighborhood.

Another very vital type of market research is "tracking," something that is done by every record company and distribution company. Airplay and sales are tracked constantly by everyone because this is how you determine whether all your work, all your expenditures and all your plans are paying off.

Tracking is far more scientific now that we have **Nielsen SoundScan** and **BDS (Broadcast Data System).** Tracking is also far more accurate now.

SoundScan was devised by Mike Shallet as the l990s started and was the most revolutionary change to hit the industry in decades. For years, chart position of the all-important *Billboard* lists was determined by information gathered manually (usually by phone) from retailers and radio stations. **SoundScan** changed all that by setting up a computerized reporting system that accurately tallied the actual sales at the cash registers of retailers and rack jobbers all over the country. The list of participating outlets was small at first, but now has grown to a size that can very accurately reflect what is really happening. Recently, Nielsen, the major player in audience tracking, bought out

Chart 14-2

Table DP-1. Profile of General Demographic Characteristics: 2000

Geographic area: Fulton County, Georgia

[For information on confidentiality protection, nonsampling error, and definitions, see text]

Subject	Number	Percent	Subject	Number	Percent
Total population..........................	816,006	100.0	**HISPANIC OR LATINO AND RACE**		
			Total population..........................	816,006	100.0
SEX AND AGE			Hispanic or Latino (of any race)...............	48,056	5.9
Male.....................	401,726	49.2	Mexican.....................	32,476	4.0
Female.....................	414,280	50.8	Puerto Rican.....................	2,925	0.4
			Cuban.....................	1,889	0.2
Under 5 years	56,819	7.0	Other Hispanic or Latino	10,766	1.3
5 to 9 years	58,129	7.1	Not Hispanic or Latino	767,950	94.1
10 to 14 years	54,118	6.6	White alone.....................	369,997	45.3
15 to 19 years	55,166	6.8			
20 to 24 years	64,660	7.9	**RELATIONSHIP**		
25 to 34 years	151,534	18.6	Total population..........................	816,006	100.0
35 to 44 years	137,850	16.9	In households.....................	784,622	96.2
45 to 54 years	109,132	13.4	Householder.....................	321,242	39.4
55 to 59 years	35,031	4.3	Spouse	119,714	14.7
60 to 64 years	24,577	3.0	Child.....................	220,401	27.0
65 to 74 years	35,759	4.4	Own child under 18 years.....................	170,511	20.9
75 to 84 years	23,649	2.9	Other relatives	59,001	7.2
85 years and over.....................	9,582	1.2	Under 18 years	23,575	2.9
			Nonrelatives	64,264	7.9
Median age (years).....................	32.7	(X)	Unmarried partner.....................	18,084	2.2
			In group quarters.....................	31,384	3.8
18 years and over.....................	616,716	75.6	Institutionalized population.....................	9,801	1.2
Male.....................	300,419	36.8	Noninstitutionalized population	21,583	2.6
Female.....................	316,297	38.8			
21 years and over.....................	579,289	71.0	**HOUSEHOLD BY TYPE**		
62 years and over.....................	82,675	10.1	Total households.....................	321,242	100.0
65 years and over.....................	68,990	8.5	Family households (families).....................	185,721	57.8
Male.....................	25,831	3.2	With own children under 18 years	92,256	28.7
Female.....................	43,159	5.3	Married-couple family	119,714	37.3
			With own children under 18 years	56,059	17.5
RACE			Female householder, no husband present.....	52,923	16.5
One race.....................	804,153	98.5	With own children under 18 years	31,109	9.7
White	392,598	48.1	Nonfamily households	135,521	42.2
Black or African American	363,656	44.6	Householder living alone	103,392	32.2
American Indian and Alaska Native...........	1,514	0.2	Householder 65 years and over	21,387	6.7
Asian	24,823	3.0			
Asian Indian	7,689	0.9	Households with individuals under 18 years	104,527	32.5
Chinese.....................	5,886	0.7	Households with individuals 65 years and over ..	51,114	15.9
Filipino	992	0.1			
Japanese.....................	1,082	0.1	Average household size.....................	2.44	(X)
Korean.....................	4,116	0.5	Average family size.....................	3.15	(X)
Vietnamese.....................	2,855	0.3			
Other Asian [1]	2,203	0.3	**HOUSING OCCUPANCY**		
Native Hawaiian and Other Pacific Islander....	346	-	Total housing units.....................	348,632	100.0
Native Hawaiian.....................	108	-	Occupied housing units	321,242	92.1
Guamanian or Chamorro.....................	69	-	Vacant housing units.....................	27,390	7.9
Samoan.....................	68	-	For seasonal, recreational, or		
Other Pacific Islander [2]	101	-	occasional use.....................	1,737	0.5
Some other race	21,216	2.6			
Two or more races	11,853	1.5	Homeowner vacancy rate (percent).............	2.7	(X)
			Rental vacancy rate (percent).................	7.1	(X)
Race alone or in combination with one					
or more other races: [3]			**HOUSING TENURE**		
White.....................	400,559	49.1	Occupied housing units	321,242	100.0
Black or African American	369,014	45.2	Owner-occupied housing units	167,119	52.0
American Indian and Alaska Native............	4,279	0.5	Renter-occupied housing units	154,123	48.0
Asian	27,704	3.4			
Native Hawaiian and Other Pacific Islander......	883	0.1	Average household size of owner-occupied units.	2.60	(X)
Some other race	26,483	3.2	Average household size of renter-occupied units .	2.28	(X)

- Represents zero or rounds to zero.   (X) Not applicable.

[1] Other Asian alone, or two or more Asian categories.

[2] Other Pacific Islander alone, or two or more Native Hawaiian and Other Pacific Islander categories.

[3] In combination with one or more of the other races listed. The six numbers may add to more than the total population and the six percentages may add to more than 100 percent because individuals may report more than one race.

Source: U.S. Census Bureau, Census 2000.

Chart 14-2 *(continued)*

Table DP-2. Profile of Selected Social Characteristics: 2000

Geographic area: Fulton County, Georgia

[Data based on a sample. For information on confidentiality protection, sampling error, nonsampling error, and definitions, see text]

Subject	Number	Percent	Subject	Number	Percent
SCHOOL ENROLLMENT			**NATIVITY AND PLACE OF BIRTH**		
Population 3 years and over			Total population........................	**816,006**	**100.0**
enrolled in school...................	**219,663**	**100.0**	Native..................................	737,387	90.4
Nursery school, preschool.....................	19,176	8.7	Born in United States	729,599	89.4
Kindergarten............................	11,791	5.4	State of residence......................	386,934	47.4
Elementary school (grades 1-8)	91,474	41.6	Different state.........................	342,665	42.0
High school (grades 9-12)....................	42,144	19.2	Born outside United States	7,788	1.0
College or graduate school	55,078	25.1	Foreign born...........................	78,619	9.6
			Entered 1990 to March 2000	50,115	6.1
EDUCATIONAL ATTAINMENT			Naturalized citizen........................	21,268	2.6
Population 25 years and over	**527,738**	**100.0**	Not a citizen..........................	57,351	7.0
Less than 9th grade	27,106	5.1			
9th to 12th grade, no diploma................	57,264	10.9	**REGION OF BIRTH OF FOREIGN BORN**		
High school graduate (includes equivalency).....	102,246	19.4	**Total (excluding born at sea)..............**	**78,619**	**100.0**
Some college, no degree.....................	97,894	18.5	Europe..................................	11,673	14.8
Associate degree...........................	24,823	4.7	Asia	20,175	25.7
Bachelor's degree..........................	140,666	26.7	Africa	6,227	7.9
Graduate or professional degree	77,739	14.7	Oceania.................................	373	0.5
			Latin America	37,231	47.4
Percent high school graduate or higher	84.0	(X)	Northern America.......................	2,940	3.7
Percent bachelor's degree or higher	41.4	(X)			
			LANGUAGE SPOKEN AT HOME		
MARITAL STATUS			**Population 5 years and over ....**	**759,179**	**100.0**
Population 15 years and over	**646,833**	**100.0**	English only............................	658,421	86.7
Never married	242,652	37.5	Language other than English	100,758	13.3
Now married, except separated	277,638	42.9	Speak English less than "very well"	47,889	6.3
Separated	19,088	3.0	Spanish	52,371	6.9
Widowed	38,552	6.0	Speak English less than "very well"	30,828	4.1
Female.................................	31,684	4.9	Other Indo-European languages	27,244	3.6
Divorced	68,903	10.7	Speak English less than "very well"	8,145	1.1
Female.................................	41,088	6.4	Asian and Pacific Island languages...........	15,825	2.1
			Speak English less than "very well"	7,554	1.0
GRANDPARENTS AS CAREGIVERS					
Grandparent living in household with			**ANCESTRY (single or multiple)**		
one or more own grandchildren under			Total population........................	**816,006**	**100.0**
18 years...........................	**17,828**	**100.0**	*Total ancestries reported ....*	*761,005*	*93.3*
Grandparent responsible for grandchildren	8,384	47.0	Arab....................................	2,713	0.3
			Czech[1].................................	1,926	0.2
VETERAN STATUS			Danish..................................	1,782	0.2
Civilian population 18 years and over ..	**616,357**	**100.0**	Dutch...................................	6,105	0.7
Civilian veterans	61,642	10.0	English..................................	64,957	8.0
			French (except Basque)[1]...................	13,744	1.7
DISABILITY STATUS OF THE CIVILIAN			French Canadian[1].........................	2,718	0.3
NONINSTITUTIONALIZED POPULATION			German..................................	59,356	7.3
Population 5 to 20 years...............	**178,266**	**100.0**	Greek...................................	2,718	0.3
With a disability	14,496	8.1	Hungarian	2,337	0.3
			Irish[1]..................................	55,810	6.8
Population 21 to 64 years.............	**502,583**	**100.0**	Italian..................................	23,909	2.9
With a disability	91,437	18.2	Lithuanian	1,197	0.1
Percent employed	56.7	(X)	Norwegian...............................	4,131	0.5
No disability	411,146	81.8	Polish...................................	11,742	1.4
Percent employed	75.6	(X)	Portuguese..............................	780	0.1
			Russian.................................	8,759	1.1
Population 65 years and over	**68,004**	**100.0**	Scotch-Irish.............................	14,496	1.8
With a disability	31,169	45.8	Scottish.................................	16,188	2.0
			Slovak	863	0.1
RESIDENCE IN 1995			Subsaharan African.......................	13,395	1.6
Population 5 years and over	**759,179**	**100.0**	Swedish.................................	5,098	0.6
Same house in 1995.........................	324,989	42.8	Swiss...................................	1,493	0.2
Different house in the U.S. in 1995	397,438	52.4	Ukrainian................................	1,621	0.2
Same county	178,091	23.5	United States or American..................	41,110	5.0
Different county	219,347	28.9	Welsh..................................	3,805	0.5
Same state	90,541	11.9	West Indian (excluding Hispanic groups)	5,664	0.7
Different state...........................	128,806	17.0	Other ancestries	392,588	48.1
Elsewhere in 1995..........................	36,752	4.8			

-Represents zero or rounds to zero.   (X) Not applicable.

[1]The data represent a combination of two ancestries shown separately in Summary File 3. Czech includes Czechoslovakian. French includes Alsatian. French Canadian includes Acadian/Cajun. Irish includes Celtic.

Source: U.S. Bureau of the Census, Census 2000.

Chart 14-2 *(continued)*

Table DP-3. Profile of Selected Economic Characteristics: 2000

Geographic area: Fulton County, Georgia

[Data based on a sample. For information on confidentiality protection, sampling error, nonsampling error, and definitions, see text]

Subject	Number	Percent
EMPLOYMENT STATUS		
Population 16 years and over	**637,017**	**100.0**
In labor force	431,553	67.7
Civilian labor force	430,872	67.6
Employed	392,627	61.6
Unemployed	38,245	6.0
Percent of civilian labor force	8.9	(X)
Armed Forces	681	0.1
Not in labor force	205,464	32.3
Females 16 years and over	**327,327**	**100.0**
In labor force	198,695	60.7
Civilian labor force	198,529	60.7
Employed	180,940	55.3
Own children under 6 years	**62,937**	**100.0**
All parents in family in labor force	34,168	54.3
COMMUTING TO WORK		
Workers 16 years and over	**385,442**	**100.0**
Car, truck, or van - - drove alone	275,363	71.4
Car, truck, or van - - carpooled	44,605	11.6
Public transportation (including taxicab)	35,939	9.3
Walked	8,628	2.2
Other means	4,110	1.1
Worked at home	16,797	4.4
Mean travel time to work (minutes)[1]	29.1	(X)
Employed civilian population 16 years and over	**392,627**	**100.0**
OCCUPATION		
Management, professional, and related occupations	170,996	43.6
Service occupations	53,021	13.5
Sales and office occupations	108,820	27.7
Farming, fishing, and forestry occupations	640	0.2
Construction, extraction, and maintenance occupations	23,508	6.0
Production, transportation, and material moving occupations	35,642	9.1
INDUSTRY		
Agriculture, forestry, fishing and hunting, and mining	1,057	0.3
Construction	20,789	5.3
Manufacturing	32,951	8.4
Wholesale trade	15,369	3.9
Retail trade	42,415	10.8
Transportation and warehousing, and utilities	23,027	5.9
Information	24,461	6.2
Finance, insurance, real estate, and rental and leasing	38,440	9.8
Professional, scientific, management, administrative, and waste management services	66,113	16.8
Educational, health and social services	59,162	15.1
Arts, entertainment, recreation, accommodation and food services	36,424	9.3
Other services (except public administration)	17,542	4.5
Public administration	14,877	3.8
CLASS OF WORKER		
Private wage and salary workers	327,507	83.4
Government workers	42,771	10.9
Self-employed workers in own not incorporated business	21,603	5.5
Unpaid family workers	746	0.2

Subject	Number	Percent
INCOME IN 1999		
Households	**321,266**	**100.0**
Less than $10,000	36,099	11.2
$10,000 to $14,999	16,923	5.3
$15,000 to $24,999	35,138	10.9
$25,000 to $34,999	35,225	11.0
$35,000 to $49,999	43,703	13.6
$50,000 to $74,999	52,961	16.5
$75,000 to $99,999	32,031	10.0
$100,000 to $149,999	34,463	10.7
$150,000 to $199,999	13,889	4.3
$200,000 or more	20,834	6.5
Median household income (dollars)	47,321	(X)
With earnings	272,492	84.8
Mean earnings (dollars)[1]	75,103	(X)
With Social Security income	56,534	17.6
Mean Social Security income (dollars)[1]	10,284	(X)
With Supplemental Security Income	13,601	4.2
Mean Supplemental Security Income (dollars)[1]	6,131	(X)
With public assistance income	11,616	3.6
Mean public assistance income (dollars)[1]	2,570	(X)
With retirement income	36,636	11.4
Mean retirement income (dollars)[1]	20,553	(X)
Families	**187,627**	**100.0**
Less than $10,000	16,199	8.6
$10,000 to $14,999	7,962	4.2
$15,000 to $24,999	18,582	9.9
$25,000 to $34,999	17,468	9.3
$35,000 to $49,999	22,120	11.8
$50,000 to $74,999	29,944	16.0
$75,000 to $99,999	20,889	11.1
$100,000 to $149,999	25,485	13.6
$150,000 to $199,999	11,279	6.0
$200,000 or more	17,699	9.4
Median family income (dollars)	58,143	(X)
Per capita income (dollars)[1]	30,003	(X)
Median earnings (dollars):		
Male full-time, year-round workers	43,495	(X)
Female full-time, year-round workers	32,122	(X)

Subject	Number below poverty level	Percent below poverty level
POVERTY STATUS IN 1999		
Families	**23,270**	**12.4**
With related children under 18 years	19,150	18.2
With related children under 5 years	9,879	22.0
Families with female householder, no husband present	**16,698**	**31.7**
With related children under 18 years	14,752	39.4
With related children under 5 years	7,517	50.3
Individuals	**124,241**	**15.7**
18 years and over	79,249	13.3
65 years and over	10,319	15.2
Related children under 18 years	43,936	22.6
Related children 5 to 17 years	30,444	22.0
Unrelated individuals 15 years and over	41,439	20.9

-Represents zero or rounds to zero. (X) Not applicable.

[1]If the denominator of a mean value or per capita value is less than 30, then that value is calculated using a rounded aggregate in the numerator. See text.

Source: U.S. Bureau of the Census, Census 2000.

Chart 14-2 *(continued)*

Table DP-4. Profile of Selected Housing Characteristics: 2000

Geographic area: Fulton County, Georgia

[Data based on a sample. For information on confidentiality protection, sampling error, nonsampling error, and definitions, see text]

Subject	Number	Percent	Subject	Number	Percent
Total housing units....................	348,632	100.0	**OCCUPANTS PER ROOM**		
UNITS IN STRUCTURE			Occupied housing units	321,242	100.0
1-unit, detached...........................	171,362	49.2	1.00 or less................................	302,260	94.1
1-unit, attached	15,171	4.4	1.01 to 1.50	10,080	3.1
2 units	9,975	2.9	1.51 or more...............................	8,902	2.8
3 or 4 units	21,451	6.2			
5 to 9 units	36,545	10.5	Specified owner-occupied units........	146,783	100.0
10 to 19 units.............................	37,047	10.6	**VALUE**		
20 or more units	55,473	15.9	Less than $50,000..........................	6,271	4.3
Mobile home...............................	1,457	0.4	$50,000 to $99,999.........................	34,067	23.2
Boat, RV, van, etc	151	-	$100,000 to $149,999.......................	20,905	14.2
			$150,000 to $199,999.......................	19,338	13.2
			$200,000 to $299,999.......................	26,840	18.3
YEAR STRUCTURE BUILT			$300,000 to $499,999.......................	25,367	17.3
1999 to March 2000	9,519	2.7	$500,000 to $999,999.......................	11,496	7.8
1995 to 1998	35,497	10.2	$1,000,000 or more..........................	2,499	1.7
1990 to 1994	33,119	9.5	Median (dollars)............................	180,700	(X)
1980 to 1989	63,177	18.1			
1970 to 1979	55,608	16.0			
1960 to 1969	56,928	16.3	**MORTGAGE STATUS AND SELECTED**		
1940 to 1959	63,627	18.3	**MONTHLY OWNER COSTS**		
1939 or earlier............................	31,157	8.9	With a mortgage	118,113	80.5
			Less than $300	511	0.3
			$300 to $499	2,877	2.0
ROOMS			$500 to $699	8,222	5.6
1 room	9,422	2.7	$700 to $999	19,083	13.0
2 rooms......................................	23,485	6.7	$1,000 to $1,499	30,498	20.8
3 rooms......................................	44,983	12.9	$1,500 to $1,999	22,248	15.2
4 rooms......................................	57,476	16.5	$2,000 or more	34,674	23.6
5 rooms......................................	58,490	16.8	Median (dollars).........................	1,462	(X)
6 rooms......................................	46,841	13.4	Not mortgaged	28,670	19.5
7 rooms......................................	31,516	9.0	Median (dollars).........................	372	(X)
8 rooms......................................	27,583	7.9			
9 or more rooms	48,836	14.0	**SELECTED MONTHLY OWNER COSTS**		
Median (rooms)	5.2	(X)	**AS A PERCENTAGE OF HOUSEHOLD**		
			INCOME IN 1999		
Occupied housing units	321,242	100.0	Less than 15.0 percent.....................	47,723	32.5
YEAR HOUSEHOLDER MOVED INTO UNIT			15.0 to 19.9 percent	25,121	17.1
1999 to March 2000	91,292	28.4	20.0 to 24.9 percent	21,575	14.7
1995 to 1998	106,138	33.0	25.0 to 29.9 percent	14,241	9.7
1990 to 1994	45,155	14.1	30.0 to 34.9 percent	8,742	6.0
1980 to 1989	37,406	11.6	35.0 percent or more	27,979	19.1
1970 to 1979	22,239	6.9	Not computed...............................	1,402	1.0
1969 or earlier	19,012	5.9			
			Specified renter-occupied units........	153,778	100.0
VEHICLES AVAILABLE			**GROSS RENT**		
None	48,859	15.2	Less than $200	11,900	7.7
1	122,741	38.2	$200 to $299	6,357	4.1
2	109,214	34.0	$300 to $499	20,148	13.1
3 or more	40,428	12.6	$500 to $749	44,179	28.7
			$750 to $999	41,361	26.9
HOUSE HEATING FUEL			$1,000 to $1,499	21,338	13.9
Utility gas	218,439	68.0	$1,500 or more	5,285	3.4
Bottled, tank, or LP gas	4,514	1.4	No cash rent................................	3,210	2.1
Electricity....................................	96,046	29.9	Median (dollars)............................	709	(X)
Fuel oil, kerosene, etc	714	0.2			
Coal or coke................................	12	-	**GROSS RENT AS A PERCENTAGE OF**		
Wood	305	0.1	**HOUSEHOLD INCOME IN 1999**		
Solar energy................................	79	-	Less than 15.0 percent.....................	26,781	17.4
Other fuel	370	0.1	15.0 to 19.9 percent	22,069	14.4
No fuel used................................	763	0.2	20.0 to 24.9 percent	20,306	13.2
			25.0 to 29.9 percent	17,422	11.3
SELECTED CHARACTERISTICS			30.0 to 34.9 percent	12,446	8.1
Lacking complete plumbing facilities	1,967	0.6	35.0 percent or more	46,447	30.2
Lacking complete kitchen facilities.............	2,229	0.7	Not computed................................	8,307	5.4
No telephone service	6,916	2.2			

-Represents zero or rounds to zero.   (X) Not applicable.

Source: U.S. Bureau of the Census, Census 2000.

SoundScan and it is now known as **Nielsen SoundScan.** In combination with BDS it is able to give the industry real numbers and real information on how well a particular piece of product is doing at retail and at radio.

A **Nielsen SoundScan** chart will give you sales for a current week as well as sales for the previous week. It also gives the record a chart position for the present week, the prior week, and the week before that (two weeks ago). It also notes the number of weeks a particular piece of product has been on the **Nielsen SoundScan** chart.

Nielsen SoundScan information can be broken down to pinpoint sales in key cities within a distribution branch's territory. This "Area of Dominant Influence Report," or ADI, gets quite specific.

BDS (Broadcast Data System) monitors airplay electronically, giving the industry information about where, how often and at what time of the day or night a record is being aired.

Since actual sales figures determine only the top 20 or so records on major charts, airplay must be factored in to create a better picture of a record's strength and potential. Thus the marriage of **Nielsen SoundScan** and **BDS** is much more accurate. When you get near the top of the charts, having actual sales figures as the reference point not only is far more reliable, but also offers a better picture of just how active record sales are each week.

However, there is other tracking that has to be done. Record company and distribution people must call individual stations and get their particular chart position on specific records. This information is vital to all companies on a day to day basis. Airplay tracking is usually done by the Promotion Department. This tracking is solely to keep up with who is playing what, and how heavy the rotation is.

Some companies pay outside firms to do this tracking, while some organizations, and this is prevalent with Nashville's country departments, hire special staffs to accomplish this.

- All this information is the "progress report" or a "report card" and is used as follows:

- By promotion with other stations since radio is not very prone to "go it alone" and requires a great deal of supportive information before adding a record to the play list.

- By sales with buyers since keeping inventories at a profitable level, while still having the right product in the stores, is the primary mandate of any buying staff.

- By publicity with consumer and trade publications since the avenues for exposure other than radio have increased tremendously in the past few years. TV, magazines, alternative newspapers, and the consumer press now offer a limitless outlet for publicity about entertainment oriented material. The public's appetite for news about record stars and their activities keeps mushrooming.

- By product management to determine advertising expenditures, and to determine its next move since it is much easier and much more economical to build on success. Chart and airplay information can predict your chances for success, not only better, but also by locale and thus fewer resources are necessary to do the job.

- By distribution to forecast pressing or duplication orders since it is imperative that the product be available for shipment when the activity starts. Having to wait too long can seriously undermine a record's chances for success.

- By distribution to make sure there is product in the stores since a number of bases must be covered to be sure the stores are "in stock" and keyed to the potential.

Everyone rejoices and congratulates themselves when reports show proper, expected or required movement, meaning upward.

However, everyone panics when progress stops short of goals or the trend reverses itself. But knowing that is happening in time makes it possible to remedy the situation and reverse the downward fortunes in many cases.

No matter how the charts are compiled, the industry lives and dies by the charts and chart action. **Chart Share not only reflects the health of individual pieces of product, but also reflects the health of the labels.** There are labels that feel that chart share in Billboard is almost as important as sales. When executives can show managers, attorneys, and major artists that their organizations know how to get chart share, it makes making deals that much easier.

There are many in the industry who are far more sensitive to chart share than to actual sales. Chart position over the long haul has a very marked impact on how well a label can attract new, good talent and records.

You have heard the adage *Don't learn from history and you perish*, this applies to the record industry also.

Summary

As the music industry grows, becomes more corporate, and realizes the benefits, it is now using market research far more than it ever did. The charts, both sales and radio play, are now compiled by accurate, electronic means that take much of the "hype" out of them.

All aspects of the industry use market research, and with the dollars that are being gambled on new stores, new artists, new ideas, it is imperative that good information be the foundation for decisions.

Terms

Focus Group: Small groups of people representing all demographics who are asked to evaluate and comment on product prior to release.

Nielsen SoundScan: Compilation of sales figures right from the cash registers in many accounts to give an accurate picture of just how well product is selling.

BDS (Broadcast Data System): Electronic monitoring of airplay to accurately count the number of times a record is played in what time slot and on which stations.

Exercises

1. What do the acronyms NARM, RIAA, and VSDA stand for?

2. The record industry showed excellent growth in 1993 and 1994. What were the increases for 1993 and 1994? How did figures for 1995 compare to the two previous years?

3. What were the factors contributing to that growth?

4. What are four factors a retail chain will consider before committing to a new store in a particular area?

5. How has Nielsen SoundScan changed the record industry?

6. How has BDS changed the record industry?

Chapter 15
Global Music Industry

Learning Objectives

After studying this chapter you should be able to:

1. Discuss the Global music industry environment

2. Identify cultural differences and problems associated with foreign market entry

3. Describe recent developments in the Global music Industry

4. Describe why Piracy is a serious Global music issue.

5. Analyze the global and regional market shares of the five major labels

6. Summarize the latest developments in the United States, Germany, Japan, United Kingdom, France

In recent years American music companies have merged with international entertainment conglomerates with related businesses in film, radio, cable, television, newspapers, magazines, internet, video, computer games, music software, electronics, and book publishing. Increasingly the means of production and distribution lie within the walls of four entertainment conglomerates. This concentration of production is mainly the result of a inter-linked economic processes called integration. Vertical integration refers to a situation where a company controls the channels of production and distribution of a particular media market. Within this structure there are two types of vertical integration, upstream and downstream. Upstream vertical integration implies broadcaster moving into production, hardware manufacturers moving into production through acquisitions and distributors buying into production. The process begins with major record labels purchase of studios, CD pressing, cassette copying plants, printing works, in-house distribution, and retail outlets. The upstream vertical integration was demonstrated in the late 1980's by Matsushita's (Japan) acquisition of MCA/Universal as well as Sony Electronics of Japan (CD) purchase of Columbia Pictures and CBS Records. Japanese companies like Sony Electronics of Japan and Matsushita (Japan) both electronic giants which have hardware expertise (camcorder, walkman, VCR etc.) need content, software and media outlets. Purchasing software company is a way of ensuring a valuable supply of music, films, movies that can be played on machines the electronic firms sell. (CD, DAT recorder, DVD etc). The recent mergers of Turner Inc. with AOL Time Warner and ABC-Disney with Fox Network is a further proof of this type of vertical integration within the entertainment industry (see Chart 15–1). Downstream vertical integration refers to producers moving into broadcasting through mergers and acquisitions and broadcasters moving into distribution. Horizontal integration exists when a company purchases the same operations of others in identical sectors. The integration of record labels has been mostly vertical but also horizontal when major labels purchase smaller profitable labels or engage in joint venture opportunities. Atlanta's music industry was stimulated in 1989 when Arista Records, a subsidiary of Bertlesmann (BMG), signed a deal worth twenty million dollars in venture capital outlay with La Face records This agreement was renewed five years later for one hundred million dollars. LaFace records produced Grammy award winning projects for Kris Kross, Usher, Toni Braxton, Toni Rich, Outkast, TLC and others.

The figure listed in Chart 15–2 indicates that Japanese companies with hardware expertise need content and purchase American owned record labels, films and program libraries. Likewise European have been acquiring American software capabilities while American companies have been exporting their programs and products as well as their knowledge concerning cable television.

Chart 15–1
Businesses at a Glance

TIME INC.
All You
Babytalk
Business 2.0
Entertainment Weekly
Fortune
FSB: Fortune Small
  Business
In Style
In Style Brazil*
In Style Germany*
In Style Greece*
In Style Korea*
In Style Spain*
Life
Money
Parenting
People
People en Español
Real Simple
Sports Illustrated
Sports Illustrated For
  Kids
Sports Illustrated On
  Campus
Teen People
Time
Time Asia
Time Atlantic
Time Canada
Time For Kids
*Published by a third party
  under license from Time Inc.

**Southern Progress
  Corporation**
Coastal Living
Cooking Light
Cottage Living
Health
Southern Accents
Southern Living
Sunset
The Progressive
  Farmer

Leisure Arts
Oxmoor House
Southern Living At
  HOME
Sunset Books

Time4 Media
Field & Stream
Golf Magazine

MotorBoating
Outdoor Life
Popular Science
Ride BMX
SaltWater Sportsman
Ski
Skiing
STN: Skiing Trade
  News
This Old House
TransWorld Business
TransWorld Motocross
TransWorld
  Skateboarding
TransWorld
  Snowboarding
TransWorld SURF
Yachting

This Old House
  Ventures
Warren Miller
  Entertainment

IPC Media
4×4
25 Beautiful Gardens
25 Beautiful Homes
25 Beautiful Kitchens
Aeroplane
Amateur Gardening
Amateur Photographer
Angler's Mail
Bird Keeper
Cage & Aviary Birds
Caravan
Chat
Classic Boat
Country Homes &
  Interiors
Country Life
Cycle Sport
Cycling Weekly
Decanter
Essentials
European Boat Builder
Eventing
Family Circle
The Field
The Golf
Golf Monthly
The Guitar Magazine
Hair
Hi-Fi News
Homes & Gardens

Horse
Horse & Hound
Ideal Home
In Style U.K.
International Boat
  Industry
Land Rover World
Livingetc
Loaded
Marie Claire
MBR — Mountain Bike
  Rider
Mini World
Mizz
Model Collector
Motor Boat & Yachting
Motor Boats Monthly
Motor Caravan
NME
Now
Nuts
Park Home & Holiday
  Caravan
Pick Me Up
Practical Boat Owner
Practical Parenting
Prediction
Racecar Engineering
The Railway Magazine
Rugby World
Ships Monthly
Shoot Monthly
The Shooting Gazette
Shooting Times
Soaplife
Sporting Gun
Stamp Magazine
SuperBike
TV & Satellite Week
TVTimes
Uncut
VolksWorld
Wallpaper*
Web User
Wedding
What Camera
What Digital Camera
What's On TV
Woman
Woman & Home
Woman's Own
Woman's Weekly
Women & Golf
World Soccer

Yachting Monthly
Yachting World

**Time Inc. South
  Pacific**
Bride To Be
English Woman's
  Weekly
In Style Australia
Practical Parenting
Time Australia
Who

**Essence
  Communications**
Essence

**Time Inc. Business
  Units**
First Moments
Media Networks, Inc.
Synapse Group, Inc.
Targeted Media, Inc.
Time Customer
  Service
Time Inc. Brand
  Licensing
Time Inc. Home
  Entertainment
Time Inc. Strategic
  Communications
Time/Warner Retail
  Sales & Marketing

Joint Ventures
Avantages S.A.
BOOKSPAN
European Magazines
  Limited

**Time Warner Book
  Group**
Bulfinch Press
Center Street
Little, Brown and
  Company Adult Trade
  Books
Little, Brown and
  Company Books for
  Young Readers
Time Warner Audio-
  Books
Time Warner Book
  Group UK
Warner Books
Warner Faith

Chart 15–1 (continued)

WARNER BROS. ENTERTAINMENT INC.

Warner Bros. Pictures
Warner Bros. Television
The WB Television Network *Kids'WB!*
Warner Home Video
Warner Bros. Consumer Products
Telepictures Productions
Warner Independent Pictures
Warner Bros. Interactive Entertainment
  Warner Bros. Games
Warner Bros. International Cinemas
Warner Bros. Online
Warner Bros. Animation
  Looney Tunes
  Hanna-Barbera
DC Comics
  MAD Magazine
  Vertigo
  WildStorm

NEW LINE CINEMA CORPORATION

New Line Cinema
Fine Line Features
New Line Home Entertainment
New Line International Releasing
New Line New Media
New Line Television
New Line Distribution
New Line Merchandising/Licensing
New Line Music
New Line Theatricals

TURNER BROAD-CASTING SYSTEM, INC.

TBS
TNT
Cartoon Network
Turner Classic Movies
Turner South
Boomerang
TCM EMEA
Cartoon Network EMEA
Toonami
TNT Latin America
Cartoon Network Latin America
TCM Asia Pacific
Cartoon Network Asia Pacific
POGO
TCM Classic Hollywood
NASCAR.com
PGA.com
Cartoon Network Studios
Atlanta Braves
CNN/U.S.
CNN Headline News
CNN International
CNN en Español
CNNRadio
CNN en Español Radio
CNN Newsource
CNN.com
CNNMoney.com
CNNStudentNews.com
CNN Airport Network
CNN to Go
CNN Mobile

Joint Ventures

Cartoon Network Japan
NBC/Turner NASCAR Races
CNN+
CNN Turk

n-tv
CNN.co.jp (Japan)
CNNj
CETV
Zee/Turner
BOING

HOME BOX OFFICE

HBO
HBO On Demand
Cinemax
Cinemax On Demand
HBO Domestic and International Program Distribution
HBO Independent Productions
HBO Video
WBTV Latin America

Joint Ventures

HBO Asia
HBO Brasil
HBO Czech
HBO Hungary
HBO India
HBO Olé
HBO Poland
HBO Romania
E! Latin America

AMERICA ONLINE, INC.

AOL
AOL Europe
AOL Latino
CompuServe
ICQ
MapQuest
Moviefone
Netscape
AOL Music
AOL Cityguide
AOL Instant Messenger (AIM)
KOL

RED
AOL Call Alert
AOL Voicemail
MusicNet@AOL
AOLbyPhone
Tegic
Winamp/Shoutcast
AOL.com
AOL PassCode
AOL Privacy Wall
Love.com
Netscape.com

TIME WARNER CABLE INC.

Time Warner Cable
Road Runner
Time Warner Cable Commercial Services
Digital Phone
Time Warner Cable Media Sales
Local News Channels
Capital News 9 — Albany (Albany, NY)
NY1 News (New York, NY)
R News (Rochester, NY)
News 10 Now — Syracuse (Syracuse, NY)
News 14 Carolina (Charlotte/Raleigh, NC)
News 8 Austin (Austin, TX)

Joint Ventures

Texas and Kansas City Cable Partners, L.P.
Urban Cableworks of Philadelphia

TimeWarner
GLOBAL MARKETING

Time Warner Global Marketing

Time Warner Global Marketing's mission is to increase the growth of advertising and marketing revenues across all of Time Warner's businesses. A catalyst for collaboration across the company, Global Marketing fully develops customized, idea-driven programs for its marketing partners by capitalizing on Time Warner's wealth of content, media platforms, consumer relationships and marketing infrastructure worldwide. In addition, it provides these marketing partners with a unique point of access to Time Warner and a commitment to a long-term partnership, as well as the ability to deliver across all the Time Warner businesses.

Chart 15-2

USA
Hardware expertise
Software expertise
Cable distribution expertise

JAPAN
Hardware expertise

EUROPE
Media outlet expansion

The advantages for international entertainment conglomerates to concentrate production and distribution strategies are power and prestige for owners and managers, influence over public opinion, dominance of markets, sharing of skills between companies merged, economies of scale, diversification of risks, innovation, control and limitation on musical content and career opportunities for employees. As a student of the global music industry you must understand the many parts of the puzzle by knowing what countries comprise the European Union, North America, Asia/Pacific Rim, Africa, Eastern Europe, Latin America and the Caribbean. Global music marketing is the performance of business activities that direct the flow of music products and services across international boundaries for the satisfaction of human needs and wants. Additionally, you must understand that the world has become a series of larger markets that have differences in culture, language, economics, laws and natural resources.

The European Union is an agreement among fifteen Western European countries to lower barriers to trade among member nations. The original EU countries of Belgium, Denmark, France, Germany, Greece, Ireland, Italy, Netherlands, Luxembourg Portugal, Spain and the United Kingdom were joined in 1996 by Austria, Finland and Sweden. People and products can travel freely across international borders within the Union and are subject to uniform tariffs. The EU has also sought economic and monetary union through the creation of a common currency and a central bank. Together the gross national products and the populations of the EU nations will exceed those of the United States. This cooperation is vital to the music industry in it's fight against global piracy.

The North American Free Trade Agreement (NAFTA) is an agreement among Canada, Mexico and the United States to phase out tariffs and other trade barriers among the three nations. Besides lifting trade barriers for goods NAFTA helps service providers by ending requirements that professionals be citizens of the country in which they practice. Consequently, U.S. banks and securities firms can operate Mexican subsidiaries and U.S. trucking firms can carry international cargo to Mexico.

The Asia/Pacific Rim is the most populous area and besides Japan has the most potential purchasing power for entertainment products. With twenty-one percent of the world's population China cannot be ignored by the world. Not only does this country have over a billion people but income is accelerating at a pace that could make China the world's largest economy by 2010. The Association of Southeast Asian Nations (ASEAN) is an agreement among Asian nations to eliminate tariffs and encourage trade among member nations. The ASEAN nations are Brunel, Indonesia, Malaysia, Singapore, Philippines and Thailand.

Another region that is significant in terms of populations is Africa, the second most populous continent. Africa/Middle East includes Egypt, Israel, Nigeria, Saudi Arabia, South Africa, Turkey and United Arab Emirates. Africa has great potential as a source of natural resources. It has laid the foundation for many types of music in the Black Diaspora with Lady Smith Black Mambazo of South Africa.

The nations of the former Soviet Union and its European allies have recently embraced capitalism. These Eastern European countries are Bulgaria, Czech Republic, Hungary, Poland, Romania, Russia and Slovakia. According to IFPI, in 2001 Russia's sales of music products increased seventeen percent.

Latin America and the Caribbean includes Argentina, Bolivia, Brazil, Chile, Colombia, Ecuador, Mexico, Paraguay, Peru, Uruguay, Venezuela, Virgin Islands, Cuba, Puerto Rico, Bahamas, Trinidad, Tobago and the Cayman Islands. These countries have lifted many restrictions on business and privatized many government enterprises. Government debt and inflation rates have declined, helping organizations become more competitive. Newly Privatized firms have boosted their financial performance making Latin America and the Caribbean an increasingly important export market for U.S. organizations. Over 40 percent of the goods imported by these countries come from the United States.

Music business students planning to do business in a foreign country should learn about the culture, which includes the belief, morals, laws, customs and their distinctive way of life. Cultural factors may indicate that changes in the marketing mix should be implemented in order to increase the acceptance of the product in foreign markets and to stimulate demand. Knowledge of and sensitivity to cultural differences apply not only to consumers but to the practices of businesses and business people. Music salespeople who want to follow proper etiquette in Asia should avoid joking around, wearing flashy clothes, giving lavish gifts and making physical contact except to shake an extended hand. In making buying decisions, Japanese business people tend to place more importance on their relationship with the merchandiser than with the product's affordability, usability and technical features.

Their relationship with the merchandiser has impact on other relationships. A female entertainment lawyer negotiating a record deal in Japan ran into difficulty because the male label representative would not talk to her. When an American male

Chart 15-3

Examples of Cultural Differences that Could Cause Marketing Problems

Body Language
- Standing with your hands on your hips is a gesture of defiance in Indonesia.
- Carrying on a conversation with your hands in your pockets makes a poor impression in France, Belgium, Finland, and Sweden.
- When you shake your head from side to side, that means "yes" in Bulgaria and Sri Lanka.
- Crossing your legs to expose the sole of your shoe is really taboo in Muslim countries. In fact, to call a person a "shoe" is a deep insult.

Physical Contact
- Patting a child on the head is a grave offense in Thailand or Singapore, since the head is revered as the location of the soul.
- In an Oriental culture, touching another person is considered an invasion of privacy, while in southern European and Arabic countries it is a sign of warmth and friendship.

Promptness
- Be on time when invited for dinner in Denmark or in China.
- In Latin countries, your host or business associate would be surprised if you arrived at the appointed hour.

Eating and Cooking
- It is rude to leave anything on your plate when eating in Norway, Malaysia, or Singapore.
- In Egypt, it is rude not to leave something.
- In Italy and Spain, cooking is done with oil.
- In Germany and Great Britain, margarine and butter are used.

Other Social Customs
- In Sweden, nudity and sexual permissiveness are quite all right, but drinking is really frowned on.
- In Spain, there is a very negative attitude toward life insurance. By receiving insurance benefits, a wife feels that she is profiting from her husband's death.
- In Western European countries, many consumers still are reluctant to buy anything (other than a house) on credit. Even for an automobile, they will pay cash after having saved for some time.

Source: William J. Stanton, Michael J. Etzel, and Bruce J. Walker, *Fundamentals of Marketing*, 9th ed. (New York: McGraw-Hill, 1991), p. 536. (c)1991 by The McGraw-Hill Companies, Inc., and reproduced by permission of the authors.

record executive was summoned by her to lead in the negotiations talks resumed. Sensitivity and knowledge of other cultures will help alleviate problems when doing business throughout the world.

In analyzing foreign markets for entry a knowledge of the following is important: Economic environment, buying power, exchange rate, political environment, agreements on tariffs and trade, laws of host nations, language, demographics/lifestyle, age distribution of population, culture and buying behavior, socioeconomic status, bribery, human rights, technological and competitive environment. The analysis of the figure below indicates the overall stability of the foreign country desirous of business investments.

Chart 15-4

Environment	Analysis Issues
Economic	• Stage of development • Buying power of consumers • Type of currency; exchange rates
Political and legal	• Political stability • Laws limiting international trade • Laws of host nations • General Agreement on Tariffs and Trade (GATT)
Social	• Cultural influences on buying behavior • Language differences • Population sizes and distribution • Socioeconomic status • Impact of marketing on the culture • Ethical considerations such as bribery and human rights
Natural	• Resources available • Impact of marketing on natural resources
Technological	• Levels of technological development • Available infrastructure
Competitive	• Degree of government involvement in competition • Ownership of competitors-local, foreign, or government

Source: Betty Jane Punnett and David A. Ricks, *International Business*, 2nd ed., (Blackwell Business). (c)1997 by Betty Jane Punnett and David A. Ricks. Reprinted by permission of the publisher.

World retail sales of recorded music (audio and video) fell by 0.4% in units and by 1.3% in value, totalling $US 33.6 billion in 2004. Music on audio formats fell by 2.6% in value, while DVD music video increased by 23.2%. Sales of CD albums dropped 0.9% in value with singles and cassettes values down 15.6% and 36% respectively.

Overview

This is the best year-on-year result achieved by the industry for five years. It reflects some positive factors including economic recovery, strong repertoire and progress in the online and mobile sectors. Including digital sales, the recorded music market would have been flat.

However, the trends vary markedly between different regions and countries. The U.S. and UK saw growth in CD sales, while in Canada, Germany and Japan the rate of long-term decline slowed very significantly. France, Spain and Sweden saw steep market falls linked to internet piracy and slow retail sales generally. Australia, Italy and Netherlands also saw falls, with DVD music video growth slowing down in these markets.

Sales Value up 2.2% in North America

The U.S. maintains a very large impact on world sales, with 36% of the global market in 2004. The U.S. saw a 2.6% growth in units and value. Sales at 'normal retail' rose 4.4% in units and 3.3% in value, but were tempered by sharp falls in direct and special markets (record club sales).

In the U.S., growth has come from a number of corners including a strengthening economy and successful releases. Music buyers have become aware of the decrease

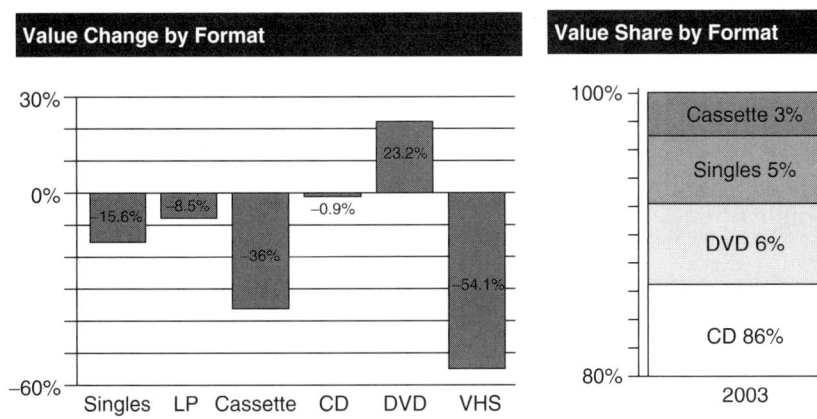

Taken from www.ifpi.org.

in retail prices as well as the increasing amount of value-added on products, including extra tracks, bonus DVDs and web-based content.

There is also a positive correlation between music consumers with digital music players and DVD players and increased CD buying, suggesting that these technologies may actually be driving CD purchasing along with DVD music video and digital tracks. Sales of the top ten albums have significantly improved in the U.S. too. Nielsen SoundScan data revealed the first climb in the combined sales of the top ten albums for three years along with a 3% increase in sales of new release albums. Catalogue albums saw an even bigger volume increase of 5%.

In the Canadian market there are signs of recovery, with the market growing 2.9% in units but falling 4.7% in value. Strong releases such as Shania Twain, Eminem, Green Day, U2 and Usher—as well as the success of several French Canadian acts—helped CD volume sales rise 3.2%. These were offset by falling retail prices, discounting and a steep drop in record club sales. Like the U.S., Canada saw better sales of top-selling repertoire—sales of the top 10 albums in 2004 were up 3% on 2003.

Slower Decline in Germany and Japan

Sales in Germany fell 4.2% in value, the most modest sales decline in three years. The slowing rate of decline reflects more optimism in the German market, fuelled by the continuing success of DVD music video and a decline in illegal downloading. The CD burning phenomenon that so sharply affected the German market over the past four years also appears to have peaked. The number of CDs burned by consumers in 2004 stayed roughly equal to that in 2003 at 327 million, though this is still more than twice the number of CD albums sold.

Sales in Japan fell 1.8% in value, a marked improvement on recent years, reflecting greater optimism and a steadily increasing number of artists signed and albums released. Japan has seen long-term decline suffering from general economic downturn, a huge growth in CDR burning and digital piracy. The market has taken time to adjust. It was previously more geared to the under 20's consumer than any other market in the world, with this group making up two-thirds of CDs sales back in 1998. That population has both fallen and turned sharply towards other entertainment, especially mobile phones.

Declines in Continental Europe and Asia/Pacific

In continental Europe, Czech Republic, Finland, France, Portugal, Spain and Sweden all saw double-digit market declines while Austria, Italy and Netherlands also dropped significantly.

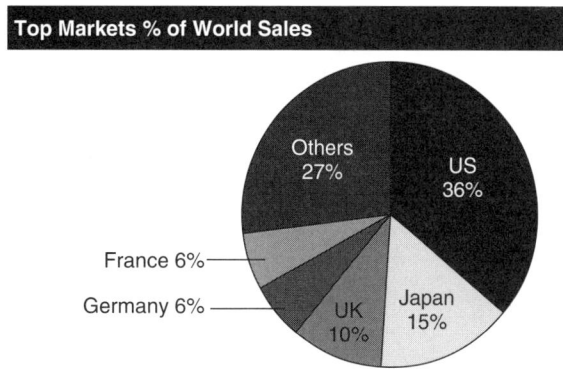

The French market fell for the second consecutive year in 2004 by 14.8%. This two-year decline follows a period of strong growth driven by local repertoire. Internet piracy has had a significant impact, correlated with rapidly rising household broadband penetration, which increased from 7% in 2002 to 20% in 2004. But it is not yet clear if the fall in the French market is temporary or the start of longer-term decline, since most of the 2004 value drop took place in the first half.

In Asia, Hong Kong, Philippines, Singapore and South Korea fell steeply. Sales have been affected by a combination of physical and internet piracy. Internet piracy is markedly having an impact on South Korea and Hong Kong. Economic difficulties and competition from other entertainment sectors have also played a part in declining sales in these markets.

China is a notable exception to the trend, showing continued growth with the market up 6.8% in units and value. Despite being the largest market in Asia after Japan, China still lags on a per-capita basis. Accession to the WTO and encouraging reforms to copyright law should stimulate further growth in the legitimate music sector.

A positive development in Asia during 2004 was the expansion of the music-to-mobile market. South Korea has established a sizeable 'ringback' tones business, while master recording ringtones have become extremely popular in Japan and increasingly in China. With the roll-out of 3G and the marketing of more advanced handsets, mobile will account for a growing share of music sales in the region.

Australia saw a 6.1% value decline in 2004 following a year of strong growth. An increasingly competitive entertainment retail environment and a significant growth in the uptake of broadband, enabling illegal downloading, were the main factors affecting sales. CD volume sales were down 5%, largely a result of a decline in the top sellers, with the top 50 album sales falling by 6%. DVD music video fell for the first time by 7%. However the format is still a source of growth and an area of focus for record companies.

Top 10 Markets Retail Value

Country	$US Million	% Change
U.S.	12,153	2.6%
Japan	5,168	−1.8%
UK	3,509	−1.6%
Germany	2,149	−4.2%
France	1,979	−14.8%
Australia	717	−6.1%
Canada	694	−4.7%
Italy	652	−7.9%
Spain	573	−12.5%
Netherlands	508	−7.4%
Top 10 Total	28,102	−1.9%
Top 10% of World	83.6%	

2004 Regional Summary

Region	Unit Change	Value Change	$US Billion
World	−0.4%	−1.3%	33.6
North America	2.6%	2.2%	12.8
Europe	−1.6%	−5.4%	12.3
EU	−3.1%	−6.6%	11.2
Asia	−3.7%	−1.8%	6.2
Asia (excl. Japan)	−4.9%	−2.0%	1.1
Latin America	9.2%	12.6%	1.0
Australasia	−5.8%	−6.2%	0.8
Middle East	−13.3%	−0.7%	0.1

UK Market Stays Vibrant

Music sales in the UK grew in unit terms including record level CD album volumes for the second consecutive year. CD album sales in the UK reached 174.6 million, up 4.5%.

The strength of UK market can be best explained by the vast amount of choice available to consumers—what to buy, where to buy, the price paid and places to hear new music. The UK releases 26,000 albums a year, increasing each year since 1998. Only the U.S. releases more records (around 33,000 per year). Value-added products have also increased, stimulating the market. In 2004, 12 albums with value-added material appeared in the top 20 during the week prior Christmas. CD album prices have fallen from an average of £10.90 in Q2 2001 to £9.50 Q4 2004.

Music retailing is also thriving in the UK. While supermarkets and internet retailers have increased their respective market shares, music specialists such as HMV and Virgin have also done well. Recent entrants such as Fopp and Music Zone have been phenomenally successful offering a well-targeted selection of music at competitive price points. Both plan to expand.

The UK media (TV, radio and print) has also played an important role in driving sales. In particular, the UK live music festival scene has contributed to the overall strength of the business. For example sales of UK signed acts Scissor Sisters and Keane increased by 50% and 30% respectively the week following their performances at Glastonbury.

Top repertoire in UK is also thriving with the top 10 album titles generating an extra million units compared to 2003. In 2004, 13 of the top 20 best-selling albums were from UK acts.

Recovery in Latin America

Latin American music sales benefited from economic recovery, increased efforts against piracy and the success of DVD music video sales, all of which contributed to a strong recovery in 2004. The region grew 9.2% in units and 12.6% in value. Most markets experienced growth in value terms. Commercial piracy is however still a huge problem in the region, reaching levels above 50% in every country.

The Brazilian market grew by 16.8% in value, overtaking Mexico as the biggest market in the region. Growth in Brazil was mostly driven by the success of DVD music video, which grew by 104% in value and now accounts for 26% of the total market. DVD music videos now account for over one in ten of all music releases in Brazil. The best-selling DVD, by local act Ivete Sangalo, sold more than 300,000 copies—this compares with 540,000 units for the best-selling album. Economic growth and retail sector recovery also contributed to 2004 results.

Major Markets Single Track Downloads 2004 (million)

US	142.6
Germany	7.5
UK	5.7
France	1.5
Total	157.3

Note: figures exclude albums and bundle downloads.
Sales including these were over 200 million

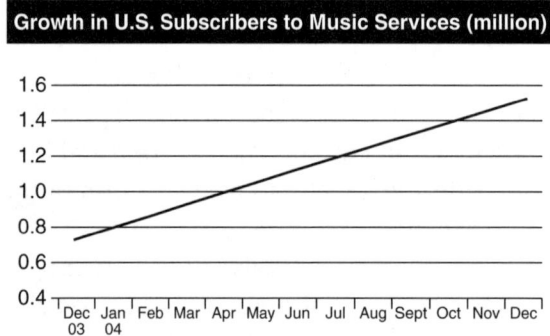

Growth in U.S. Subscribers to Music Services (million)

Source: Rhapsody, Napster, MusicNet, MusicMatch, eMusic
(public announcements)

Sales in Mexico grew 8.7% in value, attributable partly to a reduction in discounted product sales. Increased sales were driven by positive economic indicators coupled with strong releases of high-profile acts such as Luis Miguel, Alejandro Fernandez, Intocables and Paulina Rubio and strong sales of local repertoire by independent companies.

The Argentine market was badly hit by economic crisis in during 2000-2002. Recovery began in 2003 and continued in 2004 with a market growth of 33.5% in value. CDs account for 90% of sales, and although DVD sales grew, player penetration is still low at less than 5% of households.

Digital Sales Growing Sharply

Digital sales grew exponentially in 2004 with a number of key service launches and increased consumer uptake of legitimate services such as iTunes, Napster and popular national music sites. The number of digital services around the world increased four-fold in 2004 to 230, with over 150 services available in Europe alone. Music catalogues available also grew steadily, doubling to over one million tracks on the main services.

The U.S. remains the global leader in digital download sales, with over 142.6 million tracks purchased in 2004 according to Nielsen SoundScan and growth continuing strong into 2005. Downloaded tracks in the U.S. in the first two months of 2005 reached 43.9 million, more than double the 16.7 million during the same period in 2004. Sales in the top three European markets—UK, Germany and France—totalled some 15 million tracks in 2004—up from practically zero a year earlier.

Music subscription services are also growing in popularity. Paying subscribers for the major services totalled over 1.5 million in 2004—most of those in the U.S. but with growing uptake in the UK as well. The launch of Virgin Digital in the U.S. and an expanded marketing campaign by Napster in the beginning of 2005 will help to drive sales and subscriber numbers up. IFPI published its Digital Music Report in January 2005, providing comprehensive information and analysis on the digital music market in 2004 (available at www.ifpi.org).

DVD Music Video Still Growing Strongly

DVD music video grew by 24% in units and 23.2% in value globally, with big variations between countries and regions. The format is still going strong and has doubled its share of value in two years, from 4% of sales in 2002 to 8% in 2004, with global sales worth $US 2.6 billion.

The biggest selling DVD titles in 2004 were Live Aid, Britney Spears 'Greatest Hits' and Beyonce Knowles 'Live At Wembley', Queen 'Queen On Fire: Live At The Bowl', and U2 'Go Home: Live From Slane Castle'.

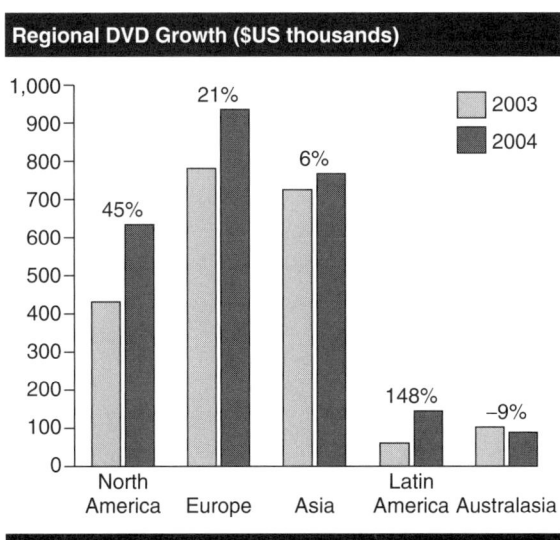

Top 10 DVD Music Video Markets

Country	$US Million	Growth 2003/04	DVD as % Market	% Global DVD Sales
Japan	589.8	6%	11%	23%
U.S.	561.0	52%	5%	22%
Germany	196.7	14%	9%	8%
France	185.4	8%	9%	7%
UK	181.5	37%	5%	7%
Netherlands	113.0	8%	22%	4%
Brazil	96.1	104%	26%	4%
Australia	78.8	−7%	11%	3%
Canada	70.9	5%	10%	3%
Spain	50.4	72%	9%	2%

Top 10 Markets Non-CD Formats ($US million)

Cassette		LP		VHS	
Turkey	88.1	Japan	22.6	U.S.	45.5
India	80.3	U.S.	19.3	Germany	12.4
Russia	79.9	UK	15.0	Japan	6.0
Indonesia	57.8	Germany	10.1	Canada	2.3
Germany	43.1	Netherlands	2.6	Taiwan	1.8
China	30.1	France	1.9	Spain	1.5
Japan	29.0	Austria	1.6	Russia	1.0
U.S.	23.7	Switzerland	1.1	South Africa	0.7
South Africa	22.8	Russia	0.7	Czech Republic	0.4
Saudi Arabia	21.1	Australia	0.5	Australia	0.4
Others	156.6	Others	1.8	Others	3.3
Total	632.6	Total	77.2	Total	75.1

Key Artists with Major Releases in 2005

50 Cent	Jennifer Lopez
Backstreet Boys	Justin Timberlake
Beck	Mariah Carey
Black Eyed Peas	Paul McCartney
Bruce Springsteen	Red Hot Chili Peppers
Christina Aguilera	Robbie Williams
Coldplay	Scissor Sisters
David Gray	Shakira
Faith Evans	Stevie Wonder
Franz Ferdinand	The White Stripes
Gorillaz	Utada Hikaru

Top 50 Albums of 2004 Based on Worldwide Units Sold

	Artist	Title	Company
1	Usher	Confessions	Sony BMG
2	Norah Jones	Feels Like Home	EMI
3	Eminem	Encore	Universal
4	U2	How To Dismantle An Atomic Bomb	Universal
5	Avril Lavigne	Under My Skin	Sony BMG
6	Robbie Williams	Greatest Hits	EMI
7	Shania Twain	Greatest Hits	Universal
8	Destiny's Child	Destiny Fulfilled	Sony BMG
9	Guns N' Roses	Greatest Hits	Universal
10	Maroon 5	Songs About Jane	Sony BMG
11	Green Day	American Idiot	Warner
12	Black Eyed Peas	Elephunk	Universal
13	Britney Spears	Greatest Hits: My Prerogative	Sony BMG
14	Gretchen Wilson	Here For The Party	Sony BMG
15	Anastacia	Anastacia	Sony BMG
16	Nelly	Suit	Universal
17	Ashlee Simpson	Autobiography	Universal
18	D-12	D-12 World	Universal

(continued)

Top 50 Albums of 2004 Based on Worldwide Units Sold (*continued*)

	Artist	Title	Company
19	Utada Hikaru	Utada Hikaru Single Collection Vol. 1	EMI
20	Kenny Chesney	When The Sun Goes Down	Sony BMG
21	Kanye West	College Dropout	Universal
22	Keane	Hopes And Fears	Universal
23	Various Artists	Now 17	EMI
24	Ray Charles	Genius Loves Company	Hear/Concord/EMI
25	OutKast	Speakerboxxx/The Love Below	Sony BMG
26	Various Artists	Now 16	Universal
27	Rod Stewart	Stardust . . . The Great American Songbook III	Sony BMG
28	Tim McGraw	Live Like You Were Dying	Curb/Warner/Sony BMG/EMI
29	Jay-Z/ Linkin Park	MTV Ultimate Mash-Ups Presents . . .	Warner
30	Norah Jones	Come Away With Me	EMI
31	George Strait	50 #1's	Universal
32	Josh Groban	Closer	Warner
33	Toby Keith	Greatest Hits 2	Universal
34	Hoobastank	The Reason	Universal
35	Jessica Simpson	In This Skin	Sony BMG
36	Gwen Stefani	Love Angel Music Baby	Universal
37	Velvet Revolver	Contraband	Sony BMG
38	George Michael	Patience	Sony BMG
39	Joss Stone	The Soul Sessions	EMI
40	Scissor Sisters	Scissor Sisters	Universal
41	Various Artists	Now 15	EMI
42	Jay Chou	Common Jasmine Orange	Sony BMG
43	Evanescence	Fallen	Sony BMG
44	Big & Rich	Horse of a Different Color	Warner
45	Nelly	Sweat	Universal
46	Twista	Kamikaze	Warner
47	Diana Krall	The Girl In The Other Room	Universal
48	R. Kelly	Happy People/U Saved Me	Sony BMG
49	Alicia Keys	The Diary Of Alicia Keys	Sony BMG
50	Joss Stone	Mind, Body & Soul	EMI

2004 World Sales—Retail

Country	Units				Retail Value			% Change	
	Singles	CDs	DVD	Total Units	USD (2004 rates)	Local Currency		Units	Local Currency
Canada	0.5	54.8	4.8	60.2	693.8	CAD	901.9	2.9%	−4.7%
USA	6.6	767.0	29.0	809.7	12,153.4	USD	12,153.4	2.6%	2.6%
TOTAL	13.0	799.1	21.5	848.1	12,575.9				
Europe									
Austria	1.6	9.7	0.6	11.0	288.6	EUR	233.8	−8.7%	−6.9%
Belgium	3.5	15.6	1.6	18.5	275.1	EUR	222.8	18.6%	−0.2%
Bulgaria	neg	0.4	0.03	0.9	5.2	BGL	8.2	−23.3%	−20.7%
Croatia	–	2.6	0.02	2.8	17.9	HRK	108.4	47.4%	−7.7%
Czech Republic	0.03	3.3	0.2	4.0	39.6	CSK	1,018.3	−8.2%	−11.0%
Denmark	0.2	9.7	0.4	10.2	187.4	DKK	1,122.7	−0.9%	−3.7%
Estonia	0.005	0.8	–	0.9	11.5	EEK	145.0	−7.0%	64.7%
Finland	0.4	9.0	0.3	9.6	133.6	EUR	108.2	−12.9%	−13.5%
France	24.3	106.4	9.0	126.6	1,979.3	EUR	1,603.3	−9.1%	−14.8%
Germany	23.5	146.6	11.5	181.3	2,149.0	EUR	1,740.7	−1.4%	−4.2%
Greece	0.6	6.9	0.3	7.6	89.3	EUR	72.4	7.2%	−5.7%
Hungary	0.04	5.4	0.2	7.6	59.1	HUF	11,973.5	48.9%	−18.4%
Iceland	–	–	–	–	–	ISK	–	Not Comparable	
Ireland	0.8	7.8	0.5	8.6	145.8	EUR	118.1	5.2%	2.7%
Italy	1.4	33.1	2.0	37.8	652.5	EUR	528.5	−11.7%	−7.9%
Latvia	0.001	0.3	0.001	0.6	4.4	LVL	2.4	−23.8%	−41.0%
Netherlands	2.7	23.2	5.3	29.9	507.7	EUR	411.3	−4.2%	−7.4%
Norway	0.9	12.4	0.3	13.1	273.8	NOK	1,845.2	6.4%	1.9%
Poland	0.1	10.5	0.6	12.3	92.0	PLZ	335.8	−1.5%	−4.8%
Portugal	1.9	9.4	0.8	12.6	127.3	EUR	103.1	−9.5%	−22.1%
Romania	–	–	–	–	–	ROL	–	Not Comparable	
Russia	0.1	58.0	0.2	118.9	490.8	RUB	14,141.2	2.9%	41.3%
Slovakia	–	–	–	–	–	SKK	–	Not Comparable	
Slovenia	–	–	–	–	–	SIT	–	Not Comparable	
Spain	1.3	34.0	3.5	38.4	572.8	EUR	463.9	−17.1%	−12.5%
Sweden	1.4	16.6	0.8	18.1	267.9	SEK	1,969.1	−13.9%	−17.5%
Switzerland	1.8	18.2	0.7	20.4	258.8	CHF	320.9	−1.0%	−7.2%
Turkey	–	14.6	–	43.5	166.2	TRL	240,737,308.5	22.0%	10.5%
UK	31.4	174.6	7.7	194.1	3,508.7	GBP	1,929.8	3.0%	−1.6%
Ukraine	0.03	7.1	0.02	15.4	41.7	UAH	221.7	−12.3%	−1.1%
TOTAL	120.4	726.8	35.1	980.1	13,122.6				
Asia									
China	–	52.0	42.3	123.6	211.8	CNY	1,754.0	6.8%	6.8%
Hong Kong	0.01	6.1	0.6	6.8	81.1	HKD	631.6	−15.4%	−12.5%
India	–	26.2	–	130.2	152.5	INR	6,913.1	−14.9%	2.7%
Indonesia	–	4.6	1.2	39.8	85.4	IDR	763,639.1	6.6%	14.8%
Japan	81.3	201.3	20.3	255.6	5,167.8	JPY	559.108.3	−1.7%	−1.8%

(continued)

2004 World Sales—Retail (*continued*)

Country	Units				Retail Value			% Change	
	Singles	CDs	DVD	Total Units	USD (2004 rates)		Local Currency	Units	Local Currency
Asia (*continued*)									
Malaysia	0.001	2.8	0.7	6.1	32.3	MYR	122.6	13.0%	−1.0%
Pakistan	-	12.3	0.2	40.1	23.5	PKR	1,412.2	5.3%	1.4%
Philippines	0.1	3.9	0.8	6.3	24.9	PHP	1,393.4	−9.5%	−8.1%
Singapore	0.02	4.0	0.2	4.2	45.6	SGD	77.1	−12.3%	−9.6%
South Korea	0.07	11.5	0.1	14.2	132.8	KRW	152,041.3	−28.4%	−21.4%
Taiwan	0.3	14.9	0.7	15.9	142.5	TWD	4,768.1	−1.8%	−1.1%
Thailand	-	11.8	15.6	35.2	140.7	THB	5,657.4	−9.5%	4.8%
TOTAL	81.7	351.5	82.7	678.0	6,240.9				
Latin America									
Argentina	0.01	12.4	0.4	13.4	83.9	ARP	244.9	18.0%	33.5%
Brazil	0.004	51.5	7.6	66.0	374.2	BRL	1,096.3	18.4%	16.8%
Central America	–	3.0	0.2	3.4	21.2	USD	21.2	61.4%	−7.2%
Chile	0.1	4.0	0.5	4.8	37.5	CLP	22,843.0	−15.5%	−9.1%
Colombia	0.007	5.6	0.3	5.9	48.5	COP	127,459.2	−14.7%	−7.6%
Ecuador	–	0.5	0.04	0.5	4.9	ECS	122,255.0	−57.0%	−31.7%
Mexico	0.3	53.2	1.6	56.3	360.0	MXP	4,063.9	−1.0%	8.7%
Paraguay	–	0.4	0.001	0.4	1.9	PYG	11,180.8	245.8%	178.5%
Peru	–	0.4	0.02	0.9	3.6	PEN	12.4	38.9%	52.9%
Uruguay	neg	0.4	0.02	0.4	4.6	UYP	132.9	68.4%	58.0%
Venezuela	–	2.6	0.06	2.7	15.9	VEB	29,985.2	263.1%	239.1%
TOTAL	0.5	134.0	10.7	155.0	956.0				
Australasia									
Australia	9.6	39.5	4.5	47.6	716.7	AUD	974.7	−6.1%	−6.1%
New Zealand	0.7	6.7	0.5	7.5	116.8	NZD	176.3	−4.3%	−7.4%
TOTAL	10.3	46.2	5.1	55.1	833.5				
Middle East									
Bahrain	–	0.1	–	0.6	3.5	BHD	1.3	−14.1%	−7.9%
Egypt	–	0.4	–	6.1	11.1	EGP	68.7	−27.6%	−18.2%
Israel	–	5.7	0.2	5.9	44.8	ILS	200.6	−4.2%	6.3%
Kuwait	–	0.2	–	1.7	8.6	KWD	2.5	−11.3%	−1.7%
Lebanon	–	0.4	–	1.1	6.8	LBP	10,307.1	−11.3%	7.5%
Oman	–	0.07	–	0.7	3.1	OMR	1.2	−1.9%	0.0%
Qatar	–	0.1	–	0.8	3.7	QAR	13.6	−9.3%	0.6%
Saudi Arabia	–	0.4	–	6.6	27.0	SAR	101.1	−5.6%	−3.9%
UAE	–	1.4	–	3.9	28.4	AED	104.3	−14.6%	−0.7%
TOTAL		8.8	0.2	27.3	137.1				
Africa									
South Africa	0.06	15.5	0.9	22.1	236.5	ZAR	1,527.9	22.1%	26.0%
Zimbabwe	–	0.2	0.005	3.6	16.5	ZWD	74,345.5	Not Comparable	
TOTAL	0.06	15.7	0.9	25.7	253.0				
GRAND TOTAL	197.8	2,114.2	179.7	2,755.7	33,613.6				

2003 World Sales—Retail

Country	Units				Retail Value			% Change	
	Singles	CDs	DVD	Total Units	USD (2004 rates)	Local Currency		Units	Local Currency
North America									
Canada	0.9	53.1	4.0	58.6	728.0	CAD	946.4	−4.2%	−2.9%
USA	12.1	746.0	17.5	789.5	11,847.9	USD	11,847.9	−7.6%	−6.0%
TOTAL	13.0	799.1	21.5	848.1	12,575.9				
Austria	2.2	10.8	0.4	12.1	310.0	EUR	251.1	−1.1%	−5.9%
Belgium	5.0	13.0	0.8	15.6	275.5	EUR	223.2	−8.5%	−10.0%
Bulgaria	neg	0.4	0.02	1.2	6.5	BGL	10.3	−32.5%	−21.7%
Croatia	0.002	1.5	0.02	1.9	19.5	HRK	117.5	37.9%	43.4%
Czech Republic	0.01	3.4	0.1	4.3	44.5	CSK	1,144.3	−5.5%	−2.5%
Denmark	0.4	9.8	0.2	10.3	194.6	DKK	1,165.8	−14.6%	−12.5%
Estonia	0.001	0.7	0.008	0.9	7.0	EEK	88.1	−34.5%	−23.8%
Finland	0.6	10.4	0.3	11.0	154.6	EUR	125.2	7.2%	2.8%
France	30.9	117.9	6.9	139.3	2,323.5	EUR	1,882.1	−9.1%	−14.4%
Germany	26.8	146.8	9.0	183.9	2,242.0	EUR	1,816.0	−14.5%	−17.9%
Greece	0.7	6.5	0.2	7.1	94.8	EUR	76.7	−5.7%	−10.0%
Hungary	0.06	3.3	0.1	5.1	72.4	HUF	14,672.6	4.5%	6.0
Iceland	-	0.8	-	0.8	17.1	ISK	1,196.8	8.0%	10.2%
Ireland	1.5	7.2	0.1	8.1	141.9	EUR	115.0	−10.5%	−15.4%
Italy	2.8	36.2	1.3	42.7	708.3	EUR	573.7	−6.4%	−4.4%
Latvia	-	0.4	0.01	0.7	7.4	LVL	4.0	1.9%	8.2%
Netherlands	3.2	24.6	4.8	31.2	548.1	EUR	444.0	−1.8%	−5.1%
Norway	1.1	11.6	0.3	12.3	268.6	NOK	1,810.5	−10.8%	−9.7%
Poland	0.1	10.1	0.3	12.5	96.7	PLZ	352.8	−11.2%	−1.5%
Portugal	0.2	11.0	0.8	13.9	163.4	EUR	132.4	−8.7%	−15.5%
Romania	-	3.0	0.009	16.9	27.1	ROL	897,779.2	4.0%	11.4%
Russia	0.2	30.3	0.05	115.6	347.5	RUB	10,010.0	1.8%	23.7%
Slovakia	0.001	1.4	0.04	1.6	10.2	SKK	330.1	22.3%	3.6%
Slovenia	0.006	1.1	0.002	1.3	13.5	SIT	2,599.2	1.7%	−14.6%
Spain	3.8	42.4	1.5	46.3	654.7	EUR	530.3	−11.4%	−9.4%
Sweden	2.4	19.1	0.9	21.0	324.7	SEK	2,386.9	−13.5%	−14.7%
Switzerland	2.3	18.6	0.5	20.9	279.0	CHF	346.0	−12.2%	−12.3%
Turkey	-	10.6	-	35.7	150.4	TRL	217,871,753.0	27.9%	19.3%
UK	36.4	167.2	6.4	188.5	3,566.6	GBP	1,961.6	−0.5%	0.1%
Ukraine	0.02	6.8	0.009	17.5	42.2	UAH	224.3	3.3%	33.8%
TOTAL	120.4	726.8	35.1	980.1	13,122.6				
Asia									
China	-	34.3	39.5	115.7	198.3	CNY	1,642.1	36.4%	21.7%
Hong Kong	0.03	7.2	0.7	8.0	92.6	HKD	721.7	−7.6%	−6.7%
India	-	15.3	-	153.0	148.5	INR	6,728.5	−10.6%	−19.7%
Indonesia	-	2.6	1.1	37.3	74.4	IDR	665,422.9	8.9%	7.6%

(continued)

2004 World Sales—Retail (*continued*)

| Country | Units | | | | Retail Value | | | % Change | |
	Singles	CDs	DVD	Total Units	USD (2004 rates)	Local Currency		Units	Local Currency
Japan	86.5	205.8	18.2	260.2	5,261.0	JPY	569,183.5	−5.3%	−9.2%
Malaysia	0.002	2.2	0.4	5.4	32.6	MYR	123.9	1.9%	8.0%
Pakistan	-	1.9	0.1	38.1	23.2	PKR	1,393.2	Not Comparable	
Philippines	0.03	3.2	1.3	6.9	27.0	PHP	1,515.8	21.6%	4.8%
Singapore	0.6	4.4	0.2	4.8	50.5	SGD	85.3	−3.7%	−3.7%
South Korea	0.1	15.6	0.2	19.8	168.9	KRW	193,489.3	−31.4%	−30.2%
Taiwan	0.4	15.1	0.7	16.2	144.0	TWD	4,821.0	−16.2%	−13.8%
Thailand	-	9.1	15.6	38.9	134.2	THB	5,397.3	−12.2%	−3.5%
TOTAL	87.7	316.8	78.2	704.3	6,355.3				
Latin America									
Argentina	0.01	10.4	0.1	11.4	62.8	ARP	183.5	85.0%	77.7%
Brazil	0.007	52.4	3.3	55.8	320.5	BRL	939.0	−25.0%	−17.4%
Central America	0.02	2.0	0.02	2.1	22.8	USD	22.8	−31.9%	−19.4%
Chile	0.1	4.7	0.4	5.7	41.2	CLP	25,131.9	−21.6%	−18.5%
Colombia	0.004	6.7	0.09	7.0	52.5	COP	137,901.8	8.5%	−17.3%
Ecuador	-	0.9	0.01	1.2	7.2	ECS	178,917.8	72.8%	−22.3%
Mexico	0.3	53.5	-	56.9	331.2	MXP	3,738.7	3.4%	−16.2%
Paraguay	-	0.1	-	0.1	0.7	PYG	4,014.7	−52.5%	−24.0%
Peru	0.001	0.7	-	0.7	2.4	PEN	8.1	59.8%	4.2%
Uruguay	-	0.2	-	0.3	2.9	UYP	84.2	94.8%	100.1%
Venezuela	0.002	0.7	0.01	0.7	4.7	VEB	8,842.1	−64.8%	−52.9%
TOTAL	0.5	132.2	4.0	141.9	848.8				
Australasia									
Australia	10.0	41.6	5.1	50.7	763.0	AUD	1,037.6	9.7%	5.9%
New Zealand	0.7	6.9	0.6	7.8	126.0	NZD	190.3	−5.7%	−3.6%
TOTAL	10.6	48.5	5.7	58.5	889.0				
Middle East									
Bahrain	-	0.1	-	0.8	3.8	BHD	1.5	−8.4%	−2.0%
Egypt	-	0.09	-	8.4	13.5	EGP	84.0	−27.1%	−27.3%
Israel	-	6.0	0.1	6.2	42.1	ILS	188.6	Not Comparable	
Kuwait	-	0.1	-	1.9	8.8	KWD	2.5	−4.5%	6.9%
Lebanon	-	0.3	-	1.2	6.4	LBP	9,585.6	−17.9%	−12.5%
Oman	-	0.06	-	0.7	3.1	OMR	1.2	−7.5%	−4.0%
Qatar	-	0.08	-	0.8	3.7	QAR	13.6	3.1%	5.1%
Saudi Arabia	-	0.4	-	7.0	28.0	SAR	105.1	−9.8%	−9.5%
UAE	-	1.2	-	4.5	28.6	AED	105.0	−5.1%	−3.1%
TOTAL	-	8.4	0.1	31.5	138.1				
Africa									
South Africa	0.2	11.5	0.4	18.1	187.8	ZAR	1,212.9	0.4%	0.1%
Zimbabwe	-	-	-	-	-	ZWD	-	Not Comparable	
TOTAL	0.2	11.5	0.4	18.1	187.8				
GRAND TOTAL	232.5	2,043.2	144.9	2,782.6	34,107.5				

Summary

Global marketing is the transaction of business activities whether movement of goods, services, capital, personnel, technology, information, data or the supervision and transfer of employees across international boundaries. The production and distribution of culture is concentrated within four major labels (Universal Music Group (UMG), SONY/BMG, EMI and WEA). This concentration results in an economic process called horizontal and vertical integration. The European Union, NAFTA and ASEAN are a few of the trade agreements between countries that contribute to the global economy. In penetrating foreign markets, knowledge of the political, legal, social, cultural, economic, competitive, technological, physical and business practices are necessary to do business in the host country. Cultural factors may indicate that changes in the marketing mix should be implemented in order to increase the acceptance of the product in markets and to stimulate demand. Global retail sales of recorded music (audio and video) decreased by 0.4% in units and by 1.3% in value, totaling $U.S. 33.6 billion in 2004. Music on audio decreased by 2.6% in value, while DVD music video increased by 23.2%. Sales of CD albums dropped 0.9% in value with singles and cassettes values down 15.6% and 36% respectively. Amazingly, this is the best year-on-year results achieved by the industry in the last five years. These trends indicate economic recovery for the industry, stronger repertoire and increases in online, mobile and digital sales.

Terms

Ad Valorem Tariffs: Tariffs levied according to the value of imported or exported goods.

Balance of Payments: Indicator of the economic health of a country, showing the net inflow or outflow of goods, services and money

Common Law Countries: Countries that have been under British influence who decide legal cases upon the bases of tradition and common practice as well as by interpretation of statues.

Common Market: Group of countries organized together to reduce internal trade barriers, establish a common external tariff, and provide a free flow of capital and labor among member countries.

Culture: Learned behavior that determines how members of a society will meet their needs and expectations.

Devaluation: An increase in the cost of converting one currency into another.

Developed Countries: High levels of economic development usually reflected in diversified economies and capital-intensive activity.

Direct Ownership: Involves an organization setting up new facilities or acquiring a foreign firm in the same line of business.

Environmental Analysis: The process of assessing the impact of uncontrollable factors such as economic conditions, business regulations, culture, demographics, technology or politics on demand and on the international firm's marketing strategy.

Exporting: Involves producing the product in the organization's own country, then shipping it to another country for sale.

Global Music Marketing: the performance of business activities that direct the flow of music product and services across international boundaries for the satisfaction of human needs and wants.

Hedging: A method of minimizing exposure to foreign exchange risk by purchasing a currency contract for a specified exchange rate.

IFPI: International Federation of Phonographic Industry (Association whose purpose is to gather statistical information worldwide on the global recording industry)

RIAA: Recording Industry Association of America (Association whose purpose is to gather statistical information on the American recording industry)

International Trade: The movement of goods and services between nations, classified as exports and imports by each country.

Joint Venture: A business arrangement in which two or more organizations share management of an enterprise

Exporting: Involves producing the product in the organization's own country, then shipping it to another country for sale.

Licensing: Granting another organization the rights to use a trademark, copyright, patented product or a process, for a fee.

Bibliography

Burnett, Robert *The Global Jukebox: The International Music Industry*, pp. 12-23, Routledge, 29 West 35th street, New York, N.Y., 1996

Stanton, William J., Etzel, Michael J. and Walker, Bruce J. *Fundamentals of Marketing*, 9th ed. (New York: McGraw-Hill, 1991) p. 536

Punnett, Betty Jane and Ricks, David A. Ricks. *International Business*, 2nd edition (Blackwell Business), 1997

National Music Publishers Association (NMPA), *News and Views*. Fall and Summer

International Federation of the Phonographic Industry (IFPI), The Recording Industry in Numbers (2002), London, England

The Recording Industry World Sales 2004 Report, Published by IFPI

The Recording Industry Interim Sales 2004 Report, Published by IFPI

The Recording Industry Piracy 2004 Report, Published by IFPI

Exercises

1. Give four reasons that foreign companies have purchased American record labels.

2. Explain horizontal and vertical integration and give music business examples for each.

3. Describe piracy and its affect on world markets.

4. What is the market share of each of the big four record labels?

Chapter 16
Other For-Profit Markets

Learning Objectives

After studying this chapter you should be able to:

1. Understand the role and responsibilities of a music publisher

2. Identify sources of income for music publishers and songwriters

3. Examine the role of music publishing as a profit center in the global music industry marketplace

4. Identify the role that clubs, TV offers, mail orders and premium sales play in the profitability of international music conglomerates like BMG-SONY, EMI, UNIVERSAL and WMG

5. Examine global piracy impact on revenues worldwide and effective measures of combating it with inter-governmental cooperation

While statistics indicate that nearly 80% of all recorded product is purchased from record stores or racked outlets, other profit centers can generate large revenue streams for major labels. These profit centers include record and tape clubs, TV offers, mail order, premium sales and publishing. One of the most profitable revenue stream for major labels is music publishing. In order to understand the intricacies of music publishing we must examine the role of the publisher. The role and responsibilities of a independent and record label publisher are:

1. Copyrighting musical compositions in the United States and abroad
2. Securing ancillary uses (stage, TV, film, recording etc) for songs in catalogue
3. Sub-distribution agreement for sheet music, folios, compilations and music books
4. Securing uses of songs for television and radio commercials
5. Suing infringers of musical compositions and negotiating settlements
6. Registration of songs with Harry Fox Agency, ASCAP, BMI, SESAC
7. Updating information regarding new technological innovations and copyright laws pertaining to its usage
8. Promoting new songs and writers
9. Negotiating fees and issuing licenses for all uses of music
10. Promoting legislation affecting music and copyright holders
11. Promoting interest in songs and writers through special projects
12. Keeping track of motion pictures, television shows, commercials and video projects in pre-production, production and post-production so that compatible songs can be submitted to producers
13. Secure commercially released recordings, CD and tapes of songs publisher controls
14. Financing and production of "demo tapes" of a writer's new composition
15. Administration of copyrights by registering, filing, auditing, bookkeeping, negotiating licenses and collecting revenue
16. Foreign promotion of catalogue and collection of royalties

Listed below are four different types of music publishing companies that are affiliated with the recording of prerecorded music products:

1. Major music publishing company and record label affiliated with an international entertainment conglomerate such as EMI of UK,

Sony BMG, Universal Music Group, EMI of the UK and WEA of AOL-Time Warner, the only American owned entertainment conglomerate. These companies have worldwide sales with substantial revenues in other related industries such as book publishing, electronics, software, newspapers, magazines, cable outlets, television stations, film, radio stations; internet

2. Independent publishing companies, fully staffed, whose "administration" is handled by a major record/publishing company

3. Publishing companies not affiliated with a major but do own administration

4. Writer-publisher owned companies

Publishers as well as songwriters derive most of their income from the following sources:

Performance Royalties

The value of the music publisher's catalog is based on the quality of the songs, frequency and nature of their use and how they are licensed. Record labels receive at least 20% or more of their income from publishing and other profit centers. One of the largest sources of royalty income is performance rights payments from ASCAP, BMI or SESAC and other affiliated societies in foreign countries. The primary types of music use that generate performance royalties are feature broadcast performances, background music on television series, specials, films, movie of the week, TV theme songs, jingles, production company and network logos, non-broadcast live venue performances, copyrighted arrangements of public domain compositions and foreign performances of U.S. writer's and publisher's works. This income is commonly referred to as Performance Based Income.

Mechanical Royalties

The second largest source of income for record label publishers is from licensing the right to produce and distribute records, tapes, CD's for sale to the public. Record manufacturers (record labels etc) are required to obtain a mechanical license in order to produce and distribute records, CD's and tapes to the public. Publishers use the Harry Fox Agency, the mechanical collection arm of the National Music Publisher's Association to negotiate and issue the license, collect the royalties, charge a service fee of 4% and forward the balance to the publisher. Synchronization (music timed to synchronize with, or relate to the action on a screen) and Transcription (covers syndicated programs, Muzak, in-flight entertainment and music library services) licensing are other sources of income.

Revenues from phono-mechanicals, synchronization/transcription and private copying is refereed to as Reproduction Based income. It is royalties collected from record companies, and others, who reproduce copyrighted compositions for distribution to the public. Royalty collections are determined by the number of units sold in a particular medium.

Other sources of income for publishers are home video, commercials, Broadway musicals, Video Jukeboxes, Lyric reprints in novels or nonfiction books, lyric reprints in magazines, monthly song lyric and sheet music magazines, public service announcements, recordings of hit songs with changed lyrics, medleys, promotional videos, greeting cards, computer and board trivia games, television commercials for motion pictures, home video television programs, home video recording artists, foreign theatrical royalties, dolls and toys, television programs and motion pictures based on songs, books based on motion pictures (lyric reprints), books about a lyricist, novelty albums, lyrics on albums, cassettes and CD packages, sheet music and folios, television and motion picture background scores, lyrics and music on soda cans, lyrics on T-Shirts and posters, audio recordings of books, special products albums, televisions sale only albums, records, clubs, key outlet marketing albums, limited edition collectibles, musical telephones, singing fish, theme parks, karaoke booth, music boxes and internet.

Distribution based income would be derived from the sale of printed music and income from the rental and public lending of CD's and videocassettes.

Challenges Facing The Music Publisher

One of the challenges facing the music publishing industry will be it's ability to adapt to the evolution of the marketplace. Publishers recognize the immediate challenge posed by the sharp increase in the availability of unlicensed music. They must work with many societies in maintaining the integrity of the art form while meeting the needs of those seeking to operate legitimate businesses in the online world. Unlicensed usage is rampant in the international territories of the Asia-Pacific rim and Latin America. In North American and Europe the dominant form of unlicensed usage is unauthorized online downloads, fueling CD-R sales. The National Music Publishers Association (NMPA) & Harry Fox Agency Inc. has a listing of over eight hundred member publishers and is the largest music trade association representing these concerns and others.

When current copyright and trademark law was passed, the realities of the digital era were yet unknown. Music publishers and copyright owners are faced with unlicensed online music, payola, piracy, file-sharing, restaurant/bar exemptions, licensing of music streaming on the internet and the consolidation of the radio industry. Piracy is a serious threat because of file sharing and CD burning. The impact of file-sharing and CD burning impacted CD sales worldwide. According to the International Federation of Phonographic Institute (IFPI) total phonorecord sales were down in 2001 by 6% with decreases in the U.S. (4%), Canada (9.6%), Germany (9.2%), Italy (8.6%) and Japan (9.4%).

The 2001 music publishing revenue report is the final one published by the National Music Publishing Association. The reporting territories collected 6.6 billion in royalty payments in 2001. This represents a decrease of 4% from the music revenues of 2000, due in part to an extraordinary gain in 2000 from a successful lawsuit filed by the Harry Fox Agency against Sony and MP3. The 4% decline in publishing revenues compares with a decrease in formats and configuration sales of 55 to $33.7 billion in 2001 as reported by the International Federation of Phonographic Industry (IFPI). The music publishing revenues of the top five territories (U.S., Germany, Japan, U.K. and France) represent 71.3% of the overall total, down slightly from 71.6% in 2000. Revenue from the top ten territories (including Italy, Spain, Netherlands, Canada and Switzerland) accounted for 85.9% of the total in 2001, down slightly from 86.5% in 2000.

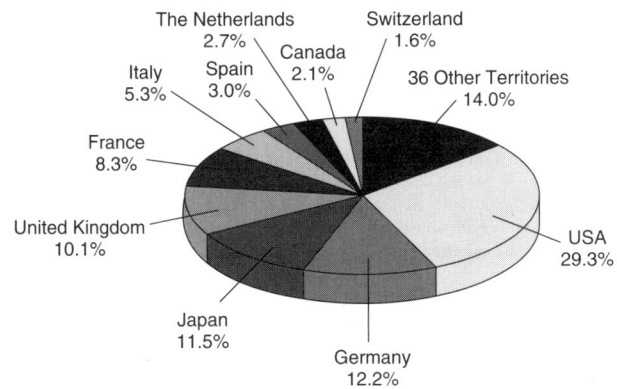

Music Publishing Revenues 1995–2001 (SM)*

1995	(57)	6,208.7	(+6.4%)
1996	(51)	6,224.5	(+0.3%)
1997	(53)	6,157.1	(−1.1%)
1998	(54)	6,440.3	(+4.6%)
1999	(53)	6,429.4	(+2.0%)
2000	(54)	6,877.3	(+6.7%)
2001	(46)	6,626.8	(−4%)

* The figures in parentheses in the second column are the number of reporting territories that year. The figures in parentheses in the fourth column are the percentage change from the previous year.

Note: 2001 figures reflect a lower amount due to an extraordinary gain resulting from settlements with MP3 and Sony.

Source for figures: NMPA International Survey

Figure 16-1
Categorization of Music Publishing Revenues

PERFORMANCE-BASED INCOME

Performance-based royalties consist mainly of those paid for the broadcast and public performance of copyrighted music, within a responding territory, regardless of the origin of the repertoire being performed. These royalties are principally collected by the major performing rights societies: ASCAP, BMI and SESAC in the U.S., for example; SACEM in France, BUMA in Holland, and PRS in the U.K.

RADIO:
In the U.S., performance societies use a system of "sampled" survey recordings or logs detailing what has been played at a local station during a defined period and/or statistical sampling, to create payment models for their member affiliates. Typically, the stations are authorized to use copyrighted musical compositions under blanket licensing agreements with the collective administrative societies.

RATES:
Royalty fees are calculated as a percentage of a station's annual advertising revenues, and distributed by a weighting process, as described earlier.

TELEVISION:
Television stations generally keep logs, or cue sheets, detailing the use and playtime of every musical composition aired. These cue sheets are forwarded to the collecting societies, which calculate payments according to usage and broadcast range (local or network).

RATES:
Like their radio counterparts, television broadcasts are covered typically by blanket licensing agreements between the copyright owners and the stations. The blanket fee is typically calculated as a modest percentage of the stations' annual gross advertising revenues.

CABLE/SATELLITE TRANSMISSIONS:
Cable and satellite TV transmissions are also licensed by the major performing rights societies, much the same way that broadcast TV is licensed. Rates are usually determined by size of the audience (transmission range) and usage.

LIVE PERFORMANCE AND RECORDED:
This category refers to recorded or live music played in a public place: nightclubs, bars, hotels, arenas, amusement parks, theaters, health clubs, etc.

RATES:
Typically, royalty fees are set according to the type of venue and whether the performance is of live or recorded music; a wide number of other variables also help determine fees. For example, for a nightclub, live performance royalties can be determined by the club's annual live entertainment costs, while in some countries, performing rights societies collect performance fees from theater exhibitors based on a percentage of box office receipts.

REPRODUCTION-BASED INCOME

Income in this category represents royalties collected from record companies, and others, who reproduce copyrighted compositions for distribution to the public. Royalty collections are determined by the number of units sold in a particular medium. The right of reproduction is typically an exclusive right provided under copyright laws subject to some variation as described below:

PHONO-MECHANICAL:
Phono-mechanical royalties refer to revenues paid to copyright owners of musical compositions for the "mechanical reproduction" of those compositions on sound recordings (audio tapes, compact discs, records and other media), which are distributed to the public for private use. For this type of activity, copyright laws around the world frequently devolve this right from an exclusive right to a mere "right of remuneration."

RATES:
Terms and conditions for the mechanical reproduction of musical compositions are frequently determined by collective bargaining between the music publishing and recording industries. Some countries, the U.S. among them, make legislative provision for so-called "statutory" mechanical rates.

Certain royalty rates are generally higher in Europe than in North America. In the U.S., the mechanical royalty rate is prescribed by legislation as a fixed-sum amount, or "penny rate."

In the vast majority of countries, however, the rates are periodically negotiated on a collective basis, and those rates are typically a percentage of the wholesale or retail selling price of the recording. These collected amounts are then distributed on a pro rata basis among the various compositions contained on the recording. The most commonly utilized agreement is known as the BIEM-IFPI contract, which is renegotiated every three years. More than 1000 record companies throughout the world are signatories to this agreement.

SYNCHRONIZATION:
Synchronization royalties are derived from the use of a musical composition in an audiovisual work, including: motion pictures, commercials, cable or broadcast television, satellite broadcast, video tapes, interactive media, etc. In these media, the musical composition is "synchronized" with the visual images which appear on the screen.

For the purposes of this survey, this category also includes transcription rights: the right to reproduce performances of a musical work in any type of electronic, magnetic or other non-phonogram recording for commercial purposes.

Also included in this category are so-called Broadcast Mechanical royalties. The legislatures and case laws in some countries provide for an additional collection of reproduction rates, on top of performance rates, when the performance takes place through a recorded sound carrier or phonogram (rather than as a live performance) which was originally licensed for private use only.

RATES:

Synchronization is one of the largest sources of income for copyright holders. Rates vary widely depending on a composition's usage and importance. In the U.S., rates for synchronization usage are not prescribed by statute, but are instead negotiated in a licensing agreement between the copyright owner and the producer and specify, among other things, the number of compositions, playing time, the type of production authorized, the geographic area of such use and the number of years covered by the license.

License fees for broadcast mechanical royalties are determined through blanket licensing agreements between broadcasters and societies representing copyright owners.

PRIVATE COPY:

While consumers in the U.S. are exempt from infringement liability for private, non-commercial home taping, under certain circumstances, songwriters and music publishers derive revenue from the payment of royalties by manufacturers and importers of digital audio recording hardware and blank digital media. Not every country represented in the survey employs a royalty (or levy) system, however. The majority of the world's countries does not provide remuneration schemes for "home copying."

RATES:

In the U.S., royalties are collected by the Copyright Office and segregated into two funds. One fund is for the persons who own or control the copyright in the musical work; the other is for the copyright owners of the sound recording and featured performing artists.

REPROGRAPHY:

These royalties are derived from the photocopying or other facsimile reproductions of musical compositions. As with home taping, the issue within a particular country is whether such "unauthorized" reproduction will affect the overall sales of the composition or printed work. In this country, the Fair Use Provisions of the U.S. Copyright Act permit consumers to make limited reproduction in certain prescribed contexts, such as scholarly use and criticism. Other countries take the view that, no matter how small or extensive the reproduction, unauthorized photocopying is a copyright infringement, and is therefore subject to a royalty payment.

RATES:

Fees are paid to collecting societies under the terms of various blanket licensing agreements with copy shops, libraries and other establishments, the theory being that much of the material being copied on these premises is copyrighted.

DISTRIBUTION-BASED INCOME:

Distribution income, as presented in this survey, includes the sale of printed music as well as the rental of sound recordings. The majority of countries participating in this survey did not report on such activities; however, NMPA will continue to broaden its coverage of this revenue category in subsequent editions of this publication.

SALE OF PRINTED MUSIC:

Printed music covers a very broad body of work, from simple popular tunes to full orchestral works; sale prices vary with the complexity of the work. These works may be published individually as sheet music, or in a wide variety of collections or folios. The works may be prepared, published and/or distributed by the original music publisher or its authorized (i.e., licensed) print agent.

RATES:

Licensing agreements are usually negotiated for a set period of time, typically one to five years. Royalty fees are negotiated between the copyright owner and the print agent, and are usually a percentage of the sales price of the score.

RENTAL (COMMERCIAL TRANSACTIONS) AND PUBLIC LENDING:

These royalties are derived from the commercial or public (from libraries and other nonprofit institutions) rental of copyrighted musical compositions, typically in the form of sound recordings. The rental may also (or instead) involve the hire of orchestral scores of printed music for group performance. Although the collection of the former is typically handled by collective administrative societies, the latter transactions are handled by those music publishing specialists who maintain their own rental libraries of symphonies, operas, ballets and the like.

RATES:

In the case of commercial rental of sound recordings, the royalty or administrative schemes are determined through collective bargaining among the various industry groups. The commercial rental of printed music is handled on a per-use basis, with royalty negotiations taking into consideration the performance audience and recording and/or broadcast applications.

MISC:

Here we present royalty collections reported by survey respondents which do not fit into any of the aforementioned enumerated categories.

CHART 2   TOTAL REVENUE BY TYPE OF ROYALTY INCOME

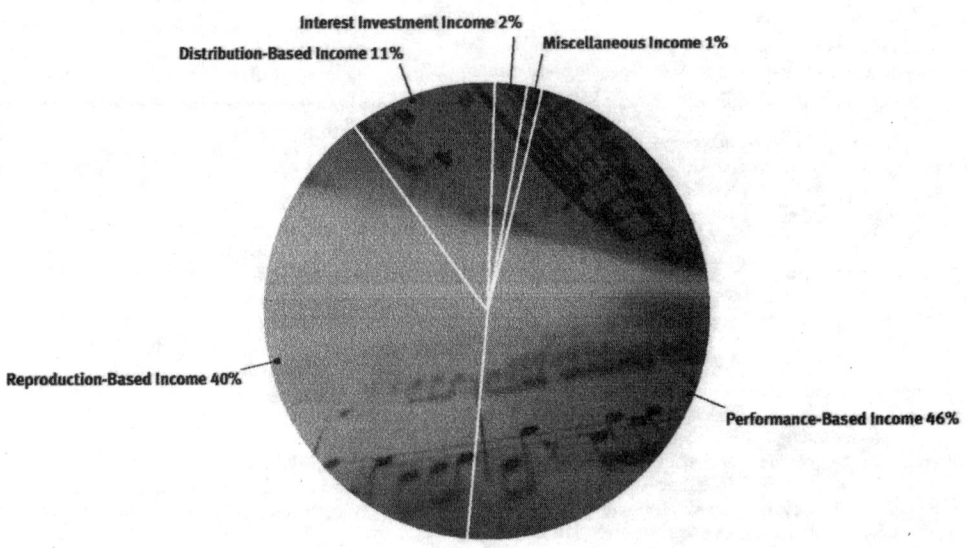

CHART 3   2000 MUSIC INDUSTRY ROYALTIES, THE LEADING COUNTRIES

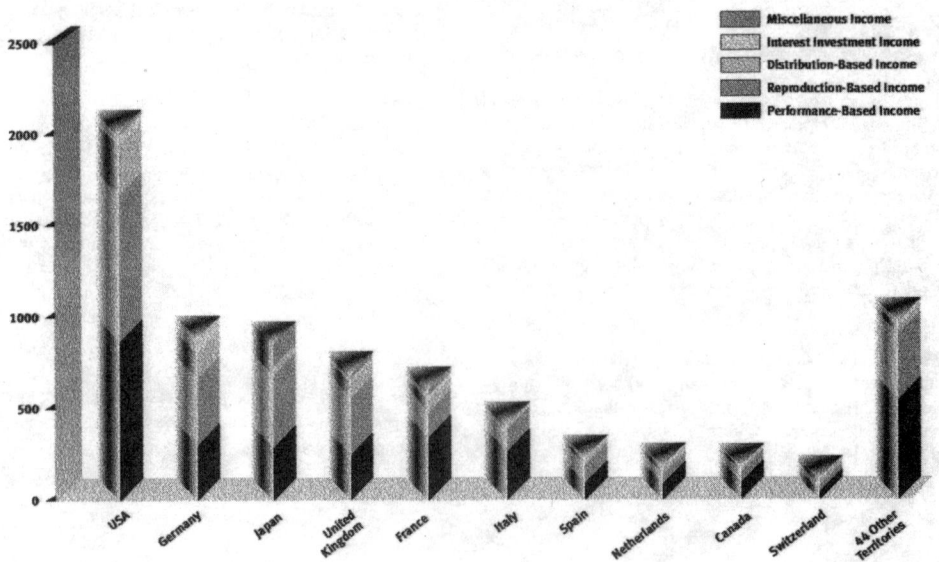

PERFORMANCE-BASED INCOME

The reported performance-based income in the world increased by 2.7% over 1999, to $3.08 billion. On a flat exchange rate, the sector recorded a 4.1% increase to $3.76 billion.

Within the performance sector, the reported income from live performance and the public performance of recorded music was the largest element, accounting for 42% of performance-based income. However, the live performance/performance of recorded music sub-sector declined in revenue by 3.4% in 2000, to $1.29 billion. Revenues from the use of music on television rose by 8%, to nearly $1.07 billion, while revenues from radio increased by 7% to $714 million.

Among the largest national markets for performance-based income, France moved up from fourth to second place, with 1999's second-largest territory, Japan, falling to fourth. Italy and the U.K. traded the fifth and sixth slots, while Canada and the Netherlands swapped the seventh and eighth positions and Spain and Argentina traded the ninth and tenth positions.

Twelve of the leading twenty markets saw the music publishing industry derive greater income from public performance than from reproduction. These were, by rank, France (where performance income was 53% of the total), Italy (73%), the Netherlands (42%), Canada (58%), Switzerland (47%), Argentina (65%), Belgium (67%), Sweden (45%), Denmark (52%), Poland (68%), Finland (63%), and Norway (59%). It is important to note that reproduction-based income figures for Brazil, the thirteenth ranked country in performance, were not available. It should also be noted that, for the first time, reproduction-based income from the U.S. and Germany (respectively, the first- and third-ranked countries in performance-based revenue) surpassed performance-based income.

In a number of territories, significant gains in performance income was reported. Canada posted a 22.7% increase over 1999 to $96.4 million; Belgium rose by 42.5% to nearly $60.3 million; and Greece increased by 59.4% to $19.5 million.

Other territories, however, saw decreases: Japan fell by 11.7% to $283.2 million, while the Netherlands declined 14.8% to $76.5 million and Argentina decreased by 10.9% to $66.6 million.

▼ *Continued on page 13*

CHART 5   PERFORMANCE-BASED INCOME   ($ MILLIONS)

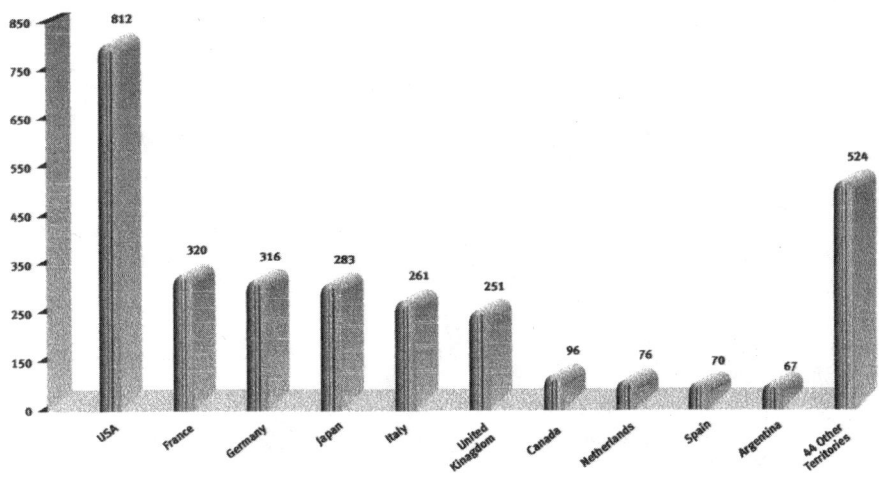

REPRODUCTION-BASED INCOME

In 2000, reproduction-based income totaled $2.74 billion, an increase of 4.1% over 1999. The rise reflects mild increases in the three main sub-sectors of reproduction-based income: phono-mechanicals, synchronization/transcription, and private copying.

Revenues from phono-mechanicals rose 5.8% to just under $2 billion, while revenues from synchronization rose 3% to $669.9 million. These totals reverse the downward trend in both sub-sectors in 1999, when phono-mechanicals declined by 1.5% and synchronization revenue fell by 13.5%. However, with the discouraging world record sales figures for 2001 released by IFPI, it is unlikely that the gains seen in 2000 will be repeated.

Revenues from private copying also rose, up 5.2 % in 2000 to $72 million. Private copying accounted for 2.6% of reproduction-based income, duplicating its share of 1999's revenue. Synchronization accounted for 24.5%

(compared with 25% in 1999) and phono-mechanical royalties 72.8% (compared with 72%).

There were few significant changes in the rates of phono-mechanical royalties paid across the world in 2000. In Continental Europe, the rate was 9.009% of Published Price to Dealers (PPD), although this was subject to various discounts negotiated at the national level. In most of Latin America, the figure was between 8% and 8.5% of PPD; Mexico's rate sets 8% of PPD for cassettes but 7.5% of PPD for CDs. Several countries in Southeast Asia (including Hong Kong, South Korea and Singapore) use a percentage of retail-selling price (RSP), with the adjusted retail price (ARP) in Japan rising from a 5.6% rate to 6%. Taiwan uses a combination of 5.4% of PPD and 6.25% of RSP. Turkey moved away from the 9.009% PPD rate to an 8% of a negotiated or deemed PPD, while Egypt changed from 6.4% of RSP to 9.35% of RSP less a 20% deduction. The United States and Canada are the only countries where the rate is calculated in cents per track rather than as a percentage of the price.

The table giving details of the Mechanical Royalty Rates for the 2000 Survey Period lists is on page 15.

Among the largest national markets for reproduction-based income, Australia/New Zealand, which had placed sixth in 1999, fell to ninth in 2000. Spain and Italy both moved up one slot, to sixth and seventh respectively, while the Netherlands, which had been twelfth, moved to the eighth slot, followed by Mexico, which in 1999 placed eleventh. Canada and Belgium, which respectively placed ninth and tenth in the 1999 survey, finished eleventh and twelfth in 2000.

DISTRIBUTION-BASED INCOME

Sales of printed music and income from the rental and public lending of CDs and videocassettes increased by 4.8% in 2000 to $768.78 million. The sector accounts for about 11 % of the world publishing market. Printed music sales worldwide rose 6.3% in 2000 to $728.9 million. The leading

CHART 6   REPRODUCTION-BASED INCOME   **($ MILLIONS)**

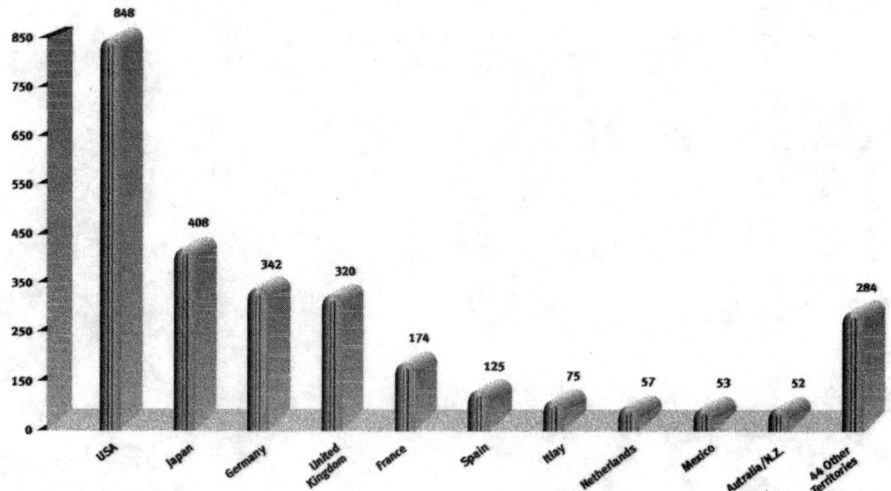

national markets for scores and song-books remained the U.S. and Germany, which collectively at $456.23 million, account for over 62% of the income from this sector. However, the total given in the Master Survey table undoubtedly understates the size of the global printed music market because there is no central source of data for this sector in many countries.

The bulk of the industry's rental income is still derived from Japan, where there continues to be a large number of rental stores. In 2000, at $30.88 million, Japan accounted for 77.5 % of revenues from this sector. However, Japan's total represents a 23 % decline from 1999, reflecting losses due to piracy, Internet downloading and increased consumer spending in other entertainment sectors.

CHART 8   COMPARISION BY REGION

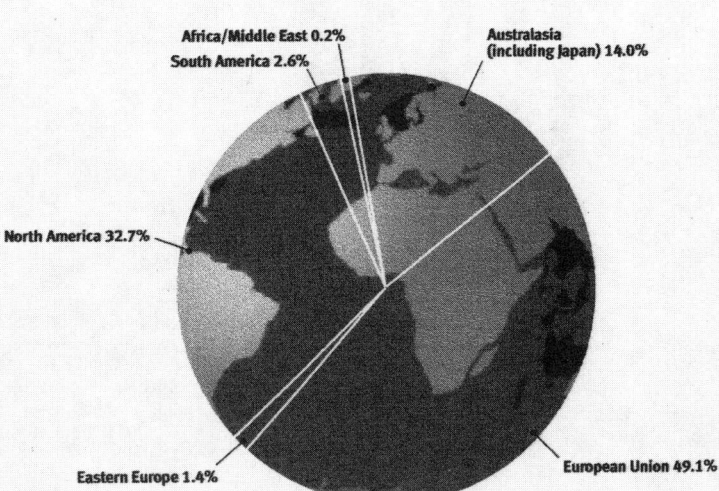

Africa/Middle East 0.2%
South America 2.6%
Australasia (including Japan) 14.0%
North America 32.7%
Eastern Europe 1.4%
European Union 49.1%

CHART 7   DISTRIBUTION-BASED INCOME

($ MILLIONS)

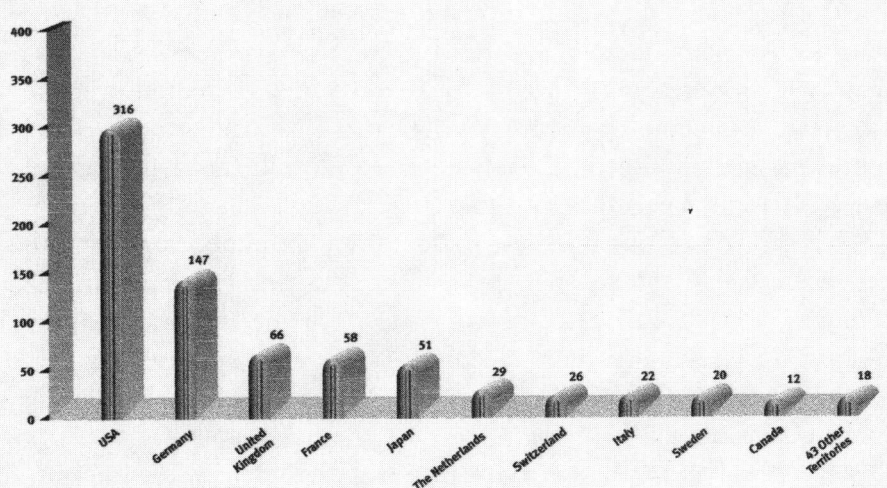

USA
Germany 316
United Kingdom 147
France 66
Japan 58
The Netherlands 51
Switzerland 29
Italy 26
Sweden 22
Canada 20
43 Other Territories 12
18

BMI

For Immediate Release

BMI POSTS WORLD'S HIGHEST PERFORMING RIGHTS REVENUES; TOPS $700 MILLION-PLUS MILESTONE

OVERHEAD RATE FALLS TO ALL-TIME LOW

NEW YORK, September 12, 2005 – BMI this week posted revenues of more than $728 million for fiscal 2004-2005, an increase of more than 8.3% over the previous year, it was announced today by Del Bryant, President & CEO of the performing rights organization. This marks the first time that any copyright organization in the world has crossed the threshold of $700 million in revenues in performing rights collections. The revenues, which represent an increase of more than $56 million over the prior year, resulted in royalty distributions to BMI affiliated songwriters, composers and publishers of more than $623 million, an increase of nearly $51 million over the prior year.

"The increase in our revenues and royalty distribution for the 15th year in a row shows the overall health of our business and our commitment to seek new areas of income and to decrease operational expenses," Bryant said in making the announcement. Operational expenses as a percentage of revenues decreased from 14.6% to 14.2%, the lowest in the company's history.

BMI's increased revenue performance was bolstered by significantly higher license fees secured in the new media and mobile entertainment areas. New media licensing revenues increased by 114%, year over year, totaling $11.4 million. Tracking the growth of the US market, fees from mobile entertainment (ringtones) accounted for the largest segment of the increase. During the year, more than 500 new digital music providers were licensed, including industry leaders such as the subscription music service Rhapsody, the streaming radio service for mobile services mobZilla, and major wireless carriers.

International revenues increased by more than 9% to more than $202.9 million while the general licensing area showed an increase of more than 12.7% due to a new contract with the Muzak background music service and the strong growth in licensing eating and drinking establishments, aerobic centers and skating rinks.

The increased revenues reflect the continuing strength of the BMI repertoire. BMI affiliated songwriters were honored with multiple Grammy Awards, CMA Awards and Emmy Awards, as well as Soul Train, American Music, Handy and MTV Awards, Tony Awards for musical theater, including the Tony for Best Musical, and the Pulitzer Prize for classical music. BMI composers accounted for 75% of the music on all network prime time shows and composed the music to the majority of the Top 10 grossing films of the past year.

Now marking its 65th year in business, BMI is an American performing rights organization that represents more than 300,000 songwriters, composers and publishers in all genres of music. With a repertoire of more than 6.5 million musical works from around the world, the non-profit-making corporation collects license fees from businesses that use music, which it then distributes as royalties to the musical creators and copyright owners it represents.

Contact: Robbin Ahrold
212-830-2502
rahrold@bmi.com

Pat Baird
212-830-2528
pbaird@bmi.com

Hanna Pantle
212-830-6328
hpantle@bmi.com

Global Piracy

Commercial piracy of physical formats once again plagued the recording industry in 2003, accounting for an estimated U.S.$4.5 billion in illegal sales worldwide.

This illegal music trade is feeding the profits of international organized crime syndicates who are involved in drugs, money-laundering and other criminal activities. It is costing governments hundreds of millions of dollars in tax revenues. It is deterring companies in intellectual property related businesses from investing in countries they fear are not adequately protecting their intellectual property rights.

It is also destroying—indeed in large parts of the world *has destroyed*—local music cultures, local record companies and the careers of local musicians. This is particularly true of the developing world where, because of the failure to enforce intellectual property rights, countries that once bred international stars now find it hard to develop successful artists even at a local level.

Commercial piracy, contrary to what commentators mistakenly think, is just as important a problem for the music industry today as internet piracy. And in several of the music industry's very largest markets—countries with low rates of broadband penetration such as Brazil, Mexico and Russia—piracy of physical discs still dwarfs its internet equivalent.

In this report we highlight ten priority countries whose governments need to take firm action against commercial music piracy. The ten are chosen for their consistent failures in anti-piracy enforcement, and yet even among these countries there are some encouraging signs which help as models for action internationally.

At the time of publication, a Congressional Commission in Brazil has produced a damning assessment of piracy in Brazil, exposing the web of crime and corruption allegedly extending through government and civil service. The report is a big step forward in a country whose once vibrant music industry has been decimated by piracy. It now needs a decisive government response. Spain, Europe's fastest-growing piracy problem country in recent years, has made good progress in enforcement and legislation—but more needs to be done given its stubbornly high levels of CD-R piracy. Meanwhile, Poland's implementation of a good optical disc law regulating CD plants has seen that country move out of the top ten priority territories. It is replaced in the list by Pakistan, a new piracy hotspot as a result of massive exports of unauthorized optical discs.

The stakes in this fight are far greater than just the health of the U.S.$32 billion recording industry. A huge entertainment and media sector worth U.S.$1 trillion, depends on governments enforcing proper laws, policies and practices in the area of intellectual property rights.

Taken from www.ifpi.org.

This report documents what the industry is doing, often with a lot of success, to fight piracy. It is impossible, however, to win this battle without very decisive support from governments. Governments of countries identified in this report need to take note of the recommendations. In addition, it is critical that the international community steps up pressure on those countries which are failing to meet international standards of intellectual property protection and enforcement. Piracy is emphatically a cross-border problem that requires cross-border, inter-governmental solutions.

"This illegal music trade is benefiting international organized crime."

In 2004, our industry's anti-piracy priorities are better enforcement, more education, effective optical disc laws proper deterrent sentencing and stepped-up international pressure on laggard countries. It is overwhelmingly in the interests of those governments' economies and cultures that they take action now.

2003 piracy statistics

This section of the report covers illegal pirate sales of music CDs and cassettes in 2003[1]. This includes pressed discs, manufactured on factory production lines; CD-Rs, where music albums are copied from a variety of sources onto blank discs using CD burning equipment; and pirate cassettes.

IFPI's value estimate is based on the prices of pirate products sold around the world. It is an estimate of the value of the pirate market, and does not equate to the losses suffered by the music industry, which are likely to be far greater.

Music piracy totals 1.7 billion units; disc piracy at a record 1.1 billion

The global pirate market for recorded music totalled 1.7 billion units in 2003. Disc piracy increased by 45 million units, a rise of 4% on 2002. The pirate cassette market fell by almost 25% as pirate discs continued to replace cassettes.

Discs: 1 in 3 worldwide is pirate

An estimated 35% of music CDs sold in 2003 were pirate products. When cassettes are included, piracy amounts to 40% of all music products sold worldwide. With declining cassette sales, over two-thirds of pirate product sold is now on disc—either an illegal factory pressed disc or a CD-R copied from an original for commercial sale.

---

[1]The rest of the report covers the period 2003 to date of publication (mid-2004)

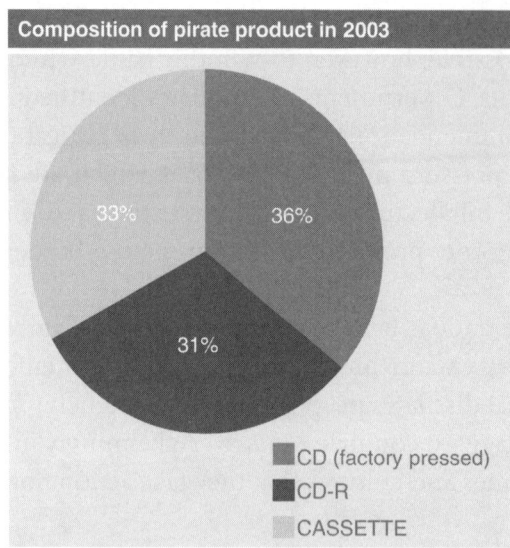

Composition of pirate product in 2003

36%

31%

33%

CD (factory pressed)
CD-R
CASSETTE

The continuing growth of CD-R piracy:

- CD-R operations are more numerous, more concealed and more portable than CD plant operations.

- While larger CD plants focus on recordings by the major international artists which can be exported, smaller scale CD-R based operations have captured the market for domestic artists' recordings.

- Pirate music sold on CD-R tends to be slightly cheaper than the pressed disc variety, which has led to a reduction in the average price of pirate discs.

The format of pirate music products varies in different regions. Pressed discs continue to dominate the pirate disc market in Asia and Russia, but CD-R accounts for the vast majority of pirate product in Latin America, North America and Europe.

The rapid spread of CD-R piracy over the past four years has created new problems for the music industry. The duplication speed of CD-R burners has increased steadily over this period and has only now begun to reach a maximum level. CD burning machines can now burn a 74 minute disc in approximately three minutes.

Global pirate sales worth U.S.$4.5 billion at pirate prices

The value of the pirate market for recorded music was an estimated U.S.$4.5 billion in 2003, meaning that pirate sales now account for a record 15% of the legitimate music market, up from 11% in 1999. The pirate sales value in 2003 was down

Domestic music piracy levels in 2003 [units]

<10%	10 – 24%	25 – 50%	> 50%
Australia	Bahrain	Chile	Argentina
Austria	Belgium	Costa Rica	Brazil
Canada	Finland	Croatia	Bulgaria
Denmark	Hong Kong	Cyprus	China
France	Italy	Czech Republic	Colombia
Germany	Netherlands	Greece	Ecuador
Iceland	New Zealand	Hungary	Egypt
Ireland	Oman	India	Estonia
Japan	Qatar	Israel	Indonesia
Norway	Singapore	Philippines	Kuwait
Sweden	Slovenia	Poland	Latvia
Switzerland	South Korea	Portugal	Lebanon
UK	Spain	Saudi Arabia	Lithuania
USA	Turkey	Slovakia	Malaysia
	UAE	South Africa	Mexico
	Zimbabwe	Taiwan	Pakistan
		Thailand	Paraguay
			Peru
			Romania
			Russia
			Ukraine
			Uruguay
			Venezuela

Source: IFPI, National Groups

slightly on 2002 due to falling prices. The global pirate music market is bigger than any individual national legitimate music market except for the USA and Japan.

Stepped-up enforcement: seizures of discs rise to 56 million

IFPI's strategy of raiding pirates at source has helped to reduce the growth in pirate product in 2003. Record quantities of discs and equipment were seized in 2003. An estimated 56 million pirate music discs—up from 13 million in 2001—were taken, while seizures of all formats, including cassettes and music DVDs,

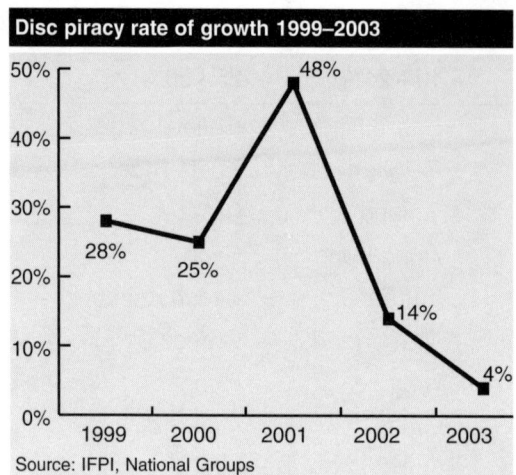

totalled 64 million units. The vast majority of seizures were in South East Asia and Latin America.

Enforcement actions are being concentrated at the source of pirate operations, where raids and seizures can result in the confiscation of manufacturing or copying equipment, with remarkable results. In 2003, IFPI seized 12,021 CD 'stampers'— the 'master copy' used to press illicit CDs. This is six times the number seized in 2002. There was also a substantial increase in the number of CD-R burners seized— 14,745 in 2003 compared with just under 5,000 in 2002.

IFPI top ten priority territories

Ten priority territories are experiencing unacceptable levels of piracy and are urged to tackle the issue as a matter of urgency. The ten territories, which are examined in detail are:

BRAZIL, CHINA, MEXICO, PARAGUAY, PAKISTAN, RUSSIA, SPAIN, TAIWAN, THAILAND, UKRAINE

CD overcapacity

Rising global overcapacity for the manufacture of discs is a key factor behind the spread of disc piracy, affecting music, film and computer software. IFPI estimates that there are now approximately 1,040 optical disc plants worldwide. It is believed that around 300 new plants have been set up in the last four years.

This is a recipe for increasing illegal pirate sales, as supply of discs far outstrips legitimate demand. It also illustrates the lack of adequate regulation by governments

Estimated pressing capacity 2003 [all formats]

Territory	Estimated Capacity (M units)	Demand (M units)	Over-capacity (M units)
TAIWAN	7,900	270	7,630
CHINA	4,900	1,100	3,800
HONG KONG	2,500	140	2,360
INDIA	1,900	400	1,500
MALAYSIA	1,860	60	1,800
SINGAPORE	620	60	560
BRAZIL	630	140	490
THAILAND	570	27	540
POLAND	500	150	350
RUSSIA*	370	30	340
TOTAL			**19,370**

Total disc manufacturing overcapacity: 19.4 billion discs annually

Source: Understanding & Solutions Ltd. Formats include CD. DVD. CD-R/W. DVD-R/W, CD Rom, DVD Rom, Video CD

*Source: IFPI estimates, CD and DVD only

of optical disc manufacturing. The ten examples below have a CD manufacturing capacity that is highly disproportionate to legitimate domestic demand. In these territories, estimated capacity outstrips local legitimate demand by no less than nine times and, in some cases, by more than 30 times.

IFPI anti-piracy 2003–2004

IFPI and its national affiliates have a global anti-piracy team of around 250 investigators, made up largely of ex-law enforcement personnel. They work in close collaboration with governments, police forces and customs departments worldwide.

Seizures of pirate product

IFPI assisted in the seizure of over 56 million pirate discs in 2003, up from 50 million in 2002 and 13 million in 2001. Highlights of these activities include:

- **Some 21 million units of pirate CD-R discs were seized in Latin America, two thirds of the total seized worldwide.** A major raid involving 1,000 police in Peru netted 1 million burned CD-Rs. In

Paraguay 40 trailers of illicit goods were seized, including more than 1 million pirate CD-Rs. Over 750,000 blank CD-Rs were seized en route from South East Asia. In Brazil, a total of 147 CD-R burners were destroyed following one raid on a laboratory in São Paolo, Brazil.

- **The vast majority of pressed pirate discs (around 80%) were found in South East Asia,** source of most manufactured discs.

- **In 2003 68 CD manufacturing lines were decommissioned globally.** This represents a production capacity of over 300 million units, bigger than any legitimate music CD market except the U.S. A significant raid in Malaysia, for example, resulted in the closure of an underground replication plant and the recovery of two replication lines, 277 stampers and thousands of infringing optical discs.

- **Seizures of CD-R burners rose to 14,745, more than twice the number of the previous year.** This represents capacity to make some 420 million pirate music CD-Rs.

- **Global seizures of blank discs and artwork inlays destined for pirate use also rose sharply.** In 2003 40 million blank discs were seized.

- **There were important actions in cassette markets.** Nearly two million counterfeit Arabic title music cassettes were recovered in the largest ever music piracy seizure in the Middle East. Egyptian police worked with IFPI and the Egyptian Central Association of Audio Producers (ECAAP) to confiscate almost two million counterfeit cassettes, one million inlays, one million tape covers, six duplication and two printing machines.

- **Other significant actions included** a major raid in Italy which led to 21 arrests and the seizure of 80 high speed CD-R burners, thousands of optical discs, inlays, printers and blank CD-Rs. A raid in Russia resulted in the closure of a clandestine DVD replication plant in Moscow, with a production capacity of 18 million DVDs per year.

Forensic analysis

IFPI uses a unique forensics laboratory that traces the manufacturing source of pirate CDs through microscopic examination and measurement. This has helped link infringing discs to source factories and resulted in many raids on suspect plants worldwide.

In 2003-2004 the forensics unit identified several new target plants actively engaged in producing infringing materials. These are being followed up with criminal actions taken in collaboration with several governments who have established their own forensic programmes.

IFPI has also traditionally cooperated with the Motion Picture Association (MPA) in the area of forensics, with a number of plants identified as having manufactured pirate DVDs containing material of MPA member companies. Since the start of 2003 IFPI's forensic laboratory has been conducting examinations on behalf of MPA and the Business Software Alliance (BSA) in addition to IFPI-related investigations.

International co-operation

IFPI works with government enforcement agencies and international crime investigation organizations. Interpol's Intellectual Property Crime Action Group (IIPCAG) was created in 2002 to respond to the growing incidence of counterfeit or copyright-infringing goods. IFPI, as part of its commitment to this group, has written an Interpol guide designed to assist police officers around the world in investigating intellectual property crimes. The guide includes details of how to recognize counterfeit products.

IFPI also maintains a crucial partnership with the World Customs Organization's intellectual property strategic group to make intellectual property protection a priority for customs authorities worldwide. The WCO IPR Strategic Group stages several training missions each year designed to educate and inform customs officers in countries where piracy either directly affects them or the neighboring region.

Organized Crime and the Industry Response

There is a well-established link between piracy and organized crime. Counterfeiting of goods is estimated to yield more than 500 billion euro a year for criminal organizations (Interpol, May 2004). Confirmed links to international drug trafficking, illegal firearms, money laundering, massive tax and revenue evasion and more recently the funding of terrorist activities have been established. In some developing areas whole economies are being distorted, leading to loss of industry and government revenue and the failure of legitimate domestic enterprise to flourish.

In July 2003 the Secretary General of Interpol, Ronald Noble, told United States House Committee on International Relations:

> "The link between organized crime groups and counterfeit goods is well established. But Interpol is sounding the alarm that Intellectual Property Crime is becoming the preferred method of funding for a number of terrorist groups. There are enough examples now of the funding of terrorist groups in

this way (intellectual property crime) for us to worry about the threat to public safety. We must take preventative measures now."

Characteristics of organized crime groups and their activities

- Collaboration by a minimum of three people.
- Criminal activity which has, or is intended to be continued over a prolonged period.
- Commission of serious criminal offences, or offences which, taken as a whole, are of considerable importance.
- Motivated by the pursuit of profit or power.
- Operations are international national or regional.
- Uses violence or intimidation.
- Uses commercial or other business-like structures.
- Engages in money laundering.
- Exerts influence upon politics, the media, public administration, judicial authorities of the economy.

National Criminal Intelligence Service (NCIS) UK

There were several important successes against organized crime in 2003–2004 including the following:

- Mexican law enforcement authorities (LEAs) and the anti-piracy group APDIF Mexico conducted two raids on targeted locations in the notorious Tepito district which led to violent clashes with criminal gangs operating in the area. During the first raid a total of 128 burners, 230,000 recorded CD-Rs, cocaine, marijuana and weapons were seized. In the second raid a total of 44 burners and 5,500 recorded CD-Rs were confiscated. Around 100 people proceeded to violently attack the police removing the confiscated material, leading to a four-hour long confrontation. It is believed that well-known crime gangs involved in illegal firearms, drugs and merchandise trafficking took part in the clashes. 39 people were arrested for disruption of the peace.

- Police in Italy dismantled a major organized ring involved in the mass duplication of music, movies and software in October 2003. The raids, in the Naples area, struck a significant blow against organized CD-R and DVD burning and distribution in the country. They followed months of investigation, and involved 50 of Italy's

Fiscal Police who located and seized six undercover burning laboratories in the suburbs of Naples. The raids netted 496 CD and DVD burners, including 200 CD burners found at one location. Nine people were arrested.

- In September 2003 a series of co-ordinated raids were conducted by the police in Athens, following a lengthy investigation by IFPI and national group investigators into the duplication and distribution of large quantities of CD-Rs. The suspects were allegedly running an illegal immigrant ring. The raids recovered over 200,000 recorded discs and 123 CD-R burners.

- An internationally traded shipment of pirate CDs—from Asia into Africa—has been intercepted by South African authorities. Africa saw its biggest ever seizure of pirate CDs when authorities intercepted the container in transit from Singapore to Nigeria containing pirate CDs and other equipment. The customs anti-smuggling team of Durban harbour and the South African Police Service (SAPS) border police decided to open the container after scanning it and found 260,000 pirate CDs featuring music by both African and international artists.

- Brazilian businessman Law Kim Chong was apprehended on June 1, 2004, when he allegedly attempted to bribe the chairman of Brazil's Congressional Anti-piracy Committee (CPI) set up in 2003 to tackle the huge problem of piracy in the country. The arrest came after two months of investigation by the Brazilian authorities. It is believed that a recent operation by CPI had dealt a severe blow to Law's business when tonnes of apparently counterfeited and smuggled goods were seized during raids in his shopping centres. Following the seizures Law was suspected of planning to bribe the CPI to keep him out of the Committee's report and leave his business intact.

CD plant education and litigation

Civil claims against optical disc plants suspected of involvement in piracy are at the forefront of IFPI's litigation strategy. For the first time ever, in December 2003, IFPI filed seven separate claims for damages totalling U.S.$1,366,600 against Moscow-based manufacturing plant, Russobit-Soft. This was followed by further compensation claims against a second Russian plant, Roff Technologies. The plants are alleged to have manufactured counterfeit CDs by top-selling artists. IFPI is awaiting action on those complaints by the Russian authorities.

Priority Territories

For the second year running IFPI is publishing a list of ten top priority territories in the global fight against music piracy. These are territories that are failing to protect and enforce intellectual property rights and tackle unacceptable levels of piracy.

This report is intended to highlight the problems of physical commercial music piracy, although many of the countries also suffer from high levels of internet piracy.

The list has been compiled considering several factors, including intelligence from IFPI's global network of anti-piracy teams and national groups, measurement of quantitative criteria, an assessment of the impact of a country's piracy activity on neighboring and international markets, and an evaluation of government action in 2003–2004.

The specific quantitative criteria reflect the relative size of each market, the extent of the piracy problem in 2003 and trends in the pirate and legitimate markets. These criteria are: U.S.$pirate market value; total legitimate market size; piracy level; pirate unit growth from 2002; and legitimate unit growth from 2002.

The following ten markets, based on these criteria, are featured in this report,

- Brazil
- China
- Mexico
- Paraguay
- Pakistan
- Russia
- Spain
- Taiwan
- Thailand
- Ukraine

BRAZIL

Pirate market value (U.S.$)	127 million
Legitimate market size (units)	58 million
Piracy level	52%
Pirate unit growth	9%
Legitimate unit growth	−25%

The legitimate Brazilian music market once again performed poorly in 2003, falling in value by 17% Units sold dropped by 25%.

Brazil remains in the list of IFPI's top ten priority territories because of the inefficiency (or non-existence) of co-ordinated police efforts at a national level, and the government's meagre resources and lack of focus on piracy compared to other criminal activities such as drug and firearms trafficking. Police corruption is rife, and court judges are slow to use criminal procedures against pirates.

The Brazilian authorities' inaction, combined with the very low cost of CD-Rs and burning equipment mainly smuggled through Paraguay, has created a strong pirate market. Of 11.2 million music buyers in Brazil, only 56% buy solely legitimate products, with the remaining 44% buying either both pirate and legitimate, or only pirate, products. The average price of pirate CDs remained approximately U.S.$1.50, with no significant change compared to 2002.

Some action has been taken in the past year—mostly promoted by IFPI's affiliated national group in Brazil (ABPD) and the music industry anti-piracy unit (APDIF)—resulting in the seizure of some 5.7 million recorded pirate CDs, 11.5 million illegal blank CD-Rs and 4,800 CD burners. However piracy continues to grow, as evidenced by the sale of 72 million pirate CDs in 2003, up from 62 million in 2002.

The success of the music industry enforcement activities is most noticeable in São Paulo, the city with the highest consumption of music but also the hub of piracy in Brazil and therefore the primary focus of anti-piracy efforts. While São Paulo accounted for 18% of the total Brazilian music pirate market in late 2001, a survey undertaken early in 2004 indicated that this fell to 12%, thanks to the reduced availability of pirate products in the streets and in illegal stores.

The most significant step in the anti-piracy campaign has come from a Congressional Anti-Piracy Commission set up to investigate piracy and counterfeit trade. The committee published a report detailing its results in June 2004, exposing a billion-dollar industry allegedly involving politicians, judges, civil servants and thousands of others. The report called for the indictment of over 100 people, including alleged heads of criminal organizations. This report has been forwarded to the Minister of Justice and the President of Brazil. Its recommendations need to be taken up decisively by the government. Among these is the immediate creation of a national anti-piracy plan, including the establishment of a centralized public organization to co-ordinate the activities of government agencies and departments.

CHINA

Pirate market value (U.S.$)	591 million
Legitimate market size (units)	76 million
Piracy level	90%
Pirate unit growth	20%
Legitimate unit growth	40%

China has huge potential as a music market, with legitimate sales growing from a small base to a level where China is now the second biggest legal music market in Asia. However, China's piracy rates are still the highest in the world; over 90% of the units sold in the market are pirate. Legitimate sales of sound recordings stood at U.S.$198 million in 2003 while pirate sales are estimated to be worth U.S.$591 million. Pressing capacity in China has doubled from 2,400 million units to 4,900 million units in one year. Moreover, the recording industry has seen no significant improvement in enforcement nation-wide since China's WTO accession.

In this context, the main concerns of the record industry are the difficulties in securing criminal prosecution and the insufficient level of enforcement actions.

Under the current interpretation of existing laws, the manufacturing, distribution and selling of pirate sound recordings in China is not a criminal offence, unless the profits made by the pirate of the total value of the operation are in excess of specified high levels. The prescribed prison terms are also too low to have any deterrent effect. Furthermore, it is very difficult for the copyright owner to participate in criminal prosecutions, as copyright owners are forbidden under Chinese law from undertaking investigations. They also face many obstacles in obtaining information and statistics from Chinese authorities regarding related enforcement actions, the status of legal proceedings and final court results.

Government bureaus and departments responsible for law enforcement rarely initiate criminal investigations and Chinese customs do not criminally prosecute the seizures of pirate goods.

IFPI recommends the following:

1. The legal thresholds for criminal prosecutions of copyright pirates should be eliminated or lowered by a significant degree, and the level of penalties should be increased.

2. Other than the amendment of the criminal code it is necessary that the Chinese Supreme Court and State Council issue new interpretations, guidelines and instructions to judges, prosecutors and police to: (a) redefine standards for criminal prosecutions (b) permit and use privately gathered evidence, and (c) direct enforcement authorities, including customs, to investigate and criminally prosecute copyright piracy.

3. Changing the law is a first step in lowering the piracy rate in China. However it will be no use, unless the Chinese government sets up and co-ordinates nationwide enforcement efforts against piracy that include the full involvement of provincial and local enforcement authorities. This could usefully include a commitment from the Chinese government in the form of a public address to the nation, ideally from a top-ranking official of the National People's Congress.

MEXICO

Pirate market value (U.S.$)	181 million
Legitimate market size (units)	56 million
Piracy level	61%
Pirate unit growth	−19%
Legitimate unit growth	3%

Piracy has robbed Mexico of its status as a top-ranking music market. In 2000, Mexico was the eighth largest music market in the world, valued at U.S.$665 million. By 2003, retail sales had fallen by nearly 50% to U.S.$346.5 million, and Mexico lost its place as the only Latin American country among the ten biggest music markets in the world.

Some 74 million illegally reproduced recordings were sold in 2003. A piracy rate of 61%, down from 68% in 2002, reflects more successful anti-piracy actions combined with a small recovery (3%) in legitimate sales. Almost 95% of pirate product is burned onto CD-Rs.

Research into pirate operations in 2003 revealed 51,000 points of sale for pirate music including street markets, street booths, public markets, and mobile vendors. To address the problem the industry initiated a unique new programme in Guadalajara. The Street Vendors' Conversion Programme seeks to turn pirate stands into distribution points for legitimate product. The programme will be of utmost importance in fighting piracy effectively in Mexico.

However piracy is still endemic; of the 17 million CD consumers in Mexico, 54% buy only pirated CDs, mostly in pirate stands, and 8% buy both pirated and original CDs. Only 38% faithfully buy original CDs, illustrating the constraints on the legitimate market. As a result, legal points of sale have fallen dramatically by more than 60% over the last five years to less than 1,000 in the country. The impact on the industry is very visible: major releases have fallen by 50% in the last few years, and in the same period the industry has laid off no fewer than 50% of its employees.

There are some important advances in fighting piracy. Under agreements with the Secretariat of the Treasury to carry out border control measures, all importers must now register their business with customs. There are only a limited number of entry points for blank CD-Rs, with anti-piracy personnel in each one of those points. Thanks to these new measures customs was able to seize over 20 million blank CD-Rs in 2003. These steps, combined with other actions taken by the local police authorities in co-ordination with the industry anti-piracy team, resulted in additional seizures of seven million units of recorded CD-Rs and sentences for over 25 pirates.

The industry recognizes these efforts, but more needs to be done. In particular the Mexican authorities are urged to:

1. Address the proliferation of pirate music street vendors The federal government should continue to support the Guadalajara conversion program and promote implementation in other key cities.

2. Reinforce border measures to reduce the importation of illegal blank CD-Rs.

3. Encourage the courts to correctly interpret the recently approved amendment to the organized crime law as it applies to piracy.

4. Approve the bill to crack down on piracy as a matter of public policy.

PARAGUAY

Pirate market value (U.S.$)	32 million
Legitimate market size (units)	0.1 million
Piracy level	99%
Pirate unit growth	−25%
Legitimate unit growth	−52%

The border city of Ciudad del Este in Paraguay continues to serve as the export centre for the significant volume of blank and recorded CD-R units shipped into Brazil. Pirate product is transported by busloads of merchants, also known as *sacoleiros,* who travel in convoys of up to 40 buses with little control from customs authorities on both sides of the border. The *sacoleiros* are estimated to be moving over 70 million blank and recorded CD-R units per year and are a major factor in the piracy problem in Paraguay and Brazil. Paraguayan companies are also fuelling the problem—local information suggests that a number of Paraguayan companies imported over 150 million blank CD-R's in 2003, mostly for export to Brazil or Argentina.

The Paraguayan authorities, with assistance from IFPI's anti-piracy staff, have conducted a number of raids against pirates that resulted in the seizure of 10 million units of recorded and blank CD-R contraband in 2003. In 2004 a major importer of blank CDs, who knowingly supplied discs to pirate organizations, was finally sentenced to seven years in prison for tax evasion and contraband. However, these actions have had little deterrence effect on the pirate market because of weak criminal penalties against pirates.

The government has taken steps to address piracy through presidential decrees that call for the following measures on the importation of blank CD-Rs:

1. An official register of importers.
2. Stricter importation documentation regarding source and product.
3. Prior import licenses.
4. Requirement for importers to identify and declare their customers and distribution networks.
5. Creation of a control unit within the Ministry of Industry and Commerce.

These requirements are being implemented and may become an important part of an overall anti-piracy campaign. However, to have any real chance of reducing piracy and ending its status as one of the major trans-shipment centres of South America, the Paraguayan government will need to:

1. Regulate the movement of the *sacoleiros* at the border to interrupt the flow of recorded and blank pirate CD-Rs.

2. Increase criminal penalties for piracy to allow the courts to issue deterrent level sentences.

PAKISTAN

Pirate market value (U.S.$)	30 million
Legitimate market size (units)	38 million*
Piracy level	59%
Pirate unit growth	−17%
Legitimate unit growth	n/a

Over the last three years, Pakistan has evolved into one of the largest manufactures and exporters of pirate optical discs in the world. The total production output of the eight known optical disc plants in Pakistan in 2003 is estimated at 180 million discs, a 50% increase compared to 2002 when output was 120 million.

With an estimated total annual domestic demand of only 20 million discs, there is evidence that the remaining plant production is being exported to overseas markets. For 2003, the average monthly export of optical discs from Pakistan was a huge 13 million discs, a quantity exceeding the demand of many developed music markets. The vast majority of these discs is illegal. Through customs intelligence and seizures in overseas markets, Pakistan has been identified as a major source of infringing products harming markets in the Middle East, Europe, Africa and the USA.

Pirate optical discs from Pakistan are exported in hand luggage, as airfreight by 'courier-services' and in bulk quantities by sea and air, and have been found in at least 45 countries worldwide. In 2004, the U.S. Trade Representative's office (USTR) placed Pakistan on the Priority Watch List under its 'Special 301' procedure, calling for the rapid introduction of an effective optical disc regulation, the effective enforcement and sentencing of Pakistan's numerous large-scale copyright pirates, and a substantial sharpening of its border controls.

The government of Pakistan has acknowledged the need to tackle this massive problem. This now needs to translate into concrete action and lasting results.

* 95% cassettes

RUSSIA

Pirate market value (U.S.$)	332 million
Legitimate market size (units)	116 million
Piracy level	64%
Pirate unit growth	−8%
Legitimate unit growth	2%

Russia is one of the world's largest producers and exporters of pirate CDs. A 64% piracy rate in 2003 has devastated the domestic Russian market, and exports of pirate Russian discs are causing serious damage to the legitimate music markets throughout Europe and the Middle East. Russian pirate discs have been traced to more than 26 countries.

In 1996 there were two known CD plants in Russia. Today there are 33 plants with more ready to come on line. Production capacity has nearly tripled over the past three years. Russia's annual manufacturing capacity now stands at 342 million CDs and 28 million DVDs, despite the fact that only 30 million legitimate music CDs were sold in Russia in 2003.

Russia's anti-piracy efforts are severely hampered by flawed legislation, ineffective enforcement by the Russian authorities and insufficient deterrent penalties in the courts. Organized criminal enterprises are involved in many aspects of optical disc piracy in Russia.

In 2003–2004, IFPI assisted in the investigating and raids on a number of suspected producers and distributors of illegal recorded material. Raids are, however, rendered meaningless when only a minimal amount of cases are submitted to court and no deterrent court decisions are taken.

The Russian government took a first step in addressing the growing piracy problem in October 2002 by establishing an Inter-Ministerial commission to combat piracy. But the commission has not met regularly and taken only small measures to address legislative reform, retail piracy, and optical disc production.

The Russian government must:

1. Immediately undertake continuous plant inspections, and shut down plants producing pirate product using the existing law—especially by withdrawing licenses for plants operating on government property. It must also implement effective border measures to stop the export of illegal product.

2. Introduce a comprehensive optical media regulatory and enforcement scheme.

3. Show significant improvement in the number and disposition of criminal investigations and raids against pirates engaged in commercial manufacture or distribution, while taking increased administrative procedures against street piracy.

4. Direct the Russian judiciary that deterrent criminal penalties are expected from the courts—this can be done via guidelines from the Supreme Court and from the relevant minister, as well as by amendments to the Penal Code.

5. Push for the necessary legal reforms in the copyright law, the criminal code, the criminal procedure code and the administrative code.

The aim is to facilitate stronger and more effective enforcement compatible with the WTO TRIPs and the WIPO digital treaties.

SPAIN

Pirate market value (U.S.$)	58 million
Legitimate market size (units)	56 million
Piracy level	24%
Pirate unit growth	−7%
Legitimate unit growth	−13%

Pirate music in Spain represented 24% of the market in 2003, approximately the same level as in 2002. There has been notable progress in enforcement by Spanish police, however. Over 2,800 people were arrested or charged with intellectual property offences, specifically those relating to the manufacture and distribution of illegal sound recordings—an increase of 44% over 2002. The number of pirate seizures increased by 12% to a total of over 4.3 million units. The number of burners seized increased by more than 150%, with 2,607 burners seized in 2003 compared to 1,015 the previous year.

There have also been improvements on the legislative side, with the amendment of the Penal Code. The amendments related to intellectual property-related crimes—due to come into force in October 2004—will increase economic and especially criminal penalties, and permit more pre-trial custody for this type of offence. This should help reduce the presence of illegal street vendors.

These efforts are hardly sufficient, however, given that thousands of illegal pirate music businesses operate in highly organized criminal networks. Penalties and deterrents are weak, and there is a patent lack of awareness or concern in Spain about the importance of intellectual property. Meanwhile the activities of street vendors persist, as criminal courts are saturated and court proceedings take a long time to produce results.

Spain's top artists have mobilized to help raise the problem to the highest level in the government. A large group of best-selling artists met President José Luis Rodriguez Zapatero in June 2004 under the slogan '*Music is dying—help us*'.

The Spanish music industry has called for the Spanish authorities to focus on the following:

1. To undertake national awareness-raising programmes to educate the public about the importance of intellectual property.

2. To apply a zero-tolerance approach to illegal street sellers and stop them from becoming part of the city landscape.

3. To speed up the trials—which currently take up to a year—in order to deter illegal street vendors and enforce imposed penalties.

TAIWAN

Pirate market value (U.S.$)	37 million
Legitimate market size (units)	15 million
Piracy level	42%
Pirate unit growth	−20%
Legitimate unit growth	−10%

Taiwan is one of the Asian markets most affected by the spread of CD-R piracy in 2003. At least four in every five pirate discs seized were burned pirate CD-Rs. Taiwan is also a large-scale exporter of pirate pressed discs in the South East Asia region. In addition, the country is having to contend with a serious internet piracy problem.

There were some positive developments in 2003. The amendment of the copyright law made piracy a public crime, while enforcement action taken by the Taiwan law enforcement agencies against night market vendors increased, resulting in a drastic drop in the number of pirate hawker stalls from 250 to less than 50 in response however, the pirates have turned to mail order, direct sales and internet orders, concluding their transactions through untraceable mobile phones or fax.

On the export front, major quantities of Taiwan-manufactured pirate CDs have been found elsewhere in the region. Industry intelligence has, for example, uncovered evidence that suggests that 1.75 million pirate pressed discs were exported to the Philippines in the second half of 2003.

More and more Taiwanese are also downloading and distributing unauthorized sound tracks through peer-to-peer (P2P) file exchanges or illegal MP3 websites. Ironically this activity has affected the physical pirate market.

Taiwan has two major P2P services, 'Kuro', which has an estimated 500,000 members in Taiwan and 250,000 members in China, and 'EzPeer', with approximately 300,000 members in Taiwan, IFPI Taiwan has brought criminal charges against both Kuro and EzPeer for abetting copyright infringement. They were both criminally indicted in December 2003 and the cases are still pending in the courts. IFPI Taiwan has also secured civil court injunctions against both sites, but these businesses are still in operation.

Meanwhile Kuro has spent vast sums on advertisements in major portal sites and in the media, and is attempting to get legislation passed that would immunise its activities by introducing compulsory license provision for online music. Such a provision would be in violation of the WTO TRIPS Agreement.

The Taiwanese government needs to curb the damage that the combination of physicial piracy and unauthorized internet music distribution is inflicting on the local industry. It must also promote a legitimate online music market that is struggling to surface. Specifically, it must:

1. Revise the flawed amendment passed in June 2003, in particular the decriminalisation of the offences committed without intending to profit from them; the unreasonable monetary or quantity threshold for criminal penalties currently set at U.S.$885 (NT$30,000) or five copies; and most importantly that judges are no longer required to impose jail terms for most offences but may impose detention or a fine instead.

2. Shut down the two major unauthorized P2P sites immediately.

3. Amend the copyright law or introduce new legislation in order to deter unauthorized internet distribution of music.

4. Expedite the legislation establishing the IPR Special Police Task Force.

5. Effectively enforce the control of pirate CD-R production.

6. Effectively implement the optical disc law regulating the manufacture of pressed discs.

THAILAND

Pirate market value (U.S.$)	28 million
Legitimate market size (units)	23 million
Piracy level	35%
Pirate unit growth	−16%
Legitimate unit growth	−20%

The enforcement efforts of the Thai government have shown some results since 2003 but despite these efforts, the piracy level for music continues to be a major cause of concern to the international recording industry. Piracy in 2003 stood at 35%, the same level as 2002, while the sale of legitimate recordings fell by 20% in 2003. Pirate music sales total U.S.$28 million annually.

The Thai government has shown some commitment to eradicating optical disc piracy and has begun establishing closer working relationships with rights holder organizations. It has also introduced an optical disc bill into the Thai Parliament. However, the bill passed by the lower house of the Thai Parliament is too diluted to be effective in controlling current levels of disc piracy. It needs to be strengthened to ensure that CD plants are obliged to abide by specific registration procedures that discourage pirate manufacturing, to use internationally recognized source identification codes (SID) and to be subject to surprise inspections.

Piracy levels have begun to rise once again, and music pirates have capitalised on the lack of a sustained nationwide anti-piracy action plan. The overcapacity of optical disc plants and lack of an effective optical disc licensing law remain key factors.

In order to maximise its efforts, the Thai government needs to urgently pass an effective optical disc law to control illegal pirate production. It must also conduct an increased and sustained nationwide crackdown on optical disc piracy.

UKRAINE

Pirate market value (U.S.$)	42 million
Legitimate market size (units)	18 million
Piracy level	68%
Pirate unit growth	16%
Legitimate unit growth	4%

Pressed CDs and DVDs still dominate the pirate market in Ukraine. A substantial number of these are imported from Russia and sold in markets, kiosks and street stalls. There are encouraging signs of increased, and geographically wider, police activity against piracy at retail level. However, this is totally insufficient to effectively reduce the availability of illegal recordings in Ukraine. Actions against sources and distribution networks feeding the retailing of these illegal materials remain rare. Border enforcement by Ukrainian Customs is also inadequate. Consequently, while the number of raids has increased, the availability of pirated materials throughout Ukraine has barely decreased.

A major reason why illegal recordings are still widely available in Ukraine is the lack of deterrent punishment of those involved in copyright crime. Prosecution, even of obvious piracy cases, is slow and cumbersome. Rights holders seeking prosecutions face time-consuming hearings, being required to testify and turn up for endless witness interrogation sessions. The piracy cases that do end up in court merely result in the imposition of administrative or criminal fines that are not even remotely deterrent. Prison sentences are very rare and are always suspended.

Despite maintained U.S. trade sanctions, which will soon enter their third year, and continued record industry pressure, Ukraine has still not adopted the necessary amendments to its flawed CD plant regulation. Some of Ukraine's optical disc plants continue to be involved in illegal production and export of pirate optical discs.

The Ukrainian music industry calls upon the authorities to:

1. Help enforcement agencies to focus more on distribution channels such as markets, kiosks and street stalls.

2. Substantially improve border enforcement, especially between Russia and the Ukraine. Customs authorities cannot continue their policy of non co-operation, refusing to share even basic information.

3. Improve the CD Plant regulation and enforce it properly. The Ukrainian optical disc law falls short of what is required to effectively prevent illegal optical disc manufacturing despite repeated explanations by copyright industries of the elements in the law that need to be revised. Moreover rights holders organizations need access to production samples of optical discs and other information currently withheld.

4. Carry out deterrent prosecution and sentencing of pirate activity, including meaningful prison terms.

In The Spotlight: South Korea

Korea has seen a dramatic rise in internet (as opposed to physical format) piracy. With government action urgently needed, Korea merits a special mention in this report.

The market in Korea for recorded music has almost halved in the past two years, down 44%. This is principally due to the exponential growth of internet piracy, fuelled by one of the highest levels of broadband penetration in the world and weak legislation to regulate e-commerce in copyrighted materials.

It has been estimated in media reports that the number of unauthorized peer-to-peer (P2P) file sharing sites in Korea may be as high as 500. The largest P2P site in Korea has an estimated 10 million members, and permits 1,000 to 15,000 simultaneous connections. In July 2002, an injunction was granted by the Korean court against P2P service Soribada, but a newly developed version is back in service. A criminal case is pending in the courts.

Another problem for the industry is the prevalence of unauthorized streaming sites. The largest streaming site, which accounts for about 55% of the market segment, reportedly has over 10 million members.

The government has begun a process of consultations to amend the Korean copyright law, releasing a Master Plan for IPR Protection by the Inter-Ministerial Joint Project, which sets out the broad intellectual property rights policy and plans to step up on law reform and enforcement.

Although the Plan on the whole is positive, it fails to address the urgent needs of the recording industry, which include ratification of the WIPO internet treaties and immediate amendment of the copyright law to accord record producers the right to control all digital transmissions of their recordings. The Plan also does not set out specific enforcement plans to tackle online music piracy.

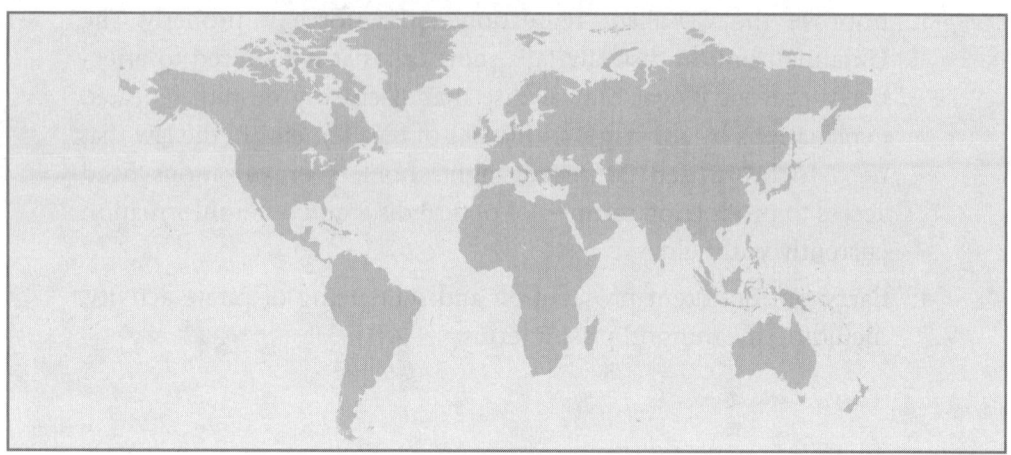

Regional Reports

European Union

Counterfeiting of sound recordings in the CD-R and DVD-R formats is most serious in Southern Europe, namely Greece, Italy, Portugal and Spain. These countries are victims of organized manufacturing and distribution of pirate CDs by criminal groups, operating within hierarchical structures.

IFPI has strong relationships with Law Enforcement Authorities (LEAs), who are now willing to initiate ex-officio actions against retailers and distributors of these products. Particular priority is given to educating the Western European judiciary about the links between music piracy and organized criminal activity. The continued lack of sentencing in piracy cases is the major problem in tackling piracy in Western Europe, and erodes the incentive of enforcement authorities to be active in this area of their work.

A key priority for IFPI will be to address the expansion of pirate trade within the European Union resulting from the enlargement of the EU and the subsequent free movement of goods between a larger group of Member States. In countries such as Poland, investigators have discovered widespread availability of pirate pre-release

Taken from www.ifpi.org.

music titles in local markets. The removal of internal borders will see these products becoming available in more Western countries. The three Baltic States—Estonia, Latvia and Lithuania, all of which recently joined the EU—also have huge piracy problems.

More positively, Poland adopted optical disc regulations that are expected to prevent its massive optical disc production capacity from being used for illegal purposes. The situation at the infamous Warsaw Stadium has improved, with the disappearance of numerous stalls selling illegal discs. As a result of these actions Poland no longer features in IFPI's list of the top ten priority territories.

The widespread growth of CD-R production in Western Europe has allowed for an explosion of piracy in the CD-R format in the region. Joint industry and law enforcement agency investigations have led to the seizure of 6.8 million CD-R discs during 2003 compared to 4.5 million in 2002.

European-wide anti-piracy legislation has been strengthened by the adoption in April 2004 of the EU Enforcement Directive, which aims to bring national legislation on civil sanctions and remedies closer in line across the 25 EU Member States. While the Directive could have gone further to help in the fight against piracy, it does extend some enforcement best practices across the entire EU region.

Gains for the all rights owners in the Directive include measures concerning the use of injunctions, the freezing of assets used in illegal activities, and guidelines to the courts on awarding damages. Importantly, the Directive allows for a presumption of ownership if a rights holder's name appears on a sound recording or other work. This measure should help record companies and other rights holders avoid expensive and pointless courtroom disputes with pirates about copyright ownership.

Under the Directive, rights holders also will be able to ask judicial authorities to order infringers to provide information on the origin and distribution of pirate goods. This should prove helpful both in physical and internet piracy cases. The Directive also contains measures to protect evidence from destruction and to allow for the use of sampling of suspected pirate product.

EU Member States now have two years to implement the Directive into national law. Since the Enforcement Directive provides for a minimum harmonisation of enforcement practices, Member States are free to go further during the implementation process.

The recording industry continues to insist on the need for strengthened criminal sanctions to help combat piracy and counterfeiting. The European Commission intends to come forward with a new proposal for EU legislation on criminal sanctions later in 2004.

Eastern Europe

Piracy levels in the Russia/CIS region remain consistently above 60%, even though the legitimate market grew in 2003 by some 24%. There has been an increase in enforcement actions targeting retailers and distributors of pirate products, but results are much fewer, with less than 25% of cases resulting in court proceedings.

The trans-shipment of pirate product from Russia, often en route to Western Europe, continues to plague the region. High quality counterfeits originating in Russia are found in markets throughout Eastern Europe, as is pre-1995 repertoire which is being reproduced in Russia where it is not yet protected by copyright. CD-R piracy continues to grow and door-to-door sales of illegal sound carriers, which are difficult to detect and control, are increasing throughout the region.

Action by law enforcement agencies remains sporadic and poorly co-ordinated. Without exception, authorities fail to show long-term resolve and a clear strategy in tackling copyright crime.

There is a serious piracy situation in Bulgaria, where enforcement has not improved since 1998. The judiciary and court system in Bulgaria have failed to actively prosecute copyright thieves or hand down deterrent sentences. The legitimate recording industry in Bulgaria is struggling to survive commercially and investment in Bulgarian music production has, as a result, shown a sharp decline.

New replication facilities in Estonia, Poland, Hungary and Romania have contributed to continuing growth in overall production capacity for optical discs in Eastern Europe. In most jurisdictions, attempts to effectively regulate optical disc manufacturing have achieved little success.

Piracy in Turkey is still very high. However, the government has recently adopted a strong anti-piracy bill, including a total ban on street sales of audio-visual products. This is expected to help eradicate the widespread phenomenon of street piracy in Turkey's main cities and tourist areas.

Latin America

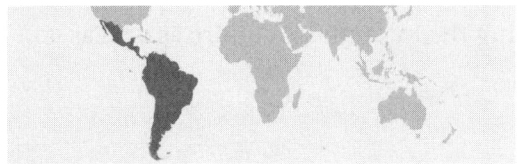

The continued decline in the legitimate market is the direct result of high levels of piracy in most markets in Latin America, resulting in a 14% decrease in value and a 10% drop in units during 2003. Last year all markets in the region sold 148 million legitimate units, compared to 243 million units in 1998–representing a drop in legitimate sales of 39%.

The trend towards recorded CD-Rs as the favoured pirate format continues, with 98% of all seized infringing products on CD-Rs. In 2003, over 150 million blank CD-Rs entered Paraguay alone from markets in South East Asia.

CD-R burning laboratories controlled by organized crime groups are able to operate with relative impunity in territories such as Brazil and Mexico, where weak legislation and ineffective policing mean there is little real threat of detection and subsequent prosecution.

Piracy levels in Mexico and Brazil have seen both countries' legitimate sales decline to the extent that these once-major markets have dropped out of the world's top ten largest markets for legitimate music.

The piracy problems of other Latin American markets such as Colombia are also in the spotlight. Legitimate unit sales in Colombia decreased in 2003 by 5% in units and over 50% in the past five years. In order to stop this continued deterioration, the Colombian government needs to conduct a consistent anti-piracy campaign throughout the country as well as increase piracy criminal penalties to allow the courts to issue deterrent level sentences.

Chile suffered a sizeable 22% decrease in legitimate unit sales. The Chilean police have been fighting piracy in Santiago for the past three years, but the campaign has not been effectively extended to other major cities. In addition, criminal penalties for piracy are too low to serve as real deterrents.

In Peru and Ecuador piracy has practically eliminated the legitimate music markets. Other than sporadic actions taken by individual authorities interested in the subject, neither country has established anti-piracy campaigns, which would ultimately help to promote the development of local artists. Piracy exceeds 95% of the total market in both countries.

As the Argentine market recovers from the economic and political collapse experienced in 2002 its unit sales of recorded music have increased. However the tools to fight piracy are inefficient as criminal penalties remain too weak to serve as a real deterrent. Moreover the Argentine government has not addressed piracy as a priority problem or recognized that it is jeopardising the local music culture as well as contributing to crime levels.

Africa and the Middle East

Political disinterest, combined with a lack of effective enforcement for intellectual property rights, continues to result in high piracy levels in this region.

In many countries the cassette remains the most popular pirate music carrier. However, CD-R piracy is growing fast.

Lebanon has the highest music piracy levels, followed by Kuwait, Saudi Arabia and Egypt. In Lebanon, with a piracy rate of 70%, the situation worsened in 2003-2004 despite promises by the government at the highest level to make copyright enforcement a key priority. Pre-raid leaks and a complete lack of ex-officio action have prevented enforcement from having any sustainable impact in the country, the only positive exception being the customs department.

In 2003, law enforcement agencies in Saudi Arabia carried out hundreds of raids resulting in the seizure of approximately 600,000 pirate music carriers. However, the absence of deterrent penalties for intellectual property violations and a total lack of transparency in the judicial system are preventing these actions from having a positive and lasting impact.

With an estimated overall piracy level of 60%, Kuwait is still one of the worst countries in the Middle East in terms of retail piracy. Even higher levels of piracy are estimated for Indian repertoire distributed in the country. Intellectual property protection is a very low priority for the Kuwaiti authorities, despite it being one of the many Middle Eastern countries to which Pakistan-based optical disc plants ship thousands of illegal optical discs every month.

Egypt still has a piracy level of close to 50%, despite the fact that enforcement has improved in the past three years. A notable even in 2003 was a massive seizure of two million pirate cassettes. However, legitimate sales decreased and the industry is struggling to revive what was once a thriving and highly creative recorded music market.

The year 2003 saw a marked increase—from three to eight—in the number of optical disc production lines now located in Africa. Although currently confined to South Africa and Nigeria, it is evident that many of the region's territories which impose no effective copyright protection, now represent an attractive haven for disc plants.

The increasing popularity of the CD as a format for music in the region has also seen increasing imports of pirate optical disc products, as illustrated by the recent seizures of discs on route to Nigeria from Singapore.

Asia-Pacific

The Asia-Pacific region maintains its position as the world's leading producer of pressed optical discs, feeding illegal music markets around the world. It is no surprise that three of IFPI's top ten priority territories are in Asia, when the region hosts nearly 50% of the world's optical disc plants. Physical piracy continues to predominate. In most countries in the region, particularly where internet penetration has yet to reach significant proportions[2].

While a number of governments within the region have exerted tighter controls on the optical disc industry—the Philippines being the latest to implement legislation on optical disc manufacturing in June 2004—such progressive moves have resulted in the shift of optical disc production lines into countries with little or no copyright protection or enforcement, for example Vietnam.

CD-R piracy is also on the increase in the region, following earlier successes in controlling pressed pirate music products in countries like Singapore, Hong Kong and Taiwan.

Malaysia continues to be a major exporter of pirated discs in the region. While the Malaysian government moved to deploy greater resources to combat pirates in early 2004, its efforts to curb piracy have been hampered by the backlog of cases in court and delays in investigations. This is partly because the relevant Ministry is also responsible for enforcing eight other consumer-related laws. The lack of a dedicated prosecution and investigation unit is another major contributing factor to the backlog which could be dealt with by creating a special intellectual property court.

Both China and Thailand have also increased government enforcement activities, but their efforts have yet to translate into a positive outcome on the ground. Elsewhere, the music industries in countries like Indonesia, India and Vietnam continue to suffer from high piracy rates. Governments across the region are urged to adopt measures to strengthen enforcement, reduce piracy levels and curb exports of illegal music products.

[2]The wider availability of connectivity in countries such as Japan, South Korea, Hong Kong and Australia has, however, led to increases in the level of illegal online distribution and file-sharing. Online music piracy is examined in the separate IFPI Online Music Report.

The Call to Governments

IFPI and its national groups are among the most active of all copyright-based sectors in taking action against piracy. The basis of the work of IFPI's enforcement teams is the protection afforded under copyright laws and the procedures and remedies available to fight against piracy. Good laws and enforcement procedures as well as a strong government commitment are vital.

Governments' top priorities in the fight against piracy can be broadly summarized as follows:

- Strong and up-to-date copyright laws.
- Enforcement rules that permit effective action against any act of infringement, including expeditious and deterrent remedies.
- Regulation of optical disc manufacturing.
- Political commitment to prosecute copyright crime aggressively.
- Stepping up international pressure on governments.

IFPI has identified three key priorities for governments to deal with physical piracy, which are:

1. Effective copyright and enforcement-related legislation

It is essential that governments provide adequate rights and protections under the copyright law against unauthorized copying, distribution and communication to the public of sound recordings. It is equally important that laws protect against the circumvention of the technological measures used to protect content (for instance copy control mechanisms applied to CDs).

Providing adequate rights is the first step in protecting recorded music. Following on from this, it is essential to provide law enforcement authorities and rights holders with effective means to enforce such rights in practice. These include effective civil, administrative and criminal procedures and measures. Key provisions in this context include:

- Damages that effectively compensate rights holders and deter infringers.
- Search and seizure orders for obtaining evidence and stopping the distribution of infringing copies.
- Right of information, for example about the extent of infringing production, sources, and distribution channels.
- Reasonable evidence rules, such as presumptions of ownership of rights, and recognition of sampling as evidence where large shipments are seized.

- Injunctions to prevent or to stop infringements.

- Deterrent-level criminal penalties against infringements that are committed for economic benefit or that cause substantial harm to rights owners.

- Effective border measures empowering customs officials to seize infringing imports, exports and trans-shipments on their own initiative.

2. Regulation of optical disc manufacturing

The replication of pressed CDs and DVDs takes place in a relatively limited number of large-scale mastering and manufacturing facilities. Anti-piracy regulation covering optical disc (OD) plants is essential in order to stop the production of infringing and counterfeit goods at source, before they are dispersed widely and hurt domestic and foreign markets.

Any country with high CD production capacity, and in particular overcapacity, should adopt OD plant regulation in order to maintain the level of transparency and business practices necessary to promote legitimate manufacturing and deter piracy. OD plant regulation is already in place in China, Macau, Hong Kong, Malaysia, Taiwan, the Philippines, Bulgaria, Ukraine, and Poland. Legislative projects for OD plant regulation are underway in Indonesia, Singapore and Thailand.

Many more countries are in need of effective OD plant regulation, based on the experience of IFPI's enforcement teams. At present, a number of countries clearly stand out as needing such regulation, particularly the Russian Federation, India and Pakistan.

3. Effective prosecution and deterrent penalties

Even where adequate laws are in place, rights are not effectively protected unless governments commit resources and political will to bringing prosecutions and deterrent penalties against copyright infringers. It is also critical that they put in place teams of prosecutors that have experience in intellectual property crimes.

The inexperience of many courts in copyright matters can also make it difficult for governments or rights holders to enforce their rights through the legal process. IFPI therefore strongly supports the creation of specialist intellectual property courts that can hear piracy cases. Whether or not such courts are established, it is essential that the judiciary treat copyright infringement as a serious matter and impose penalties that act as an effective deterrent to music piracy. This is a legal obligation on countries that are members of the WTO under the TRIPs Agreement.

Stepping up international pressure on countries which are failing adequately to enforce intellectual property rights is a vital and effective way of bringing about real change. The regular reviews conducted by the U.S. government under 301 legislation play a vital role in monitoring progress internationally. Inter-governmental pressure needs to be stepped up in several arenas, including the World Customs Organization (WCO), the World Trade Organization (WTO), the World Intellectual Property Organization (WIPO), and at regional level, for example, via the internal and external policy initiatives of the European Union.

Music Piracy—The Facts

- Freeloaders: Because of the relative low cost of the raw materials, pirate profit margins are close to 100% but the pirates add no value to the creative industries. Pirates illegally copy and sell only the recordings of the most popular international stars and local icons, pocketing the money and leaving the legitimate record business to do all the investment and to take all the risks in producing music.

- The victims: Piracy is not a victimless crime. The economic losses due to piracy are enormous and are felt throughout the music value chain. The victims include the *artists* and all those involved in the performance of music; *governments* which lose hundreds of thousands in tax revenues; *record producers,* who are forced to reduce artist rosters; and *consumers,* who get less diversity in the music that can be produced.

- Links to organized crime: Most pirates are sophisticated and organized. They are able to obtain and sell valuable intellectual property before it is even released in the legitimate marketplace. The proceeds from pirate sales fund ruthless criminal enterprises. They are encouraged by poor laws, weak enforcement and inadequate legal penalties.

- Local culture suffers: Piracy sucks the lifeblood out of local culture. Talented artists in the high piracy markets of China, India, Africa, the Middle East, Eastern Europe and elsewhere cannot get local recording contracts and have to try to make a living from touring, or move elsewhere, which means that the cultural wealth of their home country suffers.

- A global problem: Pirate operations are increasingly international and cross-border. The most effective way of fighting piracy is by inter-governmental co-operation on enforcement strategies.

IFPI represents the recording industry worldwide with over 1,450 members in over 70 countries and affiliated industry associations in 48 countries.

Record And Tape Clubs

Record and tape clubs are yet another revenue stream for major labels with publishing divisions. The clubs witnessed an increase in overall sales and market share of the business in the early 1990's. Record and tape clubs have been around since the mid to late 1950's, when they generated a great deal of animosity from the dealer structure. This reaction was not surprising to the major labels, and they did attempt to ameliorate the situation with a succession of plans that attempted to bring the dealers into the club activities via coupon, overrides, referral payments, and other gimmicks. However, none really worked and eventually the dealer structure just accepted clubs as part of the business.

Manufacturers claimed that any advertising they ran on behalf of the clubs would indirectly help anyone marketing music. They also felt that clubs served a very small part of the consumer base and most record buyers could not or would not wait for delivery, but would go to a retail outlet instead. For a few decades, this truce remained, but in the early 1990's, the dealers saw a marked increase in the amount of volume activity in clubs. From 1990 to 1994 the dealers percentage of the overall business declined 16%. Some of that volume went to rack jobbers with the resurgence of country product. That trend reversed itself with country decreasing in 1995. Leading up to 1994, a portion of the increases was club sales, which the industry felt was just part of an overall increase in "armchair" buying on the part of the consumer since catalog sales in all industries. That trend reversed itself, when a backlash developed and dealers attempted to make the major companies limit their participation in club sales, a few labels backed off from selling through clubs but most stayed. The labels that sell through clubs feel that their advertising helps everyone sell the product and that many club consumers drop their membership each year and go back to buying at retail outlets. After some profitable years, the club sales started to slide precipitously in 1994. From 1994 to 1998, club sales decreased from 15.1% of the total to only 9.1%. This decrease was a result of labels pulling back from club sales to appease the dealer structure. However, it now appears that a portion of the decrease is due to internet sales, which is another variation on "armchair" buying.

Undoubtedly, companies can make money via club activities, but it's not as easy as some would suspect. The costs of acquiring & retaining club members are astronomical since the attrition rate (90%) each year is huge. However, the clubs do not have the costs that retail and rack jobbing must bear, such as store rent, upkeep or store clerks (labor at club warehouses is usually handled via temporary workers). As with book clubs, record clubs use the "passive response" technique. You receive about fifteen notices per year and have to send back the solicitation indicating a no or you will receive the selection for that month automatically. The club operations are highly computerized and this saves costs. Clubs are able to negotiate a more favorable royalty rate because of the volume they can promise to major acts. Many a piece of product has reached the platinum level by adding in club sales. Also, knowing what your orders are before having to ship leaves you with little in the way of overstocks.

TV Offers/Mail Order

Most of the companies that run TV and magazine offers are "in house" operations of major record companies. There are some firms not owned by the record companies that go on TV with a specialty product. In just about all situations, the product is "oldies" from a few years to a few decades back. This product is licensed to the company making the offer. Once again, the cost structure is far different for these firms. Research shows that there must be a saturation of TV spots before people even think about jotting down a phone number or address to place an order. Magazine advertising is not inexpensive, but it can pinpoint an audience. When radio and TV offers started, they were usually on what was called a "P.I." basis or "per inquiry." This meant the station was paid by getting a percentage of the sale, rather than having the time purchased up front as is the case with most commercial time sales.

Once again, the retailers were not happy about these "non-traditional" offers. Soon it became very apparent that when an artist was advertised on TV, that artist's catalog sales in the stores usually increased dramatically. The industry will never forget what happened with Slim Whitman when offered on TV. Sales were sensational. Again, the syndrome of the record buyer not willing to wait the six weeks came into play. Record companies argue that everyone benefits because while some will wait the six weeks, others will go out and buy when they had no previous inclination to do so. In the case of clubs, TV and mail offers, the marketing perspective is quite narrow. The audience and media are known entities. The biggest decision is what product mix to offer.

Premium Sales

Premium sales put recorded music in an entirely different marketplace. The consumer is the same, but access comes from a desire to get a real bargain. The most prevalent premium items are the seasonal records offered by banks, oil companies and other businesses as an incentive to buy product or use their services. Premium sales are very advantageous for record companies. Usually the product comes from the vaults and has been amortized long ago, so royalty costs are nil. However, there are other advantages. The firm purchasing the prerecorded compilation or catalogue item, must place an order and pay for all items ordered. The record company can press just enough to fill that demand and not have any returns. Even better, these orders are placed long before the product will be needed and thus can be manufactured when the duplication loads on the manufacturing locations are extremely low.

Cutouts

Cutouts are a necessary evil. They are products that are in overstocks or have outlived their sales potential as either front line or budget items. Many outlets do very well with these products. The outlets are able to buy at a very low price and get a reasonable price over the counter. Product in the "cutout bins" that comes back as returns are recycled as saleable merchandise because the cost of manufacturing are non-existent. Return policies have limited cutouts but overstocks will always be plentiful when products are returnable.

Summary

Music publishing, record and tape clubs, TV offers, mail order and premium sales are yet another revenue stream for major record labels. Publishing has the potential of generating enormous profits through performance, reproduction and distribution based royalties. ASCAP, BMI, SESAC, Harry Fox and others negotiate and issue licenses for the collection of royalties. These royalties are paid directly to songwriters and publishers for use of copyrighted materials in their catalogs. The value of the music publishers catalog is based on the quality of songs, frequency and nature of their use and how they are licensed. Globally, music publishers face the challenges of unlicensed online music, file sharing, payola, piracy, radio consolidation and antiquated copyright laws.

Terms

Music Publisher: A business entity that secures commercially released recordings, CD's and tapes of songs in catalog

Catalog: A compilation of creative works and older album releases

Copyright: An original work of authorship fixed in a tangible medium of expression

Mechanicals: Royalties paid by record companies to music publishers and songwriters upon use of their songs on recordings, which requires a license to produce and distribute records and tapes to the public. Publishers use the Harry Fox Agency to issue and negotiate licenses as well as collect fees and distribute income.

Synchronization: License required to use music which is timed to synchronize with or relate to, the action on the screen

Performing Rights Societies: Organizations such as ASCAP, BMI and SESAC that collect performance royalties on behalf of songwriters and music publishers from broadcast, non-broadcast, live venues and digital transmissions.

Record and Tape Clubs: Retail selling of prerecorded music product through the mail

Television Offer/Mail Order: Specialty music product offered on Television which increases catalog sales of an artist

Premium Sales: Seasonal records, special compilations, offered by banks, oil companies and other businesses as an incentive to purchase their product or services.

Cutouts: Cutouts are products that are in overstocks or have outlived their sales potential as either frontline or budget product.

Compilation: Collection of different, often older, recordings by artist or artists compiled as a package on one or more albums or box sets.

Frontline: New album releases by current artists at the top of the industry's pricing tier.

International Federation of Phonographic Institute (IFPI)—Organization representing the international recording industry comprising of 1500 producers and distributors in seventy six countries. The priorities are to fight piracy, update copyright laws responsive to the digital era and promote the value of music in the development of economies

Recording Industry Association of America (RIAA)—Provides statistical data on the American recording industry and is a voice for their legal and technical concerns.

Spanish Society of Authors, Composer and Publishers (SGAE)—SGAE is a copyright management society comprised of nearly 68,000 music, audiovisual and dramatic creators. It's mission is the protection of its members rights for the use of their works.

Music Publishers Association (MPA)-The MPA promotes and safeguards the interests of British Music Publishers at the governmental and industry levels.

Harry Fox Agency, Inc. (HFA)- HFA is the major organization for mechanical rights administration in the U.S., licensing uses of music worldwide on records, tapes, CD's and imported phonorecords. HFA represents over 27,000 music publishers and 150,000 songwriters.

International Intellectual Property Alliance (IIPA)- IILPA is a umbrella organization of eight trade associations representing 1,500 copyright based companies in the motion picture, video game, book, music publishing, computer software and recording industries. It was organized to stimulate and augment U.S. government trade policy and actions against international piracy and to persuade foreign governments to take action against copyright, patent and trademark infringement.

International Bureau and Society of Engineering and Mechanical Reproduction (BIEM)- A confederation of mechanical rights organizations from more than thirty countries, is the most important organization for mechanical rights protection through out the world.

Japanese Society for Rights of Authors, Composers and Publishers (JASRAC)- JASRAC administers nondramatic performing, broadcasting, cable transmission, mechanical reproduction, synchronization and distribution rights in musical works.

Society of Composers, Authors and Music Publishers of Canada (SOCAN)- SOCAN is a performing rights society representing Canadian composers, lyricists, songwriters and music publishers.

Exercises

1. What are the responsibilities of a publisher and where do they derive most of their primary and secondary income?

2. The international music publisher receives income from three main sources. List, define and explain how income is derived from these sources.

3. Describe and explain some of the challenges facing the international publisher?

4. List and describe four international performing and/or mechanical rights organizations.

5. List and describe all ancillary forms of income for record labels.

6. How important is the record labels publishing catalog to its bottom line?

7. What affect does TV offers usually have on the catalog of the artists being advertised?

8. What is the most attractive aspect of premium sales to record companies?

Chapter 17
New Technology Configurations

Learning Objectives

After studying this chapter you should be able to:

1. Summarize the growth of the CD

2. Explain the growth of DVD and SACD

3. Describe Dataplay and Pressplay subscription services

4. Explain the music industry's file sharing strategy

5. Discuss how consumers may access music by mobile phones

6. Describe the technology in Apple's new iMac G5

7. Discuss Apple's iTunes 6 and it's contribution to revenues

8. Discuss Apple's new Ipod with music, video; photo features

9. Technology platforms of Snocap, Mashboxx, Qtrax, Peer Impact, Audible Magic, Overpeer, and Open Royalty

10. Mobile Services and Broadband as future revenue generators

Technology changed the industry from the introduction of radio in the 1920's to cylinder recordings, CDs, digital media and online distribution. One of the key milestones that propelled the music industry within the previous decade was in 1992 when Philips launched the digital compact disc and Sony countered with the minidisc. A year later in 1993 the CD album units outsold minicassettes for the first time. The CD album has driven growth in music sales throughout the 90s, increasing over 150% The average annual growth of the CD over the past decade was 10.8%. Although the rate of growth began to level off in the latter half of the 90's, the format demonstrated a healthy growth of 2.5% in 2000. North America increased its share of the global market by value from 31% in 1991 to over 40% in 2000. North America's CD market has driven this increasing share, accounting for over 40% of worldwide CD sales by the year 2000.

There has been much recent debate concerning where and how music will be played and listened to in the future. The arrival of digital streaming and downloading, DVD, MP3 and other mobile technologies will see music listening diversify. The majority of new music is still listened to via radio and most music is played within households, car or on portable CD players. CD player penetration is measured as the total number of CD players owned as a proportion of total households. CD player saturation is measured as the proportion of total households who own at least one CD player. In terms of household players, market penetration is gradually reaching maturity, with some markets having a penetration of 100% or greater On average, player penetration was 5% higher than in 1999 across these markets, with notable increases in Ireland, USA, UK, Austria and Switzerland. In addition, many developing music markets have relatively low levels of player saturation. These markets have a capacity for CD player sales to grow further as minicassette players are replaced and the CD format becomes more universal.

Recently manufacturers and record labels introduced three new formats, Dual Disc, DVD audio and Super Audio Compact Discs (SACDs) that they hope will replace the CD. SACDs and DVD-Audio, when coupled with the right speaker, sound superior to regular CDs. Parts of a recording buried in the music mix (drumbeat, backup vocals etc.) are now crystal clear. Both DVD-Audio and SACDs can hold several times the data contained on regular CDs. They are also multichannel (surround sound) instead of the two channel (stereo) CDs.

While CDs are more convenient and durable than vinyl they are inferior when it comes to sound. A good vinyl record will get you a little better sound of the real performance than a compact disc. When the industry transferred from vinyl to CD, warmth and the ability to record air around the instruments were lost. SACD is basically a three-dimensional experience. Music has depth, width and height and just as if you're sitting in a concert hall, you're hearing music not only coming directly at you but coming to you, and ricocheting off the walls.

The sound of DVD-Audio is comparable to that of SACDs and the format offers bonus features similar to DVDs. Listeners might watch videos or sing along to lyrics that flash on the TV screen. DVDs and SACDs are much more difficult to copy. The new discs costs about $19.00 but a DVD player is around $200.00. In order to achieve maximum benefit the consumer must upgrade their entertainment system. Sony offers bargain SACD players that also play DVD videos for about $300.00. Unlike CDs and MP3, which you can play anywhere, DVD-Audio and SACDs do not have portability. Cars, portable CD players or boomboxes don't have the technology to play them as of this date. There are three hundred albums available on DVD-Audio and four hundred and fifty on SACD format. The Sony Music Group and Universal Music Group are backing the SACD format, while Warner Music Group places its hopes on the DVD-Audio.

The newly released portable music format, called DataPlay digital media is the latest technology joining a number of choices for consumers to play their favorite music through headphones connected to palm size devices. The discs, contained in a clear plastic shell are about the size of the ring in the center of the CD, or 1/4 the size of a minidisc. They will be available in blank, recordable form as well as prerecorded, copy-protected albums. BMG, Universal music and EMI have signed agreements with DataPlay because of the copy protection.

DataPlay, a privately held company in Boulder, Colorado was founded in 1998 by its chairman Steve Volk. Initially Mr. Volk interest was in developing smaller optical discs and micro drivers for use as storage media in digital cameras. He realized that the tiny, digitally secure discs and drivers were a natural fit for the music industry, which was searching for new ways to protect and distribute recorded music. Data-Play's content is encrypted which is the kind of technology that the record labels will take a chance. DataPlay players and media may present an early stumbling block to widespread acceptance, consumer electronics retailers warn. Prerecorded Data Play discs ($18.00-$22.00) is priced more like a DVD than a CD. The price of a CD-R has decreased significantly when it is purchased in bulk. DataPlay discs, which have 500 megabytes of storage capacity or 150 megabytes less than 74-minute CD-R discs, cost $5.00 if purchased in packages of ten. The first DataPlay music player and burner, the IDP-100 is expensive at $350.00. MP3 players with 20 gigabytes of memory or forty times the capacity of a DataPlay disc are available for $300.00. The long term future of music distribution is in the music and lyrics winding through the air, captured on wireless communication equipment.

Tabe 17-1
MUSIC TECHNOLOGY CONFIGURATIONS

YEAR	CONFIGURATION
1878	Thomas Edison invents the phonograph Emile Berliner develops audio platter to replace Edison's wax cylinder
1915	78 RPM records introduced
1928	33 1/3 RPM records introduced
1947	Magnetic tape recorders enter the U.S. market
1948	45 RPM records enter the U.S. market
1958	Stereo records are produced
1965	Audio cassette tape introduced
1966	In-dash eight track tape players appear in automobiles after use in Lear-jet business planes
1969	Klass Compaan conceives idea for compact disc
1983	CD's are introduced to the U.S. market
1991	Sony announces creation of MiniDisc players and discs
2002	DataPlay player recorders & discs go on sale

Technological developments were a major force in the music industry for much of 2001. Two internet based music subscription ventures supported by the recording industry launched their companies during the last half of the year. The companies were MusicNet, which is a partnership between RealNetworks, Bertlesmann, AOL Time Warner and EMI. Pressplay another subscription service was supported by Universal and Sony music. MusicNet launched its RealOne music service in December, with 100,000 songs from its parent companies and the world's largest independent label, Zomba. Each month RealOne music subscribers are required to pay $9.95 per month to download up to one hundred songs that can be played an unlimited number of times for thirty days, and to play up to one hundred songs from an online jukebox. Pressplay features 100,000 songs from its parent company as well as EMI and Zomba, which have signed licensing deals with the service. The price range from $9.95 per month to $24.95 per month, depending on the amount of songs the consumer wishes to access.

Artists have threatened to sue companies with subscription services because the creators did not give consent for copyright usage. Record company contracts grant labels the exclusive distribution rights to an artist's catalog, which may include streaming and downloads. Universal issued a license to independent online music distributor FullAudio for the rights to a portion of its music catalog. FullAudio has negotiated the rights to a significant portion of EMI's catalog and licenses from the music publishing arms of EMI, Universal and BMG. FullAudio allows consumers to download dozens of songs to their computers for a flat monthly fee. The songs are locked on the subscriber's computer and expire after a month, but can be renewed on a month-to-month basis. On Listen.com's Rhapsody subscription service users are allowed to download and store 99% of each song on their hard drives, but must log on to Listen.com and download the remaining parts of the song before the songs can be played. Consequently, consumers cannot download music to portable devices or create their own CDs. Rhapsody is a subscription service that offers music lovers unlimited access to one of the world's largest libraries of digital music. For less than ten dollars a month, Rhapsody gives fans the ability to listen to an incredible variety of music on demand. Rhapsody is an easy to use online service that's built on the concepts of unlimited access that made the original Napster service so enticing to consumers. Rhapsody respects the interests of artists, labels and copyright owners, by providing reporting mechanisms that make it easier to compensate parties whose music they offer to subscribers. United Kingdom based internet service provider Btopenworld is testing the U. K.'s first secure music subscription service in partnership with digital distributor OD2's WebAudioNet platform. The service, at btopenworld.com/music enables secure distribution of repertoire from OD2's label partners, V2, Warner music of U.K. and BMG.

The four major labels have invested $1.99976 billion on developing digital music services. Questions as to profitability status continue to persist, with most observers predicting profitability at least several years away. While songwriters and publishers have agreed to grant publishing licenses to record labels for subscription service, the rates paid to publishers for use of their works in digital service has yet to be determined. Another question is whether operators of subscription businesses should pay both performance and mechanical royalties?

Free online music file swapping continues to be problematic. On November 19, 2001 a class action copyright infringement suit in Los Angeles was filed against MusicCity, which operates Morpheus, Grokster.com and KaZaA. These businesses are considered illegal file sharing systems. The suit follows one filed in October by RIAA and the Motion Picture Association of America, alleging that the sites encourage the unlawful exchange of music, movies, software and images. BMG plans to launch BeMusic, its onestop web destination for music commerce services, including record clubs, retail and subscriptions in 2002.

Listen.com became the first of several companies to launch new online music services offering music fans their first legal alternative to file sharing. These illicit services enabled online consumers to trade millions of copyrighted songs without compensating the songwriters, labels and copyright holders. The new legitimate services such as Rhapsody, Listen.com, MusicNet, Pressplay represents a welcomed change in the industry. Rhapsody, as well as the other services represent significant steps toward building a legal market for online music.

Another important technological development is the growing market for accessing music via mobile phones. Currently there is a booming demand for the use of music as ringtones. It has been estimated that more than $200 million has been spent by consumers worldwide to download ringtones. Japan's largest mobile phone operator, NTT DoCoMo, has estimated that some 600 million wireless phones will be in use in that country by 2010. The estimations are that twenty four percent of wireless phone users in Western Europe use personalized ringtones. Music publishers and record labels are aggressively examining this new area. EMI music publishing signed a non-exclusive global licensing agreement with the world's largest mobile phone maker, Nokia, in August 2000. U.S. based international wireless entertainment service provider Premium Wireless Service is licensing music from EMI music publishing, Warner-Chappell, Sony's publishing division, and Sony ATV to use music as part of their ringtone service. Other companies looking to enter the field include game maker Sega and Disney, whose Walt Disney Internet Group has struck deals to distribute logos, screen savers, electronic cards and ringtones in Japan, Hong Kong and Taiwan.

Increased mobile phone technology will allow users to download and play full length songs over their telephones. Universal Music France has signed a deal with local mobile phone carrier SFR to enable users to preview full music tracks on their phones, while its parent, Universal Music International, has signed an agreement with Nordic telecom Schibsted Telecom to test a pay-per-listen service via mobile phone. Ericsson, the Swedish hand set manufacturer, offers an MP3 player that can be attached to its mobile phones for listening to downloaded music, and has formed a partnership with Sony's electronics division to offer multimedia content via its wireless devices.

Apple ignited the personal computer revolution in the 1970s with the Apple II and reinvented the personal computer in the 1980s with the Macintosh. Today Apple continues to lead the industry in innovation with its award winning desktop and notebook computers, OSX operating systems, iLife and professional applications. Apple is also spearheading the digital music revolution with its iPod portable music players and iTunes online music stores. The portable player market like Apple's iPod have given consumers greater control and portability of their music collections. The growing popularity of digital players are increasing the demand for legal music services. The global portable digital player market was estimated to be worth U.S.$4.4 billion dollars in 2003 and U.S.$7 billion in 2004. Apple's iPod has over

50% share of the global digital market and is the most successful portable digital players with sales of 10 million units. In October 2004 Apple launched the first artist branded digital player, the U2 iPod, which included a discount on the option to purchase U2's entire catalogue through iTunes. The enclosed Apple new music formats are the latest in a series of groundbreaking technologies that continues to revolutionize the industry.

Apple Introduces New Technology

Seeing the Cut

Film editors cutting on non-linear digital editing systems generally see significantly less than what the cameras actually take in. But for "Dreamer," beautifully shot in 35mm film, anything less than a WYSIWYG post scenario was out of the question. The solution? An HD workflow anchored on Final Cut Pro. [Oct 21, 2005]

Apple Introduces Aperture

The first all-in-one post production tool that provides everything photographers need after the shoot, Aperture offers an advanced and incredibly fast RAW workflow that makes working with a camera's RAW images as easy as JPEG. Built from the ground up for pros, Aperture features powerful compare and select tools, nondestructive image processing, color managed printing and custom web and book publishing. [Oct 19, 2005]

Introducing the New Power Mac G5 Quad & Power Mac G5 Dual

The new Power Mac G5 desktop line now features the Power Mac G5 Quad, providing quad-core processing with two 2.5GHz dual-core PowerPC G5 processors. All Power Mac G5 models now feature dual-core processors, a new PCI Express architecture and higher performance graphics options including NVIDIA's Quadro FX 4500, bringing the industry standard for workstation graphics to the Mac. [Oct 19, 2005]

Apple Enhances PowerBooks

Apple today made its PowerBook G4 line of notebook computers even more desirable for business and creative professionals with higher-resolution displays and up to one hour more battery life on the 15- and 17-inch models. In addition, every new PowerBook now includes a DVD burning SuperDrive. [Oct 19, 2005]

Taken from www.apple.com

The New Manhattan Project

The Manhattan Producers Alliance, a co-op of accomplished composers, producers and sound designers founded in 2003, recently made the move to Power Mac G5s and Mac OS X. Its members talked to us about the new vistas of music creation this technology has opened up. [Oct 14, 2005]

Apple Unveils the New iPod

The new iPod, featuring a gorgeous 2.5-inch color screen, can display album artwork and photos, as well as play stunning video including music videos, video podcasts, home movies and television shows. The new iPod holds up to 15,000 songs, 25,000 photos or over 150 hours of video and is available in a 30GB model for $299 and a 60GB model for $399, with both models available in stunning white or black designs. [Oct 12, 2005]

Apple Announces iTunes 6

iTunes 6, the next generation of the world's most popular music jukebox and online music store, lets fans purchase and download over 2,000 music videos and six short films from Academy Award-winning Pixar Animation Studios for just $1.99 each. Customers can also now purchase and download their favorite television shows from iTunes the day after they air on TV, watch them on their Mac or PC and Auto-Sync them onto the new iPod for viewing anywhere. [Oct 12, 2005]

Apple Introduces the New iMac G5

The new iMac G5 features a built-in iSight video camera for out-of-the-box video conferencing and Apple's new breakthrough Front Row media experience. Front Row gives users a simple, intuitive and powerful way to play their music, enjoy their photo slideshows and watch their DVDs and iMovies, as well as popular movie trailers from apple.com and music videos and television shows purchased from the iTunes Music Store, on their iMac from up to 30 feet away using the new bundled Apple Remote. [Oct 12, 2005]

Apple Quarterly Results

Apple announced fourth quarter financial results, posting revenue of $3.68 billion and a net quarterly profit of $430 million, or $.50 per diluted share. These results compare to revenue of $2.35 billion and a net profit of $106 million, or $.13 per diluted share, in the year-ago quarter. Gross margin was 28.1 percent, up from 27.0

percent in the year-ago quarter. International sales accounted for 40 percent of the quarter's revenue. [Oct 11, 2005]

The iMac G5, iTunes 6 and Ipod will be discussed in much greater detail. Snow-cap, a new venture by Napster founder Shawn Fanning provides technology that recognizes songs requiring licenses on P2P networks and offers options to download legally or illegally. Mashboxx, Qtrax and Peer Impact (Wurld Media) are businesses where P2P technology is being designed to facilitate licensed file sharing with various payment options for users. Overpeer and Open Royalty Gateway have developed song-identification systems similar to Snocap.

Apple Introduces the New iMac G5

Features Built-in iSight Video Camera & Breakthrough "Front Row" Media Experience

SAN JOSE, California—October 12, 2005—Apple® today unveiled the new iMac® G5 which features a built-in iSight™ video camera for out-of-the-box video conferencing and the debut of Apple's breakthrough Front Row media experience. Front Row gives users a simple, intuitive and powerful way to play their music, enjoy their photo slideshows, and watch their DVDs and iMovies, as well as popular movie trailers from apple.com and music videos and television shows purchased from the iTunes® Music Store, on their iMac from up to 30 feet away using the new bundled Apple Remote. The new iMac G5 comes in a sleek, new design that is even thinner than its predecessor, and starts at just $1,299.

"The new iMac G5 debuts our amazing Front Row media experience, and we think users are going to love it," said Steve Jobs, Apple's CEO. "Plus, the built-in iSight video camera delivers out-of-the-box video conferencing with friends and family, as well as hours of fun with our new Photo Booth application."

Apple's breakthrough Front Row media experience uses the bundled Apple Remote to let users enjoy the content they have on their iMac—including songs from their iTunes music library, slideshows of their photo albums in iPhoto®, videos including Podcasts, iMovies and DVDs, and popular movie trailers streamed from apple.com—all from up to 30 feet away. And with iTunes 6, users can now purchase and download music videos, Pixar short films and hit TV shows such as "Desperate Housewives" and "Lost" from the iTunes Music Store and watch them on their iMac using Front Row. Front Row is easily controlled using the Apple Remote, which has only six buttons, compared to remote controls for Microsoft's Media Center which typically have over 40 buttons.

With its built-in iSight video camera, the new iMac G5 provides video conferencing right out of the box using Apple's award-winning iChat AV software. The new iMac G5 also includes Photo Booth, Apple's fun-to-use new application that lets users take quick snapshots with the built-in iSight video camera, add entertaining visual effects with the touch of a button, and share them via Mail, save them in iPhoto®, or use them as icons in iChat or Address Book.

The refined design of the new iMac G5 is now up to 1/2-inch thinner and 15 percent lighter than the previous generation. Delivering even greater value, the new iMac G5 line includes a 17-inch model with a 1.9GHz PowerPC G5 processor for just $1,299 and a 20-inch model with a 2.1 GHz PowerPC G5 processor for just $1,699. Both models now come standard with a SuperDrive™ with double-layer support for burning professional-quality DVDs, 533 MHz DDR2 SDRAM memory expandable to 2.5GB, hard drive storage capacity up to 500GB, and ATI Radeon X600 PCI Express-based graphics with 128MB of dedicated video memory for outstanding graphics performance and realistic game play. System memory is easily upgraded via a convenient access door along the bottom edge.

Offering the latest high-performance I/O, the new iMac G5s include built-in 10/100/1000BASE-T Gigabit Ethernet for high-speed networking, built-in Air-Port® Extreme for fast 54 Mbps wireless networking*, built-in Bluetooth 2.0+EDR, a total of five USB ports (three USB 2.0) and two FireWire® 400 ports. The new iMac G5 includes Apple's Mighty Mouse, featuring up to four programmable buttons and an ingenious Scroll Ball that lets users scroll in any direction—vertically, horizontally and even diagonally.

Every new iMac G5 also includes iLife® '05, Apple's award-winning suite of digital lifestyle applications; Mac OS X version 10.4 "Tiger," the world's most advanced operating system; and a collection of productivity and entertainment titles including AppleWorks, Quicken 2006 for Mac, 2006 World Book, Photo Booth, Nanosaur 2 and Marble Blast Gold.

Apple Announces iTunes 6 With 2,000 Music Videos, Pixar Short Films & Hit TV Shows

ABC's "Desperate Housewives" & "Lost" Episodes Available for Just $1.99

SAN JOSE, California—October 12, 2005—Apple® today announced iTunes® 6, the next generation of the world's most popular music jukebox and online music store. iTunes 6 lets fans purchase and download over 2,000 music videos and six short films from Academy-Award winning Pixar Animation Studios for just $1.99 each. Also, in a landmark deal with Disney, iTunes is now offering current and past episodes from two of the most popular shows on television, "Desperate Housewives" and "Lost," as well as the new drama series "Night Stalker" and the two most popular shows from Disney Channel, "That's So Raven" and "The Suite Life of Zack & Cody," for just $1.99 per episode. Customers can now purchase and download their favorite television shows from iTunes the day after they air on TV, watch them on their Mac® or PC, and Auto-Sync them onto the new iPod® for viewing anywhere.

"We're doing for video what we've done for music—we're making it easy and affordable to purchase and download, play on your computer, and take with you on your iPod," said Steve Jobs, Apple's CEO. "Right out of the gate we're offering 2,000 music videos, Pixar's short films and hit primetime TV shows like 'Desperate House-wives' and 'Lost'."

"For the first time ever, hit primetime shows can be purchased online the day after they air on TV," said Robert Iger, CEO of the Walt Disney Company. "We're delighted to be working with Apple to offer fans a new and innovative way to expe-rience our wildly popular shows like 'Desperate Housewives' 'Lost' and 'That's So Raven'."

"Apple is giving music fans a great way to own their favorite music videos," said Jimmy Iovine, Chairman of Interscope Geffen A&M. "The people at Apple fully understand the interaction between musicians and their audience."

Featured exclusive music videos are available from artists such as Beastie Boys and U2 along with more than two dozen classic music videos from Madonna. Music videos are available from hundreds of artists, including classic hits by Michael Jackson and Sting and current hits from Coldplay and Kanye West. The first ever video iTunes Originals is being released with an exclusive performance and interview from Death Cab for Cutie as well as an exclusive video album from Brazilian Girls. Music fans can also purchase the Complete Stevie Wonder digital box set, which contains over 500 songs, a full color digital booklet and three bonus videos, available only on the iTunes Music Store. Movie shorts available from Pixar include "Boundin'," "For the Birds," "Geri's Game," "Luxo Jr.," "Red's Dream," and "Tin Toy."

New features in iTunes 6 include expanded online gift options which now allow customers to give specific songs, albums, music videos or their own iTunes playlists to anyone with an email address, a public beta of new "Just for You" personalized music recommendations and the debut of online customer reviews. Now more than 10 million iTunes music fans can read other customers' reviews, post their own and rate their usefulness.

With Apple's legendary ease of use, pioneering features such as integrated Pod-casting support, iMix playlist sharing, seamless integration with iPod and ground-breaking personal use rights, the iTunes Music Store is the best way for Mac and PC users to legally discover, purchase and download music online. The iTunes Music Store features more than two million songs from the major music companies and over 1,000 independent record labels, 10,000 audiobooks, gift certificates and exclusive music not found anywhere else online.

Pricing & Availability

iTunes 6 for Mac and Windows includes the iTunes Music Store and is available as a free download immediately from www.apple.com/itunes. Purchase and download of songs from the iTunes Music Store for Mac or Windows requires a valid credit card with a billing address in the country of purchase. Television shows are available in the U.S. only, and video availability varies by country. Music videos and short films are $1.99 (U.S.) each, and television shows are $1.99 (U.S.) per episode.

Apple Unveils the New iPod

Fifth Generation iPod Now Plays Music, Photos & Video

SAN JOSE, California—October 12, 2005—Apple today introduced the new iPod®, featuring a gorgeous 2.5-inch color screen which can display album artwork and photos, and play stunning video including music videos, video Podcasts, home movies and television shows. The new iPod holds up to 15,000 songs, 25,000 photos or over 150 hours of video and is available in a 30GB model for $299 and a 60GB model for $399, with both models available in stunning white or black designs.

"The new iPod is the best music player ever—it's 30 percent thinner and has 50 percent more storage than its predecessor—yet it sells for the same price and plays stunning video on its 2.5-inch color screen," said Steve Jobs, Apple's CEO. "Because millions of people around the world will buy this new iPod to play music, it will quickly become the most popular portable video player in history."

The new iPod plays music, audiobooks, audio Podcasts, video Podcasts, home movies, music videos and popular television shows like "Lost" and "Desperate Housewives." The unrivaled combination of iPod and iTunes® 6 now provides customers with a seamless experience for buying, managing and playing video as well as audio content, including over 2,000 music videos, six short films from the Academy-Award winning Pixar Animation Studios, and five television shows from ABC and Disney Channel, including the immensely popular "Lost" and "Desperate Housewives."

The new iPod combines all of the ground breaking features that have made the iPod the best music player in the world with revolutionary new features such as the ability to view video content on a larger stunning color display. The new iPod features Apple's innovative Click Wheel for precise, one-handed navigation and the portable design is ideal for putting music, Podcasts, photos, audiobooks, home movies, music videos and popular television shows in a pocket for on-the-go viewing. iPod users can also watch their video content and slideshows of their photos on a television via optional Apple accessories.

Featuring seamless integration with the iTunes Music Store and the iTunes digital music jukebox, iPod features Apple's patent pending Auto-Sync technology that automatically downloads digital music, Podcasts, photos, audiobooks, home movies, music videos and popular television shows onto the iPod and keeps them up-to-date whenever the iPod is plugged into a Mac® or Windows computer using USB 2.0. The 30GB model features up to 14 hours of battery life for music playback and the 60GB model features up to 20 hours of battery life for music playback.*

Pricing & Availability

The new iPods will begin shipping next week for a suggested retail price of $299 (U.S.) for the 30GB model and $399 (U.S.) for the 60GB model through the Apple Store® (www.apple.com), Apple's retail stores and Apple Authorized Resellers. All iPod models include earbud headphones, USB 2.0 cable, case, dock insert and a CD with iTunes for Mac and Windows computers.

Optional accessories designed for the new iPod include: Universal Dock for $39 (U.S.), giving users easy access to a USB port for syncing, IR support to work with the Apple Remote and a variable line out and S-video connections for integration within the living room; Apple Remote for $29 (U.S.), providing wireless integration to the Universal Dock and quick and easy access to controls from across the room; Apple iPod AV cable for $19 (U.S.), enabling television viewing of video content in full-screen; the iPod Camera Connector for $29 (U.S.); and Apple Socks for $29 (U.S.) providing six vibrant color socks to dress up and protect your iPod.

iPod requires a Mac with a USB 2.0 and Mac OS® X version 10.3.9 or later and iTunes 6; or a Windows PC with a USB 2.0 port and Windows 2000, XP Home or Professional (SP2) and iTunes 6.

*Battery life and number of charge cycles vary by use and settings. See www.apple.com/batteries for more information. Music capacity is based on four minutes per song and 128-Kbps AAC encoding; video capacity is based on H.264 750-Kbps combined with 128-Kbps audio; and photo capacity is based on iPod-viewable photos transferred from iTunes.

Pricing & Availability

The new iMac G5 line will be available next week through the Apple Store® (www.apple.com), Apple's retail stores and Apple Authorized Resellers.

The new 17-inch 1.9 GHz iMac G5, for a suggested retail price of $1,299 (U.S.), includes:

- 17-inch widescreen LCD display;
- 1.9 GHz PowerPC G5 processor;
- 512MB of 533 MHz DDR2 SDRAM expandable to 2.5GB;
- 8x SuperDrive™ with double—layer support (DVD + R DL/DVD 6 RW/CD-RW);
- ATI Radeon X600 Pro with 128MB DDR memory;
- built-in iSight video camera;
- built-in AirPort Extreme wireless networking & Bluetooth 2.0 + EDR;
- 160GB Serial ATA hard drive running at 7200 rpm;
- built-in stereo speakers and microphone; and
- ships with infrared Apple Remote, Mighty Mouse and Apple Keyboard.

The new 20-inch 2.1 GHz iMac G5, for a suggested retail price of $1,699 (U.S.), includes:

- 20-inch widescreen LCD display;
- 2.1 GHz PowerPC G5 processor;
- 512MB of 533 MHz DDR2 SDRAM expandable to 2.5GB;
- 8x SuperDrive with double-layer support (DVD + R DL/DVD 6 RW/CD-RW);
- ATI Radeon X600 XT with 128MB DDR memory;
- built-in iSight video camera;
- built-in AirPort Extreme wireless networking & Bluetooth 2.0 + EDR;
- 250GB Serial ATA hard drive running at 7200 rpm;
- built-in stereo speakers and microphone; and
- ships with infrared Apple Remote, Mighty Mouse and Apple Keyboard.

Build-to-order options and accessories include up to 2.5GB DDR2 SDRAM, 250GB and 500GB Serial ATA hard drives, AirPort Express™ and AirPort Extreme Base Station, Apple Wireless Keyboard, Apple Wireless Mouse, Apple USB Modem and the AppleCare Protection Plan.

The new iMac G5 line is also available to education customers in the U.S. and Canada through the Apple Store for Education at www.apple.com/education/store or by calling an Apple education sales representative at 800-800-APPL.

*Actual speed will vary based on range from the base station, environmental conditions and other factors.

Summary

The compact disc album increased music sales throughout the 90's by over one hundred and fifty percent. While CDs are more convenient and durable than vinyl they are inferior when it comes to sound. In 1991, the mini-cassette format was 52% of global unit sales, but by the year 2000 the minicassette (MC) share had fallen to −23%, a decrease of 7% per year. The new formats are Digital Video Disc (DVD), Digital Audio, Dual Disc, and Super Audio Compact Disc which are destined to replace the compact disc. The newly released portable music format, dataplay digital media is the latest technology joining a number of choices for consumers to play their favorite music through headphones connected to palm size devices. MusicNet and Pressplay launched their companies to take advantage of legitimate subscription services. Snocap, Mashboxx, Qtrax, Peer Impact, Audible Magic, Overpeer and Open Royalty Gateway are legitimate P2P licensing services. Mobile services and broadband are technology platforms that will provide increased revenues and sales.

Terms

Broadband: High-speed access to the internet through cable modems, direct service lines (DSL) and T1/T3.

Cassette: Plastic cartridge housing a miniature reel-to-reel format of one-eighth inch tape that plays at 1 7/8 inches per second.

Compact Disc (CD): Disc measuring 4 3/4 inches in diameter with one playing side digitally encoded and read by a laser. First developed for use with computers to store large quantities of text but later modified to record sound as a alternative to tape.

Compact Disc Read Only Memory (CD-ROM): Extends CD format to store not only music but any kind of program material primarily computer applications. Can deliver text, audio, video, graphics, stills, film on personal computer.

Counterfeit Recording: The unauthorized duplication not only of the recorded sounds but also of the original label, artwork, trademark and packaging of the original recording.

Digital: Technology that reduces all material to binary data and permits a much greater range of data to be electronically captured, stored and transmitted without the serial degradation of sound quality that is typically experienced with analog formats.

Digital Audio Tape (DAT): Tape equivalent of the compact disc which was the first digital recording format made available to the consumer.

Digital Compact Cassette(DCC): New standard cassette size digital tape that offers recording and playback of high quality digital sound up to 90 minutes, and DCC players play analog cassettes.

Digital Video Disc (DVD): CD format (compatible with standard CD players) has audio and video capabilities that store up to fourteen times the amount of information of standard CDs and features increased sampling frequency which improves sound quality. It can be copied repeatedly without any loss of quality.

Downloading: The physical copying of a file onto a user's hard drive/PC from either an internet server or another person's computer.

Encoding: The conversion of a sound recording into a digital file format.

Fiber Optics: Multimode optical fibers utilized for storing, retrieval, read-only optical memory and erasable digital storage of information , audio, video and electronic distribution of products.

Gracenote: Formerly CDDB, Gracenote is a technology company specializing in music recognition, content delivery and database management. They maintain the largest online database of audio CD and song titles in the world.

Limited Download: A digital transmission of a time limited or other use limited download of a sound recording of a single musical work to a local storage device, using technology designed to cause the downloaded file to be available for listening only either (1) during a limited time or (2) for a limited number of times.

Liquid Audio: An interactive communications company that combines many technologies that they have developed into a digital music tool that enables streaming, downloading, purchasing, playback and export of secure CD-quality music from the internet in a single application.

Locker Service: An application in which a user stores digital music in a pass word protected virtual locker, rather than on a computer hard drive. The user can then access this locker from any computer with an internet connection.

Minidisc: The format is a 2.5 inch version of the micro floppy disk with similar technologies such as using a laser to read, erase and record data onto the disk. The MD has all of the features of the cassette with those of the CD, plus it doesn't skip or bounce when jolted.

MP3: Short for (Motion Pictures Experts Group) MPEG version 1 layer 3, MP3 is the most commonly available audio file format available on the internet. MP3 technology achieves compression ratios of 10:1 to 12:1. Typically, one minute of music is equal to one megabyte for stereo files.

On Demand Stream: An on demand, real time digital transmission of a sound recording of a single musical work to allow a user to listen to a particular sound recording chosen by the user at a time chosen by the user, using streaming technology, which may include but is not limited to Real audio or Windows Media Audio.

Peer-To-Peer: Also referred to as file sharing, peer-to-peer is a newly popular type of application in which, rather than accessing files from a central server, users access a common network hub and open up portions of their own computer's hard drive to the public for downloading. Well known peer-to-peer services include Napster, Gnutella and Freenet.

Playlist: Incorporated into most software playback devices, playlist let you create, save, and load groups of songs to play in the order you choose. Making a playlist is like making a digital mix tape.

Plug-In: A plug-in is an external tool that when added onto a software playback device gives the application additional features and functionality.

Ripper: An application that copies from a compact disc onto a computer's hard drive. Once ripped, the audio file can be converted into other formats, uploaded to web servers and/or burned onto another compact disc.

Ripping: The process of copying sound recordings from a compact disc onto a computer's hard drive.

Streaming: The digital transmission of a sound recording of a musical work via the internet to a user's PC a user to listen to a particular sound recording chosen by the user at a time chosen by the user, using streaming technology, which may include but is not limited to Real Audio or Windows Media Audio.

Webcasting: One of the fast growing areas on the internet, webcasting generally refers to the streaming of audio on the internet and is sometimes called internet radio. Webcasters may be internet only services that transmit several diferent genre based channels, retransmitters of traditional AM/FM broadcasts, or services that syndicate music programming as background music on Web sites.

Exercises

1. What are some of the problems associated with marketing over the Internet.

2. What are subscription services? List and discuss one company engaged in this activity.

3. Discuss file sharing and mobile phone service.

4. Discuss the latest technology formats (CD, SACD, DVD etc) and their advantages and disadvantages.

Bibliography

Apple Computer, "Apple Introduces the New iMac G5", October 12, 2005, (apple.com).

Apple Computer, "Apple's iTunes 6 with 2000 music videos, short films and Hit TV Shows, October 12, 2005", (apple.com)

Apple Computer, "Apple Introduces the new Ipod", October 12, 2005, (apple.com)

Craft, Kim. "How to Promote and Sell Your Music Online" Rhaeticus Press, Inc., Chicago, Illinois 2002

IFPI, "What Drives Digital Music", *Digital Music Report,* London, 2005

Marriott, Michel. "Reinventing the Musical Wheel" *New York Times.* August 29, 2002, pp. 2–6.

Moody, Nekesa Mumbi. "All Ears: DVD-Audio and Super Audio Compact Discs". Island Packet, October 21, 2002, p. 7–8.

Chapter 18

Internet

Learning Objectives

After studying this chapter you should be able to:

1. Historical Perspective on New Technology

2. Describe the Digital Revolution

3. Current Trends of the Digital Revolution

4. Discuss the Grokster case and it's impact on the industry

5. Internet affect on retail sales of CD's, videos, games, movies

6. Discuss mobile cellphones and ringtones

7. Describe the marriage between music, fashion, car industry, beverage industry, financial securities, cosmetics and jewelry

8. Describe the future trends of the digital revolution

9. Discuss the IFPI 2005 Report on Digital Revolution

10. Discuss internet piracy

Digital technologies such as compact disc (CD), personal computers, digital recorders, signal processors and internet have already transformed the music industry. Today it is possible for musicians to write, arrange, record and master albums on CD in their home studio at a cost less than $5,000. New technologies are harnessing the talents, resources and dollars of people worldwide in telecommunications, retail, software, finance, entertainment, media, music, education and advertising. The film and the music industry have taken legal action to try and put an end to the one hundred million people sharing songs and movies online via illegal programs and downloads. The Grokster case is an example of how difficult it is for lawmakers to make rulings regarding copyright infringement in a changing technology environment. In a recent Supreme Court ruling Grokster, a file sharing service accused of encouraging piracy, and other peer to peer software makers was found liable for assisting in the infringement that takes place on their networks. In the age of digital distribution movies, video and television are delivered to the consumer in new ways through high speed networks in the home and on cell phones. The ruling expands the powers of copyright infringement but at the same time delays the growth of new strategies that build on peer to peer (P2P) technologies. Some would argue, that defending the rights of copyright holders over the growth of new technologies, does not demand protecting outmoded ways of selling products. It may be time for the entertainment industry to accept the inevitable and refrain from using the courts to harness the growth in new media technologies. Clearly, new business models and strategies should be expanded and embraced by the entertainment industry and new media entrepreneurs.

The challenge for digital music is to make music easier to buy than to steal. In 2005 the legal digital music business moves from a niche market into the mainstream due to the following: (1) Record companies have digitized and licensed over a million songs (2) The number of online services where consumers can buy music has increased to more than 230 worldwide (3) Services like iTunes and Napster have become household names internationally (4) The digital download market increased to over 200 million in the United States, United Kingdom and Germany combined (5) Record companies first year revenues are significant from digital sales (6) Consumers awareness of, use of and intentions to use legal download services are growing (7) Anti-piracy enforcement is making a difference (8) Industry is embracing the new technology while fighting the abuse (9) Mobile phones, ringtones and broadband are increasing revenue streams (10) Portability technology with the new iPod by Apple and ATRAC3 format by Sony increases demand.

American sales of recorded music and music video products appear to be stabilizing as the industry fight piracy and promote authorized online music services. The number of CD's and other music products shipped from labels to retailers increased two percent in 2004, to 814 million units. This was the first annual increase in five years according to the Recording Industry Association of America (RIAA). Global record labels flat sales of $33.6 billion in 2004 was the industries best year in five years, according to a report by the International Federation of Phonographic Industry (IFPI).

How can the music industry compensate for decreasing CD sales due to illegal downloading and piracy? Other than legal and technological maneuvers the industry is developing new strategies and business models which would assist the industries goal of increasing revenue. Strategies include the introduction of deluxe-edition CD's, wireless downloads and cheaper ticket prices. The increased licensing of music to films, videogames, ringtones, commercials, karaoke, merchandise and fashion are all alternative sources of revenue. Another strategy is to find new talent and create a new music sound reminiscent of the days of the Philadelphia and Motown sound.

Wireless cellphone technology that can receive downloads and act as a digital player was well received by consumers. The 1.5 billion cellphone owners in the world regularly update their technology to meet the need of our changing society. Recordings, both old and new, are increasing exposure and revenue, due to cellphone providers that are using music to help sell their brands. In 2005, the sales of snippets of songs that play when cellphones ring reached $245 million in the USA, according to Broadcast Music Inc. (BMI). Ringtone sales are expected to top $500 million in sales this year. Another trend is when cellphone providers help add revenues for music labels and publishers through buying music rights to use songs in commercials. Cingular uses new music and classics in spots that are part of its "Raising the Bar" advertisement campaign. Many would argue that online subscriptions is the best way to sell music. Apple, the maker of ipod music player, has sold more than 400 million songs through itunes music stores leaving Napster, AOL and RealNetworks behind. While the number of subscribers to services from RealNetworks' Rhapsody division AOL, Napster, and others rose from 750,000 in 2003 to 1.5 million in 2004, ipod sales climbed from 4.4 million in fiscal 2004 to 17.2 million this fiscal year. Ipod sales are projected to reach 22.2 million by 2006.

Mobile Music and Ringtones

Ringtones are digitally delivered music files that play melodies for up to 30 seconds in length when users receive incoming calls on their cell phones. Consumer interest in personalizing their ring tones has resulted in a profitable source of revenue. Music on mobile phones has become a significant source of revenue for record companies. Music by mobile phone has evolved from ringtones to the use of full audio recordings in ringtones, ringback tunes, full-track downloads and other multimedia applications. With the advent of 3G technology, consumers can get a range of interactive content including music tracks and video at higher speed with better quality. Mobile phones handsets have evolved from talking devices into entertainment gadgets. Japan, which originated the ringtone format. In 2004, Japan's ringtone market was worth an estimated U.S.$100 million dollars. Label Mobile is the largest distributor in Japan with a catalogue of 80,000 tracks from nineteen record companies. In South Korea, the market has expanded beyond ringtones to full track downloads. The mobile music market was worth an estimated U.S.$158 million in 2003. China's emerging mobile music market is worth upwards of 290 million dollars. In the United States, the mobile music market has 128 million users. Ringtones are the main form of mobile music consumption. To increase sales of real recording of ringtunes operators Sprint (Music tones), AT & T (MmMode Music Store) entered into agreements with record labels. Consumers can stream songs from a catalogue of 750,000 tracks by mobile or buy single tracks which are downloaded to PC's.

Hip Hop Industry, Product Placement and Branding

Rap music has moved into the mainstream of Madison Avenue as American businesses realize that hip hop sells just about anything. Todays youth culture want to drink what rappers drink, wear what rappers wear and drive what rappers drive. Today rappers are the commercial messages to the masses or the "merchants of cool". Hip hop style has become so pervasive that it would be impossible to calculate its total impact on fashion, movies, advertising, financial securities, beverage and automotive industry. Russell Simmons has capitalized on the marketability of hip hop like none other. Simmons is the CEO of Rush Communications, a conglomerate that includes record label Def Jam, management company Rush Artist Management, clothing company Phat Farm, movie production house Def Pictures, television show Def Comedy Jam and Russell Simmons Oneworld Music Beat, magazine Oneworld and advertising agency Rush Media. No one will ever forget the fact that he coordinated the "My Adidas Deal". The industry owes a huge debt to Simmons and his entrepreneurial genius. Rapper turned executive Sean Combs oversees a clothing line that brings in $450 million in retail sales a year. His Bad Boy record label, film production company, Manhattan boutique and two restaurants places him at the pinnacle of hip hops profits. Damon Dash and Jay Z founded Roc-A-Fella records. Damon started Rocawear clothing, Pro-Keds, Roc films, Armadale vodka, American magazine and a luxury watch company Tiret. Watches at Tiret start at $18,000. Kimberly "Lil Kim" Jones started a luxury watch collection called Royalty which sells for $1,800 to $3,500. Missy Elliott partnered with Adidas to start a clothing line called "Respect Me".

Rappers are not the only artists connecting themselves and their images to products to reach a larger audience. U2 had a special edition iPod to promote Apple products and U2's single "Vertigo". The new Gap television advertisement promotes clothes, currents artists and classic songs. Artists Joss Stone, Keith Urban, Destiny's Child's Michelle Williams, Brandon Boyd (Incubus), Alanis Morrissette, John Legend covered classic songs such as "Alison" by Elvis Costello, "God Only Knows" by Brian Wilson, "Crazy" by Seal, "One Love" by Bob Marley and "Let's Stay Together" by Al Green. This promotion not only gets people interested in the Gap, but in these popular artists and more importantly in the older, classic songs.

Artists have taken advantage of product placement of lyrics in songs that promote products. Petey Pablo's "Freek-A'Leek" referenced Seagram's Gin with his lyric "Now I Got to Give a Shout Out to Seagram's Gin", because I'm drinking it and they are paying me for it. Petey Pablo's song was the number two hip hop track of the year. Busta Rhymes hit song "Pass the Courvoisier" is an example of a hit song promoting alcohol in the marketplace. Rapper Jay Z mentions Rocawear clothes and Armadale vodka in his song "All I Need", all companies of which he owns. Hypnotiq, a blend of vodka, fruit and cognac became featured in urban market videos. R. Kelly, Missy Elliott, Lil Kim, Usher, Memphis Bleek, Jay-Z and other artists contributed to 26 different tracks promoting Hypnotiz. This strategy increased sales from 10,000 cases in 2001-02 to 700,000 cases in 2003-04. Kanye West mentions nineteen brands in four songs including Geico, Toys "R" Us and Ensure. Corporate America and hip hop have become dependent on each other. The trend is moving away from the branding of luxury items to brands that shape our everyday lives.

Rappers love to give a shout-out to their favorite things. Here are the most mentined brands in the Billboard top 20 singles chart this year:

Cars

Brand	Mentions
• Cadillac	49
• **Rolls-Royce**	**42**
• Mercedes	36
• Jaguar	33
• Lexus	24

Fashion

Brand	Mentions
• Gucci	40
• **Nike**	**24**
• Victoria's secret	17
• Cartier	16
• BCBG	14

Beverages

Brand	Mentions
• **Hennessy**	**52***
• Dom Perignon	17
• Hpnotiq	17
• Seagram's Gin	16
• Cristal	16

Russell Simmons

- **Business connections:** Phat Fashions, Simmons-Lathan Media Group, Rush Visa Card, DefCon3 energy drink, Def comedy Jam
- **Background:** Founded Def Jam Recordings in 1984, unleashing LL Cool J, Public Enemy and the Beastie Boys on the world.

Damon Dash

- **Business connections:** Rocawear clothing, Pro-Keds, Roc films, Armadale vodka, America magazine
- **Background:** Founded Roc-A-Fella Records in 1995 with rapper Jay-Z.

Sean Combs

- **Business connections:** Sean John clothing, Justin's restaurants, Blue Flame Marketing & Advertising
- **Background:** Founded Bad Boy Records in 1994, launching with Notorious B.I.G. Known as Puff Daddy and P. Diddy, Combs racked up a few hits of his own, too.

*Also the No. 1 brand overall
—Source: American Brandstand/Agenda Inc.
Taken from *The Atlanta Journal Constitution.*

Entrepreneurship and New Media

The Music Industry has seen its share of entrepreneurs inventing and benefiting from new business models during the late nineties' Internet boom. After 2001's industry shrinkage, consolidations and layoffs, a new breed of entrepreneurs emerged as industry veterans reinvented themselves, capturing business opportunities in the wake of the vast changes taking root in the marketplace. During the last decade, many entrepreneurs accumulated wealth, while others lost wealth or left the music business for other industries. Throughout these changes, the impact of new media technologies on the music industry since 1999 has been more profound than in most other industries ultmately changing the traditional music industry business models.

No other art form has been impacted to such a degree by the Internet as has music. This is not to say that changes are not affecting other art forms such as movies and photography, but these other industries were not affected during such a condensed time frame. This unique situation caused a serious crisis in the music industry, an industry that has never been big on retained cash resources that could help it brave economical slopes. Moreover, the definition of a music "product" and how it is created, sold and consumed have been changing while the world economy has faced a recession. By all accounts, these have been very challenging times for the music business.

The music CD market has shrunk in recent years, a situation that pressured major label consolidations and layoffs. The effect of the latter trickled down throughout the industry all the way to music retail. New media sales today represent one of only two market segments offering fast growth for record companies (the other is music DVD sales). Sale reports show that the legal download market will grow beyond $250 million in the U.S. this year, and is projected to double yearly during the next two years. Forester Research, IDC, Jupiter Research, and other analysts have been projecting a digital music market larger than $1 billion by 2008, representing 33% of all music industry sales by decade's end. This means a major paradigm shift for the music industry as we've known it.

For decades, the music industry has modeled its product around albums sold for over $10. With 33% of sales now moving to a single-driven model at a $1 retail price point, the industry is re-evaluating its entire business model. Changes start at the A&R department level and trickle down throughout each label, affecting how recordings are marketed and sold—all the way down to the distribution arm. And since a third of sales no longer move through the distribution department—at least not in a physical form—warehouses, distribution personnel, and even CD retailers are affected. On the manufacturing side, labels have had to shrink their facilities as well. Accordingly, business emphasis—and budgets—have shifted to new media.

Despite the fast growth of new media sales, capturing the new media market opportunity is not that simple for the industry. Illegal Peer-To-Peer (P2P) services drive more than ten times the traffic of legit download services, and the billions of songs traded freely between online users on a yearly basis are believed to represent millions of dollars in lost revenues. The industry has been very aggressive in fighting illegal P2P services since Napster first appeared in 1999. But advances in P2P technologies keep appearing, and the mass market embrace of P2P technology is hard to ignore.

That said, P2P trading is apparently not for everybody: Users of illegal P2P services have to deal with inconsistent and poor file quality, viruses, industry-driven viruses (one of the ways the RIAA is fighting back), legal challenges from the RIAA in the courts, and constant RIAA litigation against individuals that up-load significant catalog volumes into P2P networks. As a result, a certain demographic trend has emerged: Young people that have little money to spend and ample time to play online tend to rough P2P networks, while older users that have more disposable money and less time to mess around with inconsistent P2P networks opt for the convenience of shopping through legit download stores like Rhapsody, iTunes and Wal-Mart. Today, fifty percent of shoppers in legit music download stores are older than 35. Growth in use, however, is seen all across the board.

Music downloads is now part of the mainstream. The proliferation of portable devices such as iPod, iRiver and Rio support the growth of this industry sector, providing a more compelling reason for consumers to spend money on digital copies of their favorite music. Portability is going to increase immensely in upcoming years with the convergence of portable music players and mobile phones—with the latter already driving significant revenues for the industry with ringtone sales. According to Baskerville Research, global ring-tone sales generated $3 billion dollars during 2003, and are forecasted to generate in excess of $4.7 billion in revenues by 2008. If the value of traditional music sales increases 2% each year, ringtones will account for around 12% of total music sales by 2008.

These vast changes also represent opportunities—some of which are pursued by the labels and by major technology companies directly, while others are pursued by creative entrepreneurs. The operational infrastructure needed to support emerging business models is so new that there are many unfulfilled needs that can be capitalized on by imaginative companies and entrepreneurs. New services are needed to "synchronize" the different business tiers involved, facilitated an efficient business process and an economy of scale, and enable all parties involved in the creation and sale of music to benefit from the emerging markets. Accordingly, dozen of start ups today support various needs up and down the food chain. Here are but a few examples:

- Virtual record companies that only sell product online and never press physical product

- New media licensing companies that help artist and labels make their music available online by aggregating catalogs and providing vast market representation (licensing to B2C, B2B, and mobile outlets)

- B2C stores that allow independent artists to make their product available online through their branded store fronts

- Virtual A&R companies that provide a bridge between unsigned artists and label A&R departments while eliminating the need for CD and cassette production and shipment

- Online promotions companies that provide marketing services to artist and labels, some involving creative artwork for online assets and properties, while others providing syndication and placement services

- Online collection agencies that help artists and labels administer copyright collection from relevant parties online and in the mobile telecom environment

- Online technology vendors that provide B2B services to different brands who want to get into the music download business through outsourcing their store to a third party

- Post-production licensing houses where one can sample music clips and then purchase post-production music delivered digitally in real time through the Internet

- Internet stores specializing in specific genres and music niches are abound, and many of these stores innovate certain aspect of their service, such as coupling download sales with community building features, music sampling and ranking features, and more

- Metadata companies that provide a unified database solution for music catalogs, artist pages, and recommendation engines— including copy, visuals and samples

- Ring tone companies that create and aggregate ring tones and provide carriers with content management services for mobile applications and services involving music

- Technology vendors that offer customized solutions supporting the creation, hosting and maintenance of private-labeled web sites for artists and labels, including e-commerce services for physical products (CDs, T-Shirts, and show tickets) and digital products (fan club subscription, ala-carte downloads, on-demand streams, and live show broadcasting)

- Hi-tech companies that continue to innovate services that enhance the music consumption experience, from enhanced Jukebox features to smart song recognition technologies

Innovation in the new media music market run the gamut from artist services, publicity, royalty tracking, and distribution, all the way to e-stores and consumer-oriented service tools. Most innovation has been driven by small businesses launched and managed by entrepreneurs with a unique business vision. But having a great idea is not enough in ensuring a company's success: Entrepreneurs must have a strong independent streak and a powerful drive to succeed against poor odds, coupled with strong business acumen that enables them to manage a business and develop it through various growth stages. To do this correctly, an entrepreneur must be well rounded and be able to learn and expand personal abilities over time—including marketing, sales, finance, human resources, and business development. Conversely, many entrepreneurs at a certain point hand over management to a more experienced manager that can help them take their vision to the next level. One must be prepared for this before starting a new business, and be prepared to do what's right for the company. Growing a business is not an easy task, and being an entrepreneur is not for everyone.

As with any other industry entrepreneurship in the music industry offers plenty of rewards as well as risks and challenges. Historically, more new businesses fail within their first five years than succeed. However, the continued paradigm shift in the music industry offers immediate and compelling rewards in a rate higher than in other industries. This opportunity won't last forever, since the market will eventually stabilize and reach maturity. Until that happens—arguably by the end of the decade—entrepreneurs in the music industry can find unique and exciting business opportunities to exploit, leading to financial and professional rewards that are rarely available in other positions in one's career.

Online Music Marketing

Artists are viewing the internet as a means to market their music and not to rely on signing a recording contract with one of the four major labels. The reality is that every aspiring artist will never sign a major label contract. Therefore, many artist are promoting their CDs and merchandise over the internet. Web marketing has come of age and the internet has become a marketing tool utilized by music entrepreneurs. Individual performing and recording artist, record labels, music publishers, performance venues, radio stations producers, distributors, retailers and just about every facet of the global music economy functions with a website and e-mail address. So what is it that the artist entrepreneurs must do or need to market his or her many products. First the music entrepreneur in order to start an online business must follow these procedures:

1. Purchase a computer with speed and memory
2. Contract a internet Service Provider (ISP)
3. Select a Web Browser (Microsoft's Internet Explorer or Netscape Navigator)
4. Set up an e-mail account
5. Access your search engine to find sites of interests
6. Create your website using Dreamweaver, JPEG, Flashcards, MP3
7. Select a web hosting site with 2.5–6.0 MB of storage space for downloading, fast connections and graphics
8. Set up a merchant card account for online shopping at your site
9. Market your site

The key to marketing your site over the internet is to research the demographics to identify who the target market is and what they are interested in. Provide visitors to site with what they are looking for and provide them with the information they want. Try to convince your potential fans to purchase your CDs. Briefly tell fans about what you think is good about the music and why they should buy it. Offer something for free and hype up the band or artist. Giveaways to loyal fans are always an effective tool. You must always have visually appealing artwork to promote the artist or group on your site.

With current technologies in recording, album production and digital formats it is difficult to find the best strategy for promoting music on a site. The three step approach involves the following: (1) Targeting the buzz (2) Targeting by site and (3) Creating long term fan base over the web. To target a buzz you will need to bring your music to the customer by placing the CD with MP3.com, a website that host free downloads, streaming play and information about all kinds of new and independent artists. By creating an official artist website fans can get complete details about the artist's music, lyrics, news, CD information, pictures, discussion boards, chat rooms and sheet music. Your official site is how you can create a new and bigger fan base and if it's frequently updated, your fans can keep up with what is going on with the artist. There is work involved and you have to be persistent in order to be successful. Web marketing involves finding out what make the music unique and what artists it is comparable to. Targeting by site involves finding your target audience over the internet and developing strategies to point them towards your music. These strategies include gearing your website towards product that your target audience is already searching for such as music in the same or similar genre. Links from fan sites to your own and search engine recognition will also help. A price strategy to attract and maintain a loyal fan base is essential. Items such as news, message boards, band and tour information, lyrics, sheet music and anything else that will keep the fans loyal are vital. Frequent updates are also a key factor providing good service to your fan base. Performing artists are now bound to stay in contact with their fan base through the internet. Resourceful websites keep fans informed of new material, tour dates, new merchandise and the latest information on the artist. Message boards are a popular hit where devout fans can interact among each other and band members. The internet allows artists to truly interact with fans on a more personal level in a short span of time. On the other hand, many argue of its cost effectiveness because the product must be given away free of charge in order to solicit and maintain a fan base. Record labels have come to love and hate the internet because marketing and promotion cost is up with cost down. Companies can cut costs in effective marketing over the internet. When companies spend an average of $60,000 to break an artist, where it may have cost better than twice that before the internet was popular to reach the same amount of consumers. Before the internet there was only a miniscule amount of piracy and sales were guaranteed if someone wanted a personal copy of music. Today, with the web, anyone can have a copy of a song without paying a dime and the amount of losses is astronomical. The internet definitely has its advantages, such as opening another marketplace for marketing and jobs, but anyone can do it therefore piracy is rampant.

The internet has provided labels with one of the most successful forms of marketing today and that is street teams. Street teams are groups of young fans that post propaganda on web message boards, pass out flyers about artists, place posters at concert venues and visit retail chains all in exchange for free items like CD's, autographs and T-shirts. This grass roots form of marketing is highly effective particularly when it comes to tours. It costs very little and ensures lots of work. Due to the internet ticket sales are up because of convenience and efficiency of pricing. For most people being able to purchase tickets in the comfort of your home is much easier than going to a retail ticket outlet. By cutting out the expense of the middleman, prices can be discounted. To many the internet has been profitable although it is sometime thought of as a factor for sale losses. The world wide web is here to stay and if you want to be effective in the global economy you must participate over the internet. The internet is becoming the number one means for marketing music. The estimates of sales suggest that music on the internet is here to stay.

Table 1

Online Music Sales by Distribution Method ($US Million), 2000–2006

	2000	2001	2002	2003	2004	2005	2006
Traditional Formats	906	1,421	2,161	3,060	3,911	4,893	5,798
Digital Downloads	6	22	86	258	584	989	1,601
Subscriptions	19	56	188	440	939	1,494	2,270
Total Online Sales	**931**	**1,499**	**2,435**	**3,758**	**5,434**	**7,376**	**9,667**

One of the problems artists face with marketing their music on the web is the fact that music delivered via the internet does not offer complete protection from hacking and tampering. The transfer of data across the internet is only as secure as its weakest link. Even with the highest encryption available there is no guarantee that the sources or recipient is secure. Because of this concern the music industry has faced and will continue to face the issue of the current state between the world of the internet and traditional record companies. Artists must be cautious of independent labels because they may not be able to deliver the service that was promised.

My Space is a very unique social networking website that is used by dedicated fans to advertise on behalf of their favorite band. Major music labels use the site to promote both new and established bands. The site is effective in promoting rock bands. The ability to design your own web page on MySpace has helped make the website an unlikely media force and a favorite marketing tool for the music industry. The 18 month old site is the 30th most visited site on the Web with 17.7 million visitors in June. 2005. News Corporation has agreed to pay $580 million dollars for MySpace's parent company, Intermix Media. The following are linkage to other companion sites. MySpace.com, vitaminic.com, GarageBand.com, CDStreet.com, Ampcast.com, JavaMusic.com, Bardscrier.com, Musicbizacademy .com, Indiebiz.com

The emergence of a successful digital business has been the single most important development in the music industry in 2004.

The Legitimate Digital Market Takes Off

The emergence of a successful digital business has been the single most important development in the music industry in 2004.

Services around the world proliferated. By the end of 2004, IFPI's global tracking on the www.pro-music.org website counted over 230 services that offer online

Taken from www.ifpi.org.

music legally, up four-fold from 50 a year earlier and 20 in January 2003. More than ten services operate in at least three markets. In Europe alone, there are over 150 online music services available in 20 countries.

The mobile market for music is also expanding rapidly, as 3G and mobile music services enter the market.

Global Brands Emerge

Brands like Apple's iTunes, Napster, Sony Connect and MSN Music, have spread internationally to multiple territories during 2004. The global leader, iTunes, unveiled its services in the UK, Germany and France in June 2004, and in nine markets in Europe during October. Apple reported sales of five million songs in the first ten weeks of operation in Europe. Globally, iTunes reached sales of 230 million tracks since launch. iTunes reached Canada in December and is expected to launch in Japan in 2005.

Napster, one of the world's most recognized digital music brands came to the UK and Canada in May 2004 and has focused on local repertoire. Sony Connect launched in the U.S. in April and in key European markets in July, while Rhapsody is expected to do so in 2005.

Microsoft's MSN Music—which first launched in 2002 through the OD2 platform in the UK, France, Germany, Italy and Australia—expanded to eight more European markets in November. Microsoft is marketing the 'Plays For Sure' message emphasizing the wide compatibility of the Windows Media Audio format with online music services and portable digital players.

A number of local services joined the market across continental Europe in 2004. These range from charity download sites to services that specialize in local repertoire such as T-Online's Musicload service in Germany, Rosso Alice in Italy and Archambaultzik.ca in Canada, which are gaining in popularity and rivalling global services. Musicload is the current market leader in Germany, reaching the one million monthly downloads mark in December 2004 (a level 80 times higher than at launch in October 2003). Other online stores are bundled with local broadband providers or linked to local music retailers.

The most advanced digital markets in Europe are the UK, with over 30 services, followed by Germany and France with more than 20 and 10 services respectively. Some of the main services in each market are shown opposite.

"iTunes really competes with piracy, not with the other services. Piracy is the big enemy. Buying music online legally is good karma." Steve Jobs, CEO of APPLE

MUSIC SERVICE LAUNCHES IN 2004

January	March	April	May	June
MyCokeMusic: UK	**Wal-Mart:** US	**Sony Connect:** US	**Napster 2.0:** UK, Canada	**iTunes:** UK, Germany, France
		MSN Music: Australia	**MyCokeMusic:** Austria	

July	September	October	November	December
Sony Connect: UK, Germany, France	**Virgin Digital:** US	**iTunes:** Austria, Belgium, Finland, Greece, Italy, Luxemburg, Netherlands, Portugal, Spain	**MSN Music:** Belgium, Spain, Norway, Denmark, Sweden, Finland, Austria, Switzerland	**iTunes:** Canada
		MSN Music: UK, France, Germany, Italy, Netherlands, U.S., Japan	**MyCokeMusic:** Switzerland **Tesco:** UK	

Key Facts of 2004:

   Available repertoire doubles to around one million tracks

   Number of sites up four-fold to 230 worldwide

   Downloads up more than ten-fold to over 200 million in the US, UK and Germany combined

Sales and Subscriptions

The U.S. remains the global leader in online music sales and subscriptions, but Europe is making headway.

Sales of single track downloads (excluding downloads sold as albums and song streams) in the U.S. for 2004 rose to 142.6 million, up from 19.2 million in the second half of 2003 (when Nielsen SoundScan began tracking downloads in the U.S.). Album downloads totalled 5.5 million.

In the UK, the largest European download market, total downloads rose from practically zero to 5.7 million (UK Official Chart Company/BPI).

Subscription services are growing steadily in the U.S.. Paying subscribers for the major services—Rhapsody, Napster, MusicNet, MusicMatch and eMusic—more than doubled in a year to some 1.5 million (December figures). Virgin Digital launched in the U.S. in September 2004—another big brand expected to boost the subscription-based sector.

Subscription services outside the U.S. are also growing; Napster (UK), Wippit (UK), Vitaminic (Europe) and E-compil (France) are examples.

Building Catalogue

The music consumer can today shop or browse in online services that offer a bigger catalogue than all but the very largest physical megastores.

Music catalogues available through online services have grown steadily. In the U.S., iTunes, Napster and Rhapsody expanded their catalogues from 500,000 tracks to over one million during 2004. In Europe, services powered by OD2 (including MyCokeMusic and Tiscali Music Club) expanded their catalogues from 300,000 to 600,000 tracks, with MSN reaching one million tracks. In Europe Napster reached one million songs, available for streaming through a subscription, after agreements with independent labels.

This is a dramatic increase in available repertoire. A catalogue of one million tracks is equivalent to around 80,000 albums—larger, for example, than most megastores.

"2004 has been a landmark year for the music industry. The digital services have given the industry the shot in the arm it needed—stimulating the public's appetite for consuming music while giving them a superior, legal alternative to the P2P sites. As broadband penetration becomes more widespread, the digital services will take even greater hold and continue their expansion into both established and emerging music markets. Through 2005 and beyond we will continue rolling out napster and our new portable subscription service 'napster to go' internationally, with carefully tailored services that cater for and respect local differences and repertoire."   Chris Gorog, Chairman & CEO of Napster

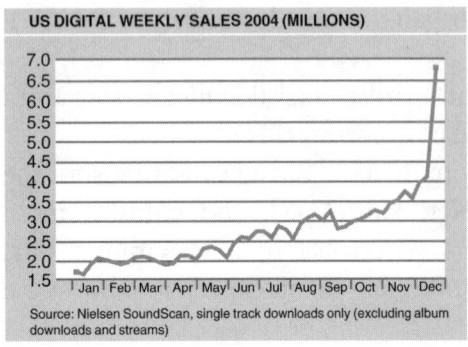

US DIGITAL WEEKLY SALES 2004 (MILLIONS)

Source: Nielsen SoundScan, single track downloads only (excluding album downloads and streams)

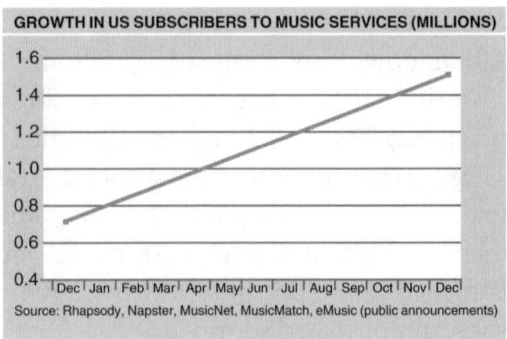

GROWTH IN US SUBSCRIBERS TO MUSIC SERVICES (MILLIONS)

Source: Rhapsody, Napster, MusicNet, MusicMatch, eMusic (public announcements)

The Business Models

Among the major brand names, two distinct business models have emerged in digital music: pay-per-download and subscription services.

Pay-per-download services meet consumer demand to 'own' music, but with greater flexibility than CDs as tracks can be selected and downloaded on the spot. Services such as iTunes, MSN Music, Wal-Mart (US) and Tesco (UK) sell downloads from U.S.$0.80 per track. Tracks are transferable to portable devices and can be burned onto disk.

Subscription services offer a very wide choice of music for a monthly fee, allowing users to access all the music they want with the option to purchase selected tracks. Services like Napster, Rhapsody and Virgin Digital offer streaming and radio-play access for a monthly fee—typically from U.S.$9.99. Downloads and burns are available for an extra per-track fee from U.S.$0.79. Some subscription services such as Napster now allows 'tethered downloads' which are transferable to portable players for as long as the consumer remains a subscriber.

Growth Outside Europe and the U.S.

Online services have expanded outside Europe and the U.S., with over 40 online music services now available. Notably, the Asia-Pacific region has seen a big increase in online services.

In Australia, NineMSN became the first OD2-powered service to launch outside Europe. In October 2004 the service launched a co-branded store with HMV offering both digital and physical music products. Meanwhile digital service provider Destra, which powers JB Hi-Fi, Sanity and ChaosMusic among others, increased its catalogue from 100,000 to 500,000 tracks during 2004.

Soundbuzz has also expanded its operations in Asia-Pacific by partnering with Singapore's Creative Technology. The partnership allows users of Creative's portable digital music players access to Soundbuzz's Digital Music Store. The Soundbuzz/Creative package has been available in Singapore since July and was rolled out in Australia, India and South East Asia at the end of 2004.

In Canada, a number of online retailers have joined existing service Puretracks by launching their own music services during 2004. These include Archambauitzik, Sympatico Music Store, Bonfire@Future Shop, Napster and iTunes.

Musica is South Africa's first online service, launched in December 2004. The service debuts with 400,000 tracks and is powered by OD2.

In Latin America, the digital music market is developing despite low broadband and portable player penetration. Brazil's iMusica is the only service provider in the region, powering MSN Brazil and iget. U.S.-based services specializing in Latin

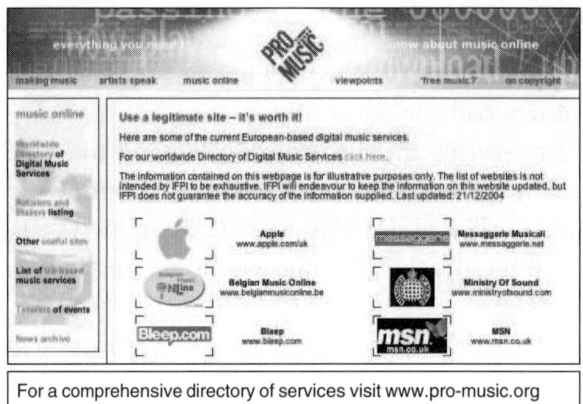

For a comprehensive directory of services visit www.pro-music.org

repertoire have developed in 2004, including emepe3.com and emusiclatino.com. Other services are due to launch in 2005, indicating growing demand for digital Latin music.

> "What sets us apart from the rest? We want to have relevant content available for consumers in all our territories. Increasingly, people will want to buy a real music product and will want to get content that's relevant. In France, for example, over half of the album chart is made up of local acts. You can't build an online service from just international content, or you won't survive in the market."   Gregor Erkel, Director of Sony Network Services Europe [Sony Connect]

Music on mobile phones is set to become a significant source of revenue for record companies.

The Mobile Music Market

Music on mobile phones is set to become a significant source of revenue for record companies. Music via mobiles has quickly evolved from ringtones, to the use of full audio recordings in ringtunes, ringback tunes, full-track downloads and other multimedia applications. With the advent of 3G technology, consumers can get a range of interactive content, including music tracks and video, at higher speed and better quality.

Mobile phone handsets have quickly evolved from talking devices into fully-fledged entertainment gadgets, and consumers are increasingly familiar with the concept of buying music through their handsets.

Taken from www.ifpi.org.

Asia Leads the Way

The mobile music market is already big business in Asia, particularly in Japan and South Korea, where 3G is advanced and handset penetration is high. There is also a wide range of products and services available in those markets, from ringtunes (launched as far back as in 2002) to dedications, ringback tunes, video and TV streaming services. In both markets, mobile music sales have easily outsold online downloads.

Japan has a ringtune market worth an estimated U.S.$100 million in 2004. Label Mobile is the largest distributor in Japan, with a catalogue of 80,000 tracks from 19 record companies. By November 2004 Label Mobile was selling a monthly average of 12 million ringtunes. Operator KDDI began offering full-track downloads to mobiles in November 2004 and was expected that the one million sales mark would be reached by the end of 2004.

In South Korea, where the market has expanded beyond ringtunes into full-track downloads, the mobile music market (including ringtones, ringtunes and full-track downloads) was worth an estimated U.S.$158 million in 2003. China is also a growing mobile music market with mobile subscribers reaching 290 million (around 20% of the population).

3G Launched in Europe

In Europe, 2004 was a break-through year with a number of key service launches and the roll-out of 3G networks. Vodafone launched a 3G music download service in November 2004 under its 'Vodafone live!' brand in 13 markets. Licensed by record companies, full-track and video downloads as well as audio and video streams are available on the service. Orange also launched 3G services in December offering

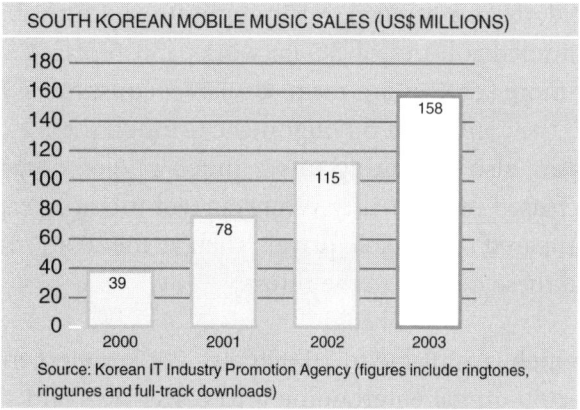

SOUTH KOREAN MOBILE MUSIC SALES (US$ MILLIONS)

Source: Korean IT Industry Promotion Agency (figures include ringtones, ringtunes and full-track downloads)

full-track downloads. UK operator '3' concentrates on 3G video services, offering music video, sports clips and news since March 2003.

Record companies have launched various initiatives in the mobile sector in Europe during 2004. EMI, for example, offered previews of Robbie Williams' music video 'Misunderstood' in partnership with '3'. The artist's latest album was also sold in memory cards compatible with handsets and handheld computers in the UK, '3' also featured streamed live concert footage of the Sony BMG act Rooster.

Also available in Europe are: O2's download service, with its own compatible portable device (Siemens SX1 Music) allowing consumers to transfer downloaded tracks from the mobile to the device; T-Mobile's 'Mobile Jukebox', available in the UK, Germany and Austria offering 90-120 second music clips; and Spanish operator Telefonica Mobile's 'Melodeo', offering some 30,000 tracks for download. Warner Music licensed its entire catalogue to Telefonica late in 2004.

US Mobile Market Emerging

In the U.S., the mobile music market is in its infancy, but growing rapidly, with an estimated 128 million mobile users. Ringtones are the main form of mobile music consumption, marked by the launch of the Billboard ringtone chart in November.

In an effort to increase sales of real recording ringtunes, various operators entered into agreements with major and independent record companies. Services launched include Sprint's 'Music Tones'; AT&T's 'MmMode Music Store' whereby consumers can stream songs from a catalogue of 750,000 tracks via mobile or buy single tracks which are downloaded onto PCs; and Verizon's 'Get It Now' offer of short audio clips. In early 2005 Verizon introduced mobile video and audio services with a range of phones capable of high-speed Web surfing.

The Future of Mobile Music

In 2005 and beyond, more advanced music applications for mobiles will emerge as a result of the continued roll-out of 3G networks and replacement of handsets. As more content and more services are made available, consumers will become much more familiar with the concept of buying music through their handsets.

Mobile phones are also beginning to see much bigger storage capacity, longer battery life and increased functionality. While current memory capacity on handsets might be small compared to portable players such as the iPod, many expect that 3G mobiles could rival these devices in the future.

"MSN Music, which is available in 20 markets, is a key element in Microsoft's vision of delivering digital entertainment to consumers and giving them the ability to easily customize their entertainment experiences. More than anything else, we've found that consumers want two things: choice and simplicity through partnerships with more than 3,000 record labels and more than 70 device makers, we]re working to meet these desires by making it fun and easy for people to find their favorite songs and listen to them on devices that fit every budget and lifestyle."   Rob Bennett, Senior Director of MSN Entertainment, Microsoft

What Drives Digital Music?

Several key factors drive the growth of digital music, including partnerships between record companies and online/mobile music services; growing broadband and mobile penetration; sales of portable players and handsets; rising consumer awareness of legitimate services; the increased flexibility that is offered to the consumer; and the fight against online piracy.

Record Company Initiatives

Digitization and licensing of music content is a key priority for record companies and essential for the development of the digital music market. Many record companies have created dedicated digital business units to distribute and market music internationally.

Majors and independent record companies have licensed their music to the big online music brands, including Apple, Napster, Microsoft, OD2, RealNetworks and AOL, as well as to a selection of smaller or niche services. There has also been a big push in licensing music to mobile operators such as Sprint, Verizon, Vodafone, Orange, T-Mobile and SKT Telecom.

Digitization has also been a priority. Universal Music, for example, has completed a two-year project to digitize its entire active European music catalogue—some 300,000 tracks drawn from more than 25,000 albums. The company now digitizes around 2,500 newly released tracks each week. Universal also launched a digital label in November 2004—UMe Digital, which will both sign exclusive digital deals with new artists and handle digital distribution deals for independent labels.

Sony BMG has created a dedicated global digital business unit to focus on global digital business development for mobile and online music. The unit also looks at antipiracy measures, new industry technologies such as CD rights-management software, and new format launches. Sony BMG has also digitized its entire active catalogue, enabling it to focus on previously unreleased titles. Over 1,600 music videos have already been digitized for electronic distribution.

Taken from www.ifpi.org.

EMI has signed hundreds of licensing agreements and spent the past few years building its global digital supply chain for both online and mobile services. Digital products can reach world markets day-and-date with its physical releases. EMI has also significantly expanded resources dedicated to digital sales and marketing in key territories. It has offered innovations such as Robbie Williams' memory-card release of the artist's album.

Warner Music has digitized and licensed the majority of its catalogue, signing licensing agreements with a number of online distributors for example, and with Verizon in the mobile sector in the U.S..

Other specialized digital marketing ventures have launched in 2004. Vital PIAS Digital, for example, incorporates dedicated digital production services, specialized sales and marketing expertise, data management and access to global digital music services for over 50 independent labels.

Record companies are also expanding into new digital channels such as 'music kiosks'. Warner Music and Sanctuary for example, both partnered Mediaport Enter-tainment Inc. to offer their catalogues in free-standing kiosk units at which people can create compilations and then either burn them to CD or transfer to portable players. EMI partnered with Starbucks in the U.S. to offer the chain's customers the ability to burn custom-made CDs instore.

2004 Marketing Initiatives

Digital only releases

Exclusive artist content available online and via mobile

Release of digital tracks prior to or simultaneously with the release of the single to radio, ahead of physical release.

Artist websites offering track downloads and exclusive materials

More information about recordings, such as composers, producers, collaborating performers etc.

Niche download sites, such as Warchildmusic.com and Bignoisemusic.com (UK), where a proportion of the price of downloads goes to charity

New digital channels, including 'kiosk services' where consumers can compile their own custom CDs.

Specialized campaigns by companies like 7 Digital Media or Recordstore.co.uk who used direct marketing to appeal to a band's fanbase

The launch of digital downloads and ringtone charts in a number of territories

Deals between broadband providers and online music services to offer 'packages' including both services for a single fee (AOL, Tiscali, T-Online)

Harnessing Peer-to-Peer (P2P)

The recording industry is working with a range of technologies that create legitimate ways of doing business in online music. It is however, totally opposed to the abuse of technology, and in particular that of certain P2P networks that facilitate large-scale copyright theft. Record companies are now examining the possibilities for using P2P in a legitimate and commercial way that pays rightholders for their works.

There are a number of publicly-disclosed projects underway. Snocap for example, a new venture by original Napster founder Shawn Fanning, provides technology that recognizes songs requiring licences on P2P networks and automatically presents users with options to purchase authorized songs instead of allowing unauthorized copies to be traded illegally. A new service called Mashboxx is reported as being developed with Snocap to offer legitimate, licensed and paid access to content in a P2P environment.

Qtrax and Peer Impact (Wurld Media) are further examples where P2P technology is being designed to facilitate licensed file-sharing with various payment options for users. Companies such as Audible Magic and Overpeer have also developed song-identification systems similar to Snocap. Some of these services plan to launch in early 2005.

Other innovative services include the 'Open Royalty Gateway' developed by Blueprint and supported by BT (UK), launched in November 2004. The system allows for a paid-for 'word of mouth' distribution. Consumers recommend tracks to friends, and are rewarded with credits for future purchases if the tracks are bought.

> "SNOCAP is pleased and proud to have come up with a technology platform that will bring the breadth of music that is currently available on unauthorized services to the paid market place. We will enable P2P services to bring rewards for everyone concerned—especially for the music fans, but also for artists, songwriters and major and independent labels alike." Shawn Fanning. Founder of SNOCAP

The Broadband and Mobile Stimulus

Many music markets are seeing rapid growth in broadband penetration rates. Broadband stimulates online music by improving download times and file quality, prompting users to download and burn more regularly. Over 90% of Rhapsody users in the U.S., for example, have a broadband connection. Forecasts indicate that broadband household connections worldwide will increase by 169% by 2008 (PWC). Latin America will experience the biggest increase (430%).

In most countries broadband penetration is still low at under 20% of households, but rates are on the increase.

Without adequate intellectual property protection, broadband can also have an extremely negative potential—the best example being South Korea, a music market which is dominated by online piracy.

Mobile penetration is also rising at a very fast pace around the world, often surpassing broadband rates, especially in Asia. In Europe mobile penetration exceeds 80% in countries such as Finland, Greece, Italy, Norway, Sweden and the UK, and is growing rapidly in other markets. The U.S. currently lags behind, but penetration is expected to rise in the coming years.

Multi-Territory Licences for Online Streaming Services

Streaming of music programmes via the internet is just one of the many new forms of digital music distribution. Webcasting is already well-established in the U.S., where there are currently 1,250 licensed services. International cross-border licensing for internet streaming has been a priority for the recording industry.

IFPI has set up a system that allows internet webcasters and simulcasters to clear the necessary rights in a multitude of countries by entering into a licence in one participating country. Such 'one-stop' licensing facilitates the entire process of setting up legitimate streaming services, eliminating the need for rights to be cleared in each individual country.

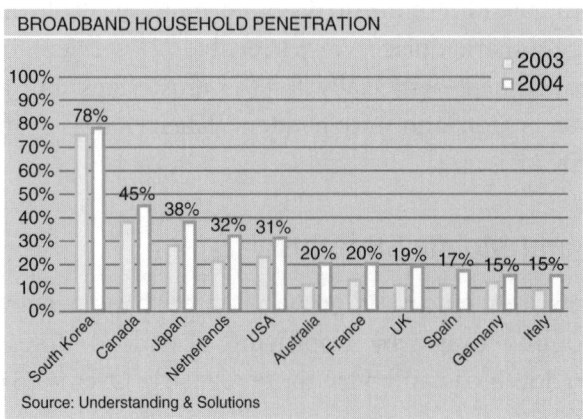

In 2004 the IFPI webcasting agreement was extended to include 17 countries, including SoundExchange in the U.S.. Simulcasting of traditional broadcasters' programming onto the internet is now facilitated by a similar crossborder agreement among producers' rights societies in 35 countries.

"We believe that the global online music market is poised for even greater growth in 2005 and 2006, as broadband becomes ubiquitous and consumers around the world grow comfortable with online services. RealNetworks will continue to work closely with the global music industry to deliver localized online services that make it easy for music fans to explore and enjoy the music they love."   Rob Glaser, Chairman & CEO of RealNetworks (Rhapsody)

Portable Music Boosts Demand

The trend towards portable technology is phenomenal. Portable players like Apple's iPod have given consumers greater control and portability of their music collections. The growing popularity of digital players, which themselves have intrinsic consumer appeal, is driving the uptake of legal music services.

The global portable digital player market was estimated to be worth U.S.$4.4 billion in 2003 and is estimated to rise to U.S.$7 billion in 2004 (IDC).

The portable player market already presents consumers with an array of choices. Apple now has a wide range of competitors including Creative (Zen product range), Rio (Karma, Carbon), Sony (Network Walkman) and others. To date the iPod, with over 50% share of the global market (including both flash media and hard-drive based players, IDC), has been the most successful portable digital player, reaching

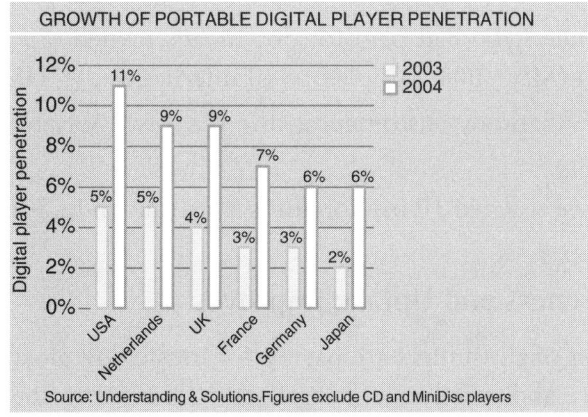

sales of 10 million units since launch in 2001. In October 2004 Apple launched the first artist-branded digital player, the U2 iPod, which included a discount on the option to purchase U2's entire catalogue through iTunes.

The market is beginning to see a convergence of portable music devices and mobile handsets, although small memory capacity and limited battery life place limits on this convergence for the time being. Many consumer technology companies, including Apple and Microsoft, are partnering mobile handset makers to offer compatible services for download or streaming to phones.

The rapid rise of different portable player systems has exposed one key problem, namely the lack of interoperability between different devices and services.

The major consumer technology companies behind the development of the major online services—namely Apple, Microsoft, Sony and RealNetworks—have developed their hardware and software using preferred or proprietary technologies. The Apple iTunes service, for example, is only currently compatible with the Apple iPod. Microsoft technologies have been used by a number of leading online services and a number of different manufacturers produce players compatible with those services, although they are still incompatible with, for example, technologies by Apple, RealNetworks and Sony. Sony Connect offers songs in Sony's ATRAC3 format, compatible only with Sony players.

Interoperability barriers between the various suppliers' products and services are confusing to consumers and ultimately could place limits on the growth of the sector. Achieving interoperability between different music services and devices is therefore a top priority both for the consumer and for the recording industry.

Portable Player Explosion—Some Key Statistics

75% of portable player owners said that they listened to music they 'most likely would not have done otherwise'—Harris Interactive (for Guardian Unlimited), UK

16% of consumers who had paid for downloads owned iPods—Entertainment Media Research (May 2004, sample of 540 internet users), UK

Nearly 50% of Rhapsody customers in the U.S. own portable digital players— RealNetworks

Sales of iPod have reached 10 million units since launch in 2001—Apple

Consumer Awareness and Uptake Improves

A growing number of consumers are paying for music downloads, more intend to do so in the future and awareness of legal services is rising sharply, according to research by IFPI as well as by third parties.

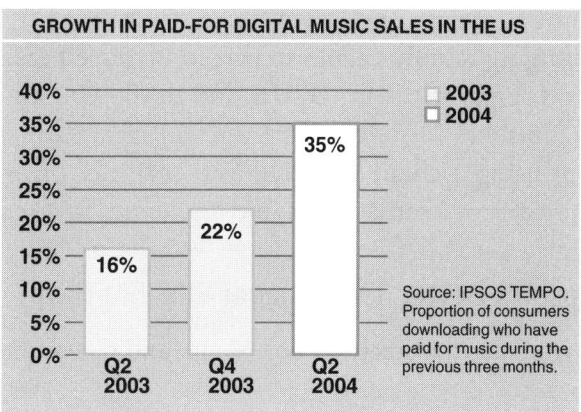

In the U.S., internet music users paying for downloads more than doubled to 35% in the year to July 2004, according to IPSOS. In the UK, 23% of downloaders said they had paid to do so at some stage (Entertainment Media Research 2004).

IFPI research indicates that the number of people buying music online legitimately appears to be rising fast—even though fewer than one person in ten in Europe regularly downloads music. A survey conducted in six European countries (Austria, Denmark, France, Germany, Italy and the UK) by GfK for IFPI in December 2004 shows that while some 44% of music downloaders used a P2P service during November 2004, a further 44% actually downloaded from either a legal service (22%) or an artist/band website (also 22%). Although legal download volumes are still low compared with P2P, the survey indicates that the number of people using legal sources is fast approaching those using P2P.

The same survey also indicates that use of legal services is likely to increase significantly in 2005. Of those who intend to download music in the next few months, almost one third (31%) stated that they are likely to download from a legal service (compared to the current level of 22%). Meanwhile, P2P use is not expected to grow, with some 38% of those intending to download saying that they are most likely to use a P2P service, compared to the current level of 44%.

Awareness of the existence of legal online music services has grown, with 29% of Europeans aware of legal online services in December 2004 (49% of 16–29 year olds), up from only 23% of Europeans (38% of 16–29-year-olds) in December 2003.

A key element of the record industry strategy is to move illegal file-sharers over to the legitimate paid-for services. For existing online music users, there appears to be a clear divide between users of legal services and people downloading illegally using a file-sharing service. In the U.S., NPD Group research, which monitors household downloads, shows that just 9% of households regularly use both legal services and file-sharing networks—it tends to be one or the other.

Younger consumers (under 25s) seem more reluctant to try legal alternatives. However this is changing rapidly, thanks in part to increased ease of payment. Napster has introduced pre-pay cards in the U.S. and in the UK, available widely from retail stores, and iTunes has introduced the use of PayPal to allow users to pay for downloads without using a credit card. The vast majority of legal online services now offer gift certificates or alternative payment schemes to credit cards.

Why Legal Shops are Better Than Illegal File-Sharing

They ensure payment to the creative community and guarantee future investment in music

They are virus and spyware free

They offer a better interface with portable music players for seamless management of music collections

They offer exclusive tracks often weeks before general release, or exclusive to the services that offer them

File quality is guaranteed

They offer quality editorial including reviews, recommendations and personalized radio stations

They are wholeheartedly supported by artists

Flexible Listening

The combination of searching, browsing, downloading and portability is transforming the experience of consuming music. Notably, it is driving demand for single tracks.

In the physical audio market, singles make up roughly 10% of unit sales compared to 90% for albums. So far, online music consumption shows an almost inverse pattern to this, with iTunes, for example, reporting that roughly only one in ten transactions are a full album purchase.

While this suggests a long-term shift in music consumption from albums to singles as digital sales increase share of consumption, the increase in digital single tracks could easily compensate for this shift. Already in the U.S., download sales outnumber physical singles by just under 20 to 1.

Digital download sales are likely to stimulate singles sales overall. In the UK the industry estimated that downloads alone would have turned a fall in singles sales of 14% in 2004, into an increase of 4%.

Record companies have responded proactively to these changes, presenting digital music in many different forms. By offering high quality audio, video, graphics and data specifically tailored to individual requirements, digital music stores can offer a much wider variety of music-related media than record stores in the physical world.

At the same time, record companies have also been enhancing the physical CD—offering special edition releases and value-added content helping sustain demand for CDs in the future.

In the longer term, digital consumption is expected to replace CD buying to some extent, since many younger music fans see their 'record collections' as digital files. Moreover, the convenience of digital is attracting new music consumers. However many people, including online music consumers, still prefer CDs for their packaging and artwork.

The Complexities of Setting Up a Legitimate Service

Digitizing content

Rights-clearance and artist negotiations

Robust technologies

Consumer-friendly DRM and 'usage rules'

Virus free services

Secure payment systems

"GERA supports the steps the music industry is taking to encourage the fast-developing legitimate online music business—the educational programmes in which we have been involved; the public promotion of all the new online services; and the decisive enforcement of the industry's rights against illegal uploaders."   Simon Wright, President of GERA (Global Entertainment Retail Association) and Chief Executive of Virgin Entertainment Group International

KEY ONLINE SERVICE PROFILES

	COMPANY PROFILE	LAUNCH	REACH
www.apple.com	Apple released the first iPod in October 2001. The iTunes Music Store followed in April 2003 and both have been a phenomenal success, helping to increase the company's revenues by 33% year-to-September 2004. The iPod, which accounted for 23% of the company's sales in 03 2004, has strengthened the Apple brand and created a 'halo-effect' on consumers, encouraging a whole economy of peripheral products	First launched in the U.S. in April 2003 and expanded into three key European markets—UK, France, Germany—in June 2004, further launches in Europe were announced in October, followed by the Canadian launch in December. The service is expected to reach Japan in 2005	15 countries
www.msn.com	Microsoft's MSN Music is driven by OD2 technology in the main European markets and by cdon.com in Scandinavia. In the U.S., the service was fully developed by Microsoft	Reached the U.S., UK, France, Germany, Netherlands, Japan and Italy in October 2004. Further European launches took place in November	20 countries
www.napster.com	Created by Shawn Fanning in 1999, Napster became world-famous for being the pioneering file-sharing network. The service was closed down in July 2001 and acquired by Roxio in November 2002, Napster 2.0 emerged in October 2003 in the US as a legitimate online service	Napster 2.0 launched in the U.S. in October 2003, and in UK and Canada in May 2004	US, Canada, UK
www.connect.com	Launched by Sony	The service was first launched in the U.S. in April 2004 and expanded into Europe in July. Plans further European expansion during 2005	US, UK, Germany and France
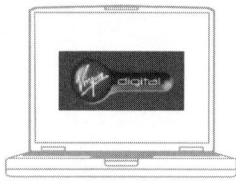www.rhapsody.com	Listen.com was the first independent service to offer content from all five majors, launching Rhapsody just before MusicNet and Pressplay. In April 2003 RealNetworks bought Listen.com and consequently Rhapsody, which started using RealNetworks technology as its primary platform. A month after Real's acquisition, RealOne Rhapsody Music Subscription was launched	Originally launched in December 2001. Re-launched in May 2003	US only, Launching in the UK and Europe in 2005
www.virgindigital.com	Service launched by the Virgin Group following the partnership between Virgin Digital and MusicNet	September 2004	US only

Taken from www.ifpi.org.

BUSINESS MODEL	MAIN PARTNERSHIP DEALS	CATALOGUE	SALES TO DATE	PORTABILITY	UNIQUE FEATURES
A la carte downloads	Partnerships announced with Motorola and Hewlett-Packard	Between one million and 700,000 songs depending on the territory	230 million by January 2005	iPods	Over 150 exclusive tracks, share playlists (iMix), stream music wirelessly to remote stereos (iPort Express), weekly free single (New Music Tuesdays), 9,000 audio books, email alerts on favorite artists (Artist Alerts)
A la carte downloads	Deal with GarageBand.com offers highlights of music and content from the community's top-rated independent artists (GarageBand.com Hub Page). MSN also has a promotional tie-in with American Express	Over one million songs	Not available	Multiple Windows Media Audio-enabled devices, including Creative Zen, Rio and iRiver	Exclusive tracks, search on which cities produced the most influential artists by decade (Map of Music), streams music videos, concert tickets
Subscription (unlimited streaming) and a la carte	AT&T Wireless will allow Napster subscribers to transfer songs to a mobile phone (Audiovox SMT 5600 smart phone). The mobile phone will be sold by Orange in the UK (Napster To Go). Tie-in with Blockbuster launched the Digital Duo card in the U.S. for sale for U.S.$20 for one month's subscription and Blockbuster Online DVD rental	Over one million songs	270,000 paying subscribers as of December 2004	Multiple Windows Media Audio-enabled devices including the Samsung Napster Player, Creative Zen, Rio and iRiver	View other subscribers' music library (Napster Community), recommend songs to other subscribers, portability with subscription plan (Napster To Go), access to service on up to three computers, email track suggestions to friends (Napster Inbox)
A la carte downloads	Promotional tie-ins with United Airlines and Intel	650,000 songs	Not available	Sony portable devices	Exclusive performances (Connect Sets), mood-specific playlists (Mood Mix)
Subscription (unlimited streaming) and a la carte	Rhapsody has partnerships with Comcast (broadband provider) and BestBuy	850,000 songs available for streaming and over 750,000 available for purchase. More than 90% of the available tracks are streamed at least once each month	625,000 paying subscribers at the end of Q3 2004 (Rhapsody & RealOne RadioPass) representing a growth of 145% on Q3 2003. The average paying subscriber streams more than 250 songs each month, the equivalent of more than 25 CDs	N/A	Radio customization, access to service on multiple computers, send playlists to other subscribers via email, add playlist links to personal 'blogs'
Subscription (Virgin Digital Music Club) and a la carte (Virtual Virgin Megastore)	Foot Locker promotional deal	Over one million songs for streaming and purchase	Not available	Multiple Windows Media Audio-enabled devices, including Creative Zen, Rio and iRiver	Service is available via the internet, in retail stores, on mobile phones and consumer electronic devices, music discovery function (Ask The Expert), detailed artist/album information (3-D Browsing)

The Industry Takes on Digital Piracy

2004 was the year the music industry stepped up its fight-back against online piracy around the world. Seven countries joined the U.S. in taking legal action against individuals illegally uploading files on peer-to-peer (P2P) networks. Information and awareness campaigns were stepped up, as were instant messaging to P2P users and deals with universities.

These activities are having an impact. Consumer awareness of the illegality of unauthorized file-sharing across Europe has improved. Trends in illegal file-sharing show the problem is being contained, helped by the growing availability of legal music downloads.

What is Internet Piracy?

Internet piracy is the act of making available, transmitting or copying someone else's work over the internet without permission. Copyright laws in virtually every country in the world make this illegal, protecting the rights of those involved in creating and those investing in creative works—writers, publishers, artists, musicians, record companies, film makers, producers, and many others. These laws acknowledge their right to choose how their work is distributed and the terms of distribution.

Authorization by the rights owner is the fundamental principle underlying copyright laws, and the key to the distinction between legitimate and illegal online music distribution. Legitimate online services have permission from record labels, publishers and artists whose music they distribute. They pay these people for the use of their works in commercial activities. Online piracy involves people or services who distribute music without authorisation.

Illegal File-Sharing and its Impact

Numerous research studies show that online piracy has a negative impact on legitimate sales of music. While other factors also affect music sales, including competition from other consumer products and general economic conditions, online piracy has contributed substantially to sales drops in recent years.

Global music industry sales declined by some 22% over five years to 2003, a reduction of over U.S.$6 billion, with some of the biggest drops in album and singles sales in countries with large or growing broadband penetration. The latest study by Forrester Research in August 2004, found that while 10% of regular downloaders

SERVICE TYPE	DESCRIPTION	WHAT IS WRONG WITH IT?
WEB, FILE TRANSFER PROTOCOL [FTP] AND LINK SITES	This 'traditional' form of online piracy remains popular in many countries. Typically the first place where unauthorized copies of a new recording appear.	These services do not attempt to obtain licenses for the use of copyrighted music. Although they may not profit directly from the distribution of music, they often generate advertising revenues and user traffic—effectively profiteering out of those who created and invested in music.
UNAUTHORIZED SERVICES	These are blatantly commercial services, generating substantial revenues from unauthorized use of music and other copyrighted content. Some services sell music directly, others receive indirect revenues from advertising, spyware and licensing. In many cases such services operate with large databases of music tracks.	Because these services do not reward those who created and invested in music, operating costs are low and financial gains can be substantial. P2P networks encourage and assist the distribution of a large number of music files between individual users ('peers') without the rightholders permission.
ILLEGAL UPLOADERS	Most users of P2P networks not only download files, but make the music stored in their computer available to others to download, thus acting as 'uploaders'. This turns individual users into large-scale distributors of unauthorized files.	P2P uploaders do not have permission to distribute music files, hence engaging in an illegal activity.

claimed to buy more music, 36% admitted to buying less. This result has been confirmed repeatedly in the bulk of all respectable third-party research.

> "We must fight piracy in any form, for the protection of intellectual property is in all our interests. It gives economic value to the most precious thing, creativity, which is the grounds of our free society."   Carlo Azeglio Ciampi, President of Italy

The Industry's Response

The recording industry is developing legitimate online music services that will displace illegal sites over time, using education, and, if necessary, law enforcement to protect its repertoire.

1. Public Awareness and Information Campaigns

Public awareness plays a critical part in introducing legal alternatives and educating consumers on risks attached to online piracy. In 2004 the music industry stepped up its educational activities to point people away from illegal file-sharing and towards legal download sites.

Schools

In Italy, a government-backed music, film and software copyright education programme has been launched to explain copyright to 14–18 year-olds in 3,000 schools. In France, a two-page copyright and anti-piracy message has been sent to one million students. In Germany, a music industry and 'Value of Creativity' campaign provides educational materials to 10,000 teachers of 10 to 15 year-olds. In the UK, a 'Respect the Value of Music' school curriculum for 11 to 14 year-olds, developed by British Music Rights, directs students to www.pro-music.org for legal downloads. A new campaign was launched in Japan in December 2004, with public statements by four major artists.

Parents and children

The Danish music industry launched a free software programme that people can use to identify and, if necessary, remove unauthorized P2P programmes and files from their computers.

Universities

In the U.S., cooperation between legal online services and record companies led to legitimate services being made available at discount to students in 24 colleges and universities.

The scheme was pioneered at Pennsylvania State University in a deal with Napster, and was followed by further deals with Rhapsody at other universities. U.S. universities have also been using anti-piracy technical countermeasures against illegal P2P file-sharing (www.educause.ed).

Companies

IFPI and its affiliates have conducted an information campaign on the copyright and security risks involved in illegal P2P file-sharing, among thousands of companies and government institutions in 21 countries. Brochures explain that these institutions are at risk of legal action if music is used illegally on their computers and that unauthorized file-sharing raises a host of security problems for institutional networks including computer viruses, firewall breaches, spyware, and exposure of confidential data. The brochures, which also explain how to tackle the risks, can be downloaded in six languages at www.ifpi.org.

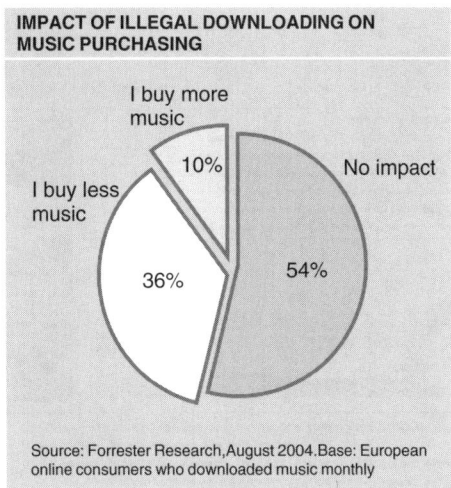

The Impact of Illegal Filesharing

28% of those spending less on music said downloading, file-sharing and burning were the main reasons—Pollara Canada, July 2004

For 2004, the potentials losses to the music industry through file-sharing could be as high as U.S.$2.1 billion—informa Media Group

36 million of the 40 million people downloading (nine in ten) in Europe are still not paying for music they download—Forrester, August 2004

"Piracy is theft–pure and simple. The government supports the principle of proportionate legal action against the worst offending uploaders"   Estelle Morris, Arts Minister, UK

Instant messages to infringing file-sharers

IFPI national groups in 10 countries have sent more than 45 million instant messages to individual users of P2P services, warning them to stop putting other people's music on the internet without permission.

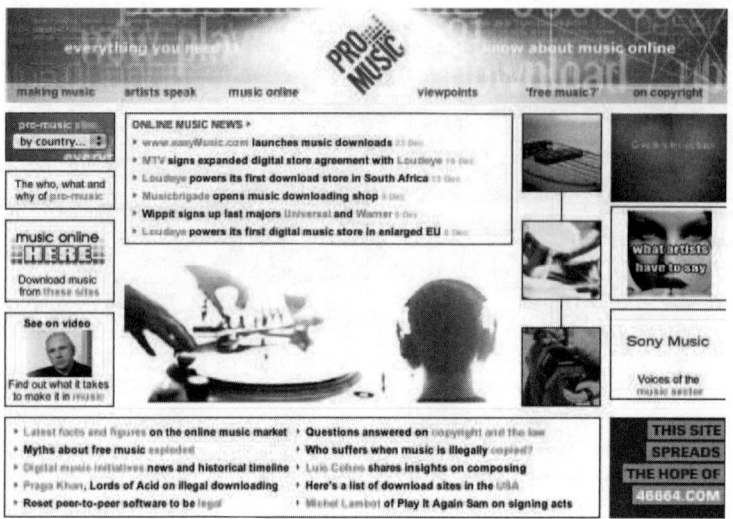

The pro-music campaign

The international cross-sector music campaign www.pro-music.org, launched in 2003, is now available in four languages (English, French, German, Italian) and includes a global directory of legitimate online services. The mission of pro-music is to promote legitimate digital music and confront the myths surrounding online music piracy.

Internet advertising

French-intitiated pro-music viral email "The Drummer" was rolled out across Europe, calling on music fans to protect those involved in creating music by downloading legally.

Artist campaigns

In the U.S., artists including Lenny Kravitz, Missy Elliot and Sheryl Crow featured in an 'I Download (Legally)' campaign. A similar project was rolled out in France in a poster campaign with 14 artists in 30 cities.

Why Not to Download Illegally

Your computer may crash
Peer-to-peer (P2P) programs write files to your hard disc and change your computer settings. These can be nearly impossible to remove and may crash your computer if you try

You can catch a computer virus

There is no quality control on the files that other people put on unlicensed P2P services. A 2004 study by security firm TruSecure found that 45% of the computer programs down-loaded using Kazaa contained a virus or other malicious code

You will get adware and pop-ups by default

Unlicenced P2P services make their money by selling advertising. The advertising comes to you via software they out on your machine—sometimes without you knowing

You may get spyware without knowing it

In many cases, the software that unlicensed P2P services distribute also contains modules that report on your file searching, web browsing or other activity. Among other things, it helps them send advertising to you

You will come across unsolicited pornographic material

Search for any popular artist's music on an unlicensed P2P service and you will also get lists of files that include a whole range of pornographic and obscene material

You will open up your computer to complete strangers

Unlicensed P2P file sharing involves giving millions of anonymous strangers access to your computer

You could be sued

Over 7,000 cases have been brought against bulk uploaders in several countries worldwide.

"We have to take responsibility, call piracy what it is and not allow to be confused with 'unlimited freedom' I believe in cultural creation and diversity, which are the victims of piracy. They need to be protected."   Renaud Donnedieu De vabres, Minister of Communication, France

Deterrence

In 2004 IFPI and its member record companies significantly stepped up the deterrence campaign against internet piracy. Cooperative work with Internet Service Providers (ISPs), litigation cases against infringing services, as well as cases against individual illegal uploaders, are all part of this strategy.

High-volume notice and takedown

Notifications are sent to ISPs, universities and companies when users are found using their systems to offer unauthorized music on the internet. ISPs are often cooperative in removing infringing web, FTP and links sites when they receive such notice. In many cases, they will also block access to P2P servers running on individuals' computers, or block pre-release music files being offered from an individual's computer. The ISPs' own terms of service typically prohibit individual users from engaging in such activities.

In 2004 IFPI's internet anti-piracy unit and anti-piracy staff in 28 national recording industry groups, secured the takedown of 60,900 infringing websites (41,000 in 2003), 477 unauthorized P2P servers (1,050 in 2003) and 1.6 billion infringing music files in 102 countries (1.6 billion in 2003).

High-profile litigation against sites and services

Where cooperation does not work, the industry pursues strategic court cases against internet sites and services that build their business on music that has not been paid for. The industry's main litigation strategy has been to stop infringement at the level of the services through which the majority of unauthorized music files are available. The bulk of the traffic on P2P networks is driven by a relatively small number of uploaders–75% of all distribution is accounted for by 15% of all individuals (NPD 2003).

Recent Cases Have Involved Claims Against:

Companies and principals related to the Kazaa P2P service (Australia)

This case, which went to trial in November 2004, alleges that the defendants violated copyright and authorized others to do so. At time of print, the judge was preparing his decision in the case.

Japan MMO

This P2P service operator was found guilty of infringement and ordered to pay ¥36.9 million (U.S.$350,000) plus interest as compensation. The court also issued an injunction against the service.

Kuro, EzPeer (Taiwan)

Taiwan courts have enjoined these subscription P2P services from offering 105 infringing tracks. Civil and criminal proceedings continue.

Weblisten (Spain)

All six civil plaintiffs have secured injunctions against this site in cases claiming that the site offered streams and downloads without licenses from the record labels. Appeals and enforcement are pending.

Legal cases against individuals engaged in 'uploading'

In 2004 it became clear that, however effective education programmes were in raising awareness, stronger action was needed to deter a significant group of 'hard core' illegal uploaders. The industry needed to show that uploaders of copyrighted music are not only breaking the law, but can be caught and made accountable. In 2004, and initial 700 legal cases were launched against bulk uploaders of music in Austria, Canada, Denmark, France, Germany, Italy and UK. In addition, more than 6,000 cases have been brought to date in the U.S., which started bringing lawsuits in 2003.

In most of the countries involved, there has been a regular flow of settlements averaging a few thousand euros. In Austria, around 50 cases were settled within three months, the highest compensation payment being EUR4,000. In Denmark and Germany, over 100 cases have been settled, with the highest individual payment of EUR13,000.

> "We know that there are millions of illegal files circulating on the internet at any given time. In the European Parliament we have dealt with this by passing effective laws to legislate for the internet age. There is no upside to illegal uploading—it undermines jobs and creativity. The law is there to be respected and enforced."   Arlene McCarthy, Member of the European Parliment

Why Fight the Battle?

The aim of the record industry's educational and anti-piracy actions is to help create a breathing space for the burgeoning online music market, to raise awareness, change attitudes and contain illegal file-sharing. Their impact in 2004 has been visible.

Increasing Public Awareness About Illegal File-Sharing

Seven out of ten people surveyed in North America and Europe are now aware that unauthorized file-sharing is illegal. Before the recording industry began its public education initiatives and anti-piracy actions against unauthorized file-sharing, this figure stood at only 37%.

Containing Illegal File-Sharing

Online music piracy has proliferated dramatically in recent years, but is being contained in the context of the dramatic increases in broadband coverage of the last two years, and rising levels of film and video piracy.

In the five years up to 2004, the number of infringing music files on the internet soared from 1 million to 1.1 billion. The problem has been largely contained since early 2003, when plans to act against illegal file-sharing were first announced in the U.S. and the first raft of legitimate online services were rolled out for consumers.

Measuring online piracy is an inexact business and often confused by the competing claims and methodologies of countless research firms. Methodologies range

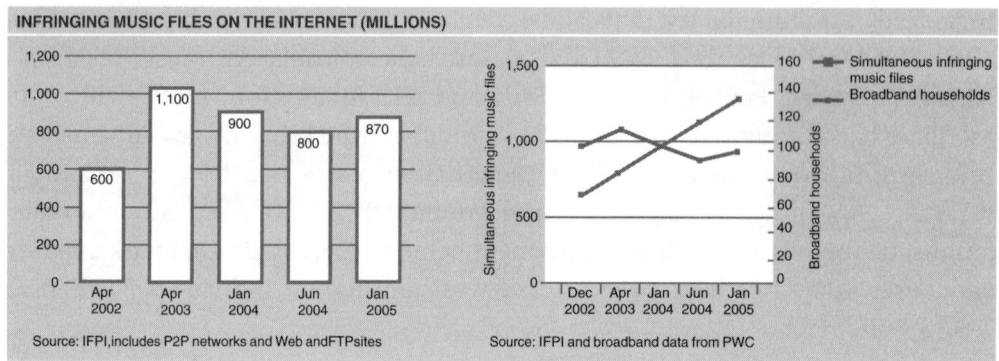

INFRINGING MUSIC FILES ON THE INTERNET (MILLIONS)

Source: IFPI, includes P2P networks and Web and FTP sites

Source: IFPI and broadband data from PWC

from counting website hits to software downloads, traffic and request data, and user sampling.

IFPI has consistently measured the number of unauthorized music files offered at any one time. This is based on the number of users per service, the average number of files per user, and the average percentage of music files versus the other files offered by users.

IFPI estimates show that pirate music online has not grown since 2004 despite a massive increase in broadband usage across the music industry's most key markets. In January 2005 there are around 870 million infringing music files on the internet at any one time (about 90% of them are on P2P networks, the remainder on FTP and websites). This is down slightly from 900 million in January 2004 (and sharply down from 1.1 billion in April 2003).

Notable trends are the decline in use of the largest service Kazaa, the rise in file-sharing of films and video and the increase in illegal file-sharing activity on new services where there has up until now been less enforcement. This led to a slight increase in the overall estimated numbers of infringing music files in the second half of 2004, from 800 million to 870 million files.

Indeed with the migration from Kazaa, use of other peer-to-peer services (notably eDonkey, Gnutella, DirectConnect and BitTorrent) rose in 2004. However, user numbers on those services increased more sharply than the number of infringing music files; this appears to be largely accounted for by a big rise in file-sharing of non-music files, such as film, video and software. Music files represent a smaller proportion of the newer services—an estimated 25% of files on eDonkey are music, for example, as opposed to an estimated 75% on Kazaa.

Stepping Up Deterrence in 2005

Legal actions against illegal file-sharing will be stepped up in an increasing number of countries in 2005. Lawsuits, which up until now have been largely focused on users of Kazaa, will increasingly target different networks, despite those services'

IFPI. "The Digital Revolution." *Digital Music Report*, London, 2005.

Kusek, David & Leonhard, Gerd. "The Future of Music." *Berkeley Press*, Boston, Massachusetts, 2005.

Oren, Shachar. "New Media Entrepreneurship." *Neurotic Media*, November 2005.

Smith, Ethan. "Advertising: Can MySpace work on Advertising Space." *Wall Street Journal*, July 22, 2005.

Glossary of Music Industry Terms

A&R (*Artist & Repertoire*)   A&R representatives are the staff at record labels that are responsible for scouting new artists and then (to some extent) helping develop those artists after a recording contract has been signed.

AC (*Adult Contemporary*)   Soft rock music, featuring current hits, and songs from the 80's, 70's.

ACB (*Advertising Checking Bureau, Inc*)   UMVD's 3rd party agency that audits all advertising claims, outside UMVD's in-house audited accounts, submitted by UMVD's account base. Upon receiving the claims, ACB will audit and then release for payment. UMVD will then issue a credit memo for the said claimed advertising.

Adtrac   UMVD's in-house mainframe advertising system. Adtrac is the database that holds all label and RDF budgets, along with all advertising that is fed from Fastrac.

Amortize   To provide for the gradual extinguishment of (as a mortgage) usually by contribution to a sinking fund at the time of each periodic interest payment.

ASCAP   ASCAP is a membership association of more than 120,000 U.S. composers, songwriters and publishers of every kind of music and hundreds of thousands worldwide. ASCAP is the only U.S. performing rights organization created and controlled by composers, songwriters and music publishers, with a Board of Directors elected by and from the membership.

Audience   The number of listeners as determined by Arbitron data and based on the average quarter hour listeners. The listening information is based on the Metro Survey Area as determined by Arbitron.

Taken from UMVD.

Authorization Number   An alpha-numeric number that is generated automatically from Fastrac. Upon submitting a request thru Fastrac, this number will be created and represented by the region abbreviation, followed by a random 5 digits consecutive number, i.e., SF20500.

BDS (Broadcast Data Systems)   BDS monitors radio and television broadcasts. Employing pattern recognition technology, BDS identifies songs played on over 1100 radio stations in the U.S. and Canada in real-time.

Bill Of Lading   A receipt listing goods shipped that is signed by the agent of the owner of a ship or issued by a common carrier Bottom of Form.

BMI (Broadcast Music Inc)   A licensing organization that lobbies licenses collects and distributes royalty fees for the publicly performed works of its membership of 100,000 U.S. writers, publishers and international affiliate societies.

Bonus Features   Additional materials included on a DVD. Bonus features are a hot selling point for DVDs and may include behind-the-scenes footage, "making of" documentaries, outtakes, deleted scenes, etc.

BPI (Branch Performance Index)   Breakdown of sales goals measured by performance.

Breached Product Credit   UMVD does not allow its accounts to return open CDs and cassettes for credit. Instead, UMVD issues a monthly credit equal to a percentage each account's gross dollar purchases of those configurations the previous month.

Canceled by MG (in reference to Adtrac)   This does not mean that Mike Gillespie canceled this ad. It's an abbreviation for management. Please contact a National Account Coordinator for further details and how this may pertain to your advertising needs.

Catalog +   A CD-Rom compendium of catalogs–Pop, Classical, by Genre, ranked by sales, etc. etc. Updated quarterly, it contains over 1200 pages of sales information in an easily printable and sortable electronic form.

CHR (Contemporary Hit Radio)   Currently popular rock tunes. This used to be called Top 40 because it featured the 40 most popular hits from the weekly Billboard Magazine list of hot songs.

CMA (Country Music Association)   A trade association of 8,000 members that promotes and develops country music worldwide and host the annual CMA awards.

Coalition   A Coalition is a network of independent music stores that provide labels with a cohesive national marketing effort for they're developing and established bands.

Combustion   A sales and marketing strategy geared for the artists not ready for frontline pricing, but deserving of a price between Listen Up and frontline. Features a $14.98 list.

Cookie   A message given to a Web browser by a Web server. The browser stores the message in a text file called cookie.txt. The message is then sent back to the server each time the browser requests a page from the server. The main purpose of cookies is to identify users and possibly prepare customized Web pages for them.

Co-op Advertising   A way for record labels to pay for media ad space with product, and is an effective way to use their inventory to promote sales. The customer is reimbursed for costs incurred by advertisements or positioning the product.

Credit Memo   A document that is sent to an account denoting the credit they received due to the advertising that they ran.

Cutout   A recording deleted from a record label's catalog, with remaining stock sold at a discount.

Dating   The date payment is due for product purchased by customers.

Day & Date   Term used when a DVD is released on the same day as the VHS. A "Day & Date" release is a great selling point for DVD.

Day-Part   A day divided into the standard segments of time which are 6am–10am / 10am–3pm / 3pm–7pm, 7pm–Midnight, Midnight–6am. This is a term referred to in radio airplay.

Deal   Discount Program, which gives a percentage off of Invoice.

Development Deal   A short-term contract and fee supplied to an artist not sufficiently developed to warrant a true contract, giving a record label or publishing company the option to sign the artist during a specified time period.

Digital Downloads   Digital music available on computer via download from the Internet.

DJ Pool   A Coalition of independent DJs who spin music in clubs and bars. DJ pools are usually regional, covering a single city and its surrounding communities. They are an effective way to quickly service many clubs in a single vinyl mailing. Good pools will provide DJ feedback on the records, as well as weekly charts on the most frequently played or requested songs.

DMA (Designated Market Area)   A. C. Nielsen's geographic market design, which defines each television market. DMA's are composed of counties and are updated annually by the A. C. Nielsen Company based on historical television viewing patterns.

DSL (Digital Subscriber Line)   This is a service that connects you to the Internet at a higher speed than modems.

DVD-Audio   The latest member of the DVD family of pre-recorded optical disc formats and is designed to be the next-generation high-quality audio format. DVD-Audio offers very high quality, surround sound, longer playing times plus additional features that are not available on CDs. DVD-Audio discs can also carry video, like DVD-Video titles, and limited interactivity. Capacity of a single layer DVD-Audio is at least 74 minutes of high quality full surround sound audio. In addition the disc can accommodate the same audio encoded as Dolby Digital for playing on existing DVD-Video players. At the time of writing, the DVD Forum is working on a hybrid version allowing DVD-Audio discs to play on CD players, but in stereo, CD quality only.

E-Commerce   Conducting business on-line. This includes, for example, buying and selling products with digital cash and via Electronic Data Interchange (EDI).

EBITDA   Earnings Positive Before Interest, Taxes, Depreciation and Amortization.

EDI (Electronic Data Interchange)   A way to electronically exchange business documents, such as purchase orders and invoices, between companies around the world.

EMO   Or "Emo-core," is a type of guitar-based typically independent music, which is emotional in content. It is very loosely defined, and encompasses a broad range of styles. The genre began to emerge in the late 80s, and became popular in the early-mid 90s as a reaction to the aggressive, male-posturing hard-core that seemed to define punk culture at the time. Weezer think they started Emo. Most people claim that Embrace's record on Dischord from the mid-80s was the first true well-known Emo record.

EPK (Electronic Press Kit)   The video version of promotional material sent to retail comprising many of the items of the printed press kit as well as interviews with the band.

Enhanced CD   An audio CD which can contain a wide range of multimedia content, including music videos and audio tracks, exclusive concert footage and interviews, biographies, etc.

EP (Extended Play)   This expression designates a recording longer than a single, but shorter than a full-length album, or LP. Often EPs are promotional releases by a new band and contain only four to six songs.

Evergreen   A song that maintains a consistent popularity over many years. A standard.

Extranet   An intranet that is partially accessible to authorized outsiders. You can access an extranet only if you have a valid username and password, and your identity determines which parts of the extranet you can view. UMVD's extranet site is UMVD.com.

Fastrac   A web based routing system for co-op advertising authorizations.

FCC (The Federal Communications Commission)   An independent United States government agency, directly responsible to Congress. The FCC was established by the

Communications Act of 1934 and is charged with regulating interstate and international communications by radio, television, wire, satellite and cable. The FCC's jurisdiction covers the 50 states, the District of Columbia, and U.S. possessions.

Firewall   A system designed to prevent unauthorized access to or from a private network. All messages entering or leaving the intranet pass through the firewall, which examines each message and blocks those that do not meet the specified security criteria.

Free Goods   A recording contract provision that provides a distributor or retailer free copies of a record, usually 15% of the total quantity ordered, for which the artist receives no royalties.

Impact   A mutual commitment between Universal Distribution and label to spotlight an artist that has shown increased sales potential and consumer awareness, in order to boost sales to the next level of gold or platinum status.

In-House Auditing   UMVD's approach to account satisfaction. By auditing particular KEY ACCOUNTS in house, UMVD can turn over claims faster and thus issue quicker credit memos.

Insight   Insight compares 2 weeks of BDS airplay information including detections, audience and daypart breakdowns, as well as Sound-Scan Album and Single sales data by market including store strata breakdowns and even overall industry sales conditions.

Intranet   (An internet) belonging to an organization, usually a corporation, accessible only by the organization's members, employees, or others with authorization. An intranet's Web sites look and act just like any other Web sites, but the firewall surrounding an intranet fends off unauthorized access. UMVD's intranet is: UMVDTools.com.

IO (Initial Order)   National sales goal on a new release.

Lankershim   An ad requested for an indirect customer. They are paid by a check as opposed to credit.

Legacy   Mainframe Operating system for UMVD that is the "backbone" for Production, Manufacturing, Inventory Management, Credit, Sales Order Processing, Accounts Receivable and Sales Reporting. User applications include SalesAction (our primary on-line Sales reporting system) and INV (for order lookup and review).

Lifestyle Account   Any account that sells a particular lifestyle (i.e., skateboarding, college, rave/clubbing), that can be used to promote an artist who defines that same lifestyle and the type of music associated with that lifestyle.

Listen Up   A program to spotlight new and developing artists that shows pre-release sales potential. Combined with label commitment, this program is designed to boost early over-the-counter sales.

Loose Pick   A loose pick quantity is any number of units of the same sku that is lees than a true box lot quantity. Most companies, including UMVD use a 30-count carton. UMVD's "loose pick charge" is assessed to any order for a single sku of between 1 and 9 units.

Make Goods   When we find that price & positioning we've paid for isn't in place— so the account will do a "make good" by extending the period a week, month, etc.

Mass Merchant   A very large retail chain that sells a variety of goods, including recorded music. Such stores include Wal-Mart and K-Mart.

MDC (Marketing Development Comp Plan)   Paid quarterly to all field positions (except regional support staff, SSM, SRCT and Latin Reps). Each individual is assigned a DMA set and a monthly list of priority product. Number of scans within a DMA set on each title is measured against the applicable genre "index" for that DMA set. If the individual meets or exceeds 90% of the number of "expected scans"—based on SoundScan's index for each DMA set—for the aggregated titles, a flat quarterly payment is made (amount of payment varies by position).

Modem   Modem is an acronym for modulator-demodulator. A modem is a device or program that enables a computer to transmit data over telephone lines. Computer information is stored digitally, whereas information transmitted over telephone lines is transmitted in the form of analog waves. A modem converts between these two forms.

Moratorium   A video title that is on "moratorium" status is no longer available to purchase. These titles will often become "active" again after a period of time.

Mp3   An abbreviation for MPEG (Motion Picture Experts Group), the electronic file format that is the current standard for transmitting electronic music over the Internet.

MPAA (Motion Picture Association of America)   The MPAA and its international counterpart, the Motion Picture Association serve as the voice and advocate of the American motion picture, home video and television industries, domestically through the MPAA and internationally through the MPA.

The MPAA Rating System:
G GENERAL AUDIENCES - All ages admitted.
PG PARENTAL GUIDANCE SUGGESTED - Some material may not be suitable for children.
PG-13 PARENTS STRONGLY CAUTIONED - Some material may be inappropriate for children under 13.
R RESTRICTED - Under 17 requires accompanying parent or adult guardian.
NC-17—No one 17 and under admitted

NAC (New Age Contemporary)   Popular light jazz, mixed with New Age music, and light rock.

NARAS (National Academy of Recording Arts and Sciences)   The academy is the sponsor of the Grammy Awards and its 8,000 members include singers, musicians, songwriters, composers, engineers, and industry professionals.

NARM (National Association of Recording Merchandisers)   Serves the music and other prerecorded entertainment software industry as the pre-eminent forum for insight and dialog in an increasingly diverse and rapidly evolving industry.

Neverouts   "Crème of the crop" catalog that retail should never be out of. Also known as "Evergreen" titles.

No Depression   No Depression- Sub Genre of Country which owes more to the traditional country of yesteryear than the big-hat, boot-scootin-boogie country of the last decade or two. Combines elements of everything from Hank Williams to The Replacements to Bob Dylan to The Byrds to Patsy Cline to Bruce Springsteen and most of all, Gram Parsons-the father of the genre. Singing & songwriting skills a must. The genre can also include other roots music genres such as, Bluegrass, Folk, Blues & others. Also known as: Alt Country. Examples of artists include: Wilco, Lucinda Williams, Whiskeytown, Son Volt, Jayhawks, Gillian Welch, Emmylou Harris, etc.

NTSC   The standard for TV/video display in the U.S. and Canada. *See also PAL.*

One Sheet   Should be 1 sheet (8 1/2″ × 11) and include:
> *Label's logo and contact information*
> *Artist Name/Logo*
> *Catalog # and UPC code*
> *List price of each available format*
> *Release Date / Street Date*
> *A brief Artist background description*
> *Selling Points*

One Stop   Carry a wide selection of major label and select independent label product, and sell to Chain Stores, Independent Stores, and miscellaneous other retail outlets that sell recorded music product. They provide a service for accounts that cannot/do not buy direct from Universal.

P&D Deal   Pressing and Distribution deal. An agreement between an independent record label and a distributor / manufacturer to make and distribute copies of recordings.

Packaging Descriptions   Slipcase—A paperboard sleeve that fits over a jewel box with one end closed by a tuck-in flap.

O-Card—A paperboard sleeve that fits over a jewel box with both ends being open. Looks like the letter "O" when viewed from the end profile.

Matrix—There is a manufacturer with this name that makes a double slimline jewel box called a "Matrix Double Slimline Jewel Box". A double slimline jewel box is the same size as a regular jewel box, but holds 2-CDs on a double sided, left hand, hinged tray.

Digi-Pak—A multi-panel paper board package that holds CDs on individual plastic trays, glued to the various panels. The package folds up to be basically the same size as a jewel box.

Amray Case—The standard 5-1/4″ wide × 7-1/2″ tall plastic package that holds a DVD. The package has a paper title sheet inserted under the clear plastic overlay surrounding the outside of the package.

Brilliant Box—A brilliant box jewel box is the same size as a regular jewel box, but holds 2-CDs on a double sided, right hand fold out, hinged tray.

PAL   A standard for TV/video display popular in Europe and Australia. *See also* NTSC.

Pan & Scan   Pan and scan is the process of cropping away portions of a widescreen movie so that the resulting image conforms to the shape of your television. In addition to cropping the sides away, pan and scan (as the name implies) also pans across the wide-screen image in an attempt to capture more of the action/elements of the original film frame.

P.O.P. (Point Of Purchase)   Materials used by retailers in stores to make consumers aware of our products. P.O.P. material include banners, posters, flats, standees, static clings, etc.

Racks   Companies that rent or lease space in large department type stores, and other mass marketing retail outlets. They usually carry only the best selling commercial product available, concentrating on major label product, and some independent label product with a strong regional presence.

Re-Issue   Renewed availability or re-distribution of an older, previously released recorded product.

Record Label   The primary job of a record label is to work closely with distribution, providing them with information on successful airplay, print media support, and live performance successes. In addition the record labels create "Distributor One Sheets", or fact sheets that include promotion and marketing plans, and list price information. The record labels also provide the distributor with "P.O.P." (Point of Purchase) items, such as posters, flyers, cardboard stand-ups etc., which can be used for in-store display.

Retail Tag   Identifying a retailer name and/or logo in advertising, ideally in exchange for "price and positioning" in their store.

Returns   Unsold records or tapes sent back to manufacturers for cash credit to buyer's account.

Returns Processing Fee   A flat, per-unit charge assessed to each item returned by the customer.

RIAA (Recording Industry Association of America)   A trade association whose members create, produce and market 95 percent of all recordings produced and sold in the United States.

RIAA Awards
Gold/500,000 Units
Platinum/One Million Units
Multi Platinum/Two Million Units
Diamond/Ten Million Units

SACD   Super Audio CD, an alternative to the DVD-Audio format developed by Philips and Sony. It is designed to play on audio CD players and Super Audio CD players by comprising two layers: one with CD-Audio the other with high quality audio. The audio encoding used is Direct Stream Digital (DSD).

Singles Credit Processing Fee   Which is not in here and will continue to exist. It would read "A flat per-unit charge" assessed to singles product which under UMVD's singles returns policy.

SKU (Stock Keeping Unit)   Refers to a configuration of a selection. For example, the cassette configuration of a particular selection is one sku; the cd configuration of that same selection is another sku.

SoundScan   The Point-of-Sale data, originating directly from the cash registers' bar code scanners, is then transmitted on a weekly basis via modem from the reporting retail locations to SoundScan for processing. Each Wednesday morning, the updated, current sales information is made available for delivery to network subscribers.

Status Codes
A = Active
B = Active Pending Cut-out (no manufacturing allowed)
C = Cut-out (returns allowed but no sales)
D = Deleted (no sales, no returns)
N = New release
X = TBD

Step Up   Sales & Marketing program designed to maximize catalog sales spikes driven by the radio and PR around that artist's new release.

Tchotchke   A toy; a small play thing; a bauble, a trinket; a gewgaw; a gadget; a little knickknack that brings joy. Etymology: Yiddish tshatshke trinket, from obsolete Polish czaczko.

Trailer   An advertisement for a movie, which contains scenes from the film. Historically, these advertisements were attached to the end of a newsreel or supporting-feature, hence the name. Doing this reduced the number of reel changes that a projectionist would have to make.

Triple AAA (Adult Album Alternative radio)   Features current albums cuts from softer rock artists frequently mixed in with folk or blues.

UAC (Adult Urban)   Soft urban music, mostly current ballads, with songs from the 70's and 80's, and no rap.

UMG (Universal Music Group)   The world's largest music company. Its global operations encompass the development, manufacture, marketing, sales and distribution of recorded music through a network of subsidiaries, joint ventures and licensees in 63 countries around the world. UMG's businesses also include music publishing, and mail order music/video clubs. UMG is the market leader in every major region, including the United States, Europe, Latin America, and Asia.

UML (Universal Manufacturing & Logistics)   The manufacturing arm of UMVD. They provide mastering, replication, printing and packaging services for all formats of compact discs including Audio CDs, CD Extra, Enhanced CDs, CD Text, CD ROMs, CD-i, Video CD, DVD Video and DVD ROM.

Value-Added   A special version of a CD that is being released (usually simultaneously) along side the regular version of a release. The "special version" may contain extra songs, a DVD, special packaging, etc. Most times it will be a limited edition release.

Venue   Any place where live music is performed, including coffee shops, bars, clubs, theaters, and major arenas.

VPN (Virtual Private Network)   This is a utility that allows you access to the Universal Network utilizing a broadband service such as DSL or cable modem. VPN sets up a "virtual network" and creates a firewall on your home computer to protect against hackers.

Web Browser   A software application used to locate and display Web pages. The two most popular browsers are Netscape Navigator and Microsoft Internet Explorer.

Widescreen   A way of watching a movie on your TV as the movie was originally shown in the theatres. The widescreen transfer process actually shrinks a movie down so that the entire visual image fits on your television screen.

Appendix

Anime On DVD
All Sources Through The Period Ending Oct. 07, 2005

Anime Suppliers	1997	1998	1999	2000	2001	2002	2003	2004	2005	Combined
A.D.V. Films			5	28	92	89	177	189	126	706
Geneon Entertainment (2)	3	6	59	45	51	61	74	85	119	503
Bandai				25	41	66	66	63	52	313
Funimation				5	26	58	59	84	71	303
Media Blasters/Kitty				10	49	63	61	64	48	295
Central Park Media	1	8	10	13	36	34	81	53	37	273
Viz Media		4	1	6	24	30	44	49	35	193
Digital Versatile/Nutech				8	31	60	33	49	1	182
AnimEigo					9	26	34	11	21	101
Right Stuf/Critical Mass				2	17	10	12	18	17	76
Manga			4	9	12	10	20	7	6	68
Tokyopop					5	17	17	13	9	61
Rhino					6	14	9	6		35
CAV–Voyager				2	5	7	8			22
Softcel						3	19			22
Adult Source Media								1	17	18
Image Entertainment (1)		2	2		3	3	4	1		15
Urban Vision				2	6	2	1	2		13
Synch-Point						2	2	2	2	8
Paramount								2	6	8
AN Entertainment							3	4		7
ANS Records							3	3		6
Broccolli/Super Techo								6		6
Buena Vista									6	6
Tai Seng								2	4	6
AV Box, Inc.									5	5
SONY Pictures						2		2	1	5
Artsmagic								2	3	5
Hirameki International								3	2	5
M2K			3	1						4
Anime Crash								2	1	3
Ardustry Home Ent.							1	2		3
Lions Gate–Trimark				1		1				2
Ariztical					1					1
Goldhil Media						1				1
Pathfinder								1		1
SONY	1									1
Total	5	20	84	157	414	559	728	726	589	3,282
Discontinued		12	13	3	25	0	0	0	0	53
Through 10/14/05	5	32	97	160	439	559	728	726	589	3,335
All DVD Titles	528	1,522	2,742	3,958	5,630	7,357	10,126	11,587	9,343	52,793
Percentage	0.95%	2.10%	3.54%	4.04%	7.80%	7.60%	7.19%	6.27%	6.30%	6.32%

(1) - Image Entertainment includes distributed lines (2) Formerly Pioneer

Reprinted from the DVD Release Report, Number 448, 2005. Taken from www.homemediaretailing.com.

Reprinted courtesy of Ralph Tribbey.

PROVIDING THE SOURCE
Retailers: Locate hard-to-find titles and genres
Indie labels: Gain access to National wholesale distribution
Key Theatrical Release Grid: October-January, 2006*

Title	Product Source	Box Office	Theatrical Release Date	DVD Release Date	ARR
Kicking and Screaming	Universal	$52,580,895	5/13/05	10/11/05	151
Kingdom of Heaven	20th Century-Fox	$47,396,698	5/6/05	10/11/05	158
Sisterhood of the Traveling Pants	Warner	$39,008,741	6/1/05	10/11/05	132
Batman Begins	Warner	$205,197,285	6/15/05	10/18/05	125
Herbie: Fully Loaded	Buena Vista	$66,002,004	6/24/05	10/25/05	123
Bewitched	SONY Pictures	$62,252,415	6/24/05	10/25/05	123
House of Wax	Warner	$32,000,834	5/6/05	10/25/05	172
Star Wars: Episode III—Revenge of the Sith	20th Century-Fox	$380,237,988	5/19/05	11/1/05	166
Charlie and the Chocolate Factory	Warner	$204,921,809	7/15/05	11/8/05	116
Christmas with the Kranks (was 3/8/05)	SONY Pictures	$73,701,902	11/24/04	11/8/05	349
Madagascar	DreamWorks	$193,136,719	5/27/05	11/15/05	172
Skeleton Key	Universal	$47,614,170	8/12/05	11/15/05	95
Stealth	SONY Pictures	$31,704,416	7/29/05	11/15/05	109
War of the Worlds	Dream Works	$233,575,986	6/29/05	11/22/05	146
Polar Express	Warner	$162,753,127	11/10/04	11/22/05	377
Mr. & Mrs. Smith	20th Century-Fox	$185,921,664	6/10/05	11/29/05	172
March of the Penguins	Warner	$75,392,512	6/24/05	11/29/05	158
Sky High	Buena Vista	$62,935,722	7/29/05	11/29/05	123
Fantastic Four	20th Century-Fox	$154,227,081	7/8/05	12/6/05	151
Dukes of Hazzard	Warner	$80,108,738	8/5/05	12/6/05	123
Cinderella Man	Universal	$61,609,400	6/3/05	12/6/05	188
40-Year-Old Virgin	Universal	$104,350,468	8/19/05	12/13/05	116
Island	Dream Works	$35,799,026	7/22/05	12/13/05	144
Bad News Bears	Paramount	$32,865,161	7/22/05	12/13/05	144
Four Brothers	Paramount	$73,617,220	8/12/05	12/20/05	130
Must Love Dogs	Warner	$43,693,219	7/29/05	12/20/05	144
Brothers Grimm	Buena Vista	$37,848,537	8/26/05	12/20/05	116
Dark Water	Buena Vista	$25,472,967	7/8/05	12/26/05	171
Wedding Crashers	New Line	$207,090,289	7/15/05	1/3/06	172

Films In Inventory

Title	Product Source	Box Office	Theatrical Release Date	Estimated DVD Release Date	ARR
Exorcism of Emily Rose	SONY Pictures	$72,130,811	9/9/05	January	
Flightplan	Buena Vista	$60,916,649	9/23/05	January	
Red Eye	DreamWorks	$57,859,105	8/19/05	January	
Just Like Heaven	DreamWorks	$43,621,756	9/16/05	February	
Transporter 2	20th Century-Fox	$42,382,658	9/2/05	January	
Tim Burton's Corpse Bride	Warmer	$42,116,028	9/16/05	February	
Constant Gardener	Universal	$31,252,269	8/31/05	January	

*Theatrical releases with a domestic box office gross of $25 million or greater.

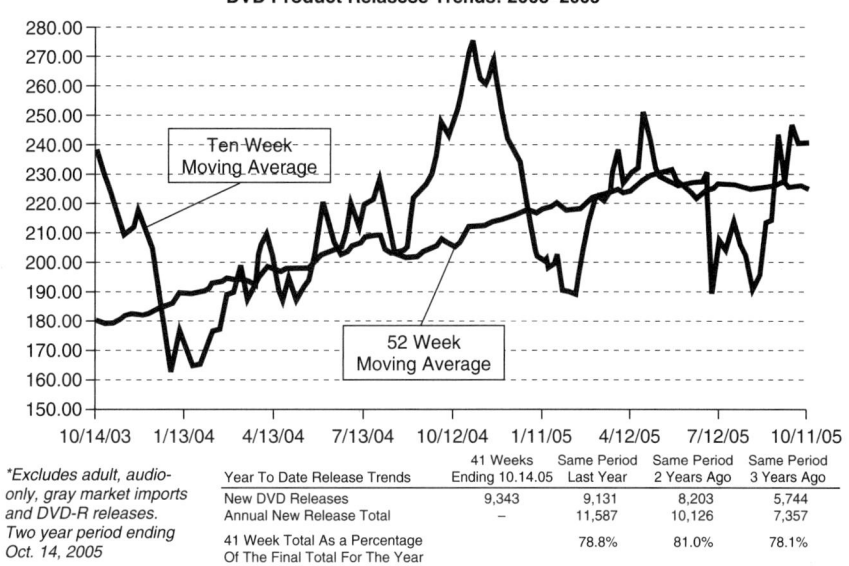

DVD Product Relasese Trends: 2003–2005*

*Excludes adult, audio-only, gray market imports and DVD-R releases. Two year period ending Oct. 14, 2005

Year To Date Release Trends	41 Weeks Ending 10.14.05	Same Period Last Year	Same Period 2 Years Ago	Same Period 3 Years Ago
New DVD Releases	9,343	9,131	8,203	5,744
Annual New Release Total	–	11,587	10,126	7,357
41 Week Total As a Percentage Of The Final Total For The Year		78.8%	81.0%	78.1%

Theatrical Releases By Box Office Levels

Through Oct. 14, 2005	#
$100 Million or greater	15
$25 Million - $100 Million	57
$10 Million - $25 Million	31
Under $10 Million	288
Combined	391

Same Period Last Year	#
$100 Million or greater	13
$25 Million - $100 Million	64
$10 Million - $25 Million	35
Under $10 Million	221
Combined	333

Same Period Two Years Ago	#
$100 Million or greater	20
$25 Million - $100 Million	57
$10 Million - $25 Million	46
Under $10 Million	243
Combined	366

DVD Releases By Format Through 10/14/05

	DVD-5	DVD-10	DVD-9	DVD-14	DVD-18	Unk.	Combined
Total 1997	353.0	167.0	8.0	0.0	0.0	0.0	528.0
Percentage	66.86%	31.63%	1.52%	0.00%	0.00%	0.00%	100.00%
Total 1998	1,192.0	192.5	137.5	0.0	0.0	0.0	1,522.0
Percentage	78.32%	12.65%	9.03%	0.00%	0.00%	0.00%	100.00%
Total 1999	2,094.0	266.5	379.5	0.0	2.0	0.0	2,742.0
Percentage	76.37%	9.72%	13.84%	0.00%	0.07%	0.00%	100.00%
Total 2000	3,142.5	200.5	602.5	0.0	10.5	2.0	3,958.0
Percentage	79.40%	5.07%	15.22%	0.00%	0.27%	0.05%	100.00%
Total 2001	4,240.5	182.5	1,193.5	7.5	3.0	3.0	5,630.0
Percentage	75.32%	3.24%	21.20%	0.13%	0.05%	0.05%	100.00%
Total 2002	5,551.5	329.5	1,392.5	19.5	4.0	60.0	7,357.0
Percentage	75.46%	4.48%	18.93%	0.27%	0.05%	0.82%	100.00%
Total 2003	7,400.5	201.0	1,992.5	16.5	7.5	508.0	10,126.0
Percentage	73.08%	1.98%	19.68%	0.16%	0.07%	5.02%	100.00%
Total 2004	8,706.0	293.0	1,914.5	8.5	25.0	640.0	11,587.0
Percentage	75.14%	2.53%	16.52%	0.07%	0.22%	5.52%	100.00%
Total 2005	6,994.5	195.5	1,695.0	13.5	51.5	393.0	9,343.0
Percentage	74.86%	2.09%	18.14%	0.14%	0.55%	4.21%	100.00%
Total	37,678.0	1,874.0	9,031.0	65.5	99.5	1,600.0	50,348.0
Discontinued	1,996.5	154.0	284.5	0.0	4.0	6.0	2,445.0
Combined	39,674.5	2,028.0	9,315.5	65.5	103.5	1,606.0	52,793.0
Percentage	75.15%	3.84%	17.65%	0.12%	0.20%	3.04%	100.00%
Sked '05	644.0	12.0	326.0	4.0	7.0	72.0	1,065.0
Percentage	60.47%	1.13%	30.61%	0.38%	0.66%	6.76%	100.00%
Sked '06	24.0	0.0	27.0	0.0	0.0	6.0	57.0
Percentage	42.11%	0.00%	47.37%	0.00%	0.00%	10.53%	100.00%
Combined	40,342.5	2,040.0	9,668.5	69.5	110.5	1,684.0	53,915.0
Percentage	74.83%	3.78%	17.93%	0.13%	0.20%	3.12%	100.00%

	UMD	Released	Announced	Total
2005		190.0	85.0	275.0

SRP By DVD Product Category: 1997–2005*

DVD Title Release Category	1997	1998	1999	2000	2001	2002	2003	2004	2005*
Animc	$27.97	$28.88	$31.31	$33.06	$29.43	$27.06	$27.93	$25.78	$26.41
Adult-Themed, Non-Feature	$24.24	$22.08	$23.47	$26.12	$21.82	$20.07	$19.30	$19.39	$18.62
Cartoon Collections	$16.23	$22.48	$22.98	$23.52	$18.98	$14.22	$9.71	$7.63	$11.51
Children's Programming, Non-Feature	$18.87	$21.93	$16.64	$18.02	$16.68	$15.45	$14.96	$13.67	$14.39
Foreign Language Feature Films	$31.33	$39.70	$35.37	$29.46	$26.21	$24.79	$23.26	$22.15	$21.87
Karoke	$24.98	$29.81	$33.79	–	$72.48	$23.84	$17.49	$19.37	$19.29
Music	$26.04	$23.66	$24.38	$22.88	$22.68	$21.46	$19.96	$18.63	$19.05
Mini Series	–	$53.99	$26.55	$45.97	$40.59	$42.51	$40.29	$33.40	$28.95
MOW (TV Movies)	$14.95	$22.17	$20.65	$21.38	$19.45	$17.41	$16.45	$16.39	$15.41
Music: Opera and Stage Performances	$32.47	$35.40	$28.23	$30.39	$31.11	$30.16	$30.53	$29.19	$30.30
Films of the Silent Era	$28.72	$24.39	$26.65	$29.33	$25.10	$21.46	$19.49	$15.27	$20.59
Special Interest	$22.80	$18.58	$21.23	$23.16	$21.72	$24.26	$23.53	$24.07	$23.47
Silent Short Compilations	$29.99	$29.99	$19.83	$28.99	$42.46	$44.26	$16.89	$34.96	$32.32
Theatrical Catalog (pre-1997)	$25.25	$25.21	$25.69	$23.46	$19.81	$17.66	$15.53	$13.87	$15.07
Theatrical Serials (1930–1956)	–	–	–	$27.98	$24.96	$9.80	$12.25	$12.41	$12.69
TV Series Programming (single disc)	$23.98	$19.43	$21.92	$21.06	$17.79	$17.24	$16.06	$11.37	$13.07
TV Series Programming: Multi-Disc Sets	–	–	$56.87	$57.11	$54.47	$58.15	$53.92	$49.80	$46.02
Direct to Video Feature Films	$19.64	$21.84	$23.40	$21.70	$19.47	$19.79	$18.54	$17.65	$19.10
New Theatrical $100 Million or greater	$27.48	$29.34	$30.44	$29.46	$28.94	$28.67	$28.91	$29.56	$30.14
New Theatrical $25 Million–$100 Million	$25.53	$28.45	$30.24	$27.91	$27.73	$28.09	$28.33	$29.01	$29.25
New Theatrical $10 Million–$25 Million	$24.98	$26.92	$27.68	$28.18	$25.59	$26.98	$26.88	$28.30	$28.92
New Theatrical Under $10 Million	$26.65	$26.15	$27.50	$27.47	$26.49	$26.99	$26.76	$26.39	$25.87
UMD Video									$23.82

*2005 results are for all titles released or announced for release as of Oct. 14, 2005 (unreleased titles through Dec. 31, 2005).

Results for each year are based upon supplier suggest retail price (SRP) at the time of a title's first entry into the market. Subsequent price revisions are not included here—this is new release pricing data only.

What a title may actually sell for at the retail level is entirely up to the retail community.

The "New Theatrical" category is presented by domestic box office gross. Excluded from the SRP results are multiple SKUs of the same title (each new film release is counted only once). Also excluded are "Collector's Editions" that may demand a premium above the mass market SKU configuration (this allows for SRP comparisons to the earlier years of the format where such configurations were not a common release strategy).

Category Grid—DVD Releases Through Oct. 14, 2005

Code	Year > DVD Title Release Category	1997 Total	1998 Total	1999 Total	2000 Total	2001 Total	2002 Total	2003 Total	2004 Total	2005 Total	Combined Active	Disc.	Total
SI	Special Interest	55	170	272	506	933	1,403	2,148	2,850	2,460	10,480	317	10,797
T	Theatrical Catalog (pre-1997)	293	575	806	922	1,105	1,221	1,661	1,773	1,073	8,721	708	9,429
V	Direct to Video Feature Films	45	145	432	744	848	1,089	1,404	1,312	959	6,382	596	6,978
M	Music	33	100	225	382	570	860	1,057	1,301	1,054	5,469	113	5,582
F	Foreign Language Feature Films	22	134	200	252	396	503	645	927	893	3,998	174	4,172
A	Animc	5	32	97	160	439	559	728	726	589	3,282	53	3,335
T	New Theatrical (1997-current)	18	165	296	334	342	397	488	497	416	2,861	92	2,953
CH	Children's Programming, Non-Feature	9	4	31	60	89	288	408	499	459	1,809	38	1,847
MOW	MOW (TV Movies)	6	36	74	129	157	229	282	293	295	1,419	82	1,501
TV	TV Series Programming (single disc)	5	9	57	125	210	184	315	352	232	1,464	25	1,489
AD	Adult-Themed, Non-Feature	20	57	100	174	276	251	196	213	123	1,305	105	1,410
TV	TV Series Programming: Multi-Disc Sets	0	0	14	28	55	113	258	445	468	1,379	2	1,381
OS	Music Opera and Stage Performances	2	12	20	49	103	79	80	125	124	592	2	594
Mini	Mini Series	0	5	15	20	37	52	75	59	80	334	9	343
S	Films of the Silent Era	4	10	42	38	44	37	45	48	26	275	19	294
CC	Cartoon Collections	4	6	10	15	13	20	44	100	46	245	13	258
K	Karoke	2	60	38	0	2	54	35	12	15	129	89	218
TS	Theatrical Serials (1930–1956)	0	0	0	10	7	11	43	47	19	137	0	137
SS	Silent Short Compilations	5	2	13	10	4	7	14	8	12	67	8	75
	Total	528	1,522	2,742	3,958	5,630	7,357	10,126	11,587	9,343	50,348	2,445	52,793

Theatrical On DVD

Asset Rollover Rate
Results Through: 10/14/05

Quickest To Market–Key Theatrical Titles 1997–2005* —$25-Million Plus

	1997		1998		1999		2000		2001		2002		2003		2004		2005		Combined	
DVD Source	#	Ave.	#	Ave.	#	Ave.	#	Ave.	#	Ave.	#	Ave.	#	Ave.	#	Ave.	#	Ave.	#	Ave.
Lions Gate/Artisan					1	159.8			1	163.3	1	167.0	1	151.0	2	144.0	3	118.3	9	133.1
SONY Pictures	2	193.0	15	201.2	7	140.0	8	144.6	16	146.4	15	140.6	14	126.5	18	114.8	9	113.7	104	142.8
MGM Home Ent.			2	147.5	1	151.0	4	179.0	4	161.5	5	159.6	5	137.6	5	141.2	3	137.0	29	152.1
Warner	9	143.2	10	165.0	9	167.2	14	157.8	10	168.3	14	159.6	11	150.6	10	156.1	12	163.9	99	159.1
New Line	1	172.0	8	164.4	4	159.8	5	163.6	4	163.3	6	168.8	6	169.7	5	155.2	6	146.7	45	161.9
Universal			5	191.6	9	165.0	15	165.0	7	174.1	13	174.5	11	170.9	15	154.9	9	136.4	84	164.7
Paramount			3	305.0	10	174.3	10	184.7	11	157.5	13	159.6	10	148.2	8	148.4	8	142.3	73	166.0
Dreamworks SKG			2	252.5	4	186.0	5	190.4	6	175.3	4	186.0	7	147.6	4	157.5	2	144.0	34	174.9
20th Century-Fox			2	242.0	8	237.0	7	194.0	9	167.3	11	185.2	13	156.0	13	147.0	9	154.9	72	175.2
Buena Vista	1	146.0	10	231.6	15	179.3	17	200.2	18	179.3	19	203.3	17	157.5	21	156.0	11	131.9	129	178.7
USA Home Ent.			2	182.5	2	217.5			2	178.5									6	192.8
HBO Home Video													1	298.0					1	298.0
Sling Shot					1	348.0													1	348.0
Total By Year	13	153.3	59	200.4	71	179.1	85	175.7	88	165.4	101	171.4	96	153.0	101	145.8	72	140.8	686	164.5

The ARR (Asset Rollover Rate) measures the length of time (in days) between a motion picture's initial theatrical release and its debut in the DVD market. Only those films released beginning in January of 1997 are included in the grid. Box Office performance and release dates have been compiled from Daily Variety and Hollywood Reporter charts published each week.

*$25,000,000+ theatrical release with an ARR of less than 365-days are defined as new. Those released after one year are considered catalog.

Theatrical Catalog/Serials On DVD

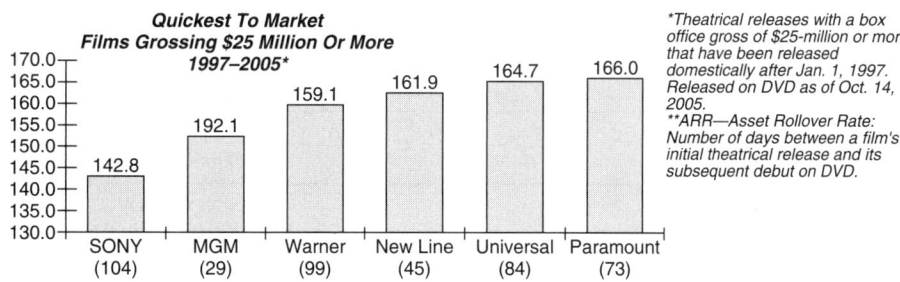

Quickest To Market
Films Grossing $25 Million Or More
1997–2005*

*Theatrical releases with a box office gross of $25-million or more that have been released domestically after Jan. 1, 1997. Released on DVD as of Oct. 14, 2005.
**ARR—Asset Rollover Rate: Number of days between a film's initial theatrical release and its subsequent debut on DVD.

*2005 results through Oct. 14—Average number of days (Asset Rollover Rate—ARR) for new theatrical releases to debut on DVD within one-year of their theatrical debut and a domestic box office gross of at least $25,000,000.

Top 25 Sources Through The Period Ending Oct. 14, 2005 By Year Of Theatrical Release

DVD Source	1930s	1940s	1950s	1960s	1970s	1980s	1990s*	Total
MGM Home Ent.	16	23	67	163	158	309	169	905
Alpha Video	264	281	109	94	15			763
Warner	52	81	89	73	115	181	168	759
SONY Pictures	12	27	57	81	75	156	198	606
Universal	17	35	27	38	67	120	137	441
Paramount	1	2	55	69	90	113	104	434
Image Entertainment	47	62	81	97	98	25	13	423
Buena Vista		9	10	37	33	57	253	399
20th Century-Fox	13	41	67	59	42	70	95	387
Anchor Bay		5	14	45	83	176	16	339
Lions Gate Home Ent.	6	24	19	4	9	60	84	206
BCI Eclipse	12	12	31	35	67	4		161
Platinum Disc	24	20	26	26	31	8	6	141
Goodtimes	18	30	42	15	14	9	12	140
VCI Home Video	3	29	24	20	37	6	1	120
Vid Tape: Pro-Active	18	32	16	18	24	6		114
Unicom/Ideal	29	31	17	13	14	3		107
New Line Home Ent.					6	13	87	106
Madacy	30	25	17	18	9	5	1	105
Catcom Home Video	17	25	24	14	22	2		104
St. Clair Vision	13	18	16	19	21	8		95
Genius Entertainment	29	28	25	11				93
Criterion	7	19	15	13	16	13	9	92
Mill Creek	19	21	32	5	6			83
Roan Group	23	29	18	3				73
Top 25 Product Sources	670	909	898	970	1,052	1,344	1,353	7,196
All Other Sources	164	214	189	236	424	193	95	1,515
Combined Active	834	1,123	1,087	1,206	1,476	1,537	1,448	8,711
Discontinued	52	61	47	67	150	160	154	713
(10/14/05)	886	1,184	1,134	1,273	1,626	1,697	1,602	9,424

	Total All DVDs	52,793
	Percentage	7.85%

*The total number of serials released is not the same as the number of SKUs released due to the confusing practice of dividing serials into two parts. VCI released three Zerro adventures on one SKU and Treeline Films released 12 serials as a one SKU release.

Direct To DVD Product Showcase

Top 25 Sources Through The Period Ending Oct. 14, 2005 By Year Of DVD Release

Product Source	1997	1998	1999	2000	2001	2002	2003	2004	2005	Total
Lions Gate Home Ent. (1)		25	42	64	87	87	113	72	60	550
Image Entertainment (2)		11	87	51	53	52	51	25	21	351
MTI Home Video			14	26	29	38	45	35	23	210
York Entertainment			12	24	56	43	30	13	14	192
Buena Vista			10	22	20	30	40	28	32	182
SONY Pictures			8	15	22	33	30	42	27	177
Platinum Disc				39	23	67	18	12	17	176
Vanguard			1	15	31	49	38	24	13	171
BCI Eclipse				1	35	31	24	50	24	165
Ground Zero Ent.				6	17	48	44	13	3	131
Ardustry Home Ent.							61	48	20	129
First Look Home Ent.					4	19	23	33	30	109
Troma		10	4	17	5	5	15	33	16	105
Universal		2	3	6	7	18	20	27	22	105
Tai Seng			10	33	27	30	2	2		104
New Concorde							54	47		101
20th Century-Fox			2		7	24	31	26	11	101
Koch	3		18	16	3	3	18	28	11	100
MGM Home Ent.		1	1	8	10	5	26	15	29	95
SRS Cinema				1	1	6	44	24	10	86
Warner Home Video (3)			1	4	8	17	15	22	17	84
Madacy				2	2	3	47	22	5	81
Trinity Home Ent.							24	35	21	80
Xenon			12	5	14	5	27	9	8	80
Ei Independent Cinema				13	15	17	12	9	13	80
Top 25 Sources	3	49	225	368	476	630	852	694	447	3,745
All Other Sources	5	19	90	198	279	377	540	618	510	2,636
Total - Active	8	68	315	566	755	1,007	1,392	1,312	957	6,381
Discontinued	37	77	117	178	45	130	12	0	0	596
Combined	45	145	432	744	800	1,137	1,404	1,312	957	6,977
All Releases	528	1,522	2,742	3,958	5,630	7,357	10,126	11,587	9,343	52,793
Percentage	8.5%	9.5%	15.8%	18.8%	14.2%	15.5%	13.9%	11.3%	10.2%	13.2%

(1) *Includes Artisan and Lions Gate.*
(2) *Includes distributed labels/lines.*
(3) *Includes distributed labels/lines.*

Music On DVD/DualDisc-DVDplus*
Top 25 Sources Through The Period Ending Oct. 14, 2005

Product Source	1997	1998	1999	2000	2001	2002	2003	2004	2005	Total
SONY/BMG (3)	12	17	38	96	107	143	158	166	138	875
Universal (1)	1		4	21	52	84	85	167	147	561
Image Entertainment	3	21	63	103	131	109	69	38	18	555
Music Video Dist.			4	17	54	60	89	115	75	414
Warner/WEA (2)	7	6	36	30	37	66	64	91	41	378
Capitol/EMI (EMD)			5	7	26	64	72	88	85	347
Naxos				15	19	33	55	68	92	282
Kultur Video			6	4	25	30	25	59	80	229
Eagle Rock Ent.				2	5	13	29	60	46	155
Geneon (formerly Pioneer)		17	27	39	33	26	4	1	3	150
Video Arts Int'L				1	11	12	23	42	35	124
Classic Rock Productions					12	33	50	14	7	116
Caroline Distribution			3	1	14	11	23	32	8	92
Cherry Red Records				4	4	10	18	26	23	85
Vestapol Videos					18	8	18	24		68
Shanachie	1	1	5	10	10	7	12	6	16	68
Passport						1	9	28	16	54
Koch					6	11	11	18	8	54
Navarre	0	0	0	0	1	13	23	3	12	52
DVD International				14	16	16			1	47
Ryko Distribution			3	5	1	0	2	20	9	40
MSI Music						36	2			38
Saint Clair							10	8	17	35
Storyville							18	16		34
Idem Home Video							31			31
Top 25 Sources	24	62	194	369	582	786	900	1,090	877	4,884
All Other Sources	2	16	31	33	72	152	237	337	294	1,174
Total Active	26	78	225	402	654	938	1,137	1,427	1,171	6,058
Discontinued	9	34	20	29	19	1	0	0	0	112
Combined	35	112	245	431	673	939	1,137	1,427	1,171	6,170
All DVD (to 10/14/05)	528	1,522	2,742	3,958	5,630	7,357	10,126	11,587	9,343	52,793
Music Share	6.6%	7.4%	8.9%	10.9%	12.0%	12.8%	11.2%	12.3%	12.5%	11.7%
DVD Music Releases	35	112	245	431	673	939	1,137	1,419	1,098	6,089
DualDisc Releases*	0	0	0	0	0	0	0	8	73	81
Combined	35	112	245	431	673	939	1,137	1,427	1,171	6,170
DualDisc Percent of Music	0.0%	0.0%	0.0%	0.0%	0.0%	0.0%	0.0%	0.6%	6.6%	1.3%

(1)- Universal - all sources, including Universal Studios and Universal Music

(2)- Warner/WEA - includes Rhino, Warner-Music and Warner Publishing

(3)- SONY - includes SONY Music, BMG Music, Red Distribution, Shout Factory & Columbia-TriStar

Totals exclude: Audio-Only, Karaoke and Theatrical Musicals

*DualDisc and DVDplus release totals exclude audio-only releases.

Special Interest On DVD*
Top 25 Sources For Special Interest On DVD*
Through The Period Ending Oct. 14, 2005

DVD Product Source	1997	1998	1999	2000	2001	2002	2003	2004	2005	Total
Image Entertainment	2	11	36	92	73	88	94	92	55	543
Goldhil - Cerebellum			10	24	20	30	47	172	157	460
A & E - New Video	0	0	0	9	25	9	26	62	170	301
Kultur			2	2	16	56	54	86	70	286
Madacy		43	33	51	58	24	12	15	9	245
Warner Home Video			11	19	20	24	47	49	53	223
L and L Publishing				2	20	55	61	39	43	220
Wellspring Media	1	4	20	45	36	34	19	36	10	205
Homespun Video						14	19	87	73	193
SONY/SONY WWE	4	4	5	11	24	43	37	34	23	185
Warner - Music/Publishing					10	75	33	50	14	182
Goodtimes					40	28	31	51	12	162
Questar			2		31	19	54	26	19	151
BCI Eclipse		2	1	10	30	19	34	13	29	138
TMW Media Group						1	31	50	55	137
Just Planes						41	34	36	24	135
Koch					23	26	22	41	22	134
Rising Sun Video							92	19	15	126
Delta Entertainment		3	2		27	23	34	21	2	112
Music Video/Eclectic			4	10	14	26	23	23	10	110
Reedswain							75	17	5	97
A2ZCDS.COM									96	96
Bennett Marine Video						22	17	26	31	96
Paramount						3	6	52	33	94
Lions Gate/Artisan Ent.				13	13	14	16	23	13	92
Top 25 DVD Sources	7	67	126	288	480	674	918	1,120	1,043	4,723
All Other Sources	11	20	101	161	418	701	1,209	1,729	1,404	5,764
Total (10/14/05)	18	87	227	449	898	1,375	2,127	2,849	2,447	10,477
Discontinued	37	83	44	57	35	28	22	10	0	316
Combined	55	170	271	506	933	1,406	2,149	2,859	2,447	10,795
All DVD Releases	528	1,522	2,742	3,958	5,630	7,357	10,126	11,587	9,343	52,793
Percentage	10.4%	11.2%	9.9%	12.8%	16.6%	19.1%	21.2%	24.7%	26.2%	20.4%
Fitness	0	1	6	18	47	129	204	302	206	913
Magic	0	0	3	3	25	89	113	158	84	475
Travel	1	6	15	16	53	42	84	118	103	438
All Other Special Interest	54	163	247	469	808	1,143	1,748	2,281	2,054	8,967
Combined	55	170	271	506	933	1,403	2,149	2,859	2,447	10,793

(1) Warner includes distributed lines.
(2) Image includes distributed lines.
(3) SONY includes WWE and Shout Factory releases

TV Series on DVD
Top 20 Sources For TV Series On DVD
Through The Period Ending Oct. 14, 2005

DVD Product Source	1997	1998	1999	2000	2001	2002	2003	2004	2005	Total
Warner (1)				4	20	36	77	93	102	332
Paramount			5	13	26	26	32	56	58	216
A & E/New Video			12	12	26	33	23	32	26	164
Image Entertainment		1	27	26	38		6	31	21	150
Alpha Video							15	47	67	129
20th Century-Fox				3	4	10	28	40	38	123
Acorn Media				6	16	17	32	24	23	118
SONY Pictures				2	2	10	26	36	39	115
BFS Entertainment				12	18	21	39	7	5	102
MPI			1	2	14	26	11	13	11	78
Universal			1		3	6	12	22	33	77
A.D.V. Films					9	11	29	17	5	71
BCI Eclipse				3		5	20	26	16	70
Buena Vista					2	4	14	25	23	68
Lions Gate/Artisan			3	5	2	4	17	15	18	64
Rhino		1		7	10	4	11	14	8	55
Platinum Disc				1	7	13	15	12	6	54
Anchor Bay					1	1	8	16	28	54
HBO Home Video				2	3	5	9	16	17	52
Delta Entertainment		3	2	1		4	8	13	20	51
Total Top 20	0	5	51	99	201	236	432	555	564	2,143
All Other Sources	2	1	17	48	57	57	140	242	135	699
Discontinued	3	3	3	6	7	4	1			27
Combined	5	9	71	153	265	297	573	797	699	2,869
All DVD (10/14/2005)	528	1,522	2,742	3,958	5,630	7,357	10,126	11,587	9,343	52,793
TV Series Share	0.4%	0.4%	2.5%	3.7%	4.6%	4.0%	5.6%	6.9%	7.5%	5.4%

Release Configurations	1,997	1,998	1,999	2,000	2,001	2,002	2,003	2,004	2,005	Total
Single Disc Compilations	5	9	58	125	210	184	315	352	232	1,490
Two Disc Sets			12	15	38	44	94	108	97	408
Multi Disc Compilations			1	13	17	69	164	337	370	971
Combined	5	9	71	153	265	297	573	797	699	2,869

(1) Warner includes distributed lines (BBC, PBS, etc.)

Foreign Language On DVD
Top 10 Foreign Languages On DVD
Through The Period Ending Oct. 14, 2005

Foreign Language	1997	1998	1999	2000	2001	2002	2003	2004	2005	Combined
Spanish		1.0	4.0	12.5	28.0	107.0	307.0	357.0	383.0	1,199.5
Chinese (1)	3.0	50.0	63.0	59.0	135.0	114.0	105.5	107.5	62.0	699.0
French		8.0	38.0	56.0	67.0	74.0	118.0	97.0	84.5	542.5
Japanese		9.0	16.0	23.0	38.0	58.0	81.0	123.0	97.5	445.5
Italian	2.0	10.0	10.0	22.5	26.0	25.0	43.0	28.5	50.5	217.5
German	1.0	2.0	8.0	18.0	22.0	26.5	36.5	24.5	24.5	163.0
Russian		3.0	3.0	6.0	18.0	29.0	10.0	27.5	16.0	112.5
Korean			1.0		5.0	12.0	13.0	13.0	39.0	83.0
Hindi			0.0	0.0	1.0	2.5	33.0	27.0	8.0	71.5
Hebrew				1.0	3.0	3.0	19.5	13.5	19.0	59.0
Top Ten	6.0	83.0	143.0	198.0	343.0	451.0	766.5	818.5	784.0	3,593.0
All Others	0.0	1.0	10.0	41.0	37.0	50.0	65.5	91.5	105.0	401.0
Discontinued	16.0	50.0	47.0	13.0	16.0	2.0	13.0	17.0	0.0	174.0
Total 10/14/05	22	134	200	252	396	503	845	927	889	4,168
All DVD Releases	528	1,522	2,742	3,958	5,630	7,357	10,126	11,587	9,343	52,793
Percentage	4.2%	8.8%	7.3%	6.4%	7.0%	6.8%	8.3%	8.0%	9.5%	7.9%

(1) *Chinese includes both Cantonese and Mandarin*

Top 10 Sources For Foreign Language Releases On DVD
Through The Period Ending Oct. 14, 2005

Supplier	1997	1998	1999	2000	2001	2002	2003	2004	2005	Combined
Tai Seng	3	48	56	45	107	88	79	75	49	550
Image Entertainment (2)	1	7	23	30	36	52	19	28	27	223
Laguna Films						28	80	56	38	202
Wellspring Media	1	18	31	41	20	20	33	18	15	197
Vanguard			1	10	17	35	34	39	32	168
SONY Pictures	1	1	12	19	24	24	38	19	12	150
Criterion Collection		7	14	11	16	16	25	28	26	143
Facets Video						2	10	31	42	43	128
Kino				11	11	12	16	38	32	120
Home Vision					4	6	15	37	24	86
Top Ten Sources	6	81	137	167	237	291	370	380	298	1,967
All Others	0	3	16	72	143	210	462	530	591	2,027
Discontinued	16	50	47	13	16	2	13	17	0	174
Total 10/14/05	22	134	200	252	396	503	845	927	889	4,168
All DVD Releases	528	1,522	2,742	3,958	5,630	7,357	10,126	11,587	9,343	52,793
Percentage	4.2%	8.8%	7.3%	6.4%	7.0%	6.8%	8.3%	8.0%	9.5%	7.9%

(2) *Image includes distributed lines*

Children's Non-Feature On DVD
Top 20 Sources Through The Period Ending Oct. 14, 2005

Children's Suppliers	1997	1998	1999	2000	2001	2002	2003	2004	2005	Total
SONY Music/Wonder	3	1	5	3	10	47	51	42	32	194
Goodtimes					4	22	26	32	29	113
Lyrick Studios/Hit Ent.			2	4		13	25	36	31	111
Paramount/PBS				4		2	16	42	46	110
Buena Vista					1	18	13	16	23	71
Warner Home Video				3	5	5	21	8	17	59
UAV	1					1	25	25	6	58
SONY Pictures		1	1	5	5	10	16	9	8	55
Lions Gate Home Ent.			1	1	6	8	3	14	17	50
Thomas Nelson Prod.					13	2	11	10	5	41
Delta Entertainment					5	22	13			40
20th Century-Fox							8	15	13	36
Warner Music/WEA						8	12	14		34
New Video						4	7	12	10	33
Image				2	3	16	11			32
Anchor Bay					1	8	4	9	7	29
Digital Versatile		1	11	14						26
Inspired Corporation					2	17		2	5	26
Koch Vision								10	13	23
Vision Video								5	18	23
Total Top 20 Sources	4	3	20	36	55	203	262	301	280	1,164
All Other Sources (138)	0	0	11	23	23	83	130	197	179	646
Total Active	4	3	31	59	78	286	392	498	459	1,810
Discontinued	5	1	0	1	11	2	16	1	0	37
Through 10/14/05	9	4	31	60	89	288	408	499	459	1,847
All DVD Titles	528	1,522	2,742	3,958	5,630	7,357	10,126	11,587	9,343	52,793
Percentage	1.70%	0.26%	1.13%	1.52%	1.58%	3.91%	4.03%	4.31%	4.91%	3.50%

The Entertainment Consumer: DVD audience

DVD buyers are slightly more male and about 5 ppts less African-American

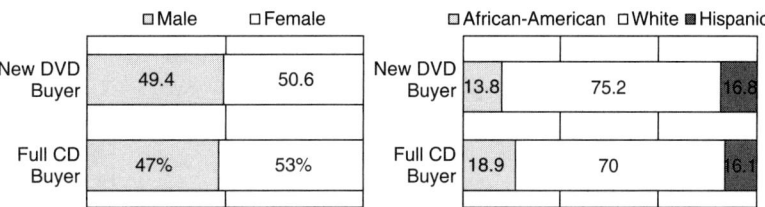

The Entertainment Consumer: Why do they buy DVDs?
In Store & Advertising Motivators—2004

Browsing is the top retail motivator for DVDs—nearly twice that of CDs. Advertisements and in-store displays are also more effective for DVDs.

Top Five Store/Advertising Motivators	DVD Sales	CD Sales
Found it while browsing	23.1	11.8
On sale	22.4	N/A
Saw a TV ad	14.0	2.9
Saw special display in store	11.9	4.6
Read a sales circular	5.2	1.9

The Entertainment Consumer: Why do they buy DVDs?
Retail Purchase Influences—2004

The number one message getting across to consumers in advertising is the collectable nature of DVDs.

Industry— 2004

Top Ten Purchase Influences	%
Add to my collection	48.8
Fan of these movies/videos	37.3
Like the actors	30.6
Good for the whole family	20.5
Saw a preview or trailer	18.9
For a child/children	16.0
Saw in movie theater	14.6
Saw the movie/show on TV	13.1
Liked previous movie/video	12.5
Recommended by friend/relative	11.0

Source: NPD Video Watch, NPD Music Watch-2004

Market Summary: Physical music and favorite artists

As other avenues for sampling music became more widespread, consumers are less inclined to take a chance on a CD by a new artist. When they do buy a CD, it's more likely that it is by a favorite artist.

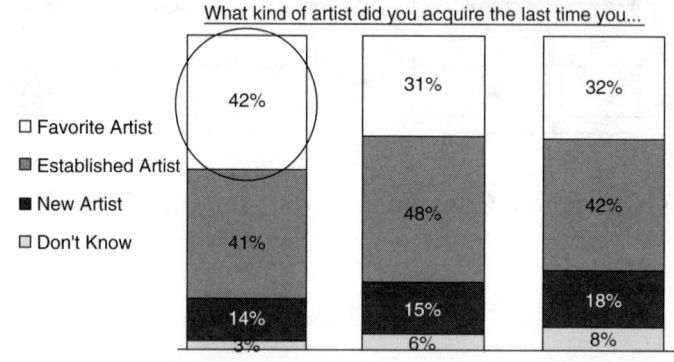

What kind of artist did you acquire the last time you...

☐ Favorite Artist
■ Established Artist
■ New Artist
☐ Don't Know

	Bought a CD	Paid for Download	Downloaded from P2P
Favorite Artist	42%	31%	32%
Established Artist	41%	48%	42%
New Artist	14%	15%	18%
Don't Know	3%	6%	8%

Source: NPD VideoWatch, NPD Music Watch-2004

Market Trends: Age Groups By Channel

The 25–34 age group is leaving CD Stores for Mass Merchants, Online and Electronics. The Electronics channel is dipping slightly among thirtysomethings and fortysomethings.

Age Group Share By Channel*

Retail Channels	13-17		18-24		25-34		35-44		45-54		55-64		65+	
	2004	▲YoY	2004	▲YoY	2004	▲YoY	2004	▲YoY	2004	▲YoY	2004	▲YoY	2004	▲YoY
Online	7.5	1.40	9.7	1.1	12.6	2.3	13.8	1.2	14.4	1.0	15.8	0.3	17.9	0.8
Mass Merchants	33.4	3.30	24.8	1.6	28.3	2.8	30.5	1.4	29.4	1.6	30.2	1.7	28.8	4.1
Electronics	20	0.90	25.4	1.3	22.8	2.5	18	(0.2)	17.4	(0.2)	13.3	0.3	10.2	(0.4)
CD Stores	23.9	(5.20)	24.5	(4.8)	20.1	(7.1)	18.7	(3.1)	16.6	(3.0)	14	(1.9)	12.3	(2.1)
Book Stores	5.8	(0.20)	6.2	0.0	6.1	(0.2)	6.2	(0.6)	7.6	(0.2)	9.1	(1.5)	7.8	(3.7)
Mem. Warehouse	1.1	(0.30)	1.6	0.8	1.8	(0.2)	2.6	0.0	3.3	0.4	3.3	(0.8)	3.3	(0.4)

*excludes "other"/non-traditional retail outlets such as Department & Convenience Stores

Source: NPD VideoWatch, NPD Music Watch-2004

The Entertainment Consumer: Wallet share competition

Music was the third most-purchased item in the entertainment category during the holiday season behind DVDs and toys. Big ticket items like TVs, DVD players and portable music players also placed on the list.

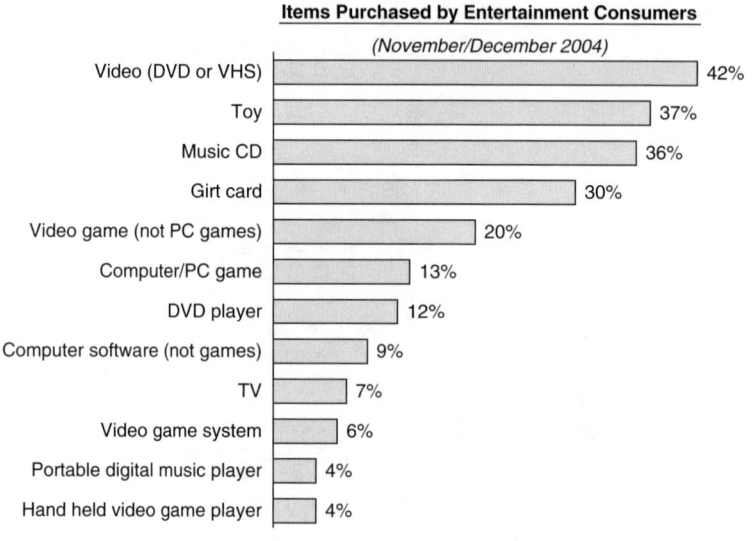

Items Purchased by Entertainment Consumers

(November/December 2004)

Item	%
Video (DVD or VHS)	42%
Toy	37%
Music CD	36%
Gift card	30%
Video game (not PC games)	20%
Computer/PC game	13%
DVD player	12%
Computer software (not games)	9%
TV	7%
Video game system	6%
Portable digital music player	4%
Hand held video game player	4%

Digital Music: Who is the legal digital consumer?

Demographic Profile Comparison of Music Buyers: Legal Downloads vs. Physical

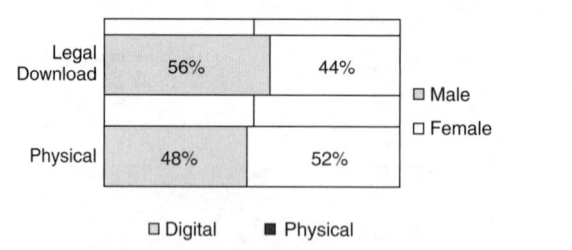

	Male	Female
Legal Download	56%	44%
Physical	48%	52%

□ Digital   ■ Physical

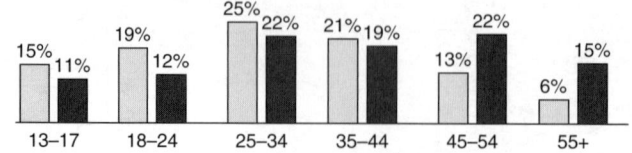

Age	Digital	Physical
13–17	15%	11%
18–24	19%	12%
25–34	25%	22%
35–44	21%	19%
45–54	13%	22%
55+	6%	15%

Source: NPD VideoWatch, NPD Music Watch-2004

Digital Music: Use per retail channel

Not surprisingly, customers of the Online channel are nearly three times as likely to have paid for digital music as Mass Merchant customers.

Channel	Percent of Customers Who Paid For Digital Music	Share of Physical Sales
Online	22%	11%
Book stores	14%	7%
Electronics	12%	22%
CD/Record Stores	11%	22%
Discount/Mass Merch	8%	29%

Market Summary: Who Buys Which Genres

Demographic Profile Comparison of CD Buyers by Genre

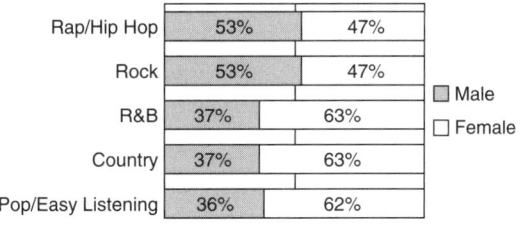

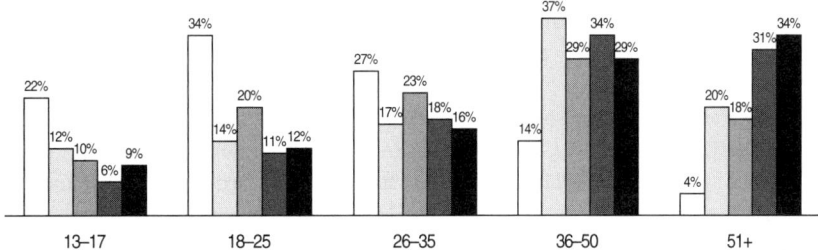

Selected Readings

Books

American Symphony Orchestra League Staff. *The Gold Book: A Sourcebook of Successful Fund-Raising, Education, Ticket Sales, and Service Projects.* American Symphony Orchestra League. [Annual]

Barrow, T. *Inside the Music Business.* New York: Chapman & Hall, 1995.

Billboard Staff. *Billboard International Buyers Guide 2004.* Garner, Bryan A., ed. Los Angeles: Amusement Business, 2003. [Annual]

Black, Henry C., et al. *Black's Law Dictionary.* 8th ed. St. Paul, MN: West, 2004.

Bolles, Richard Nelson. *What Color Is Your Parachute? A Practical Manual for Job-Hunters & Career Changers.* Rev. and updated. Berkeley, CA: Ten Speed, 2005.

Brabec, Jeffrey, and Brabec, Todd. *Music, Money, and Success: The Insider's Guide to the Music Industry.* 4th ed., updated and expanded. New York: Schirmer, 2004.

Christensen, Clayton M. *The Innovator's Dilemma.* New York: HarperBusiness, 2000.

Counseling Clients in the Entertainment Industry 2005 New York: Practising Law Institute, 2004. [Annual]

Dannen, Fredric. *Hit Men: Power Brokers & Fast Money Inside the Music Business.* New York: Random House, 1991.

Denisoff, R. Serge. *Inside MTV.* New Brunswick, NJ: Transaction, 1990.

Eargle, John M. *Handbook of Recording Engineering.* 4th ed. Boston: Kluwer Academic, 2003.

Eargle, John M. *Music, Sound and Technology.* 2nd ed. New York: Van Nostrand Reinhold, 1995.

Elias, Stephen, and Levinkind, Susan. *Legal Research: How to Find & Understand the Law.* 12th ed. Berkeley, CA: Nolo, 2004.

Eliot, Marc. *Rockonomics: The Money Behind the Music.* Secaucus, NJ: Carol Publishing Group, 1993.

Entertainment Law Institute. [Various titles and authors]. Los Angeles: University of Southern California. [Annual]

Faulkner, Robert R. *Hollywood Studio Musicians: Their Work and Careers in the Recording Industry.* Lanham, MD: University Press of America, 1985.

Faulkner, Robert R. *Music on Demand: Composers and Careers in the Hollywood Film Industry.* New Brunswick, NJ: Transaction, 1982.

Feist, Leonard. *Popular Music Publishing in America.* New York: National Music Publishers Association, 1980.

Fink, Michael. *Inside the Music Industry: Creativity, Process, and Business.* 2nd ed. New York: Schirmer, 1996.

Frascogna, Xavier M., and Hetherington, H. Lee. *Successful Artist Management.* Enl. rev. ed. New York: Watson-Guptill, 1990.

Friedman Group Staff. *No Thanks, I'm Just Looking: Professional Retail Sales Techniques for Turning Shoppers Into Buyers.* Reprint ed. Dubuque, IA: Kendall/Hunt, 2002.

Gaar, Gillian G. *She's a Rebel: The History of Women in Rock & Roll.* Preface by Yoko Ono. Exp. 2nd ed. Seattle, WA: Seal, 2002.

Goldstein, Jeri. *How to Be Your Own Booking Agent and Save Thousands of Dollars: A Performing Artist's Guide to a Successful Touring Career.* Estrin, Kari, ed. Charlottesville, VA: New Music Times, 2000.

Halloran, Mark, ed. and comp. *The Musician's Business and Legal Guide.* 3rd rev. ed. Paramus, NJ: Prentice Hall, 2001.

Karlin, Fred. *Listening to Movies: The Film Lover's Guide to Film Music.* New York: Schirmer, 1994.

Karlin, Fred, and Wright, Rayburn. *On the Track: A Guide to Contemporary Film Scoring.* 2nd ed. New York: Routledge, 2004.

Karmen, Steve. *Through the Jingle Jungle.* New York: Billboard Books, 1989.

Kohn, Al, and Kohn, Bob. *Kohn on Music Licensing.* 3rd ed. New York: Aspen Law & Business, 2002. [Also periodic supplements]

Koontz, Harold D., and Weihrich, Heinz. *Essentials of Management.* 5th ed. New York: McGraw-Hill, 1990.

Krasilovsky, M. William, and Shemel, Sidney. *More About This Business of Music.* 5th rev. ed. New York: Watson-Guptill, 1994.

Krasilovsky, M. William, and Shemel, Sidney. *This Business of Music: A Practical Guide to the Music Industry for Publishers, Writers, Record Companies, Producers, Artists, Agents.* 7th rev. ed. New York: Watson-Guptill, 1995.

Krasilovsky, M. William, and Shemel, Sidney. 2003. *This Business of Music: The Definitive Guide to the Music Industry* (9th ed. Contributions by John M. Gross). New York: Billboard Books.

Lathrop, Tad, and Pettigrew, Jim, Jr. *This Business of Music Marketing and Promotion.* New York: Billboard Books, 1999.

Leikin, Molly-Ann. *How to Be a Hit Songwriter: Polishing and Marketing Your Lyrics and Music* (3rd ed.). Milwaukee, WI: Hal Leonard, 2003.

Lindey, Alexander, and Landau, Michael. *Lindey on Entertainment, Publishing and the Arts: Agreement and the Law.* 3rd ed. St. Paul, MN: Thomson/West, 2004.

Mandell, Jim. *The Studio Business Book.* Jewett, Andy, ed. 2nd rev. ed. Milwaukee, WI: Hal Leonard, 1996.

Marcone, Stephen. *Managing Your Band: Artist Management: The Ultimate Responsibility.* 3rd ed. Wayne, NJ: HiMarks, 2003.

Martin, George, and Hornsby, Jeremy. *All You Need Is Ears: The Inside Personal Story of the Genius Who Created the Beatles.* New York: St. Martin's, 1994.

McPherson, Brian. *Get It in Writing.* Milwaukee, WI: Hal Leonard, 1999.

Music USA 2004. Carlsbad, CA: NAMM, 2004. [Annual]

Musical America International Directory of the Performing Arts, 2004. New York: Musical America Publications. [Annual]

Nimmer, Melville B. *Nimmer on Copyright.* 5 vols. New York: Matthew Bender, 1978. [Updates]

Passman, Donald S. *All You Need to Know About the Music Business.* 5th ed. New York: Simon & Schuster, 2003.

Pettigrew, Jim, Jr. *The Billboard Guide to Music Publicity.* New York: Watson-Guptill, 1997.

Pleasants, Henry. *Serious Music—And All That Jazz.* New York: Simon & Schuster, 1969.

Rachlin, Harvey. *The TV and Movie Business: An Encyclopedia of Careers, Technologies, and Practices.* New York: Crown, 1991.

Rapaport, Diane S. *How to Make and Sell Your Own Recording: The Complete Guide to Independent Recording.* 5th ed. Paramus, NJ: Prentice Hall, 1999.

Raugust, Karen. *The Licensing Business Handbook.* Rev. ed. New York: EPM Communications, 2001.

Sanjek, Russell, and Sanjek, David. *Pennies From Heaven: The American Popular Music Business in the Twentieth Century.* New York: Da Capo, 1996.

Schladweiler, Kief, ed. *Foundation Fundamentals: A Guide for Grantseekers.* 7th ed. New York: Foundation Center, 2004.

Scott, Michael D. *Multimedia: Law & Practice.* Englewood Cliffs, NJ: Prentice Hall Law & Business, 1993.

Shapiro, Carl, and Varian, Hal. *Information Rules: A Strategic Guide to the Network Economy.* Harvard Business School Press, 1999.

Siegel, Alan H. *Breaking Into the Music Business.* Rev. ed. New York: Simon & Schuster, 1990.

So You Want to Open a Music Store. Rev. ed. Carlsbad, CA: NAMM, 2000.

Steinberg, Irwin, and Greenblatt, Harmon. *Understanding the Music Business: A Comprehensive View.* Needham Heights, MA: Simon & Schuster, 1998.

Stim, Richard. *Music Law: How to Run Your Band's Business.* 4th ed. Berkeley, CA: Nolo, 2004.

Thorne, Robert, and Viera, John David, eds. *2004–2005 Entertainment, Publishing and the Arts Handbook.* Eagan, MN: West Group, 2004. [Annual]

2005 Recording Industry Sourcebook. Artistpro. Published by Hal Leonard, Milwaukee, WI.

Vogel, Harold L. *Entertainment Industry Economics: A Guide for Financial Analysts.* 6th ed. New York: Cambridge University Press, 2004.

Wadhams, Wayne. *Dictionary of Music Production and Engineering Terminology.* New York: Schirmer, 1988.

Wadhams, Wayne. *Sound Advice: The Musician's Guide to the Record Industry.* New York: Schirmer, 1990.

Weissman, Dick. *Making a Living in Your Local Music Market: How to Survive and Prosper.* Milwaukee, WI: Hal Leonard, 1990.

Whitsett, Tim. *The Dictionary of Music Business Terms.* Emeryville, CA: MixBooks, 1999.

Wilder, Alec. *American Popular Song: The Great Innovators, 1900–1950.* Reprint ed. New York: Oxford University Press, 1990.

Woram, John, and Kefauver, Alan P. *The New Recording Studio Handbook.* Rev. ed. New York: Elar, 1989.

Journals, Magazines, Newspapers, Newsletters

Advertising Age   Weekly trade publication covering agency, media and advertising, news and trends

Amusement Business   Weekly trade newspaper covering mass entertainment management including events, attendance, and spending

Billboard   Professional international news weekly for members of music and video and home entertainment industries and related fields

Broadcast Engineering   Technical monthly covering digital television technology, systems, installation, management, and maintenance

Broadcasting & Cable   Weekly business publication for broadcast and cable TV

Campus Activities Programming Magazine   Trade magazine covering college campus programming for the student and professional

Circus Magazine   Monthly consumer magazine about rock and roll

College Music Symposium   Interdisciplinary quarterly

Columbia Journal of Law & the Arts   Scholarly quarterly with articles concerning timely art law topics. http://www.columbia.edu/cu/jla/right/content/about.html

Copyright Law Reporter   Monthly with articles about today's rules, new and proposed regulations, current case law activity, and views of the regulators

Country Music   Bimonthly consumer magazine covering country music artists and the recording industry

Daily Variety   Daily tabloid newspaper of the entertainment industry

DJ Times   Business monthly with the latest technology, trends, music, and business information for DJs

Down Beat   Monthly consumer magazine covering contemporary music and aimed at seriously involved player and listener

Electronic Musician   Monthly business magazine covering electronics and computers in the creation and recording of music

Entertainment Law Reporter   Monthly covering legal developments and matters of importance to lawyers and executives in the entertainment industry

Facilities   Monthly trade magazine for the public assembly industry

Film Score   Monthly Publication providing film music reviews and composer interviews

Hit Parader   Consumer monthly with news of the heavy metal music industry

Hollywood Reporter   Daily business news and reviews of all phases of the entertainment, theatrical, and new media fields

Instrumentalist   Monthly with practical, professional information for school band and orchestra directors

International Musician   Monthly journal for members of the American Federation of Musicians

Jazz Educators Journal   Quarterly covering news and events related to jazz and popular music in education

Journal of the American Musicological Society   Scholarly articles on diversified branches of musicology, published three times a year

Journal of the Copyright Society of the U.S.A.   Quarterly dealing with domestic and foreign copyright laws, revisions, and court decisions

Journal of Music Therapy   Research-oriented quarterly for practitioners and others

Mix, the Recording Industry Magazine   Monthly business magazine focusing on contemporary music arts and audio and video music production

Modern Drummer   Monthly for the student, semipro, and pro drummer

Music & Copyright   Publication providing global reporting on the commercial aspects of the music industry, published semimonthly by the Financial Times

Music & Sound Retailer   Monthly serving owners, managers, and sales personnel in retail musical instrument and sound product dealerships

Music Educators Journal   Bimonthly dealing with all facets of study and teaching methods at all levels

Music Inc.   Business monthly providing newest trends in product merchandising, new products, industry news, and dealer and manufacturer profiles

Music Trades   Business monthly for music stores selling instruments, accessories, music, and electronic music and home equipment

NARAS Journal   Publication addressing the needs of the membership of the National Academy of Recording Arts & Sciences

Notes   Quarterly journal covering developments in music librarianship and activities of the Music Library Association

Overture   Monthly trade union paper

Post   Monthly serving the field of TV, film, and video production and postproduction

Producer Report   Biweekly newsletter covering record producer activity

Radio and Records   Weekly trade newspaper providing news, sales, marketing innovations, and airplay data

Radio Business Report   Monthly publication covering business issues, inside news on people, and company controversies

Recording   Consumer monthly focusing on all aspects of home and small studio recording

Rolling Stone Magazine   Biweekly coverage of American culture

Spin Magazine   Consumer monthly covering trendsetters in music world

Sound and Communications   Business monthly for sound contractors, engineers, consultants, and system managers

Sound & Vision   Monthly service magazine offering guidance to buyers of all types of audio equipment and the discs and tapes to be played with it

Soundtrack!   Quarterly magazine covering film music and other entertainment personalities

Symphony Magazine   Bimonthly publication with news and articles for symphony orchestra managers, trustees, volunteers, and musicians

Variety   Business weekly reporting on the entertainment industry worldwide

Wall Street Journa   Daily newspaper focusing on the business and investment communities

Professional Organizations

Acoustical Society of America (ASA)
2 Huntington Quadrangle, Ste. 1NO1,
    Melville, NY 11747-4502
(516) 576-2360
Web site: http://asa.aip.org

Actors' Equity Association (AEA)
165 West 46th St., 15th Fl., New York, NY
    10036
(212) 869-8530
Web site: www.actorsequity.org

Alliance of Motion Picture and Television Pro-
    ducers (AMPTP)
15503 Ventura Blvd., Encino, CA 91436-3140
(818) 995-3600
Web site: www.amptp.org

American Choral Directors Association
    (ACDA)
502 SW 38th St., Lawton, OK 73505
(580) 355-8161
Web site: www.acdaonline.org

American Composers Alliance (ACA)
70 W. 74th St., New York, NY 10023
(212) 362-8900
Web site: www.composers.com

American Federation of Labor and Congress
    of Industrial Organizations (AFL-CIO)
815 16th St., NW, Washington, DC 20006
(202) 637-5000
Web site: www.aflcio.org

American Federation of Musicians of the
    United States and Canada (AFM)
1501 Broadway, Ste. 600, New York, NY
    10036
(212) 869-1330
Web site: www.afm.org

American Federation of Television and Radio
    Artists (AFTRA)
260 Madison Ave., New York, NY 10016-
    2402
(212) 532-0800
5757 Wilshire Blvd., 9th Fl., Los Angeles, CA
    90036-3689
(323) 634-8100
Web site: www.aftra.com

American Guild of Musical Artists (AGMA)
1727 Broadway, New York, NY 10019
(212) 265-3687
Web site: www.musicalartists.org

Country Music Foundation (CMF)
4 Music Square E., Nashville, TN 37203
(615) 256-1639
Web site: www.countrymusichalloffame.com

Directors Guild of America (DGA)
7920 Sunset Blvd., Los Angeles, CA 90046
(310) 289-2000
Web site: www.dga.org

Dramatists Guild of America
1501 Broadway, Ste. 701, New York, NY
    10036
(212) 398-9366
Web site: www.dramaguild.com

Early Music America
2366 Eastlake Ave. E. #429, Seattle, WA.
    98102
(206) 720-6290
Web site: http://earlymusic.org

Electronic Industries Alliance (EIA)
(formerly Electronic Industries Association)
2500 Wilson Blvd., Arlington, VA 22201-
    3834
(703) 907-7500
Web site: www.eia.org

Reprinted from *Music Business Handbook and Career Guide*, Eighth Edition, by David Baskerville, (2005), Sage Publications.

Entertainment Services and Technology Association (ESTA)
875 Sixth Ave., Ste. 1005, New York, NY 10001
(212) 244-1505
Web site: www.esta.org

Entertainment Software Association
1211 Connecticut Ave., NW #600, Washington, DC 20036
(202) 833-4372
Web site: www.theesa.com

Foundation Center
79 Fifth Ave./16th St., New York, NY 10003-3076
(212) 620-4230
Web site: http://fdncenter.org

Gospel Music Association (GMA)
1205 Division St., Nashville, TN 37203
(615) 242-0303
Web site: www.gospelmusic.org

Guild of Italian-American Actors (GIAA) (formerly Italian Actors Union)
352 W. 44th St., New York, NY 10036
(212) 262-7300
Web site: www.angelfire.com/ny/giaa

Guitar and Accessories Marketing Association
P.O. Box 5488, Long Island City, NY 11105
(718) 274-3210
Web site: www.discoverguitar.com

Harry Fox Agency, Inc.
711 Third Ave., New York, NY 10017
(212) 370-5330
Web site: www.nmpa.org/hfa.html

Hebrew Actors Union
31 E. 7th St., New York, NY 10003
(212) 674-1923

International Alliance for Women in Music (IAWM)
For further membership information: slackmanl@rollins.edu. Box 2731, Rollins College 1000 Holt Avenue Winter Park, FL 32789-449
Web site: www.iawm.org

International Alliance of Theatrical Stage Employes, Moving Picture Technicians, Artists and Allied Crafts of the United States, Its Territories and Canada (IATSE)
1430 Broadway, 20th Floor, New York, NY 10018
(212) 730-1770
Web site: www.iatse-intl.org

International Association of Assembly Managers (IAAM) (formerly International Association of Auditorium Managers)
635 Fritz Dr., Suite 100, Coppell, TX 75019-4442
(972) 906-7441
Web site: www.iaam.org

International Association of Jazz Educators (IAJE) (formerly National Association of Jazz Educators)
Box 724, 2803 Claflin Rd., Manhattan, KS 66505
(785) 776–8744
Web site: www.iaje.org

International Confederation of Societies of Authors and Composers (CISAC)
20–26 Boulevard du Parc 92200 Neuilly/sur/Sein, France
(33) 1 55 62 08 50
Web site: www.cisac.org

International Federation of Actors (FIA)
Mrs. Katherine Sand, Secretary General, Guild House, Upper St. Martin's Lane
London WC2H 9EG, United Kingdom
(44) 020 7 379 0900
Web site: www.fia-actors.com

International Federation of Musicians (FIM)
21 bis, rue Victor Massé, F-75009, Paris, France
(33) 1 45 26 31 23
Web site: www.fim-musicians.com/eng

International Federation of the Phonographic
    Industry (IFPI)
IFPI Secretariat, 54 Regent St., London W1B
    5RE, United Kingdom
(44) 020 7 878 7900
Web site: www.ifpi.org

International Music Products Association
    (NAMM) (formerly National Association
    of Music Merchants)
5790 Armada Dr., Carlsbad, CA 92008
(760) 438–8001/(800) 767–6266
Web site: www.namm.com

ITA, International Recording Media Associa-
    tion
182 Nassau St., Ste. 204, Princeton, NJ
    08542–7005
(609) 279–1700
Web site: www.recordingmedia.org

League of American Theatres and Producers,
    Inc.
226 W. 47th St., New York, NY 10036
(212) 764–1122
Web site: www.broadway.org

League of Resident Theatres (LORT)
1501 Broadway, Ste. 2401, New York, NY
    10036
(212) 944–1501
Web site: www.lort.org

Los Angeles Copyright Society (LACS)
1800 Avenue of the Stars, Suite 900, Los
    Angeles, CA 90067
(310) 369–5679
Web site: http://www.copr.org

Metropolitan Opera Guild (MOG)
70 Lincoln Center Plaza, 6th Fl., New York,
    NY 10023
(212) 769–7000
Web site: www.metopera.org/guild

Motion Picture Association of America
    (MPAA)
15503 Ventura Blvd., Encino, CA 91436

(818) 995–6600
Web site: www.mpaa.org

Motion Picture Editors Guild
7715 Sunset Blvd., Ste. 200, Hollywood, CA
    90046
(323) 876–4770
Web site: www.editorsguild.com

Mu Phi Epsilon (International Music Fraternity)
International Executive Office, 4705 N. Sonora
    Ave., Suite 114, Fresno, CA 93722–3947
(559) 277–1898/(888) 259–1471
Web site: http://home.muphiepsilon.org

Music and Entertainment Industry Educators
    Association (MEIEA)
C/O Kim Wangler, 17 Pleasant St., Potsdam, NY
    13676
Web site: www.meiea.org

Music Critics Association of North America,
    Inc. (MCA) (formerly Music Critics Associa-
    tion)
722 Dulaney Valley Rd. #259, Baltimore, MD
    21204 (410) 435–3881
Web site: www.mcana.org

Music Educators National Conference
    (MENC)
1806 Robert Fulton Dr., Reston, VA 20191
(703) 860–4000/(800) 336–3768
Web site: www.menc.org

Music Library Association, Inc. (MLA)
8551 Research Way, Suite 180, Middleton, WI
    53562
(608) 836–5825
Web site: www.musiclibraryassoc.org

Music Performance Trust Funds, the Recording
    Industries (MPTF)
1501 Broadway, Ste. 518, New York, NY
    10036–5501
(212) 391–3950
Web site: www.mptf.org

Music Publishers' Association of the United States (MPA)
243 5th Ave., Suite 236, New York, NY 10016
(212) 327–4044
Web site: http://host.mpa.org

Music Teachers National Association (MTNA)
441 Vine St., Ste. 505, Cincinnati, OH 45202–2811
(513) 421–1420/(888) 512–5278
Web site: www.mtna.org

Music Video Production Association (MVPA)
201 N. Occidental St., Building 7, Unit B, Los Angeles, CA 90026
(213) 387–1590
Web site: www.mvpa.com

NABIM, The International Band and Orchestral Products Association
PO Box 5488, Long Island City, NY 11105
866–49MUSIC
Web site: www.nabim.org

NAMM Affiliated Music Business Institutions (NAMBI)
Dr. James Payne, University of Nebraska at Kearney, Kearney, NE 68849
(308) 865–8606
Web site: www.nambi.org

Nashville entertainment Association (NeA) (formerly Nashville Music Association)
P.O. Box 158029 Nashville, TN 37215
(615) 297–7320
Web site: http://nea.net

Nashville Songwriters Association International (NSAI)
1701 West End Ave., Third Fl., Nashville, TN 37203
(615) 256–3354/(800) 321–6008
Web site: http://nashvillesongwriters.com

National Academy of Popular Music (NAPM)/Songwriters Hall of Fame

330 West 58th St., Ste. 411, New York, NY 10019
(212) 957–9230
Web site: www.songwriter shalloffame.org/napm

National Academy of Recording Arts & Sciences, Inc. (NARAS)
3402 Pico Blvd., Santa Monica, CA 90405
(310) 392–3777
Web site: www.grammy.org

National Academy of Television Arts & Sciences (NATAS)
111 W. 57th St., Ste. 1020, New York, NY 10019
(212) 586–8424
Web site: www.emmyonline.com

National Alliance for Musical Theatre
520 Eighth Ave., Suite 301, New York, NY 10018
(212) 714–6668
Web site: www.namt.net

National Assembly of State Arts Agencies
1029 Vermont Ave. NW, 2nd Fl., Washington, DC 20005
(202) 347–6352
Web site: www.nasaa-arts.org

National Association for Campus Activities (NACA)
13 Harbison Way, Columbia, SC 29212–3401
(803) 732–6222
Web site: www.naca.org

National Association of Broadcast Employees and Technicians– Communications Workers of America (NABET-CWA)
501 3rd St. NW, 8th Fl., Washington, DC 20001
(202) 434–1254
Web site: http://nabetcwa.org

National Association of Broadcasters (NAB)
1771 N St. NW, Washington, DC 20036
(202) 429–5300
Web site: www.nab.org

National Association of Negro Musicians, Inc.
(NANM)
PO Box S-011, 237 East 115th Street, Chicago,
Illinois 60628
(773) 779–1325
Web site: http://facstaff.morehouse.edu/
~cgrimes

National Association of Recording Merchandisers (NARM)
9 Eves Dr., Ste. 120, Marlton, NJ 08053
(856) 596–2221
Web site: www.narm.com

National Association of Schools of Music
(NASM)
11250 Roger Bacon Dr., Ste. 21, Reston, VA
20190–5248
(703) 437–0700
Web site: http://nasm.arts-accredit
.org/index.jsp

National Association of Teachers of Singing
4745 Sutton Park Court, Suite #201 Jack-
sonville, FL 32224
(904) 992–9101
Web site: www.nats.org

National Conference of Personal Managers
(NCOPM)
964 Second Ave., New York, NY 10022
(212) 421–2670
Web site: www.ncopm.com

National Endowment for the Arts (NEA)
1100 Pennsylvania Ave., NW, Washington, DC
20506
(202) 682–5400
Web site: http://arts.endow.gov

National Federation of Music Clubs (NFMC)
1336 N. Delaware St., Indianapolis, IN
46202–2481
(317) 638–4003
Web site: www.nfmc-music.org

National Music Council (NMC)
425 Park St., Upper Montclair, NJ 07043
(973) 655–7974
Web site: www.musiccouncil.org

National Music Publishers' Association (NMPA)
475 Park Avenue South - 29th Floor New York,
NY 10016–6901
646–742–1651
Web site: www.nmpa.org

National Music Theatre Network (also known
as Broadway Dozen)
1697 Broadway, Ste. 902, New York, NY 10019
(212) 664–0979
Web site: www.broadwayusa.org

National Opera Association (NOA)
Robert Hansen, Executive Director, PO Box
60869, Canyon, TX 79016–0869
(806) 651–2857
Web site: www.noa.org

Opera America (absorbed Central Opera
Service)
1156 15th St. NW, Ste. 810, Washington, DC
20005
(202) 293–4466
Web site: www.operaam.org

Phi Mu Alpha-Sinfonia Fraternity of America,
Inc.
10600 Old State Rd., Evansville, IN
47711–1399
(812) 867–2433/(800) 473–2649
Web site: www.sinfonia.org

Piano Technicians Guild (PTG)
4444 Forest Ave., Kansas City, MO 66106
(913) 432 9975
Web site: http://ptg.org

Producers Guild of America (PGA)
8530 Wilshire Boulevard, Suite 450, Beverly
Hills, CA 90211
(310) 358–9020
Web site: www.producersguild.org

Radio Music License Committee
Keith F. Meehan, Executive Director, 9 East 53rd
    Street, New York, NY 10022
(212) 308–4311
Web site: www.radiomlc.com

Recording Industry Association of America, Inc.
    (RIAA)
1330 Connecticut Ave., NW, Ste. 300, Washing-
    ton, DC 20036
(202) 775–0101
Web site: www.riaa.com

Recording Musicians Association
817 Vine St., Suite 209, Los Angeles, CA
    90038–3716
(323) 462–4762
Web site: www.rmala.org

Screen Actors Guild (SAG)
5757 Wilshire Blvd., Los Angeles, CA
    90036–3600
(323) 954–1600
Web site: www.sag.org

SESAC, Inc.
55 Music Square East, Nashville, TN 37203
(615) 320–0055/(800) 826–9996
Web site: www.sesac.com

Society of Composers, Inc.
P.O. Box 540, New York City, NY 10113–0450
(212) 989–6764
Web site: www.societyofcomposers.org

Society of Motion Picture and Television Engi-
    neers, Inc. (SMPTE)
595 W. Hartsdale Ave., White Plains, NY 10607
(914) 761–1100
Web site: www.smpte.org

Society of Professional Audio Recording Ser-
    vices (SPARS) (formerly Society of Profes-
    sional Audio Recording Studios)
9 Music Square South, Suite 222, Nashville, TN
    37203
(615) 846–6161/(800) 771–7727
Web site: www.spars.com

Society of Singers, Inc.
6500 Wilshire Boulevard, Suite 640, Los Ange-
    les, CA 90048
(323) 653–7672/(888) 570–1318
Web site: www.singers.org

Society of Stage Directors and Choreographers
    (SSDC)
1501 Broadway, Ste. 1701, New York, NY
    10036–5653
(212) 391–1070/(800) 541–5204
Web site: www.ssdc.org

Songwriters Guild of America (SGA)
1500 Harbor Blvd., Weehawken, NJ
    07087–6732
(201) 867–7603
Web site: www.songwriters.org

United Scenic Artists, Local 829
29 West 38th St., New York, NY 10018
(212) 581—0300
Web site: http://www.usa829.org

Video Software Dealers Association (VSDA)
16530 Ventura Blvd., Ste. 400, Encino, CA
    91436–4551
(818) 385–1500/(800) 955–8732
Web site: www.vsda.org

Volunteer Lawyers for the Arts (VLA)
1 E. 53rd St., 6th Fl., New York, NY
    10022–4201
(212) 319–2787
Web site: http://www.vlany.org

Women in Film (WIF)
8857 W. Olympic Blvd., Suite 201, Beverly
    Hills, CA 90211
(310) 657–5144
Web site: www.wif.org

World Intellectual Property Organization
    (WIPO)
34, chemin des Colombettes, P.O. Box 18,
    CH-1211 Geneva 20, Switzerland

(41) 22 338 91 11
Web site: www.wipo.int

World Trade Organization
154 rue de Lausanne, 1211 Geneva 21,
    Switzerland
(41) 22 739 51 11
Web site: www.wto.org

Writers Guild of America, East, Inc.
555 W. 57th St., Suite 1230 New York, NY
    10019
(212) 767–7800
Web site: www.wgaeast.org

Writers Guild of America, Inc. (west)
7000 W. Third St., Los Angeles, CA 90048
(323) 782–4532
Web site: www.wga.org

Young Audiences, Inc. (YA)
115 E. 92nd St., New York, NY 10128–1688
(212) 831–8110
Web site: www.youngaudiences.org

2.4.1 Detailed State of the Art

The market of digital music and multimedia content distribution can be structured according to the following categories of market players:

- Technology providers, software developers;
- Content owners, music publishers, music labels;
- Copyright collecting societies;
- Content providers and distributors;
- End users (musicians, musicologists, audiophiles, music amateurs . . .)

In general these categories can present overlapping, since, for instance, a technology provider can also play the role of music publisher. Examples are Liquid Music Network and Real Networks which provides both multimedia content distribution technologies (servers, systems and models) and music download services.

2.4.1.1 Technology providers, software developers

Technology providers are innovators, know-how and software developers providing technology transfers and/or tools for the management of multimedia content and related distribution and commercialisation in the net/digital world. Here is a list of the main technologies and the related provider entity (company, research centre, institution):

- **Adobe Content Server:** Adobe Content Server (http://www .adobe.com/products/contentserver/) from Adobe (www.adobe .com) is a system for publishers, libraries, enterprises, government agencies, retailers, and application service providers to produce, manage, distribute and protect eBooks and other digital content in Adobe Portable Document Format (PDF). It integrates preparation, procurement, distribution, fulfillment, and rights management of digital content.

- **Digital World Services ADo²RA System:** ADo²RA (http:// www.dwsco.com/adora/index.html) from Digital World Services (www.dwsco.com) is a content independent digital distribution solution. It's a system that makes the creation, protection and distribution of digital content — text, music, software, games, and video — possible to access and enjoy from all mobile devices and methods.

- **DMDsecure DMDFusion:** DMDfusion (http://www.dmdsecure .com/products/dmdfusion/overview.php) from DMDsecure (www

.dmdsecure.com) is a product consisting of flexible software components and applications including Digital Rights Management and Conditional Access technologies that manages the access, usage, protection and licensing of digital content. Central to DMDfusion is the concept of a separation of layers that each performs its own tasks.

- **element 5 e-sales:** e-sales (http://www.element5.com/index .html) is the element 5 (www.element5.com) solution to perform online sales of software through unique marketing campaigns to lower distribution costs, develop new international markets, increase customer loyalty and implement new licensing models. The element 5 Control Panel enables a complete overview of online activities and sales data, to adjust sales activities at any time to meet individual needs.

  element 5 e-sales offers order processing and all associated communications, in ten major languages. It supports local payment options for various countries, and all forms of payment commonly accepted across the globe including credit cards, checks, purchase orders, cash and bank transfers.

- **IBM Digital Media Factory.** IBM Digital Media Factory (DMF, http://www1.ibm.com/industries/media/indseg/) is an open-technology framework comprised of e-business infrastructure that can help companies manage, store, protect and distribute digital video, audio and images.

- Digital media is unstructured content - video, audio and images not stored in traditional databases. The content can have intrinsic value, such as movies on demand, and business process value for managing large media files such as medical images and corporate media assets. Both uses require specially configured systems, including hardware, software and services to create the digital media, manage it efficiently and securely, distribute it and then process transactions.

  Digital media is being used in many ways across a range of industries - from retail kiosks, to government video surveillance, to wireless content distribution in the telecommunications industry.

  IBM products included in DMF are IntelliStation workstations, Electronic Media Management System, IBM Content Manager, DB2 Universal Database, WebSphere Commerce For Digital Media, IBM .server, TotalStorage solutions and IBM Global Services.

- **Inter Trust Rights | System:** Right | System (http://www.intertrust
.com/main/technology/index.html) technology from InterTrust
(www.intertrust.com) provides tools to deliver digital content
online. It supports any kind of content (music, videos, novels, articles, reports, images) and several business models (sales to subscriptions, membership clubs, pay-per-view, rentals, advertising).
Rights | System technology also adapts to explore innovative new
ways of generating revenue.

   InterTrust's Right | System technology offers a large spectrum of dis-
tribution options, including downloading from the Internet or from
a web site, streaming, CD or DVD burning, via wireless or cable links.
Its DRM forges new relationships with other members of the distribution chain, or DRM-enable the already existing relationships.

- **Liquid Audio Liquid Music Network:** The Liquid Music Network
system (http://www.liquidaudio.com/services/distribution/lmn
/index.asp) from Liquid Audio (www.liquidaudio.com) is based
on two products for final users, the Player and the Secure Portable
Player Platform (SP3), and a Server.

   Liquid Player for Windows enables streaming, downloading, purchasing, playback, ripping and CD burning of digital audio. Liquid
Plug-Ins enable third party music players to access secure music in
the Liquid Audio format.

   Liquid Audio's SP3 provides consumer electronics companies,
chipset manufacturers and embedded operating systems developers
with a digital music solution to get to market with digital audio
devices. Combined with a custom-branded version of Liquid Player
Plus software. SP3 enables the rapid development of secure digital
audio devices that are compliant with the guidelines established
using the Secure Digital Music Initiative (SDMI).

- **LockStream DRM Solution:** LockStream DRM Solution
(http://www.lockstream.com/hi_band/index.htm) from Lock-
Stream (www.lockstream.com) includes a suite of products: Secure
Package Creator Module, Secure Package Reader Module, License
Generator Module, Media Manager and Deployer.

   The Secure Package Creator Module packages up digital media into
Objects, encapsulating one or more pieces of digital content into
LockStream's proprietary format. Then it creates a license template
creating and registering DRM rules with the License Generator

Module. Finally, it turns Objects into Protected Objects by associating DRM usage rules to them.

The Secure Package Reader Module provides a set of component that developers can use to build LockStream DRM support into client applications on a multitude of client devices, platforms, and networks.

The License Generator Module issues licenses based on the DRM rule set and to manage those licenses.

The Media Manager is an executable file capable of interpreting LockStream's proprietary file formats, managing access to content encoded in the file formats, creating playlists for that content, rendering that content on computer desktops, and synchronizing the content on authorized mobile devices.

The Deployer is an ActiveX control for browser integration that manages the download and installation of software for content playback, media files used within the Media Manager, licenses issued by the License Generator and other files.

- **Microsoft Windows Media 9:** Microsoft Windows Media 9, from Microsoft, (http://www.microsoft.com/windows/windowsmedia/9series/default.asp) is a suite of programs which form a complete platform for digital media distribution.

  The Windows Media Rights Manager includes both server and client software development kits (SDKs) that enable applications to protect and play back digital media files.

  Using the server SDK, developers can create applications that encrypt (package) digital media files and issue licenses for those digital media files. A packaged Windows Media file contains a version of the file that has been encrypted with a key so that only the person who has obtained a license for that file can play it. The license is separate from the packaged Windows Media file, which means that the content and license for that content can be acquired at different times. Encrypted files can be either streamed or downloaded to the consumer's computer.

  To enable digital media playback applications to play packaged Windows Media files, acquire licenses for them, back up and restore licenses, and issue security upgrades for its DRM component, developers should use the client SDK.

- **Microsoft Digital Asset Management:** Digital Asset Management (http://www.microsoft.com/windows/windowsmedia/mediaent/dam.asp) is the Microsoft (www.microsoft.com) technology to lower operating costs and increase productivity. The search and report system locates the assets, while Windows Media's DAM allows media companies to deliver encrypted Windows Media audio and video assets to any desktop.

Windows DAM offers compression mechanism which enables asset owners to reduce bandwidth and storage costs. It allows digital distribution of video from low bit rate previews to full 720p high-definition resolutions.

- **NDS Synamedia:** Synamedia (http://www.nds.com/broadband/broadband.html) from NDS (www.nds.com) is the broadband operators' gateway to earning new video-based incremental revenues from broadband IP networks. It delivers a truly multiservice mix that lets distributors control, manage and personalize the way of providing content.

  NDS Synamedia allows broadband IP networks to offer interactive entertainment package and develop new business models around the following services: Secure digital broadcast TV, Video-On-Demand (VOD), Personal Video Recorder (PVR) functions, Pay-per-view and pay-per-use functions, Interactive applications.

- **RealNetworks Helix:** Helix (http://www.realnetworks.com/) from RealNetworks (www.realnetworks.com) is both a platform and community that enable creation of digital media products and applications for any format, operating system or device. The Helix platform combines extensive, proven digital software technology with a rich set of application interfaces. It empowers developers, information technology and consumer electronics companies to easily integrate digital media. The Helix community enables companies, institutions and individual developers to license Helix DNA platform source code in order to build Helix-powered server and client products. RealNetworks has also released a family of products built on top of the Helix DNA platform, including the Helix Universal Server.

- **STARBAK Torrent Origin Streaming Appliance:** The Torrent Origin Streaming Appliance (OSA, http://www.starbak.com/products/origin_streaming_servers.html) from STARBAK (www.starbak.com) is a network appliance. A network appliance is a specialized device that is dedicated to performing one function very well. The Torrent OSA was specifically designed to stream media. Since it is not a normal multipurpose server, it is very easy to use. The Torrent OSA utilizes web-based administration. This means that it can be controlled from any computer that has a web browser. No special software needs to be installed. It can also be administered from any location on the network.

The Torrent OSA streams all major streaming formats including Microsoft Windows Media, Apple QuickTime, MPEG-1 and MPEG-2. All formats can be streamed simultaneously from a single Torrent OSA.

- **WEDELMUSIC:** WEDELMUSIC (http://www.wedelmusic.org) is a complete system for distribution and sharing of interactive music via Internet totally respecting the publisher rights and protecting them from copyright violation. WEDELMUSIC allows publishers, archives and consumers (theatres, orchestras, music schools, libraries, music shops, musicians) to manage interactive music; that is, music that can be manipulated: arranged, transposed, modified, reformatted, printed, etc., respecting copyright. It is an innovative support for preparing performances, studying music, analysing music, learning instruments, distributing music at low cost, etc. The same music objects will be available for traditional media and Braille.

- **WebWare ActiveMedia:** ActiveMedia (http://www.webwarecorp .com/products_services_activemedia.html) software from Web-Ware (www.webwarecorp.com) provides a secure repository to manage, share, distribute, and publish rich media content, such as graphics, images, layouts, animation, video and documents. Active-Media is designed for wide-scale deployment and allows content sharing throughout global organizations among employees, partners, agencies, and distributors.

  WebWare ActiveMedia can be used as a stand-alone content management system or incorporated into an existing enterprise content management system (ECM) as the backend digital media repository. It can be implemented as installed software in-house or as an outsourced service.

- **KaZaA Media Desktop, WinMX, Morpheus:** KaZaA Media Desktop (www.kazaa.com), WinMX (www.winmx.com) and Morpheus (http://start.musiccity.com/m20/index.html) use peer-to-peer technology. This means that individual users connect to each other directly, without need for a central point of management. Users can choose which files he wants to share and how many files are allowed to be downloaded by other users at any one time. All these programs allows users to search and download the shared files. All items shared on the user network may be categorized by attributes such as category, author, description, language, etc.

Distributors
(Branch/Independent/Video)

3D Music Distribution, Inc.
954 W. Washington Blvd.
Chicago IL 60607
(312) 666-9395
(312) 666-9396 FAX
Robert Signorello

Action Music Sales Inc.
6541 Eastland Road
Cleveland OH 44142
(216) 243-0300
(216) 243-4063 FAX
Dennis Baker

Allegro Corporation
14134 N. Airport Way
Portland OR 97230
(503) 257-8480
(503) 257-9061 FAX
Joe Micallef

Alliance Entertainment
    Corp.
110 E. 59th Street, 18th Fl.
New York NY 10022
(212) 935-6662
(212) 935-6620 FAX
David Schlang

Alternative Dist. Alliance
72 Spring Street, 12th Fl.
New York NY 10012
(212) 343-2485
(212) 343-2504 FAX
Andy Allen

American Video
145 Palisade Street
Dobbs Ferry NY 10522
(914) 693-4002
(000) 000-0000 FAX
Ed Lawrence

Associated Distributors Inc.
3803 N. 36th Avenue
Phoenix AZ 85019
(602) 278-5584
(602) 269-6356 FAX
Leonard Singer

BMG Distribution
1540 Broadway, 37th Fl.
New York NY 10036
(212) 930-4000
(212) 930-4398 FAX
Pete Jones

Baker & Taylor
8140 N. Lehigh Avenue
Morton Grove IL 60053-2600
(847) 965-8060
(847) 470-7860 FAX
Stanley Meyers

Bayside Distribution
885 Riverside Parkway
West Sacramento CA 95605
(916) 371-2800
(916) 371-1995 FAX
Erik Grotte

Big Easy Distributing Co.
134-C Harbor Street
New Orleans LA 70126
(504) 241-9800
(504) 241-9866 FAX
Bob Norton

Capital Cities/ABC Video
    Pub.
1200 High Ridge Road
Stamford CT 06905
(203) 329-6412
(203) 329-6464 FAX
Abby DiCostanzo

Carolina Records, Inc.
104 West 29th Street, 4th Fl.
New York NY 10001
(212) 886-7500
(212) 643-5573 FAX
Matthew Flott

Chip Taylor Communications
15 Spollett Drive
Derry NY 03038
(603) 434-9262
(603) 432-2723 FAX
Chip Taylor

Cisco Music, Inc.
6307 De Soto Avenue, Suite C
Woodland Hills CA 91367
(818) 884-2234
(818) 884-1268 FAX
David Fonn

City Hall Records
25 Tiburon Street
San Rafael CA 94901-4721
(415) 457-9080
(415) 457-0780 FAX
Robin Cohn

Columbia Tri-Star Home
    Video
10202 W. Washington Blvd.
Culver City CA 90232
(310) 280-8000
(310) 280-1724 FAX
Paul Culberg

Dennen Sales
1870 N. Maud Avenue
Chicago IL 60614
(312) 635-4429
(312) 404-6381 FAX
Peter Dennen

Distribution North America
1280 Santa Anita Court
Woodland CA 95776
(916) 661-6600
(916) 661-7877 FAX
Ron Phillips

Distribution Video & Audio
1610 N. Myrtle Avenue
Clearwater FL 34615
(800) 683-4147
(813) 441-3069 FAX
Ryan Kugler

EMI Music Distribution
21700 Oxnard St., Ste 700
Woodland Hills CA 91367-
   3642
(818) 587-4000
(818) 999-9906 FAX
Gene Rumsey

Empire Music Group, Inc.
170 West 74th Street
New York NY 10023
(212) 580-5959
(212) 874-8605 FAX
Robert W. Stern

Entertainment Software,
   Inc.
PO Box 13789
Arlington TX 76094-0789
(817) 265-7435
(817) 275-2022 FAX
Brien Culver

Feedback Inc. Music Dist.
524 Windy Point Drive
Glendale Heights IL 60139
(800) 326-3472
(708) 545-9191 FAX
Chris Kouzes

Funkytown Music Dist.
1027 S. Western Avenue
Los Angeles CA 90006
(213) 730-4800
(213) 730-4804 FAX
Charlie Ann

Harmonia Mundi USA
2037 Granville Avenue
Los Angeles CA 90025-6103
(310) 478-1311
(310) 996-1389 FAX
Matthew Owen

Hawaii Calls Inc.
2290 Alahao Place
Honolulu HI 96819-2283
(808) 847-4608
(808) 847-4609 FAX
Donald McDiarmid, III

IMV Distributors
5850 Lakehurst Dr., Ste
   150-6
Orlando, FL 32819
(407) 352-0568
(407) 352-0568 FAX
Marcelo Fontana

Image Entertainment Inc.
9333 Oso Avenue
Chatsworth CA 91311-6019
(818) 407-9100
(818) 407-5775 FAX
David Borshell

International Marketing
   Group
1900 Elm Hill Pike
Nashville TN 37210-3712
(615) 889-8000
(615) 871-4817 FAX
Steve Kountzman

J.S.J. Distributors Inc.
6620 W. Belmont Avenue
Chicago IL 60634
(773) 286-4444
(773) 286-0639 FAX
Joseph Swiatek

JFL Distributors
2500 NW 5th Avenue
Miami FL 33127
(305) 573-7800
(305) 573-1006 FAX
Frederick Guzman

Judy S.A.
87 Boulevard Puerto Aereo
Col. Federal
Mexico, DF 15700
(525) 571-1451
(525) 786-0216 FAX
Alfonso Masri

Kandamerica Inc.
124 La Porte Street
Arcadia CA 91006
(818) 445-7700
(818) 445-0066 FAX
Toshi Fujimoti

Koch International L.P.
2 Tri-Harbor Court
Port Washington NY 11050-
   4617
(516) 484-1000
(516) 484-4746 FAX
   Michael Rosenberg

Literary Transactions Inc.
10402 Montrose Avenue
   #102
Bethesda MD 20814-4165
(301) 897-3755
(301) 897-3760 FAX
Dan Sachar

M.S. Distributing
6405 Muirfield Drive
Hanover Park IL 60103
(630) 582-2888
(630) 582-3388 FAX
John Salstone

MCS Distributing
1250 D Rankin Street
Troy MI 48083
(810) 583-4678
(810) 583-3446 FAX
Charlie Salah

MPI Home Video
16101 S. 108th Ave.
Orland Park IL 60462
(708) 687-7881
(708) 687-3797 FAX
Sam Citro

MVP Home Entertainment
9030 Eton Avenue
Canoga Park CA 91304
(818) 709-5809
(818) 709-7846 FAX
Philip Knowles

Megavizyon
Valikonaji cd. Ferah sk.
No. 15
Istanbul 80220 Turkey
902122968090
902122968095
Selguk Ogrendil

Monument Entertainment,
   Inc.
8285 Sunset Blvd. #1
West Hollywood CA 90056
(213) 650-3300
(213) 650-3331 FAX
Jeffrey Peterson

Multicultural Media
RR 3 Box 6655
Granger Road
Barre VT 05641
(802) 223-1294
(802) 229-1834 FAX
Chris Mills

Multisync Trends Inc.
540 Gotham Parkway
Carlstadt NJ 07072
(201) 842-8900
(201) 842-0666 FAX
Pradeep Khanna

Music Distributors Inc.
6504 Midway, Ste 200
Haltom City TX 76117-6699
(817) 831-2982
(817) 831-0368 FAX
Don Gillespie

Music Video Dist
PO Box 1128
Norristown PA 19404
(610) 650-8200
(610) 650-9102 FAX
Edward Seaman

Music World Distributors
PO Box 10150 NPC
Grand Cayman CAMAN ISL
(345) 945-7500
(345) 945-7500 FAX
Darrel Dacres

N.A.I.L.
17 SE 3rd, Suite 501
Portland OR 97214
(503) 746-4361
(503) 746-4364 FAX
Alicia Rose

Navarre Corporation
7400 49th Avenue North
New Hope MN 55428
(800) 728-4000
(612) 533-2156 FAX
Eric Paulson

Naxos Of America
8440 Remington Avenue
Pennsauken NJ 08110
(609) 663-4844
(609) 663-4764 FAX
Mark Miller

OR Records, Inc.
5335 N. Tacoma, Ste 3
Indianapolis IN 46220
(317) 466-1352
(317) 466-0494 FAX
Stan Denski

PDG
825 8th Avenue, 20th Fl.
New York NY 10019-7416
(212) 333-8000
(212) 603-7931 FAX
Jim Caparro

Paulstarr Enterprises
1660 Lake Drive West
Chanhassen MN 55317
(612) 361-6667
(612) 361-6936 FAX
Terrie Thompson

Pioneer Entertainment
   (USA)
2265 E. 220th Street
Long Beach CA 90810-1643
(310) 952-2321
(310) 925-2142 FAX
Yosuke Kobayashi

Platinum Disc Corporation
PO Box 2798
3160 Airport Road
Lacrosse WI 54603
(608) 784-6620
(608) 784-6635 FAX
David Thompson

Provident Music Distribu-
    tion
One Maryland Farms, Ste
    200
Brentwood TN 37027
(615) 373-3950
(615) 373-0386 FAX
Don Noes

RED Distribution
79 Fifth Avenue
New York NY 10003
(212) 337-5200
(212) 337-5252 FAX
Sal Licata

Rep Company
27 Congress Street
Salem MA 01970
(508) 744-7678
(508) 741-4506 FAX
Jim Cuomo

Reyes Records Inc.
140 NW 22nd Avenue
Miami FL 33125-5242
(305) 541-6686
(305) 642-2785 FAX
Enrique Reyes

Ringo/J.D. Whitney (B)
7503 35th Street SE, #23
Calgary, AB T2C IV3
Canada
(403) 236-4004
(403) 236-0959 FAX
Ed Brooks

Rock Bottom Inc.
6175-B Crooked Creek
    Road
Norcross GA 30092
(770) 448-8439
(770) 246-0820 FAX
Jeff Scheible

Rotz Record Distribution
2211 N. Elston Avenue
Chicago IL 60614
(312) 862-6500
(312) 862-6592 FAX
Kai Dohm

Sameach Music, Inc.
191-05 McLaughlin Avenue
Holliswood NY 11423
(718) 479-4507
(718) 479-4593 (FAX)
Izzy Taubenfeld

Scorpio Music
2500 E. State Street
Trenton NJ 08619-3318
(609) 890-6000
(609) 890-0247 FAX
John Gervasoni

Scorpius Music, Inc.
195 Nassau St., Ste 21
Princeton NJ 08542
(609) 683-1339
(609) 683-7170 FAX
Elizabeth Lyall

Select-O-Hits
1981 Fletcher Creek Drive
Memphis TN 38133-7057
(901) 388-1190
(901) 388-3002 FAX
Tiffany Phillips

Shannock Corporation
4222 Manor Street
Burnaby BC V5G 1B2
(604) 433-3331
(604) 433-4815 FAX
Bill McCartney

Simitar Entertainment
5555 Pioneer Creek Drive
Maple Plain MN 55359-9003
(612) 559-6660
(612) 559-0210 FAX
Ed Goetz

Sisu Home Entertainment
18 West 27th St., 10th Fl.
New York NY 10001
(212) 779-1559
(212) 779-7115 FAX
Haim Scheininger

Smith & Alster
5300 N. Powerline Road
Suite 200
Ft. Lauderdale FL 33309
(954) 351-0000
(954) 351-0561 FAX
Jeff Abrams

Sony Music Distribution
550 Madison Ave., 31st Fl.
New York NY 10022-9998
(212) 833-8000
(212) 833-8622 FAX
Paul Smith

Sounds of Zion
9298 S. 500 West
Sandy UT 84070
(801) 255-1991
(801) 255-1998 FAX
Doyl Peck

Southern Music Distribu-
tion
PO Box 921969
Norcross GA 30092
(770) 447-5159
(770) 447-5159 FAX
Michael Walker

Southwest Entertainment,
Inc.
5415 Bandera Road, Ste 504
San Antonio TX 78238-1959
(210) 523-2616
(210) 684-6300 FAX
Nelson H. Balido Jr.

Super Marketing Distribu-
tors
65 Richard Road
Ivyland PA 18974
(215) 674-5410
(215) 674-5459 FAX
Barbara Dwyer

Surplus Countrywide Dist.
Ent.
560 Sylvan Avenue
Englewood Cliffs NJ 07632-
3104
(201) 894-8700 Ext 0528
(201) 894-0429 FAX
Michael Maslin

Tara Publications
8 Music Fair Rd, Ste I
Owings Valley MD 22117
(410) 654-0880
(410) 654-0881 FAX
Mayer Pasternak

The Ent. Mktg Network
17 Stockholm Avenue
Box 2370
Rockport MA 01966
(508) 546-8383
(508) 546-8585 FAX
Brad Lee

Twentieth Century Fox
Home Ent.
2121 Avenue of the Stars
25th Floor
Los Angeles CA 90067-5010
(310) 369-3900
(310) 369-3318 FAX
Jeff Yapp

Twinbrook Music Inc.
227 W. 29th St. 5th Floor
New York NY 10001
(212) 947-0440
(212) 947-4567 FAX
Tom Jacobson

Unison Music Dist
3319 West End Ave., Ste. 200
Nashville TN 37203
(800)251-4000
(615) 883-7851 FAX
Rick Pritikin

Universal Asset Based
Svcs.
5000 Winnetka Avenue
Minneapolis MN 55428
(612) 504-3617 Ext 0616
(612) 504-3618 FAX
Michael Catain

Universal Music & Video
Dist.
10 Universal City Plaza
Suite 400
Universal City CA 91608
(818) 777-4400
(818) 777-8914 FAX
Henry Droz

Vidtape
200 Patton Avenue
W. Babylon NY 11704
(516) 491-4223
(517) 491-4233
Mohinder Singh

Viking Distribution Corp.
208 S. 28th Avenue
Hollywood FL 33020
(954) 926-7741
(954) 927-1940 FAX
Larry Palmacci

WEA
111 N. Hollywood Way
Burbank CA 91505-4356
(818) 843-6311
(818) 840-6212 FAX
Dave Mount

Western Record Sales
226 Linus Pauling Drive
Hercules CA 94547
(510) 741-8840
(510) 741-7060 FAX
Steve Cupples

World Trading Center, Inc.
167 Keyland Court
Bohemia NY 11716
(516) 563-8705
(516) 563-8755 FAX
Arthur Danziger

Y? Entertainment Dist. Inc.
7677 Oakport Street, Ste
1030
Oakland CA 94621
(510) 729-7347
(510) 729-7347 FAX
Ahmad Abdullah

Entertainment Software Suppliers
Branch and Independent Labels/Video and Multimedia Suppliers

32 Jazz
250 W. 57th Street, Ste 1514
New York NY 10107
(212) 265-0740
(212) 265-1067 FAX
Robert Miller

8 Ball Records
12555 Biscayne Blvd., #810
North Miami FL 33181
(954) 435-9534
(954) 435-8683 FAX
Alvin Rogers

A & M Records
1416 N. La Brea Avenue
Hollywood CA 90028-7596
(213) 469-2411
(213) 856-2693 FAX
Rich Gallo

A.D. Vision
5750 Bintliff, Ste 217
Houston TX 77036-2123
(713) 977-9181
(713) 977-5573 FAX
Craig O'Connor

Acklen Records
Belmont University
1900 Belmont Blvd
Nashville TN 37212
(615) 460-5504
(615) 460-5516 FAX
Clyde Rolston

Acoustic Disc
PO Box 4143
San Rafael CA 94913
(415) 454-1187
(415) 459-2815 FAX
Harriett Rose

Alcazar Productions
PO Box 429
Waterbury VT 05676-0429
(802) 244-7856
(802) 244-6128 FAX
Jennifer Harwood

Alchemy Records
61 Surrey Drive
Cohasset MA 02025
(617) 383-0086
(617) 383-0086 FAX
Jon Durant

Alias Records
2815 West Olive Avenue
Burbank CA 91505
(818) 566-1034
(818) 566-6623 FAX
Steve Buell

All American Music Grp/
    Scotti Brothers Records
808 Wilshire Blvd
Santa Monica CA 90401
(310) 656-1100
(310) 656-7430 FAX
Chuck Gullo

All-Star Music Corp.
9200 S. Dadeland Blvd,
    Ste 612
Miami FL 33156
(305) 670-2235
(305) 670-2236 FAX
Richard Friedman

Alligator Records
PO Box 60234
Chicago IL 60660
(312) 973-7736
(312) 973-2088 FAX
Bruce Iglauer

Alshire International Inc.
Box 7107
1015 Isabel Street
Burbank CA 91510-7107
(213) 849-4671
(213) 569-3718 FAX
Al Sherman

Alterian Records
620 West Foothill Blvd
Monrovia CA 91016
(818) 932-1555
(818) 932-1515 FAX
Cynthia Gardner

American Entertainment
PO Box 3390
Westport CT 06880
(203) 227-7473
(203) 222-8828 FAX
Rick Rogers

American Gramaphone
    Records
9130 Mormon Bridge Rd
Omaha NE 68152-1937
(402) 457-4341
(402) 457-4332 FAX
Dwight Montjar

American Multimedia Inc.
2609 Tucker Street
Burlington NC 27215
(910) 229-5554
(910) 570-2439 FAX
Tim Mallard

Amherst Records, Inc.
1762 Main Street
Buffalo NY 14208-1199
(716) 883-9520
(716) 884-1432 FAX
Leonard Silver

Anchor Bay Entertainment
500 Kirts Blvd
Troy MI 48084
(248) 362-9660
(248) 362-4454 FAX
George Port

Angel Records
810 7th Ave., 4th Fl.
New York NY 10019
(212) 603-8700
(212) 603-8648 FAX
Mark Forlow

Arista Records
6 West 57th Street
New York NY 10019
(212) 489-7400
(212) 830-2322 fax
Jordan Katz

Arkadia Records
34 E. 23rd Street
New York NY 10010
(212) 674-5550
(212) 979-0266 FAX
Bob Karcy

Art Songs for Children
73 Rudolph Terrace
Yonkers NY 10701
(914) 476-9786
(914) 476-9786 FAX
Sandra Summer

Artifex Records
1105 Myatt Blvd
Madison TN 37115
(615) 865-7909
(615) 865-8550 FAX
Peter Miller

Atlanta Int'l Record Co.
881 Memorial Dr. SE
Atlanta GA 30316
(404) 524-6835
(404) 681-0033 FAX
Norman Hunter

Atlantic Records
1290 Ave. of the Americas
New York NY 10104
(212) 707-2000
(212) 405-5455 FAX
Peter Anderson

Aureus Records
PO Box 541
Mashpee MA 02649
(508) 477-0200
(508) 477-4799 FAX
Joseph Petze

Australian Music Int'l
928 Broadway, Ste 506
New York NY 10011
(212) 253-31567
(212) 253-1521 FAX
Donna D'Cruz

Avalanche Records
12000 W. Pico Blvd, Ste 201
Los Angeles CA 90064
(310) 477-4645
(310) 477-5756 FAX
Ken Guilford

Avatar & Atlantis II Records
3716 Stonewall Circle
Atlanta GA 30339
(404) 438-7069
(404) 438-7013 FAX
Tamiko Jones

B.T. Puppy Records
155 East 29th Street
New York NY 10016
(212) 679-1092
(212) 683-8420 FAX
Rusti Wolintz

BCI/AMRIA (Amria Rec)
PO Box 120723
Nashville TN 37212
(615) 776-2343
(615) 776-5783 FAX
Boomer Castleman

BM Classics
1540 Broadway, 40th Fl.
New York NY 10036
(212) 930-4000
(212) 930-4278 FAX
Harry Palmer

BWE Music/BWE Classics
55 North 300 West, Ste 315
Salt Lake City UT 84110-
    1160
(801) 575-3680
(801) 575-3684 FAX
Dana Beren

Babylon Ent., Inc.
244 W. 54th St., #501
New York NY 10019
(212) 258-2182
(212) 307-7201 FAX
Jennifer Dellipaoli

Backbone Entertainment
243 W. 19th St., Studio I
    New York NY 10011
(212) 367-8380
(212) 367-8382 FAX
Emma Terese

Bainbridge Ent. Co.
PO Box 49628
Los Angeles CA 90049
(310) 440-4490
(310) 440-4496 FAX
Harlene Marshall

Benson Music Group
365 Great Circle Road
Nashville TN 37228
(800) 688-2505
(615) 742-6915 FAX
Mike Gay

Best Film & Video Corp.
108 New South Road
Hicksville NY 11801
(516) 931-6969
(516) 931-5959 FAX
Roy Winnick

Black Market Records
3600 Power Inn Road, Ste. F
Sacramento CA 95626
(916) 455-5441
(916) 455-5942 FAX
Cedric Singleton

Black Saint/Soul Note
Cargo Bldg 80, Room 2A
JFK Airport
Jamaica NY 11430
(718) 656-6220
(718) 244-1804 FAX
Frank Tafuri

Blackbird Recording Co.
185 Franklin St., 5th Fl.
New York NY 10013
(212) 226-5379
(212) 226-3913 FAX
Tor Elting

Blue Train
2525 Main St., Ste 205
Santa Monica CA 90405
(310) 664-1925
(310) 664-9119 FAX
Eddie Gilreath

Bowie Group Ent.
999 Haynes, Ste 325
Birmingham MI 48009
(810) 258-8808
(810) 258-8868 FAX
Dave Stevens

BoxofficeNet
3096 Cobb Hill, Ste 100
Oakton VA 22124
(703) 715-2268
(000) 000-0000 FAX
Robert Thurman

Brentwood Comm., Inc.
31344 Via Colinas, Ste 106
Westlake Village CA 91362
(818) 879-9090
(818) 879-9101 FAX
David Catlin

Bridge Records, Inc.
G.P.O. Box 1864
New York NY 10116
(914) 654-9270
(914) 636-1383 FAX
Becky Starobin

Brioso Recordings
PO Box 832
McLean VA 22101-0832
(703) 356-0730
(703) 356-0559 FAX
Tommie E. Carl

Buena Vista Home Video
350 S. Buena Vista Street
Fairmont Building
Burbank CA 91521-7198
(818) 295-5200
(818) 563-2996 FAX
Ann Daly

Butterfly Records, Inc.
1075 Bellevue Way N.E.
Bellevue WA 98004
(206) 236-4712
(206) 454-0850 FAX
Richard Fowler

CLR
1400 Aliceanna Street
Baltimore MD 21231
(410) 522-1001
(410) 675-4859 FAX
Steve Janis

CMC International
106 W. Horton Street
Zebulon NC 27597
(919) 269-5508
(919) 269-7217 FAX
Alonzo Marrow

CMI Records
PO Box 1049 GT
Grand Cayman
CAYMAN ISLANDS
(345) 947-9021
(345) 947-9021 FAX
Darrel Dacres

Cabin Fever Entertainment
    Inc.
100 West Putnam Avenue
Greenwich CT 06830
(203) 863-5200
(203) 863-5258 FAX
Rick Margolis

Canyon Records Prod.
4143 N. 16th St., Ste 6
Phoenix AZ 85016
(602) 266-7835
(602) 279-9233 FAX
Robert Doyle

Capitol Nashville
3322 W. End Ave., 11th Fl.
Nashville TN 37203
(615) 269-2000
(615) 269-2057 FAX
John Rose

Capitol Records Inc.
1750 N. Vine Street
Hollywood CA 90028
(213) 871-5391
(213) 462-7135 FAX
Lou Mann

Capricorn Records
2205 State Street
Nashville TN 37203
(615) 320-8470
(615) 320-8476 FAX
Lou Ann McClelland
Castle Communications
    (U.S.)
352 Park Ave. S., 10th Fl.
New York NY 10010-1709
(212) 985-6303
(212) 685-7184 FAX
Steven Lerner

Celestial Harmonies
4549 East Ft. Lowell
Tucson AZ 85712-1182
(520) 326-4400
(520) 326-3333 FAX
Julian Parnaby

Central Park Media
250 West 57th St. Ste 317
New York NY 10107
(212) 977-7456
(212) 977-8709 FAX
Mike Pascuzzi

Century Family Inc./
    Century Media
1453 A 14th St., #324
Santa Monica CA 90404
(310) 574-7400
(310) 574-7414 FAX
Oliver Withoeft

Cerebellum Corporation
1301 Beverly Rd., Ste 200
McLean VA 22101
(703) 848-0856
(703) 848-0857 FAX
Erik Lattig

Chesky Records Inc.
355 West 52nd St., 6th Fl.
New York NY 10019-6239
(212) 586-7799
(212) 262-0814 FAX
Norman Chesky

Chicago Records, Inc.
8900 Wilshire Blvd, #300
Beverly Hills CA 90211
(310) 967-2318
(310) 967-2380 FAX
Harold Sulman

Children's Group
1400 Bayly Street, Ste 7
Pickering ON LIW 3R2
CANADA
(905) 831-1995
(905) 831-1142 FAX
Michelle Henderson

Classic Records
1444 N. Highland
Hollywood CA 90028
(213) 466-9694
(213) 466-9825 FAX
Michael Hobson

Classic Sound, Inc.
4708 South Old Peachtree
Norcross GA 30071
(404) 729-8644
(404) 729-8624 FAX
Jim Horner

Cleopatra Records
8726 S. Sepulveda Blvd
Suite D-82
Los Angeles CA 90045
(310) 305-0172
(310) 821-4702 FAX
Brian Perera

Collectable
    Records/Gotham
2324 Haverford Road
Ardmore PA 19003-2913
(800) 446-8426
(610) 649-0315 FAX
Melissa Greene-Anderson

Collectors' Choice Music
900 N. Rohlwing Road
Chicago IL 60143
(630) 775-3300
(630) 775-3340 FAX
Gordon Anderson

Columbia Records New York
550 Madison Avenue
New York NY 10022
(212) 833-8000 Ext. 8000
(212) 833-7076 FAX
Tom Donnarumma

Compass Records
117 30th Avenue S
Nashville TN 37212
(615) 320-7672
(615) 320-7378 FAX
Garry West

Concord Records
2888 Willow Pass Road
Concord CA 94519
(510) 682-6770
(510) 682-3508 FAX
Glen Barros

Country Music Foundation
    Records
4 Music Square East
Nashville TN 37203
(615) 256-1639
(615) 255-2245 FAX
Kyle Young

Covered Bridge Ent. Inc.
    Art. Srvs
5528 Colfax Avenue South
Minneapolis MN 55419
(612) 827-8953
(612) 827-8921 FAX
Thomas Tuomela

Critique Records, Inc.
50 Cross Street
Winchester MA 01890-1257
(617) 935-7540
(617) 935-6866 FAX
Carl Strube

Curb Records/MCG Curb
47 Music Square East
Nashville TN 37203
(615) 321-5080
(615) 327-1964 FAX
Dennis P. Hannon

Cymekob Enterprises, Inc.
550 Washington, Suite 111
Daly City CA 94015
(415) 992-8858
(415) 991-4808 FAX
Yiming Mo

DM Records, Inc
1791 Blount Rd., Ste. 712
Pompano Beach FL 33069
(305) 969-1623
(305) 969-1997 FAX
Mark Watson

DTS Entertainment
31336 Via Colinas, #101
West Lake Village CA 91362
(818) 706-3525
(818) 706-1868 FAX
Sabrina Heraux

d'Note Entertainment
    Group/MK Productions
40 Platt Avenue
Sausalito CA 94965
(415) 331-2130
(415) 331-0853 FAX
Mike Kelly

da music, inc.
PO Box 3
Little Silver NJ 07739
(908) 530-6887
(908) 842-5041 FAX
Achim Neumann

Dargason Music
PO Box 189
Burbank CA 91503-0189
(818) 846-4981
(818) 846-2294 FAX
Jon Harvey

Daywind Records
128 Shivel Drive
Hendersonville TN 37075
(615) 822-4524
(615) 822-5829 FAX
Edward Leonard

Del-Fi Records
548 Norwich Drive
West Hollywood CA 90048
(310) 358-2555
(310) 358-2561 FAX
Bob Keane

Delicious Vinyl Records
6607 Sunset Blvd
Los Angeles CA 90028-7103
(213) 465-2700
(213) 465-8926 FAX
Joseph DeMeo

Delta Music, Inc.
2500 Broadway Avenue
Suite 380
Santa Monica CA 90404-
    3061
(310) 453-9504
(310) 828-1435 FAX
Michael McClain

Denon Records
200 W. 57th St., Ste 907
New York NY 10019
(212) 581-2550
(212) 581-2591 FAX
Eric Lowenhar

Docutrax, Division Music
    Central
260 West 39th St., 18th Fl.
New York NY 10018
(212) 840-3285
(212) 840-3923 FAX
Robert Fish

Domo Records, Inc.
2211 Corinth Ave., Ste 100
Los Angeles CA 90064
(310) 966-4414
(310) 966-4420 FAX
Mitch Rabin

Dove Entertainment
8955 Beverly Blvd
    Los Angeles CA 90048
(310) 273-7722
(310) 273-0365 FAX
Deborah Raffin

Dreamflight Productions
1187 Coast Village Rd,
Suite 457
Santa Barbara CA 93108
(805) 969-5654
(805) 969-9294 FAX
Patti Teel

Drive Entertainment Inc.
10351 Santa Monica Blvd
Suite 404
Los Angeles CA 90025
(310) 553-3490
(310) 553-3373 FAX
Stan Layton

Durkin Hayes Publishing
2221 Niagara Falls Blvd
Niagara Falls NY 14304
(716) 298-5150
(716) 298-5607 FAX
BJ Wood

Dutch East India
PO Box 738
Syosset NY 11791
(516) 677-5000
(516) 764-6315 FAX
Barry Tenenbaum

EMI Christian Music Group
101 Winners Circle
Brentwood TN 37027
(615) 371-6800
(615) 371-6565 FAX
Stin Fox

Eagle Records
1719 West End Avenue
Suite 612 West
Nashville TN 37203
(800) 814-3245
(615) 329-0432 FAX
Arnold Thies

Earache Records
295 Lafayette St. #915
New York NY 10012
(212) 343-9090
(212) 343-9244 FAX
Eric LeMasters

East West Communications,
    Inc.
345 North Maple Drive
Beverly Hills CA 90210
(310) 858-8797
(310) 858-8795 Fax
Doug Rogers

Eastern Front Records, Inc.
7 Curve Street
Medford MA 02052
(508) 359-8003
(508) 359-8090 FAX
Robert Swalley

Echograph Records
PO Box 1576
Santa Monica CA 90406-
    1576
(310) 264-9229
(310) 264-9208 FAX
James McKissick

Eclipse Music Group, Inc.
100 Red Schoolhouse Road
Chestnut Ridge NY 10977-
    7049
(914) 426-0901
(914) 426-1255 FAX
Alan Weiner

Edel America Records, Inc.
PO Box 7304 #343
North Hollywood CA 91603
(818) 843-4753 Ext. 2160
(818) 843-3714 FAX
Jeanne McCafferty

Electric Death Productions
130 Columbia St., Ste 11-A
New York NY 10002-1943
(212) 228-8447
(518) 346-2971 FAX
Jorge Gonzalez

Elektra Entertainment
75 Rockefeller Plaza
New York NY 10019-6972
(212) 275-4000
(212) 974-9314 FAX
Steve Heldt

Ellipsis Arts
20 Lumber Road
Roslyn NY 11576
(516) 621-2727
(516) 621-2750 FAX
Andrew Klein

Epic Records Group
550 Madison Avenue
New York NY 10022-9998
(212) 833-8000
(212) 833-4051 FAX
Jim Scully

Epitaph
2798 Sunset Blvd
Los Angeles CA 90026
(213) 413-7353
(213) 413-9678 FAX
Brett Gurewitz

Escapade Music
730 East Elm Street
Conshohocken PA 19428
(610) 825-9698
(610) 825-7329 FAX
Mitch Satalof

Espiritu Records
c/o Gibson Productions
1325 Ave. of the Americas
New York NY 10019
(212) 541-7400
(212) 541-7547 FAX
Karen Lampiasi

Essex Entertainment, Inc.
560 Sylvan Avenue
Englewood Cliffs
NJ 07632-3104
(201) 894-8700
(201) 894-8630 FAX
Andy Perl

Etherean Music
9200 W. Cross Dr., Ste 510
Littleton CO 80123
(303) 973-8291
(303) 973-8499 Ext. 9000 FAX
Chad Darnell

Evolution Records
1327 N. Adams Street
Tallahassee FL 32310
(904) 576-5588
(904) 576-6339 FAX
Andrew Tarr

Exclusive Arts, Inc.
7371 Hallcrest Drive
McLean VA 22102-2909
(703) 556-8923
(703) 556-9894 FAX
Jodi Terry Kingsley

F2-Fahrenheit/Finer Arts
   Records
2170 S. Packer Road, #115
Denver CO 80231
(303) 755-2546
(303) 755-2617 FAX
Peter Trimarco

Fantasy Records
2600 Tenth Street
Berkeley CA 94710
(510) 549-2500
(510) 486-2119 FAX
Philip Jones

Fenix Entertainment, Inc.
4530 Chermak Street
Burbank CA 91505
(818) 566-4300
(818) 840-8456 fax
James McGraw

Flip Records
524 Broadway, Ste 402
New York NY 10012
(212) 925-2527
(212) 925-2507 FAX
Jordan Schur

Folk Era Prod., Inc.
705 S. Washington Street
Naperville IL 60540-6654
(630) 637-2303
(630) 416-7213 FAX
Allan Shaw

Fonovisa, Inc.
7710 Haskell Avenue
Van Nuys CA 91406
(818) 782-6100
(818) 782-6162 FAX
Eduardo Safa

Freedom House Records
   & Production Co.
709 Woodrow Street
Columbia SC 29205
(803) 695-2082
(803) 783-0901 FAX
Jerald Field

Freeze Records
322 Eighth Avenue, Ste 1602
New York NY 10001
(212) 243-1189
(212) 243-1089 FAX
William S. Socolov

Friedman Fairfax Publishing
15 W. 26th
New York NY 10010
(212) 685-6610
(212) 685-1307 FAX
David Drachman

Front Row Entertainment
135 Fieldcrest Ave.
Edison NJ 08837-3910
(908) 225-8896
(908) 225-8268 FAX
David Sutton

GNP/Crescendo Records
8400 Sunset Blvd.
Los Angeles CA 90069-1994
(213) 656-2614
(213) 656-0693 FAX
Gene Norman

GRP Recording Company
555 W. 57th Street, 10th Fl.
New York NY 10019
(212) 424-1000
(212) 424-1007 FAX
David Steffen

Gallery Records
The Albert Building
1010 B St., Ste 425
San Rafael CA 94901
(415) 256-1440
(415) 256-1444 FAX
Gary Chappell

Geffen Records
9130 Sunset Blvd.
Los Angeles CA 90069-3110
(310) 278-9010
(310) 858-7763 FAX
Jason Whittington

Giant Records
8900 Wiltshire Blvd, Ste 200
Beverly Hills CA 90210-3800
(213) 289-5500
(213) 289-5515 FAX
Irving Azoff

Gold Circle Entertainment,
    Inc.
13906 Gold Circle, Ste 201
Omaha NE 68144
(402) 330-2520
(402) 330-2445 FAX
Mike Delich

Gospo Centric
417 E. Regent Street
Inglewood CA 90008
(310) 679-5603
(310) 677-0250 FAX
Vicki Mack Lataillade

Gourd Music
PO Box 585
Felton CA 95018
(408) 425-4939
(408) 459-7450 FAX
Neal Hellman

Grand Royal Records
3218 1/2 Glendale Blvd
Los Angels CA 90039
(213) 663-3000
(213) 663-5726 FAX
Christopher Johnsen

Grateful Dead
    Merchandising, Inc.
845 Olive Ave., Ste 110
Novato CA 94945
(415) 898-4999
(415) 898-9592 FAX
Patricia Harris

Green Linnet Records
43 Beaver Brook Road
Danbury CT 06810-6210
(203) 730-0333
(203) 730-0345 FAX
Chris Teskey

Green Meadows Produc-
    tions
PO Box 3657
South Pasadena CA 91031
(213) 223-3421
(213) 224-1908 FAX
Theodore Keyes

Griffin Music USA
PO Box 1952
Lombard IL 60148
(630) 858-7801
(630) 858-7806 FAX
Neale Parker

Grindstone/Correct
    Records
447 S. Robertson Blvd
Suite 201
Beverly Hills CA 90211
(310) 246-0779
(310) 246-0669 FAX
Michael Hamill

Guitar Recordings
10 Midland Avenue
Port Chester NY 10573-4923
(914) 935-5268
(914) 937-0614 FAX
Aida Gurwicz

H.O.L.A. Recordings LLC
    235 Park Avenue South
New York NY 10003
(212) 777-5678
(212) 777-7788 FAX
Ken Baumstein

Hal Leonard Corp.
7777 W. Bluemound Road
Milwaukee WI 53213
(414) 774-3630
(414) 774-3259 FAX
Doug Lady

Hallmark Home
    Entertainment
6100 Wilshire Blvd., Ste.
    1111
Los Angeles CA 90048
(213) 549-3770
(213) 549-3760 FAX
Doug Dohmen

Harvest Music International
8489 W. 3rd St
Los Angeles CA 90048
(213) 658-6607
(213) 658-6609 FAX
Jeffrey Soong

Hearts of Space
One Harbor Drive, Ste 20
Sausalito CA 94965
(415) 331-3200
(415) 331-3280 FAX
Leyla Rael Hill

Hemisphono Records
2782 NW 78th Avenue
Miami FL 33122
(305) 599-1190
(305) 599-1191 FAX
Jorge Jure

Higher Octave Music, Inc.
23852 Pacific Coast Hwy.
    Ste. 2C
Malibu CA 90265
(310) 589-1515
(310) 389-1525 FAX
Scott Bergstein

Hollywood Records
500 S. Buena Vista
Burbank CA 91521-0001
(818) 560-5670
(818) 563-1227 FAX
Dutch Cramblitt

Honest Entertainment
33 Music Square West
Suite 100
Nashville TN 37203
(615) 242-4452
(615) 242-4453 FAX
Carolyn Rae Cole

Horizon Records (CA)
2825 Cantor Drive
Morgan Hill CA 95037
(408) 782-1501
(408) 453-3836 FAX
Bruce Hollibaugh

Hot Hits
PO Box 41600
Nashville TN 37204-1600
(615) 259-3234
(615) 259-0930 FAX
Benny Baggott

Ichiban Records, Inc.
PO Box 724677
Atlanta GA 31139-1677
(770) 419-1414
(770) 419-1230 FAX
Ken Masters

i.e. Music
825 8th Avenue
New York NY 10019
(212) 603-1928
(212) 333-1014 FAX
Mark Wexler

Iguana Records
110 Greene Street, Ste. 702
New York NY 10012
(212) 226-0300
(212) 226-8996 FAX
Robert Stein

Imago Recording Co.
530 Broadway
New York NY 10012
(212) 343-3400
(212) 343-3344 FAX
Clay Farmer

Imprint Records
209 10th Ave S., Ste 500
Nashville TN 37203-4101
(615) 244-9585
(615) 244-9586 FAX
Roy Wunsch

In-A-Minute Records
1025 W. MacArthur Blvd
Oakland CA 94608
(510) 653-5811
(510) 652-5058 FAX
Jason Blaine

Inflight Entertainment
One Church St., Ste 550
Nashville TN 37201
(615) 248-4591
(615) 248-2835 FAX
William Byrd

Integrity Music
1000 Cody Road
Mobile AL 36695
(334) 633-9000
(334) 633-5202 FAX
Mark Powell

Interscope Records
10900 Wilshire Blvd.
Los Angeles CA 90024
(310) 208-6547
(310) 208-2427 FAX
Candy Berry

Intersound, Inc.
PO Box 1724
Roswell GA 30077
(770) 664-9262
(770) 664-7316 FAX
Donald Johnson

Island Records
825 8th Avenue
New York NY 10019
(212) 333-8000
(212) 333-8043 FAX
Wayne Chernin

JVC Music
3800 Barham Blvd, Ste. 305
Los Angeles CA 90068-1042
(213) 878-0101
(213) 878-0202 FAX
Dan Davis

Jazzmania Records
270 W. 19th Street
New York NY 10011-4002
(212) 987-7200
(212) 633-8022 FAX
Ervin Litkei

Jellybean Recordings, Inc.
235 Park Ave S., 10th Fl.
New York NY 10003
(212) 777-5678
(212) 777-7788 FAX
John Benitez

Jewel-Paula-Ronn Records
1700 Centenary
Shreveport LA 71101
(318) 227-2228
(318) 227-0304 FAX
Stanley Lewis

Jive Records
137–139 W. 25th St.
New York NY 10001
(212) 620-8790
(212) 645-3783 FAX
Tom Carrabba

John Hart Media, Inc. (A)
1314 16th Avenue
Nashville TN 37212
(615) 292-0616
(615) 292-0828 FAX
John Hart

Justice Record Company
PO Box 980369
Houston TX 77098-0369
(713) 520-6669
(713) 525-4444 FAX
Jay G. Woods

Justin Time Records Inc.
5455 Rue Pare, Ste 110
Montreal PQ H4P-1P7
CANADA
(514) 738-9533
(514) 737-9780 FAX
James West

K-Tel Int'l (US) Inc.
2605 Fernbrook Lane North
Minneapolis MN 55447-4736
(612) 559-6800 Ext. 6125
(612) 559-6848 FAX
Dennis Hoefer

Kidstyle, Inc.
PO Box 120336
Nashville TN 37212
(615) 322-9540
(615) 320-7615 FAX
Rick Horton

King Biscuit Flower Hour
    Records
18 E. 53rd Street
New York NY 10022
(212) 758-4636
(212) 758-4704 FAX
Steve Ship

Kubaney Publishing Corp.
PO Box 527950
Miami FL 33152-7950
(305) 591-7684
(305) 477-0789 FAX
Tony San Martin

Lake Street Records
298 4th Ave., Ste 392
San Francisco CA 94118
(415) 487-6240
(415) 387-5419 FAX
Allyn Rosenberg

Laserdisc Entertainment
4132-A Del Rey Avenue
Marina Del Rey CA 90292
(310) 306-5688
(310) 306-5686 FAX
Mara Epstein

Laughing Hyena
1552 E. Spruce
Olathe KS 66061
(913) 829-5200
(913) 681-1141 FAX
Arnie Hoffman

Laughing Stock Records
PO Box 724
Larkspur CA 94977
(415) 924-7814
(415) 927-3002 FAX
Elmo Shropshire

Legacy Entertainment, Inc.
340 Welland Avenue
St. Catharine's, ON L2R 7L9
CANADA
(905) 704-0049
(905) 641-8803 FAX
Wilf Wikkerink

Lifetime Classics, Inc.
1855 Air Lane Drive
Nashville TN 37210
(615) 874-9801
(615) 874-9840 FAX
Dale Nergenah

Lightyear Entertainment
350 Fifth Ave., Ste 5101
New York NY 10118
(212) 563-4610
(212) 563-1932 FAX
Arnie Holland

Lil' Joe Records
6157 NW 167th St., F-17
Miami FL 33015
(305) 362-8900
(305) 822-1122 FAX
Joseph Weinberger

Live Home Entertainment
PO Box 10124
Van Nuys CA 91406-4211
(818) 908-0303
(818) 908-0320 FAX
Sheila O'Laughlin

Logic Records
270 Lafayette St., Ste 1402
New York NY 10012
(212) 219-1838
(212) 219-2050 FAX
Thom Storr

Louisiana Red Hot Records
2001 Gentilly Blvd.
New Orleans LA 70119
(504) 948-4600
(504) 948-4422 FAX
Harris Rea

Lyrick Studios
2435 W. Central Expwy
Suite 1600
Richardson TX 75002
(972) 390-6101
(972) 390-6066 FAX
Tim Warren

MCA Records
70 Universal City Plaza
Universal City CA 91608-
   1002
(818) 777-4000
(818) 777-8998 FAX
Jayne Simon

MDG Records
PO Box 121859
Nashville TN 37212
(601) 795-6478
(601) 795-4941 FAX
Ted McClerdon

MGM/UA Home Ent., Inc.
2500 Broadway Street
Santa Monica CA 90404
(310) 449-3000
(310) 449-3026 FAX
Robert Wittenberg

Ma Ga Da Int'l Inc.
5655 Terrace Morency
St. Hubert, Quebec J3Y 6Y4
(514) 678-9980
(514) 676-4174 FAX
Robert LeMay

Macola Record Group, Inc.
115 W. Torrance Blvd
Suite 200
Redondo Beach CA 90277
(310) 937-3789
(310) 937-3793 FAX
Donald MacMillan

Madacy Music Group
1865 Trans Canada
Montreal PQ H9P-IJI
(514) 683-9321
(514) 683-7848 FAX
Amos Alter

Magnatone Records
1516 16th Avenue, South
Nashville TN 37212
(615) 383-3600
(615) 383-0020 FAX
Donald Kamerer

Major Broadcast Music
101 W. Grand Avenue
Suite 600
Chicago IL 60610
(312) 755-1300
(312) 755-1451 FAX
David Chackler

MakItRel Records
2500 81st SE Street
Mercer Island WA 98040
(206) 232-2245
(206) 232-2245 FAX
Becca Christel

Malaco Records
PO Box 9287
Jackson MS 39286-9287
(601) 982-4522
(601) 982-4528 FAX
Stewart Madison

Mardi Gras Records
3331 St. Charles Avenue
New Orleans LA 70115
(504) 895-0441
(504) 891-4214 FAX
Warren Hildebrand

Marlee Records
1515 NW 167th St., Ste 110V
Miami FL 33169
(305) 430-0656
(305) 430-0636 FAX
Jackie Ward

Mastertone, Inc.
3430 List Place, Ste 1605
Minneapolis MN 55416
(612) 926-2625
(612) 926-2815 FAX
Drew Emmer

Matador Records
625 Broadway
New York NY 10012
(212) 995-5882
(212) 995-5883 FAX
Patrick Amory

Maverick Recording Co.
8000 Beverly Blvd
Los Angeles CA 90048
(213) 852-1177
(213) 852-1505 FAX
Fred Croshal

Max Music & Entertainment
    Inc.
777 Bricknell Ave., Ste 800
Miami FL 33131
(305) 377-3100
(305) 377-2777 FAX
Alfred Picallo

Mazur Media
AM Wietzestrand 14
Wedemark 30900
GERMANY
5130790537
5130790538
Memo Rhein

Mecca Records
2999 Smith Springs Rd
Apt A-7
Nashville TN 37217
(615) 361-6725
(000) 000-0000 FAX
John Phillips

Mercury Records
825 8th Avenue
New York NY 10019
(212) 333-8502
(212) 333-8585 FAX
Jeffrey Brody

Metacom
5353 Nathan Lane
Plymouth MN 55442
(612) 553-2000
(612) 553-0424 FAX
Diane Dickmeyer

Michele Records
PO Box 566
Massena NY 13662-0566
(315) 769-2448
(315) 764-9672 FAX
Tom Gramuglia

Milan Entertainment, Inc.
1540 Broadway, Ste 28F
New York NY 10036
(212) 782-1086
(212) 782-1078 FAX
Tobias Pieniek

Miramar
200 Second Avenue West
Seattle WA 98119-4204
(206) 284-4700
(206) 286-4433 FAX
Brendan Rorem

Mixman Technologies, Inc.
850 Montgomery St., Ste
    3350
San Francisco CA 94133
(415) 403-1380
(415) 403-1383 FAX
Rob Tobias

Mobile Fidelity Sound Lab
105 Morris Street
Sebastopol CA 95472-3858
(707) 829-0134
(707) 829-3746 FAX
James Benz

Monster Music
274 Wattis Way
S. San Francisco
    CA 94080-6761
(415) 871-5650
(415) 871-1488 FAX
Thad Wharton

Moonshine Music
8525 Santa Monica Blvd
West Hollywood CA 90069
(310) 652-8145
(310) 652-8146 FAX
Sandy Skeeter

Motown Record Company
825 8th Avenue, 29th Fl.
New York NY 10019
(212) 333-8000
(212) 445-3409 FAX
Steve Corbin

Moulin D'or Recordings
1148W Pioneer Pkwy, Ste E
Arlington TX 76013
(817) 795-3177
(817) 795-3078 FAX
Doris Nichols

Mountain Apple Co.
PO Box 22373
Honolulu HI 96823-2373
(808) 597-1888
(808) 597-1151 FAX
Leah Bernsten

Music Factory N.A.
153 Waverly Place, 3rd Fl.
New York NY 10014
(212) 807-0985
(212) 807-0987 FAX
Anne Willcocks

Music For Little People/
    Earthbeat!
PO Box 1460
Redway CA 95560
(707) 923-3991
(707) 923-3241 FAX
Sheron Sherman

Music Incorporated
1012 17th Avenue S.
Nashville TN 37212-2202
(615) 327-4369
(615) 321-3863 FAX
LaQuela Scaife Barnett

Music of the World
PO Box 3620
Chapel Hill NC 27515-3620
(919) 932-9600
(919) 932-9700 FAX
Bob Haddad

Musical Productions Inc.
2090 NW 79th Avenue
Miami FL 33122
(305) 592-4836
(305) 592-4828 FAX
Antonio Moreno

Musicmasters
1710 Highway 35
Ocean NJ 07712-2996
(908) 531-7000
(732) 531-9686 FAX
Jeffrey Nissim

N2K Encoded Music
55 Broad St., 10th Fl.
New York NY 10004
(212) 378-0353
(212) 742-1775 FAX
Kent Anderson

NMC Records
PO Box 725188
Atlanta GA 31139
(770) 509-9600
(770) 590-5600 FAX
Nina Easton

NYNO Records
c/o MJI 1290 Ave. of Ameri-
    cas
Suite 602
New York NY 10104
(212) 245-5010
(212) 265-6409 FAX
Connie Kirch

Narada Media
4650 N. Port Washington Rd
Milwaukee WI 53212
(414) 961-8350
(414) 961-8351 FAX
Wesley Van Linda

Navarre Records/Digital
    Ent.
4700 49th Avenue North
New Hope MN 55428
(800) 728-4000
(612) 533-2156 FAX
    Eric H. Paulson

Naxos of America, Inc.
8440 Remington Avenue
Pennsauken NJ 08110
(609) 663-4844
(609) 663-4764 FAX
Mark Miller

Nervous Inc.
1501 Broadway, Ste 1314B
New York NY 10036
(212) 730-7160
(212) 730-7210 FAX
Sam Weiss

Nesak International
21000 Boca Rio Road, A-15
Boca Raton FL 33433
(561) 477-6422
(561) 477-3120 FAX
Martin Kasen

New World Music
154 Betasso Road
Boulder CO 80302
(303) 415-1040
(303) 415-1050 FAX
Paul Scott

New World Records
701 Seventh Avenue
New York NY 10036-1596
(212) 302-0460
(212) 944-1922 FAX
Paul Tai

Next Horizon Records
111 Westwood Pl., Ste 300
Brentwood TN 37027
(615) 661-4388
(615) 661-4084 FAX
James Berk

Ng Records
622 Broadway, Ste 3A
New York NY 10012
(212) 505-5414
(212) 505-6045 FAX
Jason Wyner

Nikki from Belgium
Vossestraat 44
PO Box 44, B-3090
Overijse 3090
BELGIUM
3226873878
3226872863
Thilo Gabler

Nimbus Records
PO Box 7746
Charlottesville VA 22906
(804) 985-8555
(804) 985-3953 FAX
Peter Elliott

No Front, Inc.
8201 Henry Ave., C-22
Philadelphia PA 19128
(215) 930-0060
(215) 930-0060 FAX
Jonas Goldstein

North Star Music
22 London Street
East Greenwich RI 02818
(401) 886-8888
(401) 886-8886 FAX
Jim Landis

Northwood Press, Inc.
PO Box 1360
Minocqua WI 54548
(715) 356-9800
(715) 356-9762 FAX
Ron Asahara

OM Records
545 Mission Street
San Francisco CA 94105
(415) 247-8800
(415) 882-4848 FAX
Kiri Eschelle

OR Records
5335 N. Tacoma, Ste 3
Indianapolis IN 46220
(317) 466-1352
(317) 466-0494 FAX
Stan Denski

Ocean Records
315 E. 62nd Street
New York NY 10021
(212) 715-0470
(212) 715-0461 FAX
Denise Pineau

Oh Boy/Blue Plate Music/
   Red Pajamas
33 Music Square W., #10273
Nashville TN 37203
(615) 742-1250
(615) 742-13603 FAX
Dan Einstein

Omega Record Group Inc.
27 West 72nd Street
New York NY 10023-3041
(212) 769-3060
(212) 769-3195 FAX
Seymour Solomon

OnQ Music
1365 Enterprise Drive
West Chester PA 19380
(610) 701-8650
(610) 701-1599 FAX
Alan Rubens

Orbison Records/Barbara
   Orbison Productions
1625 Broadway, 6th Fl.
Nashville TN 37203
(615) 242-4201
(615) 242-4202 FAX
Tanja Crouch

Order Records
441 E. Belvedere Avenue
Baltimore MD 21212
(410) 435-0993
(410) 435-3513 FAX
Joyce Klein

Orion Home Video
1888 Century Park East
Los Angeles CA 90067
(310) 282-0550
(310) 201-0798 FAX
Herb Dorfman

Our Turn Records Inc.
27520 Sierra Highway
Suite N-101
Canyon Country CA 91351
(805) 252-2740
(805) 252-1395 FAX
Eddie Pugh

PPI Entertainment Group
88 St. Francis Street
Newark NJ 07105-3515
(201) 334-4214
(201) 344-0465 FAX
DJ St. John

PR Records
1019 Via Sorella, #203
Diamond Bar CA 91789
(909) 869-0070
(909) 8699-0484 FAX
Richard Preuss

PRA Records
1543 Seventh St., 3rd Fl.
Santa Monica CA 90401
(310) 393-8283
(310) 393-9053 FAX
Ellynne Citron

Palmetto Records
71 Washington Place, #1A
New York NY 10011
(212) 673-9394
(212) 533-5303 FAX
Patrick Rustici

Pamplin Music
10209 SE Division Street
Portland OR 97266
(817) 662-0391
(817) 662-0391 FAX
James High

Pandisc Music Corp
6157 NW 167th St., F-9
Miami FL 33015
(305) 557-1914
(305) 557-9262 FAX
Bo Crane

Paradigm Associated
    Labels
67 Irving Place, 3rd Fl.
New York NY 10003
(212) 387-8900
(212) 387-8691 FAX
Dean Brownrout

Paramount Home Video
5555 Melrose Avenue
Bluhdorn Bldg
Los Angeles CA 90038-3197
(213) 956-5000
(213) 467-0171 FAX
Jack Kanne

Penalty Recordings
141 W. 28th St., Ste 1202
New York NY 10001
(212) 947-5575
(212) 947-7557 FAX
Neil Levine

Philips Media, Inc.
10960 Wilshire Blvd
Los Angeles CA 90024
(310) 444-6500
(310) 478-4810 FAX
Emiel Petrone

Phylum Records
145-C Grassy Plain Street
Bethel CT 06801
(203) 778-4873
(203) 778-0384 FAX
John Balis

Pioneer Music Group, Inc.
1420 Coleman Road
Franklin TN 37064
(615) 595-9028
(615) 790-7933 FAX
Bernie Leadon

Platinum Entertainment
2001 Butterfield Road
Suite 1400
Downers Grove IL 60515
(708) 769-0033
(708) 769-0049 FAX
Lynn Hoffman-Engel

Playboy Entertainment
    Group, Inc.
9242 Beverly Boulevard
Beverly Hills CA 90210
(310) 246-4000
(310) 246-4050 FAX
Lynn Knapp

Polygram Classics & Jazz
825 Eighth Avenue
New York NY 10019
(212) 333-8118
(213) 333-8402 FAX
David Neidhart

PopeMusic
PO Box 465
Hohokus NJ 07423
(201) 825-7900
(201) 825-0493 FAX
Gene Pope

Pow Wow Records Inc.
1776 Broadway, Ste 1206
New York NY 10019
(212) 245-3010
(212) 956-2326 FAX
Herb Corsack

Power Music
1303 S. Swaner Road
Salt Lake City UT 84104
(801) 975-7771
(801) 975-7774 FAX
Richard Petty

Priority Records
6430 Sunset Blvd
Hollywood CA 90028-7901
(213) 467-0151
(213) 856-8796 FAX
Mark Cerami

Private Music
8750 Wilshire Blvd.
Beverly Hills CA 90211
(310) 859-9200
(310) 859-1064 FAX
Stave Macon

Profile Entertainment
740 Broadway, 7th Fl.
New York NY 10003-9539
(212) 529-2600
(212) 420-8216 FAX
Sebouh Yegparian

Pure Records
79 Fairview Farm Rd.
Redding CT 06896
(203) 938-0555
(203) 938-0579 FAX
Gordon Anderson

Putumayo World Music
627 Broadway
New York NY 10012
(212) 995-9400
(212) 420-9174 FAX
Dan Storper

Quality Video and Special
    Products
7399 Bush Lake Road
Minneapolis MN 55439
(612) 893-0903
(612) 893-1585 FAX
Vickrey Ottenweller

Quicksilver Records
31312 Via Colinas, Ste 107
Westlake Village CA 91362
(818) 707-0300
(818) 707-1606 FAX
Howard Slivers

RCA Label Group (TN)
1 Music Circle North
Nashville TN 37203-4310
(615) 644-1200
(615) 664-1266 FAX
Joe Galante

RCA Records
1540 Broadway, 35th Fl.
New York NY 10036-6710
(212) 930-4000
(212) 930-4780 FAX
David Fitch

RMM Records
568 Broadway, Ste 806
New York NY 10012
(212) 925-2828
(212) 925-6154 FAX
Brenda Cora

RIOR Reachout
    International
611 Broadway, Ste 411
New York NY 10012
(212) 477-0563
(212) 505-9908 FAX
Neil Cooper

Raging Bull Records
2219 W. Olive Avenue
Suite 152
Burbank CA 91506
(818) 382-2266
(818) 382-2260 FAX
Chuck Fassert

Rawkus Entertainment
65 Reade Street
New York NY 10007
(212) 566-3160
(212) 566-5866 FAX
Jarrett Myer

Ray Lynch Productions
10336 Loch Lomond, Ste 118
Middletown CA 95461-9500
(707) 928-4082
(707) 928-1926 FAX
Ray Lynch

Razor & Tie Entertainment
    LLC
214 Sullivan St., 4A
New York NY 10012
(212) 473-9173
(212) 473-9174 FAX
Craig Balsam

Real Entertainment
2225 Colorado Avenue
Santa Monica CA 90404
(310) 449-5315
(310) 449-0025 FAX
Mike Currie

Real Music
85 Libertyship Way
Sausalito CA 94965-1768
(800) 398-7325
(415) 331-8278 FAX
Jeffrey Payne

Red Ant Entertainment
9720 Wilshire Blvd, 4th Fl.
Beverly Hills CA 90212
(310) 247-1133
(310) 247-2233 FAX
David Miller

Reference Recordings
PO Box 77225-X
San Francisco CA 94107
(415) 355-1892
(415) 335-1949 FAX
Janice Mancuso

Relapse Records
2359-A Lincoln Highway E
Lancaster PA 17602
(717) 397-9221
(717) 397-9381 FAX
Andy Hosner

Relativity Records
79 5th Ave., 16 Fl.
New York NY 10003
(212) 337-5300
(212) 337-5370 FAX
Ken Gullic

Republic Entertainment Inc.
5700 Wilshire Blvd.
Suite 525, North
Los Angeles CA 90036
(213) 965-6900
(213) 965-6963 FAX
Gary Jones

Restless Records
1616 Vista Del Mar Ave.
Hollywood CA 90028-6420
(213) 957-4357
(213) 957-4355 FAX
Tammy Kizer

Revere Records
3479 NW Yeon Avenue
Portland OR 97210
(503) 228-5113
(503) 228-6393 FAX
Devon Stross

Rhino Records, Inc.
10635 Santa Monica Blvd
2nd Fl.
Los Angeles CA 90025
(310) 474-4778
(310) 441-6575 FAX
Richard Foos

Righteous Babe Records
PO Box 95, Ellicott Station
Buffalo NY 14205
(716) 852-8020
(716) 852-2741 FAX
Scot Fisher

Rising Star Records &
    Publishers
52 Executive Park S.
Suite 5203
Atlanta GA 30329
(404) 636-2050
(404) 636-5051 FAX
Barbara Taylor

Roadrunner Records
536 Broadway
New York NY 10012-4068
(212) 274-7500
(212) 219-0301 FAX
Douglas Keogh

Robbins Entertainment
    LLC
30 W. 21st St., 11th Fl.
New York NY 10010
(212) 675-4321
(212) 675-4441 FAX
Gary Baddeley

Rounder Records
1 Camp Street
Cambridge MA 02140
(617) 354-0700
(617) 491-1970 FAX
Duncan Browne

Rykodisc USA
Shetland Park
27 Congress Street
Salem MA 01970
(508) 744-7678
(508) 741-4506 FAX
Thomas Enright

SRO Records
9548 Texhoma Avenue
Northridge CA 91325
(818) 349-2380
(818) 349-6530 FAX
Dennis White

Saban Records/
    Saban's Cool Kids
10960 Wilshire Blvd
Los Angeles CA 90024
(310) 235-5790
(310) 235-5804 FAX
Ron Kenan

Salmon Records
1369 Bobolink Place
Los Angeles CA 90069
(310) 271-1694
(310) 271-1684 FAX
Darren Blumenthal

Salsoul Records
16 East 40th St.
New York NY 10016
(212) 951-3041
(212) 779-7885 FAX
Stan White

Scarab Records, Inc.
947 Paddington Terrace
Heathrow FL 32746
(407) 333-3343
(407) 333-3288 FAX
Janet Smith

Scherling Records
PO Box 1982
Fargo ND 58107
(701) 237-3157
(701) 237-3126 FAX
Di Scherling

Sega of America
255 Shoreline Dr., Ste. 200
Redwood City CA 94065-
    1400
(415) 508-2800
(415) 802-1448 FAX
Shinobu Toyoda

Select Records
16 W. 22nd Street
New York NY 10010-5878
(212) 691-1200
(212) 691-3375 FAX
Fred Munao

Seventh Wave Productions
20 Sunnyside Ave, Ste A-197
Mill Valley CA 94941
(415) 380-9997
(415) 380-9996 FAX
Joe Anderson

Shanachie Entertainment
13 Laight St., 6th Fl.
New York NY 10013
(212) 334-0284
(212) 334-5207 FAX
Lee Goldstein

Sharp Nine Records
561 Hillcrest Ave.
Westfield NJ 07090
(908) 789-7660
(908) 654-1863 FAX
Marc Edelman

Sheffield Lab, Inc.
408 Bryant Circle, Ste C
Ojai CA 93023
(805) 640-2900
(805) 640-2901 FAX
Tom Volpe

Silva Screen Records
   America Inc.
1600 Broadway, Suite 910
New York NY 10019
(212) 757-1616
(212) 757-2374 FAX
Yusuf Gandhi

Simitar Entertainment
5555 Pioneer Creek Drive
Maple Plain MN 55359-9003
(612) 479-7000
(612) 479-7001 FAX
Ed Goetz

Sin-Drome Records Ltd.
18344 Oxnard St., #101
Tarzana CA 91356-1554
(818) 344-8880
(818) 344-8882 FAX
Christopher Roker

Sire Records Group
75 Rockefeller Plaza
New York NY 10019
(212) 275-4560
(212) 581-6416 FAX
Cindy Paul

Slab Recordings
1133 Broadway, #1220
New York NY 10010
(212) 645-1360
(212) 645-2607 FAX
Robert Chiappardi

Slow Motion Records
10507 Byron Avenue
Oakland CA 94603
(510) 639-9211
(510) 639-9212 fax
   Anthony Sterling

Smithsonian Collection
   of Rec.
470 L'Enfant Plaza, Ste 7100
Washington DC 20912
(202) 287-3787
(202) 287-3184 FAX
Bruce Talbot

Softkey International (B)
One Anthenaeum Street
Cambridge MA 02142
(617) 494-1200
(617) 494-1219 FAX
Eric Levin

Sonic Images Records
8908 Appian Way
W. Hollywood CA 90046
(213) 650-1000
(213) 650-1016 FAX
Brad Pressman

Sony Music Special
   Products
550 Madison Ave., 17th Fl.
New York NY 10022-3211
(212) 833-7060
(212) 833-7021 FAX
Harold Fein

Sound Choice
   Accompaniment Tracks
14100 South Lakes Drive
Charlotte NC 28273
(704) 583-1616
(704) 583-1871 FAX
Kurt J. Slep

Soundings of the Planet
PO Box 43512
Tucson AZ 85733
(520) 792-9888
(520) 792-0146 FAX
Dean Everson

Sounds, LTD.
17596 Corbel Court
San Diego CA 92128
(619) 485-1550
(619) 485-1883 FAX
R. B. Glassman

Sparrow Label Group
PO Box 5010
Brentwood TN 37027-5009
(800) 877-4433
(615) 371-6997 FAX
Hugh Robertson

St. Clair Entertainment
    Group
5905 Thimens Blvd.
St. Laurent, PQ H4S IV8
CANADA
(514) 339-2732
(514) 339-2737 FAX
Barb Sheppard

Start Records
17357 Tribune Street
Granada Hills CA 91344
(818) 832-3655
(818) 363-3086 FAX
Tony Muscolo

Step One Records
1300 Division St., Ste 304
Nashville TN 37203-4023
(800) 264-2054
(615) 255-6282 FAX
Jeff Brothers

Stepsun Music
    Entertainment
16 West 22nd Street
New York NY 10011
(212) 366-7200
(212) 366-4034 FAX
Bill Stephney

Inner Peace Music
212 Van Tassel Court
San Anselmo CA 94960
(415) 485-5321
(415) 485-1312 FAX
Steven Halpern

Street Gold Records, Inc.
8011 Delaware Place
Merrillville IN 46410
(219) 769-2100
(219) 769-2106 FAX
Henry Farag

Street Ready Media
406 E. Poppy
Long Beach CA 90805
(310) 423-5630
(310) 920-0766 FAX
William Odell

Strictly Hype Recordings
1001 Nicholas Blvd. Unit L
Elk Grove Village IL 60007
(847) 718-1700
(846) 718-1701 FAX
Paul Golec

Strictly Rhythm Records
920 Broadway, Ste 1403
New York NY 10010
(212) 254-2400
(212) 254-2629 FAX
Brian Ressler

Sub Pop Ltd.
1932 First Avenue, Ste 1103
Seattle WA 98101
(206) 441-8441
(206) 441-8245 FAX
Bobbi Miller

Sukay Records
3450 Sacramento St., Ste
    523
San Francisco CA 94118
(415) 751-6090
(415) 752-3559 FAX
Marc Zola

Summertone Records/Merl
    Saunders Productions
PO Box 22184
San Francisco CA 94122
(415) 759-8100
(415) 564-7798 FAX
Mariana Rosmis

Sundazed Music, Inc.
#1 Reed Street
PO Box 85
Coxsackie NY 12051
(518) 731-6262
(518) 731-9492 FAX
Bob Irwin

Sunset Boulevard Enter-
    tainment
740 N. LaBrea Ave., 1st Fl.
Los Angeles CA 90038
(213) 933-9977
(213) 933-0633 FAX
Alan Melina

Sweetfish Records USA,
    Inc.
920 Edie Road
Argyle NY 12809
(518) 638-5475]
(518) 638-5476 FAX
Rees Shad

TVT Records
23 E. 4th Street
New York NY 10003-7003
(212) 979-6410
(212) 979-6489 FAX
Steven Gottlieb

Telarc International Corp.
DBA Telarc Records
23307 Commerce
Cleveland OH 44122-5804
(216) 464-2313
(216) 464-4108 FAX
Kathleen DeJohn

Tempo
127 Peachtree Rd., Ste 250
Atlanta GA 30303
(404) 521-1800 Ext. 0014
(404) 521-3322 FAX
Robert May

Tenacious Records
PO Box 7595
Northridge CA 91327-7595
(818) 368-6479
(818) 368-3748 FAX
Alphonse Mouzon

Terrace Entertainment
    Corp.
PO Box 68
Las Vegas NM 87701
(505) 425-5188
(505) 425-5110 FAX
Robert John Jones

The Enclave
936 Broadway
New York NY 10010
(212) 253-4900
(212) 253-4999 FAX
Mike Worthington

The Mix Shop
2320 W. Moffat
Chicago IL 60647
(773) 284-9414
(773) 775-5642 FAX
Michael Bader

The Publishing Mills
1680 N. Vine, #1016
Los Angeles CA 90028
(213) 467-7831
(213) 467-0661 FAX
Geoff Schackert

The Soar Corp.
5200 Constitution Ave., NE
Albuquerque NM 87110
(505) 268-6110
(505) 268-0237 FAX
Tom Bee

Thump Records Inc.
3101 Pomona Blvd
Pomona CA 91768
(909) 595-2144
(909) 598-7028 FAX
William Walker

Time Life Music
777 Duke St., Ste 201
Alexandria VA 22314
(703) 838-6908
(703) 838-6915 FAX
Steve Janas

Tommy Boy Music, Inc.
902 Broadway, 13th Fl.
New York NY 10010
(212) 388-8300
(212) 338-8400 FAX
Steve Knutson

TopNotch Records
A Div. Of TopNotch Ent.
    Corp.
PO Box 1515
Sanibel Island FL 33957-1515
(941) 982-1515
(941) 472-5033 FAX
Vincent M. Wolanin

Touch Tunes Interactive
1204 Third Avenue
New York NY 10021
(212) 772-8762
(212) 772-6405 FAX
Rob Fenter

Touchwood Records L.L.C.
1650 Broadway, Ste 1210
New York NY 10019
(212) 977-7800
(212) 977-7963 FAX
Irv Biegel

Toy Box Productions
7532 Hickory Hills Court
Whites Creek TN 37189
(615) 876-5490
(615) 876-3931 FAX
Cheryl Hutchinson

Tribe Records
PO Box 250400
Glendale CA 91225-0400
(818) 700-3446
(000) 000-0000 fax
Marco Dydo

Triloka Records/Worldly
    Music
306 Catron
Santa Fe NM 87501
(505) 820-2833
(505) 820-2834 FAX
Mitchell Markus

Tristan Records
22 Mary Lane
Riverside CT 06878
(203) 698-2537
(203) 637-4008 FAX
Stan Snyder

Turn Up the Music Inc.
708 Colfax Avenue
Kenilworth NJ 07033-2050
(908) 620-0900
(908) 620-0911 FAX
D. Drew Matilsky

Un-D-Nyable Entertain-
    ment
875 N. Michigan Avenue
Suite 2635
Chicago IL 60611
(312) 255-2224
(312) 255-2478 FAX
Paul Wilson

Unison Music
404 BNA Dr., Ste 600
Nashville TN 37217
(800) 726-1990
(615) 883-7851 FAX
Rick Pritikin

United Multi Media Sales
Plaza Office Center
560 Fellowship Rd, Ste 422
Mt. Laurel NJ 08054
(609) 234-5555
(609) 751-3829 FAX
Paul Daly

Unity Label Group
207 Ashland Avenue
Santa Monica CA 90405
(310) 451-7313
(310) 393-7777 FAX
Robert Tauro

Universal Records
1755 Broadway, 7th Fl.
New York NY 10019
(212) 373-0600
(212) 373-0795 FAX
Marc Offenbach

Universal Studios Home
    Video
70 Universal City Plaza
Universal City CA 91608-
    1002
(818) 777-2100
(818) 733-1482 FAX
Andrew Kairey

Upaya Records
902 Broadway, 13th Fl.
New York NY 10010
(212) 388-8325
(212) 388-8400 FAX
Susan Piver

Uproar Entertainment
3663 Twin Lake Ridge
West Lake Village CA 91361
(818) 889-3757
(818) 889-3758 FAX
David Drozen

V.I.E.W. Video, Inc.
34 East 23rd Street
New York NY 10010-4483
(212) 674-5550
(212) 979-0266 FAX
Bob Karcy

V.P. Records
89-05 183th Street
Jamaica NY 11435
(718) 291-7058
(718) 658-3573 FAX
Vincent Chin

V2 Records
14 East 4th St., 3rd Fl.
New York NY 10012
(212) 673-4628
(212) 777-0764 FAX
Dan Beck

Valley Entertainment
1807 2nd Street, #101
Santa Fe NM 87505]
(505) 992-4900
(505) 992-4958 FAX
Barney Cohen

Valley Vue Records
555 Commercial Rd, Ste 10
Palm Springs CA 92262
(619) 778-6510
(619) 778-6512 FAX
Michael Dion

Vedisco Records Inc.
10475 NW 28th Street
Miami FL 33172
(305) 592-4242
(305) 592-3770 FAX
Guillermo Page

Victory Records Inc.
1837 W. Fulton Street
Chicago IL 60612
(312) 666-8661
(312) 666-8665 FAX
Anthony Brummel

Vinyl 4 Records Inc.
PO Box 701347
Tulsa OK 74170-1347
(918) 366-1100
(918) 366-1108 FAX
Scott Cox

Virgin Records
338 Foothill
Beverly Hills CA 90210
(310) 278-1181
(310) 278-6231 FAX
B. J. Lobermann

Virginia Records
422 Mamaroneck Avenue
Mamaroneck NY 10543
(914) 381-2565
(914) 381-0907 FAX
Joe Messina

Vivid Interactive/Atlantis
15127 Califa Street
Van Nuys CA 91411
(818) 908-0481
(818) 908-1324 FAX
David James

Walt Disney Records
500 S. Buena Vista Street
Burbank CA 91521-0001
(818) 973-4377
(818) 848-2610 FAX
Gina Weiss

Warlock Records
122 E. 25th Street
6th & 7th Floor
New York NY 10010
(212) 673-2700
(212) 677-2515 FAX
Adam Levy

Warner Bros. Records Inc.
3300 Warner Blvd
Burbank CA 91505-4694
(818) 846-9090
(818) 846-8474 FAX
Colin Hodgson

Warner Home Video Inc.
4000 Warner Blvd
Burbank CA 91522
(818) 954-6541
(818) 954-4758 FAX
James Cardwell

Wave Entertainment, Inc.
432 Park Avenue S., Ste 203
New York NY 10016
(212) 686-9282
(212) 252-1031 FAX
Kendall Minter

Waveform Corporation
PO Box 1310
Mill Valley CA 94942
(415) 383-8886
(415) 383-8488 FAX
F. J. Forest

Wedge Music
1674 Broadway, Ste 7-D
New York NY 10019
(212) 765-3666
(212) 765-0820 FAX
Robert Findlay

Welk Music Group
1299 Ocean Ave., Ste 800
Santa Monica CA 90401-
1038
(310) 451-5727
(310) 394-4148 FAX
Christine Hamilton

White Clay Records
536 Martin Luther King
Macon GA 31201
(912) 743-7913
(912) 743-4977 FAX
Kat Stratton

William Craig Group, Inc.
7807 E. Greenway Rd., #6
Scottsdale AZ 85260
(602) 951-2324
(602) 951-4202 FAX
William Craig

Wind Records, US Division
PO Box 7309
Alhambra CA 91802-7309
(818) 457-6250
(818) 457-6532 FAX
Patricia Chuang

Wind-up Entertainment,
Inc.
72 Madison Avenue, 8th Fl.
New York NY 10016
(212) 843-8300
(212) 843-0737 FAX
Derek Graham

Windham Hill Records
& High
Street Records
8750 Wilshire Blvd.
Beverly Hills CA 90211
(310) 358-4800
(310) 358-4801 FAX
Anne Robinson

Winter Harvest
Entertainment
1011 Woodland Street
PO Box 60884
Nashville TN 37206
(615) 227-7770
(615) 226-0346 FAX
Steve Roberts

Word Entertainment
3319 West End Avenue
Suite 200
Nashville TN 37203
(615) 457-1000
(615) 457-1185 FAX
Jim Chaffee

Xenon Entertainment
1440 9th Street
Santa Monica CA 90401-
2707
(800) 468-1913
(310) 395-4058 FAX
Tony Perez

ZYX Music Distribution,
Ltd.
72 Otis Street
W. Babylon NY 11704-1406
(516) 253-0800
(516) 253-0128 FAX
Rusty Yardum

Zero Hour Records
14 West 23rd Street, 4th Fl.
New York NY 10010
(212) 337-3200 Ext. 2250
(212) 337-3741 FAX
Ray McKenzie

Zoo/Volcano Entertainment
71 West 23rd St., 14th Fl.
New York NY 1010
(212) 367-4860
(000) 000-0000 FAX
Miles Baker

Zoom TV
1801 Century Park West
Los Angeles CA 90067
(310) 552-6510
(310) 553-4011 FAX
Dick Sowa

Suppliers of Related Products and Services

2.95 Guys
8545 Arjons Drive, Ste K
San Diego CA 92126
(800) 536-5959
(619) 566-4876 FAX
Lance Beesley

6 Head Corporation
PO Box 214
Louisville CO 80027
(303) 604-2140
(303) 604-9724 FAX
Neil McClure

A&M Marketing Group, The
483 Wellwood Drive
Shirley NY 11967
(516) 924-3384
(516) 924-6136 FAX
Philip Avelli

AGI Incorporated
1950 North Ruby Street
Melrose Park IL 60160
(708) 344-9100
(708) 344-9113 FAX
Gary Mankoff

ASR Recording Services
  of California
8960 Eton Avenue
Canoga Park CA 91307-1693
(818) 341-1124
(818) 341-9131 FAX
Jeff Schor

Advanced Comm. Design
7901 12th Avenue South
Bloomington MN 55425
(612) 854-4000
(612) 854-5774 (FAX)
Marco Scibora

Accelerated Chart
  Movement
5255 Zelzah Ave., Ste 118
Encino CA 91316
(818) 996-8973
(818) 705-7903 FAX
Rip Pelley

Allied Digital Technologies
140 Fell Court
Hauppauge NY 11788
(516) 232-2323
(516) 232-5370 FAX
Brian Wilson

Allsop, Inc.
PO Box 23
Bellingham WA 98227
(800) 426-4303
(360) 734-9858 FAX
Kristen Hollander

Alps Marketing
762 S. North Lake Blvd.
Suite 1004
Altamonte Springs FL 32701
(407) 830-1313
(407) 830-1322 FAX
James Lebedoff

Americ Disc Inc.
7575 Trans-Canada Hwy
Suite 106
St Laurent PQ H4T1V6
CANADA
(514) 745-2244
(514) 745-7650 FAX
Pierre Ranger

Ames Specialty Packaging
30 Dane Street
Somerville MA 02143
(800) 521-2637
(617) 623-8895 FAX
Judith Bright

Arion International Inc.
9311 Rush Street
S. El Monte CA 91733
(818) 443-9698
(818) 443-9598 FAX
Chen-Chen Lee

Atlantic, Inc.
10240 Matern Place
PO Box 2399
Santa Fe Springs CA 90670-
  0399
(310) 903-9550
(310) 903-9053 FAX
Don Dolliver

BASF Magnetics
  Corporation
35 Crosby Drive
Bedford MA 01730
(617) 271-4202
(617) 271-0608 FAX
Robert Baldizar

BMI-Beaux Merzon Inc.
10 Aquarium Drive
Secaucus NJ 07094
(201) 865-9330
(201) 865-9331 FAX
Larry Jacobson

Berklee College of Music
1140 Boylston Street
Boston MA 02215-3693
(617) 266-1400
(617) 247-6878 FAX
Lee Eliot Berk

Bernstein Media Research
767 5th Avenue, 20th Fl.
New York NY 10153
(212) 756-4630
(212) 756-4462 FAX
John Penney

Broadcast Data Systems
11 West 42nd St., 12th Fl.
New York NY 10036
(212) 789-3660
(212) 789-1270 FAX
Lisa Moen

Brown Innovations
51 Melcmer Street
Boston MA 02210
(773) 296-6400
(773) 296-4350 fax
Jeremy Brown

C&D Special Projects
309 Sequoya Drive
Hopkinsville KY 42240-4463
(800) 922-6287
(502) 885-1951 FAX
William MacTavish

CNA Insurance Companies
CNA Plaza 38 South
Chicago IL 60685
(800) 262-6241
(312) 755-2048 FAX
Jim Belobraydic

CRT Custom Products, Inc.
7532 Hickory Hills Court
Whites Creek TN 37189
(800) 453-2533
(615) 876-3931 FAX
Cheryl Hutchinson

Capstone Industries, Inc.
7040 W. Palmetta Park Rd.
Suite 401
Boca Raton FL 33433
(800) 725-9680
(954) 574-0609 FAX
Stewart Wallach

Case Logic, Inc.
6303 Dry Creek Parkway
Longmont CO 80503-7492
(800) 447-4848
(303) 530-3822 FAX
John Casey

Checkpoint Systems, Inc.
PO Box 188
Thorofare NJ 08086
(609) 848-1800
(609) 848-0937 FAX
Dave Shoemaker

Chicago One Stop/
    Browser Display
401 West Superior Street
Chicago IL 60610
(312) 822-0822
(312) 642-7880 FAX
Howard Rosen

Cinram, Inc.
1600 Rich Road
Richmond IN 47374
(800) 433-3472
(317) 962-1399 FAX
Hugh Landy

Clear-Vu Products
18 Sylvester Street
Westbury NY 11590
(516) 333-8880
(516) 333-7695 FAX
Grace Conte

Covenant Display, Inc.
PO Box 276
Hartsville TN 37074
(615) 374-4660
(615) 374-2828 FAX
Bill Roark

Covered Bridge Ent. Inc.
Marketing Serv
5528 Colfax Avenue South
Minneapolis MN 55419
(612) 827-8953
(612) 827-8921 FAX
Tom Tuomela

Cromico Inc.
1224 Lawrence Street, NE
Washington DC 20017
(202) 529-0363
(202) 529-0291 FAX
Candy Miles-Crocker

Cyberwerks Interactive
983 S. Josephine Street
Denver CO 80209
(303) 744-7222
(303) 744-2892 FAX
Andrea Dowdy

DNS International
6026 NE Sandy Blvd
Portland OR 97213
(503) 281-7722
(503) 281-8521 FAX
Earl Duncan

Dies & Die Cutting, Inc.
755 Wythe Avenue
Brooklyn NY 11211
(718) 802-0300
(718) 802-0444 FAX
David Kaufman

Digital Audio Disc
    Corporation
PO Box 3710
Terre Haute IN 47803-0710
(812) 462-8100
(812) 462-8755 FAX
James Frische

Digital Comm. Technologies
    Corporation
3941 SW 47th Avenue
Ft. Lauderdale FL 33314
(800) 683-3873
(305) 791-6788 FAX
Jack Brown

Digital Innovations, L.L.C.
906 University Place
Evanston IL 60201
(847) 467-2309
(847) 467-3704 FAX
Collin Anderson

Digital International Corp.
7100 Tujunga Avenue
North Hollywood CA 91605
(818) 503-8255
(818) 503-8245 FAX
Ricardo Ceja

Disc Graphics Inc.
10 Gilpin Avenue
Hauppauge NY 11788-4724
(516) 234-1400
(516) 234-1460 FAX
Donald Sinkin

Disc Manufacturing/
    Cinram
1409 Foulk Road, Ste 102
Wilmington DE 19303
(800) 433-3472
(302) 479-2527 FAX
Hugh Landy

Display Products
1 Comrac Loop, Unit 5
Ronkonkoma NY 11779
(516) 981-9788
(516) 981-9787 FAX
Glenn Jujii

Dormont Technologies Ltd
3356 Babcock Boulevard
Pittsburgh PA 15237-2422
(412) 635-9181
(412) 635-0971 FAX
Jim Quinn

Doubleware Publications
PO Box 450826
Cleveland OH 44145
(800) 871-3136
(216) 871-2242 FAX
Will Limkemann

Edelstein Diversified Co.
    Ltd.
21 Mount Vernon Street
Montreal PQ H8RIJ9
CANADA
(514) 489-8689
(514) 489-9707 FAX
Richard Edelstein

Emplast, Incorporated
950 Lake Drive
Chanhassen MN 55317
(612) 949-9311
(612) 949-1288 FAX
Scott Spell

Enso Audio Imaging
    (Division of Musak)
2901 Third Avenue, Ste 400
Seattle WA 98121
(206) 633-3000
(206) 633-6210 FAX
Bill Koenig

Entertainment Resources
    Group
Unit #1, 2320 Tedlo Street
Mississauga, ON L5A 4A2
CANADA
(905) 270-7474
(905) 270-6060 FAX
Richard Gastmeier

Eva-Tone Inc.
4801 Ulmerton Road
Clearwater FL 34622
(813) 572-7000
(813) 572-6214 FAX
Patrick Augustine

Evergreen Broadcasting/
    Marketing
99 Revere Beach Parkway
Medford MA 02155
(617) 393-7731
(617) 391-0004 FAX
David Alexander

Fuji Photo Film USA Inc.
555 Taxter Road
Elmsford NY 10523-2394
(914) 789-8100
(9140 789-8295 fax
Nick Riviezzo

Future Primitive Designs
2119 South 48th St., #J-L
Tempe AZ 85282
(602) 431-2100
(602) 431-6800 FAX
Karen Leeds

Gary Group
2040 Broadway Street
Santa Monica CA 90404
(310) 264-1700
(310) 264-7944 FAX
Dick Gary

Greater Image, Inc.
7958 Beverly Blvd
Los Angeles CA 90048-4511
(213) 658-6580
(213) 653-0482 FAX
Leanne Meyers

Guaranteed Returns
140 N. Belle Mead Road
Setauket NY 11733
(516) 689-0191
(516) 689-0197 FAX
Dean Volkes

High Level Marketing
8033 Sunset Blvd., Ste 3518
Los Angeles CA 90046
(818) 769-7700
(818) 769-7133 FAX
Ken Rubin

Hired Gun Marketing
730 East Elm Street
Conshohocken PA 19428
(610) 825-9698
(610) 825-7329 FAX
Mitch Satalof

Hypnotic Hat Ltd.
230 West 39th St., 15th Fl.
New York NY 10018
(212) 869-1024
(212) 869-1214 FAX
Howard Levy

In-Tune Music Group
71 Newark Way, Bldg 2
Maplewood NJ 07040
(201) 275-1077
(201) 275-1093 FAX
Bernie Horowitz

Infinity Development Corp.
2001 Weston Parkway
Cary NC 27513
(919) 677-8850
(919) 677-9194 FAX
Chris Aves

Inkworks
3206 Spring Forest Road
Raleigh NC 27616
(919) 873-1818
(919) 873-1825 FAX
Allan Caplan

Interactive People Systems
4557 Hwy 17 Bypass South
Myrtle Beach SC 29577
(803) 293-5979
(803) 293-6008 FAX
Grainger McKoy

International Applied   Net-
    works
8558 Palm Parkway
Orlando FL 32836
(407) 249-2030
(407) 249-2911 FAX
Kenny Bott

International Packaging
    Corp.
5601 Industrial Road
Fort Wayne IN 46825-5106
(219) 484-9000
(219) 482-8941 FAX
Gene Hull

intouch group, inc.
333 Bryant Street
San Francisco CA 94107
(415) 974-5000
(415) 974-5087 FAX
Joshua Kaplan

JVC Disc America Com-
    pany
#2 JVC Road
Tuscaloosa AL 35405
(205) 556-7111
(205) 554-5505 FAX
Jack Kiernan

John Hart Media, Inc. (B)
1314 16th Avenue
Nashville TN 37212
(615) 292-0616
(615) 292-0828 FAX
John Hart

KAO InfoSystems Company
800 Corporate Way
Fremont CA 94539
(800) 525-6575
(510) 657-8427 FAX
Peter McGiurk

KBC Music, Inc.
3408 215th Avenue
Keokuk IA 52632
(319) 838-2286
(319) 838-2286 FAX
Kirk Brandenberger

Keystone Printed
    Specialties
1 Keystone Place
Jessup PA 18434-1818
(717) 383-3280
(717) 383-2320 FAX
Martin Fischer

Kwik-Case USA, Inc.
14921 N. Applegate Road
Grants Pass OR 97527
(503) 846-9151
(503) 846-9151 FAX
Robert Broadhead

LIFT Discplay, Inc.
115 River Road, Ste 105
Edgewater NJ 07020-1009
(201) 945-8700
(201) 945-9548 FAX
Susanna Seirafi

Laserfile International, Inc.
7083 Hollywood Blvd, #303
Hollywood CA 90028
(213) 465-0840
(213) 465-1780 FAX
Andria McClellan

Leslie Dame Enterprises
    Ltd.
111-20 73rd Avenue
Forest Hills NY 11375-5532
(718) 261-4919
(718) 793-8804 FAX
Leslie Dame

Liquid Audio
2421 Broadway, 2nd Fl.
Redwood City CA 94063
(415) 572-0898
(415) 562-0899 FAX
Gerry Kearby

London International Inc.
c/o Hollicom Marketing
PO Box 126
Rosemont NJ 08556
(215) 862-9488
(215) 862-2663 FAX
Jerry Holliday

Loxys
Lotz Karoly 1
Budapest H-1026
HUNGARY
3612750030
3611762642
Sandor Ambrus

Lucasfilm Ltd.
PO Box 2009
San Rafael CA 94912-2009
(415) 662-1854
(415) 662-2334 FAX
Lucy Autrey Wilson

MNI Interactive, Inc.
501 2nd Street, Ste 350
San Francisco CA 94107
(415) 904-6222
(415) 777-2851 FAX
C. Bruce Pfander

MTI
1050 NW 229th
Hillsboro Or 97124
(503) 648-6500
(503) 648-7500 FAX
Brendan Scott

MU-6 Systems, Ltd.
39 Tel Tzur St.
PO Box 2658
Even Yehuda 40500
ISRAEL
97298997077
97298996141
Sam Goldberg

MacTec Products
19770 Bahama Street
Northridge CA 91324
(818) 773-8238
(818) 773-7495 FAX
Brian McCracken

Macey Lipman Marketing/
    Lip Service
8739 Sunset Blvd.
Los Angeles CA 90069-2205
(310) 652-0818
(310) 652-0907 FAX
Macey Lipman

Millrock Displays, Inc.
Sanford Industrial Estates
PO Box 974
Sanford ME 04073
(800) 645-7625
(207) 324-0134 FAX
Spencer Liebmann

Mob Town Enterprises
854 W. Belmont
Chicago IL 60657
(773) 279-1400
(773) 279-1419 FAX
Michael Betancourt

Music Book Services Corp.
16295 NW 13th Ave., Ste B
Miami FL 33169
(800) 555-2626
(305) 620-8484 FAX
Ben Colonomos

Music City Marketing Co.
PO Box 210437
Nashville TN 37221-0437
(615) 646-7400
(615) 662-0114 FAX
Lee Trimble

Music Marketing Network
2-40 Bridge Avenue
Red Bank NJ 07701
(732) 219-9327
(732) 219-0172 FAX
Paul Chachko

Music Sales Corporation
257 Park Avenue S., 20th Fl.
New York NY 10010
(212) 254-2100
(212) 254-2013 FAX
Steven Wilson

Music Software, Inc.
19 Birchdale Lane
Port Washington NY 11050
(516) 627-3308
(516) 627-6252 FAX
Vijay Verma

Music Sound Exchange
1221 Ave. of the Americas
26th Floor
New York NY 10020
(212) 522-3400
(212) 522-0893 FAX
Anne Blackman

Music Technology
   International
4203 Beach 42nd St.
Brooklyn NY 11224-1029
(718) 265-4700
(718) 372-4251 FAX
Ivor Kacenberg

Musicline, Inc.
1151 Sunset Vale Avenue
Los Angeles CA 90069
(310) 275-8871
(310) 275-8872 FAX
Steve Immerman

Muze
304 Hudson St., 8th Fl.
New York NY 10013
(212) 824-0300
(212) 741-1246 FAX
Gary Geller

NetRadio Network
43 Main Street SE
Minneapolis MN 55414
(612) 378-2211
(612) 378-9540 FAX
David Witzig

Nimbus Manufacturing, Inc.
PO Box 7427
Charlottesville VA 22906
(804) 985-1100
(804) 985-4625 FAX
Lorri Haney

Nordic Information Sys-
   tems
9719 Lincoln Village Drive
Suite 105
Sacramental CA 95827
(916) 856-5555
(916) 856-5566 FAX
John Bonner

OMI
111 Great Neck Road
Great Neck NY 11021
(516) 482-4907
(516) 482-4910 FAX
Ira Rosenfeld

Omni Multimedia Group
50 Howe Avenue
Millbury MA 01527-3298
(508) 581-1000
(508) 865-1853 FAX
Frank Della Rosa

P.S. Professional Store, Inc.
20135 Cheetah Lane
Estero FL 33928
(941) 498-9634
(941) 498-9757 FAX
Alan Armstrong

PICS Retail Networks
655 Montgomery St., Ste
   1410
San Francisco CA 94111
(415) 989-7427
(415) 989-7466 FAX
Laura Rodrick

PMDC
PO Box 400
Grover NC 28073
(704) 734-4219
(704) 734-4207 FAX
Henning Jorgensen

Palisades Media Group
1620 26th St., Ste 2050N
   Santa Monica CA 90404
(310) 828-9100
(310) 828-9117 FAX
Beverly Atkins

Paradise Creations, Inc.
15001 Oxnard Street
Van Nuys CA 91411
(818) 904-1424
(818) 787-6011 FAX
David Dalessandro

Photographic Specialties
1718 Washington Avenue N
Minneapolis MN 55411
(612) 522-7741
(612) 522-1934 FAX
Steve Reudelsterz

Pilz Compact Disc, Inc.
PO Box 220
54 Conchester Rd.
Concordville PA 19331
(610) 459-5035
(610) 459-5958 FAX
Edward Lack

Plastic Works, Inc.
1038 Ashby Avenue
Berkeley CA 94710
(510) 841-1001
(510) 841-6116 FAX
Tony Cole

PlayNet Technologies
One Maritime Plaza, 14th Fl.
San Francisco CA 94111
(415) 676-5700
(415) 676-5790 FAX
Jon Monday

Plus Mark, Inc.
1 American Road
Cleveland OH 44144
(216) 252-6770
(216) 252-6774 FAX
Tina Victor

Polydisc USA Inc.
54 Conchester Road
Concordville PA 19331
(610) 459-4232
(610) 459-5958 FAX
Shirley Beatty

Poly-Matrix
40 Downing Parkway
Pittsfield Ma 01201
(413) 499-3550
(413) 442-8610 FAX
David Rufo

Premium Records
706 W. Lancaster Avenue
Bryn Mawr PA 19010
(610) 520-1500
(610) 520-1505 FAX
Andrew Borislow

Professional Image
9422 East 55th Place
Tulsa OK 74145
(918) 622-8899
(918) 622-9030 FAX
Sammie King

Promotional Technologies
   International Corp.
11846 Ventura Blvd, Ste 208
Studio City CA 91604
(818) 784-9200
(818) 784-2299 FAX
Ron Friedman

RSB Disc Inc.
8400 Cote De Liesse
St. Laurent PQ H4T 1G7
CANADA
(800) 361-8153
(514) 342-0401 FAX
Richard Belanger

Recoton Corporation
2950 Lake Emma Road
Lake Mary FL 32746
(407) 333-83900
(407) 333-8903 FAX
Robert L. Borchardt

Reps Music Group
2417 Welsh Road, Ste 227
Philadelphia PA 19114
(215) 676-7377
(215) 676-7958 FAX
Jerry Ross

Rexton, Inc.
PO Box 737352
Elmhurst NY 11373-7352
(800) 343-8140
(718) 592-3934 FAX
Ted Harrison

Ringo/J.D. Whitney
#23, 7503 35th Street S.E.
Calgary AB T2C IV3
CANADA
(403) 236-4004
(403) 236-0959 FAX
Dave Jones

Ross Ellis Printing Co./
   Merlin Music
8300 Tampa, Ste L
Northbridge CA 91324-4267
(800) 447-2149
(818) 993-4760 FAX
Nina Sheldon

Roundhouse Products
3233A Donald Douglas
   Loop 5
Santa Monica CA 90405
(310) 390-7473
(310) 391-7856 FAX
Mark Chatow

Sales & Service Specialists
10749 Cypress Lake Terrace
Boca Raton FL 33498
(561) 477-4804
(561) 477-4806 FAX
Julie Sabin

San Juan Music Group
499 Ernston Road
Parlin NJ 08859-1406
(908) 727-7200
(908) 727-7240 FAX
Michael Chernow

Sanyo-Verbatim CD Co.
1767 Sheridan Street
Richmond IN 47374-1899
(317) 935-7574
(317) 935-7570 FAX
Hideo Nakai

Scene Specialties
13000 Athens
Lakewood OH 44107
(216) 228-2600
(216) 228-5228 FAX
William Getz

Screenplay, Inc.
1505 Western Ave., #110
Seattle WA 98101
(206) 625-9901
(206) 587-5368 FAX
Mark Vrieling

Secret Identitee
    Merchandising
8075 W. 3rd St., Ste 306
Los Angeles CA 90048
(213) 857-5520
(213) 939-8527
Jeffrey Kern

Seedy Software, Inc.
231 Old Bernal Rd., Ste 7
Pleasanton CA 94566
(510) 485-1445
(510) 426-7027 FAX
Raymond H. Stoll

Sensormatic Electronics
951 Yamato Road
Boca Raton FL 33431-0070
(305) 427-9700
(305) 420-2634 FAX
Bo Clucas

Shannon Display
    Merchandising Systems
46 Westland Blvd SW
Atlanta GA 30311
(404) 691-0042
(404) 691-6361 FAX
Larry Allen

Shape CD, Inc.
7380 Sand Lake Rd, Ste 350
Orlando FL 32819
(407) 351-0011
(407) 345-0888 FAX
Alan Siegel

Shorewood Packaging
    Corp.
277 Park Avenue, 30th Fl.
New York NY 10172-0003
(212) 508-5666
(212) 223-3815 FAX
Floyd Glinert

Silverman Sayre Services
2533 South Park Road
Hallandale FL 33009
(954) 989-6077
(954) 989-6133 FAX
Sydney Silverman

Softkey International
One Athenaeum Street
Cambridge MA 02142
(617) 494-1200
(617) 494-1219 FAX
Eric Levin

Sonopress Inc.
1540 Broadway, 28th Fl.
New York NY 10036
(704) 658-2000
(704) 658-2014 FAX
Dieter Baier

Sound Impressions
748 Fesslers Lane
Nashville TN 37210-4316
(615) 244-3535
(615) 255-3882 FAX
James Lenahan

SoundScan
220 N. Central Park Avenue
Hartsdale NY 10530
(914) 328-9100
(914) 328-03234 FAX
Michael Fine

Speed Graphics, Inc.
342 Madison Avenue
New York NY 10173
(212) 682-6520
(212) 986-9307 FAX
Christine Krivosheiw

SpotMagic, Inc.
1700 California St., Ste 430
San Francisco CA 94107
(415) 346-0079
(415) 346-5053 FAX
Richard Berger

Star Display
55-15 Grand Avenue
Maspeth NY 11378
(718) 386-3200
(718) 326-8251 FAX
Ronald Goldsmith

Starrbecca Entertainment
9025 E. Kenyon Avenue
Denver CO 80237
(303) 889-5995
(303) 889-5922 FAX
Steve Prust

Super Management
15104 Detroit Avenue, #2
Lakewood OH 44107-3916
(216) 221-5300
(216) 221-5348 FAX
Sheldon Tirk

Suzi Reynolds & Assoc.
200 Rector Place, Ste 7H
New York NY 10280
(212) 945-2071
(212) 786-0233 FAX
Suzi Reynolds

Synergy Direct Inc.
8008 Girard Ave., Ste 310
LaJolla CA 92037
(619) 459-7668
(619) 459-7251 FAX
Alan Sarkin

THE BOX
1221 Collins Avenue
Miami Beach FL 33139
(305) 674-5000
(305) 674-4900 FAX
Tamara Walters-Baskin

Technicolor Video Services
3233 East Mission Oaks
   Blvd.
Camarillo CA 930312-1697
(805) 445-1122
(805) 445-4280 FAX
Carrie Bissell

Technicolor Video Services
   (MI)
39000 7 Mile Road
Livonia MI 48152-1006
(313) 591-5826
(313) 591-3126 fax
Paul Chabot

Telescan Systems, Inc.
828 Mahler Road
Burlingame CA 94010
(800) 835-7072
(415) 697-9145 FAX
Jason Goldberg

The Elliott Group
1125 Main Street
Pawtucket RI 02860
(401) 772-9400
(401) 722-9410 FAX
Elliott Brodsky

The Left Bank Organization
6255 Sunset Blvd, Ste 1111
Hollywood CA 90028
(213) 466-6900
(213) 957-2311 FAX
Allen Novac

The Lucy Factor
9209 Swinton Avenue
North Hills CA 91343
(818) 894-6888
(818) 891-7077 FAX
Lucy Diaz

The NAK Group
29 E. 10th St., Ste 500
New York NY 10003
(212) 505-9290
(212) 505-9399 FAX
John Garrett

The Soundmakers
8585 Broadway, Ste 701
Merrillville IN 46410-7001
(219) 769-1515
(219) 769-1562 FAX
Richard Hutter

Time Warner Cable Direct
290 Harbor Drive
Stamford CT 06903
(203) 328-4056
(203) 328-4052 FAX
Annie Cacciato

Tomato Land Display Sys.
1640 Bohland
St. Paul MN 55116
(612) 696-9502
(612) 690-1317 FAX
Hank Fukui

Trak Systems
101 N. Plains Road
Wallingford CT 06492
(203) 265-3440
(203) 269-3930 FAX
Robert Trexler

Tribe Entertainment Serv.
201 N. Robertson Blvd,
   Ste A
Beverly Hills CA 90211
(310) 247-7830
(310) 247-7834 FAX
Paul Leighton

Trivec Inc.
290 North Plank Road
Newburgh NY 12550
(914) 562-1799
(914) 562-1676 FAX
Jerry Gerdes

Trutone Records
310 Hudson Street
Hackensack NJ 07601-6732
(201) 489-9180
(201) 489-1771 FAX
Adrianna Rowatti

Twin-Star International Inc.
6540 Via Regina
Boca Raton FL 33433
(800) 480-2388
(561) 750-8122 FAX
Mark Sofsky

U.S. Optical Disc, Inc.
1 Eagle Drive
Sanford Me 04073-4417
(207) 324-1124
(207) 490-1707 FAX
Susan DeRoy

U.S. Tape & Label
1561 Fairview Ave.
St. Louis MO 63132
(314) 4423-4411
(314) 423-2964 FAX
Nancy Lasky Rife

UMAP Distribution
PO Box 200674
Austin TX 78720-0674
(512) 260-0292
(512) 260-0092 FAX
Michelle Mayne

Unisound Marketing
    & Promotions
PO Box 8307
Van Nuys CA 91409-8307
(818) 782-1902
(818) 782-1904 FAX
Denny Stilwell

United Ad Label Co.
650 Columbia Street
Brea CA 92822
(714) 990-2700
(714) 990-2070 FAX
Beverley Kieswetter

Univenture Inc.
PO Box 28398
Columbus OH 43228-0398
(614) 529-2100
(614) 529-2110 FAX
Michele Cole

VI&A
32500 Van Born Road
Wayne MI 48184
(313) 728-4848
(313) 728-1783 FAX
Jeff Miller

Video Pipeline, Inc.
16 South Haddon Avenue
Haddonfield NJ 08033
(800) 638-4321
(609) 427-9046 FAX
Jed Horowitz

Virtual Music Entertain-
    ment
3 Riverside Drive
Andover MA 01810
(508) 688-8800 Ext. 0320
(508) 688-8824 FAX
Julie Saltonstall

Visible Ink Press
835 Penobscot Building
645 Griswold Street
Detroit MI 48226
(313) 961-2242
(313) 961-6812 FAX
Kim Intindola

Vision Information Serv.
302 South Main Street
Royal Oak MI 48067
(810) 584-4300
(810) 584-2440 FAX
Irene Correia

Visions Two Inc.
16728 SW Hargis Road
Beaverton OR 97007
(503) 627-3242
(503) 627-2225 FAX
Kevin Ilcisin

W.F. Leopold Management
4425 Riverside Drive, #102
Burbank CA 91505
(818) 955-9511
(818) 955-9602 FAX
William Leopold

WMG, Inc/World Media
    Group
6737 East 30th Street
Indianapolis IN 46219
(317) 549-8484
(317) 549-8480 FAX
Jeff Mellentine

Warner Special Products
3500 W. Olive, #800
Burbank CA 91505-4301
(818) 953-7900
(818) 953-7950 FAX
Tony Pipitone

Wings Digital Corp.
10 Commercial Street
Hicksville NY 11801
(212) 575-2022
(212) 575-1109 FAX
Ray Kissel

Young Systems Limited
6185 Buford Highway
Suite C-100
Norcross GA 30071
(770) 449-0338
(770) 840-9723 FAX
Susan Hoffman

Zenqor, Inc.
1460 SW 3rd St., Ste B-8
Pompano Beach FL 33069
(305) 946-1303
(305) 946-5103 FAX
Raj Shah

Web-Based Learning
(Session #3, Friday, April 4, 2003)
MEIEA 2003 – Loyola, New Orleans

Dr. E. Michael Harrington
Professor of Music Business
Belmont University

harringtone@mail.belmont.edu
http://schlbus.belmont.edu/mb/mbfaculty/facultyall.html

Bibliography: Websites:

Journals/Magazines/Newspapers/Search Engines/TV/Radio

Altavista.com	(http://www.altavista.com)
Arts & Letters Daily	(http://www.cybereditions.com/aldaily/)
BBC News	http://news.bbc.co.uk/
Billboard	(http://www.billboard.com)
Boston Globe	(http://www.boston.com/globe/)
Business 2.0	http://www.business2.com/
Business Week	http://www.businessweek.com/
CNET News.com	(http://www.news.com)
CNN	(http://www.cnn.com)
CNNfn	(http://www.cnnfn.com)
Google.com	(http://www.google.com)
India Times	http://timesofindia.indiatimes.com
Inside.com	(http://www.inside.com)
Ireland.com (Irish Times)	(http://www.ireland.com/)
Japan Times	http://www.japantimes.com/
National Public Radio	(http://www.npr.org)
New York Times	(http://www.times.com/)
Newsbytes	(http://www.newsbytes.com/)
Office.com	(http://www.office.com/)
PR Newswire.com	(http://www.prnewswire.com)
Public Broadcasting System	(http://www.pbs.org)
Rhythm Music Magazine	(http://www.gorhythm.com/)
RollingStone.com	(http://www.rollingstone.com/sections/home/text/default.asp)
Salon	(http://www.salon.com/)
Silicon Valley.com	(http://www.siliconvalley.com/)
Sirius Satellite Radio	http://www.siriusradio.com/main.htm
SlashDot.org News for Nerds	http://Slashdot.org/
Sonicnet.com	(http://www.sonicnet.com)
TheStandard.com	(http://www.thestandard.com)
Tech Law Journal	(http://www.techlawjournal.com/)
TechTV.com	(http://www.techtv.com/techtv/)
The Village Voice	(http://www.villagevoice.com/)
Washington Post	(http://www.washingtonpost.com/wp-srv/front.htm)
WGBH	(http://www.wgbh.org)
Wired News	(http://www.wired.com)

Yahoo.com   (http://www.yahoo.com)
ZDNet.com   (http://www.zdnet.com/)

Bibliography: Websites: Organizations/Individuals

321 Studios   http://www.copymydvd.com/
American Open Tech Consortium http://www.aotc.info/
Anti-DMCA   http://anti-dmca.org/
Audioscrobbler   http://www.Audioscrobbler.com/
John Perry Barlow - "Selling Wine Without Bottles: The Economy of Mind on the Global Net"
                                    http://www.eff.org/pub/Intellectual_property/idea_economy.article
Berkman Center for Internet & Society (of the Harvard Law School)   (http://cyber.law.harvard.edu)
Boucher Fair Use address   http://www.techlawjournal.com/intelpro/20010306boucher.asp
Boycott The RIAA   http://www.boycott-riaa.com
James Boyle   http://www.james-boyle.com)
Business Software Alliance   http://www.bsa.org/
CD Freaks   http://www.cdfreaks.com/)
Harry Hillman Chartrand   http://www.culturaleconomics.atfreeweb.com/cpu.htm
Columbia Univ. Law School...   http://library.law.columbia.edu/music_plagiarism/index2.html
Copyright Resources Online   (http://www.library.yale.edu/~okerson/copyproj.html)
Copyright Website   (http://www.CopyrightWebsite.com/)
Cornell University Law School   http://www.law.cornell.edu
Cornell IP   http://www.law.cornell.edu/topics/copyright.html
Creative Commons   http://www.creativecommons.org/
Cyberspace Law Institute   http://www.cli.org
Davenetics.com   (http://www.davenetics.com/PHT.html)
Digital Consumer   http://www.digitalconsumer.org/
Digital Consumer News   http://www.digitalconsumer.org/news.html
DMCA Primer   http://www.arl.org/info/frn/copy/primer.html
Electronic Frontier Foundation   (http://www.eff.org)
Evolution Control Committee   (http://evolution-control.com)
Fat Chuck's   http://www.fatchucks.com/
Ed Felten   http://www.freedomtotinker.com/
Findlaw.com   (http://www.findlaw.com/)
Franklin Pierce Law Center   http://www.ipmall.fplc.edu/
Free Dmitry Sklyarov   (http://www.freesklyarov.org/)
Free Expression Policy Project   http://www.fepproject.org/policyreports/copyright.html
Fritz' Hit List   http://www.freedomtotinker.com/
Future of Music Coalition   (http://www.futureofmusic.org/)
Gnutella   (http://www.Gnutella.wego.com)
Hacktivisimo News Site   http://www.hacktivismo.com/news/
Harvard Law School   (http://www.law.harvard.edu)
The Honest Thief   http://www.thehonestthief.com
Illegal Art   http://www.illegal-art.org/
Intellectual Property Mall   (http://www.ipmall..fplc.edu)
Intellectual Property Organization (www.ipo.org)
Intellectual Property & Tech...   http://infoeagle.bc.edu/bc_org/avp/law/st_org/iptf/
Intelproplaw.com   (http://www.intelproplaw.com/)
International IP Institute   http://www.iipi.org/
Internet Patent News Service   http://www.bustpatents.com
KaZaA   http://www.kazaa.com/us/index.php
Legal Information Institute   (http://www.law.cornell.edu/topics/copyright.html)
Lawrence Lessig   http://www.lessig.org/

Lessig at the USSC 02-1009	http://www.aaronsw.com/2002/eldredTranscript
Lessig at 2003 SXSW (3/03)	http://www.onlisareinsradar.com/archives/001012.php#001012
Declan McCullagh's Politech	http://www.politechbot.com/
Megalaw.com Copyright Law	http://www.megalaw.com/top/copyright.php
Musical Borrowing	(http://www.music.indiana.edu/borrowing/)
Napster	(http://www.napster.com/)
National Public Radio	(http://www.npr.org/)
Negativland	(http://www.negativland.com)
New York University Law School	http://www.law.nyu.edu/library/intprop.html
Nolo.com	(http://www.nolo.com)
Ocean State Lawyers for the Arts	http://www.artslaw.org/
Open P2P	http://www.openp2p.com/
Opposing Copyright Extension	(http://www.public.asu.edu/~dkarjala/)
Patentcafe.com	http://www.patentcafe.com/
Public Broadcasting System	(http://www.pbs.org)
Public Domain Music	http://www.pdinfo.com/
Public Knowledge	http://www.publicknowledge.org/
Pamela Samuelson	(http://ei.cs.vt.edu/~cs6604/f97/Samuelson.htm)
Samuelson Law, Technology...	http://www.law.berkeley.edu/cenpro/samuelson/index.html

Signal or Noise? Future of Music on the Net (2/25/2000 conference)

	(http://cyber.law.harvard.edu/events/netmusic_agenda.html)
Signal or Noise? Briefing Book	(http://cyber.law.harvard.edu/events/netmusic_brbook.html)
John & Ben Snyder	http://www.salon.com/tech/feature/2003/02/01/file_trading_manifesto/index.html
Richard Stim	(http://members.aol.com/rwstim/copyright/update.htm)
Brad Templeton	(http://www.templetons.com/brad/copyright.html)
Tollbooths on the Digital Highway	http://www.pbs.org/now/transcript/transcript_copyright.html
Top Secret Recipes (trade secrets?)	http://www.topsecretrecipes.com
Wendt v. Host (Kozinski dissent)	http://laws.lp.findlaw.com/9th/9655243o.html
WGBH	(http://www.wgbh.org/wgbh/)
When Works Pass Into P. D.	http://www.unc.edu/~unclng/public-d.htm
WIPO	http://wipo.org
Yahoo Intellectual Property Directory	(http://www.yahoo.com/Government/Law/Intellectual_Property/)
Peter K. Yu	http://www.gigalaw.com/articles/2002-all/yu-2002-08-all.html

Bibliography: Websites: Fair Use/Academia

Campbell v. Acuff-Rose	http://supct.law.cornell.edu/supct/html/92-1292.ZO.html
Caslon Analytics IP	http://www.caslon.com.au/ipguide19.htm
CONFU: Conference on Fair Use	http://www.utsystem.edu/ogc/intellectualproperty/confu.htm
DMCA & CTEA Primer for...	http://www.arl.org/info/frn/copy/primer.html
Fair Use (Univ. of Texas)	http://www.utsystem.edu/OGC/IntellectualProperty/copypol2.htm
Get Out Of Hell Free cards	http://www.thisistrue.com/hasbro.html
Infolibrarian.com	http://www.infolibrarian.com/cright.htm
Maricopa Community College	http://www.dist.maricopa.edu/legal/dp/inbrief/copyrighted.htm
Megalaw.com Fair Use	http://www.megalaw.com/top/copyright/copyrightfair.php
Parody (from www.publaw.com)	http://www.publaw.com/parody.html
Stanford University Libraries	http://fairuse.stanford.edu/articles/
TEACH Act (11/25/02)	http://www.copyright.gov/legislation/pl107-273.html#13301
University of Texas	http://www.utsystem.edu/OGC/IntellectualProperty/copypol2.htm
University of Washington	http://www.lib.washington.edu/help/guides/copyright.html

Bibliography: Websites: Music/World Music

African Artist Alphabetical List	(http://africanmusic.org/alpha.html)
African History and Overview	(http://www.acslink.aone.net.au/christo/geskied/biblio.htm)
African Music Encyclopedia	(http://africanmusic.org/)
African Music Resources Online	(http://www.uni-mainz.de/~bender/ama_links.html)
African Nations, List Of	http://mywebpages.comcast.net/norman-white/africalist.html
African Online Shop	(http://www.over2u.com/)
AfroCubaWeb	(http://www.afrocubaweb.com/)
All Africa	http://allafrica.com/
ArtistsDirect.com (formerly UBL)	(http://ubl.artistdirect.com/)
ASCAP	(http://www.ascap.com/)
Audiobooksforfree.com	www.audiobooksforfree.com
Beatles.com	(http://www.beatles.com/top.html)
BMI	(http://www.bmi.com/)
Boukman Eksperyans	(http://www.boukman.com/)
Brazil MPB	(http://www.adrstudio.com/search/Brazil/MPB/Search1.shtml)
Chuck D, Public Enemy	(http://www.slamjamz.com/)
Cuba (National Website)	(http://www.cuba.nl/)
Miles Davis	(http://www.milesdavis.com/)
Descarga.com	(http://www.descarga.com/)
The Doors	(http://www.thedoors.com/)
Ellipsis Arts	(http://www.ellipsisarts.com/)
Experience Music Project	http://emplive.com/index.asp
First Vienna Vegetable Orchestra	http://www.gemueseorchester.org/anfang_e.htm
Folk Alliance	http://www.folk.org/
FreeBurma.org	(http://www.freeburma.org/)
FRoots Magazine (Folk Roots)	(http://www.froots.demon.co.uk/)
Global Music Network	(www.gmn.com)
Hindu Server	(http://www.hinduonline.com/)
Jimi Hendrix	(http://www.jimihendrix.com/)
Insurgent Country	http://www.insurgentcountry.com/
Int'l Library African Music	(http://archive.ilam.ru.ac.za/home.asp)
Johnny D's Restaurant & Music	(http://www.johnnyds.com/)
Just Plain Folks	http://www.justplainfolks.org/
Leo's Lyrics	http://www.leoslyrics.com/
Luaka Bop Records	(http://www.luakabop.com/cmp/index.html)
Listen.com (Rhapsody)	http://www.listen.com/
Lyric Find	http://www.lyricfind.com/
Madagascar Cdography	(http://www.froots.demon.co.uk/madagcd.html)
Bob Marley's Bibliography	(http://www.nlj.org.jm/docs/bobbibo.html)
The Marley Store	(http://www.bobmarley.com/)
Roger McGuinn	http://www.ibiblio.org/jimmy/mcguinn/index.html
Pat Metheny	(http://www.patmethenygroup.com/)
Moontaxi	http://www.moontaxi.com/home.asp
Motown	(http://www.motown.com/)
MP3.com	http://www.mp3.com/
National Library of Jamaica	(http://www.nlj.org.jm/)
NetBeat.com	(http://world.netbeat.com/)
Notaviva.com	http://www.notaviva.com/
Okayplayer.com	http://www.okayplayer.com/
Online Classics Network	(www.onlineclassics.net)
La Plaza	(http://www.wgbh.org/wgbh/pages/laplaza/)
Pearl Jam	http://www.pearljam.com/

Pollstar.com	(http://www.pollstar.com/)
Public Domain Music	http://www.pdinfo.com/
Public Enemy	(http://www.publicenemy.com/)
Puerto Rico Governor's Site	(http://fortaleza.govpr.org/)
Puerto Rico Official Site	(http://www.puertorico.com/macie.html)
Putumayo World Music	(http://www.putumayo.com/)
Rapstation.com	(http://www.rapstation.com/)
Rhino Records	(http://www.rhino.com/)
Rhythm Music Magazine	(http://www.gorhythm.com/)
Rock & Roll Hall Of Fame	http://www.rockhall.com/
Rough Guides Music	(http://www.roughguides.com/music/index.html)
Rounder Records	(http://www.rounder.com/)
Rykodisc Records	(http://www.rykodisc.com/)
Ravi Shankar Foundation	(http://www.ravishankar.org/)
Ravi Shankar Links	(http://home.columbus.rr.com/woodstock1969/artist/ravi_shankar.html)
SESAC	(http://www.sesac.com/sesac.html
Sirius Satellite Radio	http://www.siriusradio.com/main.htm
Smithsonian Folkways Recordings	(http://web2.si.edu/folkways/)
TAXI (A & R, record deals, etc.)	http://www.taxi.com/
They Might Be Giants	http://www.theymightbegiants.com/
Tin Pan South	http://www.tinpansouth.com/index.cfm
Ultimate Band List	(http://www.ubl.com)
Caetano Veloso	(http://www.caetanoveloso.com.br/site.htm)
World Music	(http://www.worldmusic.org/)
World Music Network	(http://www.worldmusic.net/home/index.html)
Frank Zappa fansite	(http://www.science.uva.nl/~robbert/zappa/)
Frank Zappa Official Homepage	(http://www.zappa.com/)

Bibliography: Websites: U. S. Government

BALANCE Act (explained)	http://www.house.gov/lofgren/news/2002/secbysecbalance.htm
Bill Summary and Status (92nd-108th)	http://thomas.loc.gov/bss/d108query.html
CIA World Factbook 2002	http://www.cia.gov/cia/publications/factbook/index.html
Copyright Legislation 108th Congress	http://www.copyright.gov/legislation/
Digital Media Consumers' Rights Act	http://www.house.gov/boucher/docs/dmcra108th.pdf
FirstGov.gov	(http://www.firstgov.gov/)
Library of Congress Homepage	(http://www.loc.gov/)
Library of Congress	(http://www.loc.gov/library/)
Small Webcaster Settlement Act of 2002	http://www.copyright.gov/legislation/pl107-321.html
Smithsonian Institution	(http://www.si.edu/)
TEACH Act (11/25/2002)	http://www.copyright.gov/legislation/pl107-273.html#13301
United States Code	http://www4.law.cornell.edu/uscode/
U. S. Congress on the Internet	http://thomas.loc.gov/
U. S. Copyright Office	(http://lcweb.loc.gov/copyright/)
U. S. Federal Trade Commission	http://www.ftc.gov/
U. S. Patent & Trademark Office (Home)	(http://www.uspto.gov/)

U. S. Patent & Trademark Office (Trademark Information)
(http://www.uspto.gov/web/menu/tm.html)

U. S. Supreme Court Copyright Decisions
http://www4.law.cornell.edu/cgi-bin/empower?DB=SupctSyllabi&TOPDOC=0&QUERY00=copyright

U. S. Trademark Electronic Search System   ("TESS")
(http://tess.uspto.gov/bin/gate.exe?f=tess&state=pl90sd.1.1)

Bibliography: Websites: International & International Government Sites:

African IP Organization   http://www.oapi.wipo.net/index_angl.html
Australia IP Australia   http://www.ipaustralia.gov.au/
Australasian Performing Arts Association   http://www.apra.com.au/
Australian Copyright Council   http://www.copyright.org.au/
Australian Record Industry Association   http://www.aria.com.au/
Australia EFA   http://www.efa.org.au
BBC News   http://news.bbc.co.uk/
Canada Copyright Act   http://laws.justice.gc.ca/en/C-42/index.html
Canada Bill C-32   http://www.parl.gc.ca/bills/government/C-32/C-32_3/C-32TOCE.html
Canadian Coalition For Fair Digital Access http://www.ccfda.ca/
Canadian Musical Reproduction Rights   http://www.cmrra.ca/default.html
China, Constitution of the Republic of   http://www.qis.net/chinalaw/roccon1.htm
China Copyright Law   http://www.china-laws-online.com/intellectual-property-rights/copyright-law.htm
China IP Law Explained   http://www.qis.net/chinalaw/lawtran1.htm
Cultural Traffic   http://www.carleton.ca/ces/conference_fr.html
Germany Copyright Law   http://www.iuscomp.org/gla/statutes/UrhG.htm
Guardian – Internet News   http://www.guardian.co.uk/internetnews/
India Copyright Act 1957   http://www.naukri.com/lls/copyright/cpwrt.htm
International Copyright Basics   http://www.law.duke.edu/copyright/face/inatl/index.htm
International Federation of Phonographic...   http://www.ifpi.org
International IP Institute   http://www.iipi.org/
Japan Copyright Law   http://www.cric.or.jp/cric_e/clj/clj.html
Law Gazette (UK)   http://www.lawgazette.co.uk/homeframe.asp
Law Society of Ireland   http://www.lawsociety.ie/
Mechanical-Copyright Protection Society   http://www.mcps.co.uk/
Patently Absurd!   http://www.patent.freeserve.co.uk/index.html
Phonographic Performance Limited   http://www.ppluk.com/ppl/ppl_fd.nsf/home?openform
Statute of Anne (1710 copyright law)   http://edge.net/~flowers/Statute%20of%20Anne.htm
Teosto Finnish Composers' Copyright Society
                                http://www.teosto.fi/teosto/webpages.nsf/Frames?ReadForm&English
UK Patent Office (Copyright)   http://www.patent.gov.uk/copy/index.htm
UK Patent Office (Design)   http://www.patent.gov.uk/design/index.htm
UK Patent Office (Patent)   http://www.patent.gov.uk/patent/index.htm
UK Patent Office (Trademark)   http://www.patent.gov.uk/tm/index.htm

Bibliography: Websites: Music Business/Music Industry

Ads.com   http://www.ads.com
American Federation of Musicians   http://www.afm.org/
American Federation of Television & Radio Artists   http://www.aftra.org/
American Guild of Music Artists   http://www.musicalartists.org/HomePage.htm
American Guild of Variety Artists   http://americanguildofvarietyartists.visualnet.es/
AOL Time Warner   http://www.aoltimewarner.com/index_flash.adp
Arbitron   http://www.arbitron.com/home/content.stm
ASCAP   (http://www.ascap.com/)
BMG   http://www.click2music.com:80/bmg.com/
BMI   (http://www.bmi.com/)
Jeff Brabec & Todd Brabec   http://www.musicandmoney.com/index.html
Buddy Lee Attractions, Inc.   http://www.buddyleeattractions.com
Canadian Musical Reproduction Rights   http://www.cmrra.ca/default.html
Clear Channel Communications   http://www.clearchannel.com/main.html
Clear Channel Sucks   http://www.clearchannelsucks.org/

CMJ (College Music Journal)	http://www.cmj.com/
Columbia Artists Management, Inc. (CAMI)	http://www.cami.com/
Community Broadcasters Association	http://www.communitybroadcasters.com/
Consumer Electronics Association	http://www.ce.org/
Country Music Television	http://www.cmt.com/
Country Music Television Canada	http://www.cmtcanada.com/
Digital Media Association	http://www.digmedia.org/
DJ Times	http://www.djtimes.com/original/index.htm
Dotmusic.com (BT legal music service)	http://www.dotmusic.com/
Dramatists Guild of America	http://www.dramaguild.com/
EMI	http://www.emigroup.com/
Encore	http://www.celebrityaccess.com/news/
FindLaw: Tech Deals, Contracts...	http://davenetics.findlaw.com/
Fullaudio	http://www.fullaudio.com/index.jsp
Gavin	http://www.gavin.com/
Grammy.com	http://www.grammy.com/
Harry Fox Agency	http://www.nmpa.org/hfa.html
Hispanic Music Videos Television	http://www.hmvtv.com/
Information Technology Association of America	http://www.itaa.org
International Alliance of Theatrical...(IATSE)	http://www.iatse.lm.com/
International Association of Assembly Managers	http://www.iaam.org/
International Recording Media Association	http://www.recordingmedia.org/
Listen.com (Rhapsody)	http://www.listen.com/
MIDEM The International Music Market	http://www.midem.com/
Motion Picture Association of America	http://www.mpaa.org
Music Industry Association of Canada	http://www.miac.net/pages/frame.html
MusicNet	http://www.musicnet.com/
Musictoday.com	http://www.musictoday.com/
Nashville Songwriters Association International	http://www.nashvillesongwriters.com/
National Association of Broadcast Employees...	http://union.nabetcwa.org/nabet/front.html
National Association of Broadcasters	http://www.nab.org/
National Association of Music Merchants	http://www.namm.com/
National Association of Recording Merchandisers	http://www.narm.com/
National Music Publishers Association	http://www.nmpa.org/
Pollstar.com	http://www.pollstar.com/
Pressplay	http://www.pressplay.com/
Public Domain Music	http://www.pdinfo.com/
Recording Industry Association of America	http://www.riaa.org/index.cfm
Rhythm Music Magazine	http://www.gorhythm.com/)
Rock On TV	http://www.rockontv.com/
Scour Exchange	http://www.scour.com/Software/Scour_Exchange)
Screen Actors Guild	http://www.sag.org/
Secure Digital Music Initiative (SDMI)	http://www.sdmi.org/
SESAC	http://www.sesac.com/sesac.html
Sirius Radio	http://www.siriusradio.com
Sonicblue	http://www.sonicblue.com/
Sony	http://www.sonymusic.com/
Sound Exchange	http://www.soundexchange.com/
South By Southwest	http://www.sxsw.com/2001/
Star Polish	http://www.starpolish.com/advice/
TiVo	http://www.tivo.com/home.asp
Vans Warped Tour	http://warpedtour.launch.com/
Vivendi Universal	http://www.vivendi.com/vu2/en/_home/home.cfm
XM Satellite Radio	http://www.xmradio.com/
Yahoo! Music Industry Websites	http://dir.yahoo.com/Entertainment/Music/Music_Industry_Resources/

E. Michael Harrington teaches Intellectual Property Law as a Professor of Music Business (between 1985-2001 was Professor of Music Theory, Composition & Ethnomusicology) at Belmont University. He was the **1995 Jemison Distinguished Professor of The Humanities** at the University of Alabama-Birmingham, an endowed chair funded by the **National Endowment for the Humanities**, the Jemison family and UAB. He has taught at the University of Miami, the University of Massachusetts-Westfield, the University of Pittsburgh, the Ohio State University, the University of Alabama-Birmingham, and Belmont University.

He has taught training sessions for Harvard Law students and faculty at the **Harvard University Law School**, been a guest speaker at the **Boston Bar Association**, and delivered papers at 68 international, national and regional meetings of 25 different academic organizations including the College Music Society, the Music Entertainment Industry Education Association, the International Association for the Study of Popular Music, **the Experience Music Project**, the American Society for Business & Behavioral Sciences, the Society for Ethnomusicology, the American Musicological Society, the Society for Music Theory, the Center for Black Music, the Society for American Music, **the European Union Film Festival**, the Institute for Comparative Studies in Literature, Art and Culture at Carleton University (Ottawa), the Intellectual Property and Technology Forum at the Boston College Law School, the American Constitution Society at the Boston College Law School, the Music Library Association, the Guild of Carillonneurs of North America, the American Culture Association, the Popular Culture Association, the MasterCard Priceless Edge, the Grammy Foundation's Leonard Bernstein Center for Learning, Music Theory Midwest, the Music Theory Society of New York State, the American Society of University Composers, the Association of Alabama College Music Administrators, the Sonneck Society and lectured, performed and taught master classes at more than 50 universities throughout the U.S., Canada and Puerto Rico, including the Harvard University Law School, the Berklee College Of Music, the Eastman School of Music, the Boston College Law School, the Brooklyn Law School, the Suffolk University Law School, the University of California San Diego, Loyola University, the University of Miami, the University of Cincinnati, Emory University and others.

He has been interviewed by print, radio, television and Internet sources including **The New York Times, CNN, The Associated Press, National Public Radio, PC Magazine, Investor's Business Daily, Office.com, The Baltimore Sun, The Los Angeles Times, Life Magazine, Billboard Magazine, BRAVO,** CNNfn.com, CNET's www.news.com, The World African Network, Inside.com, Readers Digest, The Ottawa Citizen, The National Post, The Providence Journal, The Industry Standard, TheWhiz.com, The Atlanta Journal-Constitution, The Raleigh News & Observer, The Copley Newspapers, The Detroit Free Press, The Pittsburgh Post-Gazette, The Albany Times-Union, Aversion.com, The Tennessean, Offbeat Magazine, Wireless Flash News flashnews.com and others. His music research in popular music, world music, and copyright infringement was profiled in an article which was distributed by the **Associated Press** and the **Scripps Howard News Service** and published in dozens of newspapers throughout the U. S. in April 1995, including **The Washington Times, The Atlanta Journal Constitution, The Minneapolis Star Tribune** and **The Columbus Post-Dispatch**.

He has articles and editorials published in **Women and Music In America Since 1900: An Encyclopedia** (Oryx Press, 2002), **The College Music Symposium, Ex Tempore, Triad, The Tennessee Musician, The Birmingham Herald, The American Society of University Composers Monograph Series**, and **The Indiana Theory Review**.

Harrington has worked as an **expert witness** and **consultant** in music copyright infringement involving The Dixie Chicks, Lauryn Hill & The Fugees, Steve Perry, Collin Raye, Patty Loveless, Avril Lavigne, Mystikal, Martina McBride, Madonna, Puff Daddy, Sting, Britney Spears, the Backstreet Boys, George Clinton, Bon Jovi, 2 Live Crew, Tag Team, Duice, 95 South, D. J. Smurf, Public Enemy, Beastie Boys, Deana Carter, Kenny G, LeAnn Rimes, Crosby, Stills, Nash & Young, Bryan White, Don Schlitz, Dwight Yoakam, Mary J. Blige, MC Eiht, George Jones, Tracy Lawrence, Roger Miller, Joe Diffie, Brooks & Dunn, Lonnie Mack, Dan Penn, Chris Isaak, Billy Ray Cyrus, Sandy Linzer, Mila Mason, Robert Nix, En Vogue, the Ford Motor Company, the H. J. Heinz Company, Publix Supermarkets and others.

Index